STRAVAGANZA
City of Flowers

The *Stravaganza* series
by Mary Hoffman

Stravaganza: City of Masks
Stravaganza: City of Stars
Stravaganza: City of Flowers

STRAVAGANZA
City of Flowers

Mary Hoffman

BLOOMSBURY

Published by Bloomsbury Publishing, New York and London
Distributed to the trade by Holtzbrinck Publishers

Library of Congress Cataloging-in-Publication Data
Hoffman, Mary.
Stravaganza : city of flowers / Mary Hoffman.—1st U.S. ed.
p. cm.
Sequel to: Stravaganza, city of stars.
Summary: Seventeen-year-old Sky joins Georgia and the other Stravaganti,
"who travel between worlds and do what is required," when he leaves London
for Giglia, a city similar to renaissance Florence, and becomes involved in
ancient feuds and palace intrigue.
ISBN-10: 1-58234-887-1
ISBN-13: 978-1-58234-887-2
[1. Space and time—Fiction.] I. Title: City of flowers. II. Title.
PZ7.H67562Su 2005   [Fic]—dc22   2004055445

First U.S. Edition 2005
Printed in the U.S.A.
1 3 5 7 9 10 8 6 4 2

Bloomsbury Publishing, Children's Books, U.S.A.
175 Fifth Avenue, New York, NY 10010

Acknowledgements

Franco Cesati's book *La Grande Guida delle Strade di Firenze* and Franco Cardini's *Breve Storia di Firenze* were indispensable, as were Christopher Hibbert's *The Medici* and *Florence*. My thanks to Carla Poesio and, as always, Edgardo Zaghini, for reading the first draft, and other invaluable support. Ralph and Elizabeth Lovegrove advised on fencing and other matters. My long-suffering family endured a month of my absence in Florence, shouldering my share of the domestic load, particularly Stevie. Matteo Cristini told me wonderful things about the history of Florentine art. Santa Maria Novella and its Officina Profumo-Farmaceutica were as magical as always and an obvious destination for a Stravagante. Thanks to my editor, Emma Matthewson, who has always liked this book best, and to all the many fans who email me on the Stravaganza website, urging me to make things happen between Luciano and Arianna; I have done my best.

*For Jessica, maker of potions and expert
on Giglia*

'Non v'è città al mondo che non senta, nel bene e nel male, il peso del suo passato.'
Franco Cardini, *Breve Storia di Firenze*, 1990

('There is no city in the world which does not feel, whether for good or ill, the weight of its past.')

'Non ha l'ottimo artista alcun concetto,
ch'un marmo solo in sè non circonscriva
col suo soverchio; e solo a quello arriva
la man che ubbidisce all'intelletto.'
Michelangelo Buonarotti

('The greatest artist does not have any concept which a single piece of marble does not contain within its excess, though only a hand that obeys the intellect can discover it.'
Poem 151 in Christopher Ryan's translation,
J. M. Dent, 1996)

'È necessario a uno principe, volendosi mantenere, imparare a potere essere non buono, e usarlo e non l'usare secondo la necessità.'
Niccolò Machiavelli, *Il Principe*, 1513

('For a ruler, it is necessary, if he wants to stay ruler, to learn how not to be good and to use this power, or not, according to need.')

Contents

Prologue: Walking the Maze   15
1. A Blue Glass Bottle   20
2. The Hounds of God   36
3. Brothers   49
4. Secrets   64
5. Marble for a Duchess   76
6. Wedding Dresses   93
7. Deadly Nightshade   108
8. Two Households, Both Alike in Dignity   122
9. Angels   136
10. A Man's Job   151
11. Daggers Drawn   165
12. The Scent of Pines   179
13. Talismans   194
14. Pictures in the Walls   210
15. Visitors   227
16. Mapping the City   244
17. My Enemy's Enemy is My Friend   258
18. Flight   274
19. Flowers of the City   292
20. The River Rises   311
21. The di Chimici Weddings   331
22. Blood on Silver   351
23. Drowned City   369
24. God's Puppy   388
25. Exile   408
26. Corridor of Power   426
27. A Duel   448
Epilogue: One More Wedding   469
A Note on the di Chimici and the Medici   481
di Chimici family tree   485
Dramatis Personae   487

Prologue: *Walking the Maze*

In a black and white striped church in the north-west
of the city, a friar in a black and white robe was
waiting his turn to step on to a curious pattern set into
the floor. It was a labyrinth made of strips of black
and white marble contained roughly within a circle,
and friars came and went along it, tracing the pattern
with their footsteps. They walked in silence, but other
friars were softly chanting plainsong from the choir
stalls. It was early in the morning and the church was
empty, save for the friars, weaving their silent
patterns, moving past one another in the circle.

There were eleven circuits between the outside edge
and the centre, but each was so folded into loops that
the friars seemed to be thwarted in their goal the
closer they got to it. Still, every few minutes one or

two reached the centre, where they sank to their knees in heartfelt prayer for several moments before continuing on the path that led them out to the edge again and back into the world.

Brother Sulien was the last to step on to the maze. It was his custom and his right as Senior Friar. Sulien walked the maze even more thoughtfully than usual and by the time he reached the centre he was the only one left. The other friars had gone about their business, some to feed the fish in the cloister pool, some to dig carrots and others to tend vines. Even the members of the choir had dispersed, and Brother Sulien was left alone in the uncertain dawn light of the church's cool interior.

He knelt stiffly in the centre, on a circle surrounded by six lesser circles arranged like the petals of a flower. At the very heart was an inlaid figure that the friar's robe concealed. Indeed, an early morning visitor to Saint-Mary-among-the-Vines would scarcely have been able to see Sulien either, his hood cast over his face, kneeling in stillness at the centre of the maze.

After a long meditation, Brother Sulien rose, said 'Amen' and started the slow return out of the maze to his daily life. So began every day for Sulien, but there was something different about this one. At the end of the ritual, he pulled a threadbare carpet over the pattern, as usual, but instead of walking back through the Great Cloister to his work at the Farmacia, he sat in a pew, considering the future.

He thought about the threat to the city of Giglia and how there was trouble brewing. The great di Chimici family, on whose wealth the city floated, was busier than usual. The Duke had announced the forthcoming weddings of several younger members of the family, including his three remaining sons, all to their cousins. And no one doubted that there was more to these marriages than love.

It was common knowledge that the Duke had organised a spreading network of spies throughout the city, led by a ruthless agent of his known only as l'Anguilla, the Eel, because of his ability to get into and out of tight corners. The spies' purpose, both here and in other cities, was to sniff out all that could be known of a certain brotherhood or order of learned men and women – scientists, some people said, though others said magicians. Brother Sulien shifted on the hard wooden pew at the thought of this order, of which he was a member.

The di Chimici were resolutely opposed to the brotherhood and suspected that it was behind the resistance to their plans to expand their power throughout Talia. Duke Niccolò also believed that this brotherhood was responsible for the death of his youngest son, Prince Falco, less than a year ago. The young prince, horribly injured in a riding accident two years before, apparently committed suicide while staying at the di Chimici summer palace near Remora.

But everyone knew that the Duke believed it was murder – or perhaps something worse. Some said that the boy's ghost walked abroad, others that he was not really dead at all. When Duke Niccolò returned from Remora with his son's body, the whole city was shocked by the change in the Duke's appearance: he had aged by years and now bore a head of white hair and his beard was silver.

The funeral of Prince Falco had been a mournful if

splendid affair; the Duke had buried him in the chapel of his palazzo near the city's centre and the great Giuditta Miele herself had carved his memorial statue.

But Sulien knew that Giuditta's next commission was to come from Bellezza, the independent city-state in the Eastern lagoon. Its ruling Duchessa, the lovely young Arianna Rossi, was rumoured to be coming to Giglia for the di Chimici weddings. Despite her city's fierce resistance to all the di Chimici's attempts to overcome its independence, she was surprisingly friendly with the Duke's third son, Gaetano. He was one of the betrothed and so the Duchessa had accepted the invitation because of him.

Sulien was familiar with Bellezza, since he had only recently come from a religious house near the lagoon city to take over the friary at Saint-Mary-among-the-Vines. He saw the danger to the young Duchessa. The city of Giglia would be fuller than usual of strangers and visitors during the period of the weddings and it would be hard to afford the Duchessa the protection she needed. Indeed, he was a little surprised that her father and Regent, Senator Rodolfo, had agreed to it.

Now he gathered up the skirts of his robe and strode off to the Farmacia, as if he had come to a decision. He walked through the tranquil Lesser Cloister, with its series of chapels, and on to the Great Cloister, where a door opened into the first room, his laboratory.

As always as he climbed the two stone steps into his domain, Brother Sulien breathed its fragrant air with relief and joy. Things in the city might change but here, in Saint-Mary-among-the-Vines, certain things remained the same – the maze, which always brought calm, and the perfumes and medicines distilled here in the Farmacia now newly under his guardianship.

He passed through the laboratory, where two young apprentices, in the robes of novices, were bent over the distillery equipment. After the briefest of greetings, he took himself into his inner, private room, hardly more than a cell, and sat at his desk. He was writing a list of recipes for all the perfumes, creams, lotions and medicines made here in the monastery's church. Not forgetting its famous liqueur and the secret of making drinkable silver.

Now he pushed the parchment to one side and sat gazing at a small blue glass bottle with a silver stopper which he had taken from a shelf. Beside it he placed a silver cross, which he usually kept locked in a carved wooden box. He looked at the two thoughtfully. Then, 'It is time,' he said. 'I shall go there tonight.'

Chapter 1

A Blue Glass Bottle

Sky woke, as usual, to the smell of flowers. But it was stronger than usual, which meant that his mother was up and uncorking bottles. This was a good sign; perhaps she would work today.

Heaving Remedy, the cat, off his feet – another good sign because it meant he must have already been fed – Sky made his way to the kitchen and found his mother spooning coffee into the cáfetière. She looked bright, with a rather hectic flush on her cheeks.

'Hey, Mum. Morning,' he said, giving her a hug.

'Morning, lovely boy,' she said, smiling fondly at him.

'Why didn't you wake me? It's late.'

'It's only half past seven, Sky.'

'Well, that's late,' he said, yawning. 'There's a wash

to do before school.'

'Already on,' said his mother proudly, pouring the just-boiled water on to the coffee. Then her mood changed abruptly and she sat down at the table. 'It's not right that a boy your age should have to worry about housework,' she said, and Sky saw the telltale glitter of tears gathering in her eyes.

'Now, none of that,' he said, deliberately heading her off into a different mood. 'What's for breakfast? I'm starving.'

He didn't want one of those heavy 'We're all each other has got' scenes so early in the morning. His mother couldn't help her illness, which was so erratic that some days, like today, she would seem normal, and on others she couldn't even get out of bed to go to the bathroom, which meant he had to tend to her most private needs.

And Sky didn't mind looking after her; it was true that they were all-in-all to each other. Sky's father had never been around, except on CD covers and concert posters. Rainbow Warrior, the famous black rocker of the '80s, had been interested in fair, shy Rosalind Meadows for all of one night and that was all it took.

When Rosalind found she was pregnant, her best friend, Laura, who had dragged her to the Warrior's concert in the first place, wanted her to have an abortion, but Rosalind couldn't bear the thought. She dropped out of university and went home to brave her parents' wrath.

Although her parents were strict Plymouth Brethren they were surprisingly understanding, even when the baby turned out to be chestnut brown in colour (she hadn't said a word about his father). But when Sky was eighteen months old, they had suggested she might be happier in London, where a very pale-skinned blonde with a brown baby might attract less attention than in a sleepy Devon village. Not attracting unnecessary attention to oneself was something Rosalind's parents considered to have the force of an Eleventh Commandment.

So she had packed her bags and her baby and arrived in London with the deposit on a flat in Islington, a diploma in Aromatherapy and no other means of support. Her greatest consolation was that Laura was also in London, working as an MP's secretary, and she would often babysit while Rosalind built up some contacts in the evening with people who wanted aromatherapy.

'After all,' Laura would say, jiggling Sky inexpertly on her lap, 'he wouldn't be here at all if I hadn't taken you to that concert in Bristol.' Rosalind never mentioned that Sky wouldn't be there at all if she had followed Laura's other suggestion too.

When Sky was two, Rosalind wrote to Rainbow Warrior, feeling stupid about not knowing how to address him. In the end, she just wrote:

Dear Rainbow,
I don't suppose you remember me but I was at your concert in Bristol in '87. Your son, Sky, is two years old today. I don't want anything from you, only for you to know that he exists and to have this address, in case you ever want to get in touch with him. I enclose a photo taken a few weeks ago.

She hesitated. Should she put 'love from'? It was a

common enough empty phrase but she didn't want him to get the wrong idea, so she wrote 'Yours sincerely, Rosalind Meadows'. The letter was sent care of the Warrior's agent and marked Personal and Urgent, but the agent took no notice of that; women were always putting that sort of thing on letters to the Warrior. And it was definitely from a woman; the envelope smelt of flowers.

'Hey, Colin,' he said, waving the letter when he next saw his famous client. 'It seems you've been sowing some more of your wild oats.'

'Don't call me that,' said the singer irritably, snatching the envelope, 'and don't open my personal correspondence – how often do I have to tell you?'

Gus Robinson was one of the handful of people in the world who knew that the great Rainbow Warrior, famous across four continents, had been born Colin Peck on a council estate in Clapham Junction.

The Warrior sniffed the envelope, read the formal little letter, looked at the photo and smiled. That 'Yours sincerely' got to him the way no hysterical tear-stained diatribe would have done. Yes, he remembered Rosalind, so shy and so smitten. And the little boy was cute.

'You should get that letter framed,' said Gus. 'So you can prove she said she doesn't want any of your dosh.'

'Mind your own business,' said the singer, and that night he wrote a letter of his own, not very well-expressed and full of spelling mistakes but enclosing a huge cheque, which he could easily afford.

Rosalind had been stunned and wanted to send the money back but Laura convinced her otherwise.

'It took two, didn't it?' she demanded. 'And he should have been more careful. It must have been obvious that a goose like you wouldn't even have been on the pill.'

'But he says he doesn't want to see Sky,' said Rosalind, her tears spilling down her cheeks.

'So much the better,' said Laura firmly. 'Take the money and run.'

In the end Rosalind had used the money to pay off her mortgage and return her parents' loan; there was no denying how useful it was. She wrote to the singer again, saying that she would send a photo of their son every year, on his birthday. This time Gus Robinson didn't open the letter or all the other sweet-smelling envelopes that came from her once a year, but handed them to his richest client without a word.

Rainbow Warrior had been married three times and had fathered eight children, but no one knew about the brown-skinned laughing boy and his fair mother, except for the singer himself and his agent. And between them the subject was never mentioned.

Nor was it often mentioned between Sky and his mother. When he was old enough to understand, she showed him a picture of his father, in *Hello!* magazine. He was getting married to wife number four, a leggy Colombian model called Loretta. There were lots of children at Sky's primary school whose parents had split up, so he was not particularly disturbed by the photos of the tall dreadlocked singer and his new wife; they seemed to have nothing to do with him.

Rainbow Warrior felt much the same each year as he looked at the latest photo of his secret son. But he kept them all. Sky didn't know that his mother sent pictures of him to his father. There was a period of some months around his thirteenth birthday when he rowed with Rosalind almost every day and once threatened to find his father and go and live with him, but these violent feelings eventually went away and soon after that Rosalind fell ill.

It was the flu, and she stayed in bed for a week, with a fever and a cough that no amount of hot lemon and honey brought relief to. The week turned into months and that was when Sky began to learn how to look after himself and his mother.

ME, said the hospital doctor to Rosalind after months of visits to the GP and being told to pull herself together. No treatment – only time and rest. That had been nearly three years ago and sometimes Rosalind still couldn't get out of bed in the morning. After a year, Sky took his courage in both hands and wrote, without telling his mother, to the famous Rainbow Warrior:

Dear Mr Warrior,
I am your son and I am worried about my mum.
She has been ill for a year. Can you send her to see a
top doctor? By the way, what she has got is called
ME. She is NOT imagining it.
Yours sincerely,

Sky Meadows

He sent it to a venue where the Warrior was appearing and he never got a reply. We can manage without him, he thought bitterly. We always have done and we always will.

'When Papa dies, I shall be Duke Fabrizio the Second,' said the little prince to his tutor. He had been six years old at the time and had got a thorough spanking for it. That was how he first knew dying was a bad thing, though at the time he had only been repeating what his nurse had told him.

Now, as Prince Fabrizio walked along the gallery of his father's palace, a tall and handsome twenty-three-year-old, he felt he had learned the lesson all too well. The walls were hung with portraits of di Chimici, the living and the dead, among the latter his mother, Benedetta, and his youngest brother, Falco, taken from them so cruelly only a matter of months ago. Fabrizio stood in front of this picture for a long time.

The likeness had been made before Falco's accident and showed him standing straight and proud, very conscious of his lace collar and holding a sword that scraped slightly on the ground; he had been about eleven then.

Fabrizio was in no doubt that his brother's death would hasten his father's, though he was no longer in a hurry to become Duke Fabrizio di Chimici the Second. He felt much too young to be both head of the family and in charge of all the schemes his father had put in place. Now he wished he had been one of the younger sons and without such a weight of responsibility to look forward to.

But he squared his shoulders and resumed his walk. At least he could accede happily to one of his father's plans. Fabrizio was to be married soon to his cousin

Caterina. And she was his favourite of all the cousins, from the time they had played games together as children at the summer palace in Santa Fina. A smile played round Fabrizio's fine mouth as he thought of Caterina.

That was the one good thing to come out of poor Falco's death – he refused to think of it as suicide – all the di Chemici weddings. His two remaining brothers were to be married at the same time and his cousin Alfonso, Duke of Volana, too. There would be hardly any unmarried di Chimici left – apart from fussy little cousin Rinaldo – and it was clear that his father Duke Niccolò wanted them all to get on with breeding his descendants as fast as possible. Well, Fabrizio was willing; Caterina was a pretty and lively girl and he had no doubt she would produce a superior crop of heirs.

Sky passed a day at school that felt almost normal. He was used to being in the sixth form now, but he had never quite felt part of the school and had no close friends there.

The trouble was, he looked the part of someone cool and trendy and he knew that lots of girls were initially attracted to him. He was tall for his age and he wore his gold-brown hair in dreadlocks. But he didn't listen to any kind of rock music. It reminded him too much of his father. Rosalind sometimes played the Warrior's CDs, which were the only ones she had that weren't classical or folk, and it made Sky almost literally sick.

He used not to care about his father but, ever since the singer had ignored Sky's letter, written from the heart of despair, he had begun to hate the very idea of him. He knew that the Warrior's music was having a fashionable revival at the time, because it had featured in a film that broke box office records, but Sky didn't see the film and he never told anyone of his connection with the singer.

If he could have been interested in football, he might have felt less of a fish out of water at school. He had the physique for it but just couldn't raise the enthusiasm. He supposed it was because he had more important things to think about. He probably wasn't the only student at his school looking after a sick parent; he'd read an article once about how many carers there were under the age of sixteen – really small kids like nine-year-olds, looking after parents in wheelchairs.

Well, he was better off than they were; he was seventeen, and his mother wasn't ill all the time. But he didn't know anyone else in his position and he felt set apart, somehow marked. And it showed. Gradually, the friendly overtures had tailed off and the girls wrote him off as useless too.

There was just one girl, though, quiet and fair, whom he really liked, and if she had ever shown any interest in him, things might have been different. But she was inseparable from her fierce friend with the dyed red hair and tattoo, so Sky never got up the courage to talk to her. Still, they were all doing English AS, so at least they were in some of the same classes.

It didn't take Sky long to reach home, since his flat was in a house right next to the school. He dawdled, wondering what he would find there, whether his mother would still be feeling OK or back in bed unable to move. But he was quite unprepared for what he did find. On the doorstep to their flats stood a small blue glass bottle, with a silver stopper in the shape of a fleur-de-lys. It was empty and incredibly fragile, just sitting there on the step, where anyone might knock it over.

Instinctively, Sky picked it up and took out the stopper; a heavenly smell wafted out of it, more delicious than anything in his mother's store of oils and essences. Was it meant for her? There was no message attached to it.

He let himself in through the front door and then into their ground-floor flat. Rosalind had sold the one that the Warrior had paid for and bought this smaller one less than a year ago because she couldn't manage stairs any more. The newly converted house still smelt of fresh paint and plaster. That and the smell of flower essences greeted Sky's return.

'Mum,' he called, though she would have heard his key in the lock. 'I'm home!'

She wasn't in the living room or the tiny kitchen, and he knocked on her bedroom door with a sick feeling that something terrible had happened to her. But she wasn't there and when he went back to the kitchen, he found her note:

Gone to supermarket; there won't be any biscuits till I get back.

Sky smiled with relief; when had she last been well enough to go shopping on her own? That was usually his job, every Wednesday afternoon after school, lugging plastic carrier bags on to the bus and then putting everything away. His mother must have taken the car, though; she couldn't have managed on the bus.

Sky took the damp wash out of the machine, put it in the tumble-dryer, washed up the breakfast things from the morning and looked in the cupboards to see what he could make for dinner. Normally, he would make a start on peeling potatoes or chopping onions, but he thought he'd better wait and see what his mother brought back with her; maybe she had planned something.

He fed Remedy, because the tabby rescue cat was in danger of tripping him up by twining round his legs, then made himself a cup of tea and sat down at the table, where the little blue glass bottle stood looking innocent and at the same time significant. Remedy leapt on to the chair beside him and started washing. Sky sighed and got out his school books and read a short story for French.

Sandro was delighted with his new master. Everyone knew about the Eel; he was becoming a figure to be reckoned with in Giglia. He now had dozens of spies working for him and bringing information back to the di Chimici palace from all over the city and beyond. It was just the kind of work Sandro enjoyed, following people and hanging about eavesdropping on their private conversations. He would have been happy to do it for nothing.

Sandro was small and quick-witted and completely inconspicuous, one of those many young boys, none too clean and a bit ragged, who hung about the busy places of the city, hoping for a few cents in return for running errands. But actually he had silver in his pockets, expenses paid to him by the Eel, because he might need to buy a drink for an informant or offer a small bribe for information.

Now Sandro was tailing one of the Nucci clan and it couldn't have been easier. Camillo Nucci was so obviously on his way to an assignation that Sandro had to stifle a chuckle; the young bravo in the red cap kept looking over his shoulder as he walked past the di Chimici's grand new building of Guild offices off the main piazza and across the stone structure that was still called the Ponte Nuovo, even though it had been built two hundred years before.

A lesser spy might have lost the Nucci on the bridge, with its crush of people, its butchers' shops and fishmongers and chandlers. But not Sandro. He had guessed where his quarry was headed, anyway – the half-built palazzo on the other side of the river. The Nucci family, the only one anywhere near close enough in wealth to rival the di Chimici, had started building their grand palazzo five years before and it was still not finished.

But, if it ever was, it would be much bigger than the Ducal palazzo on this side of the river, and that bothered Sandro; he was a di Chimici man through and through. It stood to reason that his masters must have the best, the biggest and the grandest of everything. Take the coming weddings; weren't the young princes and their cousins to be married in the great cathedral by the Pope himself, their uncle Ferdinando, who was coming specially from Remora to conduct the most lavish ceremony the city had ever seen?

Camillo Nucci had reached the walls of his father's palazzo-to-be and was talking to his father and brothers. Sandro saw to his surprise that the second storey was nearly complete; it wouldn't be long before the Nucci palace was finished after all. But why was young Camillo making such a mystery of his evening stroll, since he was joined only by other members of his family? Nothing remarkable about that. But Sandro followed them into a nearby tavern anyway.

And was rewarded by seeing them joined by a couple of very disreputable-looking men. He couldn't get near enough to hear their talk, unfortunately, but he memorised every detail of their appearance to tell the Eel. His master was sure to be interested.

'Do you think this was left for you?' Sky asked his mother when he had unpacked the shopping for her.

Rosalind was looking tired again now and had flopped down on the sofa, kicking her shoes off as soon as she had got in. She looked at the little bottle in his hand.

'No idea,' she said. 'It's pretty though, isn't it?'

'But empty,' said Sky, still puzzled. 'Shall I put it with your other bottles?'

'No, it would outclass all my plastic refillables,' said Rosalind. 'Just put it on the mantelpiece – unless you want it?'

Sky hesitated. It seemed a girly thing to want a blue perfume bottle in his room, but the little phial seemed to speak to him in some way he didn't understand.

'OK,' he said, putting it temporarily on the living-room mantelpiece. 'What shall I cook tonight?'

'How about spag bol?' suggested his mother. 'That's nice and easy and we can eat it on our laps. It's *ER* tonight.'

Sky grinned. His mother loved hospital dramas but always closed her eyes during the gory scenes and operations. You would have thought she'd have had enough of doctors and nurses, but she lapped it all up.

He went away to chop onions and peppers. Later, after they had eaten and Rosalind had seen even less of *ER* than usual, because it had involved a multiple road traffic accident, Sky carried her to bed. She was very light, he realised, and she had fallen asleep before he had time to help her into her nightdress or to clean her teeth.

But Sky didn't have the heart to wake her; he left her on the bed and went to do the rest of his homework. Then he washed up, put out the wheelie bin, folded the dry washing for ironing the next day, changed the cat litter, hung his damp jeans in the airing cupboard, locked up and eventually got into bed at half past eleven.

He was exhausted. How long can I carry on like this? he wondered. True, his mother had been much better that day but he knew from experience that she would be even more wiped out than usual the next day. He started to calculate the ratio of good to bad days she had had recently. Time, the doctor had said, but how long was enough time to make her well again?

If he looked ahead to the next few years, Sky could see nothing but difficulties. His mother wanted passionately for him to go to university and have the chances she had thrown away for herself, and he was just as keen. But how could he leave her, knowing that some days she wouldn't eat or be able to shower or even feed the cat? He envied other boys his age who could leave home in a year or two and go to Kathmandu if they wanted without worrying about their mothers. He'd probably have to settle for a college in London and living at home.

Remedy climbed on to Sky's chest to purr happily. He ruffled the cat's ears. 'Easy being you, isn't it?' he said. Then he remembered the bottle. Despite Remedy's protests, he got up again and fetched it from the living room. He lay in the dark, sniffing the wonderful scent that came from it and feeling strangely comforted. The cat had stalked off in protest; these were not the kind of smells he liked and there were far too many of them in the flat as it was – give him kipper any day.

I wonder where it can have come from? was Sky's last thought before drifting off into a deep sleep, the bottle in his hand.

When Sky woke, he was not in his bedroom but in somewhere that looked like a monk's cell. There was a cross on the whitewashed wall and a wooden prayer desk and he was lying on a sort of hard cot. The bottle was still in Sky's hand and the room was filled with the wonderful smell of flowers, but he knew it wasn't coming from the bottle.

He got up and cautiously opened the door. He found himself in a dark, wood-panelled room like a laboratory, filled with glass vessels like those used in chemistry lessons. But it didn't smell like a lab; it smelled like his mother's collection of essences, only much stronger. Light was coming from a door at the side of the room and Sky could see into an enclosed garden. People in robes were digging in the beds and tending plants. What a peculiar dream, he thought. There was a lovely atmosphere of calm and freedom from pressure.

He stepped out into the sunshine, blinking, still holding the bottle, and a black man, robed like the others, took him by the arm and whispered, 'God be praised, it has found you!'

This is where I wake up, thought Sky, but he didn't.

Instead the man pushed him back into the laboratory and hurried into his cell, bending over a wooden chest.

'Put this on,' he said to Sky. 'You must look like the other novices. Then you can tell me who you are.'

Chapter 2

The Hounds of God

Sky felt as if he were sleepwalking, as he let the monk, or whoever he was, throw a coarse white robe over his head and then a black cloak with a hood. Underneath he was wearing the T-shirt and shorts he had gone to bed in, an odd detail for a dream to include, he thought.

'That's better,' said the monk. 'Now you can walk with me round the cloisters and we can talk without anyone thinking it unusual. They'll just take you for a new novice.'

Sky said nothing, but followed his companion back out into the sunshine. They were in the enclosed garden he had seen from the open door. It was a square shape, surrounded by a sort of covered walk, like the ones you get in cathedrals and abbeys in England.

'I am Brother Sulien,' said the monk. 'And you are?'

'Sky.' He hesitated. 'Sky Meadows.'

It had always been an issue for him, his hippy-dippy name, as he thought of it. And it was even worse combined with his mother's surname; it made him sound like a kind of air freshener or fabric softener.

'Sky? That isn't a name we use here,' said Sulien, after considering it. 'The closest would be Celestino. You can be Celestino Pascoli.'

Can I really? thought Sky. What sort of game are we playing? But still he said nothing.

'You have the talisman?' asked Sulien, and Sky realised he was still holding the little glass bottle. He opened his fist. A strange feeling was beginning to creep over him that this was not exactly a dream, after all.

'Who are you?' Sky asked finally. 'I don't just mean your name.'

The monk nodded. 'I know what you mean. I am a Stravagante – we both are.'

'You and me?' Sky asked disbelievingly. He couldn't see how he and this mad monk, as he was beginning to think of him, could both be anything the same at all, except human beings and black.

'Yes, we are both part of a Brotherhood of scientists in Talia.' The friar stepped out into the garden, gesturing Sky to follow. 'Look behind you.'

Sky turned and saw nothing.

'What?' he asked, confused.

Sulien gestured to the ground and Sky saw with a shock that, although the friar's shadow stretched out behind him, black as his robe, at Sky's feet there was nothing.

'The talisman has brought you here from your

world, because there is something you can help us with,' continued Sulien.

'What, exactly?' asked Sky.

'Exactly what, we don't know,' said Sulien. 'But it will be dangerous.'

*

The night before, Sandro had stayed with his quarry until he was sure there was nothing more to be gained, then strolled back to his side of the river. A short walk through the great Piazza Ducale, where the government buildings were, brought him to the left flank of the cathedral. He felt more comfortable when he could see Santa Maria del Giglio; her bulk was reassuring and the little streets and piazzas snuggled up to her like kittens seeking the warmth of a mother cat.

Sandro felt himself to be one of those kittens; he was an orphan, who had grown up in the orphanage that stood in the lee of the cathedral. Clever as he was, and resourceful too, Sandro had never learned his letters or expected to enter any profession, so he had been delighted to be recruited by the Eel.

Now he could afford to throw a few small coins to the ragamuffins who played in the street outside the orphanage even at this late hour. He had been one of them not so long ago and it made his heart swell to think how far he had come.

He stopped in the little square where people played bowls; he had a ghoulish interest in it because of the horrible murder that had happened there a generation ago. One of the di Chimici had stabbed one of the

Nucci to death; that was all the boy knew, but it fascinated him. He imagined the blood staining the paving-stones and the cries of 'Help!' as the young nobleman bled to death under the flickering torches of the piazza. Santa Maria had not been able to protect him. Sandro shuddered enjoyably.

He walked on past shops and taverns selling all kinds of delicious-smelling food and drink, feeling secure in the knowledge that he would get supper. He cut up the Via Larga, the broad street leading away from the cathedral towards the di Chimici palace. The Eel didn't live there, of course; Duke Niccolò was too canny for that. But he wasn't far away, either. He lodged close enough to the Duke to be with him in minutes if sent for.

*

'Why don't I have a shadow if we are both Strav . . . what you said?' asked Sky. 'You seem to have one.'

'I have a shadow because I am in my home world,' said Brother Sulien. 'When I stravagate to yours, as I did to bring the talisman, I am without one, just as you are here.'

Sky was beginning to understand that he had travelled in space, and almost certainly in time, but he still couldn't quite believe it. Brother Sulien explained that they were in a great city called Giglia, in the country of Talia, but it looked to Sky as he imagined Italy to be. He couldn't speak Italian, yet he understood what Sulien was saying to him – at least he understood the words; the meaning was still impenetrable.

'What do you mean by helping you?' he asked, trying another tack. 'What can I do?'

They had walked, slowly, all the way round the square cloisters, back to where they had begun, and stopped by the door into the laboratory. Again Sky felt overwhelmed by the scent coming from the room.

'What is this place?' he asked. 'Some sort of church, or what?'

Brother Sulien gestured to him to resume their walk. 'It is a friary – Saint-Mary-among-the-Vines. We have a church, certainly, a most beautiful one, which is reached through the Lesser Cloister, but also an infirmary and a pharmacy, of which I am the friar in charge.'

'Is that the same as a monk?' asked Sky. He felt very ignorant about all this. He had only ever been in churches with his mother, as a sightseer.

Sulien shrugged. 'More or less,' he said. 'It depends what order you belong to. We are Dominicans. "The Hounds of God", they call us. "Domini canes" is Talic for God's hounds.'

'And that laboratory?'

'Is where I prepare the medicines,' said Sulien. 'And the perfumes, of course.'

'Of course,' said Sky, ironically.

Brother Sulien gave him a quizzical look, but just then a bell started clanging in the tower above them and all the other friars, as Sky supposed they were, downed tools and set off towards an archway in the corner.

'Time for prayers,' said the friar. 'The Office of Terce, but today I shall miss it and take you out into the city. I want to show you something.'

The Eel was feeling pleased with himself. He had comfortable lodgings, ample pay and the best of everything to eat and drink. Most satisfactory of all, he had power. As the Duke's right-hand man, he felt himself to be only a heartbeat away from the very seat of government. And it could so easily have gone the other way; he had at one time feared that Duke Niccolò would dispose of him by having his throat cut, after that business in Remora. Instead he now wore velvet, in his favourite blue, and carried a hat with a curling plume in it, and kept a horse of his own in the Duke's stables.

In fact, the Eel did not cut as impressive a figure as he thought, being short and a bit skinny. But he was well pleased with his new life, especially his little crew of spies. He liked Giglia better even than Remora, and much better than Bellezza. In a very short time, he had memorised its streets and squares and alleys, particularly the alleys – the Eel was an alley kind of fellow, even if he aspired to boulevards and avenues. You couldn't skulk in an avenue and skulking was his forte.

*

Brother Sulien led Sky through an archway in the corner of the Great Cloister into a smaller one and then in through a door into the church. Up at the far end Sky could see quite a number of black-robed friars on their knees and could hear the low murmur of voices. His eyes scarcely had time to adapt to the gloom inside the church before they were out in the sunshine again, under a clear blue sky.

Sky inhaled deeply and looked around him. The church fronted on to a large square, at either end of which stood a strange wooden post in the shape of an elongated pyramid. There were no cars or buses or motorbikes, but across the square there was a jumble of poor-looking houses and shops and then, every block or two, a noble building standing impressive among its surroundings like a racehorse in a field of knackered nags. Definitely the past, thought Sky. Then there was the dazzling sunshine which brought a warmth unknown in an English March, sunny though they could be. Definitely Italy, he thought.

They walked briskly along a street whose gutters were overflowing with debris, and Sky couldn't help noticing an unhealthy smell of rotten vegetables and worse. Two young men rode past; they were evidently noblemen, since everyone got out of their way and they paid no attention to their route but chatted to one another oblivious of the people scattering before their horses' hoofs. Sky saw they both wore long shining swords dangling from their belts and remembered what Sulien had said about danger.

A short walk brought them to a halt in front of what was the biggest building Sky had ever seen. It was familiar to him though, from art lessons at school.

'This is Florence, isn't it?' he said, pleased to have recognised where he was.

'I believe you do call it something like that, but for us it is Giglia,' corrected Sulien patiently. 'The City of Flowers, we call her, because of the meadows around that bring her such wealth. Her and the di Chimici,' he added, lowering his voice. Then, more naturally, he continued, 'It could as easily be called the City of Wool, since almost as much of her wealth comes from sheep, but that's much less pretty, don't you think?'

This is like *Alice in Wonderland*, thought Sky. There seems to be logic in it but it doesn't quite hang together.

'And this is the best flower of all,' said Sulien, gazing up at the bulk of the cathedral. 'Even if my heart lies among the vines, I must admire Santa Maria del Giglio – Saint-Mary-of-the-Lily.'

The walls of the cathedral were clad in white marble, with strips of green and pink marble in geometric patterns; Sky thought it looked like Neapolitan ice cream but sensed it would be unwise to say so. Though he noticed that the front was unfinished, just rough stone. A slender bell-tower in the same colours rose beside it, and the whole was dominated by a vast terracotta dome, encircled by smaller ones.

'In this cathedral in eight weeks' time,' Sulien continued, 'three di Chimici princes and a duke will marry their cousins. Now let me show you something else.'

He walked Sky round to a little piazza where people were playing bowls. 'In that square,' said Sulien, 'twenty-five years ago, a member of the di Chimici clan stabbed to death a young noble of the Nucci family.'

'Why?' asked Sky.

'Because of an insult to the di Chimici over a marriage arranged between the two families. Donato

Nucci was to marry Princess Eleanora di Chimici – a fine match for him, but he was twenty and she was thirty-one. And perhaps not one of the most beautiful of her kin, though intelligent, pious and accomplished. On the day of the wedding young Donato sent a messenger to say he was indisposed. Indisposed to marry Eleanora, as it turned out, for he was also in negotiations with another family and another, younger, bride.'

'Poor Eleanora,' said Sky.

'And poor Donato,' said Sulien grimly. 'He had the gall to show himself at a game of bowls the next evening and Eleanora's younger brother, Jacopo, stabbed him in the heart.'

'What happened to Jacopo?'

'He left the city. He had only come to Giglia for the wedding; his family lived in Fortezza, another great city of Tuschia, where his father Falco was Prince. The next year old Prince Falco died and Jacopo inherited the title. Some say the old Prince was poisoned by the Nucci, but he was a good age.'

'And what happened to Eleanora – and Donato's other girl?'

'No one knows what happened to the other girl. Eleanora di Chimici took the veil and so did her younger sister. Jacopo himself married – and had two daughters, one of whom is going to marry Prince Carlo di Chimici here in a few weeks. The other will marry her cousin Alfonso di Chimici, Duke of Volana.'

Sky was beginning to see, among this muddle of names and titles, a pattern emerging.

'Is this Jacopo still alive?' he asked.

Sulien nodded. 'He will give his daughter away to the second son of this city's Duke.'

'And the Nucci lot?'

'Will be invited, of course. They are still one of the great families of Giglia.'

'Phew,' said Sky. 'Could be pretty explosive. But I really don't see why you are telling me all this.'

'Come,' said Sulien, 'a little further.'

They skirted the back of the cathedral. Among the buildings behind it was a busy, noisy workshop, ringing with the sound of chisel on stone. Sulien stopped and looked both ways.

'This is the bottega of Giuditta Miele, the sculptor,' he said. 'She is another one of us Stravaganti. And her next commission is to make a statue of the beautiful Duchessa of Bellezza, who is coming here for the di Chimici weddings.'

'Sorry,' said Sky. 'I still don't see . . .'

'The Duchessa was supposed to marry Gaetano di Chimici, the third prince. Supposed by Duke Niccolò, that is. She refused him, some think because she was too attached to a young man who was her father's apprentice. Her father is Rodolfo Rossi, the Regent of Bellezza, one of the most powerful Stravaganti in Talia. And the young man, his apprentice, did her mother, the late Duchessa, great service, and is now an honoured citizen of Bellezza, but it wasn't always so.'

'No?' asked Sky, because it seemed expected.

'No,' said Sulien. 'He was once from your world, and I think you probably know of him.'

*

Gaetano di Chimici stood in the loggia of the Piazza Ducale and everywhere he looked he saw evidence of his family's influence on the city he loved. They had built the palace that housed the seat of government, with its tower that dominated the square, they had placed the statues commemorating victories of the weak over the strong, and they had built the Guild offices, with their workshops underneath, where silversmiths and workers in semi-precious stones plied their crafts along with the less important goldsmiths.

All over the city, poor housing was being pulled down and replaced with grand buildings, columns, squares and statues. And all this was the work of his father, carrying on the tradition of his ancestors, and part of Gaetano could not help feeling proud. But he also knew how much blood stained the family's omnipresent crest of the perfume bottle and the lily, in pursuit of acquiring land and showing themselves superior to the Nucci and other feuding families of the city. And what he didn't know, he could guess.

Why, even old Jacopo, the kindest and sweetest of Niccolò's cousins, had committed a murder only a few streets away from here! Uncle Jacopo, as they called him, who had fed all the little princes sweetmeats with his own fingers and wept like a baby when his favourite hound died. Not for the first time, Gaetano wished he had been born into a family of shepherds or gardeners.

Then he and Francesca could have got up early one morning and made their vows in a country church, decorated with rosebuds. He smiled at the thought of his beautiful cousin, the love of his life, clad in a homespun dress with flowers in her hair. How different from their forthcoming marriage in the vast cathedral, which would be followed by a grand procession and surrounded by dangers in spite of all the finery of silks and brocades and silver and diamonds.

Gaetano decided to walk towards Saint-Mary-among-the-Vines and look up the friar who his friend Luciano had told him was a Stravagante, like Luciano himself and his master, Rodolfo. Unlike his own father, Gaetano was not an enemy of the Stravaganti; in fact he thought they were probably the only people who could stave off the disaster he could feel brewing.

'Lucien Mulholland?' said Sky, disbelievingly. 'But he died – about two and a half years ago. He can't be here in your city.'

'Not yet,' said Sulien. 'He lives in Bellezza. But he will accompany the Duchessa to the weddings. You will meet him. And find he is very much alive, in Talia.'

Sky sat down on a low wall. He remembered Lucien – a slim boy with black curls, two years above him at school. He vaguely remembered that Lucien was good at swimming and was also musical, but that was about it. He hadn't known him well, and when the head teacher had told the whole school in assembly one morning that Lucien had died, Sky had felt only that shock that everyone feels when death comes to someone young and familiar.

But now he was being asked to believe that this person was not dead at all but living in another world, somewhere in the past, and that he, Sky, was going to meet him. It was too far-fetched for words.

Looking around him, he noticed that he and Sulien were not the only black inhabitants of Giglia. There were not many others but there were some, which struck him as odd, if this was a sort of Italy, goodness knows how long ago. Although Sky was taking history AS, he realised that he had only the vaguest of ideas about life in Renaissance Italy. And then had to remind himself that this wasn't Italy at all. But he was glad not to attract any strange looks, except from a rather scruffy boy lounging apparently aimlessly round the food stalls.

The boy caught his eye and made his way towards Sky and Sulien.

'Hello, Brothers,' he said.

Sky knew it was because of his robes that the boy called him that, but it made him jump all the same.

'Sandro,' said the boy, nodding at Sulien and sticking out his hand towards Sky.

'Celestino,' said Sky, remembering his new name.

'Brother Celestino,' said Sandro, with a sideways glance at Sulien. 'You're new here, aren't you?'

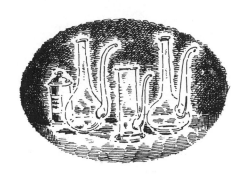

Chapter 3

Brothers

Sulien knew the Eel's boy and he hesitated about
letting his new visitor spend time with him. But the
friar couldn't continue to neglect his work at the
Farmacia and it was essential for Sky to learn his way
about the city.

'Brother Celestino is newly arrived from Anglia,' he
told the younger boy. 'He is a stranger to Giglia –
indeed he has never been to Talia before. Perhaps you
would like to show him around?' He pulled Sky to
one side and whispered, 'I have to get back. Let
Sandro teach you about the city – no one knows it
better than him, but tell him nothing of what I have
said to you, particularly about the Stravaganti – he
works for the di Chimici. And keep out of the full sun
– you can always say it's too hot for you after chilly

Anglia. When you want to leave, get him to direct you back to Saint-Mary-among-the-Vines. You must go back home without fail before sunset. The talisman will take you if you hold it while falling asleep anywhere in the city, but it's best to come and go from my cell.'

'Come and go?' whispered Sky. 'So I am coming back again?'

'Certainly,' said Sulien quietly. 'That's what Stravaganti do – travel between worlds and do what is required of them in both.'

Sky had the strangest feeling that this friar was not so mad after all and that he knew all about his life in the other world. Brother Sulien slipped off round the side of the cathedral, waving to the two boys, and Sandro, who had been cleaning his nails with an alarming-looking dagger, gave Sky a big grin.

'Ready, Brother?' he asked. 'There's plenty to see.'

And so Sky found himself being shown round Giglia by Sandro. The boy had asked no questions, except for Sky's name and if he was attached to Sulien's friary. And those Sky could just about manage to answer, though it was odd to think of himself as Celestino – or Brother Tino, as Sandro began to call him, a novice from Saint-Mary-among-the-Vines. It was like taking a part in a play or a role-playing game.

Sandro was much more interested in telling than asking. He loved explaining his city to someone so ignorant, especially someone older than him.

'This is one of the grandest streets in Giglia,' he said at the end of their wanderings, taking Sky up the Via Larga some hours later. 'The Duke has his palace just up here and my master lodges not far away.'

'What do you do?' asked Sky, amazed that someone so young could have a job; perhaps he was an apprentice of some kind? Or perhaps boys in this time – he still had no idea when it was and only the haziest idea about where – went to work much younger? He had assumed that Sandro was only about fourteen.

But Sandro just tapped the side of his nose mysteriously and said, 'What you don't know can't hurt you. Maybe I'll tell you one day when we know each other better.'

He insisted on treating Sky like a big simpleton, more naïve than himself. Sky felt his mouth curving in a smile; it was how he imagined having a little brother might be.

'Here it is,' said Sandro proudly. 'The Palazzo di Chimici. Where Duke Niccolò lives when he is in Giglia.'

Sky saw a magnificent building, much bigger than the others around it, taking up an entire block of the street. A grand pair of iron gates inside an arch allowed the two boys to look into the huge courtyard beyond. A fountain played in the middle of geometrically arranged flower beds, separated by what looked like patterned marble slabs.

'Hey there, young Sparrow,' said a voice from behind them, and an absurdly overdressed little man attempted to put his arms across both their shoulders. It was easy enough to manage with Sandro but Sky was a head taller than him and the man had to stretch to reach.

He was wearing a blue velvet suit with a lace collar and a hat with a curling feather, and Sky couldn't help noticing a powerful smell of stale sweat.

Prince Gaetano entered the gate to the Lesser Cloister of Saint-Mary-among-the-Vines; he had always liked this Dominican friary. It was here that his family's great fortune had begun, when they backed the researches into distilling perfume from flowers and gained their surname of di Chimici, meaning Chemists. But he hadn't been here recently, not since the arrival of Brother Sulien as Pharmacist and Senior Friar.

Gaetano recognised Sulien from Luciano's description. He was supervising the delivery of cartloads of hothouse irises at the back door of the Great Cloister. But he stopped and came over as soon as he saw the young prince.

'Welcome, your Highness,' he said. 'I have been expecting you.'

*

The guard at the gates of the di Chimici palace knew the Eel well and let him in with his two companions, even though a scruffy boy and a young novice were hardly likely visitors for the Duke. But the Eel was not on his way to see the Duke – not yet. He wanted to show off in front of his young apprentice and his new friend.

'Come along, Sparrow,' he said, leading the two boys into another, larger courtyard, where a bronze statue of a naked Mercury with a sword stood guard over some very elaborate flower beds. 'Who is your friend?'

'Brother Tino,' said Sandro. 'He's new. He lives up at Saint-Mary-among-the-Vines.

'Really?' said the Eel, with an unctuous grin. He was genuinely interested. That Dominican friary was one of the few places where he didn't have a spy planted and he wondered if this rather simple-seeming novice might be useful as a source of information. 'Let me introduce myself,' he said, extending a none too clean hand from his blue velvet sleeve. 'Enrico Poggi, confidential agent of Duke Niccolò di Chimici, ruler of the city of Giglia, at your service!'

Sky accepted the handshake but felt wary; this employer of Sandro's didn't seem like the sort of person a duke would have much to do with and Sky instinctively didn't trust him. But things might be different in this other world he found himself in and he was still learning the ropes.

As if summoned up by his name, a richly dressed old man walked out from under an arch, into the courtyard, deep in conversation with a less aristocratic person carrying an armful of what looked like plans. A closer look showed Sky that the nobleman wasn't as old as he first thought; he had completely white hair but his face wasn't lined. In fact he was rather handsome in a slightly spooky way.

The Duke, for it was obviously him, stopped when he saw the three intruders. He dismissed the man he had been talking to, with, 'Come back tomorrow morning with the revised drawings,' and beckoned Enrico to him.

The Eel slithered across the courtyard, bowing and smiling. Sky could see at once that the Duke regarded the man with contempt. He might be content to use him but Sky doubted very much that Enrico had more of Duke Niccolò's confidence than he thought fit to show him. Sandro had made himself invisible, in the way he had of blending in with the background. He now slouched against a column, half-concealed in the shadows.

Suddenly Sky knew exactly what Sandro did for his unprepossessing master: he was a spy!

The Duke was looking straight at Sky now, who felt very exposed and wished he had as good a gift of disguise as his new friend. He was glad that he was standing in the shade. Enrico beckoned him over. And a small cloud drifted across the sun.

'Brother Tino, my Lord,' said Enrico, presenting Sky to the Duke, like a dog offering his master a share in a particularly precious and revolting bone. 'As I said, he is based over in your Grace's old family church among the vines.'

The Duke extended a long-fingered hand, ringed with silver and rubies, and Sky went to take it, as he had Enrico's a minute before. But a small gesture from the spymaster indicated he must kiss it not shake it.

'Indeed,' said Duke Niccolò. 'It is some time since I visited there. Perhaps you, Tino – short for Celestino, is it? – would convey my respects to your Senior Friar. Who is it nowadays?'

Sky got the feeling that this vagueness was put on and that the Duke was well aware who was in charge of every institution of the city. Which was more than Sky himself was.

'I-I work with Brother Sulien, in . . . in the pharmacy,' he stammered, glad that his colouring was not susceptible to blushing.

Duke Niccolò looked hard into his face. 'Mmm. I have heard something of that friar. Perhaps I shall pay him a visit myself soon. The pharmacy of course I am familiar with. It supplies me with perfume and pomades . . . among other things.' The Duke smiled slightly, as if remembering past triumphs. Then, 'Do make your acquaintance with my palace. We have some rather fine frescoes in the chapel that would interest one of your calling. Now, if you'll excuse us, I have some business with Poggi here.'

He waved an elegant hand in a gesture that was obviously dismissal, taking in Sandro as well – so he had noticed him, Sky realised – and moved off with Enrico.

'What a piece of luck!' said the boy softly as Duke and spymaster walked into the palace in deep conference. Sky couldn't help noticing that the nobleman kept widening the distance between himself and the man in the blue velvet suit, while Enrico kept sidling up closer again.

'Luck?'

'Yes. We've more or less got his Grace's permission to snoop about his palace! He wouldn't have said that if I'd been here on my own.' Sandro was thinking how useful it was to have such a respectable companion as a novice friar. 'He's wonderful, isn't he?' he added.

'The Duke?'

'No, the Eel,' said Sandro impatiently. The Duke was so far out of his sphere that he registered him only like a piece of fine architecture; he was much better equipped to appreciate a man like Enrico. Sandro hoped that his father had been a man like that. 'Let's go,' he said now, eager to take advantage of this unusual opportunity.

The boys walked through the courtyard and Sky noticed that the paving-stones between the flower beds all carried the symbol of the lily, in its elaborate fleur-de-lys form, like the stopper to his bottle. He asked Sandro about it.

'It's the symbol of the city,' he answered. 'Giglia means City of the Lily. And the di Chimici have it on their family crest too, with the shape of a perfume bottle.'

The palazzo had what looked like its own little cemetery, dominated by a recent white marble tomb. It was topped by the statue of a young boy and his dog. Sky stopped to look at it; there was something familiar about the boy.

'That's Prince Falco,' said Sandro. 'The Duke's youngest.'

'What happened to him?' asked Sky.

'Poisoned himself,' said Sandro dramatically. 'Couldn't bear the pain any longer. He was all smashed up after an accident with a horse.'

They were both silent for a moment while Sky thought about being in so much pain you would want to kill yourself and Sandro planned how to use their permission to roam the palazzo.

On the far side of the courtyard was a broad flight of stone steps, which the boys climbed. At the top was a heavy dark wooden door, which Sandro pushed cautiously open. They found themselves in a small chapel, where two tall candles burned in even taller candlesticks on the altar. But what made both boys gasp was the paintings which covered three walls.

They were rich with silver and, looking closely, Sky

could see that some of the figures had real jewels embedded in their elaborate hats. The paintings showed a long winding procession of men, horses and dogs against a background of, he supposed, Talian countryside. Deer and rabbits and other small animals were pursued through bushes by some of the hunting dogs, and birds perched on branches, oblivious of whatever the humans were doing. At the head of the procession were three figures even more grandly dressed than the rest, with crowns instead of hats.

Something bothered Sky about it; it was familiar but somehow different. Then he realised; the painting it reminded him of had gold wherever these frescoes had silver. Sandro was up close and Sky saw to his horror that he was trying to prise a small ruby from the hat of one of the minor figures in the procession.

'Stop that at once,' he said sharply and the boy looked up, startled.

'You can't go nicking bits off a great work of art,' Sky explained.

Sandro was surprised; he didn't see it as a work of art, just a collection of coloured paints and valuable jewels, some of which would never be missed. But he realised that Tino, as a friar, might see things differently. He sheathed his dagger and shrugged. 'If you say so.'

'I do,' said Sky. 'Look how beautiful it is. But why is it silver?'

Sandro really thought Sky must be a bit touched in the head.

'Because silver's the most precious metal,' he explained patiently, as if to a child.

'More than gold?' asked Sky.

'Course,' said Sandro. 'Gold goes black – gets the *morte d'oro*. Silver just keeps on shining.' He gave one of the candlesticks on the altar a bit of a rub with his cuff. 'Nah, you keep gold for a knick-knack to give your lady love if you're not really serious about her. Silver's only for the likes of the di Chimici.'

Sandro's words made Sky think about the quiet fair-haired girl at his school. What would Alice Greaves say to a gold bracelet brought back from Talia? He didn't think she'd see it as a trinket. Then he remembered he didn't have any money here and didn't even know what currency they used. He shook his head. The small dark chapel, with its lingering scent of incense, was beginning to feel stuffy. He wanted to get out into the fresh air again. Suddenly he panicked. How long had he been roaming the city with Sandro? A gnawing feeling in his stomach told him it must be getting late. He didn't want to miss the sunset.

Sky looked at his wrist but of course his watch was on his bedside table at home. He looked up and saw Sandro regarding him with his head on one side. With his bright, alert eyes, he did look a bit like a sparrow.

'What time is it?' Sky asked, feeling really alarmed. 'I must be getting back to the friary.'

'Oh yeah, you brothers have to say your prayers every few hours, don't you?' said Sandro. 'You've probably missed some already. Do you want me to take you back?'

*

Gaetano had spent several happy hours helping Sulien in his laboratory. The young di Chimici prince was attending the university in Giglia and was interested in all new branches of learning. But he hadn't been in a laboratory for a long time and was fascinated to see how the friars distilled perfume from flowers. It would take many cartloads of irises to produce a tiny phial of the flower's intense yet delicate perfume. And Sulien was easy to work with, calm and authoritative. Gaetano fell into the rhythm of the laboratory without even noticing.

He looked at tall glass bottles containing cologne, with labels like frangipani, pomegranate, silver musk, vetiver and orange blossom. Then there were pure essences like amber and jasmine, lily-of-the-valley and violet. There was almond paste for the hands, Vinegar of the Seven Thieves for ladies' fainting fits, Russian cologne for men's beards and almond soap. There was tincture of white birch and hawkweed, infusions of fennel and mallow and lime blossom, liqueurs and compounds of willow and hawthorn.

Cupboard after cupboard full of jars of lotions and glass bottles of jewel-like coloured liquids. No wonder the place smelt like heaven! But Gaetano knew that somewhere in the friary was another, secret, laboratory, where herbs were brewed that were not so healthy – his family's source of poisons.

But for now he tried to forget about that and to lend a hand stirring and measuring and mixing and adjusting flames under glass alembics like any other apprentice. Gaetano was the only one helping Sulien; the usual novice helpers had been dismissed so that the two of them could discuss the real reason for the prince's visit.

'Luciano told me where to find you,' he said,

steadily pouring a clear green liquid from one container to another.

'And how is he?' asked Sulien. He had brought his recipe manuscript into the laboratory and was carefully recording what they were doing to make infusion of mint. 'I know Rodolfo is worried about his coming anywhere near your father the Duke.'

Gaetano sighed, concentrating hard on his task. 'My father has his reasons for not trusting Luciano too. Do you know what really happened to my brother Falco?' he asked.

Sulien nodded. 'Doctor Dethridge told me,' he said. 'He was translated, like him, but to the other world.'

'Where he lives and thrives, as far as we know,' said Gaetano. 'I miss him terribly, but it was his decision. He wanted passionately to be healed by their medicine and be whole again.'

The two of them were silent over their tasks for a while, Gaetano remembering the last time he had seen his youngest brother, miraculously grown tall and straight again, riding a flying horse in Remora. His father had sat beside him, white and rigid at what other spectators took for an apparition of the dead prince. Duke Niccolò, in his ceremonial armour, had vowed vengeance on the Stravaganti but he had not moved quickly. Gaetano wondered whether the wedding invitation to Arianna was partly a ruse to bring Luciano to Giglia.

Sulien had been thoughtful too. He knew this young sprig of the Duke's family only by reputation, but he seemed quite unlike his father and his proud brothers. He was aware that Gaetano knew about the Stravaganti, had been on friendly terms with several of them, and would not betray their secrets to the Duke. And he was handy with tongs and glass vessels, something that made a good impression on the friar.

Brother Sulien came to a decision. 'I must tell you,' he said, 'that I have today been visited by a new Stravagante from the other world.'

Gaetano put down the vessel he was holding very carefully on the wooden bench. 'But that is fantastic!' he said, trying hard to contain his excitement. 'Where is he now? Has he gone back?'

'No,' said Sulien, getting up from his stool and walking over to the door into the cloister, to assess the quality of the light. 'He should be here soon. I told him he must go back before sunset.'

As if on cue, a flustered young man in a novice's robes burst into the room from the inner door. Gaetano thought him remarkable-looking with his skin like chestnuts and his long hair like golden-brown catkins.

'I hope I'm not too late,' said Sky, casting an anxious look in the direction of Sulien's visitor. 'I lost track of time in the Duke's chapel.'

'Ah, that is easily done,' said Gaetano, smiling. 'It has happened to me often.'

Sky looked at him properly. He was clearly a noble, dressed in fine clothes and wearing silver rings. But, if it had not been for his clothes, he would have seemed rather plain. He had a big nose and a very big crooked mouth. He reminded Sky of someone he had seen recently. And then he remembered. One of the kings with a silver crown in the chapel fresco had looked like that.

'Let me present myself,' said the young man. 'I am

Prince Gaetano di Chimici, youngest surviving son of Duke Niccolò. And if you have been looking at the frescoes in my father's chapel, you have seen a likeness of my grandfather, Alfonso. I am supposed to look rather like him.' And he made Sky a deep bow.

Handsome he might not be, but he seemed so warm and friendly, and not a bit conceited, that Sky liked him immediately. He glanced towards Sulien as he replied, 'And I am Tino – Celestino Pascoli. I come from Anglia.' And he tried to copy the prince's graceful bow.

'It's all right, Sky,' said Sulien. 'Prince Gaetano knows you are from a lot further away than that. In spite of his father, he is a good friend to us Stravaganti.'

'Indeed,' said Gaetano eagerly. 'Do you come from the same place as Luciano? Or Georgia? Perhaps you know my brother, Falco?'

A strange feeling was creeping over Sky. 'Georgia who?' he asked.

Gaetano thought for a bit. 'When she was here – well, not here in this city, but in Remora – she acted as a boy and was known as Giorgio Gredi. I don't know what her real surname was.'

'I think I do,' said Sky slowly. 'You must mean Georgia O'Grady. She goes to the same school as me.'

His head was spinning. Georgia O'Grady was Alice's fierce friend, the girl with the red hair and tattoo.

'But if you know Georgia then you must know Falco!' said Gaetano, his eyes shining. He came round the bench to grasp Sky by both arms. 'A beautiful boy, not like me. A boy with curly black hair, a fine horseman and fencer . . .' His voice broke. 'He is my little brother,' he went on, 'and I shall probably never see him again. Please, if you know anything of him, tell me.'

It had been the talk of the school at one time, Sky remembered, the friendship between Georgia and the boy who fitted that description. There had been all sorts of rumours, because Georgia was in the sixth form and the boy was only in Year 10, two years younger than her. Such things were not unheard of, but it was still unusual. Still, both of them had shrugged off all comment and remained friends.

Now Sky said, 'There is a boy like that, Georgia's close friend, but he isn't called what you said. His name is Nicholas Duke.'

The image of the marble boy with the dog floated into Sky's mind, even as he said it, and he felt the world turning upside down. It was like trying to walk up an Escher staircase and finding you were going downwards, and it gave him vertigo. But Sky knew that the boy he thought of as Nicholas could be this nice, ugly prince's lost brother. But if he was, what on earth was he doing at Barnsbury Comprehensive? Then he remembered something else he knew about Nicholas. He lived with the parents of the Lucien who had died – or who was now living in Talia.

Sky felt two pairs of strong arms catch him as his knees gave way and he sank on to the bench.

'Time to go home, I think,' said Sulien. 'That's quite enough for one visit.'

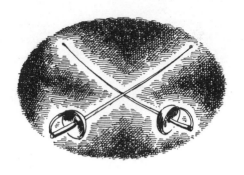

Chapter 4

Secrets

Rosalind had to shake Sky to wake him up the next morning. Normally he was first up, leaping out of bed as soon as the alarm went off and heading straight for the shower before he was really awake. But today he looked at her as if he had no idea who she was, sleep still fuzzing his brain.

'Come on, lovely boy,' she said. 'I know we live right next door to school, but you'll still have to hurry. It's quarter past eight already!'

'Mum!' said Sky, finally dragging his mind away from Giglia in the past and back to the present of his life in Islington.

'Who else?' said Rosalind, smiling. He registered that she was looking well again. That was two days in a row.

'You should have woken me sooner,' he said reproachfully, though it was himself he was cross with. 'I can't just go off to school and leave you with all the chores.'

'What chores?' said his mother. 'There's nothing urgent. Breakfast is made – you just have a quick shower and then come and eat. Everything's under control.'

Under the hot jet of the shower, Sky thought about this. It seemed to him that everything he had taken for granted about his daily life was spiralling wildly out of control. If what Sulien and Gaetano told him was true, he was a traveller in time and space, not an ordinary twenty-first-century boy with a sick mother.

The girl he fancied – yes, he acknowledged it now – was best friends with another such sci-fi traveller, whose other closest friend was a dead prince from centuries ago. And that prince seemed to have changed places with another school student who now lived in a world of magicians and duchesses, silver and treason.

He shook the water off his thick locks. He was going to have to go to school knowing that neither Georgia nor Nicholas was what they seemed. This was a much bigger secret than having a rock star for a father. But Sky had already promised to take messages between Gaetano and Nicholas; he hadn't been able to say no when he saw how moved the Giglian prince had been by the loss of his brother.

It was what everyone who had ever lost anyone to death wanted, Sky supposed. To believe that they were in a better world – and that it might still be possible to communicate with them.

Sandro was well pleased with his new friendship. A friar, even a novice one, was a perfect cover for nefarious deeds and Sandro had seen straightaway how useful Sky could be. But it was more than that; he liked the tall brown boy, so interested in everything he was told and so innocent about how things worked in Giglia. Sandro loved knowing more than someone else and telling them about it. The new friar was like a newborn lamb when wolves were about in a place like the City of Flowers. And then, secretly, he had the added satisfaction that, as a friar, Sky must know all sorts of things that he, Sandro, didn't – like all that book-learning clerics had to have.

Sandro had never had a brother, as far as he knew, but he had imagined lots of family for himself – a father like the Eel, a mother like the Madonna, a big brother to protect him and a little one to boss about. Now he felt he had found both brothers in Sky.

'Never thought he'd be a Moor, though,' Sandro said to himself. 'I wonder what the real story is there? The Eel is interested in Sulien. Maybe this Tino is the result of some secret scandal of his?'

He resolved to look into it. But not necessarily to tell his master. After all, he had always been well treated by Brother Sulien, who had more than once taken him into the kitchens at Saint-Mary-among-the-Vines and fed him, in the days before he was the Eel's man. And as for Tino, Sandro felt protective of any secret that might concern him. Even after one meeting, the strange Anglian was definitely his friend. And

Sandro had never had a friend before.

Nicholas Duke was the school fencing champion. He was legendary in Barnsbury Comprehensive, having arrived at the beginning of Year 9 with a twisted leg and able to walk only with crutches. Several operations, months of physiotherapy and a punishing training programme in the gym had resulted in a growth spurt, an athletic frame and a grace of movement that would have been unbelievable a year and a half ago.

Nicholas had been a bit of a mystery. He had been found abandoned, apparently having lost his memory. But he was clever and was soon in the top group for maths, French and English literature. Science and ICT were not his forte but he was picking them up well enough. And he was good at art and music. But the real surprise was that, as soon as he could balance and walk without crutches, he joined the fencing club and proved to be as skilled as a professional.

'You must have done this before,' Mr Lovegrove, their fencing teacher, had said.

And Nicholas had grinned, delighted. 'I suppose I must,' was all he would say.

Nick Duke had almost single-handedly made fencing fashionable at Barnsbury. He was popular with girls because of his dreamy good looks, especially now he had added height to his lithe slim figure, angelic smile and black curly hair. They were pretty annoyed that he was so obviously smitten with a girl two years above him that none of them got a look-in.

He was popular with boys too; even those who might have bullied him because of his girlish looks were impressed by his rigorous fitness training and a bit alarmed by his skills with a foil. And Nicholas was beginning to put on muscle too – he was a fine horseman and went riding every weekend. By the time he was a sixth former he was going to be a dangerous person to tangle with, even when unarmed.

The fencing club had never had so many members, male and female. Soon the school had been able to enter a team, first in the local championships, and then in the regional ones, which they won. National achievement was the next aim, and Mr Lovegrove and Nicholas Duke were training the team almost equally between them.

Now Nicholas was in the school gym, before lunch, doing a hundred press-ups. In a rare lapse of concentration, he glanced towards the door and saw a brown face encircled with chestnut locks, looking through the glass panel. And then it was gone.

'I shall move to the Palazzo Ducale as soon as the wedding ceremonies have been performed,' said Duke Niccolò. He was addressing his three sons and his daughter in the magnificent salon of his family's palace on the Via Larga. 'And I shall take Beatrice with me, of course.'

His daughter made a little curtsey. She had not been allocated a husband in the recent spate of di Chimici engagements and she did not mind. She was still young, not yet twenty-one, and she knew her father needed her. Beatrice had felt even more tenderly towards him since the death of her little brother Falco the year before. So she smiled in acceptance of the Duke's plans for her.

'I have ordered the changes necessary to give Fabrizio and Caterina a wing of the Palazzo Ducale,' continued the Duke, nodding to the architect Gabassi, who was clutching his usual armful of plans.

'I trust that meets with your approval?' Niccolò said to Fabrizio, but it was a formality. No one in the room dreamt of raising any objection to their father's plans. The only di Chimici prince to defy him now lived in another world, though only his brother Gaetano knew that.

'Carlo and Gaetano will live here in the Palazzo di Chimici, of course,' said the Duke, inclining his head towards his second and third sons, 'with their wives Lucia and Francesca. It is a large enough palace in which to raise children, I think.'

The Duke was looking forward to his grandchildren, lots of them. He believed with all his heart that it was the destiny of his family to rule all Talia, and he wanted all twelve city-states secured by having their titles in family hands. Preferably in his lifetime, but if not, he wanted to know before he died that there was a good supply of di Chimici princelings and dukelets in waiting.

Fabrizio was content. To live in the Palazzo Ducale was fitting for a prince of his family and future. And he would have more opportunity to study his father's ways of doing things, feel more like the Duke-in-waiting. The palazzo in the Piazza Ducale had been commissioned and paid for by the di Chimici, but no member of the family had ever lived in it. It was the seat of Giglian politics, where the city Council met, but a very grand building and quite large enough to house a Duke and his heir. And it would help with achieving his father's political plans to be living right above the place where the laws were passed.

If Fabrizio was heir to Duke Niccolò's title and political ambition, Prince Carlo was his natural successor in financial acumen. The di Chimici had made their fortune initially from perfecting the art of distilling perfume, but over the years it had grown through their role as bankers to the great families of Talia and the crowned heads of Europe.

'And our business meetings, Father?' Carlo now asked.

'Will continue as normal,' said Niccolò. 'It does not matter whether here or in the Palazzo Ducale.'

Gaetano said nothing. There was, as far as he knew, no part for him in his father's plans. He had feared once that he would be forced into the Church and groomed to be the next Pope when his uncle Ferdinando died. But then Niccolò had ordered him to propose to the beautiful Duchessa of Bellezza. Arianna had turned him down but encouraged him to ask the woman he really loved, his cousin Francesca. Gaetano's father had raised no objections to their marriage, so presumably he had given up the idea of his third son as a celibate priest, but doubtless he had something in mind for the young prince; Niccolò had a plan for everyone.

Sky waited until quite late to go into lunch, once he had checked that Nicholas was in the gym. He knew that Alice always had lunch with Georgia and most days Nicholas joined them. Sky timed his entry into the cafeteria so that he was about three people behind the two girls and could see where they chose to sit. There was no sign of Nicholas yet, but he guessed they'd choose a table with room for at least a third person.

And he was in luck. When Georgia and Alice had settled on an empty table for four, Sky moved swiftly in and asked to sit with them. It didn't escape his notice that Alice coloured up as soon as he approached, but he had a different quarry today; it was Georgia he had to speak to. And he had to get her on her own.

Georgia was regarding him with hostility; she had noticed Alice's blush too. But she wasn't actually rude – just someone with no small talk, Sky realised. Overcome with shyness, Alice got up.

'I forgot I meant to pick up some fruit,' she said, escaping for the counter.

This was Sky's chance, now that he and Georgia were alone, but he had no idea how to begin. Should he say, 'I know you're a Stravagante. I'm one too'? Somehow in the very ordinary surroundings of Barnsbury Comp cafeteria, with people munching chips and slurping Coke, it seemed absurd.

And as he hesitated, they were joined by Nicholas Duke.

'Who's your friend?' Nicholas asked Georgia, pleasantly enough but with a confidence that irritated the older boy.

'Sky Meadows,' said Georgia tersely.

'Sky?' said Nicholas. 'Unusual name, isn't it?'

This was Sky's chance. 'Almost as rare as Falco,' he said quietly.

The effect on the other two was absolutely electrifying. Georgia's fork crashed on to her plate and Nicholas dropped his drink, splashing orange juice over the table.

Alice arrived with her apple to find them all mopping up the mess with paper napkins and thought immediately that there had been some sort of row. She sighed. She really liked Sky, and they were both so shy that this was the first time he had made any sort of approach to her. She had left him and Georgia on their own so that they would have to make some sort of conversation. Alice was never going to get anywhere with Sky unless Georgia could be made to accept him. But it looked as if Alice had made the wrong decision.

'What on earth did you say to him?' she whispered to Georgia.

'Nothing,' said Georgia, white-faced and tight-lipped. She had never thought to hear Falco's name again unless she or Nicholas uttered it in one of their many conversations about the past, so it had come at her like a bolt of lightning. Now all she could think of was how to get rid of dear, sweet Alice and find out what Sky knew.

In the Ducal palace of Bellezza, a much better feast than chips and Coke had been consumed. It was the last night of Carnival in that great city and the guests all wore their best clothes. Even outside in the square, the revellers, who had eaten their own feast, were brushing crumbs and wine splashes from dresses gorgeous with lace and velvet or cloaks and doublets of slashed silk. Both sets of partygoers wore masks, the men as well as the women, and all restraint was thrown aside for this last night of the week-long celebrations.

Inside the palazzo, the Duchessa and her court were preparing for the ball. The Duchessa herself, being still only seventeen, wore ivory silk and got away with it. Her mask of white peacock feathers was echoed by the same design on her skirt and bodice, with every eye of the bird's brilliant display embroidered in silver and sewn with diamonds.

She started the dancing with Senator Rodolfo, her father, in his usual black velvet. His black mask was in the shape of a hawk's head and beak and carried blue-black feathers of its own.

'You are very lovely tonight, my dear,' he said, expertly guiding her round the dance floor as more and more couples joined the whirling throng.

'Thank you,' she said, smiling. Arianna loved to dance, as she loved to run or shout or swim or scull a mandola through the water of the Bellezzan canals, but all the other occupations were almost memories. Only on grand occasions like the Carnival ball could she lose herself for a while in the sheer joy of physical action.

'I must soon give you up to a younger partner,' said Rodolfo, smiling too. 'You are too energetic for an old man like me.'

'Will you choose a staid old woman to dance with

instead?' asked Arianna, teasingly. She had already spotted her mother, in her midnight-blue dress, masked like a silver leopard, and knew where Rodolfo's feet would lead him next. Arianna was now used to the risks her supposedly dead mother took every time she exposed herself to recognition on occasions like this; she knew how incapable her parents were of staying apart for long, even though one lived as Regent in Bellezza and the other kept up an alias as a rich widow in Padavia.

Arianna's mother Silvia took the floor now with a slim young man, whose long black curls were tied back with a purple ribbon. He was a good dancer, almost as good as his partner, and she was quite out of breath by the time they moved near to Rodolfo and Arianna.

'Time for my staid old woman,' murmured Rodolfo, taking his secret wife in his arms and whirling her away.

They did not break the rhythm of the music for a moment, Luciano and Arianna, but danced together smoothly and effortlessly, as if used to holding one another.

'You last wore a mask like that in Remora,' Luciano said. 'When Georgia won the Stellata.'

'I'm surprised you remember,' said Arianna. 'You had eyes only for her at that time.'

'You were at the window of the Papal palace,' said Luciano, 'looking down into the Campo. But even a glimpse of you remains in my mind always.'

'You are becoming quite poetical,' she said, laughing.

She always does this, thought Luciano. Just when I

try to say something serious about how I feel, she always turns it aside with a joke. How can I ever get her to understand? But he was used to Arianna's moods and always took his tone from hers.

'I wonder what Georgia is doing now?' he said now, skilfully guiding the Duchessa through the dancing throng.

But Arianna was not jealous of the girl Stravagante tonight.

'I hope she's having as nice a time as we are,' was all she said.

'Meet you both outside the school gate at half past three,' hissed Georgia to Sky and Nicholas.

Somehow she was going to have to give Alice the slip; she couldn't wait any longer to find out what Sky knew about Nicholas and how he had come by the name of Falco.

Chapter 5

Marble for a Duchess

Rosalind Meadows was pleased and surprised when Sky let himself in with two friends in tow; she often worried that he didn't seem close to anyone in school. After making them all tea, she made an excuse and took herself out, leaving them the flat to themselves.

Georgia was looking round the living room and sniffing. 'This flat is brand new, isn't it?' she asked. 'It still smells of paint.'

'Yes,' said Sky. 'We moved in a few months ago.'

'Who lived here before?' she pursued. 'Was it all one house?'

Sky shrugged. 'Yes, but I don't know who lived here – some old lady who died, I think my mum said.'

'That's it!' said Georgia, turning to Nicholas. 'This

must be the house my horse came from! Mr Goldsmith said it came from the great-niece of an old lady who died in a house near the school.'

'And Luciano said his notebook came from there too,' said Nicholas.

Georgia looked at Sky for a long time, as if deciding just how much to trust him. 'Our school is on the site of William Dethridge's Elizabethan laboratory,' she said eventually. 'Or a part of the school and perhaps a part of this house. Whenever a Stravagante comes to England in our time, they seem to end up here. We think that's why two of us were found by the talismans.'

'Three,' said Sky quietly.

'I knew it!' exclaimed Nicholas, jumping up and pacing the small living room. 'Where do you go? And what is your talisman?'

Sky went into his room and came back with the perfume bottle. Georgia smiled when she saw the bubble-wrap. It brought back memories of her own stravagations. But Nicholas was beside himself when he saw the blue glass bottle.

'That's Giglian!' he said. 'You go to Giglia, don't you?'

'Well, I've only been once,' said Sky. 'Last night.'

'Who did you see? Who told you about me?' asked Nicholas eagerly. 'Was it Gaetano?'

The two brothers, so different physically, were very alike in one thing, thought Sky. They were equally devoted to each other and eager for news.

'Yes,' he said to Nicholas. 'I saw him. He asked me to seek you out and give you messages. I think he wants to use me as a go-between.'

Nicholas looked as if he wanted to climb into Sky's mind and grab everything in it relating to his old life, but Georgia stopped him. Sky was impressed by the influence she had over the younger boy.

'Do you know why you've been chosen?' she asked Sky now.

'No, not exactly. I found myself in a sort of a monastery, with a pharmacy attached to it.'

'I bet it was Saint-Mary-among-the-Vines!' cried Nicholas.

Sky nodded. 'That's where I met your brother,' he said. 'But not at first. The first person I met was Brother Sulien. He . . . he told me we were both Stravaganti and that I was needed to help the city. He said there was danger coming from all sides. I think it's linked with the weddings in your family, Nick.'

'Oh, who is getting married?' he asked in an agony of curiosity. 'Gaetano, I know, is to marry our cousin Francesca, but who else?'

Sky saw that Georgia had gone quite pale.

'It's your other two brothers,' he said. 'Marrying some more cousins. I'm afraid I don't remember their names. And your cousin Alfonso, the Duke of Volana, is marrying yet another relative. You have a big family.'

He saw Georgia relaxing and heard her breathe out.

'And the Duchessa of Bellezza is coming to Giglia for the weddings and the Nucci clan could be plotting something, but that's pretty much all I know so far.'

'Arianna,' said Georgia, and Sky saw to his amazement that there were tears in this tough girl's eyes. 'And where Arianna is, there Luciano will be too. You know about Luciano?'

'Sulien told me. But what he said seemed too fantastic to be true. It wasn't until Gaetano told me about you two that I began to believe it.'

'And is Gaetano well? Is he happy?' burst out Nicholas.

'He seemed well,' said Sky. 'And happy, apart from missing you. He said to tell you that he has a new horse, a grey stallion called Apollo.'

He felt a bit silly passing on this message but both Nicholas and Georgia were listening intently, clearly horse-mad.

'Will you tell him about the fencing championships?' said Nicholas. 'I think he'd like to know I am still good with a sword.'

A bullock cart was delivering a piece of marble to Giuditta Miele's bottega. She had chosen it herself in the quarry at Pietrabianca, running her hands over the white stone as if sensing something locked within it. Now she was supervising the unloading, while the white bullocks sweated and shivered.

With her broad shoulders and muscular arms, she looked as if she could heave the marble off the cart herself, but she left it to the team of workmen. A space had been cleared in the middle of the sculptor's workshop, where soon the piece of quarried marble stood upright. Giuditta was slicing the ropes off the sacking that covered it before the workmen were out of the door.

Then she walked slowly round and round the

revealed white stone, getting to know it all over again. Her apprentices watched in silence, used to her methods; it would be days before she took a chisel to the block of marble.

Giuditta was remembering her visit to Bellezza, when she had met the young Duchessa. Titles and honours were of no significance to the sculptor; she saw all people as shapes and volumes, curves and relations between lines. Young and beautiful subjects rarely held much interest for her, since she had left her own youth behind and was now more interested in character and the way it stamped its mark on features and bearing.

Her last portrait statue had been of young Prince Falco and for that she had had no model. But she had seen the boy on several State occasions and been struck by his delicate beauty. And something underneath that – a kind of steel that made him interesting to her in spite of his youth. The funeral statue of Prince Falco was already attracting visitors to the palace in Giglia, as its fame spread. A slight boy with his hand resting on the head of a favourite hound, his gaze attracted by something in the distance. It was intimate, informal, domestic, as different as possible from the classical statues that lined the loggia in the Piazza Ducale.

And now the Duchessa. Giuditta grunted, looking at the copious sketches she had made. It was hard, this business of works of art commissioned by nobles. You had to show them still and dignified. She would have liked to sculpt Arianna in full flight, running forwards with arms raised and one foot off the ground, her hair tumbling loose down her back, like an Amazon or a nymph. But that would never do for the ruler of a great city.

My next statue, thought Giuditta, will be of a peasant in his eighties.

*

In Bellezza, a formal ceremony was taking place in the Senate. The Regent, Rodolfo, and his daughter the Duchessa were conferring an honour and title upon a young man.

'I wish to announce to the Senate,' said Rodolfo, 'that my late wife, the previous Duchessa of our great city, was subjected to an earlier assassination attempt, on the night of the Maddalena Feast two years ago. It was kept quiet at the time because it failed and the Duchessa wanted to find out more about who was responsible. Alas, the second attempt was successful, as you know, and we have concluded our investigations without finding definite proof of the identity of those who wished to rob us of her gracious presence.'

He paused to let the other twenty-three Senators take in the new information.

'In the need to keep our investigations secret, it was also necessary to keep from public knowledge the name of the person who prevented the first attempt on the Duchessa's life.'

He motioned Luciano forwards.

'But it is now possible to identify him as my apprentice, Luciano Crinamorte.'

There was enthusiastic applause from the Senate.

'In token of the great service he did to our city, I

hereby release him from his apprenticeship. And the Duchessa, honouring the memory of her late mother, bestows upon him the title of Cavaliere of Bellezza.'

Luciano knelt at Arianna's feet and she put over his head a purple satin ribbon with a large silver seal with the city's emblem of a mask embossed on it.

'Arise, Cavaliere Luciano Crinamorte,' she said in her clear, musical voice. 'Serve your city well and it will always serve you.'

The three teenagers sat in Sky's flat, quite exhausted. They had talked themselves to a standstill. Each was now wrapped in private thoughts.

For Sky it was still all too fantastic to take in. Yesterday he had been an ordinary Barnsbury student, living next to the school in a little flat with his sick mother. Today he was a time and space traveller, living over an alchemist's lab from more than four centuries ago. And his mother seemed to be getting better; could these two things possibly be linked?

They had pooled information and Georgia had told him that Luciano had always felt well in Talia. And Falco had taken the enormous step of becoming Nicholas in order to be healed. Yesterday Sky had arrived in a place of healing, which also produced perfumes. What did that mean and why had he been chosen? Only more visits to Giglia would tell.

Georgia was in a whirl of emotions. She hadn't been back to Talia since the previous September, nearly six months ago, when she and Nicholas had made a dramatic stravagation to Remora together and he, as Falco, had ridden the flying horse around and above the Campo. She hadn't seen Luciano on that occasion, hadn't seen him for over a year and a half in fact, because Falco's death in his old life and his new identity as Nicholas had caused the gateway between the two worlds to destabilise, so that more than a year had passed for her but not for her friends in Talia.

And she and Nicholas could travel only to Remora, while Sky had been chosen to stravagate to Giglia, Nicholas's home town. But if Luciano was coming to that great city, then that was the only place she wanted to be. She shook her head. This was madness. She had taught herself to do without Luciano after they had said goodbye in the Campo of Remora so long ago. He lived in a world she couldn't inhabit, only visit, and then in the wrong city. And he did not love her, except as a friend. His heart was given to the young Duchessa of Bellezza, beautiful, clever and brave, who was going to Giglia in spite of all the dangers that awaited her there.

Nicholas, too, was deeply unsettled. Like Georgia, he had learned to give up what he loved – his family, his city, all his old life. And he had adapted well. His physical health was the great prize he had surrendered everything else for and the sacrifice had been worth it. He had a comfortable home with Luciano's parents, lots of friends, and Georgia.

He was completely in thrall to her. Not just because of her bravery and daring, although that had been the initial attraction. It was her otherness, her coming from the magical world of the twenty-first century, which had not diminished now that he knew other people from the same time. And she had rescued him, had brought him here to the world and time that had cured him, so that he could ride and fence and, best of all, walk again without help. She had given him back his life and he would always adore her for it.

But it didn't alter the fact that she was nearly seventeen and he fifteen and such relationships were frowned on in their school, although there would have been no objections in Talia to his being engaged to a woman much older than Georgia. All he could do was settle for a close friendship and hope that things would change in time. He was ashamed at feeling secretly glad that Luciano was safely trapped in the other world of centuries ago.

And now everything had changed; Talia had thrust itself back into the foreground the minute he had heard his old name. Just thinking that Sky might see his brother again in Giglia that night made this new world of school and cafeteria and gym seem thin and insubstantial.

'Goodness, you're all quiet!' said Rosalind when she got back in. 'I thought there was no one here.'

'Sorry, Mrs Meadows,' said Georgia, snapping out of her thoughts. 'We've been . . . talking about the fencing championships.'

'Call me Rosalind, please. I didn't know you were interested in fencing, Sky.'

'I am,' he said quickly. 'Nicholas here is the captain of our team. I wondered if I could learn.'

Nicholas played along straightaway. It was instinctive the way they all wanted to protect both Sky's mother and themselves. Their strange bond was as vulnerable as a newborn infant and they jumped at a chance to defend it and prolong its life.

'I think Sky could be good,' he said now. 'We've been arranging for me to give him some lessons.'

And if Rosalind wondered why that made them all so solemn, she said nothing.

Sulien was expecting Sky when he arrived in Giglia the next morning. It was early, because the boy had gone to bed early in his own world, eager to visit Talia again. He woke already dressed in his black and white novice's robes.

They were both in Sulien's cell, but the door was open into the laboratory and through that Sky could see the other door, open to the cloister. The early morning sun steamed through and he stepped out into its light, without greeting the friar. He turned and checked: no shadow.

And then he spoke to Sulien. 'Tell me about William Dethridge,' he said.

*

Duke Niccolò had spent a busy morning with his architect in the Palazzo Ducale. The plans for the conversion of the private apartments were developing well. Now he turned into the neighbouring piazza, to visit the workshops under the Guild offices. His new quarters and Fabrizio's must have furnishings and ornaments worthy of princes.

In the bottega of Arnolfo Battista, he stopped to order tables inlaid with marble chips and semi-precious stones. From the silversmith's next door, he ordered an epergne in the shape of a dragon with wings spread. And then in the jeweller's, four thick ropes of rubies and pearls for his two nieces and two young girl cousins, as wedding gifts.

Well pleased with his arrangements, the Duke strolled through the cathedral piazza on the way to his old palace. And stopped outside Giuditta Miele's bottega. It brought back painful memories, faintly tinged with pleasure. She had sculpted a lifelike statue of his boy, Falco, that was at once touchingly familiar and a great work of art. The Duke respected art and he respected Miele, though his opinion of her would have been far different if he'd known she was a Stravagante.

Now he decided to call in on the sculptor. He found her apparently doing nothing, gazing at a block of white marble. It took her a few minutes to register her illustrious guest. One of the apprentices, who were all busy bowing and doffing their caps, tugged at her sleeve to rouse her out of her reverie.

'Your Grace,' she said in her deep voice, making a curtsey, although her rough work clothes hardly lent themselves to the action.

'Maestra,' he said, raising her graciously to her feet. 'I was just passing.'

An apprentice had been busy brushing stone dust off a stool and rushed forwards to proffer it to the Duke.

'I do not keep much in the workshop,' said Giuditta. 'But I can offer your Grace a cup of wine.'

'Thank you, most kind,' said Niccolò, repressing his fastidiousness to sit on the stool and accept the pewter mug. He sipped cautiously and had to disguise his surprise at the quality of the drink.

'Mmm,' he said. 'Bellezzan red. And a fine vintage too. You have a good wine merchant.'

'It was a gift,' said Giuditta. 'From the Duchessa.' She couldn't help her eyes moving to the block of marble. All the time she was exchanging pleasantries with the Duke, she could be spending time with it, getting to know the figure trapped inside.

Duke Niccolò's quick mind made the connection straightaway.

'Ah,' he said pleasantly. 'You are perhaps commissioned to sculpt her?'

Giuditta nodded. 'I have travelled to Bellezza to make my sketches and the Duchessa will grant me several sittings while she is here in Giglia.'

'Would that be before or after the weddings?'

'Before, your Grace.'

'So she is expected soon? I must hasten to send her appropriate gifts as an honoured guest to Giglia,' mused Niccolò. 'I should like her statue to show her holding in her hand a scroll of the treaty I hope she will make with my family.'

It irked him that this artist knew more about the Duchessa's movements than he did. What was the Eel's spy network up to?

But he didn't show his irritation. Instead he finished his wine and stood up, resisting all temptation to brush the seat of his velvet breeches, and walked over to the piece of marble. He hadn't seen the young Duchessa since the death of Falco and her rapid departure from Remora, but he thought about her often.

Arianna Rossi was unfinished business. She had

defied his wishes when she refused his son, just as her mother had always defied him in her resistance to any alliance with the di Chimici, and he must find a way of dealing with her. The white marble reminded him of the Duchessa's creamy unblemished skin, and he left the sculptor's workshop musing on youth and innocence and how little it could do in the long run against age and experience.

*

Sulien took Sky to walk the maze with him. At first the twenty-first-century boy was sceptical. It seemed a bit New Age-y to him, all this chanting and meditating and pacing slowly in silence. But it worked. He had stepped on to the black and white stone labyrinth with his mind all a-jangle.

Sulien had first explained to him about William Dethridge. 'He was the first Stravagante, an Elizabethan alchemist who was trying to make gold and instead, after an explosion in his laboratory, found the secret of travel in time and space.'

'And his laboratory was where my school and my house are now?'

'So it would appear,' said Sulien. 'When I brought your talisman, on the advice of both Doctor Dethridge and Rodolfo, I left it on the doorstep of what must be your home.'

Sky smiled at the thought of the friar in Islington. But monks and nuns and people like that still wore robes in Sky's time, so he probably wouldn't have attracted that much attention.

'You say that Dethridge and Rodolfo advised you,

but how did you speak to them? You said they both live in Bellezza now, and you don't have telephones yet.'

Sulien had then shown him a plain oval hand-mirror in which Sky saw not his own brown face reflected but a dark panelled room with a lot of strange instruments in it. Sulien passed his hand over its surface and closed his eyes, concentrating. And then there was a face, thin and bony, with hawk-like eyes and silvered black hair.

'Maestro,' said Sulien. 'Let me show you our new brother.'

He had encouraged Sky to look full in the mirror and he found himself face to face with Rodolfo. It had been an unsettling experience. Apart from his actual travelling between the two worlds, Sky had not encountered anything in Talia that could be described as magic until that moment.

Rodolfo was nothing but warm and welcoming, but Sky knew that he was talking to a powerful Stravagante – and doing it through an enchanted mirror. When he had stepped on to the maze a few minutes afterwards, his thoughts were a jagged and swirling mess.

When he left it twenty minutes later, he was quite calm. Sulien was five minutes behind him.

'Incredible,' said Sky.

'It was here when I arrived,' said Sulien. 'I found it under the carpet one day but the other friars didn't know how to use it. You don't have to believe it – just do it. I walk the maze every morning and evening, just so that I can find the centre whenever I need it.'

Sky looked alarmed.

'Don't worry,' said the friar. 'I don't expect you to do it that often. Only when you feel the need. I just wanted to show it to you.'

Sky was relieved. But a part of him knew he did want that experience again.

*

The Eel was waiting for his master outside the gates of the Palazzo di Chimici in the Via Larga. There was a new guard on duty that day who didn't know him. But he knew the Duke all right, and was apologetic when Niccolò arrived and waved the unprepossessing little man in after him.

'I wanted to talk to you about your contacts in Bellezza,' said Niccolò.

'That's a coincidence, your Grace,' said Enrico. 'That's what I've come to tell you. I've had a report from my man Beppe that the Duchessa will soon be in the city.'

'Buzz, buzz,' said Niccolò irritably. 'I learned that myself today. The point is I should have heard of it sooner.'

'And she is going to have her likeness made,' continued Enrico, unabashed.

'By Giuditta Miele, yes, yes,' said the Duke. 'Tell me something that I do not already know.'

'That her young paramour will accompany her?' hazarded Enrico.

'Paramour? You mean the old wizard's apprentice?'

'Yes, her father's favourite – and hers too, if rumours are true.' Enrico dared a familiar leer.

Everywhere he turned his thoughts or laid his plans,

Duke Niccolò seemed to come up against Rodolfo or his mysterious apprentice. He knew they were in some way connected with the death of his youngest son, which he believed was not a true death, even though he had held the lifeless body in his own arms and seen it laid in coffin and tomb. It was why he needed to persecute the Stravaganti. The very thought of the one young man alive while the other lay in a marble vault crowned by Giuditta Miele's statue, filled him with a wild rage that threatened to overturn his reason every time he entertained it.

Enrico read the signs; he wouldn't have mentioned the Bellezzan boy if the Duke hadn't known all his other information. Now he saw that he must try to direct his patron's thoughts to happier subjects.

'If I might ask, your Grace,' he said, 'how are the preparations going for the weddings?'

A long silence from Niccolò, then, 'Well. They are going well. I spent this morning ordering furniture and jewels for the young couples.'

Enrico decided to take a big risk. 'I wonder that your Grace doesn't think of taking a second wife yourself. Why should the young ones have all the fun? The princess Beatrice will one day need a husband herself, and a fine lord like your Grace needs the companionship of a good woman in his declining years.'

The gaze the Duke turned on him was terrifying.

'Not that your Grace is anywhere near declining yet,' spluttered Enrico, realising he had miscalculated. The Duke waved him aside, clutching at his throat, as if having trouble breathing. Then he regained control and looked at his spymaster with a new expression.

'You may leave,' he said. But after the Eel had gone, he said to himself in a ghastly voice, 'He is quite right. I shall take a wife. And I know just the woman.'

Chapter 6

Wedding Dresses

'Now we need to get out of the city,' said Sulien, when he and Sky had left the maze. He led the boy through the two cloisters to where a cart stood harnessed to two patient old horses in the cobbled yard.

'Where are we going?' asked Sky, surprised when Sulien motioned him up on to the seat and prepared to drive himself.

'To visit some more brothers up on the hill in Colle Vernale,' said Sulien, flicking the reins. 'We have plants to collect.'

It was an hour's ride, on the flat at first, but harder as they climbed the winding road round a steep hill to the north-east of Giglia. The views were fantastic from the city side of the hill, the whole of Giglia dominated by the great Cathedral of the Lily and its huge dome.

The air was a lot fresher than in the valley too and Sky breathed in the scent of flowers from the fields around.

He had never made a journey pulled by horses before; it made the whole pace of life seem slower and, as the cart moved steadily up the hill, Sky had the strangest feeling that his heart rate was slowing too, as it had in the maze. Sulien gave him a quizzical sideways look.

'How are you finding life in the sixteenth century?' he asked. 'We do things very differently from in your world, if the glimpses I've had of it recently are anything to go by.'

'It's weird,' admitted Sky. 'I'd have expected to find it a bit tame, but there seems to be so much going on. Tell me more about the dangers.'

'We take a long time to learn,' said Sulien, shaking his head. 'Family vendettas like that between the Nucci and the di Chimici go on for generations, sometimes bubbling underground, sometimes bursting out into violence and murder. At the moment the whole city feels like a cauldron, heating up to boiling point. These weddings provide the perfect opportunity for crime. The city will be full of strangers, the bridal procession will be through streets thronged with spectators, well-wishers and citizens, and no amount of city-guards could possibly keep an eye on all the crowds. It will mean that a single man armed with a dagger would be able to settle old scores.'

'And where do the Stravaganti come in?' asked Sky.

'There will be at least six in the city,' said Sulien. 'You, me and Giuditta and the three from Bellezza – Rodolfo, Luciano and Doctor Dethridge himself. It is our job to do what the guards cannot – protect the Duchessa of Bellezza and try to keep the peace for everyone else. And keep out of the Duke's way as much as possible, since he is against the Stravaganti.'

'And what am I supposed to do that you others can't?'

'That I do not know. Keep your eyes open and wait for the right opportunity,' said the friar. 'I'm sure it will come – otherwise you wouldn't be here – and I'm almost certain it will be at the weddings.'

*

Francesca di Chimici and the young Duchessa had rather surprisingly become good friends. The first time they had met had been when the young princess from Bellona had been forced to stand against Arianna in the election after the old Duchessa's 'assassination'. Forced too into marrying old Councillor Albani, from whom she had later been freed by the Pope's annulment.

But when they had next met, during the visit of Prince Gaetano to court the Duchessa in Bellezza, Arianna had softened towards the young woman she had been taught to think of as an enemy. It was clear that Francesca was both very unhappy and in love with Prince Gaetano herself, and Arianna had done everything she could to put the two cousins in each other's way.

And when Gaetano, acting under his father's orders in Remora, had finally brought himself to ask Arianna to marry him, she had been happy to refuse and glad to see the light in his eyes as she sent him off to ask

Francesca instead. Arianna liked Gaetano very much, something that made her more open to the idea that there were sympathetic di Chimici, but she didn't want to marry him.

Arianna and Francesca had travelled back to Bellezza at the same time and had become friends during the time that the di Chimici princess was packing up her belongings and extricating herself from Albani's house, before going back to Bellona.

And now she was in Bellezza again, as the Duchessa's guest. They never talked about politics and Francesca had no idea that Arianna's mother was still alive; even Gaetano didn't know that. Instead, they were in deep discussion about clothes.

'I didn't get a proper wedding last time,' said Francesca. 'And I hoped for something rather splendid in Giglia, but now we have to share the day with Gaetano's two brothers and cousin Alfonso, it's going to be a bit of a circus. Four couples – can you imagine? It would not have been my preference to share the day with three other brides!'

'But you will be the prettiest, I'm sure,' said Arianna, adjusting her green silk mask.

'Oh, as to that, I don't care,' said Francesca, tossing her black hair as well as she could for its pins and braids. 'But Gaetano and I will be the least important couple in the cathedral. And I did so want it to be special.'

'Nonsense!' said Arianna firmly. 'You will be the most important to each other – and to me. I don't know the Duke of Volana or his duchess-to-be and I've met Prince Fabrizio and Carlo only briefly and never seen their brides. I'm sure they are all very good-looking and important, but you and Gaetano are the only di Chimici who are my friends.'

Francesca flashed her a grateful smile.

'I've had an idea,' said Arianna. 'What were you planning to wear?'

*

Sulien and Sky drew into a small village, the horses sweating and panting. 'It will be a lot easier for them on the way back,' said the friar. 'It will be downhill all the way and my plants make one of the lightest loads for a beast of burden.'

After a few minutes' rest, he urged the two nags up a steep side path out of Colle Vernale to a friary at the very top of the hill. From the quiet grassy terrace outside, the view over the countryside was spectacular. Sky could see not only the city and its cathedral dome, snug in the valley, but the great river Argento which fed it, snaking down from the distant mountains. If he screwed up his eyes, Sky could trace the blue thread of it right back up to its source.

'The Argento is running high for this time of year,' said Sulien, following the line of his gaze.

'It's fantastic up here!' said Sky. 'Everything so far away but so clear. I feel as if I could touch the campanile of the cathedral if I just reached out a bit.'

Sulien smiled. 'Not yet,' he said. 'You are still a very new Stravagante.'

A brown-robed friar came bustling out to greet them.

'Welcome, welcome,' he said. 'Welcome to San Francesco.'

The friar must mean his Friary of Saint Francis, Sky thought. So Dominicans wore black and white and Franciscans wore brown. Just how many more religious orders were there to learn?

After introductions and instructions to a novice of his own to look after the horses, Brother Martino led them into his little church, which was cool after the sunshine and smelt of incense and candlewax. But they didn't linger there, crossing rapidly to a door into a cloister. When Brother Martino opened it, Sky was blinded by the light, overwhelmed by aromatic scents and almost deafened by the sound of birdsong.

The cloister was a herb garden. It was smaller than even the Lesser Cloister at Saint-Mary-among-the-Vines, and arranged around a fountain, whose spray sparkled in the sunlight. Low hedges clipped firmly into shape surrounded the herb beds. The wall nearest the church was one huge aviary, in which little birds like finches twittered and flew, singing at full throat.

Martino stopped to pull a pouch of seed from his belt of white rope and filled the feeders. The tuneful song immediately turned to squawking and squabbling.

The friars left the noisy cloister and entered the refectory, where Martino offered the Giglian visitors cold grape juice from a terracotta pitcher. Sky gulped it thirstily.

When they were refreshed, they went out to a yard behind the friary, where the horse cart was being loaded up by young friars. Hessian sacks gave off pungent and spicy scents.

'Fennel,' said Sulien, consulting a list. 'Lemon balm, valerian, pennywort, mallow, mint, burdock, borage, dandelion, bergamot.' He walked around the cart, crushing dried leaves between his brown fingers, and tying sacks tighter.

Sky was feeling dizzy. The smells reminded him of home and his mother's herb-based oils. What was he doing here, high up above a Renaissance city, wearing a friar's robe?

'The flowers are brought to me from all the meadows around Giglia,' said Brother Sulien. 'But the herbs I collect from Colle Vernale myself. I trust no one else to bring them to me with their properties undiminished.'

*

'Will you let me help you?' Arianna asked Francesca. 'My grandmother lives on one of the islands and makes exquisite lace. She makes it for all the most beautiful wedding dresses in the lagoon and can create any design. Shall we go there and ask her to make yours? I should love to give you your dress as my wedding present. And I haven't been to Burlesca for a long time.'

*

Camillo Nucci had an interest in herbs and plants himself, at least the poisonous variety. He had been brought up to hate the di Chimici family and he saw himself as the natural avenger of all his clan's insults and slights at their hands, not to mention the murders for which Duke Niccolò's family were responsible. It didn't bother Camillo that the di Chimici were growing in power and spreading over Talia; he wasn't interested in politics. All he wanted to do was even the score.

The upcoming weddings would provide perfect cover for an attempt on the di Chimici; the city was already filling up with merchants and pilgrims for Easter, and the public celebrations for the princes' marriage would only increase the numbers. Who could say whether a particular poison introduced into a di Chimici dish had come from within the city or from one of their many enemies from beyond Giglia?

Now he was closeted with an old monk from Volana, discussing with him the properties of the wild mushrooms that grew in the fields and forests around the city. But he had not noticed a scruffy street boy, who had trailed him to the family's old palazzo up near Saint-Mary-among-the-Vines and was now listening through a crack in the door.

'Now why does Camillo Nucci want to know about poisonous mushrooms?' Sandro asked himself. He made a mental note to pass this on to the Eel, then set off in search of Brother Tino.

*

The boatman rowed the Duchessa and her friend out across the lagoon to Burlesca. He was doing double duty as a guard, and the Duchessa also had a young Cavaliere with her, armed with a wicked-looking merlino-dagger. Luciano carried his weapon openly, but only he knew that Arianna had one of her own tucked into a garter. Her foster-brothers, true to an old promise, had given it to her when she turned sixteen, and Luciano had no doubt that she would use it if attacked.

'I came here with Gaetano last year,' said Francesca, happy at the memory.

Luciano looked at her curiously. Francesca never referred to the fact that her husband-to-be had been courting another woman the previous summer, a woman who was rapidly becoming her closest female friend. He himself had been all too aware of it, during the weeks when he had been in Remora, unsure whether Arianna would accept the di Chimici prince. His feelings about it hadn't been uncomplicated either, since he liked Gaetano, and had been having his own adventures with Georgia, the Stravagante. Not romantic ones, but their shared status as Stravaganti made their relationship special and had given him an insight into why the company of a Duke's son might be pleasant to a Duchess.

'Look, there's their house,' said Arianna. 'The white one among all the colours.'

The boat moored in the harbour and the young people moved through the village, receiving interested glances. Two good-looking women, richly dressed, both masked, were bound to attract attention.

'That's the young Duchessa,' was the whisper. 'Come to see her grandparents, no doubt.'

Paola Bellini sat outside her whitewashed cottage as usual, with her lace cushion. She had been mother and grandmother to a Duchessa, but had no desire to live anywhere grander than the little white house that had been her home for the last fifty years.

'Grandmother,' called one of the slender masked young women, hastening towards her. 'We need lace for a wedding dress!'

Paola's black eyes snapped towards Luciano but he met her glance with a slight frown.

'For my friend, Francesca,' Arianna continued smoothly. But she had seen the look and a flush crept up her neck.

*

Burlesca wasn't the only place where wedding dresses were being discussed. In Fortezza, the Princesses Lucia and Bianca were plaguing their father to death on the subject.

'Daughters, daughters!' Prince Jacopo exclaimed to his wife, Princess Carolina. 'Why did you give me nothing but daughters? I shall go mad if I hear another word about satin, silk, velvet or brocade!'

'What about taffeta?' asked Carolina, unperturbed. 'And I was of the impression that *you* gave the daughters to *me*.'

She was perfectly aware that Jacopo was devoted to his girls and, even if he was sad at the thought that his title would pass to the son of another di Chimici, he would not have exchanged them for all the boys in Talia.

'Tell them they can have what they like, as long as I don't have to hear about it,' said the prince, caressing the ears of his water-spaniel.

'But what about jewels?' asked the princess. 'They must have something special for their wedding day. Remember, Bianca will become a duchess and Lucia will be the Princess of Remora one day.'

'Haven't we enough in the palace treasury to kit

them out without ordering more?' asked Jacopo. 'You hardly ever wear the things.'

Carolina sighed. 'Fashions change, my dear,' she said. 'The gems I had at our wedding belonged to your mother and your grandmother before her. I didn't mind, but young women today are quite different. They may want something specially set in Giglia, where all the fashionable jewellers are.'

'Then let cousin Niccolò buy them,' growled Jacopo. 'He seems intent on masterminding these weddings.'

Princess Carolina let the subject drop. She knew how her husband felt about having their daughters married in the cathedral in Giglia. It had unfortunate associations for him. But she hadn't been his wife for thirty years without knowing how to manage Jacopo's moods. She would make discreet enquiries of Niccolò's daughter, Beatrice, and find out if he intended gifts of jewellery. If not, she would order something suitable for her daughters herself.

*

Rinaldo di Chimici was a changed man. At his powerful uncle's urging, he had entered the church. He was now Father Rinaldo, with good prospects of a cardinal's hat before long. Of course he was not a parish priest; he was far too grand for that. He had left the family's palace in Volana and become the Pope's own chaplain in Remora. It suited him very well to be so close to the Head of the Church in Talia, who was his uncle too, and he found the life of a clergyman in the Papal palace comfortable and easy.

And he had at last got rid of Enrico, who had gone to Giglia to spy for the Duke. Now Father Rinaldo was practising forgetting his life as an Ambassador when he had ordered the death of a woman, the last Duchessa of Bellezza, and was looking forward to assisting the Pope at the forthcoming di Chimici weddings.

Both his brother and sister were getting married – Caterina to Prince Fabrizio, who would one day be Duke of Giglia and head of the di Chimici family. Rinaldo was pleased with how his life was working out. He dreamed of a future in which he would be brother-in-law to Duke Fabrizio the Second and maybe Pope himself. It was a sweeter prospect than had faced him when he had failed to bring Bellezza into the family fold and had let that black-haired boy slip through his fingers. And if he were Pope it would put him in a position of power higher even than his older brother Alfonso.

*

In Volana, Duke Alfonso was closeted with his sister Caterina, also discussing the weddings. He was as relieved as Rinaldo that she was marrying so well within the family, so much so that he hadn't minded being assigned Bianca, Old Jacopo's younger daughter, even though she didn't bring a title with her. Besides, Bianca was very pretty and Alfonso had been a bit lonely in his castle since he had inherited the title four years before.

His mother, the dowager Duchess Isabella, had thrown off her widow's weeds and was entering into the spirit of the forthcoming celebrations.

'We must find out what your cousins are planning, my dear,' she said to Caterina. 'As bride to the Duke's heir, you must be the most splendid, mustn't she, Fonso darling?'

'My own bride must not be neglected, however, Mother,' the Duke said mildly. 'How would it look if the new Duchessa of Volana were cast into the shade by her sister-in-law?'

'These are delicate matters,' said the dowager, now in her element. 'But the weddings will be in Giglia, where the "figura" of their prince will weigh more than ours.'

'Still, we must do honour to our family too,' said Caterina, who secretly had no objection to outshining her new sister-in-law, though she had no reason to dislike Bianca herself. 'Perhaps we should take advice from Duke Niccolò?'

Her mother snorted in a most unducal manner. 'I think we've had quite enough advice from him.' Isabella would have preferred her son to marry the Duke's daughter, rather than the Fortezza girl, but she had seen the wisdom of going along with his plans for her family. And she quite understood that Niccolò was not ready to part with his Beatrice yet, after his recent bereavement.

Isabella sighed. She did not relish losing her own daughter to Giglia, even though it was such an advancement for Caterina. The dowager must learn to make do with her daughter-in-law.

*

'Brothers!' called Sandro when he saw them descending from the cart. 'Where have you been?'

'Collecting herbs,' said Sulien. 'And I must unpack and store them quickly, so perhaps you two would like to get yourselves something to eat in the kitchen.'

The two boys were drawn into the warmth of the kitchen, where Brother Tullio wielded the knife and ladle, assisted by two nervous novices. He was disposed to be cross till he heard Sulien had sent them.

'Ah, so the pharmacist is back,' he said. 'Brother Ambrogio, take him some refreshment to the storeroom. He won't stir from there till all his herbs are stowed. And as for you two, well, boys must be fed, I suppose.'

He gave them bread and sheep's milk cheese and tomatoes and hard little pears which were as sweet as they were tough.

'You know what he does with his plants?' said Sandro casually, as they took their booty out into the cloister and picnicked sitting on its low wall.

'Makes medicines, of course,' said Sky. He didn't want always to know less than Sandro.

'And?' persisted the little spy.

'Well, he makes perfume from the flowers, I know,' said Sky. 'And all sorts of lotions and potions.'

Sandro tapped the side of his nose. 'Close,' he said. 'But not just potions – poisons too.'

*

When they got back to the Palazzo Ducale in Bellezza, Arianna was tired but pleased with the day. She was sure that Francesca's dress would be magnificent.

Luciano left her at the door and returned to his home with Doctor Dethridge and Leonora, while Francesca went to change her dress for dinner.

Arianna and her maid Barbara were chatting about lace in her private room when Rodolfo came to see her. His expression immediately spelt trouble; she had rarely seen him look so disturbed.

'We have had another message from Duke Niccolò,' he said abruptly.

'He has no sons left unengaged to sue for my hand,' said Arianna, more lightly than she felt.

'It is not a marriage proposal this time,' said Rodolfo. 'It is a request to know your measurements. Niccolò di Chimici wants to send you a dress to wear at the weddings.'

Chapter 7

Deadly Nightshade

Sky found concentrating on his school work very hard the next day. Sulien had urged him to stravagate home early and he hadn't been reluctant. Sandro's information had knocked Sky for six. Could the friar possibly be a poisoner? Or at least a maker of poisons? It didn't make much difference really; if you made them, you knew what they were going to be used for.

Sky tried to remember what Brother Sulien had said to him in the Great Cloister on his first visit. 'The laboratory is where I prepare the medicines – and the perfumes, of course.' He hadn't said anything about poisons. Sulien was a good man – Sky was sure of it. But were good and bad the same in sixteenth-century Talia as now in London?

He was glad that school was breaking up soon for Easter. Georgia had warned him that he would get very tired during the day if he spent every night stravagating to Talia and today he understood what she meant.

Nicholas Duke was as good as his word and was waiting for Sky in the gym in the lunch break. Georgia had come along to watch. Nick handed Sky a mesh mask to protect his face and a foil with a sort of button on the end.

'You won't need padding for a trial session,' he said. 'I promise not to hurt you.'

Arrogant little prat, thought Sky, I'll show you.

But Nicholas was good, very good, and Sky couldn't get his foil anywhere near the younger boy's body. By the end of the session, he was sweating and panting and Nicholas seemed as cool as at the beginning. As Sky towelled his streaming face he was very glad that Alice hadn't joined Georgia to watch them.

'Good,' said Nicholas. 'You'll be a good fencer.'

Sky stopped, astonished. 'What do you mean? I was rubbish.'

'What do you think the point of fencing is?' asked Nicholas, looking at him intently.

'To slice your opponent,' said Sky.

'No,' said Nicholas. 'It is to prevent him from slicing you. Only assassins fight to kill the other person.'

Great, thought Sky. That's all I need – another younger kid to tell me what's what.

'It's true you didn't touch me,' continued Nicholas. 'But you didn't let me touch you many times either –

your defences are instinctive and that's good to work with.'

'Look,' said Sky, turning to Georgia for support. 'I'm not really going to learn to fence, am I? I just made that up to explain our being together.'

To his surprise, Georgia didn't back him up.

'Nick and I think it might not be a bad idea for you to learn,' she said. 'True, it will give us an excuse to spend time together – I often watch him in practice and matches – but we also think it might be useful for your protection in Talia.'

Sky felt the hairs on the back of his neck rise.

'What? You think someone may try to kill me?'

'Why not?' said Nicholas with a shrug. 'You're a Stravagante, aren't you? Let's go and get some lunch. I'm starving.'

Rodolfo, Luciano and Doctor Dethridge worked together late into the night in Rodolfo's laboratory in Bellezza. Luciano had been an apprentice to both older men and had learned a lot. Although he had been released from his apprenticeship and was supposed to be going to university the following year, he still felt he had much to learn. Now they were working together to see whether it would be possible for Stravaganti from the other world to travel to cities in Talia other than the ones their talismans came from.

'Wee coulde sende more thane one talismanne to eche Stravayger,' Doctor Dethridge had suggested, 'but it does not seme ryghte to mee to do such a thynge.'

'Nor to me,' agreed Rodolfo. 'But it does limit the usefulness of other-world Stravaganti to be able to travel to only one city. Luciano we now have with us always and everywhere and we are heartily glad of it, but he is one of our Talian Brotherhood now and no longer a traveller from the other world. Suppose we needed Georgia in Bellezza? Or this new one, Sky, might need to come here from Giglia.'

'Sky?' said Luciano, interested. There had been only one person with that name at his old school. He could just remember the young Sky Meadows from Year 10, but of course more than a year had passed since he had been 'translated' to Talia and then there had been that time lurch when Falco had died in Remora. Sky must be in the Lower Sixth now, he calculated, with Georgia.

'I saw him through Brother Sulien's mirror,' said Rodolfo. 'This time it is a young man and he is a Moor, like Sulien. I am very glad that Sulien has brought us another Stravagante. There is trouble brewing in the city.'

'Aye,' said Dethridge. 'Where the chymists have their home there will always bee daungere. In especial where the Duke ys to bee founde.'

'We had a message from him today,' said Rodolfo carefully, not looking at Luciano. 'He wants to send Arianna a dress to wear at the weddings.'

Luciano felt uneasy. 'Is that usual?' he asked.

'He has sent gifts before,' said Rodolfo. 'It is common between Heads of State. But he intends her to wear this garment and it is a much more personal gift than ever before.'

'Well, what does that mean?' asked Luciano.

'Yt meyneth somethinge ill, yow canne be certayne,' said Dethridge.

Luciano was used to the Elizabethan's antiquated way of talking by now and agreed with him that anything Duke Niccolò was planning would be bad news.

Alice was waiting for them in the cafeteria and seemed surprised that the chance meeting of the day before had already led to fencing lessons for Sky and a friendship among the three. But she didn't mind. It gave her the chance to get to know Sky better.

'Does Alice know about you two?' Sky asked Nicholas quietly as they walked back to lessons.

'What do you think?' said Nicholas. 'Would you ever have told anyone about Talia, if you hadn't known I came from there?'

'It must make it hard, though,' said Sky. 'Doesn't she wonder about your friendship?'

'Georgia told her she felt responsible for me,' said Nicholas, his face suddenly creased with pain. 'And Alice believes her, because Georgia was supposed to have found me in this world and taken me to Luciano's parents – Lucien, as you knew him.'

Sky saw how it was with the younger boy and felt sorry for him. Nicholas was obviously devoted to Georgia but feared she would never feel more than concerned friendship for him.

Quickly he changed the subject. There wasn't long before afternoon school and their lessons were in different buildings.

'Did you know Brother Sulien in your old life?' he asked. 'Do you think he could possibly be involved in making poisons?'

To his surprise, Nicholas continued to look agonised. He shook his head.

'No, I didn't know him then. There was a different friar in charge of the pharmacy when I last was there. But I know that Saint-Mary-among-the-Vines does supply poison. There is a second, secret laboratory somewhere in the friary. My family has got poison from there in the past.'

Duke Niccolò took Carlo into his confidence first. They had finished their weekly business meeting and were eating a private lunch together in the small dining chamber of the old palazzo, with only one servant.

'The weddings are less than two months away now,' said the Duke. 'On their eve, I shall make an important announcement.'

Carlo looked expectant, helping himself to polenta. He took a generous helping of wild boar stew but refused the dish of mushrooms proffered by the servant.

'The legislation is already in place,' said Niccolò, allowing the servant to add mushrooms to his much smaller helping. 'I intend to adopt the title of Grand Duke of all Tuschia.'

Whatever Carlo had expected, it was not that. 'Can you do that?' he asked, rather tactlessly.

His father raised his eyebrows. 'I don't see why

not,' he said. 'We have family members ruling in all the main city-states of the region of Tuschia – Moresco, Remora, Fortezza – and they would not dispute my claims to create such a title, as head of the family.'

'Of course not, Father,' said Carlo hastily. 'I'm sorry. I was just surprised, that's all.'

And the two men began to eat their meal in silence, each occupied with his own thoughts.

It took Sky a long time to stravagate that night. Normally he had no trouble sleeping; the busyness of his life at home ensured that. But that night he tossed and turned, thinking about poisons, fencing, unrequited love and all sorts of other things. Eventually, he got up and fetched some water from the fridge. He carried Remedy back to bed with him and settled down again with the cat in the crook of his arm and the glass bottle in his hand.

Then he had second thoughts and moved the tabby down to his feet; it would never do for Brother Tino to turn up in the friary with a miniature tiger in tow.

As soon as he arrived in Saint-Mary-among-the-Vines, Sky could see from the light that it was about midday. Sulien wasn't in his cell or the laboratory or the pharmacy. Sky wandered out into the cloisters; all was eerily quiet. He could hear the faint sound of chanting coming from the church.

And then a messenger burst into the Great Cloister from the yard. He took Sky for a novice and grabbed him by the arm.

'Where is Brother Sulien? He is urgently needed in the Via Larga – Duke Niccolò has been poisoned!'

*

Sandro was having his lunch bought for him in a tavern near the market. The Eel was in an expansive mood, as a result of soup and pasta and a large quantity of red wine.

'The Duke is up to something,' he was saying. 'You mark my words, Sparrow. There'll be an announcement soon.'

A flutter of movement in the corner of the market caught Sandro's eye. Black and white robes flapped as two figures ran through the square at an undignified pace.

'Look,' said Sandro. 'There go Sulien and Tino. What on earth can they be doing?'

'Only one way to find out,' slurred the Eel, throwing silver on the table. 'Come on!'

The two spies, master and boy, hurried after the friars. It was clear where they were heading. The great palazzo on the Via Larga almost backed on to the market and the square provided a short cut to it from the friary.

By the time Sulien and Sky had reached the palazzo gates, a small knot of people had gathered outside; news travelled fast in Talia and the rumours were already flying. The Duke was dead, the di Chimici had all been poisoned; the weddings were off.

Sky hadn't had any time to think. When the Duke's servant had arrived with his alarming news, Sky had found Sulien in the church and hurried with him to the pharmacy to collect bottles of medicine, before running all the way to the di Chimici palazzo. Now another servant led them, panting, up the great staircase to the Duke's bedroom, where he had been carried after his collapse.

The room had a foul stench of vomit and the figure on the bed was thrashing around on soiled sheets, in paroxysms of agony. His sons stood beside him wringing their hands, though the only one Sky recognised was Prince Gaetano. And he supposed the young woman trying to bathe the Duke's face was his daughter Princess Beatrice.

Brother Sulien took command as soon as he entered the room.

'Who was with the Duke when the poisoning took place?'

'I was,' said one of the young men. 'We were having lunch together.'

'Did you eat the same things?' asked Sulien, who had already crossed to the Duke and was trying to take his pulse.

'I didn't have the mushrooms,' said the prince, 'I don't like them. But Father had some.'

'And when did the signs of poisoning come on?'

'Almost immediately. He complained of stomach pains while we were eating some fruit. And then he started to vomit.'

'Can you hold him down, please?' said Brother Sulien. 'I'd like to examine his eyes.'

Sky was impressed by how the friar was taking

over; there were no 'your Highnesses' or ceremonious bows. He could see that speed was essential if the Duke's life were to be saved.

'I'll need clean linen and plenty of water heated up,' said the friar, after looking into the Duke's eyes, which kept rolling alarmingly back into his head. 'And warm coverings.'

He sniffed the bowl by the Duke's bed. 'Open the windows and air the room,' he ordered.

Princes and servants alike hurried to do the friar's bidding.

'Will he live?' asked the princess, pleading.

'It is not certain,' said Sulien. 'But if he can be saved I promise I shall do it. Now, Tino, hand me the phial with the purple liquid.'

Sky rummaged in the bag and found the right phial.

'I'll need a small glass of clean drinking water,' said Sulien, and Beatrice poured the water with an unsteady hand.

The friar took the stopper from the phial and added four or five drops of the dark purple tincture to the water, which turned a purplish black. It reminded Sky of the water he cleaned his paintbrushes in at school.

'He has to drink all this,' said Sulien. 'It's not going to be easy.'

The Duke was still racked with spasms and his teeth were bared in a ghastly rictus. It took all three princes and Sky to hold him still while the friar forced the purple liquid into his mouth. Niccolò struggled like a wild cat and Sky wondered if he thought he were being poisoned anew. After what he had heard from Sandro, the awful thought crossed Sky's mind that Sulien might actually be trying to finish the Duke off.

But he thrust it away again as he watched the Stravagante straddling the poisoned Duke on the bed, determined to get the antidote into the Duke's failing body.

Within minutes Niccolò di Chimici's struggles ceased and the whole room seemed to be holding its breath. The friar got off the bed and smoothed his robes down. The glass was empty.

'You can let him go now,' said Sulien. The princes rested their father back gently against the pillows. His white hair was plastered to his head and his eyes were staring, the pupils hugely dilated, but he lay still and the spasms seemed to have stopped.

'It is a miracle,' said Princess Beatrice, crossing herself.

'Just science,' said Sulien. 'I have given him extract of belladonna to calm the spasms. The poison was one of the muscarines found in some species of mushrooms. He will need rest, and no nourishment but water and some warm milk for twenty-four hours. You must see that he is washed and given clean linen and kept warm and that the room is well aired.'

'Of course,' said Beatrice. 'I shall wash him myself.'

Brother Sulien motioned to the princes to follow him into the next room, while the princess and servants fussed around the now apparently sleeping Duke. Sky followed his master, still dazed by what he had taken part in.

'We are eternally grateful to you, Brother,' said the handsomest of the princes, rather stiffly but with genuine emotion.

'Thank you, your Highness,' said Sulien, reverting

to the usual courtesies. 'May I present my assistant, Brother Celestino? Tino, this is Prince Fabrizio, the Duke's heir, and this is Prince Carlo, his brother. Prince Gaetano you have already met.'

Sky bowed to each in turn and they to him. 'We are grateful to you too, for your help,' said Prince Fabrizio.

Prince Carlo suddenly slumped into a chair. 'I thought he was going to die,' he said, dropping his head in his hands. 'It was terrible to see him.'

'Who made the dish with the mushrooms, your Highness?' asked Sulien gravely.

'I don't know,' said Carlo. 'I assumed it was made in the kitchens.'

'And who served it? Does the Duke not use tasters?'

'Usually,' said Gaetano. 'Did he today, Carlo?'

His brother shook his head. 'We lunched alone, with only one servant.'

'Which one?' asked Fabrizio.

Carlo shook his head as if trying to clear it. 'I don't know. I don't think I noticed.'

Sky wondered what it must be like to have so many servants that you didn't notice which one was on duty. Did these princes even know the names of any of the palace servants?

'We must find out,' said Gaetano. 'And about who cooked the dish. Could it have been an accident, Brother Sulien?'

'It is not impossible,' said the friar. 'Mushrooms are treacherous. You would need to know when and where they were gathered or whether they were bought from the market. But it is also possible that muscarine was introduced into the dish in the kitchens or by a servant, using ordinary mushrooms to disguise the taste.'

'The Nucci are behind this, without doubt,' said Prince Fabrizio, still white-faced with shock.

'Your Highness knows best,' said Sulien calmly. 'But I should think that it would be wise to conduct some investigations among the palace household before any public accusations are made.'

'Quite right,' nodded Fabrizio. 'It shall be done.'

'What else must we do for Father?' asked Gaetano.

'I shall leave this phial,' said Sulien. 'Three drops only, in water, to be given night and morning. No more. I shall return tomorrow to see how the Duke progresses.'

'Saint-Mary-among-the-Vines will be the richer for your work here today,' said Prince Fabrizio, shaking the friar's hand.

*

Sandro and the Eel got through the palazzo gate easily enough but a guard barred their way up to the Duke's chamber. So they had to cool their heels in the courtyard with the bronze nude statue. Enrico was consumed with curiosity about his master's state.

'Why did they let that friar up?' he fumed, pacing up and down. 'And that greenhorn of a novice, your friend, when they won't let me anywhere near him?'

It was about half an hour before Sulien and Sky came down the grand marble staircase.

'What happened?' Enrico asked eagerly. 'How is the Duke?'

'He will live,' said Sulien. 'At least, this time. He

was poisoned by a dish of mushrooms.'

Sandro remembered the discussion he had overheard between Camillo Nucci and the monk from Volana. He decided to tell Enrico as soon as he could.

'Can I see the Duke?' asked Enrico.

'I can't say,' said Sulien. 'That is up to his guards and the family. But he is sleeping now. I don't think he will see anyone for a while.'

Enrico set off, determined to try his luck with the guards again, but told Sandro to wait in the courtyard. Sulien went over to the fountain to splash cold water on his face.

Sky whispered to Sandro, 'You see he is no poisoner. He saved the Duke's life with something called belladonna. It stopped the spasms straightaway.'

Sandro was looking at him oddly.

'What?' asked Sky.

'Nothing,' said Sandro. 'Only belladonna is a poison, too. Deadly nightshade is its other name. I'm just wondering why Brother Sulien had a supply of it to hand.'

Chapter 8

Two Households, Both Alike in Dignity

Sky was silent over a late Saturday breakfast, wondering what on earth he should tell Nicholas about what had just happened in Giglia. How would *he* feel if someone brought him news of his mother from another world and he had to hear that she had been poisoned?

'How's the fencing going?' asked Rosalind.

'Fine,' said Sky, snapping out of his reverie. 'It was really good, actually. I mean, I wasn't very good, but Nicholas thinks I can be if I train hard.'

'Is he serious about teaching you?' she asked. 'If you're really keen, shouldn't we get you some paid lessons?'

'It's very expensive, Mum, and he's very good,' said

Sky. 'We're lucky that he's willing to do it for free.'

Sky got up and cleared the breakfast away, automatically loading the dishwasher and wiping the table. Then he checked Remedy's food and water bowl.

'What will you have for lunch?' he asked, opening the fridge. 'I'm going to meet Nicholas for another lesson – shall I make you a sandwich to eat later?'

'No, darling. I'm all right today. I can make something myself when I'm hungry.'

Sky looked at his mother. It was true; she did seem all right. He sat down at the table again, taking one of her hands in his.

'Are you really all right? You do seem a lot better.'

His mother nodded. 'I don't know why, but I feel as if I am coming to the end of a long tunnel. And it has been a long one, hasn't it? I don't know what I would have done without you.'

Sky escaped to meet Nicholas at the local gym, not wanting to stay and listen to her gratitude. If his life had stayed normal, he would have been feeling light-hearted now. His mother was getting better, the days were warming up and it would be the Easter holidays in a few weeks. But as a Stravagante, he found everything getting complicated. He had seen the most powerful man in Talia nearly die from poisoning and he was no longer sure who could be trusted.

It was a matter of honour to Camillo Nucci, the eldest of the young generation of his family, to loathe every di Chimici, and it was his dearest wish to avenge the murder of his uncle Donato, which had happened before he was born. His father, Matteo, was the richest Nucci so far and had commissioned the most splendid palace on the far side of the river, mainly to annoy Duke Niccolò. It was bigger than either the Palazzo di Chimici in the Via Larga or the grand Palazzo Ducale in the city's main square.

The Nucci were as old a family as the di Chimici and nearly as rich. But the two clans had been at war for as long as anyone could remember. It had most likely begun two hundred years previously when the first Alfonso di Chimici had been friends with the first Donato Nucci. The two young men had both courted the same young woman, the beautiful Semiramide. She was as haughty as she was lovely and the two suitors were less highly born than her.

It was the time when the two families were accumulating their first fortunes, the Nucci from wool and the di Chimici from distilling perfume. Each young man brought a gift for Semiramide. Donato's was a woollen shawl, warm and soft but not particularly elegant. Alfonso's was a crystal phial of lily cologne.

Semiramide was vain, it was summer, the shawl was set aside, the perfume applied to her wrists, and Alfonso's suit was favoured. For generations afterwards, when a Nucci met a di Chimici in the street, one would hold his nose and the other bleat like a sheep. The di Chimici's star rose rapidly; the money they made selling their perfumes and lotions brought them such riches that they were soon acting as bankers to half the royal houses of Europa and charging high interest on their loans.

Alfonso died in his sixties and his eldest son, Fabrizio, declared himself Duke of Giglia within eighteen months. The Nucci's fortune grew too and their acres of sheep farms ensured their continuing prosperity. But they could never catch up with the di Chimici, who gave themselves airs and wore fine clothes and acquired titles the way other men bought boots.

The Nucci could have rallied their supporters to form some kind of opposition to the di Chimici in Giglia. But they chose instead to brood over their wrongs and school their young people in hatred of the perfumiers and bankers.

Still, they were almost social equals, being richer than any other Giglian family, and it seemed as if the old enmities would be forgotten when young Donato was offered the hand of Eleanora di Chimici. But the original feud sprang up again a hundred times more fiercely after the insult to Eleanora and Donato's murder.

So it was with undisguised pleasure that Camillo received the news of the Duke's poisoning. His informant was a man who had removed his di Chimici servant's livery and run straight from the Via Larga to the Nucci's old palazzo.

'You stayed to see him taken ill?' pressed Camillo.

'Yes,' said the man. 'I served him with the mushrooms myself, the young prince having none, as you said would be the case. Then, when the main course was cleared and they were eating fruit, the Duke started to clutch his stomach. I waited until the vomiting began, then thought I should make myself scarce.'

'They will investigate the cook first, I don't doubt,' said Camillo. 'I should not like to be in his shoes.' He handed over a purse full of silver. 'Well done. And now I suggest you should take a little holiday – perhaps in the mountains – for a few weeks.'

*

Camillo would not have been so happy if he had seen Duke Niccolò a few hours later, sitting up in bed in a snowy nightshirt, his eyes glittering and his mind and body unimpaired.

His sons were around him and his daughter waited on his every need, but there was to be no deathbed scene – not this time.

'What did the cook say?' he asked Fabrizio.

'He swore that the mushrooms came from his usual supplier and were wholesome when he sent up the dish,' said the prince.

'And did you torture him to make sure his answer was honest?' asked the Duke, as he might have said, 'Are you sure it's not raining?'

'Yes, Father,' said Fabrizio. 'Not personally, of course, and not much. It was clear he was telling the truth. He has been in the family's service a long time.'

'No one is incorruptible,' said the Duke. 'No one. But I expect you are right. What about the footman?'

'No one has seen him since the meal was served,' said Prince Carlo. 'It is most likely that the poison was introduced by him. We have men out searching the city.'

'And what are they looking for?' said the Duke. 'A

man. That's all we could remember about him, isn't it?'

Carlo was silent.

'Let us waste no more time on the servant,' said the Duke. 'It is the master we want. I know I have many enemies, but this is not the work of the Stravaganti. Their methods are more subtle. It is to the house of Nucci that we must look for the origin of this attempt on my life.' He looked ready to leap out of bed and bring the culprit to book himself.

'Rest now, Father,' said Beatrice. 'You are still weak and must sleep in order to recover your strength.'

'Don't we need some proof before accusing the Nucci?' asked Prince Gaetano. 'It is only a guess that they were behind it.'

'Find proof, then,' snapped the Duke. 'But in the meantime, if I still have three sons loyal to their father, I shall expect this crime to be avenged.'

Sky waited till he and Nicholas were showering after their fencing lesson before telling him about the Duke. It was the only time he could be sure Georgia wouldn't be around. He didn't think she would approve of his passing on such disturbing news.

'Poisoned?' said Nicholas, standing still under the spray. 'Is he all right?'

'Yes,' said Sky. 'He's going to be fine. Brother Sulien gave him an antidote.'

'But who did it?'

Sky shrugged. 'No one knows.'

'It was the Nucci, I bet,' said Nicholas, as they

towelled themselves in the changing room. 'I can't bear it. I must go there.'

'To Giglia?' said Sky, surprised.

Nicholas sighed. 'But I can't, can I? My talisman comes from Remora and would take me to the City of Stars. I could ride to Giglia from there but it would take me at least half a day and I'd have to get back to Remora in the same day to stravagate back here.' He tugged his wet hair in frustration. 'And it's not that easy, going back. But I must. It drives me mad to think of my family in danger. What if someone tried to kill Gaetano?'

Carlo didn't consult his brothers. He took a dagger from the chest in his room and hid it down the side of his suede boot. Running down the steps of the palazzo, he bumped into the man he knew Duke Niccolò used as a spy.

'Come with me,' Carlo hissed at him. 'Take me to where the Nucci will be.'

Enrico knew vendetta when he saw it. He made no attempt to calm or dissuade the prince. If a di Chimici wanted to kill a Nucci that was family business. If Enrico could help they would be grateful, and whether the attempt failed or succeeded, he would have a hold over another di Chimici family member.

The two men left the palazzo, trailed by an inconspicuous street boy. The Eel recognised his young apprentice and smiled to himself; it wouldn't hurt at all to have another witness.

The Nucci would be at their palazzo near Saint-

Mary-among-the-Vines, Enrico thought, though that was a bad place to carry out revenge. He recommended waiting nearby till one came out. It was nearly dusk, and once the torches were lit, all of Giglia's fashionable families would dress in their best and join in the 'passeggiata' round the city's main squares.

Carlo was a complete amateur; he wanted to stab the first Nucci who appeared, in full sight of the people already gathering in the square with the two elongated pyramids, outside the friary church. But Enrico managed to restrain him until the little band of Nucci brothers – Camillo and the younger Filippo and Davide – had come out and were a good distance from the palazzo.

The three young men walked down an alley, taking a short cut to the Piazza Ducale. The two older Nucci walked on ahead while Davide, only eighteen years old and proud to be able to stroll out with his big brothers, stopped to caress a stray dog.

'Now!' hissed Enrico and Carlo felled the boy with a single thrust. Davide Nucci had no time to cry out. He felt the blade withdrawn from between his ribs and his life blood following it. Before his eyes closed, he saw the young prince's gloating smile and heard his feet padding away over the cobbles.

Camillo noticed that his younger brother had fallen back. 'Hurry up, Davide,' he called. 'The young ladies will be waiting!' He turned and saw a crumpled body at the far end of the alley.

Camillo and Filippo raced back to where their little brother lay dying. They did their best to staunch the blood but could see straightaway that the wound was fatal.

'Who?' demanded Camillo, cradling Davide in his arms. 'Who was it?'

'Di Chimici,' was the last thing Davide ever said. A small dog licked his blood from the cobbles while his brothers howled their grief to the darkening sky.

'What have you been saying to Nicholas?' whispered Georgia. 'He's in a very funny mood.'

As quickly as he could, Sky filled her in on the poisoning.

'You shouldn't have told him,' said Georgia.

'How could I just not tell him when he asked me what happened in Giglia last night?' asked Sky. 'It was upsetting for me too, you know, seeing a man nearly die of poison.'

'Yes, but it wasn't your father,' said Georgia, and immediately regretted it when she saw Sky's expression. She knew he had a single mum, knew vaguely that there was some mystery about his father and that he never talked about him; all the girls in their year knew that. She had put her foot in it. And it wasn't as if she didn't know what it was like to be fatherless. Even though her stepdad, Ralph, had become like a real father to her, she understood about families and the private sufferings they could conceal.

She put her hand tentatively on Sky's arm. 'Sorry,' she said.

And that was when Alice saw them. It hit her all at once that Sky was not interested in her at all; he just wanted to get to know her in order to get close to her best friend. She turned away, her cheeks scarlet.

'Damn!' said Georgia, catching sight of Alice. 'I'm getting everything wrong today. I'm just so worried about Nicholas. He says he wants to go back to Talia. I think he's regretting coming here.'

'You feel responsible for him?' asked Sky.

'Yes. If it hadn't been for me – and Luciano – he wouldn't be here. We tried to persuade him that he would miss his family too much but I can't tell you how determined he was. I've never met anyone with a will as strong as Nick's. And he was just a kid then.'

'Is that all it is?' Sky was surprised at his own boldness. A few days ago Georgia had seemed remote and intimidating; now he was asking her if she fancied a boy two years younger than her.

Georgia didn't flare up. 'No. It isn't all. I think Nick and I will always be together, because he's the only one who knows what it was like for me in Talia. You can't have an experience like that and just live the rest of your life normally as if nothing had happened. I know the real him and he knows the real me; it's as simple as that.'

'Not simple for him,' said Sky.

'It isn't simple for anyone, is it?' said Georgia. 'Why don't you ask Alice out?'

Sky was gobsmacked. It wasn't where he thought the conversation was going at all.

'You've wanted to for ages, haven't you?' asked Georgia. 'And she likes you, you know.'

Sky suddenly felt as if the sun had come out and all the birds were singing. His lungs felt too full of air to breathe properly. He grinned at Georgia and she smiled back at him.

'Go on, then,' she said. 'She's over there. Do it

before she gets the wrong idea about you and me. But I'll want to talk to you about Nick again.'

All was chaos in the Nucci palace. The brothers had carried Davide home, his blood staining their fine clothes, and laid him in the family chapel. Now their mother and sisters had begun to lament and their cries were heard through all the surrounding streets. The men left the body to the women and were huddled in Matteo's study. Servants brought wine and Camillo was drinking deep.

In a corner of his grief-maddened brain, he knew that he was in a way responsible for Davide's death. No di Chimici would have stabbed the boy if Camillo hadn't poisoned the Duke. But he simply couldn't afford to think like that. The only way to retain his sanity was to tell himself that the hated di Chimici had struck again. They had killed his little brother, just as they had killed his uncle, and only shedding more of their family's blood would make him feel any better.

The servant pouring wine for Matteo Nucci whispered something in his master's ear. The merchant started and fixed his eyes on his eldest son.

'I hear there was an attempt on Duke Niccolò's life today,' he said, slightly slurring his words.

'Hah!' snorted Camillo. 'Rather more than an attempt, I should say.'

'You had better say nothing!' snapped his father. 'The Duke lives. And my boy lies in the chapel.'

Camillo gaped. 'Impossible!'

The mild evening when Camillo had gone

swaggering out into the square, puffed up with his success in ridding the city of an arrogant tyrant, had turned to a black night of despair.

'You seem to know a lot about it,' said Matteo. 'But you don't know that the Duke has been healed by the Senior Friar at the church here. Don't you know better than to try and poison a family named for being chemists? They have remedies at their disposal that no one else has. And do they bother with poisons now? No, they avenge their wrongs with a knife.' And the old man wept.

'Forgive me, Father,' said Camillo, in anguish. 'But I shall avenge him. I shall avenge Davide's death. I shan't rest till the streets of Giglia run with di Chimici blood!'

'And what good will that do?' came a voice from the doorway. Graziella Nucci had already donned the black clothes she would wear for the rest of her life. 'Will that give me back Davide? No. All you will achieve is more deaths in both families, more lamenting women, more work for priests and gravediggers. I envy Benedetta di Chimici her place under the earth, where she no longer has to fear for the death of her children.'

Camillo loved and honoured his mother, but even as he respected and shared her suffering and promised her that he would not pursue the vendetta, he had every intention of breaking his word.

*

Sandro was rattled. He had never seen a man die before and this one was not much older than him. He picked up the little dog and carried him back to his lodgings. He didn't feel like eating much himself and was glad to give the animal half his dish of liver and onions. The dog wolfed it down and wagged his tail.

'You're as bad as me, I reckon,' said Sandro. 'Just a street stray, ready to do anything for a meal.'

He knew that it had been Prince Carlo who struck the blow, but he had seen the Eel lead him to the place and give him the nod when the boy got separated from his brothers, like a wolf singling out a vulnerable lamb.

So his master was a murderer as well as a spy. Well, he should have known. Giglia was a violent city, used to such things. Hadn't he himself always been fascinated by the stabbing in the little square? But now that he had actually seen blood spilt on the cobbles, Sandro's ghoulish imagination had drunk its fill.

The little dog was dozing on a rug.

'It's all the same to you, isn't it?' said Sandro. 'Blood and gravy. But that was a real boy, like Tino. Someone with a mother and father who loved him. Not like us. I don't reckon anyone would miss either of us.'

He was surprised to find tears running down his cheek. He rubbed them away fiercely with his sleeve. But he was glad not to be on his own that night. Even a scruffy stray dog was better than no company at all. He stretched out on the rug beside the sleeping dog.

'It looks as if we're stuck with each other,' he said, yawning. 'I'd call you after that young Nucci, but I don't know his name. Still, he was someone's brother. I'll call you Fratello.'

*

When Sky returned to Talia that night, he found Sulien pacing his small cell in deep thought.

'It has begun,' he said. 'The Nucci tried to kill the Duke and now someone has succeeded in killing the youngest Nucci. From now on, Giglia will be in a state of civil war.'

Chapter 9

Angels

Over the next few weeks tensions rose in Giglia. There were no more deaths but plenty of fights between the Nucci and di Chimici factions. It wasn't just family members; the majority of the city took sides with one clan or the other. Over the generations, hundreds of people had owed their livelihood to one of the two warring families. Now every night in the city bands of young men roved around, looking for trouble, and when rivals met, jeers and insults broke out. By day, many youths sported black eyes, bandaged heads and bloody noses.

The old Nucci palace was fortified with an ancient tower; many palazzos had such towers, left over from earlier days when life in Giglia had been even more violent and unpredictable. Now, ever since Davide had been buried, Matteo Nucci and his two remaining sons had been building up a supply of weapons to defend their family, in case those days returned.

Family members had gathered from all over Talia, rallying round the bereaved Nucci and filling the palazzo with strong young men. Di Chimici too would soon be assembling in the city for the weddings. Rumours were flying round that the Nucci would avenge the loss of Davide as soon as their period of mourning was ended.

Sandro's spying tasks increased but he wasn't happy about it; he kept out of the Eel's way as much as possible, just giving his reports and leaving. He no longer wanted to hang round Enrico and certainly no longer wished he had a father like him. Sandro passed most of his days up at Saint-Mary-among-the-Vines, which was convenient for spying on the Nucci and meant he could spend more time with Brother Tino.

Sky was relieved when the Easter holidays came and his mother was still getting better. It meant he could lie in late in the mornings like a normal teenager, which made up a bit for his nightly trips to Talia. His social life was becoming more normal too. He had taken Alice out twice before the end of term, once to the cinema and once just to a coffee bar, when they had talked for hours and really begun to relax with each other. Now he was looking forward to spending more time alone with her.

But a new problem had developed; Georgia, Alice and Nicholas often did things together and didn't mind Sky tagging along, but when he was with them he was torn between wanting to be with Alice and responding to frantic signals from the other two to tell them the latest news from Giglia. Seeing them on their own was difficult to organise too. Thank goodness for fencing! Alice was bored by it and had never come to watch Nicholas practise. Now that they couldn't use the school, Nicholas and Sky booked regular times at the local gym and it was natural for Georgia to come and watch. Meeting up in the cafe afterwards was their best time for exchanging news.

Nicholas was in a permanent state of agitation about his Talian family. Although Sky had assured him that the Duke had suffered no ill consequences from the poisoning, it had made the boy restless and the news about the stabbing of Davide Nucci had only made things worse. 'How is Gaetano?' – always his first question – had acquired a new urgency.

And worse was to come. Georgia dropped the bombshell at their first fencing session. 'You know I'm spending Easter in Devon with Alice? My parents are going to Paris.'

'What about Russell?' asked Nicholas.

Georgia snorted. 'As if I'd stay in the house with him!' Two terms at Sussex University had slightly improved her stepbrother but she still wouldn't want to spend any time with him. 'Anyway, he's back off to Greece. I think he's got a girlfriend there.'

Sky was stunned. No Alice and no Georgia. He tried out in his head the thought, 'My girlfriend's going away.' At least it sounded more normal than, 'My fellow Stravagante won't be around.' And he would still have Nicholas. But a day or two later even that ground was cut away. Nicholas had been down to Devon with Georgia before, where they all rode horses, and Alice had asked if he'd like to join them that Easter. The Mulhollands had no objections and Nicholas couldn't think of a convincing excuse, so he was going too. Sky was a bit hurt that Alice had asked Nicholas and not him.

Rosalind noticed that Sky was unusually quiet. 'What's up?' she asked, after he'd got off the phone with Nicholas.

'Everyone's going to Devon this holidays,' said Sky, trying to look positive about it. 'First Alice and Georgia and now Nick too.'

Rosalind was thoughtful. 'Perhaps it's time we visited Nana?' she said.

Giuditta Miele was virtually unaware of the mounting tension in Giglia. When she was beginning a statue, she thought of nothing else, day or night. She had made her first cautious cuts with the chisel on the Duchessa's block of marble. The young woman was in there somewhere, she knew, and her job was to uncover her. In spite of Duke Niccolò, the Duchessa would be portrayed as a symbol of her city's independence and autonomy.

Giuditta had decided to carve her almost like a ship's figurehead, standing at the prow of her state barge, as she did after her Marriage with the Sea. Arianna would be masked, with her cloak and hair streaming out behind her as she faced her city, returning to it after the ceremony that ensured its prosperity for the forthcoming year.

Now the sculptor worked all day, gradually excavating the statue she could already envisage. Her young apprentices watched and kept her supplied with food and drink. They were supposed to be working on a marble sarcophagus of a simple but effective design. It was like a large basket with rope handles – a style made fashionable by a tomb of a di Chimici ancestor in their family church of Sant'Ambrogio. It wasn't difficult and it kept them occupied, but there wasn't a would-be sculptor in the workshop who wasn't more interested in what Giuditta was doing.

'Come here, Franco,' she said to the best-looking of them now. 'Stand straight, looking towards the window. Pretend you are on the open sea at the front of a ship.'

Franco posed diffidently, trying to look like a sailor.

'No, no,' said Giuditta impatiently. 'You are a young woman. Don't plant your feet so sturdily. You are graceful, dignified, but also wild.'

It was a tough assignment but young Franco did his best. His skin was pale and his hair an unusual silvery blond; his mother came from northern Europa. He was much in demand by Giglia's many painters as a model for angels, but he was far from angelic and not effeminate at all. He adored Giuditta, who was the only artist he had met who was completely impervious to his charms.

'Mm,' said the sculptor. 'What would you do with your hands?'

'Grasp the ship's rail, Maestra?' hazarded Franco.

'Good,' said Giuditta, snatching up her pile of drawings and swiftly making some strokes with a piece of charcoal. 'You can go back to your basketry now.'

Then, to herself, 'I need the Duchessa here.'

*

The next time Sky arrived in Giglia, he found Sulien smiling.

'What's happened?' said Sky.

'Reinforcements,' said Sulien mysteriously. 'Can you manage to stay later tomorrow? It would mean sleeping through the morning in your world.'

Sky thought about it. It wouldn't be too difficult. Rosalind had a client the following morning, her first for ages, and she had arranged to have lunch afterwards with Laura, who still worked in the House of Commons. It would be perfectly easy to say that night that he wanted to sleep in.

'I think so,' he answered. 'Why?'

'Duke Niccolò wants us to come to dinner at his palazzo,' said Sulien. 'I think he wants to thank us for saving his life. And he will have some important visitors.'

But he would say no more, however hard Sky pressed him.

'Today I need your help in the laboratory,' said the friar. 'We are going to distil perfume from narcissus flowers.'

*

The Duchessa of Bellezza was entertaining some dear friends when the messenger arrived from Giglia.

Doctor Dethridge and his wife Leonora, the woman Arianna had been brought up to believe was her aunt, had arrived with Leonora's great friend, Silvia Bellini, Arianna's mother. The disguised former Duchessa had often sat in this same reception room, entertaining important foreign visitors. But plain Silvia Bellini did not miss the days of State occasions and gorgeous gowns. Now mask-less, she enjoyed a freedom that she had given up for twenty-five years in order to rule the city.

This little group and less than a dozen others were the only ones in Talia who knew that the old Duchessa still lived. Now they were drinking the blond sparkling wine for which the city was famous and catching up with the news. Silvia's constant companion, a tall red-haired servant, hovered behind her chair.

'Wants to give you a dress?' Silvia was saying, when the messenger was shown in. 'He never sent me one.'

Guido Parola coughed over her last words, so that the palace servant wouldn't hear them. Silvia was getting careless. The messenger being shown in was carrying a long box. He bowed as best he could and then presented the box to the young Duchessa.

'With the compliments of my master, the Duke of Giglia,' he said. 'His Grace, Duke Niccolò, asks that you wear this unworthy garment at the forthcoming nuptials of his sons.'

Arianna's startled eyebrows appeared above her rose-coloured mask. So soon? she thought. But she courteously thanked the messenger and sent him to get refreshment, while Barbara, her waiting-woman, took the box. The little group of people was expectant.

'Shall I open it, your Grace?' asked Barbara.

The tasselled silver cord was undone and the lid lifted, while Arianna resisted an urge to get down on her hands and knees and rummage in the tissue paper herself. Barbara lifted the dress out reverently; it was very heavy. 'Oh, milady!' she whispered.

It was an extraordinary garment. The cloth was a stiff silver brocade but it was almost invisible under the gems stitched into it. The wide skirt was criss-crossed with lines of pearls and amethysts, so that the whole dress sparkled and shone like the moon at dusk. The bodice was tight and the neckline cut low and square, the tops of the sleeves high in the Giglian style.

'It's beautiful,' said Leonora.

'The gemmes do matche thine eyes,' agreed Dethridge.

'You'll not be able to sit down in it,' said Silvia, casting a practised eye over the jewel-encrusted dress. 'But you'll look wonderful in it – fit to have your portrait painted.' She shifted her direct gaze to Arianna's eyes, so like her own.

'What do you really think?' the young Duchessa asked.

'I think you should contact Rodolfo and Luciano as soon as possible,' said Silvia.

*

Rodolfo and Luciano were already in Giglia. They entered the city as quietly as they could, but all visitors had to give their names in at the gates at a sensitive time like this, and news soon spread that the Regent of Bellezza and his assistant had arrived. They went first to their lodgings then set out to call on Giuditta.

The sculptor met them abstractedly and Luciano was immediately overawed by her. He had seen her just briefly when she came to sketch Arianna in Bellezza. She was the only female Stravagante he had met, apart from Georgia, and she was as different from the twenty-first-century girl as could be. Giuditta was tall and well-built, deep-bosomed and broad-shouldered. Her brown hair was streaked with grey – though whether from age or marble dust it was hard to tell – and was tied loosely back just to keep it out of her eyes. Her coarse working clothes made her look like a washerwoman rather than an artist and possessor of occult knowledge.

'Greetings, sister,' said Rodolfo, and Luciano saw a kind of transformation creep over the sculptor. Her spirit swam up to the surface of her eyes and it was as if she had suddenly woken from a deep dream.

'Rodolfo!' she exclaimed, smiling, and Luciano saw that she was attractive, with a lively intelligence and that total self-confidence that all Talian Stravaganti seemed to have. 'Does this mean the Duchessa is here too?'

'Not yet,' said Rodolfo. 'You remember my apprentice, Luciano, from your visit to Bellezza? He is a Cavaliere now and works with me as my assistant. We have come first, to ensure the city is safe for her.'

'I am told the city isn't safe for anyone,' said Giuditta, her eyes flicking back to the marble even as she spoke to them.

'Is that it?' asked Luciano. 'Arianna's statue?'

'It will be,' said Giuditta. 'I am still trying to find

her, but I know she's there. Go on, touch it. You know her. See if you sense the Duchessa inside.'

Luciano went and laid his hands on the white marble. It was cold and rough; only the polished marble of finished statues was smooth and shiny. He closed his eyes and thought of Arianna; it wasn't hard to do. But he saw only the warm, laughing girl of their first friendship, and this statue would have to be of the formal, public city-ruler who was still a stranger to him.

'No,' he said, opening his eyes. 'I'm sorry.'

'That's all right,' said Giuditta. She seemed quite amused. 'It doesn't mean she isn't there, only that you are not a sculptor.'

*

Sulien was still being mysterious when Sky arrived the next morning. It had been easy enough for him to feign tiredness when he had gone to bed in his own world; he had spent a lot of the day fencing and training and Nicholas was a hard master.

'I'm knackered, Mum,' he had said, scooping Remedy up to take him to bed. 'Is it all right if I don't set my alarm?'

'That's fine,' Rosalind had replied. 'I won't see you till late tomorrow afternoon. Remember I'm having lunch with Laura and she always has a lot of gossip to pass on.'

Now Sky was wondering what on earth dinner with the Duke would be like and what else was on the agenda besides.

'Come,' said Sulien. 'It is time you met another Stravagante.'

Luciano and Rodolfo were in their lodgings and the older Stravagante had unpacked his mirrors. He was adjusting them now, focusing the first, as always, where he believed his wife to be.

'Silvia does not seem to be in Padavia,' he said, frowning.

'You know how often she goes to Bellezza,' said Luciano. 'She takes awful risks.'

Rodolfo sighed. 'It is her nature and always has been.' He paused. 'Arianna is very like her, you know. Impetuous, certain her choices are right, and liable to walk into danger.'

'Do you think that's what she'll be doing here?' asked Luciano. He couldn't forget what it had been like when they had left the Duke in Remora after the death of Falco. Niccolò had been unconscious when they had removed hastily from the city, and this wedding invitation was his first overture to Bellezza since then.

'You know I would not let her do that,' said Rodolfo. 'But I shall not always be here to guide her. One day she must learn to make the right choices on her own. I can form my own opinion and advise her about any dangers, but she must be the one who decides if it's right to come to Giglia or not.'

Luciano saw the Ducal palace in Bellezza coming into sharp relief in one of the mirrors. Twisting the knobs and levers underneath, Rodolfo roved through the rooms of the palazzo until he found what he was looking for.

Bingo! thought Luciano, as the mirror showed

Arianna, her maid Barbara and Silvia in the Duchessa's private chamber. They were all looking at something which could not be seen in the mirror, and appeared worried. Rodolfo bent close to the glass surface and then focused another mirror on Leonora's house in the Piazza San Suliano. Immediately William Dethridge's large face swam into view.

'Maistre Rudolphe!' the Elizabethan's voice crackled. 'I was juste aboute to seke thee myselfe.'

'What is it?' asked Rodolfo. 'I have seen both Duchesse and they look worried. Has something happened?'

*

Sky couldn't believe his luck, getting into Giuditta's bottega. He had been interested in sculpture for a long time but didn't dare think about studying it, because it would mean a Foundation Year in art school, followed by at least another three years doing a degree, and he didn't think Rosalind could afford it. Whenever they talked about university, she assumed he'd do a three-year course in a subject like English.

But as soon as he walked into the bottega, Sky's heart leapt. He envied the apprentices who worked on their own projects while Giuditta's monumental work was created under their eyes. The workshop was full of maquettes and copies. In one corner stood a carved wooden angel holding a candle sconce, painted silver. Sky jumped when he looked from the angel to one of the apprentices; he had the same face.

The floorspace was dominated by a huge block of white stone on which Giuditta was working. She was chiselling furiously at the back of it and Sky wondered if she were making another angel; something very like wings seemed to be emerging. The sculptor's face appeared round the block of stone, whitened by the dust she was creating. Her hair too was like that of one of her statues, stiff and moulded to her head. When she saw the two friars, she climbed down from her ladder to meet them.

'You have come for your angel?' she asked Sulien, and Sky had the strangest feeling that if these two Stravaganti had been alone in the room together they would not have bothered to use words.

'And brought you the sky,' said Sulien. 'This is Celestino – Brother Tino, we call him. He comes from far away.'

Giuditta looked at him closely. If it had been anyone else, he would have been embarrassed.

'You have a good face,' she said, and he suddenly felt his chin grasped by her chalky fingers and his face turned towards the light.

'I like its planes and angles,' she said. 'But it is not a monk's face. And it would be a shame to trim all that hair to a tonsure.'

Sky felt thoroughly seen through, recognised as a Stravagante and fake friar and one with very unreligious thoughts about girls. But he didn't mind; Giuditta reminded him of Georgia, in a funny way. She had no small talk, just said what was on her mind. And he knew instinctively that she was honest and reliable.

'I wish I could be your apprentice instead,' he said truthfully, and was aware of suppressed laughter from the four young men who had downed tools and were watching him with curiosity.

'Art and religion?' said Giuditta. 'We don't separate them here. Come and look at this marble,' she said, and took him over to the block she had been working on.

'Is it another angel?' asked Sky.

'No,' said Giuditta. 'Those aren't wings. That's the Duchessa's hair and cloak.' She walked him round to the other side of the statue. 'Now, put your hands here, about halfway down. Can you sense her?'

Sky hesitantly put his hands on the marble. He had never seen Arianna but Georgia had told him about her. He guessed that he was touching the marble somewhere at the level of her middle. He expected to imagine sliding his hands round her slim waist, a strangely intimate gesture to make to someone unfamiliar and important, even though it was only a statue.

He frowned. Clear in his mind was a pair of white hands almost pushing him away. He opened his eyes, unaware that they had been closed till then. He found himself looking straight into the brown gaze of the sculptor.

'She resisted me,' he said. 'Her hands are here,' he indicated, 'pushing me away.'

Giuditta smiled. 'They are resting on a ship's rail,' she said. 'But only I know that, I and the apprentices. And now you too, Brother Tino. I think you must be an artist of our kind.'

Sulien and Sky carried the wooden angel with its candlestick back to the friary. It was wrapped in a bundle of sacking but still about the size and shape of a person, if you didn't count the wings. It made Sky feel as though they were carrying a corpse through the streets of Giglia.

*

'Yt is the dresse,' said Dethridge. 'Yt has arrived. And yt is worth a fortune. The Dutchesse asked me to telle thee. She is afeard. And so is her lady mothire. They thinke it bodes ille.'

Chapter 10

A Man's Job

Sky left Giuditta's bottega feeling ten feet tall. She really thought he could be a sculptor, like her! And that mattered so much that it took a while for him to realise that they had something else in common: they were both Stravaganti.

'You are quiet,' said Sulien, smiling, as they carried the angel home. 'I think our visit has taught you something?'

'Yes,' said Sky, 'but it just makes me want to find out more. I mean, what does it mean that you and I and Giuditta are all, you know, of the same Brotherhood? You're a friar, she's a sculptor, I'm a schoolkid. How does that make us the same and how are we like this mysterious Rodolfo and a boy who used to live in my world? Or Georgia and

Falco, who is now Nicholas?'

'Not all Stravaganti are practising scientists,' said Sulien quietly, checking that they were not overheard. 'Rodolfo, yes, and Doctor Dethridge, but many others of us follow other professions. In Remora, for example, there is a Horsemaster, and there is a musician in Volana. But we all know the ones in Bellezza and we communicate by means of a system of mirrors. As for the ones from your world, all we know is that the talismans seem to choose potential Stravaganti who are for some reason not happy there.'

He stopped and turned from his end of the angel to look in Sky's face. 'I feel that was true of you when the talisman found you. But I don't know if it still is.'

*

Rodolfo had asked William Dethridge to visit the Duchessa again and to get her to hold the dress up in front of the mirror in her chamber. He and Luciano were now staring at it.

'She can't wear that,' said Luciano decisively. 'She can't accept such an expensive present from the Duke. Or anyone, except perhaps you.'

'I couldn't afford it,' said Rodolfo grimly. 'Just look at those jewels! She's going to be more richly dressed than any of the di Chimici brides.'

'You don't mean she should wear it to the wedding?'

'I don't see how she can avoid it, without offending the Duke,' said Rodolfo. 'And with things the way they are, we must be very careful not to offend the Duke.'

'Is that why we're going tonight?' said Luciano. 'I really don't see why we have to go and meet him in his own palace – he might poison us both.'

'He might,' agreed Rodolfo. 'He is perfectly capable of it and would have the means, but I don't think he will. Remember, he is still fascinated by our Brotherhood and he wants to know all our secrets. He is much more likely to torture us than kill us.'

'Great,' said Luciano. 'Nothing to worry about there, then.'

*

Sandro was waiting back at Saint-Mary-among-the-Vines. He looked rather forlorn, lounging round the Lesser Cloister, watching friars weed the garden.

'No work today?' asked Sulien.

Sandro shrugged. 'Nothing new,' he said.

'Would you like to do something for me?' asked Sulien. 'Brother Tino and I are going to make liqueur.'

Sandro's eyes brightened. He would be in the laboratory, which had always fascinated him, and the Eel couldn't tell him off for that.

Enrico had asked him to find out what he could about the pharmacist-friar. But Sandro resolved not to tell his master about anything he found out.

Sulien's work on his list of formulas was progressing slowly. He was now making a new batch of the liqueur Vignales, for which the friary was famous, and whose recipe was a secret from all except the other friars. Sandro and Sky both felt honoured to be entrusted with even a part of the mystery.

'How do you know how to make it if you don't

have a recipe already?' asked Sky.

'It has been handed down through several pharmacist-friars to me,' said Sulien. 'I made it under the supervision of old Brother Antonino, my predecessor. More than once. But it's never been written down before.'

It took hours, filling a sort of cauldron with sugar, alcohol fermented from grapes and the various herbs and spices that Brother Sulien instructed the boys to supply from colourful ceramic jars. It soon became obvious to Sky that Sandro couldn't read and that Sulien was careful to instruct him in ways he could understand – 'please bring me the blue jar on the far left of the bottom shelf,' or 'the aniseed is in the tall green jar with the pink stopper,' and so on. To Sky he just said, 'I need cinnamon,' or 'fetch the ginger root.'

The pile of parchment, with recipes for perfumes, lotions, elixirs, tinctures and tisanes was growing slowly, but Vignales was an important addition. The three worked steadily and quietly for several hours until the cauldron steamed with a thick sticky blue liquid that smelt to Sky a bit like cough mixture. Still, Sulien assured them both that it was a highly prized and expensive drink, and they could certainly attest to the strength of its fumes. Sandro, who had eaten nothing all day, was beginning to stagger.

'Enough,' said Sulien. 'We can leave it to cool now and bottle it tomorrow. It must be getting late. Now, Brother Tino and I have to dine with the Duke but you, Sandro, look in need of a meal nearer home. Go to Brother Tullio and say you have been helping me all afternoon and I said to give you something to eat.'

Sulien took a bottle of the blue Vignales from a shelf. 'From my previous batch,' he explained. 'The Duke will be pleased to get it as a gift.'

'Here's one I made earlier,' murmured Sky.

'He's wonderful, isn't he?' Sandro said to Sky, and Sky was surprised that the scruffy urchin, so tough and hard-bitten when they were out exploring the streets of Giglia, was so impressed by the gentle and scholarly friar.

'I thought you said he was a poisoner?' he whispered.

'I don't really think he can be, do you?' Sandro whispered back. And Sky just had time to shake his head before they had to leave for the Via Larga.

*

'Why are we entertaining these Bellezzan charlatans?' asked Prince Fabrizio, brushing an invisible speck of dust from his white ruffled shirt. 'I thought they were our bitter enemies.'

'If you think diplomacy is about entertaining only people you like, then you have learnt nothing from me at all,' said his father, severely. 'It is true that Rodolfo is a Stravagante and that there is something sinister about his assistant, as he is calling him now. I haven't forgotten his involvement in Falco's death – how could I? But at the moment, we have problems nearer home than the Stravaganti. It was not they who tried to poison me.'

'The Nucci are planning something, I'm sure,' said Fabrizio. 'They'll not let Davide's death go unavenged for long.'

Both father and son knew who was responsible for that death but they would not say a word about it, even when alone with other family members. The expression 'walls have ears' might have been invented to describe the di Chimici palace in the Via Larga.

'Besides,' said the Duke, as if he had no thought of the Nucci, 'I must treat the Duchessa's Regent with due respect.'

'Huh!' said Carlo. 'It's not as if she showed us much courtesy, turning down Gaetano and rushing away from Remora the minute poor Falco died.'

Niccolò rounded on him and Carlo wondered if he had gone too far.

'I won't have a word said against the Duchessa,' the Duke said. 'And I shall expect you all to behave to her father with the same civility you would show to the lady.'

Gaetano remembered how hard he had needed to persuade his father that Arianna had intended no slight either in refusing the offer of a di Chimici marriage or in hastening back to her own city. For himself, he would have no trouble at all in being civil to Luciano, who was his friend, and he had a deep admiration for Rodolfo.

He couldn't help wondering what his father was up to.

*

Sky felt nervous walking to the di Chimici palazzo with Brother Sulien. It was one thing to explore it with Sandro, which he had done more than once, or to run there in an emergency as on the day Niccolò di

Chimici had been poisoned, but to enter it as the Duke's invited guest was quite another. The guard at the gate ushered them into the courtyard with the bronze Mercury, where another flunkey escorted them to the Duke's private reception rooms.

Sky had not seen them before and was overawed. The servant opened the double wooden doors and ushered them into a room more magnificent than anything the twenty-first-century boy had ever seen. But his awe soon turned to fascination. It was obvious that the Duke was a great patron of the arts.

Every wall was covered in paintings, of the kind Sky's art teacher had taught him were called trompe l'oeil, 'eye-deceivers'. Pillars, columns, staircases and balconies all appeared to grow from the walls but were two-dimensional painters' effects. Gods and goddesses leant from the balconies and nymphs danced round the columns, chased by satyrs. Sky stood open-mouthed until a cultivated voice cut through his reverie.

'I see your novice is a lover of the arts, Brother Sulien,' the Duke was saying.

'Indeed, your Grace,' Sulien replied. 'He is most impressed by all the great beauties of your family's city.'

Sky saw that Duke Niccolò was completely recovered. It was the third time he had seen him and he was an impressive figure, tall and well built, with the typical noble features of well-defined cheekbones and a thin bony nose. His white hair and silver beard were cut short and rather suited him. He was dressed in a crimson velvet robe over a lace-trimmed shirt and black breeches, 'like an aristocratic pirate,' thought Sky.

The young princes and the princess were now introduced to the friars, as if they had not met in that mad scramble to save the Duke's life. As indeed they might not have, so different were they now in their elegant clothes, with their composed manners. Sky soaked up every detail to tell Nicholas back home: Princess Beatrice, so dignified and graceful in her low-cut black satin (still in mourning for her brother), Fabrizio haughty and handsome but perfectly polite, Carlo rather nervous and Gaetano as ugly and charming as ever.

The Duke led the way into a second equally elaborately decorated room and Sky saw two figures waiting to meet them there.

'May I introduce Senator Rodolfo Rossi, the Regent of Bellezza?' said the Duke. 'Senator, I should like to present to you one of our most distinguished scientists, Brother Sulien of Saint-Mary-among-the-Vines – and his novice Celestino. You may have heard what signal service they did me recently when I was indisposed after a poisoner's attack.'

There were bows and polite murmurings, even though Rodolfo and Sulien were actually old friends.

'And this is my assistant, Cavaliere Luciano Crinamorte,' said Rodolfo, presenting him to the two friars. 'I think that he and Brother Tino are not far apart in age.'

'And close in age to my youngest son, Gaetano, too,' said the Duke.

Sky saw the little crease of pain that crossed Niccolò's face as he hesitated over the word 'youngest', but Gaetano quickly corralled him and Luciano and, under the excuse of taking them to admire a fine painting, got them away from the others, while servants brought wine.

So this was Sulien's surprise – for Sky to meet the mysterious Lucien! The two boys recognised each other straightaway, though one was dressed as a Dominican friar and the other as a Bellezzan nobleman.

'This is bizarre, isn't it?' said Luciano, as Gaetano pretended to explain the painting to them.

'Incredible,' said Sky.

It was the old Lucien Mulholland, all right, alive and well. He seemed at ease in his grand surroundings and to be on friendly terms with Gaetano, who now asked the usual question, 'How is my brother?'

'He's well,' said Sky. 'He's teaching me to fence.'

'Good idea,' said Luciano. 'You need to be careful here. Gaetano won't mind my saying that his father and brothers are dangerous people – even if they are on their best behaviour tonight.'

Gaetano shook his head sadly. 'But it's not just my family. The Nucci are gathering in their old tower and I dread what they might be planning for the weddings.'

'How's Georgia?' asked Luciano. 'You do know her as well as Falco, don't you?'

'She's fine,' said Sky. 'Off to Devon with her friend Alice. They're both going, her and Nicholas, I mean. You know that's Falco's new name?'

'Yes,' said Luciano. 'Georgia dreamed it up when we were planning his translation. I still find it hard to believe we actually pulled it off. It was mainly Falco, of course. It would all have fallen apart if he hadn't been so determined.'

'He's still that,' said Sky. 'In fact he's desperate to come here and see his family. But that would be madness, wouldn't it? Even if his talisman could bring him to Giglia, he'd be recognised. And he's supposed to be dead!'

'It would be wonderful to see him again,' sighed Gaetano.

'Rodolfo and I are working on the talisman problem,' said Luciano, 'with Doctor Dethridge. You know who that is?'

'The Granddaddy of them all,' said Sky, ruefully.

'We have so much to catch up on,' said Luciano. 'Can I come and see you at the friary tomorrow?'

Sky just had time to say yes, when dinner was announced and the Duke led the way into a dining room, even grander than his salon. Just the sight of the table made Sky feel nervous. Meals at home were eaten in the kitchen with Rosalind or on their laps in front of the television, and now here was a long, marble-topped table, with silver candelabra, wine goblets and a huge silver ornament in the middle.

Luckily he was shown to a seat between Luciano and Gaetano and opposite Beatrice so, although he couldn't talk about the things most on his mind, his position wasn't too terrifying. Rodolfo spent most of the meal in conversation with Sulien and the Duke, and Sky knew that the two older Stravaganti were under the same constraints as him and Luciano, which made him feel better.

Servants kept the red wine coming and Sky sipped his cautiously, noticing that the other young men knocked it back easily. He wasn't sure he liked it, but there was nothing else to drink and some of the dishes were quite salty. He noticed an extra servant, who stood permanently at the Duke's right elbow and who tried every dish and the wine too, before Niccolò allowed himself anything. His taster, presumably. What a frustrating job, thought Sky. Either you clutched your throat and fell down with agonising stomach pains, or the food and drink were perfectly OK and you couldn't have more than a sip or morsel of them.

The food was more recognisable than Sky had feared. There was a green soup which Gaetano said was made from nettles, but which was surprisingly tasty, and then a kind of white fish which was cold and soused in vinegar. That was not so nice but Sky was hungry. The next dish was a risotto with what turned out to be duck. But startlingly it was decorated with little pieces of silver foil – not the sort you'd wrap round a turkey in Sky's world but more like the thin slivers he had sometimes seen on Indian sweets. By the time that the servants brought a sort of sweet pizza, with raisins and sugar and cinnamon, and a dizzyingly sweet wine to go with it, Sky was quite stuffed.

He noticed that Luciano's attention was distracted. What had the Duke just said? He had asked after the Duchessa, Sky thought, but his brain felt a little fuddled, even after a small amount of wine.

'My daughter is very well, thank you,' Rodolfo was now saying.

'Charming young woman,' said Niccolò. 'It was a great disappointment to me that she refused to become part of my family.'

Luciano and Gaetano both tensed and Gaetano

started to blush.

'Not that I am not perfectly happy for Gaetano to marry his cousin,' the Duke continued smoothly.

'Indeed, Francesca di Chimici is also a very lovely young woman,' said Rodolfo.

'I have sent her a gift,' said Niccolò.

'Francesca?' asked Rodolfo, as if he didn't know all about it.

'The Duchessa,' said Niccolò. 'A paltry garment, which I hope she will do me the honour of wearing to the wedding.'

'The honour will be hers, I am sure,' said Rodolfo.

'Tell me,' said the Duke casually, 'do you think the young Duchessa would be equally averse to all members of my family?' Everyone round the table was surprised. Sky thought the Duke might be going to suggest yet another nephew or cousin of his, but all the others knew that the choice of di Chimici suitors would be very limited. The forthcoming weddings would tie up most eligible di Chimici males.

'I have been thinking,' continued the Duke, 'of re-marrying myself. 'And I think perhaps I erred in sending the Duchessa so young and inexperienced a suitor to court her, fond though I am of Gaetano. It perhaps proves the truth of the saying "Never send a boy to do a man's job." What do you think your daughter would say to the suggestion of becoming my Grand Duchess?'

There was silence around the table, but Sky had seen Rodolfo's eyes move straight to Luciano and the boy was fixed in his place only by the intensity of the message that gaze was sending. Both Rodolfo and Luciano had turned quite pale but it was Brother

Sulien who spoke first.

'Does this mean you are taking the title of Grand Duke, your Grace?' he said. 'May we offer our congratulations?'

It was clear that most of his children hadn't known what the Duke was intending; only Carlo looked less than amazed.

'I shall make a public announcement of my intention the night before the weddings, at the feast,' said the Duke. 'That is, as far as my new title is concerned. I think the time is right to become Grand Duke of Tuschia.'

'Then we must congratulate your Grace,' said Rodolfo diplomatically, raising his goblet as if in a toast. 'As for my daughter, I'm sure she will hear your suit with the honour due to it when she arrives in Giglia.'

Fabrizio was very torn. He had no objections to inheriting an even grander title when his father died, but Niccolò's plan to marry again appalled him. He didn't want a stepmother younger than himself, however beautiful, and he could see that Gaetano and Beatrice at least shared his view. None of them had any doubt that their father's courtship would succeed. Who could refuse such a man and such a title?

For Luciano, the rest of the evening was sheer torment. He couldn't wait to get out of the palace. In fact, the four Stravaganti left the palace together, after much tedious ceremony, and Gaetano had time only to whisper that he would meet the others at the friary the next day.

Sky knew that Luciano was still being restrained by the silent force of his master's will until they were well away from the Via Larga. But as soon as that control was relaxed, Luciano exploded.

'So that was what the dress was all about! And the grand dinner! We're supposed to be impressed. But I'll never let Arianna marry that monster. I'll kill him myself first!'

Chapter 11

Daggers Drawn

Sky woke up in the middle of the afternoon with a mini-hangover. He was surprised to find he could still taste the sweet dessert wine that he had gulped down in his nervousness at the Duke's announcement. He got up and showered and brushed his teeth extra thoroughly and drank two glasses of water before Rosalind got in.

He was just wondering what to eat and what meal to call it when he heard his mother's key in the lock. She was in a good mood but tired.

'Tea!' she moaned, falling into her chair in mock exhaustion.

'How was your lunch?' he asked, as he made Rosalind tea and himself toast and marmalade.

'Good,' said Rosalind. 'Laura's always a tonic. She's

a Councillor now, you know. I bet she'll end up an MP herself one day, instead of looking after them.'

'Perhaps she'll be Prime Minister?' suggested Sky. 'Imagine – there'd be laws making it illegal not to have parties every weekend.'

Rosalind giggled. 'I don't know where she gets her energy from. I used to think she'd stolen some of mine. Is that your breakfast, by the way? I know you said you wanted a lie-in, but I hope you didn't mean till four o'clock.'

Sky just grinned. 'Want some?' he asked. He couldn't decide if he felt tired because of spending a day and most of a night in Giglia or refreshed by having spent nearly sixteen hours in bed.

The phone rang. It was Nicholas. Sky took the phone into his bedroom. 'How did it go, dinner with my family?' was Nick's first question.

'OK, I suppose,' said Sky. 'I mean, no one got poisoned and I didn't spill my soup. But I still feel a bit drunk.'

'Who else was there?'

'Luciano and Rodolfo. Luciano recognised me straightaway.'

'He's nice, isn't he?'

'Yeah. I can see what Georgia saw in him.'

There was an awkward silence at the other end of the line.

'You know that, then?' said Nicholas quietly.

'Pretty obvious, I'd have thought.'

'Like you and Alice?'

'Touché,' said Sky. 'Don't worry – there's no future in it, with him stuck in the past, if you see what I mean.'

'I wouldn't be too sure,' said Nicholas. 'She's as keen as I am to go back, if something could be worked out about the talismans.'

'Luciano said something about that. I think Rodolfo and Doctor Dethridge are on the case.'

'I think the only thing that stops her is that Luciano is in love with Arianna,' said Nicholas.

'Um . . . about that,' said Sky. 'Your father made an announcement at dinner that didn't go down too well with Luciano.'

Sandro hadn't gone back to his lodgings. He had hung about the friary with his dog, feeling left out while Sulien and Tino were at the di Chimici Palazzo, and had eventually curled up in a corner of Sulien's laboratory, wrapped tightly in his thin cloak, with Fratello sleeping on his feet. The pharmacist found them after Sky had stravagated back home.

Brother Sulien covered the boy with his own thick black robe and didn't wake him then or when he got up early to walk the maze. Sandro was only beginning to stir when the friar came back from the church.

'Breakfast?' asked Sulien, and took the boy to the refectory for porridge and honey and milk still warm from the friary's goats. Fratello was banished to the yard but Sandro begged a bone for him from Brother Tullio.

It was only when they had both satisfied their appetite that they spoke.

'You seem to have moved in,' remarked Sulien conversationally.

'Only for one night,' said Sandro. 'I've got to be back outside the Nucci place tomorrow, so I thought why go home?'

'Where is home?' asked Sulien.

Sandro shrugged. 'Don't really have one. Not family, anyway. Just lodgings, up near where you were last night.'

'I know you were found by the orphanage near the Duomo,' said Sulien. 'Was there never any search for your mother?'

'Not that I know of,' said Sandro. 'She was probably glad to get rid of me. I expect she was an unmarried girl – or a whore, I suppose.'

'You are still bitter about it,' said Sulien. 'Come with me. I'd like to show you something, if you don't have to go on duty straightaway.'

They picked up Fratello and walked in the direction of the Duomo, but branched off left into a little piazza, called Limbo. It was quiet and deserted, with a tiny old church in one corner. In front of it was a little graveyard, full of small white stones.

'You know what this is?' asked Sulien.

'Yes, it's where they bury the babies.'

'The unbaptised ones, whose souls are in limbo,' nodded Sulien. 'They were born dead or died too soon after their birth to be given their names and welcomed into the church.'

'What are you trying to tell me?' said Sandro.

'There are lives which have a bad start, like yours, and there are those that don't start at all, like those of these innocent children,' said Sulien. 'But we are all in limbo unless we choose to let our lives begin and take us somewhere.'

'I must be getting back to the Nucci now,' said Sandro. But Sulien had given him something to think about.

'I don't believe it,' said Georgia flatly. 'If she wouldn't have Gaetano, who's a really nice guy, she won't take the Duke. Arianna hates the di Chimici – him most of all.'

But even as she said it, a little green devil lodged in her brain was thinking, But if she did marry the Duke, that would take her out of Luciano's reach for ever.

'I know that,' said Sky. 'But Rodolfo seems to think she can't just turn him down. And he's going to make himself Grand Duke now, whatever that means.'

'It means that my family will be even more important in Tuschia,' said Nicholas stiffly.

They were in Sky's room, discussing his latest visit to Talia.

'I'm sorry, Nick,' said Georgia. 'But you've got to stop thinking of them as your family. Vicky and David are your family now, not the di Chimici, and I can't pussyfoot around your feelings every time we talk about them. You know what your father is capable of.'

'It is not easy to stop thinking of those who are in Talia just because you can't see them any more,' said Nicholas, staring at Georgia till she changed colour.

'The point is,' said Sky patiently, 'I think it's going to mean more trouble. Luciano won't give her up without a fight – literally. Rodolfo was able to control him yesterday but that won't last for long. Arianna'll be in the city soon, for sittings with Giuditta the sculptor, and things will come to a head then.'

'What does Gaetano think?' asked Georgia.

'I don't know,' said Sky. 'He's coming to see me tomorrow. So is Luciano.'

'This is unbearable,' said Nicholas. 'I must find a new talisman and get back to Giglia. Can't you bring me something? You could have picked up a spoon or something at my father's table.'

Sky had a vision of what the Duke would have said if he had caught him smuggling silverware out of the palace.

'Don't be so stupid, Nick!' said Georgia, really angry. 'You know that Sky isn't trained to do that – only the Talian Stravaganti bring talismans from world to world.'

'You did it for me,' said Nicholas.

'It wasn't the same,' said Georgia, exasperated. 'That was the eyebrow ring I had with me all the time in Talia. But, while we're on the subject, I did it because you were so desperate to come here, remember?'

It was the closest Sky had ever seen them get to a row. Nicholas was flushed, his hands clenched, and Georgia looked as if she wanted to slap him.

'And now I'm desperate to go back!' Nicholas retorted. 'And so are you, admit it!'

Luciano hadn't slept all night. He tangled himself in the bed covers, thinking of what he would do if Arianna even pretended to listen to the Duke's offer.

He drove himself mad with visions of her as Niccolò's Grand Duchess, wearing dresses every day like the jewel-encrusted monstrosity she had been sent for the di Chimici weddings.

Ever since she had become Duchessa, the Arianna he had known and explored the canals of Bellezza with had seemed to be drifting away from him. She was still friendly and warm towards him, even flirtatious sometimes, but her many official duties and her necessarily grand lifestyle made her seem more and more remote in his eyes. And what was he? A Cavaliere of Bellezza, waiting to go to university. He didn't have a real aristocratic title, like a di Chimici, or even a job that would make him rich.

Now he longed to ride back to Bellezza and grab Arianna's hand and lead her, laughing, into a rowing boat and take her to empty her foster-brothers' lobster pots on Merlino or to eat cakes in her grandparents' house on Burlesca.

But it was no good. In a few days, the Duchessa would be here in Giglia, escorted by Dethridge – and Silvia, who could never keep away from where the action was, or from Rodolfo, for long. And here Arianna would have to be every inch the Duchessa, with her maids and her dressmakers and her hairdresser and her footmen and her bodyguards, and Luciano would be just another admirer she had to fit into her schedule.

He got up and dressed, and went downstairs, where he found Rodolfo already sitting having an early breakfast, served by their landlord.

'So, you couldn't sleep either?' said his master. 'I'm not surprised. These are deep waters we are in.'

The landlord, catching the last words, said, 'Indeed, masters, the Argento hasn't run so high in spring for a hundred years, or so people are saying in the city. It's the heavy winter rains we had. They reckon there's a real danger of flood by Easter.'

'Then I hope it drowns the Duke,' said Luciano gloomily.

The landlord looked shocked to hear such seditious words in his house.

'Take no notice of my young friend,' said Rodolfo. 'He drank too freely of the Duke's wine last night. And now he needs coffee and eggs.'

The man backed out hastily.

'Be careful what you say, Luciano,' warned Rodolfo. 'The city is full of spies.'

*

Francesca's wedding dress was finished. A frothy confection of white lace over a satin bodice and full underskirt, in which she would look every inch a princess. She was trying it on in Arianna's grandmother's parlour and the two young women and the old one were all admiring the effect.

'Gaetano is a lucky man,' said Arianna, smiling. 'No one will have eyes for any bride but you.'

'And what shall you wear, Arianna?' asked Paola Bellini, who had heard about the Duke's present.

'Oh, Nonna, I don't know,' said Arianna. 'If only I could just please myself and forget about diplomacy.'

'Then you would wear one of your old cotton frocks and go barefoot, I expect,' said Paola.

'Your uncle has sent me a dress, Francesca,'

explained Arianna. She hadn't mentioned it to her friend before. 'And it is much too grand and expensive for me to accept without granting him some favour in return. And the favour he has in mind is for me to sign his treaty with Bellezza – of that I am sure.'

'But you won't, will you?' said Francesca.

'No, I can't. It is what my mother spent her life resisting and I owe it to her and the city to continue the fight,' said Arianna. 'And yet, if I don't wear the dress, the Duke will be offended and that is undesirable too.'

'I see,' said Francesca. 'You have a dilemma.'

'It's too hard for me to decide,' said Arianna. 'I don't want to wear it but I can't do just what I want any more. I'm going to ask my father and Dottore Crinamorte what they think.' And my mother too, she thought to herself.

*

It was not long after Sky arrived back in Giglia that Luciano turned up at the friary. They were both short of sleep and went out to sit in the sunshine on the wall of the Great Cloister. Luciano looked at his own single shadow and sighed.

'I wish sometimes I had never been given the notebook,' he said bitterly.

'Notebook?' asked Sky.

'It was my talisman – the thing that brought me to Talia,' said Luciano.

'But, if it hadn't, wouldn't that mean . . .?' Sky hesitated.

'That I would be dead?' said Luciano. 'Yes. But I

think that may be going to happen anyway. I can't see how I can get out of this situation alive. If the Duke tries to marry Arianna, I will kill him – I would say "or die in the attempt" like some corny hero, except that in my case it will probably be "and" not "or", and I'm no hero.'

'You care about her that much?' asked Sky. 'So much you would die for her?'

Luciano didn't answer straightaway. 'Can you imagine what it was like to give up my family and my life in your world?' he asked finally. 'To leave everything I had ever known and be flung back over four centuries to live in the past in this world?'

'Not really,' said Sky. He had seen how comfortably the old Lucien seemed to fit into life in Talia and only now thought about what his feelings must have been when he had to leave his previous life.

'Oh, I know it gave me a second chance, that I *had* a life instead of what was going to happen to the old me,' said Luciano. 'And I'm not ungrateful, believe me. But I've had to become a different person, with a different future to look forward to, and it's only the people here who have made that possible. Arianna most of all. If I thought she was going to become the Duke's wife, I really think I would go mad.'

'But you don't think she'll accept him, do you?' asked Sky. He couldn't imagine a girl of seventeen preferring a white-haired man in his fifties to the good-looking Luciano, but he didn't know Arianna and he guessed a Duchessa couldn't always do what she preferred.

'I think it's unlikely,' said Luciano. 'But not impossible.' He couldn't forget how Gaetano's suit had not been turned down out of hand when it was first made. 'But if she does refuse him, then all our lives will be even more in danger, here in the di Chimici stronghold, with everyone armed and ready for a fight.'

A figure stepped out into the sunlit cloister to join them. It was Gaetano. 'What's this about fighting?' he asked.

*

The Eel was feeling pleased with himself. Word had flown around the palace that Duke Niccolò was going to marry the beautiful young Duchessa of Bellezza and Enrico lost no time in taking the credit for putting the idea into his master's head. He was pleased about the Duke's plans for a new title too; now he would be able to boast of being right-hand man to the Grand Duke. And once Bellezza had entered the fold, it would not take long for the remaining Talian city-states to follow suit. Enrico was quite sure that the Grand Duke would be king of a united Talia one day. If not this Grand Duke, then the next.

He made a mental note to cultivate Prince Fabrizio. The only fly in Enrico's ointment was that his spy network wasn't operating as efficiently as he would like. He wanted hard information about what the Nucci were planning. After all, they had made an attempt on a di Chimici life even before their Davide was killed, so they must be plotting something now. The only question was whether they would wait for the weddings when all the di Chimici would be in the city, or show their hand before.

This was the kind of work Enrico relished, collecting information, following suspects and perhaps having the chance to slide a knife between someone's ribs and be well rewarded for it. He had made himself indispensable to the Duke and looked forward to a rich future. True, he seemed to be losing his influence over his youngest spy, who had become sulky and elusive, but he had lots of others.

There was only one thing missing in the Eel's life and that was the comfort and companionship of a woman. Ever since his fiancée, Giuliana, had so mysteriously disappeared in Bellezza, Enrico had sworn off women. It had been inexplicable; they had been due to marry in a matter of days, Giuliana had ordered her dress and was apparently very excited about the wedding. Then, without a word or a note, she had vanished.

The only explanation he could think of was that she had met someone else and run off with him, someone who was such a good prospect that she had been prepared to leave not just Enrico, but all her family, without any farewell. So complete had been her deception that her father had come round and threatened Enrico for having taken his daughter away.

But that was some time ago and Enrico had been influenced by the Duke's decision to marry again. If a grieving widower could do it, so could a jilted spy, and Enrico was now open to the idea of another romance.

*

'You don't mean it,' said Gaetano. 'You're just upset. It may come to nothing.'

'I don't say what I don't mean,' said Luciano. 'I'm serious. I will kill him if he tries to marry her. I'm sorry he's your father, but I will do it.'

The three boys were still in the cloister. Sky was impressed by how close Luciano seemed to the di Chimici prince. He had heard something of their history together in Remora from Georgia and he knew that what had happened with Falco had forged a strong link between them.

'What do you think, Sky?' asked Luciano.

'What do I know?' he said. 'I've never known my father. I can't imagine what it's like for Gaetano to hear you threaten his.'

'I'm more afraid for you than the Duke,' said Gaetano. 'If you cross him, he can have you eliminated in an eye-blink. He wouldn't even let you get near him.'

'Perhaps Luciano should have fencing lessons too,' said Sky. He was joking, trying to lighten the atmosphere. But both the others turned to him eagerly.

'Could you teach me, Gaetano?' asked Luciano.

'Of course,' said the prince. 'Have you tried before?'

'A little, in Bellezza,' said Luciano. 'I've done a bit of rapier and dagger with Guido Parola.'

'Who's that?' asked Sky.

Luciano smiled for the first time since the Duke's dinner.

'He's a reformed assassin I happen to know,' he answered, remembering the first time he had met the red-haired Bellezzan, when he was trying to kill the previous Duchessa. 'He works for Rodolfo's friend, Silvia.'

'Well, he sounds like a good teacher,' said Gaetano. 'But we should start straightaway. I'll go and get a couple of rapiers and meet you back here.'

'Are you sure you don't mind?' asked Luciano. 'Remember that I shall want to use everything you teach me on the Duke.'

Gaetano smiled crookedly. 'Let's hope it doesn't come to that,' he said. 'But I want you to be able to defend yourself.'

Sky didn't stay late in Giglia; he was too tired. So he caught up on several hours' sleep and woke only when the telephone rang in the morning. He could hear Rosalind answering it and then she knocked on his door.

'That's all settled, then,' she said, coming into his room. 'Cinderella shall go to the ball!'

'What are you on about, Mum?' asked Sky, rubbing the sleep out of his eyes. But he was pleased to see her looking so happy.

'We're going to Devon tomorrow – for Easter,' said Rosalind. 'To visit Nana. And you can see your friends while we're there. Alice's house is less than twenty miles away. What do you think?'

Chapter 12

The Scent of Pines

The Nucci palace across the river was nearly finished. In the last few weeks, extra workmen had been hired to make sure that the second storey was complete, and others were busy laying out the extraordinary gardens, with their fountains, grottoes and radiating walkways. The city was about to see a display of di Chimici wealth at their family weddings and Matteo Nucci was determined not to be outshone.

Word had spread that the new palace was going to be bigger and better than anything owned by Duke Niccolò and people had taken to hanging about watching the workmen. The moving-in day for the Nucci had been announced for the day after the di Chimici weddings and already some of their furniture was being moved into the ground floor, while workmen finished tiling the roof.

Among the watchers was Enrico, who was not looking forward to telling the Duke what he had seen. Sandro had brought his master to see how rapidly the new palace was nearing completion.

'It's a deliberate snub to his Grace,' said Enrico. 'A way of saying that the Nucci are better than the di Chimici and at least as rich. The Duke won't like it.'

'It's a better way of saying it than killing people, though, isn't it?' muttered Sandro. 'Building a bigger and better house.' He bent down to stroke Fratello's ears.

'Now just you listen to me, young Sparrow,' said the Eel. 'Don't think that because they're building a house the Nucci have given up ideas of killing. They'll get their revenge for Davide, don't you worry.'

*

The Ducal carriage was drawn up on the mainland opposite Bellezza, waiting for the Duchessa. Some feet behind it was another less grand carriage with a red-haired footman standing by the door. Inside it sat an elegant middle-aged woman in a travelling cloak, with her personal maidservant.

'Another journey, Susanna,' she said. 'And this the most dangerous yet.'

'Yes, milady,' said Susanna. 'The Duke in his home city and not distracted by a dying son will be much more vigilant than he was in Remora.'

'Then I must be even more vigilant,' said Silvia. 'I want to know what he's up to, particularly as far as Bellezza is concerned.'

'Here comes the Duchessa,' said Susanna, who had been alerted by Guido Parola.

The red and silver barcone was beaching on the shore. The mandoliers who had rowed it now started carrying trunks over the shingle to the baggage carriages. And a white-haired man handed a slender figure on to a walkway of planks up to the road. Then came a small company of bodyguards. They were followed by the Duchessa's maid, Barbara, who was organising the luggage and scolding a burly young mandolier carrying a long silver box.

William Dethridge and Arianna stopped by the Padavian carriage and Guido Parola opened the door.

'Good morning, my dear,' said Silvia. 'And to you, Doctor. I trust you left Leonora well?'

'Excellently welle, good ladye,' said Dethridge. 'Bot a littil troubled by my voyage with the yonge Dutchesse here. Shee likes it not whenne I am from home.'

'You are fortunate in your marriage,' said Silvia a little pensively.

'Let's hope the di Chimici will be equally blessed,' said Arianna. 'I am sure that at least Gaetano and Francesca will be happy together.'

'If the Duke's ambition lets them,' said Silvia.

'I'm looking forward to seeing Giglia, anyway,' said Arianna. 'Gaetano spoke so highly of it.'

'Wel thenne,' said Dethridge. 'Lette us bee awaye. There is a longe road ahead.'

*

The Duke received Enrico's report in silence but he

sent for his architect straight afterwards.

'What progress on the palace?' he asked as soon as the man was shown in.

'Excellent, your Grace,' said Gabassi. 'The rooms are ready and I was going to say that we could start moving the new furniture in.'

'Good, good,' said Niccolò. 'Then let us begin. I shall move in with Prince Fabrizio and my daughter before the weddings and we shall host the celebrations in the piazza outside.'

When Gabassi had gone, the Duke went to a window that overlooked the main courtyard. 'Avenues and grottoes, indeed,' he muttered. 'Nucci is a farmer at heart and wants to bring the countryside into the city. I shall show him how a real nobleman uses his wealth.'

He rang the bell to call Enrico back. The Eel had not gone far.

'I want you to help Prince Fabrizio to move his apartments to the Palazzo Ducale,' said the Duke. 'And Princess Beatrice. I should like us to be in our new residence by the end of the week.'

'Certainly, your Grace,' said Enrico, rubbing his hands. This was his opportunity to make himself useful to the Duke's heir. And to the beautiful Principessa. She hadn't shown herself to be very warm to him in the past but perhaps that could be made to change.

*

Gaetano met Luciano at his lodgings, carrying two rapiers. They had tried a few passes the day before in

Sulien's cloister but now the real training began. They walked to a nearby piazza, where there was plenty of space to practise. The piazza took its name from the elegant Church of the Annunciation which made up one side of the square with its porticoed loggia. The square itself was amply big enough for swordfighting, if you stuck to the area between the two elaborate fountains, and a small knot of people had soon gathered to watch the two young men.

'Take no notice of them,' said Gaetano, driving Luciano hard back towards one of the fountains. 'You'll always have something to distract you if you are attacked. It won't be nicely organised, following rules of courtesy.'

'It's not them I'm bothered about,' gasped Luciano, who hadn't realised swordfighting was such a demanding activity. 'It's you. You're too good. Can we have a breather?'

Gaetano put up his weapon. 'Very well,' he said. 'Five minutes.'

They sat on the edge of the fountain, dipping their handkerchiefs in the water, and the small crowd dispersed.

'It's true I'm good,' said Gaetano, not boastfully. 'But my father's good too. And so are all the armed men you might encounter. Nobles in Talia are brought up to fight from a very young age – think of Falco – and assassins do it as if they've learned it as soon as they were weaned off their mother's milk.'

'Then there's not much hope for me, is there?' said Luciano, dripping the cool water on to his face. 'Whatever happens here is going to come about in the next few weeks. Even if we practise every day, I won't be able to catch up.'

'All we're trying to do,' Gaetano explained patiently, 'is teach you how to defend yourself. If you are attacked, your blood will run hot and your courage, together with the moves you have learned, may save your life.'

'Adrenaline,' murmured Luciano.

'But that doesn't mean you should lose your head,' added Gaetano warningly. 'If you lose control, you will certainly be killed.'

'But what about if I want to attack someone?'

'My father?' said Gaetano. 'I don't recommend it. Not with a sword, anyway.'

'Well, what else can I do? Poison? He has tasters, as I've seen, and besides, it seems cowardly compared with fighting face to face.'

'You can't really expect me to advise you how to kill my own father,' said Gaetano. 'Whatever he has done or is thinking of doing. Wouldn't it be better to talk to Arianna and find out what she thinks about the marriage?'

'The Duke hasn't even asked her yet,' said Luciano. 'But she'll be here in a day or two and I expect Rodolfo will tell her what your father is planning as soon as she gets here. Still, it's not easy. She didn't say anything to me all the time when you were courting her. I think a di Chimici proposal counts as politics with Arianna, not as an affair of the heart.'

'I think it probably counts as politics with my father too,' said Gaetano grimly. 'I doubt if he would be able to tell Arianna from one of his own nieces if she were not presented to him as the Duchessa of Bellezza.'

A scruffy boy with an even scruffier dog on a string was watching the two young nobles as they talked. He had noticed them fencing as he walked through the square on his way from his lodgings to the Piazza della Cattedrale. Then he had recognised one as the ugly di Chimici prince and his curiosity had been piqued.

Sandro was familiar with the Piazza of the Annunciation. He was fascinated not by the church but by the huge orphanage on one of the square's other sides. The Ospedale della Misericordia had the same porticoes as the church, but in one of them was the famous Ruota degli Innocenti, the Wheel of the Innocents, and that was what drew Sandro.

A wide, open window-space held a horizontal metal wheel, operated by a handle at the side. Desperate mothers with too many mouths to feed or no husband would come, usually at night, and place their babies on the wheel and crank the handle till their pathetic bundles vanished inside the Ospedale. The baby's cries would eventually rouse the nun on night duty and the infant would be accepted into the orphanage.

Occasionally one would be lucky and a rich woman with no children of her own would come and select a healthy smiling baby, usually a boy-child, and take it off to a life of leisure and luxury. That hadn't happened at Sandro's orphanage. Such women always went first to the sisters of the Misericordia. Time and again he had wondered why his mother had left him in the loggia of the Piazza della Cattedrale instead of on the Wheel of the Innocents in the city's only other orphanage. Was she saying she didn't want another mother to have him?

Such thoughts would make Sandro avoid the Piazza of the Annunciation for weeks, but he would always be drawn back to it like a tongue to a hurting tooth. Today he waited a little to see if the prince and his friend would start fencing again before he gave up and headed back to the Nucci's new palace.

Sky managed one snatched meeting with Nicholas and Georgia before they took the train with Alice to Devon. Nicholas had brought round a pair of foils.

'Bring them for us, since you're going by car,' said Nicholas. 'And we'll use them whenever we can meet up. Alice's place is huge.'

'She's not going to be too pleased if I turn up there and then spend all my time fencing with you though, is she?' said Sky. But he put the foils under his bed.

'Have you found out any more about the talismans?' asked Georgia. 'Are Luciano and Rodolfo any nearer to making them work for other cities?'

'I don't know,' said Sky. 'I haven't seen Rodolfo since the dinner at the Duke's, and Luciano seems to have other things on his mind.'

'Arianna,' said Georgia softly.

'More the Duke, actually,' said Sky. 'Gaetano's teaching him to fence, just like you and me, Nick.'

'My brother is teaching Luciano to fight my father?' asked Nicholas. His huge brown eyes were open wide. Sky smiled.

'Well, not specifically. I think he hopes it won't come to that. But Luciano is already quite handy with a weapon. He says that some bloke in Bellezza called Parola taught him.'

Georgia snorted. 'That would be Guido the assassin. He was trying to murder the Duchessa when Luciano met him.'

'Arianna?' asked Sky, surprised. He couldn't imagine Luciano making friends with anyone who had tried to hurt her.

'No. Her mother, the last Duchessa. He works for her now – as a sort of bodyguard-cum-footman.'

Georgia had told Nicholas ages before about how the mysterious Silvia she had met in Remora was really the Duchessa whom the di Chimici's second assassin was supposed to have blown up in her own audience chamber, but Sky hadn't known she was still alive.

'You can bet she'll turn up in Giglia too,' said Georgia. 'Just look out for a glamorous middle-aged woman somewhere near Rodolfo. That'll be her.'

'Who's a glamorous middle-aged woman?' asked Rosalind, putting her head round the door. 'Not me, I'm guessing.'

'No one you know,' said Sky quickly.

'We must be going,' said Georgia. 'Do you want to come and see Alice off at the station tomorrow?'

'No,' said Sky, suddenly embarrassed. 'I'll call her on her mobile.'

Sandro was waiting for Sky when he walked out of Sulien's cell the next morning in Giglia.

'Come and see how the new Nucci palace is getting

on,' he said straightaway. 'If Brother Sulien can spare you.'

Sandro's scruffy dog, Fratello, was waiting outside, tied to a metal ring in the wall. He jumped up and barked with pleasure when he saw his master and included Sky in his welcome too.

'What are those two wooden columns for, Sandro?' asked Sky. 'I've often wondered.'

'They're . . . ob-e-lisks,' said Sandro, trying hard to get the word right. 'We use them for markers when there are carriage races round the piazza.'

'Carriage races?' said Sky. 'I'd like to see that.'

The two boys and the dog walked through the centre of the city in the bright spring sunshine. Sky had got used to the smell of rubbish in the gutters and the juxtaposition of rickety wooden houses and grand palaces. They both looked up at the dome of the great cathedral with equal affection. It was so huge that you could see it from almost every street in Giglia, but the massive bulk of it was still always a shock up close.

They dipped down a side street off the square to pass through the Piazza Ducale, where there was quite a bustle round the Ducal palace. Workmen were carrying bundles of tapestries and pieces of furniture from carts in through the imposing front entrance.

'The Duke's moving house,' said Sandro. 'The next time he asks you to dinner, it will be here.'

'Why is he moving?' asked Sky. Sandro shrugged.

'Wants to live above the shop, with Prince Fabrizio, to keep a close eye on all the new laws being made. And he'll be able to keep an eye on the Nucci from here too – they'll be just across the river.'

They continued past the Guild offices and jewellery workshops, across the Ponte Nuovo. Sandro paused in the middle of it, letting Fratello sniff round the butchers' shops and fishmongers that lined both sides. The smell of blood was awful. Sky went to stand in one of the curved balconies in the middle of the bridge, looking out over the river. The water level was very high. Sandro came and stood beside him,

'The Argento will flood this spring,' he said knowingly.

'What? Into the city?'

'It happens often,' said Sandro. 'Though usually in the autumn. This bridge used to wash away in the old days, when it was made of wood. That's why they built this new stone one.'

'It doesn't look very new,' said Sky, looking at the grimy bricks and blood-stained cobbles and ramshackle food shops.

'It's been here two hundred years or more,' said Sandro. 'Stood up to floods all that time.'

They walked on to the street on the other side of the river, past one of the many small churches that punctuated the districts of Giglia. Within a few streets they were in sight of the surrounding countryside. Only the huge Nucci palace and its formal gardens separated the city from the fields around.

Sky was impressed. It was bigger and showier than either of the Duke's palaces. And, although it was built in a style he recognised as Renaissance architecture, it was so obviously modern and new that it suddenly made the grandeur of the di Chimici residences, with their frescoed chapels and trompe l'oeil reception rooms, seem outdated and stuffy.

Here too workmen were busy moving in furniture and hangings.

'Let's go into the gardens,' said Sandro.

'Is it allowed?' asked Sky.

'No one notices boys like me,' said Sandro. 'Or friars.'

They walked past the grand front face of the palace, at the top of a natural slope, and on towards what would one day be a gated side entrance to the gardens. Here all was innovation – radiating avenues of freshly planted trees encircling small lakes with fountains and statues. And every now and then the boys would come across an elaborate grotto, surrounded by vines and creepers carved from stone and bursting with statues of gods and nymphs.

They walked the whole circuit, following the upward slope of the ground, until they were at the back of the great house. In one direction the cupola of Saint-Mary-of-the-Lily dominated the blue sky; in the other lay fields of jonquils and asphodel. The air was fresh and laden with the scents of flowers and the mature pine trees that lined the avenue behind the palace.

'Wow!' said Sky.

'They've done it this time,' said Sandro. 'I don't think the Duke will let them hang on to it for long.'

*

The Duke was standing at the window of his new apartments at the top of the Ducal palace. It overlooked the river and from here he had a clear view of the newly risen Palazzo Nucci and its extensive gardens. Even from here he could see the bustle of activity that indicated the wool-merchant family were beginning to take possession of their new home. He was impressed and disgusted in equal measure but had no intention of showing the former emotion.

'There they are, the sheep-farmers,' he sneered. 'At least there'll be no shortage of mutton for their table. Their own grazing must start practically at the edge of their vulgar gardens.'

'Indeed, my Lord,' said Enrico, joining the Duke at the window. 'I hope it doesn't spoil your view.'

'I like to see the ants building their nest,' said Niccolò. 'But from here it feels as if I could tip a pan of boiling water over the whole colony. Just let them try anything else against my family and I will.'

'Fabrizio is here, Father,' said Beatrice, coming into the room. 'Shall I send for him to come up or do you want to take him to his rooms?'

'I shall come down and escort him myself,' said Duke Niccolò. 'This is a great day for the di Chimici family. We have moved to the centre of the city, where we belong. Let the Nucci play in their gardens, like the rustics and bumpkins they are. Politics are conducted in Council chambers, not in meadows.'

*

Sky lay in the as yet un-mown grass under the pines, breathing in the sharp and musky scent. Sandro and Fratello had flopped down beside him, glad of the shade in the warm mid-morning sun.

'I saw the young prince fencing yesterday,' said

Sandro conversationally.

'Which one?' asked Sky, though he thought he knew.

'The ugly one,' said Sandro.

'Gaetano?'

'Yeah,' said Sandro. 'He's the best of them, I reckon. Though the kid wasn't bad either, the one that died.'

'You knew Prince Falco?'

'Not to say knew,' said Sandro. 'Boys like me don't get on very close terms with princes. But he was all right. Fond of animals, especially his horses, till he had that accident. Complete wreck after that, of course.'

Sky wondered what Sandro would think if he could see Nicholas now.

'Anyway, his brother, Gaetano, the one that was closest to Falco, was teaching a young nobleman to fence. Don't know what sort of noble he was, mind you, that came from a family where he needed to be taught – probably a foreigner – but he's picking it up all right.'

'I expect that was Luciano, the Bellezzan,' said Sky cautiously. 'I met him when Sulien and I went to the Duke's.'

'Oh, Bellezza,' said Sandro, as if that accounted for it. 'I've heard they don't even have horses there. No wonder their nobles need helping by Giglians. They must be quite uncivilised.'

Sky rolled over on to his stomach, away from the boy with the dirty face and ragged clothes, to hide his smile.

'Shame, though,' said Sandro. 'He was much better-looking than our prince, though I can't imagine a

Bellezzan girl would have him if he needs so much polishing up, unless their girls are equally rough.'

'That's what the Duke thinks,' said Sky. 'He's planning to offer himself to the Bellezzan Duchessa, though I think she's far from rough. And I think she'd prefer Luciano.'

'Do you?' said Sandro, sitting up. 'That's very interesting.'

And Sky hoped he hadn't given too much away.

Chapter 13

Talismans

Lucia di Chimici was a redhead with fair skin, like her father Prince Jacopo, so she did not want to get married in pure white.

'Next to you I would look like a corpse,' she told her sister Bianca, who was dark like their mother. 'I shall wear gold.'

It was a bold choice for a Talian, because gold was a lesser valued metal than silver in their world and there was a danger of looking cheap. But there would be nothing cheap about Lucia's wedding dress. The gold taffeta would be oversewn with emeralds and she would wear her long dark red hair part loose and part plaited with gold and green ribbons.

She would look more dramatic than Bianca, whose choice was simple white satin rendered sumptuous by the addition of diamonds and pearls. Their father shuddered a little when he heard the cost, but he was proud of his girls' beauty and didn't take much persuading by his wife.

'They will be the two most beautiful brides,' said Carolina. 'And the honour of Fortezza is at stake.'

During the many fittings, the sisters had plenty of time to talk about their forthcoming marriages. At first they were too excited about the grandeur of the ceremony, with all its attendant celebrations and opportunities for fine gowns, to think of anything but the day itself. But as time went on, the seriousness of their lives' changes began to sink in. Neither girl had ever lived outside Fortezza and now they would both leave home together. Bianca would live in Volana with Alfonso, as his wife and his new Duchessa. And Lucia would be in Giglia with Carlo, living as she had been told with her cousins Gaetano and Francesca in the di Chimici palace on the Via Larga.

She had the advantage over Bianca, in that she and Carlo had always been fond of each other, from when the cousins were all small and played together in the summer palace at Santa Fina. At twenty-three, he was only one year older than her and they were well-matched. She wasn't exactly in love with him, but he was good-looking and clever and fitted the role of husband well enough to content her.

Bianca, at twenty, was seven years younger than her husband-to-be. The gap had seemed enormous during those long summers, when Alfonso and his skinny brother Rinaldo had been the two eldest, and she was still a bit in awe of him.

But he too was good-looking and had shown

himself perfectly willing to marry her, which was an excellent recommendation. And she was glad Duke Niccolò's choice had hit on him and not on Rinaldo when picking out a husband for her, as Bianca would have had to obey, whatever his decision.

All that spring the two princesses talked about their future in the di Chimici dynasty, imagining the children they would have and the city-states they would rule over.

'Duke Niccolò means Gaetano to have Fortezza when father dies,' said Lucia. 'I'm sure that's why we're getting such well-titled husbands. So that they won't contest Fortezza for themselves.'

'It is sad for Father to think on,' said Bianca. 'His line dying out in his own city. I hope we have boys, don't you?'

'I don't see why girls shouldn't inherit a title,' said Lucia. 'Look at Bellezza, where they always have Duchesse.'

'But they are elected,' said Bianca. 'The title isn't inherited like the ones in our family.'

'Still, this one's the daughter of the last one, isn't she?' said Lucia. 'It comes to the same thing.'

There was no way that Rosalind could drive all the way from Islington to Devon, even though she was much better. It was doubtful that their car would have made it, anyway. The dented Fiesta had belonged to Rosalind's father. When he had died four years earlier, her mother had given it to Rosalind, but life in London was harder for the car than in a Devon village and it was now the worse for wear.

Laura was going to drive them all in her new Rover; conveniently, she was visiting her family too.

'If I get frantic, tell me I can come and stay with you, darling,' she said to Rosalind as she drove very fast along the M4, window down and chain-smoking.

'Of course,' said Rosalind, smiling round at Sky. 'We wouldn't mind.'

He knew what she was thinking. Nana Meadows didn't approve of Laura and never had. 'Fast' and 'flighty' were her two favourite ways of describing her. Sky had once heard his mother stop his grandmother in her tracks by saying calmly, 'It's funny that you're so rude about my best friend. Particularly when you consider that I'm the unmarried mother and she's the one with a respectable job and decent income.' Of course, she hadn't known Sky was listening.

Laura had baulked a bit at their luggage, especially when she saw Sky's box of foils. But nothing ever fazed her for long and she had cheerfully re-packed the boot, piling the extras in the back with Sky.

'It's time you learned to drive,' she now shouted at him over her shoulder, sending clouds of smoke into the back of the car. 'I'll start teaching you in Devon, if you've got your provisional.'

It so happened that Sky had. And he had passed his theory and his hazard tests. But that was as far as it had gone. His mother couldn't afford driving lessons and she hadn't been fit enough until recently to think of teaching him herself.

At the next service station, Laura bought another packet of cigarettes and a pair of big red Ls for Sky; she never let the grass grow under her feet. Rosalind was feeling well enough to drive the next bit and Sky sat in the front with her, while Laura stretched out in the back. She was instantly asleep, looking much younger curled up on bits of luggage and without a cigarette in her mouth.

'What kind of a driving instructor do you think she'll make?' Sky asked his mother.

'Interesting,' said Rosalind, and they both laughed. 'Oh, I'm looking forward to this break,' she went on. 'I feel as if I haven't breathed any proper air for years. I bet I wouldn't have been so ill if we hadn't lived in London.'

'You don't want to move back to Devon, do you?' asked Sky, surprised.

Rosalind shook her head. 'No way,' she said. 'It may have better air, but a few days with your nana makes me long to be back in the smoke.'

'She's not so bad,' said Sky.

'Not to you. You're her blue-eyed boy – which is very strange, considering they're brown!'

It was true. Rosalind's parents had been appalled when she had told them she was expecting a baby, even though it wasn't unusual for unmarried girls any more. Then the golden boy with his chestnut curls had won Joyce Meadows over and it broke her heart when they moved to London. That had largely been Geoffrey Meadows's idea and his widow had often hinted she would like them to move back.

Up till now, Sky had thought that would be a disaster, but here he was speeding towards Devon and the girl he really liked and the two other people who now meant most to him in his life. And until as recently as a few weeks ago he had never spoken to any of them.

'It's enormous!' said Arianna, looking at the cathedral cupola. Fine as the Basilica of Santa Maddalena was in Bellezza, with its silver domes and mosaics, it couldn't rival Saint-Mary-of-the-Lily for size and grandeur.

She was staying at the Bellezzan Embassy in the Borgo Sant' Ambrogio. It was uncomfortably close to the Palazzo di Chimici in the Via Larga, and it was with relief that she learned that the Duke had moved further in towards the city's centre. Her Ambassador had refused as diplomatically as he could, on Arianna's behalf, all the offers for her and her retinue to stay at either palace, on the grounds that it was the first visit of a Duchessa of Bellezza to Giglia for nearly twenty years and that the Embassy must have the privilege of entertaining her.

She stood on the balcony of the Embassy's most splendid bedroom, looking down the Borgo towards the cathedral. In a few weeks she must attend the splendid weddings there and she still did not know what to do about the Duke's dress. Barbara was unpacking it even now, smoothing out invisible creases in the jewel-encrusted skirt, although it really was too stiff to crumple, even on a long journey.

There was a tap at the door. 'May I come inne?' said Doctor Dethridge, putting his grizzled head around it. 'Youre visitours have arryved.'

He was followed by Rodolfo and Luciano, and

Arianna's heart lifted to see them both. Her visit to Giglia might be a diplomatic quagmire but at least she was to be surrounded by people she loved, who were Stravaganti into the bargain. She would be much more comfortable with her father and Luciano living in the Embassy.

*

In another part of the city, two more Stravaganti were talking about the Duchessa's safety. Giuditta Miele was visiting Brother Sulien in his laboratory, drinking a tisane of mallow.

'Rodolfo has called a meeting of members of the Brotherhood for this afternoon,' Sulien was saying. 'With Doctor Dethridge now arrived in the city, there will be five of us. Six if you count young Celestino.'

'That will not be enough,' said Giuditta. 'You know my apprentice, Franco? The pretty one?'

Sulien nodded.

'He has been posing for Bruno Vecchietto, who has been painting angels all over the Nucci's new palace. And he told Franco there is definitely trouble brewing. Their armoury is stocked full of weapons, and they are not a military family.'

'But there is no reason to suppose their violence will be offered to the young Duchessa, is there?' asked Sulien. 'It is the di Chimici who are their enemies, and since Bellezza is opposed to the Duke's plans, I should have thought the Nucci would be on Arianna's side.'

'Violence is never tidy, Sulien,' said Giuditta. 'All it takes is for young men armed with swords and daggers to get their blood up and there could be a massacre. Can you be sure Arianna will be safe in such a mêlée?'

'What would you have us do?' asked the friar. 'Rodolfo will be open to suggestion.'

'If only there were another strong faction who could help keep order,' said Giuditta.

'The Nucci could have been useful,' said Sulien thoughtfully, 'but not since the death of Davide. If they see the opportunity to attack the di Chimici they will be caught up in that, not looking out for the Duchessa.'

'We need more Stravaganti here,' said Giuditta. 'I would have Rodolfo summon others of the Brotherhood from all over Talia. If it comes to a fight, it is not swordsmen we need, but those who can communicate without words and surround the Duchessa with their thoughts rather than their muscles.'

Sky moved into the little boxroom he always slept in at his grandmother's. It looked smaller than ever this time.

'Good heavens!' said his grandmother, looking in on him. 'You'll be bursting at the seams. I had no idea you had grown so tall!'

'Growth spurt, Nana,' said Sky. 'Don't worry – I'll be fine.'

'Next time, I'll put you in the back bedroom and let Rosalind sleep in here,' said Mrs Meadows. 'We can't have you cramping your young limbs. Are you sure you can fit in that bed? It's not even a full-size single.'

It was nice to be fussed over for a while but Sky was itching to get to see Alice. Next morning, after breakfast, he got Rosalind to drive him over to Ivy Court in Laura's car. Laura's parents lived within walking distance of Nana Meadows and Rosalind was quite happy to drive short distances on roads she knew well.

It was a fine spring day and the scent of flowers was in the air. It reminded Sky of Giglia. Particularly when they turned into the drive of Ivy Court and he caught the unmistakable scent of pine trees.

'Crikey,' said Rosalind. 'Your girlfriend must be loaded!'

Sky scarcely noticed that she had called Alice his girlfriend for the first time. His heart had sunk. Ivy Court was a red-brick Elizabethan farmhouse with imposing chimneys and a circular gravel drive. There seemed to be a lot of outbuildings as well. Nicholas had said that Alice had plenty of space but he had been very casual about it. Now Sky thought that it was all very well for Nicholas, who had been a prince in another life.

But it was Georgia who came round the corner; she was flushed and rather pretty – something Sky had never thought before.

'Oh, hi,' she said, smiling. 'Hello, Rosalind. We've just been for an early ride.'

'You obviously enjoyed it,' said Rosalind.

'Yes, it was great. There's something about the air down here. Come in and meet Alice's dad. I'll make us some coffee. Alice and Nick are still rubbing down the horses.'

Horses? thought Sky. She has more than one? He

moved into the house like a zombie.

Paul Greaves was sitting in the kitchen, reading the paper. He was relaxed and friendly and immediately started chatting to Rosalind while Georgia filled an enormous kettle and put it on the hotplate of a cream Aga. It was a comfortable, untidy room but Sky knew that it meant money. He thought of their kitchen at the flat, where they ate their meals. There was a wooden table and chairs in here too, but he was pretty sure that this house would have a proper dining room as well.

Georgia made six full mugs of real coffee and set out hot cross buns, and, by the time she was done, Alice and Nicholas had come in, smelling slightly of horse and with their hair ruffled and their faces glowing. Sky couldn't have felt less at home. But Alice gave him a beaming smile and he thought again how lovely she was and how lucky he was that she liked him.

'Did you bring the foils?' asked Nicholas, under his breath.

'They're still in the car,' said Sky, feeling glad that at least they had turned up in the new Rover and not his granddad's old Fiesta.

'Good,' said Nicholas. 'We'll start after coffee.'

'Start what?' asked Alice. 'Don't tell me you two are going to spend the holiday fencing?'

'Fencing?' said Paul. 'Are you another swordsman, Sky?'

'Not as good as Nick,' said Sky. 'But I'm learning.'

'He's obsessed,' said Rosalind. 'Every spare moment.'

'It's a good sport,' said Paul. 'I wish I could do it. It

always looks so glamorous and dashing.'

Alice laughed. 'You want to be dashing, Dad?'

Now it was Paul's turn to blush a little, and Sky saw where Alice got her looks from. He also noticed his mother looking appreciative, which alarmed him a bit.

'You know what an old romantic I am,' said Paul, putting his arm round Alice. 'It comes of being a country solicitor, who lives in the house he was born in,' he explained. 'I often think how unadventurous my life must seem from the outside, though I do like my job.'

'And it's a wonderful house,' said Rosalind.

'Alice tells me you were born round here too,' said Paul, and then the two adults were off on one of those 'Where-did-you-go-to-school and did-you-know-so-and-so?' conversations that meant the others could escape.

'You're not really going to start fencing, are you?' asked Alice. She was longing to be alone with Sky.

He felt torn in two. Insecure and lacking in self-confidence all over again, he would have liked to be on his own with Alice, too. But he also needed to talk to Nicholas and Georgia, who were obviously keen to quiz him about what was going on in Giglia.

'Come on, Nick,' said Georgia, coming to his rescue. 'Let's give them some space. I'm sure Alice would like to show Sky round.'

'We do need to get more Stravaganti here,' said Rodolfo, agreeing with Giuditta.

'Then send messages to Remora, Bellona and all the

other city-states,' she said. 'The brothers in Fortezza, Moresco and Volana could get here quickly too.'

'There is another way,' said Rodolfo. 'And one that wouldn't leave all the other cities vulnerable. It is bad enough that Bellezza is undefended.'

'Wee have been essaying to altir the nature of the talismannes,' said William Dethridge.

'How?' asked Sulien.

'You know how they bring Stravaganti from my old world always to one city?' said Luciano. 'It's a restriction we've been trying to overcome.'

'So that Celestino could travel to Bellezza, for instance?' asked the friar.

'Yes, though it's here he'll be needed,' said Rodolfo. 'But there are two others we could bring here.'

'Then you have succeeded?' said Giuditta.

'No,' said Rodolfo. 'Not yet.' He walked over to the window. He and Luciano had moved into the Embassy, to be closer to Arianna, and he was holding his conference of Stravaganti in one of its elegant reception rooms.

Luciano wondered if his old master had told Arianna about the Grand Duke's marriage plans. He hadn't been able to bring himself to ask; Rodolfo seemed so preoccupied with the safety of his daughter at the weddings.

'You sense the tensions in the city?' Rodolfo was asking Sulien and Giuditta. 'I don't think we can depend on the success of our experiments. I think you will have to take two new talismans yourselves.'

Rosalind stayed to lunch at Ivy Court. She couldn't remember how long it had been since she had liked someone as much as she did Paul. And it wasn't just because he was an attractive man. He was warm and friendly and willing to be interested in her and eager to show her round the house and grounds, not because he was showing off but because he loved them.

Lunch turned out to be a scrappy affair of things dug out of the freezer and larder. Sky was the best cook among them, which was not saying much, but they ended up eating a surprisingly satisfying concoction of rice and peas with what Sky said was chilli con carne. It was quite hot and Paul brought up cold beer from the cellar – it was the kind of house that would have a cellar. And his freezer was well-stocked with large tubs of ice cream – apparently a stipulation of Alice's when she was coming to stay.

'You'll need to get more with four teenagers in the house,' said Alice.

'I shall order a daily cartload,' said Paul grandly, and Sky felt pleased that he had been so easily accepted as just another friend of Alice's who was going to be around. But he was still reeling from his tour of the house and grounds. OK, it wasn't like a di Chimici residence, but it was still the grandest home he had been in outside Talia.

After lunch, Rosalind reluctantly said she must be getting back to her mother's. 'What time shall I collect him?' she asked Paul.

'Oh, don't worry,' said Paul. 'I'll drop him back whenever you want him.'

'Thanks. It'll be easier when Sky can drive,' said Rosalind. 'He's supposed to be having some lessons this holiday, so you mustn't let him spend all his time here.'

'I could give you some lessons, Sky,' said Paul. 'There's space for you to pick up the basics in the grounds, without going out on the road. It's an awkward stage, isn't it?' he said to Rosalind. 'Before they're quite old enough to drive but they're old enough to go out on their own and you end up ferrying them everywhere.'

Rosalind didn't feel quite comfortable agreeing; she knew that made it sound as if she was always doing things for her son, when it was usually the other way round.

'Now,' said Nicholas to Sky and Alice. 'If you love-birds are willing to be unstuck, Sky and I could do some fencing.'

Georgia nobly left them to it while she went off to talk to Alice and the two boys were able at last to talk about Giglia.

'I didn't go last night,' said Sky. 'And I'm hoping it will work OK stravagating from my nana's. I'll try tonight.'

'Georgia was able to get to Remora from here,' said Nicholas. 'What happened the last time you went?'

'Not a lot,' said Sky. 'I saw the new Nucci palace. It's huge.'

'The Nucci?' said Nicholas. 'They have a place up by Saint-Mary-among-the-Vines, don't they? The one with the tower?'

'They do. But they're moving to this swanky new one on the other side of the river. I don't think the Duke's too pleased about it.'

'I bet,' said Nicholas. 'He thinks swank is his prerogative.'

He was still holding a foil but not making any attempt to fence. He was too thoughtful.

'How am I going to get there?' he asked. 'I must be able to see what's going on for myself.'

'But wouldn't you be recognised?' asked Sky. 'Even if something could be done about the talismans?'

'I'll grow a beard!' said Nicholas.

They both laughed. 'You'd better start now, then,' said Sky. 'Do you even shave yet?'

'Just for that, I'm going to whip your ass,' said Nicholas. '*En garde!*'

The statue of the Duchessa was complete apart from the hands and face. She stood in Giuditta's studio, looking like a bird poised for flight, her marble cloak and hair streaming out behind her in the invisible wind.

'It's wonderful,' said Arianna. She was wearing a grey velvet cloak with a hood pulled up over her masked face and was accompanied by Barbara and two bodyguards. Franco the angelic apprentice was looking at Barbara in admiration, unperturbed by the two armed Bellezzans.

'I have never sculpted a face with a mask before,' said Giuditta.

'It's a pity,' said Arianna. 'But that's how I must appear, in a public statue.'

'Still, I should like to see your face,' said the sculptor. 'It would help if I knew what I was covering up.'

'Then everyone else must look away,' said Arianna.

'My guards know the penalty and would exact it.'

Giuditta gave the order and her apprentices turned away, watched over by Barbara and the guards. Arianna untied her mask and Giuditta looked long at her face, sketching swiftly with a stick of charcoal. She walked round the Duchessa for twenty minutes, drawing her face from several angles.

At last she said, 'It is enough for today. Thank you, your Grace.'

Arianna felt dismissed. She could tell that Giuditta was itching to get back to work on the marble. She re-tied the mask and put on her cloak. The tension in the studio lifted and she was sure she saw one of the apprentices wink at her maid.

When she had gone, Franco came over to look at the sketches.

'It can't be forbidden even to look at a drawing of her face,' he said, and the other apprentices clustered round.

'She's as beautiful as they say,' said one.

'She's OK,' said Franco. 'But I like the maid better.'

'How can you tell? She was masked too.'

But Giuditta took no notice of their chatter. She was concentrating on the macquette she was going to make of the Duchessa's head. It was taking her mind off the other thing she had agreed to do.

Chapter 14

Pictures in the Walls

Sky took the blue glass bottle in his hand with some trepidation. He had not stravagated the night before – the first time he had missed a night since his Talian adventures had started. He found it difficult to believe that he could arrive there just as easily from Devon as from London.

Everything felt different down here – the visit to Ivy Court had unsettled not just him. His mother had been unusually animated that evening, chattering about Paul and Alice, while he had retreated more into himself. He could see in his mind's eye the sort of boy Alice was supposed to get serious about – blond, rich and having ridden a horse practically as soon as he could walk – and Sky didn't fit any of the criteria.

It would be a relief to turn to his new friends in

Talia and his alternative identity as a novice friar and secret Stravagante with some serious involvement in politics and strategies. For weeks now he had been leading two parallel lives, and no one who knew him in his everyday world, apart from Georgia and Nicholas, would have believed that this lanky teenager with the long dreadlocks spent his nights striding round a mighty Renaissance city, dressed in black and white robes.

At the beginning, it had been like a game for Sky – a kind of dressing-up and play-acting that gave scope to his more flamboyant side that had been suppressed for years. And it had been a welcome break from being the only fully functioning person in his family. But as Rosalind continued to get better and some of the burdens had lifted at home, Sky had got more and more involved in what he was doing in Talia. It wasn't just adventures and role-playing; he had been sent there on a mission. Only he wasn't yet sure what it was.

The more time Sky spent with Brother Sulien, the more he came to respect and admire him. He could see that Luciano practically worshipped Rodolfo and wondered if that was always how it was with Stravaganti. Georgia hadn't said much about the one she met in Remora, but Sky knew that he was called Paolo and that Georgia still missed him and his family.

Still, it wasn't just the heady company of fellow Stravaganti that Sky enjoyed. He liked Prince Gaetano, who actually made him feel less uncomfortable than Alice's father, even though he lived in palaces and was rich beyond Paul Greaves's wildest dreams of a son-in-law. And then there was

Sandro, at the other end of the scale, with not much more status than the mongrel dog who trailed round after him. A novice friar was as much above Sandro as a prince was above Sky; the boy couldn't even read.

But he was Sky's friend nonetheless, because he liked him. Sky wondered, as he lay wide awake holding the bottle, whether Sandro ever wondered where he, Sky, had come from. He never asked. Just accepted that he was there. That was one of the things that was comfortable about Sandro.

Sandro had in fact been wondering about exactly that. He had been spending more and more time hanging round Saint-Mary-among-the-Vines and less and less with the Eel. Ever since the night of Davide's murder, his former admiration of his employer had started to wane. Certainly Enrico fed him and gave him lodgings, or at least gave him the silver that bought these things. But that was just payment for Sandro's services. Brother Sulien gave him food and shelter without wanting anything in return and Sandro loved him for it. And there was more; Sandro had a secret. Ever since the day he had helped Sulien and Brother Tino make Vignales in the laboratory, Sandro had been trying to learn to read.

Sulien was teaching him his letters from a big illuminated Bible. Sandro loved the pictures that went round the letters at the beginning of each chapter. 'A' for Adam, with its pictures of the first man and woman and the apple and the serpent, just like another picture in a chapel he had seen on the other side of the river. Sandro hadn't understood the wall paintings then, but now Sulien told him the stories that went with all the pictures.

The first man and woman had been very unhappy; Sandro understood that. When they had disobeyed their Lord they had been banished from their garden for ever. An angel barred the way back, and that began with an 'A' too. Sandro also knew what 'S' looked like because it began the name of King Solomon, as well as Sulien and Sandro. And, even more amazingly, his name began with an 'A' as well, because it was short for Alessandro. He was rapidly unwrapping the mysteries of language and the excitement of stories. And if he imagined the temple of Solomon as being rather like Saint-Mary-of-the-Lily, perhaps it did not matter very much.

No one had ever told Sandro stories before. The nuns in the orphanage had been too busy; they had taught him his catechism, so that he knew the words, but he had never known what any of it meant. Or that it related to something about which there were stories. His lessons with Sulien were nothing like those with the nuns anyway.

The pharmacist, having taught him a letter, would show him how to find it on his pots and jars. And, when Sandro's eyes were weary of letters, he would take him into the church and tell him stories about what was painted there. There were two paintings that Sandro knew now, about the poor man who had been nailed to a cross of wood. One was on a huge painted cross that hung down between the friars' stalls and the congregation's pews. It was so sad, with what looked like real drops of blood trickling from the hands and feet.

Sandro preferred the other one, which was a wall painting, showing the same melancholy scene, but with the man's father above him and a dove between the two of them. Sandro thought it must be a comfort for the red-headed man on the cross to have them there while he suffered.

'It's not just a comfort for him,' said Brother Sulien, 'but for all of us. You see, that Father is yours and mine, too.'

'Nah,' said Sandro. 'I haven't got a father – you know that.'

'You've got that one,' said Sulien. 'We all have. And he gave his own Son's life for us.'

'Not for me,' said Sandro.

'Yes, even for you,' said Sulien.

Then they would go and look at something more cheerful, like the frescoes in the Lady Chapel, showing the miracle wrought by the church's patron Saint. The first Alfonso di Chimici, when already a wealthy perfumier, had been taken ill one day during Mass and been carried through to where the infirmary now stood. The friars had not known how to help him, but a vision of the Virgin had appeared to the pharmacist-friar of the day and advised the administration of unripe young grapes from their vineyards. Within days, Alfonso was cured and gave a large sum of money to the church to build an infirmary.

Sandro liked this story, because it was about a friar curing a di Chimici. 'Just like you and the Duke,' he told Sulien. And it had a happy ending – unlike most stories about the di Chimici.

*

When Sky at last arrived in Sulien's cell, he sighed with relief. The friar wasn't there; the room was still and quiet and Sky lay on the cot for a few minutes letting his pulse slow. He stretched his limbs in his novice's robes and felt himself adapting to his Giglian role. Brother Tino. A young man without family, history or responsibilities. He suddenly felt ravenous and set off for the refectory.

There he found both Sulien and Sandro, tucking into bowls of frothy warm milk with cinnamon and freshly baked rolls.

'Ah, Brother Tino, come and join us,' called Sulien, moving along the bench. Most of the other friars had finished eating, so there was plenty of space.

'What news?' asked Sky, pouring himself some milk from an earthenware jug.

'Niccolò di Chimici has given us a farm,' said Sulien.

'Really?' said Sky. 'Why?'

'Because we saved his life,' said Sulien. 'Prince Fabrizio sent me the deeds. It's only a little homestead, on the other side of the Argento, but Brother Tullio is pleased, because he can grow more vegetables there.'

Wow, thought Sky. Fancy being so rich you could just hand over a farm as a thank-you present!

'And the Duchessa has arrived,' said Sandro, who had been bursting to tell what he knew. 'I've seen her.'

'What's she like?' asked Sky.

Sandro shrugged. 'Hard to say. She wears a mask. But she's got a pretty figure and lots of hair.'

'You shall see for yourself, Tino,' said Sulien. 'We

are invited to the Bellezzan Embassy for morning refreshment. Don't eat too many rolls now.'

'But "we" 's not me,' said Sandro, wiping his mouth with his sleeve. 'I haven't the manners for it. I'll see you later.'

*

Rodolfo was waiting when they arrived at the Embassy. He introduced Sky to William Dethridge and the Elizabethan held out both hands to the boy and studied him carefully, in much the way that Giuditta Miele had done.

'Aye,' he said at length. 'Ye'll do. Tell mee, how fares yonge George?'

It took Sky a moment or two, thrown by Dethridge's way of talking, to realise that he meant Georgia.

'She's fine,' he said. 'But anxious to get back to Talia. Almost as keen as, you know, Falco,' he added under his breath. 'Any luck with the talismans?'

It was Sulien who answered. 'We are to go to your world again, Giuditta and I, taking new talismans for Georgia and the young prince. Ones that will bring them here.'

'The only problem,' said Rodolfo, 'is that they will need to give up their old ones. How do you think they will respond to that idea?'

'I think that Georgia will not like it,' said a low voice, and Sky realised that the Duchessa had silently entered the room. He jumped to his feet, confused.

A beautiful young woman in a green silk dress was approaching. He had no doubt that she was beautiful, in spite of her mask. Behind it, violet eyes sparkled, and her glossy hair – lots of it indeed, Sandro, thought Sky – tumbled in carefully arranged long curls over her shoulders. She was followed by a woman Sky didn't recognise, an elegant middle-aged one, who stopped to talk to Rodolfo.

'Your Grace,' stammered Sky, attempting a bow.

'Call me Arianna, please,' she said, taking his hand and leading him to a new seat beside her. 'You are a friend of Georgia and Falco and a member of the same Brotherhood as my father. You are welcome in Talia.'

'Yow moste ask the yonglinges,' said Dethridge. 'Ask them if they wolde give up their olde talismannes to make the journeye to this grete citee where they are needed.'

'But they aren't in London at the moment,' said Sky. 'They are on Easter holiday with me, in Devon. I've come from there tonight – I mean today.'

'Easter?' said Sulien. 'I never thought to ask. Is it Easter in your world already?'

'It was Good Friday there today,' said Sky. 'When is it in Talia?'

'Not for another four weeks,' said Rodolfo.

'Is that because there's been another time shift in the gateway?' asked Sky.

'No,' said Sulien. 'It is because of the fact that Easter is a movable feast and your world is more than four hundred years ahead of ours. It would have been unlikely for the dates of Easter to match.'

'I can still ask the others about the talismans,' said Sky. 'But you mustn't stravagate to my world until we're back in London.'

'It is an unwelcome delay,' said Rodolfo. 'It means

we shall have less time to accustom them to this city before the wedding.'

'But it cannot be helped,' said Sulien. 'When do you all return home?'

Sky calculated. 'Four days,' he said. 'I'll come and tell you, the night we get back, and then you can come the next day. I can look out for you,' he added, feeling peculiar at the thought of the friar and the sculptor turning up on his doorstep. He must make sure Rosalind was out.

Just then, Luciano was shown into the room, his eyes sparkling and his cheeks glowing. Sky knew immediately that he had been swordfighting with Gaetano.

'Hi!' he said to Sky, and then made a more formal greeting to the others, first raising the Duchessa's hand lightly to his lips.

'You look well,' she said, smiling under her mask.

'I feel well,' he said simply.

Sky looked at them and felt sorry for Georgia. What a mess.

'What do you think, Luciano?' asked Arianna, as if reading his thoughts. 'Would Georgia give up her flying horse for a new talisman?'

'It would be hard for her,' he said. 'She loves horses and it's her only link with Remora and Merla.'

'We can but try,' said Rodolfo. 'We need her here. I am not so sure about Falco. It's a risky strategy. If he is recognised by any member of his family, except Gaetano, who knows his choice, there's no telling what might happen.'

'Yet he is the one more likely to accept a new talisman from here,' said Luciano. 'Giglia is his city, after all – not Remora.'

Luciano walked back to the friary with Sky and Sulien.

'Why does Doctor Dethridge talk like that?' Sky asked.

'Like what?' asked Sulien.

'It's because Tino and my foster-father come from the same world, centuries apart,' explained Luciano. 'I've got used to it, but to other English speakers from our world, Doctor Dethridge sounds as if he's speaking a very old-fashioned language.'

*

Arianna was going to change her dress but Rodolfo stopped her.

'There is something else I must tell you,' he said, but he waited so long to say what it was that Arianna thought he had forgotten she was there. Silvia had her eyes fixed on Rodolfo, waiting for his news.

At last he took Arianna's hand in his and, sighing, said, 'Duke Niccolò is going to ask you to marry him.'

Arianna felt numb. This was not like hearing that Gaetano was going to propose; this felt like being a small bird with a hawk circling in the air above her and she could see no way of escape.

'If you wear the dress he sent, at the weddings, he will assume you look kindly on his offer,' said Silvia.

'When?' said Arianna. She could scarcely find her voice. 'When is he going to ask?'

'I should think the night before the weddings – or perhaps the wedding feast itself, so that he can make the announcement in front of all his family,' said Rodolfo.

'Then I am trapped,' said Arianna bitterly. 'What will he do when I refuse him?'

'Not so hasty,' said Silvia. 'You don't have to refuse him outright.'

'Silvia!' said Rodolfo. 'You are not serious.'

'I am completely serious,' said Silvia. 'At least about getting my daughter and my husband out of this city alive. It may be necessary for Arianna to seem to go along with his plans. It will buy us time to work out what to do.'

Arianna shuddered. The Duke was repulsive to her. He was not unhandsome, even though so much older than her, and he was a cultured, civilised man, who valued art and literature and music. He was fabulously wealthy and could give her anything she might ever want. Except her freedom and the freedom of her city. But he was a murderer. And she did not, could not, love him. But her own mother was suggesting that she should not turn his proposal down out of hand.

Worst of all, Arianna guessed that Luciano knew of this development and had said nothing. What else was all this fencing about? It was pathetic; she didn't know whether to laugh or cry. Luciano against the Duke. She wished with all her heart that they had never come to Giglia.

Next morning, Paul himself came to collect Sky; the young people were out riding, he explained. He also explained that only one horse was Alice's, the one called Truffle. He was looking after Conker, the horse that Georgia rode, for a friend, and she and Nicholas had to take turns when they were both down together.

He clearly saw nothing odd in Georgia's friendship with the younger boy and nothing odd about his daughter's fondness for Sky either. He sat in Nana's parlour as much at his ease as in his own kitchen, chatting about horses and drinking her coffee, which was much less nice than at Ivy Court. Sky decided that he liked Alice's dad very much; he was the sort of person who was at home everywhere and accepted everyone on their own terms.

Paul hardly spoke to Rosalind, but he looked at her often and Sky wondered what he was thinking. He tried to see his mother as she might appear to Paul. A thin, pale-skinned, very fair woman in her late thirties, with a ready smile and expressive dark blue eyes. He wondered if she looked as fragile to Paul as she did to him. Sky suddenly felt fiercely protective of her. In all his seventeen years she had not dated anyone to his knowledge. Was it going to happen now? And with Alice's father, of all people! Sky couldn't imagine how that was going to affect his own relationship with Alice.

When they reached Ivy Court and found the others still out, Paul offered Sky the chance to drive his Shogun in the grounds. It felt enormous, sitting behind the wheel, but Sky managed to drive it without stalling and even changed gears with only one crunch. He was still in the driving seat when they finished a complete circuit and returned to the front of the house. Alice was waiting with her thumb stuck out.

'Any chance of a ride?' she smiled at him.

'Not till you've had a shower,' said Paul. 'I don't want my car reeking of horse. I have to drive it to my office, you know.'

But, horsey or not, Alice gave Sky a quick kiss when he got out of the car and, since it didn't seem to bother her father, Sky put his arms round her and kissed her back.

'You can go and get your sword-fighting out of the way while I shower,' she said. 'Nick says he's not going to bother till after – he'll only need another one after you've finished. He's waiting for you in the yard.'

Sky went round to the back and found Nicholas still talking to Conker. Sky himself was a little nervous of horses, never having had anything to do with them, and this one struck him as huge. But he was a handsome beast, with his arched neck and long mane. Seeing Nicholas with him reminded Sky of how little he knew about Georgia's stravagation and the time when the di Chimici's youngest prince had made his fateful decision.

'I miss having my own horse,' said Nicholas, looking up. 'I mean, I used to have them around all the time, before my accident.'

'But at least you can ride again now,' said Sky. 'And you would never have been able to do that if you had stayed in Talia. Or fence, come to that.'

'That's why I did it,' said Nicholas, but he sighed so deeply that Sky decided to tell him about the Stravaganti's plans straightaway.

'I'd be sorry to give back Merla's feather, of course,' said Nicholas, his eyes shining. 'But I'd do it if your friar could bring me something from Giglia.'

'That's what I thought,' said Sky.

'When are they coming?' asked Nicholas eagerly.

'As soon as we get back to London,' said Sky.

'So I could be back home in less than a week?'

'I guess.'

'Brilliant!' Nicholas punched the air, then stopped. 'What about Georgia?'

'Well, do you think she'd be willing to give up her talisman?' asked Sky. 'You know her better than I do.'

'I think it would be very hard for her,' said Nicholas. 'It was stolen twice, you know – by her awful stepbrother. The first time he broke it and the second time he kept it for nearly a year. We couldn't go back and it was agony. She was so happy when the horse came back. It means a lot to her.'

'More than seeing Luciano again?' asked Sky softly, but Nicholas couldn't answer that.

Giuditta had finished the macquette of the Duchessa's head. The hair was only suggested, because she had already sculpted it; it was the face she had made it for.

'Remarkable,' said Rodolfo, who had accompanied Arianna to her latest sitting. 'You have caught her to the life.'

'Will you hold on to the back of this chair, your Grace?' asked the sculptor. 'I should like to sketch your hands as if holding a ship's rail.'

Arianna was quite happy with this arrangement, which left her free to talk. Giuditta was taciturn as always, but her workshop was, unusually, empty, so

Arianna and Rodolfo were free to speak to her about private matters.

'Is it true that you are going to Luciano's old world?' Arianna asked the sculptor.

'Yes. Please don't tighten your fingers. Thank you.'

'Giuditta has of course been before, more than once,' said Rodolfo. 'But not to take a talisman for another Stravagante.'

'What will it be?' asked Arianna and saw Giuditta's dark eyes glance up, startled.

'I don't know yet,' Rodolfo answered for her. 'It must be from Giglia and Giuditta must choose it herself.'

'Do you think that Georgia will come?' Arianna asked Rodolfo.

'I think she will want to,' he said, looking thoughtful. 'And she is brave and loyal. But it would mean giving up her connection with Remora, and that will not be easy for her.'

Giuditta was listening, though she appeared to be totally concentrated on her work. So this girl she had to fetch was going to be difficult to persuade. Giuditta had hoped that, since Georgia was already a Stravagante, her work would be almost done. Now she could see this was far from true.

'Give up the flying horse?' said Georgia. 'Why on earth would I want to do that? They must have gone mad!'

'It's the only way to get you to Giglia at the moment,' Sky explained. 'And they all seem to think you'll be needed there. As well as Nicholas.'

Georgia was flattered, but the enormity of what she would need to do overwhelmed her.

'Can't I just take the other talisman and leave the horse here?' she asked.

'It doesn't work like that,' said Sky. 'Don't ask me why. They all know more about that sort of thing than I do. If Doctor Dethridge says that's the way it is, I'm not going to argue.'

'And they'll be here in a few days, as soon as we get back to London?'

It cast a shadow over the three of them for the rest of the weekend, making them edgy and anxious. Alice picked it up but had no explanation for it. Her time with Sky had started so well but now, inexplicably, he seemed to want to be with Nicholas and Georgia more than with her. And Georgia herself was remote and scratchy; the only times when things felt right were when they were out riding.

As for Nicholas, he was moodier than Alice had ever known him. Normally they got on well; it had been hard at first to accept him, but he and Georgia were so close that, over time, Alice had come to like him in his own right. But now he had become just a monosyllabic teenage boy and whenever they were all together, no one had anything to say except Alice. Paul was hardly ever there; he seemed to be spending a lot of time with Sky's mother.

In the end, Alice could think of only one reason for their behaviour, and she decided to confront them. It was the afternoon before they were due to go back and the weather had turned very warm. The boys had finished their fencing practice and were flopped on the lawn at the back of the house. Georgia had been watching them as usual. And Alice had been watching them all, from her bedroom window.

The three of them were talking quite animatedly. What did they find to talk about when they would say nothing to her? As soon as she reached the garden, the others fell silent.

'There's no need to stop,' said Alice. 'I've worked out what it must be. If you two want to be together,' she said to Sky and Georgia, 'then that's all right.'

Then she turned and walked back to the house, so that they wouldn't see she was crying.

Chapter 15

Visitors

Luciano's swordsmanship was improving. Twice he had managed to disarm Gaetano and hold a rapier to his throat. He was naturally quick and light on his feet and getting better at predicting his opponent's moves. When he wasn't practising in the piazzas and parks of Giglia, he often fought imaginary assailants with invisible weapons, whirling and twisting in the largely empty rooms of the Bellezzan Embassy. Many were the innocent statues and mirrors menaced by his increasing skill.

'You are quite alarming, even without a sword,' said Arianna, coming upon him alone on one such occasion.

He stopped, confused. They had hardly been alone together since Arianna had come to Giglia and he felt self-conscious. Here, in the Embassy, she was still very much the ruler of her city, and he felt more distant from her than ever. He still didn't know whether Rodolfo had told her about Niccolò's marriage plans and couldn't bring himself to ask.

'Why are you doing all this?' she asked now. 'I know Gaetano has been teaching you to fight. Do you know of some danger you are keeping from me?'

Luciano said nothing. If Rodolfo hadn't told her, then he had his reasons. Or if he had told her perhaps she didn't see it as a danger. In the old days, he would just have asked her, but now that she was Duchessa, he had to think before he spoke.

'Of course if you think it is safer for me not to know . . .' she said, turning her head away so that he should not see the sadness in her face. It pained her that Luciano no longer confided in her; the old Luciano of their early friendship in Bellezza would not have been capable of keeping anything a secret from her. She was longing to share her fear of the Duke's proposal with him but she couldn't raise it herself, couldn't talk to Luciano, of all people, about being asked to marry another di Chimici.

'It is nothing,' said Luciano stiffly. 'Just that, you know, Rodolfo and Doctor Dethridge and Sulien all seem sure that something bad will happen at the weddings. Even Gaetano seems to think the same. I just want to be ready if there's trouble.'

'And that's why they want more Stravaganti here? Even though bringing Falco back would be such a risk?'

'Yes,' said Luciano. 'I think Sulien and Giuditta are going to take the new talismans tomorrow.'

'Together? That's unusual, isn't it?'

'I don't think it's ever been done, but Giuditta hasn't taken a talisman before and she's a bit nervous, so Sulien offered to go at the same time.'

'Giuditta – nervous?' Arianna laughed, and Luciano smiled too.

'I know,' he said. 'It's hard to think of her being scared of anything.'

'I find her quite terrifying,' said Arianna. 'I'm glad she's on our side.'

'Me too,' said Luciano. 'She makes me feel about five years old. But I don't think she means to – it's just that she's so involved with her work that she doesn't see anything else as being important.'

'Well, she must think stravagation is important, or she wouldn't have done it.'

'How's the statue going?'

'Pretty well, I think,' said Arianna. 'We have only a few sittings left before the weddings.'

'Will you go back to Bellezza straight afterwards?' asked Luciano.

'Yes. I have invited Gaetano and Francesca to come back there for their honeymoon. It was where their courtship began – even though Gaetano was supposed to be wooing me at the time.'

'Did you ever consider accepting him?' asked Luciano. He had never dared to ask before but now he really needed to know.

'I had to *consider* it, Luciano,' said Arianna seriously. 'As Duchessa I have to think for my city, not for me,' she added, thinking of the coming proposal more than the last.

It wasn't an answer that Luciano found reassuring.

Carlo had been jumpy ever since the murder of Davide. He was unnerved by the apparent lack of reaction of the Nucci clan and he kept a bodyguard with him at all times. His bride was due to arrive in the city in a few weeks, with her sister and parents, and his uncle Jacopo would demand to know how his daughters were to be kept safe. Carlo didn't know the answer.

Several Nucci would be present at his wedding to Lucia, when the four couples would process into the great cathedral. Each couple would have their own entourage and it would be possible to introduce some armed guards into the procession; the bridegrooms themselves would all wear swords as part of their ceremonial dress. But it was unimaginable that they should be drawn in the cathedral. The very thought of it brought Carlo out in a cold sweat.

'I wish these accursed weddings were over and we were all married!' he said to Fabrizio.

'That's no way to talk about your approaching nuptials,' laughed his brother. 'Lucia wouldn't find it romantic at all.'

'You know what I mean!' said Carlo. 'I've no objection to marrying Lucia, but the more I hear about Father's plans for the occasion, the more certain I am that the Nucci will strike then.'

'Still, what would you have him do?' asked Fabrizio. 'Three di Chimici princes and a duke all marrying on the same day cannot be a jug of wine and a plate of olives affair!'

'I know, but Father has decided to make it the

biggest exhibition of di Chimici wealth and power in the history of Talia! And if he can also announce the Grand Duchy and his betrothal to the Duchessa of Bellezza at the same time . . .'

'I know,' said Fabrizio. 'I have the same fears as you. It's just going to provoke the Nucci and their allies. But Father's chief spy is working to find out what he can and he will be in charge of our safety at the weddings.'

'The Eel?' said Carlo, uneasily. 'I hope he knows what he's doing.'

Sky was utterly miserable. He had tried to explain to Alice that he had no interest in Georgia and they had sort of made up. But he couldn't give her any reason for why he needed to spend so much time with Georgia and with Nicholas. It wasn't just his secret, so he made a poor fist of being convincing. Their sunny holiday had fizzled out in suspicion and jealousy.

And to make it worse, Rosalind hadn't noticed anything wrong and had chattered happily about Paul Greaves all the way home. Laura seemed almost as peeved as Sky about this. She knew Paul's ex-wife Jane, Alice's mother; they were councillors together in Islington and had sat on several of the same committees. Since Jane was Laura's friend, she couldn't believe that Paul could possibly be a good person.

'You know why they got divorced?' she demanded, driving too fast as usual, with the window open, so that she had to shout over all the noise.

'Because he was a serial killer? He held orgies at Ivy Court? He beat her up?' suggested Rosalind, stung by Laura's know-all attitude.

'Because he was controlling and didn't want Jane to lead her own life,' said Laura. 'He was always sure he was right about everything.'

'Alice says it was because they were too different,' said Sky. Wretched as he felt about his own relationship, he didn't want Laura to squash his mother's happiness. He couldn't remember when he had last seen her as carefree and relaxed as she had been over this long weekend.

Rosalind had been exhausted by the time they got back to London though and had gone straight to bed. After a not very satisfactory phone call with Alice, Sky had followed suit and hurled himself towards Talia for a quick dip into his Giglian life – just long enough to tell Sulien that they were back.

The next morning he was up early, making breakfast, determined to be first to the door when the Talian Stravaganti arrived. He didn't know how he was going to get his mother out of the flat. Remedy wound round his legs, torn between pleasure at having him back and indignation at having been fed by a neighbour for so long. Sky picked him up and held his long, purring body over his shoulder. The doorbell rang.

It was Nicholas and Georgia. Rosalind came into the kitchen, looking young and tousled, in her dressing gown.

'Oh, hello, you two,' she said, smiling. 'Can't keep away, can you? Alice not with you?'

Everyone mumbled something uncomfortably and

Sky smoothed the moment over with offers of coffee and toast, while his mother went off to shower.

'I don't know how I'm going to get rid of her,' he said. 'She's so tired after yesterday's journey. I can't just shove her out of the house.'

'Perhaps we should wait outside for them,' suggested Georgia.

'It'll look a bit odd, won't it?' said Nicholas. 'Us just hanging around on the doorstep all day.'

'It wouldn't be all day,' said Sky. 'They're going to get here some time this morning.'

There was a muffled knocking from the front door in the hall.

'Too late,' said Georgia. 'I bet that's them.'

Sky came out of the flat and listened. He could hear voices outside the front door of the house and then it opened. His neighbour, Gill, from upstairs, the one who had been feeding Remedy, was letting herself in. She had a newspaper under her arm and a paper bag from the local patisserie in her hand; he could smell the warm, fresh croissants.

'Sky,' said Gill. 'There's a sort of priest here, asking for you. Shall I let him in?'

Beatrice was adapting to her new home in the Palazzo Ducale. She had a much larger chamber than her old one in the Palazzo di Chimici and a pretty little sitting room with green silk on the walls, next to her father's suite of rooms and sharing its view of the river. Her life was busier than ever, turning the lofty, elegant rooms into something that felt like a home, and she would soon have guests to welcome at the old palazzo in the Via Larga. Members of the di Chimici family would be converging on Giglia from all over Talia, to celebrate the weddings.

The last time so many family members had been together in the city had been for Falco's funeral, and Beatrice was determined to chase that memory away with the warmth of their welcome for the happier occasion. She wondered if her father had the same idea as she heard more about his elaborate plans for the celebrations. Three days of feasting, tournaments, pageants and processions were being prepared for, and the princess, as the only female di Chimici of the Giglian branch, had to oversee everything as hostess.

She had very few moments to herself and, though she was glad of the help she was offered by Enrico, her father's confidential agent, she wearied of the way he seemed always to be there, one step behind her.

On this day, a week after having moved into her new home, Beatrice stood at the window of her sitting room, enjoying a few minutes of solitude. The year was warming up; it would be April soon and the weddings were just over three weeks away. The river was running very high, she noticed, remembering how wet the winter had been. At least the rains seemed to be over now; it would be an awful shame for the brides to have their finery drenched, she thought. She looked across to where the new Nucci palace stood and its grand gardens beyond.

Beatrice sighed. She didn't understand why things had got so bad between the two families; she could remember a time when they visited with one another reasonably civilly. Although rivals with a bloody history, they were the two wealthiest families in the city and that meant at least some social intercourse. A smile played round her mouth as a day came back to her from childhood when the three Nucci boys and their two sisters had visited the di Chimici in the Via Larga. The grown-ups had been interminably talking and drinking wine and the children had all been turned out like puppies into the courtyard. Camillo Nucci and her own brother Fabrizio had devised a plan to clothe the bronze Mercury in the middle of the flower beds.

It had been Beatrice who had fetched the scarves and necklaces and a petticoat from her mother's room, but Camillo, Fabrizio and Carlo had done the draping, while the little princess had looked on with Filippo Nucci and the little boys and girls. It had been before Falco was born and Davide had been no more than a toddler in his big sister's arms, thought Beatrice, looking back fondly on how ridiculous the Mercury had looked in his finery and how the Duke and Matteo Nucci had scolded them.

And now Davide and Falco were both dead and the families were bitter enemies. On the few occasions when Beatrice had passed any of them in the street, they had looked sternly ahead, even though Graziella had sat and mourned with them after Falco's death and Beatrice had sent words of sympathy on their own bereavement.

A knock at the door roused her from her reverie.

'The confectioner is here, your Highness,' said Enrico. 'Wanting to speak to you about marzipan.'

'I shall come directly,' said Beatrice.

It would take a quantity of sugar to sweeten the

inevitable coming together of the two families.

Sulien and Giuditta stood on the doorstep. Brother Sulien looked just like a monk or friar from any modern monastery or friary; his robes were a kind of uniform that hadn't changed over more than four centuries. But Giuditta did not look as if she belonged in the twenty-first century at all. She wore a long green velvet cloak with its hood flung back over her ordinary working clothes, and Sky was sure he could see marble dust in her hair. But she was as calm and impassive as she was in Giglia, with the stillness of one of her own statues.

'Can we come in?' asked Sulien, and Sky couldn't think of any way of saying no.

They walked along the short passage to the kitchen and suddenly he found himself introducing four Stravaganti to one another. Giuditta recognised the young di Chimici prince, changed though he was, but Nicholas had not met Giuditta before. The Giglians were looking round the kitchen with interest when the freshly showered Rosalind came in and saw them.

'Good heavens,' she said, startled. 'We are having a lot of early visitors this morning. Who are your friends, Sky?'

Sky had no cover story ready; he had been banking on getting his mother out of the way before the Stravaganti arrived. But it was, surprisingly, Giuditta who handled the situation.

'I am Giuditta Miele, the sculptor,' she said, holding out her hand. 'And this is Fratello Suliano Fabriano.

He brought your son to my studio and I saw that he was interested in sculpture.'

It was one of the longest speeches Sky had ever heard her make and he could see it was full of holes. But his mother was nothing if not polite and she latched on to the bit she could understand.

'Yes, he's very good at art; it's always been one of his favourite subjects. Can I offer you some coffee, Ms Miele? And Frat . . .'

'Please call me Sulien,' said the friar, with a winning smile. 'Sky always does. I'd love some coffee.'

Sky was already busy washing up the cáfetière.

'Should I know your work, Ms . . .?' Rosalind began to ask Giuditta.

'Giuditta,' said the sculptor. 'I doubt it. It is in another place.'

'Italy, is it?' asked Rosalind. 'Your English is very good, both of you.' She was struggling to incorporate these two strangers into her frame of reference. How could this handsome friar have taken her son to the sculptor's studio if it was in Italy? And how did Sky come to know him? They seemed old friends.

Nicholas came to the rescue. 'She has a wonderful reputation,' he said. 'Giuditta Miele is one of the most famous artists in Europe.'

'Really?' said Rosalind. 'Please forgive my ignorance.'

Georgia had been sitting dumbstruck, appalled by the awkwardness of the situation. She wondered what she would have done if Paolo the Horsemaster, 'her' Stravagante in Remora, had ever turned up at her house and sat drinking coffee in the kitchen. Remembering how her mother Maura had got the wrong end of the stick about her relationship with the old antique dealer who had sold her the talisman of the flying horse, she began to feel hysterical laughter rising in her throat.

Nicholas kicked her under the table and she turned it into a cough. The phone rang and Rosalind went to take the call in the living room.

'Thank goodness,' said Georgia. 'I thought I was going to burst. You can't get away with this, Sky. She's bound to smell a rat. You don't just have friends who are sculptors and friars who live in Italy without ever mentioning them to your mother.'

'I can make her forget all about meeting us if you like,' said Sulien. 'If you think it would be less worrying for her?'

'You don't mean with one of your potions, do you?' asked Sky apprehensively.

'I would never administer anything that could harm her,' said Sulien gravely. 'But no, I meant something simpler.'

Rosalind came back into the room looking pink and pretty. 'I'm awfully sorry, but I'm going to have to go. A friend is unexpectedly in town and wants to see me. I'm sure Sky will look after you.'

To Sky she whispered, 'It's Paul. He came up on the night train last night. He wants me to meet him at his club. Will you be all right here?'

'Of course,' said Sky. Then said, 'His club?' with a quizzical look.

Rosalind suppressed a giggle. She went to get her bag and jacket, then took her leave of the group in the kitchen. As she shook hands with Sulien he gazed into her eyes and said some words that no one in the room, except perhaps Giuditta, could understand. Rosalind shook her head slightly, her blue eyes suddenly cloudy. Then she said goodbye to the three teenagers, as if there were no one else in the room, and left.

'Phew,' said Sky. 'That was horrible. Thank goodness for Paul.'

'We are wasting time,' said Giuditta. For all her apparent confidence, she did not yet feel at ease out of her own world.

'Prince Falco,' said Sulien. 'I have come because I hear you are willing to try stravagating to Talia again.'

'More than willing,' said Nicholas eagerly. 'I'm dying to go back.'

'But the talisman you have takes you only to Remora,' said the friar. 'Do you have it with you?'

Nicholas pulled a glossy black feather, about the size of a swan's, out of his jacket and laid it on the table. It was beautiful. Sulien took from his pocket what at first looked like an identical feather and put it beside the first one. Then Sky saw it was in fact a very fine quill pen. Nicholas took it up and admired it; it had a bluish sheen.

'You understand that if you take it, you have to give up the other talisman?' said Sulien. Nicholas nodded; he seemed mesmerised by the quill. Sulien took the black feather and stowed it in his robes.

'Simple, isn't it?' said Georgia, and Sky saw that she was glaring at Giuditta. 'I suppose you now offer me something and I'm supposed to hand over my flying horse?'

She took a bubble-wrapped package from her pocket and began to open it. Giuditta said nothing. She had said nothing to Georgia at all so far. At last the winged horse stood on the table between them. Sky had never seen Merla, the miraculous horse with wings that both Georgia and Nicholas had ridden in Remora, but he could see how much the little figure meant to Georgia; she was fighting tears as she said, 'What can you offer me to set beside that?'

'Nothing,' said Giuditta. 'The exchange can be made only if the Stravagante is willing. I did bring a new talisman for you, but if you do not want to give up your right to travel to Remora, I cannot make you.'

This was not what Georgia had been expecting. She struggled with her curiosity to see what the sculptor had brought and her desire to keep the little horse. But it seemed churlish to ask to see the new talisman when she had no intention of accepting it.

Giuditta took something from a pocket in her work-dress and put it, wordlessly, on the table. It was an exquisite figure of a ram.

'I made it myself,' she said impassively.

'For me?' asked Georgia. Giuditta nodded. 'Can I hold it?'

Georgia took up the small animal. It was quite different from her original talisman – Renaissance in feeling beside the Etruscan figure, more sophisticated in its detail, with the tiny curved horns and woollen curls meticulously sculpted. And it touched her that this gifted, if severe, artist had made it specifically for her.

'It's beautiful,' she said simply, handing it back.

'But you are not going to take it?'

Georgia shook her head, miserable.

'Georgia,' said Nicholas, taking her hand. 'If you

took it, we could be in Giglia together tonight! I could show you my city. And we could see Gaetano again. You'd like that, wouldn't you?'

Georgia was crying, silently.

Giuditta stood up. 'Do not attempt to compel her,' she said sternly. 'An unwilling Stravagante would be no good to us in time of danger. Sulien, I think we should leave.'

She put the ram away but Sky did not think she was offended; if anything, she seemed to be on Georgia's side. Giuditta asked if she could lie on his bed to stravagate back to Talia and he led her to his room; Sulien would follow as soon as the sculptor had disappeared. When Sky got back to the kitchen, he found Sulien spooning honey on to a piece of toast and making Georgia eat it.

'You are trembling, my dear,' he said. 'You have been through an ordeal and must have something sweet to restore you.'

'Please don't be so nice,' said Georgia, her mouth full of crumbs and stickiness. 'I know I'm spoiling all your plans. And the ram was really lovely. But I just can't give up the horse.'

'Then we must just make some new plans,' said Sulien.

While Beatrice spoke of sweetmeats and silvered almonds, the Duke was giving a very special commission to a jeweller from the nearby workshops. The Grand-Ducal crown of Tuschia was to be kept a secret, on pain of death. It was to be a circle of silver with the Giglian lily in front, bearing a great oval ruby that was already in Niccolò's possession. All the way round rose points of silver, every other one terminating in a miniature lily, and the whole was to be set with gems, square-cut and round.

And the jeweller had a second even more secret commission: a smaller crown, for a Grand Duchess, a copy of that to be worn by her lord and master. And if he wondered who was to wear it, since the Duke was a widower, he valued his own life far too much to voice the thought. And he was going to be busy; the Duke had also ordered a choker of pearls and diamonds, a sleeve pendant in the shape of a Bellezzan mandola and two silver collars, 'large enough for a big dog.'

'Any particular dog, your Grace?' hazarded the jeweller. 'Such as I might measure?'

'They are not for dogs at all,' said Niccolò haughtily. 'I have ordered two spotted cats from Africa; the collars are for them.'

'It doesn't matter, really,' said Nicholas for the umpteenth time, but Georgia was inconsolable.

Sulien and Giuditta had both gone. Sky had been feeding Georgia sweet tea for shock but she was still in a terrible state.

'I do want to go to Giglia with you, more than almost anything,' she was saying. 'It's just that I can't give up the chance of going back to Remora and seeing Paolo and Cesare again and their family – and the horses. It was what stopped me going mad all that time when Russell was bullying me.'

The doorbell rang again and Sky went to answer it.

'I understand, honestly,' said Nicholas. 'I didn't mean to make it harder for you. You know I wouldn't do anything to upset you.'

Someone was following Sky into the room; it was the last person he had expected to find on his doorstep.

'Hello, Georgia,' said Luciano.

Chapter 16

Mapping the City

The Pope was feeling testy. He was accustomed to being treated as less important than his older brother, the Duke; it had been going on all his life. But he was Pope, after all, and Prince of Remora into the bargain, and he did think he might have been consulted about the arrangements for these weddings, especially since he was going to officiate at them. Now his chaplain, his nephew Rinaldo, was telling him that he would have to travel to Giglia soon after celebrating Mass in the cathedral of Remora on Easter Sunday, in order to be there in time for a great tournament the next day.

In truth, much of his bad humour came from the fact that it was nearly four weeks into Lent and Ferdinando di Chimici hadn't had what he considered a decent meal since Shrove Tuesday. Easter Sunday's dinner was something he had been looking forward to. The Pope was a great trencherman and Lent was a sore trial to him.

'I shall have terrible indigestion if I travel by coach after dinner on Easter Sunday,' he complained.

'But, your Holiness,' said Rinaldo, who was well aware of his uncle's weakness, 'you would not wish to miss any of the feasts planned by your brother the Duke. He has told me himself of the splendour and magnificence of the banquets. Perhaps if you took a light lunch after Mass on the Sunday, you could travel in comfort? I am sure the Duke will entertain you sumptuously when you reach Giglia.'

The Pope was mollified. 'Tell me about the banquets,' he said.

Georgia was quite hysterical.

'I know why you've come!' she hissed at Luciano. 'They thought you could persuade me to swap talismans. I bet you've got that ram with you, and I know it's beautiful, but I'm not going to take it. It's not fair to ask me!' And all the time she was thinking, It's Luciano, after all this time, and I'm all red-faced and teary – I must look a sight.

'I'm not going to ask you,' said Luciano calmly. 'I came to tell you I've thought of another way. I haven't got any ram.'

His voice was husky, as if his throat hurt, and Georgia was suddenly seized with remorse, as she remembered how hard it was for him to stravagate in this direction. She wondered if he'd had to go first to his old home and whether his parents had seen him.

'Give him some of your sweet tea,' she said to Sky. 'He looks as if he needs it.'

Luciano accepted the tea and looked admiringly at Nicholas, while Georgia escaped to the bathroom to repair the damage done by all the crying.

'You look amazing, Falco. I should hardly have recognised you.'

'Thanks,' said Nicholas. 'Do you think I'll be recognised in Giglia? I mean, I'm a whole year older than I should be, as well as being alive when I'm supposed to be dead.'

'I think you'd be fine,' said Luciano, 'except with members of your family. They'd know you but they'd have to see you up close.'

'I told Sky I'd grow a beard,' said Nicholas. 'But I can't wait for that. I want to go to Giglia tonight.'

'Without Georgia?' asked Sky.

Nicholas paced the small kitchen. 'Of course I don't want to go without her! But you'll be there, won't you? And it doesn't look as if she ever will.'

'That's why I've come,' said Luciano.

Georgia came back; she was calm now and ready to listen to his idea.

'It's simple really,' said Luciano. 'Although we thought there wouldn't be time for you to get from Remora to Giglia and back within one night's stravagation, there's something we've all been forgetting.'

They all looked blank.

'We've been thinking of doing it by carriage or horse, using the road between the two cities,' he continued. 'It would take several hours each way on the sixteenth-century highway – it's not like a motorway. But the distance between Remora and Giglia is not so very great – at least, not as the horse flies.'

Georgia saw it in an instant, although the other two were a few steps behind her. She flung her arms round Luciano, no longer embarrassed, and he smiled into her radiant face.

'Brilliant!' she said. 'That's it! I could go to Paolo's and see Cesare and the family and then fly to Giglia on Merla. And then do the same in the opposite direction before darkness falls in Talia. I could keep my talisman and still come to Giglia!'

Now she hurled herself at Nicholas and made him dance round the kitchen with her. Everyone was grinning. Suddenly it seemed as if they were all about to embark on an exciting and glamorous holiday.

'When can we go?' asked Nicholas.

'Hang on,' said Sky. 'We've got to plan this properly. If I understand it, you've both got to have proper clothes waiting at the other end and Nick's at least will have to be some sort of disguise. And how is Georgia going to land a flying horse in the middle of a city? They don't exactly have airfields in Giglia, and she hasn't been there before – how will she know where to meet us?'

That slowed everyone down a bit.

'We can contact Paolo and tell him about Georgia going to Remora,' said Luciano. 'Rodolfo can do it through his mirrors. And I'm sure we can make some arrangements in Giglia, but Sky's right; you can't go tonight, Falco. Your disguise and cover story are going to take a bit of planning.'

'How about him being another novice, like me?' said Sky. 'My black robe has a hood, which he could pull up over his face if there was anyone around who might recognise him. And Sulien could organise that.'

'Where will I arrive?' asked Nicholas. 'The only time I've done it before, I turned up in Paolo's stables, because my talisman was Merla's feather, but I don't know where the quill comes from.'

'I think Sulien brought it from his cell,' said Luciano. 'But I'll check on that and on the novice friar idea. I can tell Sky when he stravagates tonight.'

'Oh, this is too frustrating!' said Nicholas. 'I have the talisman and I still can't go! How long is it going to take?'

'Not more than a day or two,' said Luciano. 'I must tell Gaetano, and we Stravaganti need to talk about where you should go and where you should be during the weddings. And Paolo will need to organise some clothes for Georgia. Nicholas isn't the only one who has changed since he left Talia.'

Georgia felt a blush beginning. Luciano hadn't been in Remora when she and Nicholas had made their dramatic stravagation there six months ago and found that their worlds had been separated by an extra year. She knew she was no longer the awkward, flat-chested girl who had harboured a secret crush on Lucien Mulholland. The constant admiration of Nicholas and the increase in her confidence that her adventures in Remora had given her had turned her into quite a different person. In all respects but one. Just seeing Luciano sitting in Sky's kitchen, wearing the simplest white shirt he could find and undisguisably black velvet trousers, she was overtaken by a wave of the old despair. The only boy she had ever really loved was separated from her by hundreds of years and a dimensional barrier she couldn't begin to understand. And yet he had come back to tell her his idea himself, when he could have just explained it to Sky in Talia.

'I wore one of Teresa's dresses when I went back last time,' she said quickly, to hide her feelings. 'I expect I could do that again.'

Luciano nodded. 'We could organise that.' He passed a hand across his face, suddenly weary. 'I'd better get back. Can I lie on your bed, Sky, to stravagate home?'

'Help yourself,' said Sky, showing him the way. 'It's been like an airport terminal in there today.'

When Sulien stepped off his maze the next morning he found two colourful figures waiting silently in the pews. A young man and woman, tall, with long dark hair, wearing the vivid, be-ribboned clothing of the Manoush. Sulien gestured to them to follow him into the cloister. He hadn't met these two before but he knew others of their tribe; now he realised that the man was blind. The woman said, 'Brother Sulien? Rodolfo sent us.'

Sulien nodded.

'I am Raffaella,' said the woman. 'And this is Aurelio. Rodolfo thinks you may need us.'

Before he could ask why, a rather dishevelled and tired-looking Luciano joined them; clearly he knew the Manoush. Aurelio raised his fine head towards him as soon as he heard Luciano's voice. But before they had finished exchanging greetings, Sky too had appeared. The five of them moved to Sulien's laboratory.

Luciano laid out the problems about getting Georgia from Remora to Giglia.

'She will come on the zhou volou?' asked Aurelio. 'We can look after the horse for her while she does whatever you need her for in the city.'

'Where could she land?' asked Sky. 'She doesn't know Giglia.'

'There are fields all round the city,' said Raffaella. 'We just need to agree a suitable place. It must be somewhere where we can keep the flying horse safely hidden until Georgia comes back for her.'

'It also has to be somewhere she can find by easy landmarks,' said Luciano. 'You could draw her a map, Sky, showing her what to look for.'

'The river and the cathedral are the two main landmarks she will be able to see clearly from the sky,' said Sulien. 'They will guide her course when she flies in from Remora.'

'And what about the new Nucci palace?' suggested Sky. 'I bet that's visible from quite high up.'

'Is it safe to land near there?' asked Aurelio. 'Is it not from the Nucci that you fear danger?'

'From what I've heard,' said Sky, 'they aren't moving into that palace until the day after the di Chimici weddings. Until then they'll be living in their home near here. Besides, we have a little farm there. It used to belong to the di Chimici family but Niccolò gave it to the friary recently. Georgia's Merla could be kept safe there.'

He fetched paper and pen and unrolled a parchment

with a map of Giglia on it. They all contributed ideas, until there was a rough sketch that Sky could memorise and reproduce for Georgia.

'What about, you know, Nicholas?' he asked Sulien warily, looking at the Manoush. He didn't know quite what to make of these new people, but the friar seemed to trust them and Luciano obviously knew them.

'Do you know what happened to Prince Falco?' Luciano asked them.

'We know it was not what was given out,' said Raffaella. 'Our friend Grazia, in Remora, told us that she saw him win his own memorial Stellata, on the zhou volou.'

'Many there said it was a ghost who rode in that race,' said Aurelio. 'But the Manoush can tell spirits from living people. I would guess he now lives in the other world – the one known to you Stravaganti.'

'You are right,' said Sulien. 'But he, like Georgia, will come back here to strengthen our numbers in the troubled times ahead. I myself took him a new talisman to bring him here – one of my own quill pens. He will arrive here, Sky. You can stravagate together.'

*

Rodolfo and Paolo faced each other in the mirror. Arianna and Silvia watched in silence.

'So we shall see her again, our little champion?' said Paolo.

'Not for long,' said Rodolfo. 'She will take Merla, if you are willing, and leave you swiftly for Giglia. There will be no time for her to linger in Remora.'

'It will still be a pleasure, if a fleeting one,' said Paolo. 'And it will not be a single stravagation, if I understand you.'

'She will need to learn the city, if she is to be of use to us when danger strikes,' said Rodolfo.

'And she will need clothes?' asked Paolo.

'A young woman's costume, as before,' said Rodolfo. 'Luciano tells me she has grown up.'

'So,' said Arianna, when Rodolfo turned away at last from the mirrors. 'Georgia is coming back.'

'Do you mind?' he asked.

'Not if you need her,' said Arianna.

'I need them all,' said Rodolfo. 'And even with them, with eight Stravaganti in the city, I still don't know if it will be enough.'

'I wish it were all over,' said Arianna. 'And that we were back in Bellezza and out of the Duke's clutches.'

'As to that,' said Rodolfo, 'have you decided what to do about the dress?'

Rosalind had looked very pleased with herself when she returned from her meeting with Paul. If she remembered that her kitchen had been full of Stravaganti when she left, she said nothing about it.

'How was the *club*?' Sky teased.

'It was OK,' she said. 'But we didn't stay there. Paul was supposed to be meeting a work colleague in London, but after we'd had coffee, we went out and ended up having lunch together in Soho.'

'You really like him, don't you?' said Sky.

'I do,' said Rosalind. 'Does that make it difficult for you and Alice? I've noticed you seem to be, well, having problems.'

'It's not because of you,' said Sky. 'Though it is a bit weird when your girlfriend's dad fancies your mum. We had a misunderstanding in Devon. Alice thought I preferred Georgia.'

'I'm not surprised,' said Rosalind. 'You do spend an awful lot of time with her. But aren't she and Nicholas together? I've often wondered.'

'It's not that simple,' said Sky. 'Sorry. There are things I can't tell you because they're not my secrets.'

Rosalind didn't press him. But Sky wasn't happy. The new developments in Talia meant that he was going to be spending even more time with Georgia and Nicholas and their shared secrets were going to grow. How could he explain it to Alice? She was already suspicious and, try as he might, he couldn't see how he was supposed to have a normal relationship with a girl while he spent every night stravagating to another world.

The first problem arose the next day. He was round at the Mulhollands, reporting to Nicholas on the progress of plans for getting him to Giglia. Georgia was there too, and the two boys were trying to draw her a map of the city. But Sky was trying to remember Sulien's sketch and Nicholas kept telling him he was getting things wrong.

'Geography homework in the holidays?' asked Vicky Mulholland, seeing them all bent over the dining table. 'You are keen.'

'Vicky,' said Nicholas. 'Have you got any maps of Italy?'

'Somewhere,' said Vicky. 'Let me think. Yes, up in David's office. Do you want me to get them?'

'I'll find them,' said Nicholas. 'Thanks.'

'I'll come with you,' said Georgia.

'Would you like some coffee, Sky?' offered Vicky and he went with her into the kitchen.

Now that Sky had met Luciano, he was fascinated by Vicky Mulholland. She had the same black curly hair as her son but she was small and energetic. Nicholas towered over her and so did Sky. As he watched her deft movements about the kitchen, grinding beans, assembling mugs, tipping biscuits on to a plate, he wondered how on earth she had coped with losing one son and gaining another so mysteriously.

What would Rosalind have done if he had died and, a year later, a Sky lookalike had turned up, in need of a home?

'How's the fencing going?' Vicky was asking.

'What? Oh, yes, very well, thanks,' said Sky. 'I'm nowhere near as good as Nick, of course, but he's a good teacher.'

'I'm glad to hear it,' said Vicky, pouring the coffee into mugs. 'He's been a bit, well, restless lately. I'm glad he's got something to occupy him.' She hesitated. 'You know how he came to live with us?'

Sky felt wrong-footed. He had just been thinking about it and what he knew was very different from the Mulhollands' view of events. 'He was abandoned, wasn't he? By asylum-seekers or something?'

'I don't think exactly abandoned,' said Vicky slowly, 'but it was something like that. He had been badly injured and I think mentally scarred too. He had lost his memory. Only – well, it's silly really – I don't like to ask him about it in case it upsets him, but lately I've been wondering if he has remembered something – if he's been thinking about his old life.'

She looked at Sky with her big dark eyes, so like both Luciano's and Nicholas's, and he felt very uncomfortable indeed; she was closer to the truth than she realised.

'Has he said anything to you?' she asked.

He was saved from answering by the return of the others, triumphantly waving a handful of maps. They had struck gold and found one of Italy and an old battered one of Florence. They took their coffee into the dining room and spread the maps among their bits of paper. Vicky disappeared with her mug, looking a bit wistful. It was another complication, but Sky had to push it to one side as they pored over the outline of the city that both was and was not Giglia.

'Florence is almost due north of Siena,' said Georgia. 'So, if Giglia and Remora are in the same positions as them, I'd need to set my course and fly virtually straight till I reach the city walls.'

'And you'll see the river running almost across the middle,' said Nicholas, 'with Saint-Mary-of-the-Lily on the far shore.'

'The Manoush think you should land before you reach the river, though,' said Sky. 'There's a breach in the southern wall between the fields and where the gardens of the Nucci palace begin. They'll meet you there if we agree on a day and time.'

'And they'll look after Merla?' she asked.

'Yes, they offered. They seemed to know all about her,' said Sky.

'They were there when I won the Stellata,' said Georgia, remembering. 'And Cesare flew over the Campo on Merla. I'm sure Aurelio saw her, even though he's blind. I'd rather trust her to them than anyone else outside Remora.'

'Now, you need to know how to get from there to a place you can meet us,' said Nicholas. He was flushed and excited, trying to trace the lines of his old home under the sprawl of the modern city. 'Oh, this is so frustrating! It isn't Giglia at all!'

'Of course not,' said Sky. 'It's Florence. It's a different city in a different world over four hundred years later. What did you expect?'

But Nicholas ploughed on. 'Just walk past where Sky says this new palace is, towards the river, and you'll come to a stone bridge – the Ponte Nuovo.'

'Just follow your nose,' said Sky. 'It stinks. It's full of butchers and fishmongers.'

'Then cross the river and turn right and you'll come to a square on your left,' said Nicholas, ignoring him and closing his eyes, visualising a walk he had done many times when he was little. 'That's where the silversmiths have their workshops, under the Guild offices. Turn left and walk through that square to the next one – it's huge. That's the Piazza Ducale with all the statues.'

'That must be where the Piazza della Signoria is today in Florence,' said Sky, pointing it out to her on the map.

Gradually they pieced out a route from Georgia's landing place to the piazza with the great cathedral in it.

'I think we should meet in Giuditta's bottega,' said

Sky, 'if she'll let us.'

Georgia squirmed. 'Must we? She probably despises me for making it all so difficult when I could just have stravagated straight there with her model of the ram.'

'It's central,' said Sky firmly. 'And right by the one thing in Giglia you can't miss. It's on the north side of the big bit of the cathedral – where the little domes are. And it's Stravaganti territory – near neither the Nucci nor the di Chimici, so we should be safe.'

Georgia committed it all to memory. She was getting excited now too. She didn't expect to love this city the way she had Remora, but it had been Nicholas's home when he was Falco and it was where Luciano was now.

Someone came in and they didn't look up, assuming it was Vicky. But it was Alice. They had been talking so animatedly that they hadn't heard the doorbell.

'I think it's time you told me what's going on,' she said quietly, and they all looked up, as guiltily as if they'd been caught planning a bank robbery. 'There's something that you're all in on,' said Alice. 'And I'm not leaving till you tell me what it is.'

Chapter 17

My Enemy's Enemy is My Friend

'So you and Georgia are time travellers and Nicholas is from another dimension?' said Alice coolly. 'Like something out of *Buffy*?'

'More *Roswell High*, really,' said Sky. 'The site of our school was where the first Stravagante had his laboratory in the sixteenth century. That's why the talismans always end up near it.'

'Well, thanks for clearing that up,' said Alice. She seemed so calm that it took a while for the others to realise that she was in a white-hot rage. 'Now would you like to tell me what's *really* going on?'

When she had arrived at the Mulhollands' and demanded an explanation, it had taken only a few exchanged looks before they decided there was no way out but to tell her the truth. And now she didn't believe them.

'I don't blame you for not believing us,' said Georgia. 'I wouldn't if I were you. But it's true. I found my talisman in Mortimer Goldsmith's antique shop nearly two years ago. I started travelling to Talia then and I met Nicholas there – Falco, he was then.'

'I decided to come here because I couldn't walk in that world,' said Nicholas. 'You remember what I was like before I had my operations? I'd had a terrible accident with a horse and I couldn't be cured in Talia.'

'And I pretended to find him outside this house,' continued Georgia.

'And you're seriously trying to tell me that you kept all this Talia stuff from me all the time we were becoming friends?' said Alice.

'I didn't want to,' said Georgia. 'But you wouldn't have believed me – you don't believe me now. Or any of us!'

'Let me show you the talisman,' said Nicholas suddenly, taking the quill pen out of his shirt.

A few moments passed and Georgia took the winged horse out of her pocket. Sky followed suit with the perfume bottle. The three talismans sat on the table among the sketch maps and the coffee mugs. Alice was visibly shaken.

'I don't understand,' she said. 'All these come from the other world, according to you. But Nicholas doesn't go there, does he? If what you told me is true, he came from there to here. His talisman should be a – I don't know – a GameBoy or something!'

They all smiled at that, even Alice herself. She suddenly sat down.

'I don't know why I'm even trying to bring logic

into this,' she said. 'It's too crazy even to discuss.'

They explained about how Nicholas had used Georgia's old silver eyebrow ring to stravagate from his old world and had been back to it only once, using a feather from the flying horse. And how the quill was a new talisman, to take him to Giglia.

'You're saying they came here – two travellers from this other world?' asked Alice.

'That's how the talismans always get here,' said Sky. 'Stravaganti bring them from Talia so that we can go there. I know it sounds fantastic, but it's true. That's why I've spent so much time with Nick and Georgia. I found out about them while I was there.'

'OK, then,' said Alice. 'Prove it. Take me with you the next time you go.'

'You can't just come with us,' said Nicholas. 'We've explained that a talisman has to be brought by a Stravagante from Talia before someone from here can travel there.'

'Then how can I believe anything you've said?' said Alice. 'If I can't see it for myself?'

'Well, I could ask Sulien, I suppose,' said Sky. 'When I go there tonight. We hope that Nicholas and Georgia will be able to go back tomorrow.'

'You mean you're going there tonight?' said Alice.

'Yes,' said Sky. 'I go there nearly every night, for as long as I can.'

'He won't let you bring another talisman,' said Nicholas.

'How can you be so sure?' said Alice. 'How come you and Sky and Georgia are so special but I'm not worthy to have one of your little trinkets? Why shouldn't I be a Stravagante? Oh, God, I can't believe

I'm even asking this. It can't be anything more than a crazy story you've made up.'

'Why would we make up a story to keep you out?' said Georgia. 'Look, the talismans seem to find people who are unhappy, or ill, even. The first person to go from our school was Lucien – the Mulhollands' son – you know, the boy I told you about. And he was so ill he died.'

'But you're telling me he's still alive in this Talia of yours?' said Alice.

Georgia looked round nervously. 'Keep it down,' she said. 'You don't want Vicky to hear. She doesn't know anything about it.'

'Well,' said Alice bitterly. 'If you have to be unhappy, then I qualify. How do you think it feels to have a boyfriend who's always busy seeing your best friend or playing sword games with her . . . whatever Nicholas is? And when you ask for an explanation, all you get is fantasy fiction.'

Sulien showed Sky the second set of novice's robes he had ready for Nicholas.

'When he stravagates, you should both arrive here,' the friar said. 'I'd like him to walk the maze before you take him out into the city. I think from what I saw of him in your world he will be too excited to be careful and I want him to leave here in a calm frame of mind.'

Sky nodded. He had walked the maze himself a few times now and it always steadied him; it would do Nick good. He wished he could do it himself now, after the row with Alice. But there was too much to organise and he wasn't quite ready to tell Sulien about her.

'It's going to get crowded in your cell of a morning,' he said. 'Especially if Sandro is hanging around too.'

Sulien smiled. 'He certainly spends a lot of time here.'

'What shall we call Nicholas while he's being a novice?' asked Sky. 'He can't be Brother Falco!'

'No, nor Brother Niccolò, really. What do you think?'

'I'll ask him,' said Sky. 'Is everything ready in Remora? And with the Manoush?'

'There is no reason why you should not all make your first trial stravagation tomorrow,' said Sulien. 'You can meet at Giuditta's workshop as planned.'

'It will be so odd to have them both here,' said Sky. 'I sort of think of it as my place now.'

'The young prince will help you know it even better,' said Sulien. 'But Georgia will need you both to help her find her way around.'

'She needs a Sandro,' said Sky.

'I've been meaning to talk to you about Sandro,' said Sulien. 'Do you think he knows about you?'

'I don't think so,' said Sky. 'He's never said anything about anyone being a Stravagante.'

'But he knows Prince Falco by sight,' said Sulien. 'And it will be difficult to keep the two of them apart. Yet I would rather that Sandro were on our side than working for the di Chimici. He's very observant.'

Sky had been putting it off too long. 'There's been a bit of a complication in my world,' he said.

It was the Warrior's fiftieth birthday. April the first – April Fool's Day – and he felt the irony. Loretta was giving him a party to which, bizarrely, she was inviting all his ex-wives, girlfriends (at least the ones she knew about) and his many children and grandchildren.

'That woman is a saint,' said Gus, getting rather sentimental over the champagne. 'To put up with you and all your brood.'

The singer just grunted. He knew how lucky he had been with Loretta but he wasn't going to agree with Gus about anything that didn't involve a contract.

'Only it's not quite all, is it?' said Gus, nudging the Warrior in the ribs. 'There's one Colin sprog she doesn't know about.'

The Warrior shot him an evil look. 'Don't call me that!' he said automatically. But Gus had got him thinking. He had been a rotten father to most of his children, but to Sky Meadows most of all; he had never even met him. It had been Sky's seventeenth birthday recently and he had a new photo of his secret son. The boy was old enough to be a father himself, he thought; the Warrior had certainly made his own first kid at that age, even though he wouldn't recommend it.

He was suddenly overwhelmed by the feeling that he was getting old.

'Loretta,' he said to his wife that night, when all the visitors had gone home and the guests who were staying over in his Hollywood mansion had gone to bed, 'I want to go back to England. There's someone I want to see.'

'That is a complication, indeed,' said Sulien when he had heard Sky out. 'I don't think anyone has ever volunteered to be a Stravagante from your world to ours before. I'll have to ask Doctor Dethridge about it.' He didn't seem fazed by the idea of Alice turning up in Giglia.

'Wouldn't it be too dangerous, though?' asked Sky. 'I mean, she can't fight and you all seem to think there's going to be trouble coming.'

'It's dangerous for all of you,' said Sulien. 'She won't be as experienced at stravagating as you or Georgia and she won't know the city as well as Falco does but, if the others agree, she'll have more than two weeks to get used to it before the weddings.'

'She might not want to keep coming,' said Sky doubtfully. 'It's just supposed to convince her that we're telling her the truth.'

'I don't think Doctor Dethridge will agree to taking a new talisman for just one journey,' said Sulien. 'But stop looking so worried. Nothing can be decided until I've spoken to the others.'

It was so unusual for Sky and Sulien to be on their own together these days that Sky decided to ask him about something else. They were in Brother Sulien's cell and the friar had been working on his collection of recipes and formulas when Sky arrived. It looked nearly finished. Sky looked at what he had been writing down; it was a cure for tiredness.

'I shall need some of that soon,' he said, trying to smile. 'All this stuff with Alice and coming here every night is wearing me out.'

Sulien scrutinised his face. 'If it gets too much for you, you must tell me,' he said seriously. 'We can't have you getting ill.'

'I'm all right really,' said Sky, embarrassed. 'And my mum is so much better. I wanted to ask you – is that because of my visits here? Could that be helping to cure her of her ME?'

Sulien was thoughtful. 'I don't think so,' he said at last. 'After all, she doesn't come here herself. We don't have the illness you speak of in Talia, unless it is like the sleeping sickness. But from what you have told me about it, I gather that it can get better quite suddenly, after a period of years?'

'That's what the doctors kept saying,' agreed Sky. 'Just give it time, they said.'

'And that is what has happened,' said Sulien. 'Just be thankful. Now, why don't you go and find Sandro?'

Sky was glad to get out into the city. He found Sandro and Fratello in their usual position loitering outside the Nucci palace. The boy's face brightened when he saw Sky.

'Ciao, Tino!' he said.

'What's happening?' asked Sky.

'Nothing,' said Sandro, lowering his voice. 'None of the Nucci have come out yet today.'

'Do you have to stay and wait for them?' asked Sky.

Sandro shrugged. 'There aren't any rules about it. As long as I keep bringing little bits of information back to my master.'

But at that moment, Camillo came out of the palace and looked in their direction.

'Quick,' said Sandro. 'Pretend I'm talking to you.'

'You are talking to me,' said Sky, smiling.

'No, I mean about something serious!' said Sandro. 'So he doesn't think I'm watching him.'

Camillo Nucci glanced around him, focused for just a moment on the little dog, frowning, and then set off towards the cathedral.

'Come on!' said Sandro. 'We'll follow at a distance.'

The two boys strolled along the busy streets and Sky felt his worries over Alice lift. The sky was the same blue it always seemed to be in Talia and the sun beat warm on his robes; it was almost too hot. At every window and doorstep, window boxes and flowerpots spilled pink and red petals and trailing greenery. And the scent of flowers hung in the air, covering up the worse smells coming from the gutters and the streets.

Sandro picked a bloom from one of the plants and stuck it in his cap. When they reached the cathedral square, they were just in time to see Camillo disappear into the door of Saint-Mary-of-the-Lily.

'We can't take Fratello in there, surely?' said Sky.

'Come with me,' said Sandro mysteriously.

They walked further round the cathedral, towards Giuditta's workshop, and stopped by a side door. Sandro tied Fratello to a rail and the little dog immediately sank down with his nose on his paws. Sandro slipped through the door, beckoning to Sky to follow. But instead of going into the body of the great echoing building, he led Sky up a stone staircase. They climbed until they were both out of breath, pausing only once, at a sort of landing, before resuming the upward curve of the steps. Just when Sky thought his lungs would burst, they were out on a narrow balcony that ran round the base of the dome. There was only a wooden banister between them and a sheer drop to the floor of the cathedral.

Sandro leaned casually on the banister. 'All right?' he asked.

Sky's heart was pounding. From up here he could see the floor of the cathedral, inlaid with designs so that it looked as if it were covered with marble carpets. They reminded him of Sulien's maze. There was no service at present but there were always visitors in the cathedral. The people seemed tiny from here and he noticed how few of them looked up. It was the perfect place for a spy. Sandro nudged him.

'See Camillo,' he whispered, pointing to the Nucci's distinctive red hat.

Camillo seemed to be measuring the length of the aisle from the cathedral door to the high altar, pacing it out. It wouldn't have looked odd from ground level but from up here it seemed clear that he was planning something.

'This would be a good place to position archers,' said Sandro.

'During a wedding?' said Sky.

'That's when the di Chimici expect the attack to come,' said Sandro. 'They'll have archers up here, all the way round, mark my words.'

Camillo seemed to have finished his measuring.

'Do you want to go right up to the top?' asked Sandro.

'Can you get further?' asked Sky.

Sandro led him round half the circumference of the dome's base and through another door. The steps began again and Sky realised that they were climbing up inside the dome itself, up hundreds of stairs – so many that he lost count – until they emerged inside the white stone lantern at the very top.

The two boys sat hanging on to the wooden rails, with their legs dangling over the side. Sky wished he had brought some water. His robes were sticking to him after the hot climb. But there was a welcome breeze up here and the view made it worth it.

The whole city was spread out beneath him. He could see the Piazza Ducale and the river and the new Nucci palace on the other side and the stretch of green that was their gardens. He could even see the avenue of pine trees where he had been with Sandro just over a week ago. And beyond that, the city wall and the meadows of flowers that surrounded the city, alternating with green fields dotted with white blobs that were sheep.

Tomorrow, if their plans worked, Georgia would land somewhere over there on Merla. Sky wondered if he would ever get the chance to see the flying horse.

Rainbow Warrior had two homes in England: a mansion in Gloucestershire, where he spent hardly any time but which he felt was an important part of his image to keep up, and a flat in Highgate. Whenever he went on tour in the UK, he spent a bit of time in north London and it was here he decided to stay for a few days shortly after his birthday. On the spur of the moment, he asked Loretta to accompany him; he was nervous of telling her about Sky but even more so about the prospect of meeting his son on his own.

It would be unusual for him to be back in the country of his birth without having any gigs to play. He could visit his mother, of course. She had taken a lot of persuading to leave the estate where he was born and had spent only a few years in the house he bought her in Esher before needing to go into a residential home. She was wandering in her mind a bit now and scandalised some of her fellow residents with the language she sometimes came out with.

But there were his brothers and his sister as well and he didn't look forward to their knowing he was in town. The Warrior had given them a lot of money over the years and none of them had made anything of their lives. One brother had a half-hearted career as a record producer; the other was unemployed and always asking for handouts. His sister was a bitter woman, jealous of his success, which had made her discontented with her job as a nurse, her husband and the house her brother had bought her in Clapham.

She sneered at him for the articles in *Hello!*, his many marriages and his regular albums. But she bought the magazines, accepted flights out to the weddings and boasted to her friends when the albums sold well.

Sometimes the Warrior thought that the only person he had ever met who had never asked him for money was Rosalind, who had been prepared to bring up a child on her own. He had sent money, though, a lot of it the first time. But neither she nor her son had ever expected anything from him and that intrigued him.

He told his PA to book the flights straightaway.

'Can I ask you something?' said Sky when he was alone with Brother Sulien.

'Of course.'

'You said when I first came that Duke Niccolò di Chimici was dangerous and hated all Stravaganti.'

'That is still true.'

'But he seems to be more of an enemy of the Nucci at the moment. Does that mean that we and the Nucci are on same side?'

'If the Nucci knew anything about us, it's true that they might want us to help them in their vendetta against the di Chimici,' said Sulien. 'But the Stravaganti are not to be used in such feuds. We are only on the opposite side from Niccolò because we believe that he wants to take over all Talia. The Nucci long ago ceased to care about the government of Giglia, let alone Tuschia or Talia as a whole. They just want all the di Chimici dead, because of Davide.'

'I can see that it would be a bad thing for Niccolò to rule all Talia, because he's a bad man,' said Sky, frowning. 'But would it be a bad idea for Talia to get together under someone? I mean, in my world Italy is one country, not lots of little dukedoms and so on.'

'I know it must seem to you as if we are interfering in politics,' said Sulien. 'But it is not like that. We are protecting the gateway to your world from the uses the di Chimici would make of it.'

'What uses, exactly?' asked Sky.

'If Niccolò had the secret of travel in time and

space, he would not respect the rules we have developed,' said Sulien. 'He would take cheap gold from here and use it to buy weapons and drugs that have not been invented here.'

Sky could just see it – di Chimici with swords and daggers were bad enough, but the thought of them with an arsenal of chemical weapons was terrifying.

'There's nothing I can do till the Stravaganti have made their decision,' Sky told Alice on the phone next day.

'But you're all still going tonight – you and Nick and Georgia?'

'Yes, it's all arranged,' said Sky.

'Then I'm at least going to be at Georgia's while she stravagates,' said Alice.

'You do believe us, then,' said Sky.

'I don't know,' said Alice. 'I want to. I don't want to think you would lie to me. But it just seems too incredible.'

As soon as she got off the phone to Sky, Alice called Georgia and went round to her house.

Maura O'Grady was used to finding Alice in her house when she got home from work, and if she thought things were a little tense between the two girls, she put it down to teenage hormones and worries about the coming term's exams. She certainly had no objection to Alice staying the night. In fact she was relieved that Georgia was spending more time with her best female friend; it bothered her how often her daughter was with Nicholas.

After a supper of takeaway Chinese – much to Georgia's relief because Maura was a dreadful cook – the girls had an early night. They said they were going to watch videos in Georgia's room.

'So how exactly does it work, then?' asked Alice. 'Do you just hold the talisman and say "abracadabra"?'

'No,' said Georgia, a bit reluctant to go into details. 'You have to fall asleep with it in your hand, thinking of where you're going in Talia.'

'And what will it look like when you've gone?'

'Just the same, I think. My body will still be here. I have another body in Talia, one without a shadow.'

Alice shook her head. 'So you won't be able to prove that you've been anywhere?'

'I'll tell you everything about it when I get back,' said Georgia. 'And you can ring Sky first thing and check it all with him. Then you'll know we're not making it up.'

But she secretly wished that Alice were not there. It was going to be hard getting to sleep with her best friend watching her.

Early next morning Cesare was in the stables as usual but he kept glancing up at the hayloft. He hummed under his breath as he filled the horses' water troughs from a bucket and mucked out the dirty straw. Arcangelo, the big chestnut, was restless and bent his great neck to huff in Cesare's ear.

'I know, boy,' he said, grinning. 'She's coming back.'

His father, Paolo, came in with a bundle of clothes.

'Any sign yet?' he asked.

Cesare shook his head. A small grey cat wound its way round the stable door and leapt on to the ladder to the loft. There was a rustling sound and the cat paused, its ears pricked. The trapdoor was raised and a tawny head appeared.

'Giorgio!' said Cesare, then stopped, confused. 'I mean, Georgia. It's good to see you!'

Chapter 18

Flight

While Alice slept and Georgia crossed worlds, Sky was spending the night at the Mulhollands'. Nicholas was so excited about stravagating back to Giglia that he kept them both awake talking about it. And then he fell silent and Sky, anxious that Nicholas was going to arrive in Giglia before him, tossed and turned a lot longer, unable to give up the hold on consciousness that was preventing him from slipping into his other life.

Gaetano had arranged with Sulien to come to the friary early so that he could be there when his brother arrived. It had been over six months since Falco had died in Talia. Gaetano had seen him a month later, riding the flying horse, and he had been told that, for Falco, a whole extra year had passed. Yet he did not know what to expect. There was so much that he didn't understand about the gateway between the two worlds, and he found it hard to believe that his little brother had caught up on him by a year and was now fit and well, able to walk unaided and to ride. But Gaetano clung on to one thing: Falco was coming back.

Sulien was awake and waiting in his cell. It was a bare room – just a cot of a bed, a chest, a table and a chair – whitewashed and dominated by a large wooden cross. The bed was empty and Sulien was sitting in the chair. He rose when the prince entered but Gaetano gestured him back.

'I shall sit on the floor,' he said, and settled himself with his back to the wall. 'How long do you think it will be before they come?'

'It depends on how hard they find it to fall asleep in their own world,' said Sulien. 'It perhaps will not be easy for your brother. It may be that Sky will arrive ahead of him.'

The two of them sat in silence, waiting. Gaetano rested his arms on his knees and cast his cloak over his head. He must have dozed a little but was woken by a sigh. On Sulien's bed lay a figure stretching and yawning, a young man with curly black hair, worn loose and rather long. He swung his long legs over the edge of the bed and stood up tall and straight.

Gaetano got to his feet, stiff from the wait. Sulien left the cell as the brothers embraced.

*

Georgia had greeted every horse in the stable. Most of them knew her – Arcangelo, Dondola, Starlight and the miraculous Merla. The black winged horse was now fully grown, glossy and well-muscled. Georgia had no doubt she would be able to carry her to Giglia.

'I have ridden her that far and further,' said Cesare. 'And I weigh more than you do.' He couldn't stop smiling; he was so pleased to see Georgia again.

'I wish I could stay and catch up with all your news,' she said, longingly. 'But I must leave straightaway if I'm to meet the others in Giglia. I'll see you tonight, though.'

Paolo and Cesare led Merla to the meadow where she could take off. The horse was glad to be out so early in the warm spring morning and was already flexing her wings. Georgia was going to ride bareback, so she was glad of a leg-up.

Once astride Merla's back, she looked down on her friends' faces, sad to be seeing them so briefly but exhilarated at being back in Talia and the prospect of another flight on the winged horse.

'Go safely,' said Paolo.

And Cesare slapped Merla on the rump.

The young mare broke into a trot, then a canter and was at full gallop before she unfurled her mighty wings. With a few lazy flaps she was aloft and Georgia saw the rose-coloured City of Stars dwindling beneath them. She clutched Merla's mane, ready for their next adventure.

*

When Sulien re-entered his cell the two brothers were sitting on the bed with their arms round each other. He smiled at them.

'Welcome, Prince Falco,' he said.

'Alas, I am that no longer,' said the new Stravagante, slipping back into his former way of speech.

'What shall we call you?' asked Gaetano. 'You'll have to have a new name while you are here.'

'How about Benvenuto?' said the boy. 'If I am really welcome.'

'Brother Benvenuto indeed,' said Gaetano.

'And now we must give you your disguise,' said Sulien, opening the chest and taking out a set of robes.

'I hope they fit him,' said Gaetano. 'He is taller than me now.'

When he was dressed in the robes, Nicholas looked the part of a Dominican novice. He tried pulling the hood up over his face and Gaetano said, 'No one would recognise you now – even the family. You are so much taller, and of course they would not be expecting to see you.'

'You made it all right, then?' said Sky and they turned and saw him, already robed, on Sulien's cot.

The two novices faced each other. Nicholas couldn't wait to get out into the streets of Giglia, but he also wanted to spend time with his brother, and the others had to remind him how dangerous it would be to be seen with the prince.

'You may look very different from when you left,' said Sulien, 'but you don't want anyone to make the link because of seeing you two together.'

Gaetano stayed with them for breakfast and they met Sandro in the refectory. The boy showed no signs of recognising Prince Falco.

'Another novice?' he said suspiciously, when Sulien introduced him to the new 'Brother Benvenuto'. 'How many are you going to have?'

'As many as are called,' said Sulien. 'There is always room in God's house.'

Sandro was disposed to be jealous of the new novice. He regarded Brother Sulien as his personal property and wasn't at all pleased that he had to share him with another young friar. And this Benvenuto seemed much too friendly with Brother Tino, who was also Sandro's own discovery.

When the prince left and the two novices went out into the city, Sandro trailed alongside them, as his dog trotted after him.

'Where are you going?' he asked.

'We have a commission to Giuditta Miele, from Brother Sulien,' said Sky. 'Why don't I meet you later, back up here?'

Sandro recognised that he was being got rid of and remained, sulking, in the piazza outside Saint-Mary-among-the-Vines.

*

It was a glorious day and the sun warmed Georgia's right side as she flew north on Merla. She was wearing a russet-brown dress of Teresa's and it felt awkward riding with a full skirt. But she had bunched it up around her and left her legs bare to the sun. They flew over fields and meadows, the people of Tuschia tiny beneath them, tilling the earth and pulling vegetables like the little figures in a book of hours. The countryside was gently undulating, with small green hills crowned by cypresses and brick farmhouses with terracotta roofs. She could see miniature cattle and sheep and the blue threads of streams winding between green banks.

After about three quarters of an hour of Merla's steady flight, Georgia began to see in the distance the signs of a great city, much bigger than Remora. It was surrounded by meadows of flowers of every colour; Georgia could detect their scent even from this height. Strong defensive walls encircled the city and Georgia looked out for a gap in them, which would show her where to land.

She whispered in Merla's ear and the flying horse began her descent. She landed on the edge of a meadow of bluebells, where two figures waited, as colourful as the flowers. Georgia climbed off the horse, shook out her skirt and clasped hands with the Manoush. Merla whickered a greeting and went with them happily.

'We shall take good care of her,' said Aurelio, stroking the horse's nose. 'We are taking her to a small homestead that belongs to the friary.'

He pointed out to Georgia a cluster of buildings in a field, then Raffaella took her as far as the road.

'It's that way to the river,' said Raffaella. 'You know how to go from there?'

'Yes,' said Georgia. 'Thank you. I'll be back well before nightfall.'

She walked towards the city. On her right stood the great edifice of the Nucci palace, gleaming in its newness, with its vast fringe of gardens. It was her first glimpse of Giglia and she was impressed. Past the little church, she set foot on the stone bridge and smiled as its smells assailed her. She stopped and looked out over the river. It looked like a picture postcard of other people's Italian holidays. But there was no time to look longer; she had to get to her meeting place.

Giglia was very different from Remora, full of grand buildings and squares. Georgia followed the map in her mind and crossed the great piazza with its statues. Soon she reached the cathedral, whose cupola dominated the city and had beckoned her here to its centre from a great distance. She skirted it warily, following it round to the east end. How was she to tell which was Giuditta's bottega among this jumble of little buildings?

*

The statue of the Duchessa was finished. Sky and Nicholas gazed at it in admiration. Nicholas had never seen its subject; he had already been unconscious when Arianna came to Remora. And Sky had met her only once so far. And yet both of them knew the statue was a masterpiece.

Two of Giuditta's apprentices were polishing the marble of the white figure. Arianna stood oblivious of their caresses, grasping the rail of her ceremonial barge. She looked proud and independent, most unlikely to yield to persuasion or intimidation. Her creator stood opposite her, almost a mirror image of determination.

'She's made the Duchessa look like her,' whispered Nicholas.

'Only more beautiful,' said Sky.

'Perhaps,' said Nicholas. 'But Giuditta is beautiful too – in her own way.'

'Don't let her hear you say that,' said Sky. 'I shouldn't think she likes to be flattered.'

'That reminds me,' said Nicholas. 'I wonder if Georgia's all right?'

'I'll go and look for her,' said Sky.

It had been Nicholas's first test as Benvenuto, walking to Giuditta's workshop, and no one in the streets had given him a second glance. He thought that one of Giuditta's apprentices – a blond boy with angelic curls – had stared at him a little too long, but put that down to natural curiosity. Now Nicholas gazed at Giuditta, fascinated. He knew that she had sculpted his memorial statue and it made him feel very peculiar to think about it.

Sky stood outside the workshop in the lee of the cathedral, making sure to stay in the doorway so that his absence of shadow would not be seen. He was soon rewarded by the sight in the distance of a familiar figure with a head of red, white and black hair. He could not greet her out loud, as it would hardly be seemly for a novice to hail an attractive young woman in the street, but he closed his eyes and concentrated his thoughts on her, using the fact that they were both Stravaganti to guide her to him.

He opened his eyes to see Georgia coming towards him, a relieved look on her face. He beckoned her inside the workshop. Franco looked up appreciatively at this new arrival and Sky suddenly saw Georgia through the apprentice's eyes. A tall and quite graceful figure in a simple russet dress, with her dramatic hair colouring, she could be an aristocrat in disguise or a woman of the streets. Either way, she didn't look like a suitable friend for two young novice friars. Giuditta must have thought the same, because she shooed all the apprentices out of the workshop and told them to take a long break.

The Stravaganti were alone together. But not for long. A well-dressed middle-aged woman entered from the street before they could even greet one another properly. She had the air of a wealthy woman who had wandered in to commission a portrait bust of her late husband, perhaps, and was accompanied by a tall red-headed servant. Sky had a vague half memory of having seen her somewhere before. His heart sank at the interruption but Giuditta made no attempt to get rid of the woman.

And the woman went straight up to Georgia and said, 'I don't think we could pass you off as a boy now, Georgia,' and embraced her.

Sky and Nicholas stared at each other. Then light dawned on them simultaneously: this could only be the previous Duchessa of Bellezza, Arianna's mother, who was supposed to have been assassinated by a di Chimici agent in her own audience chamber. And Sky remembered where he had seen her: in the Bellezzan Embassy, with Arianna and Rodolfo. Georgia made the introductions. Silvia took Nicholas's hand in hers and scrutinised his face.

'We have something in common, Prince Falco,' she said in her low, musical voice. 'We are both supposed to be dead. I hope your disguise will be as effective as mine.'

Then she turned to Sky. 'And you are the new

Stravagante,' she said. 'You have joined us at a time of great danger.'

'I know,' said Sky. 'The Nucci and the weddings.'

'And the new threat to the Duchessa from the Duke,' said Silvia, nodding at the statue. 'You have caught her perfectly, Giuditta. Helmswoman of the ship of state.'

'Or figurehead,' said a voice from the door. Guido Parola's hand moved to the hilt of his sword, as a white-haired figure entered. Nicholas shrank into the shadows, pulling his hood up over his face.

'Good morning, Maestra,' said the Duke to the sculptor. 'Good morning, Brother Celestino. I trust your master is well? Good. Won't you introduce me to your charming patroness, Giuditta? Clearly she knows something of the beautiful ruler of Bellezza.'

'This is Signora Silvia Bellini,' said Giuditta, almost truthfully. 'From Padavia. I believe the Signora has seen the Duchessa on a visit to the city.'

'That is so, your Grace,' said Silvia, suddenly playing the part of a flustered and foolish woman thrown into confusion by the presence of the great man. She curtseyed and gestured to her servant to bow to the Duke. 'My late husband had connections in Bellezza and I have seen the young Duchessa there on State occasions.' She placed her hand to her heart as if it were fluttering at the honour of being in the Duke's presence.

'Delighted,' said the Duke, putting Silvia's other hand to his lips. 'Pray don't let me disturb your discussion with the maestra – I came merely to look on the work she has created, whose reputation is already spreading in Giglia.'

Thank goodness Luciano isn't here, thought Sky. He would probably try to run the Duke through. As it was, Guido Parola still had his hand on his sword. Duke Niccolò walked over to the statue and caressed its white marble cheek. The tension in the workshop was unbearable.

'So,' he said. 'She is clearly *not* holding a treaty.'

'I made her as I saw her, your Grace,' said Giuditta.

'I have finished my business here, my Lord,' said Silvia, gesturing silently to Sky to leave.

'And so have I,' Sky said, taking his cue. 'We shall return to the friary.'

'And what about the other charming lady?' asked the Duke, not taking his eyes off the statue. So he had noticed Georgia.

'She is one of my models,' said Giuditta. 'You can take a break now and come back when the apprentices do,' she told her.

Slowly they all left the workshop, backing out of the Duke's presence, leaving him alone with the sculptor. As soon as they got outside, Silvia beckoned the others to follow and took them into a nearby tavern. As they collapsed on to wooden benches, she ordered red wine, even though it was only the middle of the morning, and they all drank deeply when it came.

'That was awkward,' she said pleasantly, but Sky saw that the hand holding her goblet was shaking. Parola took his wine and stood by the door. Now that Nicholas had thrown back his hood, his face appeared white and frightened.

'I would not have recognised him,' he said. 'I would have said it was here that extra years had passed – he looked so old.'

'It was young Prince Falco's death that did it, they say,' said Silvia quietly.

'Thank goodness he didn't notice Nicholas,' said Georgia.

'He didn't mention him,' said Silvia. 'But that is not the same thing at all.'

In the middle of the night Alice woke suddenly. She was sleeping in Georgia's bed and Georgia was in a sleeping bag on the floor. She looked across at the body of her friend, her chest rising and falling gently with her breath. Georgia had told her that there would be nothing to see when she stravagated, but Alice peered carefully at her all the same.

Then she found it hard to get back to sleep. She lay for what felt like hours, imagining the three others in their secret world; it was too fantastic to believe that their bodies lay sleeping in this world while three alternative ones had adventures in another. She wouldn't – couldn't – believe it unless she experienced it herself. And yet, if it were true, it made her feel afraid. Talia seemed to be such a dangerous place. Sky hadn't told her everything, but there had been enough about stabbing and poisons to make it sound thoroughly alarming.

Alice wondered what would happen if she tried to shake Georgia awake; she felt terribly lonely.

A meeting of the Stravaganti was held at Silvia's

lodgings that afternoon. Sky felt guilty that he was neglecting Sandro but he couldn't miss out on the meeting. And he was beginning to see that he couldn't really turn up at the friary with Georgia in tow; for the first time, his novice's disguise was a hindrance.

Silvia felt it too; she offered Georgia a red scarf to hide her hair. But not before she had been caught in a bear hug by William Dethridge and greeted by Rodolfo and Sulien. Best of all for her, though, was the embrace from Luciano, a long heartfelt hug even though only one between friends.

'Eight of the Brotherhood in one room,' said Rodolfo. 'It is an honour to have you all here. We can hope to save the city in its time of danger.'

'Um,' said Sky. 'Would it be even better to have nine?'

Sulien had already heard about Alice, and of course Georgia and Nicholas knew about her, but that still left four to convince that they should bring yet another talisman to their world. Luciano at least knew who Alice was, but the others were surprised at the idea of someone volunteering to come to Talia.

'It's the only way I can convince her that we're not lying,' said Sky. He felt terribly embarrassed at having to talk about his girlfriend with these distinguished grown-ups. Georgia came to his rescue, emboldened by being with Luciano again.

'Alice is my best friend,' she said simply. 'And she was very unhappy because she thought that Sky had something going on with me. He's been spending a lot of time with me and Nicholas, what with the fencing and all the talk about Talia.'

'So it is our secrets and our problems that have brought about your own difficulty?' asked Rodolfo. 'You are prepared to risk your life in Talia to save others and yet we have done nothing for you. I think we should grant your request. What does everyone else think?'

'The more the merrier, as far as I'm concerned,' said Luciano, rather wildly. He felt that the whole business of Stravaganti from his world was getting out of hand; was the whole of Barnsbury Comp going to turn up here? They could charter an inter-dimensional bus at this rate.

'Hold harde,' said Dethridge. 'If the mayde is to stravayge, who is to take hir talismanne? Shee can not arrive in a house of brothires of Saint Francis.'

'It must be me then, I suppose,' said Giuditta. 'I have done it before.'

Georgia felt most uncomfortable. Everyone in the room knew that she had rejected Giuditta's talisman and she couldn't bear the idea of Alice having the ram that had been made for her.

'I shall take her something from my workshop,' continued the sculptor. 'And she will arrive there. But my counsel is that she should come for only one stravagation, to confirm the truth of her friends' story.'

*

Sandro was bored with spying. He no longer believed that there was any danger from the Nucci, in spite of their defensive tower and their many weapons. Their attempted poisoning of the Duke and the loss of their youngest family member were in the past now and he thought they might be a spent force. Now he was tired of hanging about outside their old palace; he would have far rather been out exploring the city with Brother Tino.

Then he remembered that Tino had gone off with the new novice without even a backward glance, and felt annoyed. Fratello was his only real friend after all, thought Sandro, and he bent to ruffle the dog's ears. And found himself looking at a pair of feet in black shoes with silver buckles. An unpleasant scent in the air and the growl in Fratello's throat alerted him to the presence of his master.

'How is it going, little Sparrow?' said Enrico genially. 'Anything happening with our friends over there?'

'Nothing,' said Sandro. 'Nothing to report at all. Can't I go somewhere else?'

'That's the minute something will happen, if I know anything about it,' said Enrico. 'What about at the friary? Anything interesting going on there?'

The most interesting thing in the friary as far as Sandro was concerned was that he was learning to read there, and he didn't want the Eel to know that.

'There's a new novice,' he said instead. 'Brother Benvenuto.'

'Another one?' said Enrico. 'They'll have more novices than full friars soon. Perhaps you'd better keep an eye on this one – let me know if there's anything fishy going on. I'm never quite sure whether that Sulien is loyal to the di Chimici or not.'

Sandro said nothing. He knew now what being loyal to the ruthless di Chimici might involve and he also knew that it wasn't a good idea to be found wanting.

*

'Now,' said Rodolfo. 'Alice or no Alice, we must plan our strategy for the days of the wedding.'

'*Days?*' said Georgia. 'You mean they take more than one day to get married?'

'The ceremony itself takes not much longer than an ordinary Mass,' said Sulien. 'But there will be a grand tournament the day before, with a banquet in the evening, various pageants and processions on the day itself, and a final party the day after.'

'And we moste kepe vigillant atte all these tymes,' said Dethridge.

'How, exactly?' asked Nicholas.

'A circle of strength,' said Giuditta. 'If all eight – or even nine – Stravaganti are together, we can surround the likely targets with our linked minds, see where the danger is coming from and protect them from harm.'

'And who are the likely targets?' asked Sky.

'I'm afraid that is what we don't know,' said Rodolfo. 'My daughter is my main concern, but any member of the di Chimici and Nucci families is at risk.'

'And if vyolence comes,' said Dethridge, 'thenne every one and eny one canne be harmed. Inne a church or a square – wheresomever there are crowdes – a small acte with a blade canne lead on to mayhem overal.'

'Wait a minute,' said Georgia. 'I can see about the circle of minds, I think, though I'd like to practise it. But what if we do see a threat coming from a

289

particular person. What can we do about it? Can the Stravaganti disarm an armed man with their thoughts?'

'No,' said Rodolfo. 'That is why Luciano has been learning to fight. We and our allies have to be ready to defend ourselves and others.'

'Gaetano will be ready,' said Luciano.

'But he will be getting married,' protested Georgia. 'How much use can he be? You surely don't expect him to break off the ceremony to fight a bit and then carry on with it.'

'We shall all go armed to the wedding,' said Giuditta.

'And Guido here won't be getting married,' said Silvia. 'He is a handy fellow with a blade.'

Sky realised that this was the assassin Luciano had told him about.

'I don't think you will be invited to the wedding, Silvia,' said Rodolfo, smiling. 'The Duke doesn't know you, and you should be grateful for it.'

'As to that,' said Silvia, 'I met the Duke only this morning and I think he was disposed to be charmed by me. But what do I care for invitations? I shall be at these weddings, invited or not.'

*

Sandro and the Eel walked into the centre of town, though Fratello was careful to keep on Sandro's side, as far away from Enrico as possible. As they neared the cathedral, the spy suddenly clutched at the boy's sleeve.

'Is that him?' he hissed.

Two young Dominican friars were coming out of a palazzo.

Sandro nodded. 'That's the new one, with Brother Tino.'

The novices were followed out of the building by a striking-looking young woman with stripy hair. And then Luciano and Rodolfo, the two Bellezzans, with an older white-haired man whom Sandro didn't recognise. Finally Giuditta Miele came out of the door, in conversation with Brother Sulien.

'Now that is something worth reporting,' said Enrico. 'What are they up to? And who exactly is that new brother?'

He had pulled Sandro back into a doorway. They hid as the party from the palazzo passed on the opposite side of the road.

Enrico gasped. 'Look!' he said. 'Look at that new novice! He has no shadow. And, come to that, nor does your Brother Tino! I think the Duke might be very interested in that.'

Chapter 19

Flowers of the City

Georgia woke feeling stiff and disorientated. She had flown back to Remora soon after the meeting of Stravaganti, spent a few sweet moments with Cesare and his younger sisters and brothers, and fallen easily asleep in her old hayloft. It took her a few minutes to adjust to being back in her room.

'At last,' said Alice when she saw that Georgia's eyes were open. She herself was already showered and dressed. 'Do you know what time it is? Your parents have already gone to work.'

Georgia sat up blearily. 'Give me a minute,' she said.

'Sweet dreams?' asked Alice.

Georgia wasn't sure she liked this new aggressive version of her friend. But as far as Alice was concerned, she still needed to be convinced that what the others had told her was true and that she could still trust Sky. Georgia decided to let it pass.

'I went to Remora, flew to Giglia and met the others there,' she said. 'I saw the old Duchessa in the sculptor's workshop and then Duke Niccolò came in. We had a meeting of Stravaganti at Silvia's place and then I did the journey back.' She stretched. 'Can I go and have my shower now?'

'Did you see, you know, Lucien?' asked Alice.

Georgia nodded. 'He's one of the Stravaganti who was there. But I don't want to talk about it.'

'Fair enough,' said Alice. 'I'll get us some breakfast, shall I? And then we can go round to Nick's.'

Sandro was feeling uneasy. He hadn't taken kindly to the idea of sharing Brother Tino and Sulien with anyone else, but he didn't want the new novice to fall foul of the Eel; he knew what his master was capable of. But he was puzzled by the business of the shadows. That wasn't natural, surely? Everything had a shadow – even Fratello. Sandro separated from Enrico as soon as he could and went straight to Saint-Mary-among-the-Vines.

The friars were all at prayer; it was the hour of Vespers. Sandro was not allowed to take his dog into the church, so he waited outside the main door until he heard the chanting stop. Then he put his head round the door and called softly. Sulien heard him and came towards him.

'You are troubled?' he said straightaway, seeing the

boy's distress.

'What does it mean, Brother, when a man has no shadow? Is it the work of the Devil?'

Sulien didn't answer directly. 'Tie your dog up and come inside,' he said.

Not all the friars had left the church. Sandro watched as Sulien walked over to a side aisle and pulled back a threadbare carpet to reveal a strange circular pattern of black and white. Meanwhile, a line of friars was forming, waiting to step on to the circle. Sandro had never seen this before.

Sulien came over to where Sandro sat in the pews and said, 'Watch what they do. I want you to walk the maze just before me.'

'Why?' asked Sandro. 'What does it do?'

'You can tell me that yourself afterwards,' said Sulien.

The girls walked round to the Mulhollands' house in silence. Vicky let them in.

'I'm afraid they aren't up yet,' she said. 'Shall I call them?'

'Well, if you're sure,' said Georgia.

'It's late,' said Vicky. 'It's time they were up. Why don't you put the kettle on?'

Twenty tense minutes later, Nicholas and Sky joined them in the kitchen. To the relief of all, Vicky had gone shopping. The boys were tired but, after a few cups of tea and a lot of toast, were willing to talk. By then Alice was ready to explode.

'Well?' she asked Sky. 'I've heard Georgia's version

of last night. What's yours?'

He could scarcely recognise her; she seemed so cold.

'Nick got to Giglia first,' he said. 'And when I got to Sulien's cell, he was already there with his brother. We walked to Giuditta's workshop and then Georgia came. And Silvia, Arianna's mother, turned up.'

'With her bodyguard,' added Nicholas.

'And then the Duke arrived,' said Sky.

'My father,' said Nicholas. Alice saw that he had dark circles under his eyes. 'He had come to look at Arianna's statue.'

'And then we all went to a tavern and drank wine,' said Sky. 'It'd been a bit of a shock, meeting the Duke like that.'

'We had a meeting of Stravaganti in the afternoon,' said Nicholas.

'And we asked them about you, Alice.'

'Oh yes, what did they say?'

'They were pretty much OK about it,' said Sky. 'Giuditta said it would have to be her who brought you the talisman.'

'Well, congratulations,' said Alice. 'Your stories match perfectly.'

'They're not stories,' said Georgia. 'They're accounts of what we actually did. And I for one am getting fed up with you not believing us.'

Alice looked surprised.

'How often do I have to tell you that I'm not the slightest bit interested in Sky as a boyfriend?' said Georgia, warming to her theme. 'Why would I invent all this about Talia? Why would any of us?'

'Stop it, both of you!' said Nicholas suddenly. 'I can't take any more of you two arguing about whether my country exists or not! My father was poisoned there and the other members of my family may be attacked at any time. I can't waste any more time on this stuff with Alice. Believe us or not, as you like. I want to talk about going back.'

'Well, we can go back tonight,' said Sky.

'No,' said Nicholas. 'I don't mean tonight. I mean permanently.'

Sandro put one foot tentatively on to the maze. He didn't understand why Sulien wanted him on it, but gradually, as his feet traced the pattern of the marble, he felt himself calming down. He looked down, shuffling slowly forwards behind the black and white robed friar in front of him, till the colours of the maze and the colours of the robes blurred. When he found himself in the middle, he sank to his knees, suddenly tired. He would have liked to stay there for ever.

He became aware that Sulien had joined him. The last of the other friars had finished walking out from the centre. Sandro realised that he was kneeling on the figure of a woman. Her robes and hair were outlined in black against the white marble and she had a sweet, loving face that made him want to cry. There were twelve stars around her head. Sandro got to his feet and silently, slowly, traced the path back to the outer world. By then the light was waning in Talia and the sky outside the church windows was darkening.

'I must get Fratello,' he said to Sulien. 'He'll be lonely.'

'Bring him in through the cloister,' said the friar.

'You can both sleep in the laboratory tonight.'

'Then will you explain about the shadows?' asked Sandro.

'I will,' said Sulien.

*

'I just wondered, my Lord,' said Enrico, 'whether there's any chance that the Nucci could be in alliance with other enemies of yours.'

'More than likely, I would have thought,' said the Duke. 'Which enemies did you have in mind?'

Enrico wasn't quite sure how to proceed. When he and his master had returned from Remora after the young prince's memorial race, the Duke had been obsessed with a group of people led by the Regent of Bellezza. Enrico knew they were called 'Stravaganti' but he didn't know what that meant. He believed they were a powerful Brotherhood of magicians and he feared what Senator Rodolfo might be able to do to him.

He knew that the Senator's young assistant, Luciano, had learned more than science from his master, and he feared the young man too. There had once been something unnatural about him but that was so no longer. Enrico had captured Luciano with his own hands and knew that at one time he had been without a shadow.

The Eel's old master, Rinaldo di Chimici, had been most interested in that fact, even though it had crumbled to dust when brought to the attention of a People's Senate in Bellezza. Enrico had never known what it meant; it was one of those things he pushed to the back of his mind, like the disappearance of his fiancée. Luciano certainly had a shadow now and so did Rodolfo. It must be something to do with their magic powers. But now Enrico had seen two more people without shadows in Giglia and they were both connected with the Moorish friar who had saved the Duke from poisoning.

So had it been a double bluff? Was Sulien softening the Duke up for a later occasion when he would finish him off? This was the sort of thing the Eel was supposed to know and normally would have been happy to investigate. But any suggestion of magic unnerved him; he was afraid of the evil eye.

'Well?' said the Duke. 'Have you information or not?'

'There is a new novice at Saint-Mary-among-the-Vines, my Lord,' said Enrico hesitantly.

'That is hardly momentous,' said the Duke. 'I think I may have glimpsed him with young Brother Celestino in the sculptor's workshop. What of him?'

'How sure is your Grace of the loyalty of the friars up there?' asked Enrico.

'Tolerably certain,' said the Duke. 'Brother Sulien did save my life recently.'

'It's just that . . . well, neither this new novice – Benvenuto, he's called, according to my information – nor that Brother Tino seems to have a shadow.'

The Duke was silent. His memory of the events in Remora was clouded – by grief and, he suspected, by sorcery. But he knew that there was something deeply significant in this information. Something connected with his son's death. He had never believed that Falco had killed himself. That Luciano and his stable-boy friend who seemed to have disappeared had something to do with it. But the Duke had a private plan of his own for how to deal with Luciano.

'Look into it,' he said abruptly. 'Find out all you can about this Benvenuto and bring the information direct to me. Speak to no one else about it.'

Nicholas's announcement had stunned them all.

'I'm tired of being Nicholas,' he said simply. 'I don't even want to be Brother Benvenuto. I want to be Falco again, living in my own city, with my own family.'

'But you can't just turn back the clock,' said Georgia. 'You're dead and buried in Giglia – with a statue by the great Giuditta Miele on top.'

'How do you know I can't?' asked Nicholas. 'When I was translated here, this world leapt forward a year. Perhaps if I went back, it would move in the opposite direction.'

'But wouldn't you end up just the way you were before?' asked Sky, 'with your leg all hurt?'

'It's worse than that,' said Georgia, who had seen it all in a flash. 'He'd have to die in this world. Are you really prepared to do that to Vicky and David, Nicholas?'

'There may be a way to make it work out all right for them,' he muttered.

'Stop it!' said Alice. 'You three are freaking me out! OK, I believe you about this other world of yours. There's no need to go on about dying.'

'Look,' said Sky. 'You're tired and it must have blown your mind to be back in your world. We can go back tonight – every night if you like. But you can't just go back to live in Talia as if nothing had happened.'

'Have you ever wondered about where Brother Tino came from?' asked Sulien.

'Anglia, you said it was,' said Sandro.

'And that is true,' said the friar. 'In a way. But both he and Benvenuto come from an Anglia that is in another world – and from a time hundreds of years ahead of us.'

Sandro made the Hand of Fortune, to ward off the evil eye. Such talk was the last thing he expected to hear from a man of the church. Sulien smiled.

'There is nothing to be afraid of,' he said. 'They are good people. And they belong to the same Brotherhood as I do.'

'The Hounds of God?' asked Sandro.

'The Stravaganti,' said Sulien.

'What's that?'

'Travellers,' said Sulien. 'Travellers in time and space. There are several gathered in the city at the moment. They – we – have plans to save it from bloodshed at the approaching wedding festivities.'

'So Brother Tino isn't really your novice after all?' asked Sandro. 'Is he even a friar?'

'No,' said Sulien. 'I'm afraid that was a story to give him a reason for being here.'

Sandro felt strangely pleased. 'Tell me about the shadows,' he said. 'You said you are one of these travellers, but you have a shadow. I've seen it.'

'We have a shadow in the world we live in because that is where our real bodies are. It is only in the world we travel to that we are without our shadows.'

'So where do you go?'

'To Tino's world,' said Sulien. 'And there I have no shadow. I am just a visitor.'

'Could I go?' asked Sandro.

'Who knows?' said Sulien. 'Maybe one day. But you couldn't take Fratello with you – dogs can't be Stravaganti. Anyway, what I have told you is a secret. It would be very dangerous for us if anyone else knew it – particularly the di Chimici.'

'Even Prince Gaetano?' asked Sandro.

'No,' said Sulien. 'Gaetano knows about us. But you mustn't tell anyone else. I have told you our great secret, because I believe you can be trusted. You have changed in the last few months and I don't think you are as much of a di Chimici man as you used to be. You wouldn't do anything to put Brother Tino and myself in danger, would you? But you must be careful in front of that man up at the palace, the one who works for the Duke.'

'He already knows about the shadows,' said Sandro, anxious to show himself worthy of Sulien's trust. 'We saw you all coming out of a palazzo in the city today. Tino and that Benvenuto came out first and Enrico spotted that they didn't have them.'

'Then we are already in danger,' said Sulien. 'I must tell the others.'

Nicholas was so restless that the four of them left the

house and walked back to Sky's flat. Georgia was really worried about Nicholas. There had always been a danger in letting him go back to Talia but she had never thought it would hit him as badly as this. All the anxiety about him and the problems with Alice were spoiling her enjoyment at having been back to Talia herself. She longed for the old days when no one else knew about stravagation but her.

Sky let them in and heard his mother talking to someone. But the last person he expected to see at their kitchen table was Giuditta Miele. His heart sank; what on earth had the two of them found to talk about?

'Oh, hello, darling,' said Rosalind. 'You have a visitor. We've been waiting for you. Hello, you lot. Make yourselves at home – I'll get another chair.' She went off to the bedroom to fetch one.

'Alice,' said Sky. 'This is Giuditta Miele. I've told you about her.'

'It's Alice I've come to see,' said Giuditta. 'I've brought something for her.'

She took out a piece of paper, smaller than A4, with a red crayon sketch on it.

'Oh, that's Georgia, isn't it?' said Rosalind, coming back in with a chair. 'It's very good.'

'Thank you,' said Giuditta.

Alice took up the sketch, which showed Georgia hiding from the world's gaze behind a long sweep of tiger-striped hair.

'You made her look sort of Renaissance,' said Rosalind, 'in spite of the hair. How did you do that?'

'I drew what I saw,' said Giuditta simply.

'Well, I must leave you all to it,' said Rosalind. 'I

have a client to visit. Sky will look after you.'

'Is that my talisman?' asked Alice when she had gone. 'The drawing of Georgia?'

'Yes,' said Giuditta. 'It will bring you to my workshop in Giglia.'

'And I'm to go tonight?' said Alice, stunned. She no longer had any doubts that her friends had been telling the truth and she wasn't sure that she wanted to go to Talia any more. It seemed to bring nothing but trouble. But the others were all looking at her eagerly, as if something wonderful had happened, so she just said, 'Thank you.'

Wherever Beatrice went, her father's agent was at her elbow; she was beginning to think that the Duke had ordered this man to be especially helpful to her and she wished fervently that he had not. Enrico had a rank body odour – as if he rubbed himself with onions – and he stood too close. She took to applying more of the cologne that came from the pharmacy in Saint-Mary-among-the-Vines, so that she moved in a cloud of her own scent. But although it kept something of the man's smell at bay, it did not get rid of the man himself.

Today she was trying to arrange what would be necessary by way of flowers for the weddings, and it was no small task. Beatrice set off for the Garden of the di Chimici, a large tract of ground near their old palace, where Dukes as far back as Fabrizio the First, a hundred years ago, had grown flowers in the heart of the city. She had a key to the iron gates in the bunch hanging from her girdle, so she let herself into the garden, reluctantly allowing Enrico in after her.

'Paradise on earth!' he exclaimed. 'Just look at those colours!'

'I like it for its sweet scents,' said Beatrice.

'Never had much of a sense of smell myself,' said Enrico cheerfully. 'But I like flowers. You get plenty of them in this city but I've never seen anything like this garden.'

The garden was full of bees and butterflies. Gardeners worked in beds of all shapes – crescents, circles, octagons, diamonds, trefoils – divided by gravel paths. But Beatrice walked straight to the glass hothouses, where she knew the head gardener would be. Here were plants which would normally flower later in the year, like roses and carnations and lily-of-the-valley, brought on to bloom early and grace the Duke's dinner table. Here too were the exotic flowers collected by her father, not her favourites, because of their fleshy petals and their absence of scent. But they needed specialist care so the senior gardeners looked after them.

'Principessa!' said the head gardener, coming towards her wiping his hands on a sacking apron. 'We are honoured. What can I do for you?'

'I have come to talk about the wedding flowers,' said Beatrice.

'I think I'll wait outside, if you don't mind, your Highness,' said Enrico, mopping his brow with a lace handkerchief. 'It's too hot for me in here.'

Beatrice watched him go with relief. It was indeed stifling in the hothouse but it was worth it just to be rid of the man's presence.

'We need flowers for each bride, of course,' said the princess. 'And for their attendants. The cathedral itself must be a mass of blossoms and we shall need more flowers for the palazzo and the procession to the Church of the Annunciation that comes after the wedding ceremony.'

'We cannot supply so many from our own beds,' said the gardener. 'But the brides' flowers and those for the banqueting table, those we can provide from among our finest blooms here. The rest will come from the meadows outside the city, picked fresh on the day.'

Beatrice bent to smell a white orchid with purple splotches: no scent, as usual. She had a sudden vision of her father's own wedding, perhaps only a few months away, to the beautiful young Duchessa. He would want her to wear these waxy, lifeless flowers, as like real ones as statues to living, breathing people. And what then? Would the Duchessa look after Niccolò the way his own daughter had?

Beatrice feared there would be no place for her in the Grand Ducal palace once it had its Grand Duchessa; it pained her to think of her little riverside sitting room turned into a dressing room for a stepmother some years younger than herself. Best to leave for a new home of her own, with a husband. But who? The only unmarried di Chimici cousin left after the coming weddings would be Filippo of Bellona, Francesca's brother, unless you counted cousin Rinaldo. Beatrice's mouth curled up at the very thought. But Filippo was all right, thought Beatrice, a kind man and not unhandsome. She would try to find out if her father's plans tended that way.

All this flashed through her mind in the time it took to sniff an orchid.

They were all going to stravagate separately that night. Alice had reasoned that, since she wouldn't arrive in the same place as Georgia, there wasn't much point in their leaving together. And she felt shy about being watched. Giuditta had promised to have clothes waiting for her in the workshop, but she hadn't much confidence in what they might be like.

Her relations with Sky were still strained and Georgia was obviously worried about Nicholas, who was still muttering darkly about translating back to Giglia full time. Alice was happy to spend some time on her own. But she found an unexpected complication.

It was one of the rare evenings when Jane Greaves didn't have a committee meeting and she was disposed to stay up late and chat. Normally this would have made Alice happy, but she wanted to get an early night in case the stravagating took a long time to get the hang of. Giuditta had said she must arrive in the workshop before the apprentices were up and she didn't want to be late.

'What's the hurry?' asked her mother. 'You've got another week off school. You can lie in after I've gone to work – lucky you. Besides, we haven't talked properly for ages.'

It soon emerged that what she wanted to talk about was Rosalind Meadows.

'I gather your boyfriend's mother made a big hit

with your dad,' she said, a little bit slurrily, since she was drinking her way through a bottle of red wine.

'Well, she's nice,' said Alice defensively.

'I'm sure she's lovely,' said Jane, waving her glass. 'She's Laura's best friend, you know, the one who's on the same scrutiny committee as me? Known each other since they were at school. She told me about Sky's father.'

Alice was burning to ask about him but thought she shouldn't; Sky would tell her when he was ready, she supposed.

'Doesn't it make it a bit awkward for you, though, his mother and your father being together?' asked Jane.

'Don't exaggerate, Mum,' said Alice. 'They're not "together" like that – they just got on well in Devon. That's all.'

'Not what I heard,' said Jane. 'I spoke to Laura this evening and she told me they spent last night at Rosalind's flat. Sky was out or something.'

Yes, thought Alice; he was at Nick's, stravagating to Talia. It made her feel very peculiar to think of her father and Rosalind as a couple, and she wondered what Sky would say. Her brain was buzzing with thoughts. What was her father doing in London without contacting her? Was he going to be here all weekend? And where had he been when they called round at Sky's flat this morning? Had he left before Giuditta arrived?

'I'm sorry, Mum,' she said. 'I'm dropping. I really must go to bed.'

Giuditta was always up before her apprentices. She was still working on the Duchessa's statue, polishing, chipping minute fragments off it, polishing it again. It was always hard for her to decide when a piece was finished. Sometimes she felt that something was complete only when it left her workshop, collected by the patron who had ordered it. At other times the finishing point was the moment when she started something else. Certainly, she didn't yet feel that her connection with Arianna was over.

She stoked the fire that heated the stove in her little kitchen at the back of the workshop and put on a pan of milk to simmer. Giuditta had a bedroom of her own above the workshop, but the apprentices slept on the floor among the statues and blocks of stone. She had stepped over them on her way to the kitchen and none had stirred. She made a mental note that Franco was not among them – catting about with one of his many conquests in the city, she supposed.

Giuditta was about to sit down in the kitchen's one chair, when an ethereal figure materialised in it. A fair, slender girl in a long blue shift with the mysterious word 'fcuk' written on the front of it, solidified in the chair. She looked terrified.

Giuditta silently gave her some warm milk and stirred honey into it. Alice drank it gratefully, thankful too that she recognised this large, calm woman as the sculptor who had brought the drawing of Georgia, which Alice was still clutching, rolled up in her hand.

'I am in Talia?' she whispered.

Giuditta nodded. 'Stay quiet here,' she said. 'I'll fetch you some suitable clothes. And don't go in the workshop – there are boys sleeping in there.'

She was back soon, holding a simple blue cotton dress. 'My niece's,' she said, helping Alice into it and giving her a pair of dark blue ankle boots. 'You and she are much of a size, as I guessed.'

The dress had a complicated bodice with laces and Alice suspected she might look a bit like the soppy love interest in a pantomime, but there was no mirror in Giuditta's kitchen and at least now she could go out into the street.

'I must give the boys their breakfast,' said Giuditta. She seemed almost motherly, warming bread in the oven and pouring spiced milk. Alice helped her carry bowls and platters into the workshop. One apprentice was opening the shutters and letting in the bright morning light. The other two were stretching and yawning. A fourth boy, older than the others, slipped in through the door and was cuffed round the head by Giuditta before being given his breakfast.

They were all amazed by the sight of Alice.

'My new model, Alice,' said Giuditta, only she gave the name three syllables – Ah-lee-chay. She gestured to Alice to keep out of the sun; the girl jumped back quickly when she saw she had no shadow.

She was suddenly ravenous and ate bread and butter and a delicious preserve made from berries. They all breakfasted in silence, but when the apprentices were rolling up their bedding, Sky and Nicholas arrived. Alice had never been so glad to see anyone before.

Giuditta gave them a sheaf of drawings and said,

'Please take these to Brother Sulien. Alice, you can go with them and bring me back any comments he has.'

The three Stravaganti waited outside the workshop for Georgia to arrive. Alice flung her arms around Sky.

'I'm so glad you're here,' she said. 'It's all so strange.' She was gazing up at the vast cathedral, unable to accept that she was here and not in her bedroom at home.

'It'll be stranger still if anyone catches you embracing a friar,' said Nicholas. 'I think we'd better work out a different cover story.'

Chapter 20

The River Rises

After that once, Alice never stravagated again. Sky and Nicholas and Georgia all looked at home in Talia, as if they understood their role there. But she felt out of her depth the whole time. They took her to meet the other Stravaganti and they were perfectly welcoming. But Alice felt nervous of them; she was acutely aware of being an intruder into someone else's world.

She didn't like the way the city and its people smelt, the fact that all the men carried swords or daggers unnerved her and, worst of all, she had the feeling all the time of arriving in a play where she hadn't seen the earlier acts. Everyone seemed tense and worried about these weddings and she still couldn't sort out everyone's names and which person was getting married to which.

'Even my talisman isn't really for me,' she told Georgia the next day. 'It has your face on it.' And she took Giuditta's sketch and had it framed and hung it on her bedroom wall.

At least the tension had gone out of her relationship with Sky and the others. She was in on their secret, which would prove useful in providing future alibis, and she now understood why they all spent so much time together. She was included in their conversations and even joined Georgia when she watched the boys fencing. It no longer seemed boring now that she knew why they needed those skills.

Gradually, as they went back to school and started revising for exams, Alice felt her world swivel so that from being an outsider she became someone who was included, who could be told secrets that no one else in the world, literally, would understand. She didn't want to go back to Talia herself but she wanted to hear all about what was going on there. And with a part of herself she knew that the life the others were leading in the City of Flowers would come to a climax in less than two weeks' time and, for good or ill, Sky's role there would be over. And she would still be here, waiting for him.

In Talia, preparations for the big di Chimici event were in full swing. An additional kitchen was being built on to the back of the Palazzo Ducale in order to cope with all the planned feasting. The tournament on the day before the weddings was going to be held in the great Piazza Ducale, followed by an open-air banquet, and one of the main worries of the Duke's steward was the weather.

For the first two weeks in April, it rained steadily in the city, causing the already swollen river to rise even higher. The Duke's men were erecting a wooden platform on one side of the square, which was to hold tables seating hundreds of guests. It was to have a canopy bearing the di Chimici arms, but the weather was too wet to put it up yet.

When Arianna walked through the square, the sight of all the preparations made her heart sink. So far she had met only two or three times with the Duke and he had said nothing of his intentions towards her, but by the time the banquet was held he would surely have made his proposal formally and she would have to give him an answer. And she still didn't know what to do about the extravagant dress.

She picked her way through the puddles, attended by Barbara and her bodyguards, glad of a break in the rain to get out of the Embassy and visit her mother. The sky was still dark with rain clouds.

'If I believed in augury,' said Silvia after their greetings, 'I would think the gods were against at least one of these marriages.'

'Well, it wouldn't be that of Gaetano and Francesca,' said Arianna. 'I never met such a lovesick swain. Gaetano hasn't stopped talking about her since I arrived. I'll be glad when Francesca gets here herself, so that she can look after him.'

'And give you more time to look after your own swains?' asked Silvia.

'What do you mean?' asked Arianna. 'You are surely not referring to the Duke? He's a little old for a swain, I think.'

'Well, he is one of them, though he has made no declaration yet,' said Silvia. 'And I wish you would pay some thought to what you will say to him when he does.'

'I think about it all the time,' said Arianna. 'But to no avail.'

'Perhaps because your affections are already engaged?' suggested Silvia. 'That need not determine how you handle the Duke.'

'But he has no feelings for me,' said Arianna, exasperated. 'It is my city he wants, not me. It's all politics.'

'So it must be dealt with politically,' said her mother. 'Not romantically at all. It must not matter that he doesn't care for you – or that you don't care for him.'

'How could I care for him? He was behind the plot to kill you and as far as he knows he was successful. I think he was also involved in killing that young boy in the Nucci family and goodness knows how many others.'

'All the more reason to be careful how you refuse him,' said Silvia. 'You know what a dangerous man he is. And if he suspects that it is because you prefer another, that person's life would not be worth a scudo.'

*

Enrico hadn't been able to find out anything about the new novice, and it bothered him. Sandro had been quite useless in bringing him information on Brother

Benvenuto, or anything else at the friary recently, come to that. Though he was still keeping an eye on the Nucci.

Saint-Mary-among-the-Vines niggled at the back of Enrico's mind whenever it wasn't occupied by the arrangements for the wedding, helping the Principessa or spying on the Nucci. He knew that the pharmacy used to be the seat of the di Chimici's experiments, which were only partly into distilling perfumes. It was common knowledge that the family continued to be supplied with poisons from there for generations. But what about now? Enrico couldn't quite see Brother Sulien handing out deadly potions to the Duke if he asked for them. And yet he had no reason to suppose that the friar wasn't loyal. He had been prompt enough to save the Duke in his hour of need.

No, and besides, Sulien definitely had a shadow; Enrico had checked. He could not be one of those occult masters that the Duke feared and hated. So why did he entertain two novices who were under suspicion of belonging to that secret Brotherhood? It was one of those things that irked Enrico – like what had happened to his fiancée.

The Warrior had been in London for nearly two weeks and had not yet plucked up the courage to go and see Sky. Loretta knew he was worried about something and wisely said nothing. She had known what she was taking on when she married him and knew that if they were to have any future she mustn't be jealous of his past.

They had been married for six years now and there had been no babies, which was a sadness for her; she had long passed the youthful stage of thinking that children would ruin her figure and would have liked one of her own now. But she could see that Rainbow, as he liked to be called, was not exactly broody. He had so many children of his own already.

It was a mild spring in London, with the parks full of daffodils and no likelihood, as so often, that they would end up battered under a layer of late snow. Loretta filled the flat with flowering plants until it was full of the scent of hyacinths and the exotic blooms of orchids and hibiscus. And she waited.

One warm April morning while they were drinking cappuccinos outside the Café Mozart and the Warrior had signed just the right number of autographs to keep him happy – he was still a celebrity but didn't want his privacy disturbed – he said, 'Loretta, there's something I've got to tell you.'

At last, she thought, and took another bite of sachertorte.

The State coach of Fortezza, with its crest of the lily crossed by a sword, rumbled into the Via Larga late in the evening of Maundy Thursday. Princess Beatrice, who had spent all day supervising the making up of beds and airing of rooms, was first to greet Prince Jacopo and his family. Even though the di Chimici palazzo was large, she was glad that she and the Duke and Fabrizio had already moved into the Palazzo Ducale; there were more visitors expected. Francesca would be brought from Bellona by her brother Filippo, who would be giving her away. And cousin Alfonso would arrive next, from Volana, with his sister and mother. Thank goodness, thought Beatrice, that Uncle Ferdinando had a Papal residence in Giglia too, where he and cousin Rinaldo would stay; the di Chimici palace would be stretched to its limits, particularly since the bridal couples must be kept strictly apart.

'Welcome, welcome!' she said now to Jacopo and Carolina, receiving hearty kisses on both cheeks, and hugging Lucia and Bianca with genuine affection. Beatrice had always been fond of that branch of the family and intimate with these two cousins, who were distant in blood but near to her in age. These weddings were going to bring everyone closer.

'Little Beatrice!' growled Jacopo, gripping her like a bear. 'Why no husband for you in the cathedral next week? You are as pretty as your mother and shouldn't keep the young men waiting.'

'Father is not ready to part with me yet,' said Beatrice, blushing. 'He will be here soon, to greet you. Fabrizio too. Let me show you to your rooms.'

Liveried servants, of both the Fortezzan and Giglian branches of the family, carried the considerable baggage of the brides-to-be and their parents up the staircases, while maids scurried to bring heated water and lighted candles.

'Come and talk to us while we change, Bice dearest,' said Lucia.

'We want to show you our wedding dresses,' said Bianca.

'And I want to see them,' said Beatrice.

'Will Carlo be at dinner?' asked Lucia.

'Yes, yes,' said Beatrice. 'He is anxious to see you. And Alfonso will be here on Saturday,' she told Bianca, 'and Francesca. By the day after tomorrow all four couples will be able to sit down to dinner at the same table, even though you know you must not be alone together.'

'That's all right,' said Lucia. 'After next Tuesday, we will have a lifetime of being alone together.'

*

Sandro was watching the di Chimici palace from the street with Enrico. The Eel thought it was part of his young spy's education to show him the family members as they arrived. Sandro shuddered when he saw Prince Carlo came back with his father and older brother; Fratello growled softly.

'Now, you are straight about which prince is going to marry which princess?' asked Enrico. 'The little redhead who came from Fortezza tonight gets Carlo.'

'Poor her,' said Sandro under his breath.

'What was that?' asked Enrico.

'Which one is the dark sister going to marry?' asked Sandro, to distract him.

'Duke Alfonso of Volana,' said Enrico promptly. 'He's coming on Saturday. His sister is Caterina.'

'The one that Fabrizio is going to marry?' asked Sandro.

'Well done,' said Enrico. 'And their brother is?'

Sandro shook his head. 'No idea.'

'My old master, Rinaldo,' said Enrico. 'I worked for him when he was Ambassador to Bellezza. A real pansy. He works for the Pope now. They won't be here till Monday because the Pope has to say the Easter Mass in his own city of Remora.'

'The Pope's the Duke's brother, isn't he?'

'His younger one, yes. Now, who is Prince Gaetano's bride?'

'Francesca of Bellona,' said Sandro, screwing up his face with the effort of remembering. 'He's always talking about her.'

'Right then, you know all our lot. Now how about the Nucci? How many are there at the tower now?'

'Well, you know about Matteo,' said Sandro, 'and Camillo and Filippo. There are at least eight others – cousins I think or uncles – whose names I don't know.'

'But you know them by sight? You'd recognise them?'

Sandro nodded.

'Good lad,' said Enrico. 'You'll be useful on the day of the weddings.'

*

Sky had a second disguise in Giglia now. Gaetano had given him a set of clothes to keep up at the friary; they were the plainest he had and yet they still made Sky feel the part of a young nobleman. Now he was Brother Tino within the walls of Saint-Mary-among-the-Vines and ordinary Messer Celestino when he went out into the city. In this way he could consort with Georgia without comment and, if they usually had another young friar with them, that lent more respectability to their association. Nicholas continued to need his disguise and the abandonment of Sky's identity as a novice wasn't without its dangers. He had to be careful not to be seen by Nicholas's brothers or the Duke. But the nobles were all involved in the wedding preparations and it was good to stride about the city in clothes that accommodated a sword and dagger at his belt.

On the day after the Fortezzas arrived, Good Friday in Giglia, Sky and Nicholas set out to meet Georgia at Giuditta's workshop a bit later than usual. As novices, they had been required to attend a special service before leaving the friary. In their own world they had been back at school a week and hadn't missed a night's stravagation to Talia. They were tired, their senses a little dulled in both worlds, or they might have been quicker to realise what was happening in the narrow street off the Piazza della Cattedrale.

Most of the streets around the piazza were deserted, since the majority of the people who would normally have been out were still attending a long service in the cathedral. Gaetano and Luciano had used the emptiness of the Annunciation piazza for an early-morning practice with the foils.

They too were on their way to meet Georgia at the sculptor's workshop when they suddenly found their way barred by a small group of the Nucci faction. It was Camillo and two of his cousins and all three were armed to the hilt. Luciano didn't know any of them and was taken by surprise when these obviously hostile youths started to hold their noses and jeer the name di Chimici. He didn't know that the traditional response was to bleat like a sheep and crow 'Nucci!'

Gaetano was not responding; he and Luciano were

outnumbered and he had no desire to provoke a fight so he said nothing.

'See what lily-livers these lily boys are!' cried Camillo. 'They don't like a fair fight, these flower-arrangers! They prefer secret stabbings in an alley!'

'I have no quarrel with you,' said Gaetano finally, as evenly as he could manage. 'I am sorry for the death of your brother, but it was not my doing.'

'Maybe so,' sneered Camillo. 'But you can't deny your family had a hand in it.'

'I am not my family,' said Gaetano. But it was no use. His attitude was incomprehensible to red-blooded Giglians. In the City of Flowers family was everything. The three Nucci came closer until Camillo's face was only centimetres away from Gaetano's. Meanwhile one of the others gave Luciano a shove. The prince glanced sideways for an instant at his friend and that was time enough for Camillo to draw his dagger and aim it at Gaetano's ribs.

But Gaetano had excellent reflexes and blocked the blade with his left arm and hit him smartly in the face with his right fist. Luciano backed off and drew his rapier and soon his new fighting skills were being used in deadly earnest.

That was when Sky and Nicholas turned the corner and saw what was happening. They both rushed into the fray, Sky drawing his sword awkwardly and Nicholas launching himself at Camillo's back and pinning his arms. Suddenly the odds were against the Nucci. Camillo was disarmed, with Gaetano's blade at his throat, and his cousins found themselves faced by two other armed and ferocious young men, even though one of them was a friar.

'Call off your men,' said Gaetano, and Camillo nodded gingerly. His cousins sheathed their swords and at a further sign from Camillo retreated into the distance. Gaetano lowered his weapon.

'Go back to your family,' he said. 'I say again I have no quarrel with you and nor do my friends.' He signalled to Nicholas to release his hold and Camillo Nucci loped off after the others, cursing all di Chimici as he went.

'You're bleeding,' said Nicholas to Gaetano, as the others put up their weapons.

They were fortunately near Giuditta's workshop by then and took the wounded prince in.

'It's not a bad wound,' said Gaetano. 'The dagger just glanced off my arm.'

'Just a scratch, I suppose?' said Georgia hysterically. She realised that they had all been in mortal danger.

Giuditta sent her to boil water on the stove, while she eased off Gaetano's doublet and shirtsleeve. The apprentices crowded round; this was better entertainment than they had expected on the long penitential day of Good Friday.

It was indeed only a flesh wound, though it bled impressively. Giuditta tore up a cotton sheet to bandage it.

'Will it heal by Tuesday?' asked Gaetano, not so much worried about it impeding his wedding as about whether he would be able to fight then if called upon.

Giuditta nodded. 'It will knit together well enough in a few days if you do not use it. I don't recommend your taking part in the tournament on Monday.' She pulled his shirt and doublet back on gently and made a sling from more of the sheet.

'So I shan't be able to conceal today's encounter,' he said wryly.

'Be thankful it was not worse,' said the sculptor. 'And that you had friends at hand.'

'But it irks me that Gaetano has taken hurt while the Nucci walked away unscathed,' said Nicholas, surprising the apprentices. They would not have expected a novice friar to be so bloodthirsty.

*

Beatrice was with her other family members in the church of Sant'Ambrogio, and had no idea what had happened. But her thoughts were not altogether concentrated on the service. Because of the religious obligations of this day and of Easter Sunday, there was effectively only Saturday left in which to finish getting everything ready for Monday's tournament and banquet, which would lead rapidly on to the weddings themselves. And Francesca and Alfonso and their wedding parties would arrive on Saturday and need housing and entertaining.

Thank goodness I'm *not* getting married on Tuesday too, she thought, or nothing would be ready in time.

By the time they left the church, it was again raining heavily in the city and the di Chimici party had to make an undignified run to the palazzo.

When Sky returned home after school the next day, there was a red sports car outside his flat. He didn't think for a moment that it had anything to do with him and let himself in as usual. But in his kitchen sat a very glamorous couple. A middle-aged black man with greying dreadlocks and a silk suit, and a stunning long-legged bronzed young woman, sitting perched awkwardly on a kitchen chair with Remedy on the minimal lap of her very short skirt. Rosalind was looking dazed.

But she didn't need to make any introductions; Sky remembered the *Hello!* article when he was eleven. He felt his hackles rising.

'Hi there, Sky,' said the Warrior awkwardly.

Sky couldn't say anything. What could he say after seventeen years? He moved instinctively close to Rosalind, remembering how the singer had ignored his appeal of three years ago.

Loretta held out a perfectly manicured hand with scarlet nails and Sky took it, fascinated.

'I've only just heard of your existence,' she said to him. 'Yesterday, in fact. I'm sorry. If Rainbow had told me, I would have invited you to visit us in the States.'

'I wouldn't have come,' he said instantly, appreciating her forthrightness. 'I wouldn't have left Rosalind.'

'I understand,' said the Warrior. 'You don't want anything to do with me and I don't blame you. But I didn't want to die never having met one of my sons.'

'Are you dying, then?' asked Sky rudely. 'Why should I care? You didn't seem that bothered when Rosalind was ill.'

They all looked at him equally blankly.

'You know, when I wrote you that letter?' he added. 'Asking you to find her a good doctor.'

The Warrior shook his head. 'I never got no letter,'

he said. 'You never told me you'd been ill,' he said to Rosalind.

'I'm getting better now,' she said. 'It was tough on Sky for a while – it was ME.'

It was clear from the Warrior's face that he didn't know what she was talking about. Sky felt something beginning to unknot in his stomach. But he was puzzled by the singer's attitude. It sounded as if he and Rosalind had kept in touch, which was not what Sky had been told.

'I'm sorry,' said the singer. 'Sorry I didn't get the letter, sorry that your mum's been ill – sorry for being such a rotten father. But she did say that she wanted to bring you up on her own. And I'm not dying – I just wanted to see you in the flesh. All these photos are great but it's not the same.'

He took an envelope from his inside pocket and tipped out a cascade of photographs on the table. Sky saw his whole life spread out in random order, from chubby brown baby to six-foot teenager. The pictures were all tatty round the edges, particularly the older ones, as if they had been handled and looked at often.

For the first time, he saw that he looked like his father.

It rained the whole of the rest of that weekend in Giglia. Then, miraculously, on Easter Sunday in the afternoon, the sun came out and the city began to steam in the spring heat.

'God be praised!' said the Pope, in his carriage on the way from Remora.

'Goddess be thanked!' said the many workmen and tradesmen busying themselves about the weddings. They worked late into the night, Easter Sunday or not, carrying tables out into the Piazza Ducale, plucking and arranging flowers, spreading ornate cloths and di Chimici banners, creating fantasies of sugar and marzipan in the kitchen.

Monday dawned fair and clear, to the relief of grooms and armourers and all the young men taking part in the tournament. Sky and Nicholas got to the piazza early, meeting Luciano and Georgia in the loggia with all the fine statues. They wanted to get a good view of the tournament, even though their own favourite, Gaetano, would not be taking part.

He had greeted his bride two days before, with his arm still in its sling. Francesca had cried out when she saw him but he had reassured her that it would be better by Tuesday and that he would marry her with two strong arms. The Duke had been furious to hear of the Nucci attack, but Gaetano and Beatrice had prevailed on him not to take any revenge before the weddings.

'You got visitors, Gloria,' said the care assistant.

'Mrs Peck to you,' said the old lady. This was one of her better days.

Sky wasn't at all sure about this. His other grandmother, Rosalind's mum, had been a part of his life as long as he could remember. But this tiny black woman seemed to have even less to do with him than the ageing rock singer did. He would have appreciated

Loretta's company on the drive down, but there was room only for two in the sports car and she had stayed to talk to Rosalind.

So Sky had been enclosed in a small space with the man he could not think of as his father. He supposed it hadn't really been any more awkward for him than for the Warrior. But he had no intention of making it any easier.

'I really never got that letter, you know,' said his father, as soon as they were heading south.

'I believe you,' said Sky. 'It's OK.'

'Your mum always writes care of my agent, Gus,' he went on. 'And I've always got her letters – the ones with the photos. Regular as clockwork, once a year.'

'I didn't know she was doing that,' said Sky.

'I expect you hate me, don't you?' said the Warrior, after a long silence.

'No,' said Sky, thinking about the way the Nucci felt towards the di Chimici. 'I don't hate you. I just don't know you. I don't feel as if you have anything to do with me.'

The Warrior winced. 'Fair enough,' he said. 'But there is a connection. I mean, blood's thicker than water, isn't it?'

'Is it?' said Sky. 'I don't think we've got anything in common except our DNA. I may look more like you but Rosalind's the one I'm really like.'

'Only because you've been with her all this time,' said his father.

Sky shook his head. 'I don't think so,' he said.

'Well, then, I suppose I'll just have to settle for the DN whatsit,' said the Warrior.

'It'd be useful if you ever needed a kidney or a bone

marrow transplant,' said Sky, but even as he said it, meaning to be sarcastic, he thought of all those episodes of *ER* he had watched with Rosalind and couldn't help smiling.

'You taking the piss?' asked his father, glancing sideways at him. 'Nothing wrong with my kidneys.' Then he relaxed just a bit. 'Might need some liver one day though – used to drink like a fish before Loretta took me over.'

'She's nice,' said Sky and meant it.

'Yeah, she's a real diamond,' said the Warrior.

'Nice car, too,' ventured Sky.

'You want a go?' he asked. 'Have you got your licence yet?'

'Only the provisional,' said Sky. 'I'm only just seventeen.'

'Course not,' said the Warrior. 'It's different in America. Kids can drive as soon as they're fifteen in some states. But I tell you what. Have a spin round the grounds of the home after we've seen your granny – OK?'

Sky wasn't quite sure how he'd been talked into this visit. The Warrior had asked if he'd go with him to see his old mum in a home in Surrey and Sky had the strangest feeling that the singer wanted someone with him to act as a buffer. He had explained that the old lady sometimes got a bit confused.

She seemed bright as a button when Sky first caught sight of her, her eyes darting back and forth between them.

'Hello, Mum,' said the Warrior, bending over to kiss her. They had stopped on the way to buy flowers and he now presented her with a huge bouquet of hothouse roses.

'There now, Mrs Peck – isn't that lovely?' said the care assistant before taking them away.

'Say hello to your granny, Sky,' said the Warrior.

Sky didn't feel he could kiss a perfect stranger. He held out his hand to her. A puzzled look crossed the old woman's face.

'Is it Kevin's boy?' she asked her son.

'No, Mum,' said the Warrior. 'This is my son, Sky. You haven't met him before. Nor had I till today. He lives with his mum.'

'Another one?' said Sky's grandmother. She didn't seem very pleased to meet him. 'He looks like you, Colin. And your dad – poor bugger.'

Sky didn't know if she meant him or his grandfather. But he was amused to discover that the millionaire Rainbow Warrior was really Colin Peck, with an old mum who stood no nonsense from him. He felt a bit sorry for him, really. What with his feisty mother and Loretta taking him in hand, it seemed as if the glamorous rock star was a bit henpecked.

'What you laughing at?' said Mrs Peck. 'Let's have a proper look at you. Mum's white, I see.'

Sky nodded. He wasn't going to discuss Rosalind with this woman.

'Well, you've got the looks. I suppose you want to be a singer too?'

'No,' said Sky. 'I want to be an artist. I don't even like his kind of music.'

Then he realised he was being unnecessarily rude. They were both staring at him. He suddenly had a very strong feeling that he was young and had all his choices ahead of him. This old woman, who was biologically his grandmother, looked as if she didn't have much of her life left. And the Rainbow Warrior wasn't a bad man; he'd just led a very different life from Sky.

'There – don't they look lovely?' said the care assistant brightly, bringing back the roses arranged in a glass vase. 'Would you like me to make you all a nice cup of tea?'

Chapter 21

The di Chimici Weddings

The young Stravaganti sat on the steps of the loggia, watching the preparations for the tournament. The loggia itself was filling up with food stalls for all those not fortunate enough to have been invited to the banquet. Luciano bought them all thick slices of frittata between pieces of coarse bread and a jug of cold ale to share. Nicholas sat slightly apart, his back against one of the statue plinths and his hood pulled up to shade his face.

The di Chimici party came out of the Palazzo Ducale. A special stage had been built for them to sit on and watch the games. All four di Chimici bridegrooms escorted their brides, and there was also the Duke, Princess Beatrice, the Duchessa of Bellezza and her father the Regent, and the Pope himself, who stood and gave his blessing on the crowd before the games began. Prince Fabrizio announced his bride to the spectators as Queen of the Tournament. As future wife of the di Chimici heir, Princess Caterina of Volana merited that honour. And the crowd were delighted to see the pretty young woman blushing as the prince placed the wreath of olive leaves on her golden hair.

The tournament began with a great procession of bullock wagons carrying models of all the cities that were under di Chimici rule – Remora, Moresco, Fortezza, Volana, Bellona – finishing with a perfect model of Giglia itself, complete in every detail (apart from the marked absence of the new Nucci palace) and dominated by the miniature of the great cathedral. By then the edges of the square were full of spectators.

'No Bellezza, you see,' Luciano whispered to Georgia. And he knew that Arianna, sitting in splendour across the piazza, was thinking the same. 'You'll never see a model of the City of Masks carried on a cart to glorify the Duke in Giglia.'

Not unless Arianna accepts his proposal, thought Georgia, but she carefully kept that thought to herself.

When the last wagon had rumbled past the Palazzo Ducale, two men came and set up a quintain at the south-east end of the L-shaped piazza. It was a stuffed dummy of a man with a shield in one hand and a weighted whip in the other. Riders ran at it with a lowered lance and once they had struck the shield had to jink out of the way to avoid the whip as it swung round. The first two or three were easily knocked off their horses.

Nicholas was on his feet booing with the rest of the crowd. 'I was very good at this,' he told Sky. 'Oh, if only I had a horse and a lance!'

Fabrizio, Carlo and Alfonso had left the wooden stage now and entered the lists. They were wearing only light armour and no helmets. Gaetano scanned the tops of the surrounding buildings carefully for archers but the only bows he could see were di Chimici men, archers from the Duke's private army. He was almost as frustrated as Nicholas that he couldn't tilt at the quintain but Francesca held him tightly by the hand.

The flower of Giglian youth was at the tournament – not just di Chimici and Nucci but every family that had any claim to ancient lineage in the city. The Aldieri, the Bartolomei, the Donzelli, the Gabrieli, the Leoni, the Pasquali, the Ronsivalli and the Salvini were all represented, and each family was in allegiance with either the perfumier-bankers whose weddings were being celebrated or the wool merchants and sheep farmers who were their enemies.

The young men were lining up to try at the quintain while in other parts of the square jugglers and acrobats and musicians entertained the crowd while they waited for the main joust. And not just nobles; every boy and youth, no matter what their estate, was in the square, greedily absorbing the sights and sounds. Sandro and Fratello were on the edge of the crowd, watching.

Prince Fabrizio won the quintain and was rewarded by Caterina who bestowed his prize of a silver chain round his neck. He whispered in her ear as she put it over his head and the crowd roared their approval.

For the main joust, the combatants all put on metal helmets. Sky couldn't believe that he was going to see real riders and horses charge at one another with metal-tipped lances. But for the others, who had seen the excesses of the Reman Stellata, it was not so surprising. The clash of lance on shield and sword on sword rang round the square and no quarter was given, even though this was supposed to be a wedding celebration.

The jousting lasted for hours until only Camillo Nucci and Carlo di Chimici were left in the lists. By then many young men were nursing broken limbs or bleeding from sword slashes. Fabrizio and Alfonso had both retired with minor wounds because their brides-to-be insisted on their remaining in one piece for the next day.

'Surely someone will get killed?' said Sky.

'Not usually,' said Nicholas.

Camillo and Carlo thundered towards each other along the short run the piazza permitted. Their lances both made contact and both riders were unhorsed. The loose horses charged on, stopped only by the fearless grooms who caught their harness. The two young men leapt to their feet, swords drawn. Camillo had dropped his shield but was thrown another by his brother Filippo.

The combatants circled each other like gladiators while the crowd bayed for blood. This was the pinnacle of the day's entertainment for most of them. Georgia found herself cheering 'Carlo! Prince Carlo!' and then stopped, wondering why. The only di Chimici she liked were Gaetano who wasn't fighting and the translated Falco who was standing beside her dressed as a friar and yelling for his brother to win, in a most unecclesiastical way.

'What do you reckon?' Sky whispered to Luciano.

'They're pretty evenly matched as to size and skill, I'd say,' Luciano replied. 'But it's not like fencing. Look at the weight of those swords!'

The two armoured men stood and exchanged blows. There was not much space between the metal plates to inflict a wound, but that wasn't what the endgame of a tournament was all about. It was enough for one to disarm the other or force him to the ground. They were both nimble and good at swordcraft but the weapons were heavy and it was not a subtle contest.

'That's for my brother,' hissed Carlo, lunging at Camillo's neck.

'And this for mine,' retorted Camillo, deflecting the blow with his shield and aiming one of his own.

After twenty minutes, Camillo had wearied his opponent into submission and Carlo sank to his knees. The joust-master stopped it there, seeing that Camillo would have pulled off Carlo's helmet and inflicted a final blow. So the prize was awarded to a Nucci, which left half the crowd howling for revenge and the others crowing with delight.

To her distaste, Princess Caterina had to bestow a handsome silver and bronze war helmet on her family's enemy. The di Chimici applauded politely, their smiles painted on. As he came down the steps Camillo very lightly pinched his nose, provoking more cheers and catcalls. The exhausted Carlo was sitting on the steps of the loggia, his helmet off and drinking a cup of ale. As Camillo passed him he saw a ragged boy and his dog that he had often spotted hanging round outside their family's palace.

The boy and dog were hurrying across the piazza to where the next event was going to take place. Their route took them past Carlo, but the dog suddenly swerved and barked at the prince. It was over in an instant, with the prince cursing at the dog and the boy dragging him away on his piece of string, but at that moment, Camillo Nucci remembered where he had seen the mongrel before. And he knew which of the di Chimici had killed his brother.

But then it was time for the fencing and half a dozen pairs of young men were suddenly ferociously thrusting and parrying all over the square.

'Come on!' said Luciano to Sky. 'Let's have a go!'

A groom gave them a couple of bated weapons and they fought together for the first time. For Sky it was the most exhilarating moment of his journeys to Giglia so far. The sun was shining on their weapons, they were young, alive and well-matched and he was just another well-dressed Giglian noble taking part in the city's great day of rejoicing. But the sixteenth-century rapier was so much heavier than the fencing foils that Sky was used to that Luciano was soon able to beat his weapon out of his hand. As Sky went back to sit with the others, Georgia grabbed him by the arm.

'What on earth did you think you were doing?' she railed at him. 'Imagine if you'd won the whole thing and had to collect a prize from the princess. I suppose you think Giglia's so full of black brothers with dreads that the Duke wouldn't have realised you're the one who's supposed to be a friar!'

But she wasn't listening for an answer. Luciano was now fighting with Filippo Nucci and she was in agony that he might get hurt. Several of the fencers had lost the buttons off the end of their rapiers and there were cries as sharp blades met flesh. But Filippo pressed Luciano hard and soon disarmed him, catching Luciano's weapon on the elaborate cross-guards of his own rapier.

Luciano came back to join them, out of breath. They watched as a revived Prince Carlo saved the honour of his family by defeating Filippo Nucci in the final encounter. His soon-to-be sister-in-law smiled much more happily as she gave him his prize of a silver drinking cup. Nicholas applauded loudly. Georgia shuddered; all these encounters with sharp weapons brought home to her the fears everyone had expressed for the next day's wedding ceremonies.

'I'm glad Alice isn't here,' she whispered to Sky.

'Me too,' he said. He realised that he wouldn't be able to concentrate on what the Stravaganti had to do the following day if he had to keep one eye on his girlfriend. He had distractions enough at home without having them in Talia too. Deliberately he thrust the thought of his father to the back of his mind and concentrated on what was going on across the square.

The di Chimici were leaving the wooden stage and going back into the palazzo. Swarms of servants were finishing laying the tables for the banquet on the platform in the north-west corner of the piazza. Others brought out bowls of warm water scented with rose petals or lemon peel so that the arriving guests could wash their hands. The platform had been constructed to encompass the fountain with its central statue of Neptune and its basin spiked with cologne so that there was a continuing fragrance and the sound of purling water throughout the meal.

The canopy was now in place, made of turquoise cloth threaded with silver and hung with swags of greenery and hothouse roses and lilies. Escutcheons with the di Chimici crest hung on every supporting pole. Guests were divided into male and female, young and old, so that the brides were all at one table with Beatrice and Arianna while the grooms sat at another with the two Nucci sons and various other nobles. Theirs was the most tense gathering at the feast.

Isabella, the dowager Duchessa of Volana, presided over the table of older women, which included Francesca's mother Princess Clarice of Bellona, Princess Carolina of Fortezza, and Graziella Nucci. At a very lavishly decorated table near the fountain sat the Pope in his grandest robes, with his brothers, the Duke of Volana and Prince of Bellona, and his cousin, Prince Jacopo of Fortezza. Rodolfo sat there too and Matteo Nucci and it was of course presided over by the Duke himself.

'Aha, what have we here?' said the Pope as the first course was brought in.

'Capon in white sauce, your Holiness,' said the servant, who had been instructed to serve him first. 'And those are silvered pomegranate seeds.'

Bronze cauldrons filled with water kept cool the greenish wine from Santa Fina while the bottles of Bellezzan and Giglian red had warmed gently in the afternoon sun.

The young Stravaganti, none of whom were invited

to the banquet, quelled their hunger with sugared pastries and watched the comings and goings across the square, like spectators at a theatre.

'That will go on for hours,' said Sandro knowledgeably, coming to join them on the steps of the loggia. Nicholas ruffled Fratello's ears. Ever since Sulien had told him about the Stravaganti, Sandro had spent more and more time with them. They were aware that he knew their secret and that Brother Sulien trusted him.

'I must leave long before the end,' said Georgia regretfully. The next day was a school one and she couldn't risk oversleeping. And, unlike the boys, she had a long flight before she could stravagate back.

'I'll tell you all about it tomorrow,' said Luciano, giving her one of his heart-stopping smiles.

'Me too,' said Sandro. 'I'll name you all the dishes. Enrico will know them all, even though he's not grand enough to sit down with dukes and princes.'

'Or clean enough,' said Luciano. 'They'd have had to fill the fountain with every perfume in Sulien's pharmacy if he'd been invited.'

It bothered Luciano that Sandro was still working for the Eel, even though it was Sulien who had advised the boy not to break off his connections with the di Chimici. Luciano knew what Enrico was capable of, including murder, and he didn't like the idea of the boy risking exposure as a sort of double agent.

Georgia left the square as the candles were being lit in the di Chimici silver candlesticks and the lanterns hanging from the canopy. Sky and Nicholas stayed just long enough to watch a great confection being carried in of spun sugar in the shape of a giant perfume bottle surrounded by lilies. Then Sky had to drag Nicholas back to Saint-Mary-among-the-Vines.

Luciano sat on in the darkening square with Sandro, while the sated guests nibbled silvered almonds and figs and listened to the band of musicians who played on the balcony of the palazzo. When the music stopped, the speeches began, and Luciano realised he must have dozed off, because Sandro was shaking him awake.

'The Duke's making some big announcement,' he said.

The two of them got up and strolled closer to the banqueting platform, which was now an island of light and flowers in the dark. Duke Niccolò, resplendent in a fur-trimmed scarlet velvet doublet, was standing holding a silver goblet full of red wine. His speech was slightly slurred and he swayed a little but he was still very much the master of the feast.

'My brother, his Holiness the Pope, Lenient the Sixth, here to celebrate the union of eight of our closest family members in the cathedral tomorrow, has conferred upon me the honour of a new title.'

The Pope also rose, even more unsteadily than his brother, and took the new crown from a page who had borne it to the platform on a purple velvet cushion.

'By the powers invested in me as Bishop of Remora and Pope of the Church of Talia,' he said, 'I here declare Duke Niccolò di Chimici, Duke of Giglia, to be the first Grand Duke of all Tuschia.'

He placed the Grand-Ducal crown, which looked rather like one of the kitchen's finer confections, on his brother's white head.

The new Grand Duke adjusted it as the applause rose from all the tables.

'This crown I hope to pass on, with the title, to my heir Fabrizio and his descendants,' said Niccolò. His eyes sought out one person among his guests. 'And now, before we adjourn to the palazzo for dancing, I ask you to join me in one final toast, to our most welcome guest, the beautiful Duchessa of Bellezza!'

There was some whispering among the diners at that; such a signal honour coming straight after the announcement of the Duke's new title must mean something of significance. Luciano gripped Sandro's shoulder tightly. But there was no further announcement; the Grand Duke had no secret understanding with Arianna. The most important guests were moving into the central courtyard of the Palazzo Ducale for dancing, and Arianna passed out of Luciano's view.

'Would you like me to stay here and wait for her to come out?' asked Sandro.

Luciano was touched. 'I think I'll stay myself, thanks,' he said.

'Then I'll keep watch with you,' said Sandro.

The servants were clearing the platform, so they went and sat on the edge of the scented fountain and soon found themselves partaking of leftovers from the feast – even Fratello got some fragments of goat liver that had fallen from the tables.

In the piazza outside Saint-Mary-among-the-Vines, carriage races were being held round the wooden obelisks but Sky was not there to see them.

In all the other piazzas of the city bonfires were lit in celebration of the new Grand Duke and of the weddings on the morrow. Silver coins were thrown into the crowds by Niccolò's men and the people cried, 'Long live Grand Duke Niccolò! Long live the di Chimici!'

*

In the courtyard of the Ducal palace, couples were forming for a dance. Arianna sought out her father for a quick conference but was forestalled by the Duke himself.

'Ah, your Grace,' he said, bowing rather carefully and unsteadily. 'Please do me the honour of being my partner.'

Arianna was quite startled till she realised he was just referring to the dancing. All round the first floor of the inner courtyard ran a loggia, to which the musicians had now removed. Torches flickered in iron brackets fixed just under this gallery and the players themselves had their music illuminated by many-branched candelabra. The air was heavy with the scent of lilies and high above the dancers the stars came out. It was the perfect night for romance.

The four couples who were to marry the next day clearly thought so and so, alarmingly, did the Grand Duke.

'I have a present for you,' he said to Arianna, as they executed the formal movements of the dance.

'Your Grace has already been more than generous,' she said.

The Duke took from his doublet a black velvet bag.

Goddess save us, thought Arianna, not during the dance with everyone looking. But it was not a ring. It was a silver sleeve-pendant in the shape of a mandola, encrusted with precious stones.

'It's lovely,' said Arianna. 'But –'

The Duke held up his hand. 'That is a word I do not care for,' he said. 'There are no conditions to accepting it – let us call it a gift from Giglia to Bellezza.'

'Then Bellezza thanks Giglia,' said Arianna.

'Here, let me pin it to your sleeve,' said the Grand Duke, and they stepped aside from the other dancers so that he could fix it to the left sleeve of her blue satin gown. When that was done, he signalled to a servant and led her into a small side chamber. She looked frantically around for Rodolfo but he was nowhere to be seen.

'There is something more,' said Niccolò.

A servant led into the room two beautiful spotted cats, the size of boarhounds. Each wore a silver collar of entwined fleur-de-lys with a long chain attached. Arianna couldn't help showing her pleasure; she loved animals.

'You may touch them, my Lady,' said the servant. 'They are quite tame.'

Arianna stroked their magnificent fur and admired their large brown eyes, which were underlined with black, like those of the most fashionable Giglian ladies. Her own eyes were shining and the Duke looked pleased.

'Are they really for me?' asked Arianna, like the girl she still was.

'Another token of Giglia's esteem,' said the Grand Duke. 'And a sign of the closer friendship I hope will develop between our two cities.'

Completely captivated by the glamorous cats, Arianna was quite heedless of the way this encounter was moving. Niccolò was beginning to feel jealous of the caresses lavished on the animals and ordered his man to take them away.

'You heard my announcement after dinner,' he said, showing no signs of wanting to rejoin the dance.

'Indeed,' said Arianna.

'And saw my crown?'

Arianna noticed that the crown was displayed on its velvet cushion on a small table in the chamber. Niccolò clicked his fingers and another servant brought in a second crown. It was smaller and more delicate but equally sparkling with gems.

'Can you guess who this is for?' he asked.

Arianna said nothing.

'I had it made for my Granduchessa,' said Niccolò, taking the slender silver crown from the servant. 'I should like to see if it would fit your Grace.'

Arianna protested. 'I couldn't wear it,' she said, adding, 'and I know not how to address you, my Lord, under your new title.'

'Niccolò is my name,' he said, lifting the small tiara of diamonds from her hair and putting the crown in its place. 'There! A perfect fit, I would say. It looks well on you, my dear – Arianna, as I would call you. Won't you honour me by wearing it always and being my Granduchessa?'

It has happened, thought Arianna, and it feels like one of those dreams when you try to run and your legs won't move and everything slows down. At that moment a battery of rockets went up and stars of purple and green and gold exploded above the courtyard, so she was excused from speech. Not as good as Father's, she thought, but they came just at the right moment.

The new Grand Duke looked annoyed. Arianna took off the crown and restored her tiara. 'Do let us return to the courtyard to see the fireworks,' she said, as calmly as she could manage.

'There is no need to answer straightaway,' said Niccolò, raising his voice over the sound of Reman candles. 'You can tell me tomorrow, after the weddings. I'd like to make an announcement in the evening. In fact, you do not have to tell me. Just wear the dress I sent you and I will know your answer is favourable.'

At that moment, all Arianna could think of was getting away from him. 'Yes,' she said. 'That would be acceptable.'

Then she hurried out of the room, leaving Niccolò to look at the pair of crowns. Among the crowd whose upturned faces were illuminated by the fireworks was Rodolfo, and Arianna almost ran to his side, she was so relieved to see him. He put his arm round her.

'He has asked me,' she said simply and pressed herself close to her father's side, suddenly shivering in the warm night air.

'I hoped I had let off the rockets in time to prevent it,' he said.

'They saved me from having to give him an answer now,' said Arianna. 'But the fireworks aren't yours, are they?'

'I was taking a professional interest,' said Rodolfo, with the ghost of a smile. 'Unfortunately for the firework master, I set off the display a little ahead of time.'

Arianna was exhausted and, as they made their excuses and farewells and slipped out into the night, her bodyguards closed up around her, carrying torches to light her back to the Embassy. The fireworks continued to explode over the Palazzo Ducale and Luciano, waiting in the square, saw that Arianna's face was bereft of all colour except what their light shed on her.

*

Next morning the Palazzo di Chimici on the Via Larga rang with the cries of ladies' personal maids calling for warm water, curling irons, hairpins and combs, as four brides were arrayed for their weddings. In the Piazza della Cattedrale a baldachino of blue velvet studded with silver stars was erected to provide a covered walkway to the cathedral's east door, and a red carpet decorated with silver fleur-de-lys was unrolled underneath it to reach right to the end of the piazza, where the princesses would descend from the Ducal carriage.

The cathedral itself was filled with lilies – and soldiers. Members of the Duke's private army lined the walls, and up in the gallery above the High Altar, a body of archers encircled the base of the dome. In the vestry the Pope was being helped into his silver brocade cope. All morning guests kept arriving and filled up the pews of the body of the building.

Rodolfo and Sulien were invited but not Dethridge, Giuditta, Luciano or Sky. And certainly not Nicholas or Georgia, who weren't even known to be in the city. So two Stravaganti would be inside the cathedral and the remaining six outside among the celebratory crowds. Silvia and Guido would also be among the observers. Many Giglians had been up since dawn establishing their viewpoints and bringing their own food and drink. Every window and balcony that overlooked the Piazza della Cattedrale was filled with spectators.

In the Embassy, Arianna was in a panic of indecision. The cursed di Chimici dress was laid over her bed alongside the equally elegant – and much more comfortable – green and blue brocade she had brought from Bellezza. She paced up and down in her lace shift, her chestnut hair loose and tangled about her shoulders, to the despair of Barbara the maid, who was trying to dress it.

Arianna had not slept the night before and was glad of a mask to wear to conceal the dark circles under her eyes – but was it to be the diamond-studded silver one sent by the Grand Duke to match the dress or the green and blue shot-silk one that went with her Bellezzan gown? Rodolfo had advised against wearing Niccolò's present, once he had heard about the proposal and this way of giving an answer. But Silvia thought not wearing it would provoke a dangerous diplomatic incident at the weddings.

'How can you be so unsure, my Lady?' asked Barbara, who was about Arianna's age and on very confidential terms with her mistress. 'I would love to have the chance to wear that diamond one.'

Arianna stopped her pacing. 'That's it!' she said. 'You shall, Barbara! Why not? My mother used a double often enough and you and I are much of a size. If I wear the dress, the Duke will take that as my consent to his proposal. But if I can later say it wasn't myself in it, I will have bought myself a little more time. Say you'll do it!'

*

The Grand Duke was visiting the young brides in the Via Larga. There was a flutter of screens and towels and dressing gowns when he put his head around their doors. But the Duke just laughed; he was in an excellent mood and all these pretty young relatives of his just served to remind him that he might have a young bride of his own soon. He had brought them their wedding chests, each cassone painted with the scene that was soon to take place at Saint-Mary-of-the-Lily, of the four couples entering the cathedral under the di Chimici baldachino.

And inside each were the thick ropes of pearls and rubies he had ordered as their wedding gifts. The princesses were thrilled with the jewels and held them up against their wedding dresses, kissing the Duke with their hair still loose about their shoulders. He left their rooms in high good humour.

*

The guests in the cathedral craned their necks to see the lovely Duchessa of Bellezza enter on the arm of her father and take a seat of honour near the High Altar. She was resplendent in a dress of silver so oversewn with pearls and amethysts that the brocade could scarcely be seen between them. A silver veil covered her hair and she was masked as usual, but that did not stop the Giglian crowd from declaring her the most lovely young woman they had ever seen.

The Grand Duke, sitting in his place of honour, saw her come in wearing the silver dress and smiled. He sat back and prepared to enjoy the weddings; it would not be long before there would be another, even more important one, in his family.

The Duchessa was attended by a maid in a plain but rich dark green gown, who was herself remarkably pretty, though she wore her hair twined in a double plait around her head and no jewels in it. The Pope and his attendants entered, taking their places at the altar with the Bishop of Giglia who was to assist at the ceremony.

Outside the cathedral the Ducal carriage had arrived at the edge of the square and a great flurry of dresses and veils was gradually emerging from it. Four nervous bridegrooms waited on the red carpet to receive their brides. First to extricate herself from the carriage was Caterina, in a dress of silver and white brocade. Then came the two Fortezzan princesses, the redhead in her green and gold and the brunette sister in her pure white satin scattered with white jewels.

Finally came Francesca in her Bellezzan white lace with her black hair full of pearls. Each groom thought his bride the loveliest, which was quite as it should be. They took hands under the baldachino and processed slowly into the cathedral, the three Giglian princes preceding their cousin Alfonso.

At various points around the cathedral the Stravaganti linked minds with the two of their

Brotherhood who sat inside it. Power flowed back and forth among them, creating a force-field which held the great building suspended in their protection. The wedding procession music came to an end and the Pope intoned the opening words of the Nuptial Mass.

Camillo Nucci, sitting with his parents and his brother and sisters looked up at the gallery and saw the archers, their bows already strung and arrows nocked. 'Not here, then,' he murmured to Filippo.

It took an hour and a half to marry the di Chimici nobles to their brides. By the end of the ceremony, the young Stravaganti were exhausted by their concentration on their task. As the bridal couples stepped out on to the red carpet and the crowd cheered and the silver trumpets blared and the bells rang from the slender campanile, they allowed their minds to relax.

And at that moment a dark rain cloud blotted out the sun.

Chapter 22

Blood on Silver

The Church of the Annunciation was a traditional place of pilgrimage for newly-weds. It sat at right angles to the orphanage, in the square where Luciano had fought so often with Gaetano. Three hundred years earlier a monk had painted on one of its walls a fresco of the Angel appearing to Mary with news of her expected child. At least, he had started to. The Virgin was depicted at a prayer desk and there was the body of a winged angel on the left, carrying a sheaf of lilies. But the unnamed monk didn't know how to paint the Angel's face.

The legend was that he had prayed for help and in the night the Angel himself had come and finished the picture. Over the generations a custom had developed for just-married couples to take bouquets of flowers to lay in front of the miraculous picture, so that the Angel would bless their union with children. If he did, they were fruitful and, if not, well, there was always the orphanage nearby, where there would be a supply of babies to fill the gap.

The di Chimici were no less superstitious than any other Giglian and the Duke was anxious to have grandchildren, so it had always been a part of the wedding plans that the four couples would go in procession to the Church of the Annunciation and lay their wedding flowers before the Angel. It was only a short walk from the cathedral.

The narrow street linking the two squares was lined with cheering citizens, and more hung out of the windows, greedily soaking up the sight of the fine dresses and jewels. Since the church was much smaller than the cathedral, only some selected guests followed the young people, the rest going on to the Palazzo Ducale, where another banquet was in preparation. The first fat drops of rain started to fall as the bridal procession left Saint-Mary-of-the-Lily.

Rodolfo and Arianna were among the procession, the Duchessa still accompanied by her maid. But it was a nightmare for her bodyguards in that narrow street. A thought-message from Rodolfo sent Sulien and the other Stravaganti running up the parallel side roads, so that they could reach the Piazza of the Annunciation before the wedding party. They were joined there by Guido Parola, sent on by Silvia, who was alarmed at seeing her daughter disappear up the narrow Via degli Innocenti. The square was full of spectators – all the people who couldn't get into the Piazza della Cattedrale had crowded in and were perching on the fountains and lining the arched loggias of the church and orphanage.

Among them was Enrico the spy. He hadn't been invited to the wedding, the blessing or any of the banquets and he was feeling a bit peeved about it. Hadn't he been involved in all the safety precautions and kept the Duke informed every step of the way? He could see now that the procession was virtually unguarded and he shrugged. Amateurs, he thought.

The red carpet that had been laid all the way from the cathedral to the church was darkening with the rain and the brides were jostled by the crowd as servants tried in vain to cover their heads against the worsening weather. The archers and soldiers from the Duke's private army streamed into the piazza, pushing spectators out of the way, aware that they had been held up by the crush on the way there.

Sulien and Dethridge tried to marshal the Stravaganti into a new circle of strength, but the rowdiness of the crowd, who had been drinking from their wineskins since early in the morning, and the confusion developing round the procession, made it hard for them to concentrate. Sulien could feel the younger ones slipping out of the link.

*

To the east of the city was a tributary of the river Argento. It had been filling all winter and the rains of earlier in the month had taken it to the top of its banks. As the di Chimici couples had left the cathedral in the city below, a thunderstorm had broken out and the tributary had overflowed. The Argento, already full to the brim, could not sustain any more water and broke its banks. Waves of turbulent river water spilled out over the city, hurrying through the centre.

*

The di Chimici newly-weds were glad to get into the safety and cover of the church. They filed along the aisle to the fresco in a chapel to the side of the High Altar, where they were greeted by the priest in charge. The Grand Duke, the Pope, the Duchessa and many other notables, including the Nucci, crowded into the church behind them. But there was not enough room for all the di Chimici armed men and many of them were stuck in the atrium outside the church's front door.

And that was when the Nucci struck. Camillo had been seething ever since he had seen the little dog snarl at Carlo in the Piazza Ducale. He had sat all through the long wedding service, watching the man he was now sure was his little brother's cold-blooded killer, while he smiled at his pretty bride, surrounded by all the pomp and splendour the di Chimici coffers could provide. And now he was being blessed by another priest with the promise of children. Where was the bride for Davide and the hope of his descendants? Locked in the grave.

As the couples walked slowly back up the aisle, accepting the greetings and congratulations of their friends, Camillo leapt in front of Prince Carlo and stabbed him in the chest.

The church erupted. Lucia snatched a candlestick from a side chapel and brought it down hard on

Camillo's head. Fabrizio, who had been just in front of them, swiftly slit the Nucci's throat. Filippo Nucci, howling with rage, hurled himself into the fray. And then all was a confusion of knives and swords.

More soldiers pushed into the little church. But Sky, Nicholas and Luciano, alerted by the cries from within, were before them. The Grand Duke and Fabrizio were both fighting with Filippo but he wasn't without supporters. There had been more Nucci and Nucci-sympathisers in the church than anyone had realised. The priest and the Pope and his chaplain were trying to herd the women up to the altar and away from the fighting, but Luciano arrived in time to see a young man strike at a slender figure in a pearl and silver dress.

Luciano ran through the crowd, his rapier drawn, but a red-haired figure had already tackled the assailant and was engaging him in fight. Before Luciano had reached them the Duchessa's maid had whipped out a merlino-dagger and stabbed her mistress's attacker.

Out of the corner of his eye the Grand Duke saw the famous silver dress, stained with bright blood, and saw its wearer collapse in the arms of two young men. He had time only to notice that one of them was the black-haired Bellezzan who had been Falco's friend, before he had to fight off the opponent who pressed him.

Fabrizio and Alfonso were also in single combat with Nucci. Nicholas snatched up a fallen blade and went to fight beside them. Guido Parola left the wounded woman with Luciano and ran to the side of Lucia, who was lying over the body of her dead husband, and dragged her with him back to the altar. She was hysterical. The clergymen were having the greatest difficulty keeping Caterina and Francesca out of the fray.

When the frantic Georgia at last managed to get into the church, ducking between blades, she saw a scene of chaos. She ran to Luciano, who was uninjured, but stricken, holding the body of Arianna in her fantastic dress.

'She isn't dead,' said the Duchessa's maid in a familiar voice and Georgia found herself looking into violet eyes. 'She mustn't be dead,' repeated the maid, who was not Barbara at all. Luciano continued to hold the inert body of the real Barbara, who was still breathing. Arianna in the maid's dress was holding a wicked-looking blade, still dripping with blood.

'We must get you both out of this madness,' said Georgia.

She could see Sky fighting beside Gaetano, the two of them assailed by three Nucci, and Gaetano went down even as she watched. And then Rodolfo was there, wielding a sword that she had assumed was merely ceremonial, defending Sky and wounding two of the attackers.

But gradually the Nucci riot was put down, as more and more di Chimici men got into the church. The remaining Nucci, including old Matteo, were held; they had suffered many casualties. Camillo was not the only one dead and Filippo was seriously injured. But the di Chimici had lost Prince Carlo and both Fabrizio and Gaetano were badly wounded. It looked as if three of the new brides could be widows before the day was out.

The Grand Duke strode round the church from body to body, blood welling from a gash on his forehead. Flowers lay trampled and stained underfoot. Sulien came and stood by his side, laying a hand on his shoulder.

'All my sons,' said the Duke wildly. 'They want to take all my sons!'

'Prince Carlo I cannot save,' said Sulien. 'But trust me with the others. Let me take them back to Saint-Mary-among-the-Vines and I will do all I can.'

But by the time litters had been made for the wounded and they had been carried out into the square, they found it inches deep in flood water – and rising rapidly. All the spectators had left, running back to save what they could of their own property. But such had been the noise and chaos within the church that no one had heard the shouts of warning outside.

'Quick,' said Giuditta, who had been out in the square with Dethridge and had organised everything. 'We must get the survivors to the upper floors of the orphanage.'

The door of the Ospedale was already open and the nuns waiting to help nurse the injured. One by one they were carried up – Fabrizio, Gaetano, the Duchessa and even, at the insistence of Beatrice, Filippo Nucci. Four soldiers carried the dead prince and laid him in a room on his own. The body of Camillo Nucci was tossed unceremoniously into a corner. The walking wounded followed, including Sky and the Grand Duke, but not before the latter had ordered any surviving Nucci to his dungeons, even the women.

The Pope brought the four brides up too, since there

was nowhere else safe to take them in time, above the level of the swirling waters. So, gradually, all the remaining guests at the most splendid weddings the city had ever seen found their way to the upper floors of the orphanage. Babies were crying, temporarily abandoned by their nurses, who were all needed to tend the wounded.

Giuditta corralled the shocked Georgia into tearing up bandages, cutting away clothes and fetching basins of warm water. Silvia materialised as if from nowhere, ashen when she heard that Arianna had been wounded.

'Where is she?' she asked, tight-lipped.

'Luciano is with her and her maid,' whispered Georgia. 'I think they swapped clothes.'

Silvia closed her eyes and Georgia thought for a moment she was going to laugh. But she just hugged her and said, 'Goddess be thanked!'

Sulien was going back and forth among the wounded. Fabrizio, Gaetano and Filippo were the most seriously injured and were unconscious. Sky had a slash on his arm that hurt like hell but he knew he had been lucky.

'Have you seen Nick?' he asked the friar.

'No,' said Sulien. 'Is he not among the uninjured?'

Duke Alfonso of Volana, though he had fought bravely, had suffered no hurt and had been put in charge of the women and of the other unwounded who had been taken up to the top floor.

'I'll go and look,' volunteered Sky. 'How's Gaetano?'

Sulien looked worried. 'They are all badly hurt. I don't know how I'm to help them if I can't get back to my pharmacy.'

'How bad do you think the flood will get?' asked Sky. 'When will we be able to leave here?'

'Not today,' said Sulien. 'We have had many such floods in the city before. Some are worse than others – usually the spring ones are less severe than the autumn ones. But even they can rise to six feet or more.'

Sky knew that would mean he and Nicholas couldn't stravagate back from the friary but he decided not to worry about it yet. He had more pressing worries, such as where Nicholas was.

*

In the Piazza Ducale the water had risen above the level of the loggia steps and invaded the banqueting platform. Servants had carried all they could into the palazzo as soon as the flood hit the square, and wedding guests who had not been invited to the Annunciation blessing had taken shelter inside the building, swarming up the great staircases to the upper floors. They now looked down over the wreckage of the feast and the shining surface of the waters, where only the day before young nobles had jousted in the sun.

Some startled guests came face to face with two large spotted cats who had been brought up to the roof by their handler. But the beasts were well-behaved and chained to a pillar by their silver collars. They shared a side of meat that the cooks had provided.

The soldiers who had been entrusted with the Nucci had not been able to march them back to the palazzo, whose dungeons were anyway flooded. The squad had broken up into a second riot as soldiers and prisoners scrambled for their lives out of the way of the incoming waters. Matteo and Graziella ran with their daughters and remaining supporters to a nearby tower of the Salvini family, who were sympathetic to their faction. They hammered on the doors for entrance, the water now up to their waists. Ladders were let down from an upper floor and they climbed up, the women hindered by their sodden wedding finery. But at last they were all safe, at least until the waters went down, and could give way to their grief for Camillo and their fears for the only remaining Nucci son.

*

Arianna tended Barbara herself, undoing the fastenings on the dress that had betrayed her into danger. Luciano refused to leave them, even though the maid was now in her shift and her white breast exposed, with an ugly bleeding gash in it.

'It was my fault she got hurt, Luciano,' sobbed Arianna. 'I didn't mean anyone but the Duke to think she was me. He said if I wore the dress, he'd know my answer to his proposal.'

'So he did ask you, then?' said Luciano, thinking how odd it was to be talking about this while people lay dying and the waters swirled through the city.

'You knew he was going to?'

Luciano nodded.

'It was last night, during the dance. He put the vile crown on my head.' She shuddered. 'And now Barbara may die because I was too much of a coward to say no straightaway.'

'Not if I can help it,' said Sulien, coming to the girl's bed. He examined the wound carefully and asked one of the nuns to bring him the remedies he needed. 'It's not too deep,' he said. 'A little lower and the blade would have pierced her heart. The attacker cannot have had a clear aim.'

'Parola foiled him,' said Luciano. 'But Arianna finished him off.'

Arianna was shaking. Her mother ran to her and caught her in her arms. 'You are all right?' she asked.

Arianna nodded. 'As you see,' she said, 'Barbara took the blow meant for me.'

'Quickly,' said Silvia. 'Get into that wretched dress and lay the maid's one across the bed.'

'Why?' asked Arianna.

'Because we don't know who attacked you and why,' said Silvia.

'It was one of the Nucci,' said Luciano. 'I saw him.'

'And you know a Nucci sympathiser from a di Chimici agent?' asked Silvia. 'The Grand Duke must have taken your wearing the dress as assent, Arianna. Let him go on thinking that for a while.'

Silvia helped Arianna out of the plain green gown and into the Grand Duke's gift. Her daughter hated it even more now that it was slashed by a dagger and stained with blood.

'Don't just stand there,' Silvia said to Luciano, who was trying to keep up with the turn of events. 'Get Arianna's hair out of those plaits, while I try and turn Barbara back into a maid.'

Arianna's hair tumbled down as Luciano uncoiled and released the braids. He passed her the silver mask and veil while Silvia undid the elaborate coiffure Arianna and Barbara had constructed together a few hours earlier. While she gently teased out the curls of it, Barbara revived. She looked at Silvia out of cloudy eyes.

'Brave girl,' said Silvia. 'You have saved the Duchessa's life.'

'And Parola saved hers,' said Luciano. 'He deflected the blade.'

'Did he now?' asked Silvia, interested. 'What a remarkable young man he is. Sulien, what can you do for the girl?'

Brother Sulien was bathing the wound with an infusion of herbs brought by the nun.

'This will help,' he said. 'But I'll need to sew the wound together. It will hurt, so I must give her a soporific. But I am greatly hampered by not being able to fetch things from my pharmacy.'

'I'll go,' said Luciano. 'Make me a list.'

'It's too dangerous,' said Arianna. 'The flood waters are still rising. How will you get there?'

'Don't worry – I'll find a way,' said Luciano.

*

Georgia ran into Sky on the stairs up to the higher floor of the Ospedale.

'Thank God,' she said. 'You're all right?'

'I've got a slash in my arm,' he said. 'But not too bad. Did you see what happened to the others?'

Georgia nodded. She didn't want to think about the bodies which she had seen carried out of the church.

'How's Nick?' she asked instead.

'I'm looking for him,' said Sky. 'I'm hoping he's upstairs with the uninjured people.'

They clung together for a moment on the stairs.

'It was so horrible,' said Georgia. 'I don't think I'll ever be able to forget it – the blood and the smell.'

'Me neither,' said Sky, patting her back awkwardly. He thought again how glad he was that Alice had decided not to return to Giglia. It hadn't been exciting and glamorous when the wedding attack came. It had been the most horrible quarter of an hour of his life. And in the end the Stravaganti had been powerless to stop it.

'Do you know if Gaetano is going to be OK?' asked Georgia.

'No,' said Sky. 'I reckon if anyone can save him, Sulien will. But he's cut off from his medicines.'

They walked up to the top floor, where Duke Alfonso had organised some fortified wine for the women and the other people who had not been hurt. His bride, Bianca, clung to his arm, terrified. He was the only uninjured groom and she could not believe that he had survived unscathed. His mother fussed over all the girls, especially her own daughter, Caterina, whose new husband lay badly hurt on the floor below.

Lucia, who had fought so bravely to save Carlo, though in vain, sat shocked and cold on the far side of the room. There was no sign of her parents, Jacopo and Carolina. Guido Parola had put his cloak over Lucia's shoulders and was trying to get her to sip the wine. The Pope, revived by the strong drink, turned to Alfonso.

'We must get them warm. They are all soaked and

shocked. Where are all the nuns?'

'Tending to the wounded, I expect,' said Alfonso. 'Perhaps Cousin Beatrice could help?'

'I'll find her,' said Sky. 'I know what she looks like.'

'Well, I have no idea who you are,' said the Pope. 'But if you can find my niece, I'll be grateful.'

'Have you seen a young Dominican friar anywhere?' asked Georgia. 'He was fighting in the church and we don't know if he's all right.'

But no one had seen Nicholas.

They found Beatrice with the Duke, who was sitting, dazed, while she bound his head. Sky ducked out of Niccolò's view and Georgia delivered the message.

'I'll come,' said Beatrice. 'Will you be all right if I leave you, Father?'

'I shall go to my sons,' he said, his voice slurred, as if from strong drink.

'That's probably where Nick is,' said Georgia to Sky. 'With Gaetano.'

They followed the Duke at a distance to a separate cell. Gaetano and Fabrizio lay very still on beds next to each other. Sulien stood over them with a grave face. But there was no sign of Nicholas. They looked into the room next door and Georgia could not suppress a cry. There was just one bed in this cell and on it lay the body of Prince Carlo, his wedding finery soaked in blood. Curled up between the bed and the wall, looking like a bundle of black and white rags, lay Nicholas.

*

Enrico's first instinct when the flood waters had entered the square was to climb up to the top of the orphanage. From the roof he had seen bodies and wounded people carried out of the church and he knew that everything had gone horribly wrong, even though he couldn't tell who had been hurt. His first thought was that he might be held to blame – his intelligence hadn't helped to prevent a slaughter. But he didn't even know if the Grand Duke had survived; he waited alone on the roof for some time before deciding he would have to find out.

Cautiously he descended the stairs, looking into a room which he at first thought was full of nuns. But they had curled hair and their pale faces still bore rouge and they wore jewels at their throats. It was the princesses, who now looked like the widows they might be, for all Enrico knew, clad in black robes brought for them by the nuns. Their sumptuous wedding dresses lay crumpled and sodden on the floor, including one that had once been of gleaming white lace. It reminded Enrico of the one his Giuliana had ordered for their wedding.

His eye was drawn to the little red-headed princess; she was being comforted by a similar-looking tall young man, who must be some relative. The only prince in sight was Alfonso, who seemed to be all right. Enrico sighed with relief; there was one di Chimici bridegroom left standing at least. There was no sign of the Grand Duke.

He went down another flight, to the first floor. There, the large dormitory, usually full of babies and children, had been cleared and the wounded laid on their beds. Enrico couldn't see any of the di Chimici princes. Sulien was busy among the wounded. A flash of silver suddenly caught the Eel's eye. He moved slowly into the room.

A screen was partially obscuring the bed beside which the Duchessa sat and she was surrounded by bodyguards, but Enrico could see that, although the silver and gems of the dress she was wearing were encrusted with blood, the Duchessa herself did not seem hurt. She was holding the hand of her maid, who clearly *was* wounded. The squeamish spy stuffed his fist in his mouth when he saw the mutilated breast. There was another, older woman, sitting by the bed, whom he scarcely registered. But his mind was racing. Why would the maid be hurt and the Duchessa be unharmed? And why was the Duke's gift-dress so stained if no one had attacked the Duchessa?

*

Luciano didn't leave Arianna until Silvia had rounded up the remnants of her bodyguard and posted them round the bed where her daughter sat, holding her servant's hand. Then he went to look out of the window and was shocked by what he saw. The piazza where he had so often fenced with Gaetano was a sheet of water. The tops of the two fountains stuck up out of it and gave him some idea how deep the flood was. About five feet, he calculated, and probably still getting deeper.

The tops of the buildings were all full of people waving and shouting in a kind of parody of the way they had behaved when the wedding procession entered the square. Luciano couldn't believe how much had changed in such a short time. But, in spite of his promise to Sulien, he didn't see how he was to get to the friary, collect medicine and bring it back here.

He went out on to the landing and met Georgia and Sky, with Nicholas slung between them like a sack of potatoes.

'What is it?' he asked. 'Is he badly hurt?'

'I don't think so,' said Sky, lowering the boy to the floor and wincing as his arm took the weight. 'He was with Carlo.'

'We think it's shock,' said Georgia. She was shaking herself. Suppose the Duke had gone next door to see his dead son and found two of them!

'I'll fetch Sulien,' said Luciano.

The friar was busy. He had left the two princes for the moment, having their wounds bathed by nuns, and was attending to Filippo Nucci, but he came straightaway when Luciano told him about Nicholas. He lifted the boy and took him over to the stairs, where he examined him for signs of injury.

'He has a wound much like yours, Sky,' he said. 'But I think his mind has closed down. He has seen one brother killed and two others wounded. He needs rest and medicine.'

'I'm going to the pharmacy,' said Luciano. 'Have you got that list?'

As Sulien gave him a scrap of parchment, Georgia asked, 'How are you going to get there?'

'Swim, I suppose,' said Luciano, trying to smile.

'Don't be daft,' said Sky. 'We need to find some kind of a boat.'

'We?' asked Luciano. 'Are you coming too?'

'Of course he is,' said Georgia. 'It was probably what he was sent here to do.'

'Oh my God,' said Sky. 'I'm hallucinating.'

He pointed outside the window and they all saw the black wings of the flying horse, with a brightly dressed Manoush on her back.

Chapter 23

Drowned City

Sandro hadn't been at the wedding or the blessing either. He had drifted back to the Piazza Ducale, pleased that there hadn't been any attack and hoping to find some more scraps for him and his dog when the next feast started. He was hanging around the platform when the rain began and minutes later the flood water came swirling into the square.

He ran, then, up the steps of the loggia and sat at the top, hugging the scared Fratello and sheltering from the rain. He didn't think that it would last for long. Sandro had heard a lot about floods in Giglia but hadn't seen one in his short life. The little dog was trembling but Sandro himself was not frightened.

At least not then. The water was only inches deep. But then he saw wedding guests hurrying into the palazzo and the water still rose. And later, citizens came splashing through the piazza shouting about an attack. They hadn't stayed to hear what had happened in the Church of the Annunciation but rumour spread through the city: all the di Chimici had been assassinated; the Grand Duke was dead, stabbed by the Duchessa of Bellezza with his own sword.

Sandro thought he would let the news settle down like the flood water and leave a silt of truth he could sift through later. But the water had now reached the top of the steps and Sandro couldn't swim. He tucked Fratello under his arm and began to climb on to the back of a lion sculpted by one of Giuditta Miele's ancestors.

*

Georgia ran up to the roof with Sky and Luciano. Never had she been so glad to see anyone as Raffaella and the flying horse. It had been nagging at the back of her mind that she didn't know how she would get back to Remora by nightfall if she couldn't get to Merla on the other side of the river. But she had felt bad even for thinking about it when she didn't know if Gaetano would survive his injuries.

Sky stood gazing at the winged horse in wonder. In spite of everything he had been told about Merla, the reality of her was so much more overpowering than any description.

Rafaella dismounted.

'Aurelio sent me,' she said. 'He seemed to know where you would be.'

'Can you help us?' asked Georgia. 'We need to get

medicine from Saint-Mary-among-the-Vines. Is the whole city flooded?'

'Certainly between there and here,' said Rafaella. 'But I can take Merla up again and look for a boat.'

'Do you think she'd carry both of us?' asked Georgia. 'Perhaps I could bring one back?'

No one liked the idea but Georgia persuaded them on the grounds that she was the lightest and the best rider.

'It's not the riding I'm worried about,' said Sky. 'It's the dropping into a boat.'

He and Luciano watched the two young women take off on the flying horse.

'She's got guts, all right,' said Luciano.

From the air the city looked like a dreamscape: only the biggest buildings seemed the same. But the piazzas were lakes and the streets canals; fountains and statues and pillars poked up above the water like drowning people waving desperately for help. The river, no longer defined by its banks, had spread like a stain into every corner of the city.

But in the end Georgia did not have to be dropped into a boat. Raffaella landed Merla on the Ponte Nuovo. The horse didn't like it: it was narrow and dangerous for her wings and the water rose over her hoofs. But it was only inches deep here and Georgia was able to splash through it down to where boats bobbed on the surface of the flood, tugging at their painters tied far below the water. Raffaella cut the rope of one with a dagger from her belt, as far under the surface as she could reach.

'I'll take Merla back to the orphanage roof,' she said. 'You'll still need her to get back to Remora tonight.'

Georgia nodded. She was struggling with the boat. She had never rowed one before, except once on the Serpentine in Hyde Park, and everything was wet. Her dress and hair were soaked, the bottom of the boat slopped with rainwater and the oars were slippery and very heavy. A cold wind lashed the flooded river into waves and she couldn't at first see where she was going for her wet hair whipping into her face. And she hadn't quite got the hang of travelling backwards and was scared of bumping into hazards she couldn't see.

But gradually she managed to steer the boat up between the pillars of the square where the Guild offices were. The city was eerily quiet and she shivered as she rowed awkwardly into the Piazza Ducale. It was so weird to think her boat was sliding forwards nearly her own height above yesterday's tournament lists. The last thing she expected was to hear her name shouted.

It was Sandro, sitting on a stone lion with his little dog clutched in his arms. Cursing under her breath at this new complication, Georgia tied the boat to the lion's leg and coaxed him down into it. It was doubtful whether Sandro or the dog was more alarmed by the rocking motion of the boat as they got into it. But Sandro's teeth were chattering and he had been very frightened, alone with no prospect of the water withdrawing.

'I'll take you to the orphanage,' said Georgia. 'That's where all the others are.'

'What happened?' asked Sandro, trying to warm the dog inside his jerkin.

'Where do I begin?' asked Georgia, casting off again. 'Do you know how to row?'

'I can try,' said Sandro.

Georgia looked at his skinny arms and undernourished frame.

'No, it's OK. I can manage till I get there. But then I'm leaving it to Luciano and Sky.'

'Brother Tino?' asked Sandro. 'What are they going to do?'

'They're going to the friary to fetch medicine for Brother Sulien,' said Georgia. 'You know the Nucci attacked at the church?'

'I heard people shouting something,' said Sandro. 'But I was stuck on the loggia and couldn't find out anything.'

'Lots of people have been killed or hurt,' said Georgia. 'Gaetano and his oldest brother are seriously injured and Prince Carlo is dead.'

Sandro jumped so violently it rocked the boat. 'I'm not sorry,' he said. 'He was a murderer.'

'But Gaetano isn't,' said Georgia. 'And we must do what we can to save him.'

They had reached the drowned Piazza of the Annunciation. Sandro helped Georgia navigate past the fountains and up to the orphanage. The front door was still open and the ground floor flooded in spite of the steps leading up to it. They had to pull the oars in while the boat slipped through the door, but once inside they were able to tie it up to the stone banister of the staircase. Fratello leapt out of the boat, shaking himself, and ran gratefully up the steps, looking back to check that Sandro was following.

Sky was amazed to see the little spy, particularly when he told him how he had got there. Georgia soon appeared, looking very bedraggled. Sulien was relieved to see her but still anxious to get what he needed for his patients.

'I'd go myself,' he said. 'But I am needed here. You're sure that you and Luciano will manage, Sky?'

Sky's arm had stiffened up and was really hurting. He didn't think he'd be much use at rowing but he knew where to find most things in the pharmacy. And Luciano was the least afraid of water of any of them; he was a first-class swimmer and lived in a city where the streets were canals.

'Take this key,' said Sulien. 'The most important thing I need, and the one I can't replace quickly, is in a locked cupboard in my cell. The jar says "argentum potabile" and it's the only thing that will save the young princes.'

'Right,' said Sky, more confidently than he felt. He put the key in his pocket.

'Let me come too,' said Sandro. 'I'm not heavy and I know where everything is.'

Sulien agreed. 'Take him,' he said. 'He might be very useful.'

'Only look after my dog,' said Sandro. 'He won't want to get back in that boat.'

'I'll look after him,' said Georgia, taking the sodden length of string round Fratello's neck. She suddenly felt exhausted, but there was plenty of work left to do in the orphanage and Giuditta needed her.

The boys ran down the staircase to the drowned hall. Luciano took the oars and Sky sat at the other end, with Sandro crouched damply in the bottom of the boat.

They glided out into the piazza as Luciano struck out west from the orphanage, trying to find a navigable street that would take them south to the Dominican church. Saint-Mary-among-the-Vines lay even closer to the river and had been one of the first areas to be flooded. When they reached the piazza in front of it, they could see just the tops of the wooden obelisks sticking up through the water.

'The cloisters will be flooded,' said Sky, 'and the pharmacy will be under at least five feet of water. What are we going to do?'

'We've got to try,' said Luciano. He manoeuvred the little boat through an archway beside the black and white church and steered right into the Lesser Cloister.

The arched cloister was underwater and Sky realised that all the plants and vegetables would be ruined. They had to take the boat across to the far corner of the cloister and steer it along a corridor, with their heads almost grazing the ceiling. But then they were through and out into the Great Cloister where the pharmacy and Sulien's cell were. Sandro cried out when he saw the devastation caused by the water.

The door from the cloister to the laboratory had been open when the flood came. Alembics and crucibles floated about, and bottles and jars had been smashed by the force of the water pouring in.

'This is hopeless,' said Luciano after a few minutes' fruitless search. 'There's nothing in one piece from his list.'

'How about the stuff in his cell?' asked Sky. 'The medicine in the locked cupboard might be OK.'

But here was a problem: the door between the laboratory and Sulien's cell was closed, with a weight of water holding it shut. They manoeuvred the boat back out into the cloister.

'Look,' said Sandro. 'There's a skylight I could climb through.'

It was true. There was a small, glazed fanlight that led into Sulien's cell, and neither of the other two would have been able to wriggle through it. Luciano smashed the glass with an oar and Sandro took the key from Sky. They watched as he climbed in, then heard a splash and a cry as he landed on the other side.

'Oh God, don't tell me he can't swim!' said Luciano.

*

Enrico flitted from room to room in the orphanage. He had seen the body of Prince Carlo and the near-corpses of the other two princes. But something else was niggling at the back of his mind and preventing him from concentrating on the present scene. Something to do with the Duchessa and her maid.

He was jolted out of his trance by the Princess Beatrice.

'There you are!' she said, for once pleased to see him. 'I need you to help me.'

Beatrice, Giuditta and Georgia had formed a sort of nursing team with the nuns, carrying out instructions from Sulien and Dethridge. There were all the orphans to look after as well as the injured and the roomful of traumatised princesses. The nuns were also in a great flutter at having the Pope himself under their roof, not to mention the Grand Duke of Tuschia. They kept

Enrico busy running up and down stairs on errands. It was not long before he found himself taking wine to his master, and he didn't know how he would be received.

But Niccolò did not hold Enrico responsible for the attack; he knew very well whom to blame. Had he not seen with his own eyes Camillo Nucci stab his second son? Enrico recognised the feverish look in his master's eyes; the Duke had been the same when young Falco was dying. Now the only thing consoling him for Carlo's death was the thought of the revenge he would take on the Nucci. It didn't seem the right moment for the Eel to tell his master that the young Duchessa hadn't been wearing the expensive dress he had given her; he would try to let him know later that it was the maid who had been hurt. But perhaps he wouldn't mention that she had been impersonating the Duchessa at the time. Enrico had a feeling that information would make the Grand Duke very angry, even though he was too distracted at the moment to think of courtship.

*

Sandro surfaced, spluttering. He was terribly afraid. The water was cold and his feet couldn't touch the bottom. He flung out an arm and found himself clutching the top of the wooden crucifix on the wall. He held on to it as to a lifebelt; he knew what it was – the suffering man, like the one who hung in the church. The princes were suffering too and perhaps he, Sandro, could save them. He waited, floating on the top of the water, anchored only by his hand on the cross, getting his bearings in the little room.

A face looked anxiously through the skylight. Sandro waved with his free hand and then saw the cupboard. It was a triangular wooden one high up in one corner. It had a keyhole and a wooden knob in the door. Sandro launched himself across the room, sank again, resurfaced and grabbed at the knob. It surprised him how little purchase you needed on a fixed point in order to stay afloat. He had the key clutched in his hand. The water came up nearly to the keyhole but he was able to unlock it and wrench the door open.

The shelves inside were full of packets and bottles, Sulien's most precious remedies. 'Ar-gen-tum pot-a-bil-e,' Sandro spelt out from the label on one bottle; he had no idea what it meant.

'He's got it,' said Sky outside the fanlight.

Sandro thrust the hand with the bottle in it as far towards the little window as he could. He pushed himself as far away from the cupboard as he could manage without letting go of the door. There was still a gap of about six inches. Sky reached his arm through, cutting it on the broken glass.

Suddenly Sandro thought, It doesn't matter if I drown. What matters is getting Sulien's medicine to the people who need it.

He thrust away from the cupboard. Sky grabbed the bottle as the boy sank.

*

The rain had stopped. The water in the city was no longer rising, though it would be a while before it began to sink. The friars at Saint-Mary-among-the-Vines had taken shelter on the upper floors. Brother Tullio looked out over the drowned cloister, shaking his head. How was he to feed the brothers with all his produce underwater? He just hoped something had been saved at the new farm across the river, which was on slightly higher land.

Tullio blinked. There was a boat in the cloister, rocking dangerously just under a broken window. His first thought was looters, then he saw that although the two young men in it appeared to be nobles of the city, one of them was young Brother Tino.

He watched while they poked an oar through the window and a bedraggled, wretched figure appeared clutching the end of it. It was clearly a rescue mission, not a burglary.

*

Sandro had panicked when he went down and found himself on the floor of Sulien's cell. But the water was not far above his head. He opened his eyes and saw he was just by the wooden chest in which Sulien kept robes. He managed to get one foot up on it and push his head above the water, shaking his hair out of his eyes. And there was the oar. Sky pulled him towards the fanlight, nearly capsizing the rowboat in the attempt. But once Sandro had reached the window frame, he wriggled through and collapsed in a wet and shivering heap on the floor of the boat.

'Tino! Brother Tino!' shouted a voice from above them. Brother Tullio stood waving from a window on the upper floor. Luciano rowed over until they were underneath it.

'Where have you come from?' said Tullio.

'From Brother Sulien,' explained Sky. 'There has been a terrible fight at the blessing ceremony and there are people badly injured. He sent us for medicines but everything is ruined in the pharmacy and the laboratory. We've only got what Sandro managed to find in his cell.'

Brother Tullio peered down. 'Is that drowned rat young Sandro?' he asked. 'What does Sulien want?' he continued. 'The brothers brought everything up to the top floors that we could salvage.'

It wasn't long before a basket full of medicines was lowered to the boat and the boys were able to make the voyage back. Sky put the precious bottle in the basket with the other remedies and just then realised how lucky they were to have it.

'You read the label,' he said to Sandro and the street-boy grinned, trying not to let his teeth chatter.

*

It was beginning to get dark, and Georgia was wondering how much longer she dare stay in Giglia. But she didn't think she should leave with Nicholas still unconscious. How was he going to get back to his own world? Sky and Luciano had brought back the medicines, and a delirious Fratello had hurled himself at the filthy wet bundle which was Sandro. Sulien was even now administering his precious 'Drinking Silver' to the most seriously injured patients. There was very little of it because it was so costly and time-consuming to make; it was a secret process, taking months. He gave five drops each to Fabrizio and Gaetano and then made his way to where Filippo Nucci lay moaning and feverish.

'I forbid you to give it to that wretch,' said the Grand Duke.

But Sulien took no notice and measured out a dose for Giuditta to administer to the young man. Princess Beatrice herself restrained her father's hand or he might have attacked the friar in his grief.

'Very well,' he said, struggling to collect himself. 'Let him live. There will be one more Nucci for me to hang.'

Sulien went next to the Mother Superior's room, where he had hidden Nicholas, and gave him a drop of the valuable liquid. The boy's eyelids fluttered and Sulien breathed a sigh of relief. But he could not rest. Now that his medicines had arrived, he moved among the patients, stitching wounds and giving soporifics to ease pain.

By the time Georgia climbed wearily up to the roof, everyone who needed treatment had received some. But there were a lot of cold, wet and exhausted people for whom there was no food; all the stores had been on the ground floor and only a few bottles of wine were still usable. Merla was waiting for her, her wings drooping. She didn't like the water. Raffaella sat patiently with her, soothing the horse with one of her strange-sounding songs.

The two of them lifted off on Merla as she made her run off the roof, relieved to be heading back out of Giglia and towards dry ground.

*

It took all Sky's powers of persuasion to get Nicholas to leave with him. As soon as he was awake, the boy was determined to stay and see his brothers recover.

'Look,' said Sky. 'It's already getting dark outside and we're going to have to leave from here rather than the friary. Who knows if we'll even arrive back in the right place? And what do you think it'll do to Vicky if she finds you unconscious in the morning? Don't you care about your new family at all?'

'I won't be able to go to sleep anyway,' said Nicholas. 'Not with Gaetano and Fabrizio like that.'

'You can't be with them,' said Sky. 'You'd be recognised by your father or sister. And you can come back tomorrow.'

'I'll give you both something to help you sleep,' said Sulien. 'You do have your talismans with you? All you have to do is think of your home in the other world. And I promise you I shall do everything in my power to keep your brothers alive until you return.'

'What on earth have you done to your arm?' said Rosalind when she went to wake Sky up. She thought he had just overslept but of course he had stravagated back late. Sky was so relieved to find himself in his own bed that it took him a few minutes to register what she meant about his arm. There was a very un-modern looking bandage round it and he could see the flesh round it was swollen.

'I cut it fencing,' he said, which was the best he could manage.

'Well, why didn't you say something last night?'

demanded his mother. 'Let me see if it needs stitches. We must get you to the hospital if it does.'

'It's been stitched, Mum. Don't fuss,' said Sky. He felt awful – deathly tired and his arm was throbbing – but he had to find out what was going on at Nicholas's and somehow get through a day at school.

'What do you mean?' asked Rosalind. 'When did you go to the hospital?'

He was saved any more questions by the phone ringing. He sat up groggily, nursing his arm. Remedy came and head-butted him. Sky felt like bursting into tears – delayed shock, he supposed. He was just beginning to realise that he could have been killed in Talia, stabbed like Carlo. He couldn't get the image of the dead prince out of his mind.

'Well, that's that!' said Rosalind from the doorway. 'No more fencing for you! That was Vicky Mulholland on the phone. She says that Nick's been injured too and won't tell her how it happened. You're both going to have the day off and we're taking you to the doctor. I want those stitches looked at – Nick told Vicky he'd had some as well.'

She let him have breakfast first though, and he was ravenous. Sky managed to ring Alice on her mobile.

'How was the wedding?' she asked.

'Awful,' he whispered. 'We're all right, but Nick and I were both wounded and his brother Carlo was killed.'

'Wounded?' gasped Alice. 'Are you OK? What happened?'

'I'm OK but Mum's suspicious. Other people were hurt too – I can't say any more now. Mum and Vicky are taking Nick and me to the doctor. Get Georgia to tell you everything and I'll see you after school.'

Silvia looked out of the orphanage window over the dark city. She was no longer worried about Arianna; even Barbara was sleeping peacefully, her wound having been stitched. But it was going to be a long night, with no lights in the city and no warmth in the orphanage and very little food. And then she blinked, unable to believe what her eyes were seeing.

Prince Jacopo was standing in the prow of a large boat, lit with torches and laden with supplies. At the other end stood a tall dark figure holding aloft a glowing red stone.

'Rodolfo!' said Silvia and ran down to meet him.

The barge was too big to get in through the main door, so the little rowboat found by Georgia was used to ferry people and provisions into the orphanage in stages. Jacopo left his men to unload and demanded to be taken to his daughters. Lucia flung herself into his arms and wept properly for the first time. It shocked Jacopo to see her and Bianca dressed as nuns, reminding him of his sisters. He knew that Lucia's bridegroom was dead but he was relieved to see Alfonso alive and looking after Bianca.

'Where are the other princesses?' he asked Beatrice.

'With their husbands,' she answered. 'Oh, Uncle, we don't know if Fabrizio and Gaetano will last the night.'

'We have brought food and drink and dry clothes and blankets,' he said. 'The Regent of Bellezza has been helping. You must all take heart. Things will look better in the morning.'

'Not for me,' said Lucia. 'Nothing will ever be better again.'

Rodolfo went from room to room, placing his firestone in hearths and warming whole wards of patients. He found Arianna sleeping fitfully on the floor beside Barbara's bed and covered her with a warm blanket. Her bodyguards were still on duty around the screen. All those who were awake were given food and wine. Sulien was still working, his face looking grey with fatigue in the candlelight. The Grand Duke and his daughters-in-law kept vigil over the unconscious princes.

Rodolfo and Silvia made Sulien sit down and have something to eat. Dethridge, Giuditta and Luciano joined them.

'You have done all you can tonight,' said Rodolfo.

'And yet we failed,' said Sulien. 'Eight Stravaganti and we could not stop the slaughter.'

'Perhaps it would have been worse without us,' said Giuditta.

'And you and Doctor Dethridge were marvellous about getting this place turned into a hospital,' said Silvia.

'Thatte was just physicke,' said Dethridge. 'Brothire Sulian is righte. Wee sholde have bene able to forestalle the murthers.' He cast his cloak over his head.

'Do not despair, old friend,' said Rodolfo. 'There is work yet to do and other deaths we may prevent. The Duke will need restraining even if both his remaining sons survive.'

Doctor Kennedy was completely perplexed by the two sword wounds.

'They have both been expertly stitched but with very out-of-date materials. Where was this done?'

Neither Sky nor Nicholas would answer.

'I doubt if the wounds were even sterile,' she said, frowning. 'Were you given anti-tetanus?'

The boys shook their heads and were both given shots by the nurse. Doctor Kennedy wrote out prescriptions for antibiotics and strong painkillers.

'Just to be on the safe side,' she said. 'But it would cause more trauma than it's worth to restitch the wounds. Whoever was responsible for this bit of fancy embroidery knew what he was doing.'

The boys would say nothing more than that they had both been hurt fencing, however much the women nagged them. Sky couldn't explain the scratches on his other arm, from the broken glass, and Nick had the beginnings of a black eye.

Vicky said she was going to phone the school and complain to Mr Lovegrove but Nicholas stopped her.

'We weren't in school,' he said. 'It was an accident.'

Even that cost him a lot, letting Vicky and Rosalind think that they had done this to each other when all their injuries were the fault of the Nucci. The two women didn't know what to make of it, but it seemed clear to them that there was no hard feeling between Sky and Nicholas and that it was safe to let them be together. The two boys spent the rest of the day at the

Mulhollands' house. Their foils were taken from them and locked in a cupboard, though Vicky was surprised to find them unstained and still bated.

Chapter 24

God's Puppy

Dawn broke in Giglia over a dismal scene. The flood waters had retreated and the fine city was filled with evil-smelling sludge and mud. For the new Grand Duke, however, it was a welcome sight. He didn't want to sit by his ailing sons' beds any more; he had lived through that experience once before. He had a city to organise. And Enrico was at hand to help him.

Beatrice was left in charge of the sick and injured at the orphanage while her father strode about giving orders, marshalling his army to collect sodden debris into heaps that could be dried out in the sun and then fired. Then every bucket and broom in Giglia was commandeered to bring well water and wash the squares and streets. The bodies that had been left in the Church of the Annunciation were brought out –

those of the Nucci faction to be hung by the heels on display in the Piazza Ducale, those loyal to the di Chimici washed and clothed in silk and laid in the chapel of the palazzo in the Via Larga. And first among them Prince Carlo.

The Pope was dispatched to purify the church itself from the bloodshed within, but not before he had gone to his Residence for a change of clothes and a large breakfast.

Damage to houses was less than it would have been in an English city; very few people had carpets or soft furnishings on the ground floor. And the Talian sun, which had so often been absent of late, was now back in full strength, shining into doors and windows, dispelling all mustiness from the wet floors and walls. The whole city seemed to steam in the morning heat.

Guido Parola had been sent by Silvia to the Bellezzan Embassy, for the State carriage, and he came back to the orphanage to collect Arianna and the wounded Barbara. Silvia went with them and Luciano rode on top with Parola. Gradually the nuns were losing their unexpected guests and were able to concentrate on cleaning up and looking after their usual charges.

A fleet of Ducal carriages took the exhausted princesses back to the Via Larga, to be tended and cosseted by their maids and their families. Soon the only ones who were left at the Ospedale were the two di Chimici princes and Filippo Nucci, being nursed by Beatrice, Giuditta and Sulien. Rodolfo and Dethridge had volunteered to go to the friary to see whether it could be made suitable to receive the patients. Sulien was anxious to have them near his supplies of medicine, depleted though they were.

He administered a second dose of Drinking Silver to the three injured young men but there was little of the precious liquid left. Both princes had intermittently regained consciousness, but not Filippo, who had lost even more blood than they had.

It did not take long for the Grand Duke to realise that his prisoners had escaped. He sent one team of men to comb the city for Nucci; they went from palazzo to palazzo and tower to tower of those families known to be sympathisers. It would be only a matter of time before they were brought to justice.

The new palace, into which the Nucci should have moved on that very day, had escaped damage altogether. It had been built on raised ground on the far side of the river and the flood water had not reached even up to its front gate.

Matteo Nucci doubted that he would escape with his life, let alone be allowed to take possession of his new home. He knew that they would not remain safe for long in the Salvini tower. He didn't fear so much for himself – what had he to live for now if all his sons were dead? – but he couldn't be sure that Graziella and his daughters would be spared Niccolò's wrath.

'Go now, my dear,' he told his wife. 'Take the girls and leave the city with what you stand up in. See if you can get to Classe and my brother's family. Amadeo Salvini will lend you some money, I'm sure.'

But Graziella wouldn't hear of it. 'With Camillo's body and perhaps Filippo's too still lying unburied in Giglia?' she demanded. 'Am I a mother or a monster? I am going nowhere, unless the . . . Grand Duke of Tuschia,' she spat, 'chooses to dispatch me.'

Alice and Georgia went round to Nicholas's after school, where he and Sky were still recovering from the Giglian battle. Alice couldn't rest until she'd seen their wounds.

'It's all right,' said Sky. 'Sulien did a good job of stitching us up and we've got all sorts of pills from the doctor.'

'That's more than my brothers have,' said Nicholas. He was very pale.

'But that stuff Sky brought back from the friary must be pretty good,' said Georgia. 'I'd back Sulien against Doctor Kennedy any day.'

'Really?' said Nicholas. 'I seem to remember I had to give up my entire life in Talia because no one there could cure me and your doctors could.'

Georgia was really worried about Nicholas. Ever since his first stravagation to Giglia and his wild idea about translating back, he had been a different person. She and Sky had both talked endlessly to him about the craziness of this idea, about the hurt he would inflict on the Mulhollands, the danger that his disability would return, the impossibility of taking up his old life in Giglia. And he had seemed to listen to them and accept what they said.

But now that he had seen his family attacked, it was different. There was a hardness and determination about him that reminded Georgia of his stubbornness when he had first decided to leave his world and come where he could be cured. Only this time she was not in his confidence; he said nothing to her about what he was planning and that made her very uneasy. And she didn't like to admit how hurt she was that he could think of abandoning her so easily to return to his family. Georgia had got used to being all-important to Nicholas.

'Are you going back tonight?' asked Alice.

'Of course,' said Nicholas, though it was Sky she had been asking.

Niccolò agreed to let his sons be moved to Saint-Mary-among-the-Vines, once he had inspected the infirmary. He had sent some of his own men to help with clearing up the mess left in the friary and its church. But he did not want Filippo Nucci to be nursed with them. In this, however, he was completely overruled by Beatrice.

'He is a young man as precious to his people as Fabrizio and Gaetano are to us,' she said firmly. 'Don't you remember how our two families played together when we were children? Why, Mother herself used to take him on to her lap and tell him stories. Where is his own mother now – dead or missing? For pity's sake, we should care for him, as we would want others to care for my brothers if we were not by.'

Niccolò was not used to this fierce side of his daughter and he let her have her way. But Sulien did not trust him and ordered three of his friars to keep a round-the-clock watch by Filippo's bed.

Giuditta had at last made her way back to her workshop, where she found that her apprentices had made a start on the clearing up. Their bedding was hung out to dry from the balcony outside her bedroom and the kitchen stove had been re-stocked with dry logs. The mud had been swept and washed from the tiled floor of the studio. But they had not touched the statues, which were all stained with a muddy high-tide mark, even the beautiful white Duchessa of Bellezza. Fortunately, she was on a raised plinth and looked as if she had been gazing out over the flood waters from her state barge.

'Maestra,' said Franco. 'We are glad to see you safe. We didn't know what had happened to you – there were rumours of bloodshed in the Piazza of the Annunciation.'

'Not rumour,' said Giuditta. 'Cruel fact. I have been tending the wounded.'

Stories about the slaughter had spread through the city. The bodies of the Nucci hanging in the Piazza Ducale and the black ribbons on the doorknocker at the Palazzo di Chimici had told some of the tale, and it was soon embroidered. But nobody expected the sight that was to be seen in the late morning. Matteo and Graziella Nucci, still in their bloodstained and muddy wedding finery, walked proudly from the Salvini tower to the Palazzo Ducale to demand the body of Camillo Nucci. It was not among the corpses displayed in the piazza, much as it grieved them to see nephews and brothers hanging there.

The Grand Duke himself came to the door when he heard who his petitioners were.

'It is not often that the fox comes willingly back to the trap,' he said, when he saw Matteo Nucci.

The old man knelt then in the muddy square.

'Do with me what you will,' he said. 'I care not. But

let us first bury our son and tell us whether there be another body, that of his brother, to bury with him. Then you will have robbed us of all our sons and we shall be ready to join them.'

'*I* rob *you*?' said Niccolò, incensed. 'I have a son of my own lying dead in my chapel and a daughter-in-law made a widow on her wedding day. And two more whose husbands' lives are in the balance, all because of your murdering boy. But you shall have his body, if someone cares to remove it from where my soldiers threw it in the orphanage. And as for the other, he lives and may yet survive to feel my vengeance.'

Matteo Nucci stood. 'I offer myself as hostage,' he said, 'if you will let my wife visit Filippo.'

'You are in no position to bandy terms with me,' snarled Niccolò. 'I could have you and your beldam hanged beside your relatives here, to make food for crows – yes, and your daughters too!'

'But you will not,' said the Pope, appearing beside his brother on the steps of the palazzo. 'There has been enough killing. Camillo Nucci must have his funeral rites, and these other poor wretches too. And I shall myself take Signora Graziella to see her son at the friary. As for Signor Matteo, there is no dungeon here dry enough to put him in. I suggest that he and his daughters and any of those remaining who took part in the attack surrender themselves to my authority. I shall house them at the Papal Residence under guard until they can be brought to trial.'

The Grand Duke could not show how displeased he was. His brother was Pope, after all, and ruled as Prince over the most important city in Talia, even if

Niccolò was head of the di Chimici family. Never had Ferdinando defied him before – and in public too.

Rosalind was at her wits' end. Just as she was feeling physically better than she had for years and was embarking on her first proper relationship with a man since Sky had been born, his father had suddenly appeared out of nowhere. And now Sky seemed to be going off the rails. It perhaps wasn't surprising that he hadn't wanted anything to do with the Warrior. But this business of injuring Nicholas, and getting hurt himself, in what had obviously been a no-holds barred fight, and then clamming up about who had treated their wounds – well, that was completely unexpected.

He had been a model son for the last three years, devoted and coping cheerfully with all the extra demands that her illness had placed upon him.

'Perhaps that's why,' she said to Vicky Mulholland, the day they took the boys to the doctor. 'It hasn't been a natural life for a teenager, never going out and having all that extra responsibility. Perhaps, now I'm getting better, he'll break out with all the stuff he's been suppressing for years.'

'But that doesn't account for Nick,' said Vicky. 'He's younger, of course, but David and I have never had any trouble with him until the last few weeks. He's been so – I don't know – depressed, somehow, and he never was through all that dreadful treatment and the operations.'

'It's a good thing they've got each other,' said Rosalind. 'And I would have said it was a good thing they had their fencing – until this morning. What do you think happened there?'

Vicky shook her head. 'I honestly don't know.' She hesitated. 'You'll think I'm crazy, I know, but there's always been something a bit, well, inexplicable about Nicholas.'

The Bellezzan Ambassador to Giglia was more than a little startled when his footman told him there was a man at the door with two leopards.

'He says they belong to the Duchessa,' explained the servant.

'Oh, my cats,' said Arianna. 'The Grand Duke gave them to me. They are not exactly leopards, but they are quite tame. Perhaps I could house them in your stables until I return to Bellezza?'

Enrico entered the audience chamber, without waiting for permission, with the two spotted cats on their leashes.

'Pardon the intrusion, your Grace,' he said. 'My master, the Grand Duke, asked me to deliver these to you, and a message to say that he would call on you this afternoon to see how your Ladyship is and to talk about his other gift.'

Arianna, blushing fiercely under her mask, hid her confusion by stroking the magnificent beasts. They already recognised her and rasped her hands with their rough tongues. She couldn't believe that the Grand Duke would pursue his suit while he had one son lying in state and two others on the brink of death. But then she remembered how he had ordered

Prince Gaetano to propose to her when poor Falco lay dying. He was as unstoppable as the flood.

'Take them to the stables,' ordered the Ambassador. 'And tell my people how they are to be fed and exercised.'

*

Nicholas and Sky were relieved to find that they were not under several feet of water when they stravagated back to Giglia that night. Sulien's cell was greatly damaged but more or less dry. They found Sulien himself with the wounded in the infirmary.

'It's over then, the flood?' asked Sky, while Nicholas went to his brothers. They were sleeping more naturally now.

'The waters have retreated,' said Sulien. 'But it will be some time before everything is back to normal. I'm glad you are both here. How are the wounds?'

He made them roll up their sleeves to show him. Nicholas was in his novice's robe, but it was damp and muddy. Sky was still in Gaetano's old clothes and they were stained with both blood and flood water.

Sulien nodded approvingly. 'You are healing well, with no fever. But you can't wear those wet clothes. All the robes in my chest were ruined, but go to Brother Tullio and he will kit you both out in dry ones. He rescued so much from the ground floor. Then come back to me – I have an errand for you.'

Brother Tullio had laid all the logs for his ovens out to dry in the sun in the Lesser Cloister; there had been no porridge for the friars that morning. But there had been beer saved from the barrels that floated on the flood and a great deal of Easter bread consumed. Sandro was eating some of it on the cloister wall, sunning himself beside his dog.

When Sky and Nicholas were newly clad as novices in clean dry robes, he joined them. Sandro had no desire to find his official master or to go back to the orphanage, where he had seen dead bodies. All his instincts kept him tied to the friary and the life-giving Sulien.

Sulien told them that Brother Tullio had rescued his parchment with the precious recipes and kept it safe on the top floor. Now he wanted Sky to go up to the Franciscan friary in Colle Vernale above the city and collect fresh herbs to restock the pharmacy.

'Do you think you could drive the cart?' he asked.

Sky hesitated just a little; he was honoured to be entrusted with such a mission but he really was not comfortable with horses.

'I can,' said Nicholas.

'And I know the way,' said Sandro eagerly. 'I'll go with them.'

So the three boys and the small dog left the city and rose above the smells and the factions and up the hillside to the friary. Sky couldn't believe how much had happened since he had first gone there with Sulien less than two months before. Giglia lay spread out beneath them, calm and beautiful in the sunshine. From here there was no sign of the violent events of the day before; it was hard to think that so few hours had elapsed since the outbreak of carnage and the flood that had overtaken it.

They rested the horses in the village and Sandro

dropped off the cart to race Fratello to the top of the hill.

'I love it up here, don't you?' asked Sky.

'Yeah,' said Nicholas. 'You can forget what a stinking mess the city is and just enjoy the beauty.'

'Are you all right, really?' asked Sky. 'I'm sure your brothers will get better. Sulien knows his stuff.'

'No,' said Nicholas. 'I'm not all right. Look, could you drop me off before we get back to the friary? The horses will know the way and I want to see Luciano. I guess he'll be at the Embassy with Arianna.'

*

Arianna was longing to get back to Bellezza but she couldn't leave while Gaetano's life was in danger. Both Francesca and Barbara needed her; her friend was in an agony of fear for her new husband's life and her maid was still in a lot of pain.

'Whatever I put my hand to seems to bring disaster,' Arianna said to Rodolfo. 'I should never have become Duchessa. It is too hard.'

'We are in a tight corner now, I agree,' said her father. 'But we have been in tight corners before and come out of them. You have to be brave a little longer – just long enough to refuse the Grand Duke without offending him.'

'And do you think he'll just accept my answer and let me go back home without taking any revenge?'

Rodolfo was silent. He had believed that he and all the other Stravaganti would have been able to prevent the kind of attack that had followed the di Chimici weddings. True, Arianna was safe, but many others had died or been injured. Could they still keep her safe if Niccolò di Chimici turned against her?

He pressed her hand. 'You'll have me and Luciano and Doctor Dethridge. Once you've refused the Grand Duke we won't leave your side till you're back in Bellezza.'

'His Holiness Pope Lenient the Sixth and the Grand Duke of Tuschia,' announced the footman.

*

Luciano was in the courtyard at the Embassy, making a few desultory passes with a rapier at a statue in the middle of a fountain. It was mud-stained up to its middle. He was relieved when the figure of a tall Dominican novice was shown into the court.

'Your technique isn't quite right,' Nicholas told him and took the weapon from him, showing him how to improve his grip. 'That's why Filippo Nucci was able to disarm you.'

'How is Filippo?' asked Luciano. 'And your brothers?'

'Sulien thinks they will all recover,' said Nicholas.

'That's wonderful. You must be so relieved.'

'Yes, of course,' said Nicholas. 'But that's not what I wanted to talk to you about. Luciano, do you ever feel homesick?'

Luciano was taken aback. 'Sometimes, yes,' he said. 'Is this about you? About wanting to come back?' Georgia had filled him in a bit.

'Not just me,' said Nicholas. 'It's about your parents too – Vicky and David, I mean.'

Luciano had never asked Nicholas about his living

arrangements in the other world; it was too painful.

'What about them?' he said, his face closed.

'They haven't got over it, you know,' said Nicholas. 'Losing you, I mean. I'm a good substitute but that's all I'll ever be. It's not like being their real son.'

'Why are you saying this?' asked Luciano. 'You know there's nothing I can do.'

'That's just it – there is,' said Nicholas. 'I've got a plan.'

*

Upstairs in the Embassy, the Bellezzan Ambassador was serving the famous red wine of his city to his most illustrious guests. The Pope was interested in the almond cakes that the Duchessa had brought with her from Bellezza; he was a great authority on sweetmeats.

'I have never been in the Embassy before, Ambassador,' he said good-humouredly. 'Perhaps you would care to show me around? I could bless any parts damaged by the flood. My chaplain here has a phial of Holy Water.'

'Certainly, your Holiness,' said the Ambassador. 'I would be honoured.'

'Won't you join us, Regent?' the Pope said to Rodolfo. 'I believe you were acquainted with my nephew when he was Ambassador to Bellezza, before he found his present vocation?'

Rodolfo and Rinaldo exchanged the thinnest of smiles; there had been no love lost between them at that time.

Rodolfo did not want to leave Arianna with the

Grand Duke but she motioned him to go. She wanted to get the forthcoming audience over with and she didn't believe she would be in immediate danger. After all, she had killed a man since Niccolò made his proposal. Arianna shuddered, remembering the feeling as she had plunged her dagger into the chest of the man attacking Barbara. There was no doubt that she had killed him, and she had no idea who he had been. For a moment she had understood what it must be like to be Grand Duke Niccolò di Chimici and to regard another human being as completely expendable.

But even while she was thinking these thoughts, the Duchessa of Bellezza had already asked after the princes and seen that Niccolò was genuinely concerned about them.

'I shall be happy to entertain your Grace's daughter-in-law Francesca here as long as I am in the city,' she said.

'That is most kind,' said the Grand Duke. 'And only what I would expect from such a gracious lady. I believe one of your own retinue was also injured. I am greatly relieved to see that you yourself are unhurt.'

'My maid took the force of the blow intended for me,' said Arianna. 'She will make a complete recovery.'

'I was honoured to see you wear my gift at the wedding,' said Niccolò. 'May I take it that you look kindly on my proposal? Of course we must delay the announcement until after Carlo's funeral and until Fabrizio and Gaetano are quite recovered, but it would give me great joy to be able to look forward to it.'

'What would you expect to happen to my city if I were to be your Grand Duchess?' stalled Arianna. Her mouth was dry and her heart pounding.

The Grand Duke was delighted; this was going better than he had hoped. 'Well, my dear,' he said confidentially, 'you would of course live here with me in Giglia. Perhaps the Regent could look after Bellezza for a while, but he will not live for ever. And your city is used to a female ruler. I thought perhaps my daughter the Princess Beatrice could become its Duchessa in due course.'

'So it would be a di Chimici city,' said Arianna softly. 'And I a di Chimici bride. Forgive me, but that does not seem a very safe occupation this morning.'

'Nowhere is safe in Talia,' said the Grand Duke. 'Least of all Bellezza if it stays out of alliance with my family. Come, my dear, it is time to put aside all enmity – what is your answer?'

'I prize the independence of my city too much to put it in your hands,' said Arianna.

'But you wore the dress,' said the Grand Duke impatiently. 'The dress was to have been your answer.'

'I did not wear it,' said Arianna. 'That was my maid. And she suffered for it. The blow was meant for me.'

'Ah, I understand now,' said Niccolò. 'You fear for your life if you marry me? Be assured that I shall look after you. No harm will come to my Granduchessa.'

'You could not protect Carlo,' said Arianna, more bluntly than she had meant to. The Grand Duke flinched. 'But that is not my only reason,' said Arianna, bracing herself. 'I cannot marry where I do not love.'

'That is a girl's answer, not a ruler's,' said Niccolò impatiently. 'I am not offering love, but good political sense.'

'I am a good ruler of my city,' said Arianna. 'But I am a girl too. And I am in love with someone else. If I can't marry him, I shall stay single.'

Niccolò was furious but remained icily polite. 'Might I ask who is my rival for your Grace's hand? Who can equal the offer of a Grand Duke of Tuschia?'

'That is a matter for my own heart,' said Arianna. 'There is no other offer and no engagement. I am very sensible of the honour you do me but I must decline. I cannot marry without love.'

And then it was over. The Grand Duke swept out of the room, white-lipped with rage. Arianna was shaking. She had always known that she could not accept his offer but she hadn't known how to do it. And in the end she had been on her own, without Rodolfo or Luciano to support her. She had gone head to head with the most powerful person in Talia and had no doubt that he would exact a terrible revenge.

*

Sandro and Sky got the cart safely back to Saint-Mary-among-the-Vines and unloaded Sulien's supplies. While the sacks of dried herbs were being used to restock the unbroken jars in the pharmacy, the Eel wandered in.

'Good day, Brothers,' he said, doffing his rather bedraggled blue velvet hat. 'I came to enquire after the princes. But I see my little Sparrow is here helping you. Good, good.'

'The princes are recovering well,' said Sulien. 'And I am grateful for the loan of the boy – Sandro has been most useful. Indeed, if it had not been for his efforts yesterday, I doubt the princes would have lived to see this day.'

Enrico was surprised. He couldn't imagine what Sandro could have done that would be medically useful, but he made a mental note that the boy was well regarded by the pharmacist-friar.

Sandro looked from Sulien to Enrico and made a decision. He was not officially apprenticed to the Eel; no papers had been signed. What he knew of his master was that he had taken Carlo to find a Nucci to murder. And he didn't doubt there were other murders in the Eel's past. But all his experience of Sulien was of healing and care for others, even to the point of teaching a street boy his letters and telling him stories. Sandro didn't want a life of running errands and telling tales for the Eel.

'I'd like to stay here,' he said to Enrico.

'Good idea,' said Enrico. 'You can bring me messages as to how the princes are getting on. And I want that Nucci kept an eye on too,' he added, lowering his voice.

'I don't mean that,' said Sandro. 'I mean I want to be a friar here at Saint-Mary-among-the-Vines.'

Sky and Sulien were as surprised as the Eel.

'But you can't even read or write,' said Enrico. 'How could you be a friar?'

'I think you'll find that he can read,' said Sulien. 'And we can teach him to write. That is, if you are serious about this, Sandro?'

'I am,' said Sandro. 'I want to be a Brother, like

Tino and you.'

Enrico didn't like it. He felt in some way that he had been robbed. But he made no objection; somewhere under the layers of his years of crime he had a glimmer of conscience that told him Sandro had made a good choice.

*

'You are seriously insane!' said Luciano, throwing aside his rapier and pacing up and down the courtyard. 'There is so much wrong with that idea, I don't know where to begin.'

'Why?' asked Nicholas. 'We've both done it before. And it would make everything right for our families.'

'Let's see, shall we?' said Luciano, ticking off reasons on his fingers. 'We'd both have to die again – I can't believe I'm even saying this – my parents would have to lose their foster-son and all my friends here would have to lose me. Then, if it did work, my parents and I would have to move away somewhere so that they didn't have to explain how come their son who had been dead for two and a half years had suddenly turned up again. And, oh yes, Prince Falco would also have suddenly risen from the dead, much to the delight and surprise of his family in Giglia. Good God, Nick, this is la-la land!'

'Not really,' said Nicholas. 'Talia is much more open to the supernatural than England is. I could probably get away with it here. I agree you couldn't pull it off in Islington, but I bet Vicky and David would be willing to move away if it meant they got you back.'

Luciano couldn't deny that.

'And perhaps it would get my father off the Stravaganti's back?' said Nicholas. 'He's never really believed our cover story about my suicide.'

'But what about my mum and dad?' said Luciano, tugging at his hair. 'I wouldn't even think of putting them through that again.'

Nicholas looked at him calculatingly. 'I could tell them,' he said.

'Tell them?'

'Yes. They know you're alive in another world. You told me yourself that they've seen you stravagate back a few times. I could tell them the whole plan. Just think about it, Luciano. You must want to see them again properly.'

And the awful thing was, although he still thought the whole idea was madness, Luciano knew that Nicholas was right. He did want to see his parents again – very much.

Chapter 25

Exile

The Pope's men brought the body of Camillo Nucci to the church of Saint-Mary-among-the-Vines and laid it out in a chapel, alongside five other Nucci corpses recovered from the Piazza Ducale. Graziella Nucci and her daughters found it there after they had visited Filippo in the infirmary. A friar had been sitting by the Nucci's bed when the women entered. Gradually Filippo was surfacing from his death-like sleep. Brother Sulien had given him the last few drops of the *argentum potabile*. And the Princess Beatrice was helping to nurse him as well as her brothers.

Graziella had shed tears of joy to see her last remaining son returning to life. But it was another matter when they were taken into the church.

'We shall have them all washed and anointed,' said

Sulien. 'The Pope has authorised it. They shall receive decent burial wherever you wish.'

Graziella bent over Camillo. 'Let him be buried with Davide in the same grave,' she said. 'And the others in the same chapel. Who knows how many of us shall join them?'

But she and her daughters stayed to help with preparing the bodies; it was the last thing they could do for their kinsmen.

*

The new Grand Duke was in a slowly simmering rage. He barked at his servants and wouldn't wait for his tasters but tossed back many goblets of wine and sent for Enrico. He had lost another son, been overruled by his brother and his daughter and now had been turned down by a chit of girl in favour of a youth a third his age. Niccolò had no doubt who was meant when the Duchessa had referred to 'someone else'. Who could it be but that black-haired Bellezzan youth, the Regent's assistant, who seemed to dog his every step?

And the Duchessa preferred this callow boy to a mature man with all the wealth and prestige of his house to offer her! It made him livid to think of the silver dress, the African cats and the costly brooch. Not that he wanted his gifts back; he would disdain to have them. He was not mean. But he was proud, and the slight to his honour and his person was more than he could bear.

Still, as he drank more, his angry mood settled into an equally dangerous calm. It was not that he had failed to anticipate this. He had always known that

Arianna might refuse him for this reason and he had a plan for how to turn it to his advantage.

'You sent for me, my Lord?' said Enrico.

'Yes,' said the Grand Duke. 'I want you to take my glove to that Bellezzan boy at the Embassy and challenge him to a duel.'

*

Arianna slipped out of the Embassy, accompanied by Guido Parola and her bodyguards, to visit Giuditta. The sculptor's apprentices were still cleaning her statue.

'It looks as I feel,' said Arianna. 'Stained.'

'The stain can be removed from marble,' said Giuditta. 'What has tainted the original?'

'I am ashamed of what happened to Barbara,' said Arianna. 'She is weak and in pain from a wound that should have been mine. But there is something else – the Grand Duke made his proposal a few days ago and I refused him finally today. He made it very clear that his offer was not motivated by love, and yet I fear he is deeply offended and therefore dangerous.'

'Did you give him a reason?' asked the sculptor.

'I gave him one I thought he would understand – that I was in love with someone else. But that is not all. He wants to take my city from me – the city my family has fought so hard to keep free and independent of the di Chimici.'

'Did you tell him who the other person is?' asked Giuditta.

'No, but I fear he will guess. Now I am worried that I have put Luciano in danger. It will be like Barbara all over again – maybe worse. It always seems to be others who suffer the consequences of my actions.'

'Why are you telling me this?' asked Giuditta. 'Why not talk to your mother or Rodolfo?'

'My mother thinks only of politics and they are both too concerned with my safety. I thought perhaps, as a Stravagante but not a politician, you might advise me.'

'I think it might be advisable to leave the city – at least for Luciano, if not yourself.'

'But don't you think he will be watched?' asked Arianna.

Their conversation had been conducted quietly, only Parola standing near enough to hear them, but now Giuditta raised her voice.

'I think we had better make arrangements for carrying your Grace's statue back to Bellezza,' she said.

Georgia had not stravagated to Talia the day after the weddings. She wanted to give Merla a rest, since the horse had made some of her journeys with two riders. And Georgia herself felt weary to her bones. She just couldn't face another night without sleep and full of exhausting adventures in Talia. So the two boys had gone with the pledge that they would tell her all about it the next day, which was Saturday in their world.

Georgia's parents were going to be out for the day so they were all going to meet at her house – Alice too. On the Friday, Georgia had an early night, leaving the model of the flying horse on her chest of drawers, where she could see it but not be tempted to hold it.

But in spite of these precautions, she dreamed about Giglia, reliving the moments in the Church of the Annunciation – the screams and the blood and the sight of people she knew and trusted turned into sword-wielding nightmares. And people she had always feared like Niccolò di Chimici appeared even larger than life in her dreams. He was standing with a bloody sword over the body of Luciano.

She woke in the middle of the night, sweating, and wondered whether to stravagate after all, just to check that Luciano was still alive. But she lay in the dark instead, thinking about him and about how little progress she had really made in getting over him since he had walked away from her in the circular Campo in Remora over a year ago.

The Pope had prevailed over his brother about the Nucci's lives but they were not to get away with their crimes unpunished. The Grand Duke issued a proclamation that anyone bearing the name of Nucci and any known to have fought by their side at the Church of the Annunciation were banished from Giglia in perpetuity and their property sequestrated.

'I see their new building was unaffected by the flood,' said Niccolò. 'Send Gabassi to me,' he ordered a servant. 'I shall take their palace in payment for Carlo,' he told the Pope. 'I no longer wish to live in the Palazzo Ducale. It has unpleasant memories. I shall live in the Nucci's extravagant folly and let

Fabrizio have this place. And I shall get Gabassi to build me a covered walkway above the city, elevated over any future flood waters, that will take me from the seat of government here to my new home there. It can cross the Guild offices and the bridge.'

'That is reasonable,' said his brother. 'I agree that Matteo Nucci should forfeit his property and be driven into exile. But let the wife and daughters remain until Filippo is fit enough to be moved from the city.'

'Very well,' said Niccolò. 'But they must stay in their old palazzo; I won't have them take possession of the new one. And I want another proclamation issued that Camillo Nucci was a murderer and would have been executed publicly if he had not already had the penalty exacted by Prince Fabrizio. I want that family disgraced and their name wiped from the memory of this city, except as the felons they are.'

*

Luciano was waiting for Arianna when she got back to the Embassy.

'I must talk to you,' she said.

'Me too,' he said.

She dismissed her guards. The two of them sat in silence for a while in the blue salon of the Embassy. Arianna was wearing one of her simplest dresses and a white silk mask, which she now took off. The Duchessa of Bellezza went unmasked only with her personal maid and her nearest family members; it wasn't often that Luciano saw her face now that she was ruler of a great city. It made him feel sad to see how tired she looked and so full of cares, compared with the light-hearted girl he had met in Bellezza.

But her beauty moved him as it always had, and the vulnerability she showed in unmasking before him made him feel even more protective of her than usual.

'You go first,' she said.

He took her hand.

'Nicholas has come to me with a strange proposal,' he said. 'He wants us to change places. For him to become Falco again and for me to go back to my parents.'

It was the last thing she had expected. But it made her shiver.

'Would that work?' she asked, playing for time. 'I mean, with the extra year's difference and everything? And wouldn't he be crippled again? And you, would your disease of the Crab return?'

'Is that what you would care most about?' asked Luciano, holding her hand tightly and looking her straight in the eye. 'That I would be ill again in my old world?'

It wasn't. But it was too much of a shock for Arianna to say what she really thought. Why was he telling her this unless he was seriously thinking of doing it? And how could he even think of leaving her if he felt as she had always hoped he would?

'What do you think?' persisted Luciano.

'I think you should talk to Rodolfo,' said Arianna shakily, 'and Doctor Dethridge and any other Stravagante. I'm sure there must be rules against translating back, or the Doctor would have suggested it after – you know – what happened to you in Bellezza.'

It was not what Luciano wanted to hear. He wanted her to beg him not to go, to say she couldn't live without him.

'What did you want to tell me?' he asked.

'The Grand Duke came for his answer,' she said.

'And what did you tell him?' he asked.

'I told him that I could not accept him, that I could not let Bellezza become a di Chimici city – he wanted Princess Beatrice to rule it.'

She did not repeat the other reason she had given Niccolò; she could not bring herself to say it now that she knew Luciano was considering leaving her for ever.

And so they parted at cross purposes and Luciano was completely unprepared for Enrico's visit.

He had glimpsed the Eel on more than one occasion in Giglia and always kept well out of his way. He aroused memories of the worst days of Luciano's life, when he had been kidnapped in Bellezza and held beyond the time he should have stravagated back to his own world. Well as the old Lucien had adapted to his new life, the Bellezzan Luciano could not look back on that time without pain.

And now his kidnapper had turned up at the Embassy, cool as a lettuce, and walked straight up to him and struck him in the face with a long leather glove! Luciano raised one hand to his smarting cheek and his other flew to the hilt of his weapon.

But Enrico raised his own hand to stop him.

'Hold there,' he said pleasantly. 'The blow was not from me and should be repaid to him who sent it. The Grand Duke Niccolò di Chimici challenges you to defend the insult given to his honour. He will meet you at dawn on Friday in the grounds of the new Nucci palace. You may bring two seconds.'

Luciano felt as if he were having a bad dream.

'What insult? There must be a mistake. I have not spoken to the Grand Duke since I dined with him a month ago. And I have never knowingly insulted him.'

'Too bad,' said Enrico. 'The Grand Duke has issued his challenge and if you refuse it you will be branded as a coward and subject to his persecution.'

'That's completely senseless,' said Luciano.

'So you refuse the challenge?' asked Enrico.

Luciano suddenly felt reckless. He had said he would kill Niccolò if he asked Arianna to marry him and now he had the opportunity to do it legitimately. It didn't matter that she had refused the Grand Duke; she had done it for the wrong reason. He would kill him anyway.

'Tell your master I'll be there,' he said.

Sky stravagated back to his world early that night, without waiting for Nicholas. He was as exhausted as Georgia and wanted to catch up on some sleep. He was confused about his role in Talia now. The Stravaganti hadn't prevented the deaths at the weddings, he had done what he could to help the injured and he no longer knew why he was supposed to be visiting the other world.

Perhaps it had all been to save Sandro from the Eel? The boy certainly wouldn't have offered himself as a novice friar, Sky was sure, if he hadn't befriended 'Brother Tino' and become closer to Sulien. Georgia had warned him that the reason he had been brought to Talia might be different from what he thought. She had believed she was needed in Remora to help Falco translate into Nicholas, but in the end she had replaced Cesare in the mad horse race and struck a further blow for the independence of Bellezza. But Sky didn't see what that had to do with him and his visits to Saint-Mary-among-the-Vines. In fact it made his brain hurt even to think about Talia. It had all got so complicated.

It had been much more straightforward when it had just been him and Sulien in the friary, and now it was all tangled up with Nicholas and Georgia, and even Alice. It had been much easier at the beginning to separate his daily life from his nightly journeys to the other world. Now they seemed to be sort of leaking into one another.

He woke early and set out for Georgia's house as soon as he reasonably could. Paul was going to be in town again and Rosalind was singing while she washed her hair. It seemed to Sky that being an adult was much less complicated than being a teenager – particularly a teenager who was a Stravagante.

When Sky got to Georgia's house it was Alice who opened the door. He put his arms round her, burying his face in her hair; it smelt good. He wondered if she had sung in the shower at the thought of spending the day with him.

'Are you OK?' she asked.

'Pretty much,' said Sky. 'My arm's a lot better and I came back early last night – I was so knackered.'

Georgia let them in and the three of them waited for Nicholas to arrive. Her parents had already left and the house felt calm and quiet. They made mugs of instant coffee and took them out into the garden with slabs of a chocolate cake Maura had bought. It was sunny and still warm, as it had been in Devon, and tulips were beginning to come up in the flower beds among the daffodils. They sat at the wooden pub table where barbecues were eaten in the summer and Georgia shared her worries about Nicholas.

'He's shutting me out,' she said. 'I've always known what he was thinking and planning before, but all I know now is that the signs aren't good.'

'Do you think he still wants to go back to Giglia?' asked Alice. 'Even though he's been stabbed there?'

'I think he wants it more than ever,' said Georgia. 'He's seen what his family has been through the last few days and it's bound to make him want to be with them.'

'I'd have thought he was well out of it,' said Alice, shivering in the warm sunshine. She couldn't wait for her friends to finish their Talian adventure. She just didn't understand the fascination it held for them.

'Georgia's right,' said Sky. 'I think he has got some sort of plan. He went to see Luciano today, after he'd checked his brothers were doing OK.'

The doorbell rang and the three of them jumped guiltily.

A body of the Grand Duke's soldiers accompanied Matteo Nucci and a dozen of his followers to the north-east gate of the city. He was glad that his route to Classe did not take him past the new palace where he and his family would never live. He had been allowed only the clothes he wore and the horse that would take him away from Talia. But Matteo Nucci had money in cities other than Giglia.

Graziella had accompanied him as far as the gate, promising to bring Filippo and the girls on to Classe as soon as possible.

'Believe me, I shall not stay a minute longer than I have to in this city,' she said bitterly. 'I can think of nothing better for us now than to live in a city where the di Chimici do not rule.'

They embraced then and parted.

*

In another part of the city, a young boy was being robed as a Dominican novice. He had to make his preliminary vows in the church; then he would be entitled to eat all his meals and spend all his nights quite legitimately at Saint-Mary-among-the-Vines.

'But you must give up swearing, gaming and keeping loose company,' said Brother Tullio solemnly.

'And you won't be able to keep the dog,' said Brother Ambrogio. 'Friars aren't allowed to have pets.'

Sandro looked absolutely stricken.

'Don't tease him,' said Sulien. 'Fratello sounds like a friar already. He shall be Brother Dog and live in the kitchen with Tullio. We need something to keep down the rats. Now, are you ready to take your vows?'

Sandro looked round; he wished that Brother Tino and Brother Benvenuto could be there to see him through the ceremony, but he understood that they could not be in Giglia at night-time; it was all to do with their shadows and their lives in the other world. But the encouraging smiles he was getting from Sulien and the others were enough to make him feel he belonged. He was going to get a family at last – not the kind of brothers he had once imagined and neither the Father nor Mother were where he could see them. But it was enough.

'I'm ready,' he said.

It was much worse than any of them had thought. Nicholas hadn't wanted to discuss it at first, but of course Georgia had wanted to know everything about his seeing Luciano, since she had missed a day in Giglia.

'Well, he told me he has to fight a duel with my father,' said Nicholas. It was true, but he had found this out only later. If possible he was going to keep from the others the plot he hoped Luciano would agree to. But this news was startling enough.

'A duel?' said Georgia. 'But surely he can't beat Duke Niccolò?'

'*Grand* Duke Niccolò,' Nicholas corrected her. 'It's true that Gaetano won't be able to help him. It will be weeks before he's strong enough to hold a sword. But Sky can be one of his seconds. He's allowed two.'

'How can you be so calm about it?' demanded Georgia. 'Even if Luciano could beat Niccolò in a fair fight – which I doubt – how can we be sure the Grand Duke will fight fair?'

'Why has he challenged Luciano now?' asked Sky.

'You'd have thought he'd be grateful for what he did when we got the medicine.'

'Luciano said his challenge was about an insult to his honour,' said Nicholas. 'But he didn't know what.'

'Maybe Arianna turned Niccolò down,' suggested Alice.

They all turned to her in horror; what she said made a kind of sense. If Niccolò was jealous, challenging Luciano to a duel was just the sort of thing he would do.

Georgia felt a pang – would Luciano fight the Grand Duke if Niccolò had proposed to her? Then the absurdity of the very idea overtook her and she laughed, a bit hysterically.

'He'll be killed, for sure,' she said. 'And there'll be no other life for him this time.'

Nicholas couldn't bear to see her so upset; he thought he would be able to console her.

'I wouldn't be so sure,' he said.

*

Niccolò di Chimici took possession of the palace over the river the next day. But Giglians kept the name for it; though generations of di Chimici grand dukes and princes would live there and no member of Matteo's clan ever set foot in it again, it was never known as anything other than the Nucci palace.

Niccolò had a good reason for moving in; his sons were recovering and he wanted them back under his own eye. The Palazzo Ducale felt tainted to him; he would always connect it with the remnants of wedding-feast finery washed up against the steps, his public humiliation by his brother and his proposal to the Duchessa on the night before the weddings, which had been all in vain.

The Nucci palace, undamaged by the flood, represented a new start, and the Grand Duke was good at new starts. He walked through the fine reception rooms, admiring the taste and wealth behind their decoration and furnishings. He ordered all the Nucci portraits to be taken down and representations of his own family put in their place; the Nucci coat of arms was also hacked off the stonework and hastily painted wooden escutcheons with the arms of the Giglian di Chimici fixed in their place.

Enrico walked through the palazzo too, a few steps behind his master and the architect Gabassi. The Eel was also in need of a new project and he was as taken with the grandeur of the palace as Niccolò was. He had a vision of becoming the Grand Duke's steward in his new home; what vistas of opportunities for skimming off silver into his own pocket were opening before him!

They moved up the grand staircase to the upper floors. The rooms were all furnished, the cupboards and chests full of linen and the library full of codices and manuscripts. All this was now di Chimici property because of the blow struck by Camillo Nucci in the Church of the Annunciation. The Grand Duke allocated bedchambers for himself and Beatrice and temporary ones for Fabrizio and Gaetano and their brides. They would keep Fabrizio here until he was well enough to go back to the Ducal palace and Gaetano until he could return to the Via Larga, where he would live as planned with Francesca.

Poor Carlo would have no more need of a palace and Niccolò made a mental note to talk again to Lucia. She would presumably want to go back to Fortezza with her parents, but she would go as a widowed di Chimici princess, one robbed of her future role as wife of the ruler of Remora.

He had already thought about Remora – Gaetano must have that title now and there would have to be another plan for Fortezza. The weddings had been such a promising scheme for increasing the number of di Chimici heirs, but the family had been robbed of two of its young men and both Fortezza and Moresco were without males to inherit their titles.

'A husband for Beatrice,' mused Niccolò to himself. 'Perhaps she could marry the ruler of one of the city-states we have not yet won. If Bellezza can't be brought into the fold just yet, then I shall concentrate on treaties with Classe and Padavia.'

*

Silvia had sent for Guido Parola. He was not far; since the day she had taken him into her service as his punishment for trying to assassinate her, he had never been very many paces from her side. When he entered her presence, she gave her maid Susanna permission to leave.

'Ah, Guido,' she said, scrutinising him carefully. 'You are looking pale. Are you quite recovered from your hurts?'

'Yes, my Lady,' said Parola. 'I was very fortunate and took only slight flesh wounds.'

'Sit down, Guido,' ordered Silvia, indicating the

place beside her on a chaise longue.

'My Lady?' asked Parola hesitantly.

'Stop being my servant for a moment,' said Silvia. 'I want to talk to you properly and you are much too tall for me to do it if you don't take a seat. You're making my neck ache.'

He sat nervously on the edge of the chaise.

'Don't look so worried, Guido,' said Silvia. 'I am very pleased with you. You saved the life of that girl Barbara and, as far as I am concerned, the life of my daughter, since she was the one intended for that blow.'

'Do you think it was the Nucci?' asked Parola. 'I went back to the church the next day, but I couldn't say which of the bodies was the man the Duchessa dispatched.'

'I think it was,' said Silvia. 'Not even Niccolò di Chimici would engineer an attack on his family to provide cover for assassinating Arianna. Besides, he hadn't then been told that she wouldn't marry him, and his plan was to take Bellezza by matrimony, not violence.'

'And the Nucci thought the Duchessa might accept him?'

'I doubt if they even knew about the proposal,' said Silvia. 'But she was an honoured guest of the di Chimici and wearing his handsome gift, as they thought. You can be sure that he himself had spread the rumours that Bellezza was about to form an alliance with Giglia. And he isn't the sort of man to keep quiet about the lavishness of his presents. So as far as the Nucci were concerned, she was a fair target.'

They were silent a few moments, reliving the horror

of what had happened in the Church of the Annunciation.

'Guido,' said Silvia. 'I am going to release you from my service.'

He looked stricken, and started to protest, but Silvia held up her hand.

'Let me finish. You are a nobleman. I know your family's fortune was gambled away by your older brother, but you should be at university completing your education as a gentleman, not acting as a footman to me. You have paid many times over for your original crime – which was one of intention rather than commission – but you are now fully pardoned and should be making your own way in the world.'

'But I don't want to leave your service, my Lady,' said Parola. 'Don't dismiss me. I want to go on protecting you.'

'I am not dismissing you, Guido,' she said gently, taking his hand. 'I am, very regretfully, letting you go. You will have an ample financial reward for all that you have done for me. I forgive you for trying to kill me and I want you to regard me now as a sort of godmother. You can escort me back to Padavia. But after that, what would you say to going to university in Fortezza?'

Chapter 26

Corridor of Power

Rinaldo was nervous about remaining in Giglia. He
had not carried a sword at the di Chimici weddings –
he was a priest now, after all – but it had been
frustrating, brought up as he had been, to be unarmed
in the midst of such slaughter. He had helped his uncle
get the women, including his sister Caterina, first to
the sanctuary of the High Altar and then into the
orphanage. But not before he had seen people killed
and wounded.

Now he was anxious to get back to the comfortable
life he lived in the Papal palace in Remora. His uncle
and master, the Pope, was not loath to leave Giglia
either, but he would not go until the young princes
were out of danger. The Grand Duke too was in a
strange mood. He had been thwarted of the bloody

revenge he wanted to take on the Nucci, and this idiotic plan to move out of the Ducal palace after only a few weeks was part of his frenzy. The Pope wanted to keep an eye on him and sent Rinaldo across the river to see how his cousins were faring.

He was walking near the great cathedral when he glimpsed a tall figure he thought he recognised coming out of one of the palazzi. He had noticed him before in the Church of the Annunciation, fighting and later taking care of the Princess Lucia, but in the chaos of the slaughter and its aftermath during the flood he had forgotten all about him. It niggled at the back of Rinaldo's mind, the sight of this red-headed youth; he knew he had seen him somewhere before but couldn't think where.

*

Luciano was waiting for Sky and Nicholas at the friary when they stravagated to Giglia. He had bumped into Sandro, almost unrecognisable in robes just a little bit big for him.

'So you are Brother Sandro now?' asked Luciano, smiling.

'Yes,' said Sandro. 'And Fratello is Brother Dog. He works in the kitchens. You are waiting for Tino and Benvenuto?'

Luciano nodded. He had to remind himself that Benvenuto was Nicholas, who once had been Falco. Was he going to be Falco again? Luciano thrust the thought down. He needed to talk to them both and to Brother Sulien.

The boys arrived within minutes of one another and

came out to find Luciano and Sandro in the cloister. They went together to the infirmary and found Gaetano sitting on the edge of his bed. There were no other friars about so Nicholas threw his arms around his brother.

Sandro suddenly realised who he was. He had seen the memorial statue of Prince Falco many times but never made the connection until he saw 'Benvenuto' in Gaetano's embrace. He turned to Luciano, eyes wide, but the Bellezzan just put his finger to his lips. Sandro understood. He was a friar now, not a spy, and was going to have to learn how to keep secrets, not pass them on.

'Gaetano!' said Nicholas. 'You really are all right? Where is Fabrizio?'

'Gone with Sulien and Beatrice to Father's latest palace. I shall join them soon. You know that we have taken over the Nucci place?'

'I wanted to talk to you about that,' said Luciano. 'Your father has challenged me to a duel tomorrow and he wants us to meet in the gardens of the Nucci.'

Gaetano looked horrified. His arm was in a sling and his head was bandaged but he made as if to grab his sword, then realised he didn't have one.

'A duel?' he said. 'But why?'

Luciano shrugged. 'What does it matter? He's made up his mind to fight me. I don't think anyone refuses a challenge from the Grand Duke.'

'This is terrible,' said Gaetano. 'I won't be able to lift a rapier for several weeks.'

'But you've given me lots of lessons,' said Luciano. 'I'm not going to learn any more in a day. I'm either ready to meet him or I'm not.'

Georgia was not going to miss another day in Talia. And she had the idea that she might be better able to persuade Nicholas out of his crazy idea if she could get him on his own in Giglia and show him how impossible it would be to return there as if nothing had happened. But the awful thing was, although she knew it was a fatally flawed plan for Nicholas, she couldn't get it out of her mind that it could work to save Luciano's life – which would certainly be at risk if he fought this duel with the Grand Duke.

If Vicky and David were somehow made to understand, they could be ready to take their restored son away somewhere far from Islington. And one day Georgia could go and find him, wherever he was. It would put him for ever out of the reach of Arianna, just as she would have gone out of Luciano's if she had accepted the Grand Duke. And who else in the world would the new Lucien turn to if not Georgia?

There was so much wrong with this picture that Georgia knew it was really a fantasy, and yet she couldn't shake it out of her head. There was only one thing to do: she must talk to the Stravaganti about it, the way they hadn't when she and Luciano had helped Falco translate across worlds.

She started with Giuditta, who was beginning to pack up Arianna's statue when Georgia arrived at her workshop that morning. The head, with its streaming hair, was still poking out of the layers of straw and sacking, the Duchessa's masked face staring out defiantly. Georgia felt a bit guilty about her thoughts;

she had come to admire Arianna, even if she could never stop feeling jealous of her.

'Good morning,' said Giuditta. 'I think we can stop for a while, boys. You can have half an hour's break.'

When they had gone, Franco lingering to give Georgia a lascivious backwards look, the sculptor boiled a pan of water on her kitchen stove and made a tisane of lemon verbena for them both.

'You look as if you need it,' she said to Georgia. 'Drink it while you wait for the others to get here.'

Georgia was grateful. 'There's something I want to ask you about,' she said. And then she told Giuditta Nicholas's plan.

*

'We should go and meet Georgia,' said Sky to Nicholas, when Gaetano had been removed to the Nucci palace.

'I'll come with you,' said Luciano.

The three of them walked in silence to Giuditta's bottega. The cleaning-up operation was continuing in the city, helped by the cloudless sky in which the sun burned as if rain were an unknown phenomenon. Sky had to admit that the Grand Duke was a good administrator. Everywhere they went they saw bands of citizens and soldiers working together to burn debris, clean monuments and repair damage. Their route took them through the Piazza Ducale and they saw that the banqueting platform had been taken down as quickly as it had been erected; there was no sign of all the canopies, flowers and lanterns that had adorned the square the night before the weddings.

Notices had been pasted to various columns proclaiming the exile of the Nucci and the sequestration of all their lands, houses and goods, even down to the least lamb in their flocks, by the house of di Chimici in compensation for the treasonous uprising against their authority and the loss of Prince Carlo. An idealised woodcut of Carlo appeared on the handbills but Nicholas scarcely noticed. He walked, head down, with his hood pulled over his eyes.

When they reached the Piazza della Cattedrale, unusually Giuditta was waiting for them outside her bottega, with Georgia.

'I want Luciano and Brother Benvenuto to come with me,' she said seriously. 'Georgia and Tino can meet us later. We are going to the Bellezzan Embassy.'

So Sky and Georgia were left on their own, making an odd couple – the friar and the artist's model. In order to escape curious looks, they went into the baptistery and sat one behind the other. It was a much smaller building than the cathedral, and the clearing up from the flood had finished there, so that they could talk relatively undisturbed.

'She's going to see if the other Stravaganti can make them see sense,' said Georgia.

'Them?' asked Sky. 'I thought it was only Nick who wanted to do it. Luciano's surely too sensible?'

'Yes, well, you'd have thought so, but with this duel hanging over him, I think Nicholas is going to try to persuade him to take the easy way out,' said Georgia. 'Drink poison in Giglia and stravagate to Islington before it works. Nicholas does the same, maybe with sleeping pills, in the Mulhollands' house. Then, Bob's your uncle: they both end up with real bodies, complete with shadows in the worlds they started from.'

'I never heard anything so ridiculous,' said Sky. 'Surely Luciano would never buy it? I mean he's got a lot going for him here, if you know what I mean.'

'Yes,' said Georgia calmly. 'You mean Arianna.'

'Among other things,' said Sky. 'And what would people say here?'

'That he killed himself rather than face the Grand Duke in a duel,' said Georgia. 'That part would be just about believable, at least by outsiders.'

'But what about Nick? What would Vicky and David tell everyone, even if they were in on the swap?'

'That he had been depressed and difficult lately,' shrugged Georgia. 'He wouldn't be the first fifteen-year-old to kill himself.'

'I don't buy it,' said Sky. 'I mean, they're pretty attached to him, aren't they?'

'But just imagine if he were giving them the chance to have their own son back. I bet they'd consider it.'

'There isn't time for all this anyway,' said Sky. 'Nick would have to explain it all to them and get them to agree tomorrow, if Luciano was going to – you know – take poison before the duel.'

'I think,' said Georgia slowly, 'that if they both agreed to do it, it could just about work as far as the time is concerned. But the Stravaganti would have to give their blessing within the next few hours.'

'And you said Giuditta was against it, so they're not likely to give their blessing, are they?'

'I would have said not, but Sky, if Luciano doesn't do this, he might be killed by Niccolò tomorrow. With no second chances. Finito!'

'He's asked me to be one of his seconds,' said Sky. 'I think he means to go through with it.'

'And who else?' asked Georgia. 'It can't be Nicholas – it's too dangerous.'

'Or Gaetano. You couldn't expect him to support someone against his own father. I think he might be going to ask Doctor Dethridge.'

*

'Here are the rapiers you asked for, my Lord,' said Enrico. 'They are well balanced and matched to perfection.'

'Ah, yes,' said Niccolò. 'We must be seen to be scrupulously fair.' He showed his teeth in a humourless smile. 'What about the poison?'

'The poison, my Lord?'

'Yes, man, poison,' he said. 'Am I to go and ask Brother Sulien for it myself? To say, "Thank you so much for saving my sons' lives with the medicine Cavaliere Luciano helped bring through the flood and now can I have some poison to make sure that I kill him?" No Sulien must not know.'

'I see, my Lord,' said Enrico, scrambling to keep up and trying to be indispensable. 'Of course you have none here?'

The Grand Duke gave him a quelling look.

'No, no, let me think,' said the Eel. 'Yes, I think I know where to get it.'

'Then do so,' said Niccolò. 'Immediately.'

'No,' said Rodolfo. 'I absolutely forbid it.'

He had summoned Dethridge and Brother Sulien to the Embassy to meet Giuditta and the boys. But it wasn't till they were all together that the sculptor told them what it was all about. It was just the six of them in the blue salon; Giuditta had asked for Arianna and Silvia not to be included yet.

Nicholas was standing stubbornly in the middle of the room, his Dominican hood thrown back, revealing his unmistakeably di Chimici features. Luciano was looking at the floor. All he wanted at the moment was to have the decision taken out of his hands.

'Wait,' said Sulien. 'Do we know if this is even possible? What do you say, Doctor?'

'Yt has nevire bene assayed before,' said Dethridge. 'Any sich translatioune is perilous – bot two atte one tyme!'

'But we've both done it before,' said Nicholas. 'Doesn't that count? And if he doesn't do it, Luciano will surely die tomorrow.'

'There are other ways to save him,' said Rodolfo. 'I could contest the Grand Duke's right to challenge, someone else could offer to represent him – me for example – or we could smuggle him out of the city. Don't do this because you think you have no other choices, Luciano.'

When the Eel had gone, Niccolò sent for Gabassi again; the architect did not get much peace from the restless Grand Duke at the moment.

'Have you brought the sketches for my walkway?' asked his master as soon as the man got into the room.

'Yes, your Grace,' said the architect, rolling out his drawings on the table.

They showed an elegant roofed corridor zigzagging from the Palazzo Ducale across the top of the Guild offices and over the Ponte Nuovo to the Nucci palace.

'Excellent!' said Niccolò. 'I'd like you to start straightaway. My son Fabrizio and I can walk from here to the government seat or the other direction, above the noise and dirt and smells of the city. Quite right for people of our importance.'

'There may be a problem with smells from the shops on the bridge,' said Gabassi. 'You see that most of them are butchers or fishmongers.'

'Then we'll change the shops,' said Niccolò. 'I'll give orders moving all food shops out to the market. Then the silversmiths and gemstone workers, who lost so much in the flood, can move their workshops to the bridge. Any other problems?'

'No, my Lord,' said Gabassi. 'If your Grace will give me the funds and the authorisations I need, I can start building tomorrow.'

*

When Sky and Georgia met them later up at the friary, Nicholas looked morose and Luciano drawn and anxious. The others guessed that the Stravaganti had vetoed the plan and Georgia was relieved that the decision had been made. Brother Sandro greeted them in the cloister and dispelled some of the tension by asking Luciano straight out, 'Shouldn't you be practising for your duel?'

It jolted Luciano out of his torpor and sent him off back to the Embassy to find rapiers and some clothes of his own for Sky and Nicholas to wear; there was no way they could fight in robes.

'They said no, then?' Sky asked Nicholas.

'It was all the same stuff I've heard before – we don't know if it would work, too dangerous, not Luciano's only option,' said Nicholas. 'I'm sick of it. There's so little time left, and if we don't do it, Luciano is a dead duck tomorrow.'

'Don't say that,' said Georgia.

Sandro didn't ask about the forbidden option or who 'they' were who had said no. He felt a great respect for the Stravaganti, especially this startling-looking young woman. As far as he was concerned, if Sulien was one, then these time travellers were a good thing. And, as for Luciano, he held him in awe and some fear, since the friar had told him that this handsome young noble had died once and been reborn in Talia. Now he had guessed who 'Brother Benvenuto' really was, there were clearly great and frightening mysteries afoot, about which Sandro realised he wasn't qualified to talk.

But he understood Georgia's terror about the next day. Niccolò di Chimici was a fearsome opponent.

'Perhaps there is something that could put the Grand Duke off his guard?' he suggested tentatively, looking at Nicholas.

Nicholas looked at the little novice, light dawning.

'You're right!' he said. 'I think if my father saw me

and knew me, he might fall into a swoon or something. At least it would give Luciano the chance to disarm him. Thanks, Sandro.'

'We should all be there,' said Georgia. 'All the Stravaganti. Our circle failed at the weddings but we'd have only one person to protect this time. Surely seven of us could save the eighth?'

She was beginning to see some hope.

'I'll have to be there anyway,' said Sky. 'I'm one of his seconds. And Doctor Dethridge is going to be the other.'

'But how can Nick and I be there?' asked Georgia. 'Or the others?'

'I think you will find there will be quite a crowd of spectators,' said Sulien, joining them. 'Rumours are flying about the city that the Grand Duke is going to fight at dawn, and Giglians are not likely to pass up on such a spectacle.'

*

'Fight the Grand Duke?' said Silvia, when Rodolfo told her. 'What new devilry is this? You must stop it.'

'Luciano is determined to fight this duel,' said Rodolfo. 'I can't stop him or get him out of the city. But if we are all there we should be able to protect him.'

'Should?' said Silvia. 'Will that satisfy Arianna?'

'I think that Luciano and Arianna are not in each other's confidence at present,' said Rodolfo. 'They seem unhappy about more than the Grand Duke.'

'But that doesn't mean she wants Niccolò to kill him!' said Silvia.

Rodolfo sighed.

'I'll have one more try to persuade Luciano to leave the city,' he said. 'There's no need for Arianna to know anything about the duel yet.'

*

Barbara was feeling better. Her wound still hurt but Brother Sulien had promised to come and take the stitches out the following week and she could feel that the flesh was knitting together. She now had the novel experience of sitting up in bed, being waited on by her own mistress. The Duchessa was so mortified by what had happened that she brought her maid tempting morsels of food or fortifying drinks every hour.

'I can't just lie in bed doing nothing, my Lady,' said Barbara. 'Give me something to occupy my hands.'

'I'm sure that nothing is exactly what you should be doing,' said Arianna. 'Oh, if only I hadn't asked you to wear that hateful dress!'

'I was happy to wear it for your Grace. It made me feel like a real lady – it was so beautiful. What will happen to it now?'

'I should like to burn it,' said Arianna bitterly. 'But I can't do that because of its value. As well as the great tear where you were stabbed, I don't think the blood will ever come out of the brocade – the Embassy staff have tried. I suppose all the gems will have to be unpicked.'

'Then let me do that, at least,' said Barbara. 'That will not be taxing and, in spite of everything, I'd love to see it again.'

'Really?' said Arianna. It made her shudder to touch it and she hadn't even been the one wearing it. But she ordered the dress to be brought and Barbara bent over it assiduously with a tiny pair of silver scissors, snipping at the rows of embroidery that kept the stones in place. Each pearl or amethyst was put in a bowl as it was released and the pile grew steadily as the young women talked.

'It might be easier to clean when all the jewels and silk embroidery are off,' said Barbara. 'And the tear could be mended.'

'Well, if you will undertake the repair, you may have the dress if you want it,' said Arianna. 'It would make a fine wedding dress – if you have a sweetheart.'

Barbara blushed. 'I do have a young man who keeps asking me,' she said.

Arianna was surprised. 'Well, then, I promise to have some of these stones set for you into wedding jewellery,' she said. 'As a thank you for saving my life. And if you don't want this dress, you shall have another, at my expense.'

'Thank you, my Lady,' said the girl, quite happy to bear the scar of her wound in return for such a lavish gift. It made Arianna feel more ashamed.

'I shall miss you, Barbara,' she said, her eyes filling with tears. 'Who shall be my maid if you marry?'

'Oh, I don't want to leave you, my Lady,' cried Barbara. 'My young man is Marco, one of your Grace's footmen at the palazzo. We would both want to continue in your service, I'm sure.'

'Good,' said Arianna, blinking her tears away. 'How old are you, Barbara?'

'I am eighteen, your Grace – very late to marry, I

know,' said Barbara. 'But we have been saving.'

'You are less than a year older than I am,' said Arianna.

Barbara was horrified. 'Oh, your Grace, forgive me. I did not mean to insult you. It is different for nobility. Take no notice of my silly chatter.'

'That's all right, Barbara,' said Arianna. 'We do marry young in the lagoon. Two years ago, I would have expected it myself, when I lived on Torrone. Now, as you say, it is different. I have many duties to perform that are not compatible with romance.'

She fetched such a deep sigh that Barbara said, 'I am sure there is no need to worry about the young man.'

'What young man?' asked Arianna.

'Why, Cavaliere Luciano,' said Barbara. 'They say he has been having fencing lessons and may well defeat the Grand Duke.'

Arianna jumped to her feet, spilling bright jewels all over the floor.

'Defeat the Grand Duke? What are you talking about?'

*

Now that he had seen the red-headed man once, Rinaldo caught glimpses of him everywhere. But he never had a moment to think about where he knew him from. The Pope kept him constantly busy with errands between the Residence, the Via Larga, the Palazzo Ducale and the Nucci palace.

On one of these journeys he bumped into his old

servant Enrico. He was not someone that Rinaldo wanted to spend time with, but the man was friendly enough.

'How is your Excellency keeping?' he asked.

'I am that no more,' said Rinaldo. 'Can't you see I am a man of the cloth now?'

'Of course!' said Enrico. 'But how should I address your Lordship now?'

'Father will do,' said Rinaldo primly. 'I am only a priest. But the Pope's chaplain too,' he couldn't help adding.

'Oh yes, Uncle Ferdinando,' said Enrico with a leer. 'Not long till there's a Cardinal's hat in it, I shouldn't wonder.'

Rinaldo shuddered at the man's familiarity.

'It's amazing what you can get pardons for now, isn't it?' said Enrico conversationally. 'Kidnapping, murder. Confession and absolution are wonderful things.'

'What are you implying?' said Rinaldo. He had a feeling that this horrible little man might be trying to blackmail him.

'Implying?' said Enrico innocently. 'Nothing, Father. Just thinking of all the terrible things you have to listen to in the confessional. All the dreadful sinners you have to deal with. It must be a sore trial for a virtuous man.'

'I'm afraid I must bring this delightful encounter to an end,' said Rinaldo. 'I am taking a message from the Grand Duke to the Pope.'

'Maybe it's about tomorrow's duel,' said Enrico. 'You might want to come along to that. One of them will be in need of a priest by the end. And if it isn't the

Grand Duke, it will be a young man that you and I know rather well, if you get my meaning.'

He tapped the side of his nose and went on his way, whistling. Inside his jerkin was a phial of deadly poison bought from a certain monk from Volana. But even without knowing about that, Rinaldo was profoundly unsettled by their meeting.

*

'That's better,' said Nicholas. He and Sky had both pressed Luciano till all three of them were hot and panting. But Luciano had kept his defences up and even touched them lightly once or twice. He wasn't as good as Nicholas but he was better than Sky. Nicholas soon adapted to the heavier Talian rapier, which was what he used to use before his translation, but Sky still found it awkward and unwieldy. Luciano took comfort from the fact that he was a great deal younger and fitter than the Grand Duke.

'Let's stop for a bit,' said Sky.

They were in the kitchen yard at Saint-Mary-among-the-Vines, watched by Georgia, Sandro and Brother Dog. The little animal had got very excited when the boys first started fighting, but had calmed down a bit. He was still shivering in Sandro's arms, but had stopped barking.

'I can't believe you're going through with this,' Georgia said to Luciano, while the boys flopped on to the ground and Sandro went in search of some cold ale from Brother Tullio.

'Thanks for the vote of confidence,' said Luciano, breathing heavily, his dark curls wet with sweat. 'I thought I was doing rather well.'

'You are. But there's no reason to suppose the Grand Duke will fight fair.'

'Who will his seconds be?' asked Sky.

'One of them will be that man they call the Eel,' said Luciano. 'I know him of old. He was the one who kidnapped me in Bellezza. He was the one who kidnapped Cesare too, Georgia, and stole Merla.'

'A nasty piece of work,' said Nicholas. 'We need to watch him as closely as my father.'

*

The di Chimici princesses were assembled once more, in the Nucci palace. Francesca and Caterina were in attendance on their husbands, who were getting stronger with every hour. Bianca was visiting with her husband Alfonso. Lucia drifted through the empty rooms on the first floor in her black widow's weeds as if searching for something.

Princess Beatrice found her and brought her to the others.

'Come and live with me in Fortezza, Bice,' Lucia said impulsively, when she saw the other three couples. 'We can be old maids together.'

'We'll all come and visit you often,' said her sister Bianca. 'You won't be alone, I promise. We just have to get through this funeral of Carlo's today and then you can return with your mother and father to Fortezza. They will be a comfort to you.'

The thought of returning to her childhood home, husbandless, instead of living happily in Giglia with Carlo in the Via Larga, caused fresh tears to roll down

Lucia's cheeks. Much as she had dreaded leaving Fortezza for her strange new life, this ending was much worse. She was still in a state of shock from seeing her bridegroom murdered beside her just after their union had been blessed. That image haunted her dreams and so she had not slept properly for two nights.

'If there is anything I can do for you,' said Duke Alfonso, 'please tell me. Perhaps you would like to come to Volana with Bianca and me? My mother would look after you as tenderly as your own.'

'You are very kind,' said Lucia. 'But I think I will do best in my own city.'

Francesca sat holding Gaetano's uninjured hand. She pitied Lucia with all her heart, and not least because it was only providence that had saved her from the same fate. It could so easily have been Gaetano lying cold in the di Chimici chapel, waiting for his burial.

*

'I think I'll stravagate back early this afternoon,' said Nicholas. 'That is if you don't need any more practice, Luciano.'

'I'll be OK,' said Luciano. 'At least, I think I've done as much as I can. It's up to fate now – or the Goddess.'

Georgia was watching Nicholas closely. She slipped off the wall and signalled to Sky to follow her lead.

'I'll go back, too,' she said. 'I could do with a bit more sleep. And we'll all need early nights tomorrow if we're to be back here at dawn.'

'I'll walk with you to the city wall if you like,' said Sky. 'I'd like to see Merla again.'

'Can I come?' asked Sandro.

But Sulien came and called him into the pharmacy.

'You are a real friar with work to do, Brother Sandro. You cannot spend your days gadding about with Tino and Benvenuto, let alone with such an enchanting young woman as Georgia.'

While Sandro turned and trotted off obediently after Brother Sulien, Georgia suddenly flung her arms around Luciano.

'Take care,' she said, hugging him tightly.

He hugged her back.

'I'll be fine,' he said. But he looked pale and worried.

Nicholas went off to Sulien's cell to stravagate and Georgia walked through the cloister with Sky. She waited till they were out of the friary before voicing her fears.

'I don't trust Nick,' she said. 'I wouldn't put it past him to do something stupid. I want to get round to his house early and keep an eye on him.'

'Do you want me to come too?' asked Sky.

'Would you? I'd be happier if there were two of us. We'll need to watch him all day.'

'I'll stravagate back as soon as you've gone,' said Sky. 'And I'll ask him round to my flat tomorrow night.'

Georgia stopped outside the church.

'Listen,' she said. 'What's that music?'

There was a sound of muffled drums coming from beyond the Piazza della Cattedrale. A passer-by said,

'They are burying Prince Carlo.' Georgia and Sky stood still, their heads bowed for a few minutes.

Then they walked over the Ponte Nuovo. Gabassi the architect and a man Sky recognised as the Grand Duke's steward were arguing with a large butcher. They stopped to listen before heading towards the Nucci palace.

'A walkway across the river?' said Sky. 'And he doesn't want any bad smells as he walks along. Is there no limit to the man's arrogance?'

'He thinks the di Chimici are above the likes of ordinary people,' said Georgia. 'And he doesn't like it when he doesn't get what he wants. That's what this duel is all about, isn't it? He proposes to Arianna, she turns him down, so he wants to kill Luciano because he thinks he's his rival.'

'It's hard to believe it's going to happen here in the Nucci gardens in less than a day,' said Sky.

They skirted the gardens and turned off left down to where Merla waited with the Manoush in the little homestead. She sensed Georgia's approach and whinnied from far away, running up to the fence round the field. Sky caught his breath at the sight of the magnificent winged horse. If only there were time to get to know her.

Aurelio was whittling a recorder out of pearwood. He lifted his sightless eyes as they came up to the fence.

'This is Sky,' Georgia said. 'He is another Stravagante from my world.'

Aurelio bowed in Sky's direction, touching his breast and brow with both hands.

'You are troubled about something,' he said to

Georgia. 'What is wrong?'

'Luciano is going to fight a duel with the Grand Duke at dawn tomorrow,' she said. 'In the gardens of the Nucci palace. And I am afraid he will lose.'

Chapter 27

A Duel

Rodolfo had been so insistent that Luciano had agreed to talk to him again about the duel.

'You understand that you can't agree to this crazy plan of Falco's?' said the older Stravagante.

Luciano was silent.

'What is it, Luciano?' asked Rodolfo gently. 'Do you want to go home so badly? Do you not feel at home here in Talia with us? With Arianna?'

'She doesn't care about me,' said Luciano bitterly. 'She could have asked me to stay.'

'She refused the Duke's proposal,' said Rodolfo.

'But not for me,' said Luciano. 'For Bellezza. She cares more about her city than she does about me.'

'Do not throw your life recklessly away in this duel,' said Rodolfo, and he looked stern. 'I can get you out of the city. Promise me that you will not fight.'

'I can't promise,' said Luciano, moved by Rodolfo's concern. 'But I will think about it.'

*

At dawn the next day, many people converged on the Nucci gardens. The Grand Duke was last to arrive with his two seconds, Enrico and Gaetano, who had to lean on Francesca. Luciano was already there, with Doctor Dethridge and Sky. Georgia and Nicholas arrived at almost the same time; Nicholas had stayed at Sky's flat that night and stravagated soon after him.

Georgia was very relieved to see him; she had stuck to him all Sunday in their world until Sky took over and took him home. Now they mingled with the substantial crowd. Georgia saw Silvia standing near Rodolfo with Guido Parola. She scanned the gathering for a sight of Arianna but there were too many people present to see properly.

Sky was feeling very nervous about his role.

'Fyrste wee most assay to have the encountire annulled,' explained Doctor Dethridge. 'Wee most entire negotiatiounes with yonge Cayton and yondire villayne Henry.'

He means Gaetano and Enrico, thought Sky.

'Yf thatte fayles, thenne wee inspecte the weapouns to insure they are alike and notte tampered with. Yf that wee are contente, thenne the conteste most beginne.'

The four seconds approached and began to debate the issue of settling the quarrel without a fight.

All this time Luciano and the Grand Duke stood at some distance apart, not exchanging as much as a look. Luciano scanned the crowd for friends and saw a reassuring number of Stravaganti manoeuvring themselves into position so that they took up points on a circle. The first person he saw was Rodolfo, and he felt bad that he hadn't been able to take his advice. Sulien, Giuditta, Georgia, Nicholas – they were all there. He was surprised to see Gaetano as one of his father's seconds. That meant that three of the seconds were Luciano's friends, even though Gaetano could hardly take any action against his father.

Francesca was there to support her husband, Silvia could be located by the tall red-headed young man beside her and Luciano also caught a glimpse of the multi-coloured clothing of Raffaella the Manoush. It seemed as if almost everyone he knew in Giglia had come to support him. Almost. There was no sign of the slight masked figure he most wanted to see. Yet this duel was for her, at least as far as Luciano was concerned. He still didn't know exactly why the Grand Duke had challenged him. But with every pass he made with his foil, Luciano would be thinking about Arianna and venting the anger he had felt for a month, ever since the Duke's dinner party when Niccolò had announced his intention of marrying her.

Niccolò himself had a more complicated agenda – as always. He wanted to hurt the Duchessa, to punish her for continuing her mother's resistance to a di Chimici alliance and for slighting his offer. But this contest was also for Falco. He had wished a thousand times that he had put Luciano and his accomplice to death in Remora when his boy had died so mysteriously. It was only his grief and the befuddlement of his senses by witchcraft that had stopped him.

The witchcraft of Rodolfo. All the recent strife with the Nucci had deflected Niccolò from his other purpose: persecution of the Stravaganti. The Bellezzan Regent was one of that Brotherhood, he knew, and he suspected that Luciano was being trained in the same arts. This duel might flush out some more of them. The boy's seconds, for instance. That old man, he knew to be Luciano's father, or foster-father, but what about the young Moorish friar? The Eel had found no evidence to confirm that he was Brother Sulien's illegitimate son, so he was another potential Stravagante. Unlikely in a friar, and Niccolò owed Sulien thanks for his role after the Nucci attack and at the time of his own poisoning. Still, he was a friend of Luciano's, so a possible suspect. And there had been another young friar seen in their company. But there was no more time to wonder about him now, as the duel was about to begin.

Enrico refused to accept any peaceful settlement on his principal's behalf even though his own fellow second supported it. The Grand Duke was mortally offended, he said, that the Bellezzan had interfered with his suit to the Duchessa, poisoning – Enrico emphasised the word – her mind against him. He demanded full satisfaction.

Interfered with his suit? thought Luciano. So Arianna *did* say something about me when he proposed. Niccolò is jealous! It gave him fresh heart, but there was still no sign of Arianna in the crowd.

So they proceeded to the inspection of weapons. Enrico brought out the two rapiers in a long case, lined with black velvet. He offered Luciano first choice and the Bellezzan took the weapon further away from him, just in case his seconds had missed anything. He balanced it in his hand, took the tip and slightly bent it in a curve to test the blade; it was an elegant, even beautiful weapon. The Grand Duke took the other.

Sky swallowed. His mouth was dry. He felt that he would be making every pass and parrying every blow with Luciano. He didn't know how his friend could stand there so coolly, testing the rapier when, in a few moments, he would be fighting for his life. Neither weapon was bated and there were no face-guards or body padding; this was supposed to be a duel to the death.

There was a slight commotion in the crowd and the Duchessa of Bellezza appeared and stood beside a well-dressed middle-aged woman. Luciano met her violet eyes and made the slightest nod in her direction before taking up his guard. This is for you, he thought silently. If I get out of this alive, I'm going to tell you how I feel. He held his weapon in front of him as if making her a salute and with it a promise. The Grand Duke saw the gesture and followed his gaze to the masked figure in the crowd. His lip curled with disdain. So the lagoon slut was here to support her lover? Let her take him away in pieces or infected with a poison beyond cure!

He didn't press Luciano at first, letting the boy get over-confident. But it surprised Niccolò to see how good his opponent was. Nothing that would trouble the Grand Duke, but the Bellezzan would die valiantly.

Rinaldo di Chimici watched nervously. His uncle would win, of course, but Rinaldo, like everyone else, was caught up in the excitement of the contest. And there was a great deal of support for the underdog. He looked at the crowd. There was that red-headed fellow again – near the young Duchessa and an older woman, clearly his employer. Something about the association of the man with Bellezza made the necessary link in Rinaldo's brain and at that moment he knew who Guido Parola was.

Enrico was watching the young Duchessa too. The fight wouldn't get interesting for a while yet. She was a fetching little thing, he thought, sentimentally. It was a pity she was going to lose her inamorato – such eyes were not meant for tears. Perhaps she would recover one day and marry. But not the Grand Duke; he was much too old for her. Enrico allowed his mind to wander to his old love, his fiancée Giuliana, who had disappeared from Bellezza at the time of the old Duchessa's assassination. Would he ever find a woman to replace her? He still could not understand what had happened to her.

Rinaldo no longer had any attention to spare for the duel. Guido Parola owed him money; he had taken half his fee for assassinating the Duchessa, botched the job and disappeared. Now Rinaldo wondered if he could set Enrico on to him.

Luciano was beginning to sweat. He had been parrying as skilfully as he could but had never got close to touching the Grand Duke. The hilt of the rapier was getting slippery in his hand. He muffed the next blow and felt Niccolò's blade pierce his left shoulder. It was not a deep cut but the seconds halted the duel to attend to it. Both men were brought wine to drink while they rested.

Sky helped Dethridge clean and pad Luciano's wound with cotton strips. Rinaldo took the opportunity to approach Enrico.

'See that red-headed fellow over there?' he hissed. 'That's the man I paid to kill the Duchessa on the night of the Maddalena feast in Bellezza. I want you to catch him and make him give back what he owes me.'

Enrico didn't really want to be distracted now. This break gave him the opportunity he needed to smear the point of Niccolò's rapier with the poison he had with him. Rinaldo was standing between him and the onlookers, providing a perfect screen. And the other three seconds were all looking at Luciano.

'Funny he's with the new Duchessa now,' said Enrico, applying the poison. He knew Rinaldo wouldn't stop him – even if he was a priest now, he had no love for the boy who had fooled him in Bellezza.

'He's not with the Duchessa. He's a servant of that other woman – the good-looking middle-aged one,' said Rinaldo.

Enrico looked where he was pointing. And Rinaldo looked again.

'Yt is time to beginne agayne,' said Dethridge. 'Yonge Maister Lucian is fitte to fyghte.'

Enrico passed his master the poisoned blade, as Rinaldo gripped his arm.

'That's her!' he hissed. 'The Duchessa!'

'I know it is,' said Enrico. 'Now get back to the crowd. We have a duel to finish.'

'No,' said Rinaldo urgently. 'The old one!'

But he was pushed back among the other spectators and Luciano and Niccolò faced each other again.

The man's losing his mind, thought Enrico. How could the assassin be with the old Duchessa? I killed her myself. Lobbed a bomb at her in that crazy room of mirrors she had.

Nicholas didn't like the way the duel was going. Luciano's confidence had been weakened by the hit to his shoulder, even though the wound was not serious. Nicholas decided it was time to try Sandro's idea. He moved through the crowd until he was positioned where his father could see him, even though it meant breaking out of the circular formation with the other Stravaganti. Then he let his hood fall back.

Enrico was troubled by his conversation with Rinaldo and found it difficult to concentrate on the duel. Someone had died in the Glass Room, and if it hadn't been the old Duchessa, then who was it?

Suddenly, the Grand Duke sank to his knees, clutching his chest.

'Oh, Goddess save us!' muttered Enrico. 'Don't have a seizure now!'

He rushed to his master's side. Gaetano was raising his father and giving him more wine. 'Falco!' whispered Niccolò. 'I saw him, Gaetano. Over there!'

Enrico looked round but there was no one special to be seen in the crowd. Where the Grand Duke pointed was a young friar, one of Sulien's novices, with his face hooded.

But Prince Gaetano seemed disturbed. 'We should

stop the fight, Enrico,' he said.

'No, no,' said the Grand Duke, passing his hand over his face. 'It's nothing – a hallucination. Give me another mouthful of wine. I'll fight on.'

The Duchessa was pressing forwards to see what was going on.

'Is it over?' she called out. 'Does the Grand Duke concede?'

Sky was the second nearest to her. He shook his head. Arianna made to move forwards but the duel was about to resume. It was going to be dangerous if she got near the foils.

'Silvia,' he called. 'Guido! Keep her back.'

Silvia. That was the old Duchessa's name. Enrico saw the middle-aged woman and the assassin together restrain the young Duchessa. Rinaldo had been right. This was Silvia, the Duchessa of Bellezza.

Enrico lived in sixteenth-century Talia, so he had never seen a slow-motion sequence in a film. But that was just like what he was experiencing. If the old Duchessa of Bellezza was still alive, he thought again as he picked up the two foils, then who had died in the Glass Room that day when he had planted the explosive?

And then all of a sudden he knew exactly what had happened to his fiancée. If the old Duchessa was alive, she must have used a substitute. She had done it before. And the person she had used was Enrico's fiancée, Giuliana.

When Enrico passed the foils to the duellists, he made sure that Luciano got the poisoned one. It was the decision of a moment. As Enrico realised that he had killed his own fiancée, blown her into little pieces, a hatred like nothing he had ever experienced welled up inside him.

He would deal with Rinaldo later, and maybe the old Duchessa herself, for tricking him by using a double – but for now he wanted to kill the Grand Duke, the man who had ordered the assassination. If it hadn't been for him, Giuliana would be alive. Enrico's first instinct was to stab the man himself. But no, there was a perfect way to do it – they were in the middle of a duel, after all, one that the Grand Duke himself had rigged. It would be very satisfying to see Luciano kill him.

And if by any chance the Grand Duke managed to kill Luciano with the unpoisoned sword, well then Enrico would stab Niccolò himself and take the consequences.

The two duellists feinted, circling each other warily. The Grand Duke lunged, forcing Luciano backwards. Nicholas stepped forwards and pulled back his hood again. The Grand Duke faltered and Luciano struck. It was a light thrust but the point went in and his man was down.

The Duke's seconds went to him. 'You must stop it now,' said Gaetano to Enrico. 'Look at him. He's not fit to continue.'

The Grand Duke did indeed seem a lot worse than the strike warranted. Luciano had lowered his weapon, puzzled. Enrico took it from him. Brother Sulien came out of the crowd to offer his healing skills. But the Grand Duke was racked with spasms. In his agony he grabbed a red flowering bush in a pot by the path and was showered with crimson petals. It was obvious that Luciano's weapon had been poisoned. But both weapons had disappeared and the Grand Duke's second with them.

Niccolò di Chimici was dying in front of their eyes.

'Poison,' he said to Sulien, clutching his robes. 'I had one of the foils poisoned. They must have been switched.'

'What poison?' asked Sulien urgently. 'Tell me the name.'

But the Grand Duke shook his head slightly. 'I don't know,' he whispered. 'Enrico got it for me.'

'I can't help him,' said Sulien. 'If I had any of the Drinking Silver left . . . but I gave the last drops to Filippo Nucci.'

Nicholas pushed his way through the people clustered round the Grand Duke where he lay on the ground. 'Father,' he whispered, from within the folds of his hood. 'Forgive me.'

And those who were nearby thought it was the Grand Duke speaking, asking absolution of a priest.

Niccolò's eyes fluttered open. 'Bless you, my son,' he whispered.

And the onlookers thought the words were offered by the young friar to the dying man. At least that was the story that circulated in Giglia in days to come. That Niccolò di Chimici had died in a state of grace.

The Grand Duke's body was carried into the palazzo. Luciano stood stunned. Arianna ran to him as if to comfort him but stopped short of touching him. Dethridge took him in a bear hug. Sky was holding Nicholas back from going after the body and its followers. Georgia came running up to them and saw Luciano and Arianna gazing into each other's eyes. Her heart lurched. All was confusion.

'I killed him,' said Luciano stupidly.

'No,' said Nicholas, white-faced. 'I did.'

*

Prince Fabrizio was startled when servants burst into his room and knelt to him. It took some time for him to understand that they were addressing him as Grand Duke and that meant his father was dead. But Gaetano came in soon after, leaning on Francesca's arm, to confirm that Niccolò had indeed been killed in the duel. The two brothers, still weak from their own wounds, were taken by their wives to see Niccolò laid out on his high bed.

'I don't understand,' said Fabrizio. 'There is hardly any blood. How did he die? Could you not save him, Brother Sulien?'

'He told me that he had poisoned his foil and the weapons may have been switched,' said Sulien. 'But his man, Enrico, had disappeared, and the Grand Duke could not tell me what kind of poison had been used. He died before I could administer any remedy.'

Fabrizio bowed his head. It was only too likely that his father had sought to rig the duel and inadvertently brought about his own downfall. Was there to be no end to the disasters brought on his family? But now he must become its head and inherit his father's wealth and title. He would be not Duke Fabrizio the Second of Giglia, as he had imagined when he was a little boy, but Grand Duke Fabrizio the First of Tuschia.

The Pope entered the bedroom, summoned hastily from the Residence by Rinaldo. He approached the bed with his censer and intoned the first words of the prayer for the dying: 'Go, immortal soul . . .'

'Send to have all the bells tolled,' Grand Duke Fabrizio said to his brother Gaetano. 'The greatest of the di Chimici is dead.'

*

The Stravaganti were all at the friary, where Brother Tullio gave them all warm milk laced with brandy. Rodolfo had taken them there while Sulien attended the Grand Duke.

'I don't understand,' said Luciano again. 'I barely wounded him.'

'The foil was poisoned,' said Nicholas dully. 'That man Enrico must have switched them.'

'But why?' asked Sky. 'He was the Duke's right-hand man.'

'Perhaps he was a double agent,' said Georgia. 'Maybe he was in the pay of the Nucci?'

'He is a bad man,' said Sandro, who could not be kept out of the kitchen. 'I know he did murders.'

Rodolfo said, 'I think it was something Sky said that made Enrico swap the foils.'

They all stared at him.

'Me?' said Sky. 'What did I say?'

'I'm only guessing,' said Rodolfo. 'But I think he heard Sky call Silvia's name and then he realised that Arianna's mother hadn't been killed in the Glass Room.'

'You mean he was the one who planted the explosive?' asked Georgia.

'If he was, then he must have realised that he had killed his own fiancée,' said Rodolfo. 'That would have been enough to make him want revenge on the Grand Duke.'

'Will the new Grand Duke – Prince Fabrizio, I suppose – take some revenge on Luciano?' asked Georgia. All this stuff about the old Duchessa had rather gone over her head. The explosion in the Glass Room had happened before she had ever visited Talia.

'Let us say it would be a good idea for Luciano to leave the city soon,' said Rodolfo. 'Even though he was unaware of the Grand Duke's deceit and killed him in a fair fight.'

'But it wasn't a fair fight,' said Nicholas. 'I distracted him. Luciano might not have got him if I hadn't.'

'You weren't to know the foil was poisoned,' said Georgia. 'It wasn't your fault. You were just trying to save your friend.'

But it was as if Nicholas hadn't heard her.

The bells of the campanile in the Piazza della Cattedrale started to toll. Saint-Mary-among-the-Vines followed suit. Soon all the bells in the city had taken up the solemn note and Giglians knew their ruler was dead.

Sulien joined them and went straight to Nicholas. 'Come with me,' he said. 'You too, Sky, and Luciano.'

He took them into the church and set them on the maze, Sky leading the way. 'I'll go last,' said Sulien.

When Sky reached the middle he waited until the other three joined him. He hadn't really thought that Nicholas would walk it properly; he seemed so dazed and wretched. There was room in the centre for all of them to kneel and they did. It seemed hours before Sky was ready to step back out into the world.

Luciano followed him, slowly. Finally, Sulien helped Nicholas out, the boy leaning heavily on his arm.

'Now, listen,' said Sulien. 'You did not kill your father. Nor did Luciano. Or that wretch Enrico, come to that. Niccolò died by his own hand, as surely as if he had drunk that poison. There was nothing anyone could do to save him. He was your father and you loved him, but he was a man who killed his enemies and in the end that was what took his own life.'

He turned to Sky. 'I want you both to go back now. It will still be night in your world. I will give you both a sleeping draught, and when you wake up at home, look after Nicholas. He will need you. And Georgia. She must go too.'

Georgia opened her eyes in her own room; she was clutching the flying horse. It felt as if she had woken from an awful nightmare. Yet the person she used to care most about was unhurt. She could not get out of her head the sight of Luciano and Arianna staring into each other's eyes. But she realised she was more worried about Nicholas. Before she left Talia, she had arranged with Sky that she would come round to his flat in the night and ring once on his mobile. She would have to risk Rosalind hearing Sky let her in.

She dressed hastily in the dark and let herself quietly out of the house. The stars were out and the night was very still. As she walked through the dark streets of Islington, she remembered doing this once before, when she was making arrangements to stay in Talia for the Reman horse race. How simple it had been then! Scary, but easy. All she had had to do was stay on a horse for a minute and a half. Now she had no idea what to do, but Nicholas needed her.

Sky came to the door quickly and quietly and they passed through his flat and into his room. Nicholas lay on the bed fully dressed, his eyes open, but not focused. She sat beside him and took his hand.

'How are you?' she asked softly.

He turned his gaze on her and clung on to her hand.

'Let me go back,' he said.

In spite of how much he had grown up since then, he reminded Georgia of the boy he had been when he decided to leave his world.

She took the flying horse out of her pocket.

'Give me the quill,' she said gently.

Reluctantly, Nicholas drew it out of his jacket. Georgia took it from him and put it with the horse on Sky's mantelpiece, next to the blue glass bottle.

'You can't go back,' she said. She thought about the way Luciano had looked at Arianna after he had killed the Grand Duke, then she put her arms round Nicholas and took a deep breath. 'If you like, we'll destroy them both – both talismans. We have to live here, Nicholas. The other life is just a dream.'

The boy looked at her as if he were still half in Talia and scarcely knew who she was. She would have to try harder or she would lose him. He would go back somehow or would lose his mind in the attempt. And Georgia realised that she couldn't bear to be without him.

'Help me, Sky,' she said. 'We've got to make him see that his life is here.'

Sky was feeling only half-sane himself. He'd been

thinking about what Rodolfo had said. If he was right, then Sky had perhaps completed what he had been called to Talia to do. But it looked as if it had been to bring about Nicholas's father's death. How was he to console his friend?

'Nick,' he said quietly. 'I'm sorry. Really sorry about your father. And especially if it had something to do with me. I'm sorry about all the things we got wrong in Giglia – all the deaths and injuries. But Georgia's right. You belong here now, not in Talia.'

'I feel as if I don't belong anywhere,' said Nicholas dully.

'You belong with me, Nicholas,' said Georgia. Something shifted in her heart and she knew it was true. Nicholas was a real flesh and blood boy she could love. In fact she loved him already. Luciano was the dream, someone she had loved from afar. But she and Nicholas knew each other as they really were.

'I'm going to live here,' she said. 'I'm not going to go back to Talia again. There are some choices you can only make once. You can't go back to where you made a choice and then take the other one.'

Nicholas was looking at her intently now.

'I'm doing now what I should have done ages ago; I'm choosing you over Luciano. What do you choose?'

*

Paul Greaves whistled as he shaved. He wasn't going back to Devon until the afternoon and he was going to take Rosalind out to lunch. He hadn't been so happy for years. Of course it was early days; he had known her exactly a month. But already he felt they were meant to spend the rest of their lives together.

He frowned slightly at his reflection. What would Alice think about that idea? Or Sky? He realised it could make things awkward for them. But he brushed the thought aside. He liked Sky and hoped the feeling was mutual. It would be interesting to have a son, thought Paul. Then he smiled at himself, knowing he was letting his imagination run away with him.

Rosalind was making coffee in the kitchen when she noticed the time. She went and knocked on Sky's door.

'Wake up, sleepyheads,' she called. 'You'll be late for school.'

Sky came round the door very carefully, closing it behind him. He put his finger to his lips.

'Nick's not well,' he said. 'He's had a terrible night. I don't think he should go to school.'

'What's wrong?' asked Rosalind. 'Shall I go and talk to him?'

'No, Mum, he's sleeping. I'll ring Vicky.'

'But you have to go to school. I'll ring her, but I need to know what's wrong with him.'

Sky was saved by Paul coming out of the bathroom.

'Morning, Sky,' he said cheerfully. 'Mmm. That coffee smells good.'

'Better than my mother's,' said Rosalind. 'Well, look – you go and get showered, Sky, if you're going to get any breakfast.'

When he'd gone, Paul kissed her. 'You're looking particularly pretty this morning,' he said.

'Thank you,' she said, smiling. Then, 'Sky says Nicholas is sick and can't go to school this morning. But he wouldn't say what was wrong. I know Vicky's been very worried about him.'

They went into the kitchen. 'You don't think it could be drugs, do you?' said Rosalind, lowering her voice. 'I know they can get hold of them in school. But I'm sure Sky's never taken anything.'

'You're worrying about nothing,' said Paul. 'Nick's much too much of an athlete to mess around with drugs.'

'That's not logical,' said Rosalind. 'Athletes are always in the news for taking drugs.'

'Not that kind,' said Paul, smiling.

Georgia could hear them talking from where she stood behind Sky's door. Nick was at last in a deep sleep and it was safe to leave him. But she didn't know how she was going to get herself out of the flat and to school without being seen. She had left Maura a note saying she was going for an early run and might not see her before she went to work, so that end was sorted. But she hadn't reckoned on Paul being here for a leisurely breakfast with Rosalind. Only she was going to have to get out of Sky's room soon; she was busting for the loo.

Sky came back from the shower, damp and wrapped in a towel, so Georgia saw her chance. It was just her bad luck that the doorbell rang at that moment and Rosalind came out of the kitchen to answer it.

Sky and Georgia froze in the doorway. There was nothing they could think of as an explanation for why she was coming out of his room at that hour. In the end she just said, 'I'm sorry, Rosalind.' And bolted for the bathroom.

'Get dressed, Sky,' said Rosalind, more calmly than she felt. 'I must see who's at the door.'

It was the Warrior.

Georgia wondered whether to go straight to school. But she couldn't leave Sky to face the music on his own. She went into the kitchen and found Rosalind and Paul sitting with the man whose image stared from thousands of teenage bedroom walls. Sky's father.

'Who's this?' he said. Then, when Sky joined them, 'Oh, I see. You're taking after your old man at last.'

'No I'm not,' said Sky rudely. 'I'm nothing like you. Georgia's just a friend.'

'Call round for you early, did she?' asked the Warrior.

'They're both over the age of consent,' said Paul. 'They can do what they like.' But he didn't look very happy; he was disappointed in Sky.

'It's not what it looks like,' said Sky. 'I didn't spend the night with Georgia – not in the way you mean, anyway.'

'She spent it with me,' said Nicholas. He came into the kitchen, looking like a ghost.

The Warrior clapped his hands. 'Even better – a threesome!' he said.

'Will you stop being such a – sleazebag!' said Sky, furious.

Anything less like an orgy than the ghastly night they had passed was impossible to imagine. Georgia had held Nicholas in her arms while he had raved and wept and Sky had lain on the floor unable to sleep.

'I'm going out with Paul's daughter, Alice, if you must know,' he told his father.

'Coz-ee,' said the Warrior.

'I don't know exactly what has been going on,' said

Rosalind. 'But I really don't think it's any business of yours, Colin.'

'Colin?' said Georgia. She started to giggle. It was like finding out that P. Diddy was really called Sean.

Nicholas sat down suddenly. 'Can I have some coffee?' he asked. 'There's nothing going on,' he said as Rosalind poured him some. 'Nothing you'd understand, anyway, and nothing to do with sex. And it's over now – sorted.'

'That's all right then, isn't it?' said the Warrior. 'Everybody's happy. Look, Sky, I came to say goodbye. Me and Loretta are going back to the States. It's been nice meeting you.'

Sky couldn't answer. He felt hugely relieved that his father was going and wasn't insisting on being a part of his life.

'It's a bit awkward saying this in front of an audience,' said the Warrior. 'But if ever you want to come and visit, you know you're welcome. Just let me know and I'll send you a ticket. And I've told your mum I'll stump up for your university. She says you want to do sculpting or something.'

Sky looked at Rosalind in amazement. Then he felt rather rotten; his father could certainly afford it but he didn't have to. And he was holding out this peace offering in front of quite a roomful of people. Sky looked at Nick, who had just watched his own father die in agony.

He swallowed hard.

'Thanks,' he said. 'That's very good of you. I'll think about coming on that visit.'

Epilogue: *One More Wedding*

In the black and white church attached to the friary of Saint-Mary-among-the-Vines, Brother Sulien was performing a wedding ceremony. It was the day after the duel and there were not many guests – Brother Tino, Brother Sandro, Giuditta Miele and Doctor Dethridge were the only people gathered in the Lady Chapel when the principals and their two attendants arrived.

'This has to be the strangest wedding that ever was,' said Luciano.

'Stranger for me,' said Arianna, smiling at him through her white lace mask. 'They are my parents, after all.'

'And married already, don't forget,' said Luciano. 'What will Sulien do about that?'

'I'm sure he has thought of something,' said Arianna.

'Dearly beloved,' began Brother Sulien.

And married Rodolfo Rossi, Regent of Bellezza, to Silvia Bellini, a widow from Padavia. Sulien knew their history and knew how important it was to find a way for them to live together publicly. Signor Rossi would return from Giglia with a new wife, and if she looked rather like the first, well, Bellezzans knew that men often ran true to type. He was a great favourite with citizens, known as a fair man with a tragic personal history, and they would be happy for him.

The little party afterwards was a low-key affair, held in the refectory of the friary, with no di Chimici present. The city was officially in mourning for a period of thirty days, in honour of its Grand Duke. Giglia had suffered many devastating blows, with the Nucci slaughter followed by the flood and the fatal duel.

But the wet weather, followed by a period of intense sun, had brought on all the late spring flowers early and the city was filled with the scents of lily-of-the-valley, sweet peas and stocks. Silvia had carried a spray of early white roses, from a tree carefully nurtured by Brother Tullio over the kitchen door of the friary.

Two brightly dressed figures joined the company. They made obeisance to the bride and groom and then Aurelio raised the Duchessa's hand to his lips. 'I am honoured to make music for you and your parents,' he said.

Aurelio played his harp, accompanied by Raffaella on the recorder he had made. The first tune was achingly sad, more suited to a wake than a wedding, and the guests listened to it, remembering the dead of the last week. But then the music became lively and Rodolfo led Silvia into a dance.

'It will be odd for me to live in the Palazzo Ducale again,' she said to him.

'It will be bliss,' he said, smiling. 'Just think, we never had the chance to live together as man and wife and we have been together more than twenty years and have a grown-up daughter.'

'Don't,' said Silvia. 'You'll make me feel old.'

'You are as beautiful now as when I first met you,' said Rodolfo, tightening his hold on her. 'And this time all the world will know that we are married and nothing shall ever separate us again.'

There were few women at that party, but Dethridge led Giuditta on to the floor and Raffaella stopped playing to dance with Sky. She was vividly beautiful and danced with the flamboyance of her people, which rather embarrassed him.

The friars found it highly amusing that one of their novices should have such an exotic dancing partner, even though most of them knew by now that Sky was not a real friar, but an important visitor in disguise. The liveliness of the music caused even Brother Tullio to take to the floor. He grabbed Brother Sandro by both hands and whirled him round, Brother Dog barking excitedly as they twirled round the refectory.

'They look happy, don't they?' said Luciano.

'Sandro and Tullio?' asked Arianna.

'Rodolfo and Silvia, silly,' he said, smiling down at her.

'Is it wrong to be so happy after so many people

have died?' she asked. 'You and I have both killed someone and yet I feel better than I have for a long time.'

But before Luciano had time to answer, Gaetano burst into the refectory.

'I'm sorry,' he said. 'I don't want to break up the party, but Fabrizio has just issued his first arrest warrant. And it's for Luciano.'

*

Franco the apprentice was driving a cart out of the city gate that opened on the road to Bellezza. He had a flagon of wine at his feet and a pretty girl beside him on the box. The guards had orders to stop all those leaving the city and search their vehicles for any signs of the traitorous Cavaliere Luciano of Bellezza who had killed the Grand Duke by foul means.

'Good evening,' said Franco politely to the largest of them, a man he recognised. Franco was well known for his exploits within and without the walls of the city and had a night territory the size of a tomcat's.

'Ah, Franco,' said the guard. 'What might your business be on the road so late?'

'I am transporting a statue for my mistress, Maestra Miele,' said Franco honestly. 'It is the statue she made of the beautiful young Duchessa of Bellezza. Perhaps word of it has reached you? Another masterpiece.'

'Are you taking it to Bellezza?' asked the guard.

'Indeed,' said Franco. 'And you see I have found another little masterpiece to accompany me on the road.'

'A masterpiece of the street, certainly,' said the man, and his companions all joined in the coarse laughter. 'You won't mind if I take a look at the load?'

Franco jumped down and untied the canvas cover that had been roped over the cart. There was a massive packing case of light wood, packed in by blankets to stop it from being jolted.

'Big girl, that Duchessa,' joked one of the guards.

'Like the woman who made her,' said another. 'Did you ever see the size of her? Keep a whole company of us warm, that one would.'

Franco wanted to punch him on the nose; he adored Giuditta. But he kept quiet. He was a man on a mission and had no desire to cause trouble.

'I should get you to open her up,' said the guard Franco knew. There was a crowbar in the cart for when the statue reached its destination.

Franco sighed. 'You can't believe how long it took us to pack her up,' he said in the grumbling tones of apprentices the world over. 'Sacking, straw, more sacking. That's why I'm setting off so late. It took three hours to get the Duchessa in her box. Everything has to be done just so for Giuditta Miele.'

'Otherwise you're for it, I suppose?' said one of the guards.

'I wouldn't mind if she wanted to spank me,' said another.

More laughter. Franco had an idiotic grin fixed on his face.

'Oh well, let be,' said the chief guard. 'I trust you. Look at that face,' he told his men. 'Can't imagine an angel like that lying, can you?'

'Can't imagine an angel doing lots of things that

one gets up to,' said one of them, setting them off again.

Franco gritted his teeth behind his angelic smile.

'I appreciate it,' he said. 'It's a long way to Bellezza.'

At last the cart was through the gate and Franco was on his way.

Inside the wooden crate, Luciano sighed with relief. He had his arms round Arianna and, if she was cold and unresponsive, it was because she was only a statue.

*

After Gaetano had broken up the wedding party and the Bellezzans had all left, Sky had a long talk with Sulien before stravagating home. Georgia and Nicholas had been true to their new pact and not stravagated back to Giglia again. And Sky felt that his mission in the city was over. There was a sad autumnal feeling in the air, even though summer had not yet begun.

'My father turned up,' he said to Sulien, as they walked slowly round the Great Cloister.

The friar looked at him closely. 'And how do you find him?' he asked.

Sky shrugged. 'He's OK, I suppose. Generous with his money, anyway, trying to make up for lost time. But I don't know him. I feel I know you better than I do him.'

'But you have made a start,' said Sulien. 'Surely that is better than wondering about him?'

'He wants me to visit him in America, where he lives,' explained Sky. 'And I've said I'll go. It looks as if everything is going to be different from what I thought. My mother is getting together with my girlfriend's father and it looks as if I'll be able to study sculpture after all.'

'Then you will be an apprentice of Giuditta's, in a manner of speaking,' said Sulien.

'Maybe,' said Sky. 'But I won't be able to come here and do it properly. I think perhaps I should stop visiting Giglia. I've felt torn in half for too long. At first I had no father and now I seem to have acquired two.'

Brother Sulien put his arm round Sky's shoulder. 'There will always be a third here for you if you need one,' he said. 'You have done whatever was asked of you here and we should do whatever we can for you.'

In the school cafeteria four friends sat together. Sky was telling the others about the wedding and the party after it. Alice was enjoying it; this was much more the sort of thing she liked – not duels and murders.

'At least you got through one wedding in Talia without anyone getting stabbed then,' she said.

Sky had just been going to tell them about Gaetano and the news of Luciano's escape from the city hidden in Giuditta Miele's cart. Then he noticed that Georgia and Nicholas were holding hands under the table. He decided not to mention Luciano.

Sky turned to Alice. 'What do you think about your dad and my mum?'

'It's weird,' said Alice. 'Weird for us, I mean. But I think they make a great couple. She's nice, your mum.'

'Yes,' said Sky. 'She is, isn't she?'

'You're supposed to say – "he's nice, too", Sky,' said Alice.

'Well, he is,' said Sky. 'I like him. But it would be a bit peculiar having him as a stepdad.'

'Do you think it will come to that?' said Georgia, seeing that Alice was dumbstruck.

'What would that make you two?' asked Nicholas. In spite of all that had happened he was feeling light-headed with happiness. He had accepted his fate. And Georgia was holding his hand.

'Close relations,' said Sky.

'That doesn't sound so bad,' said Alice shakily. 'I think I could handle that.'

'I don't think it will happen till we've gone to university, anyway,' said Sky. 'I think they'll wait till then to make it easier on us.'

'Are you definitely going to take up your dad's offer, then?' asked Georgia.

'Yes,' said Sky. 'And I'm going to do part of my degree in California and live with him and Loretta for a year. He's offered to pay for that too and I think I owe him that much.'

'You won't be able to stravagate from there,' said Nicholas.

'Well, I've been thinking about that,' said Sky. 'And I think I'm going to give it up. Hang up my talisman and my friar's robes. I'd better concentrate on my exams if I want to get into university.'

At a staging post on the road between Giglia and

Bellezza, some very grand carriages were drawn up at an inn. The Duchessa of Bellezza, her father the Regent and his new wife, and their many bodyguards and servants were all being entertained by a flustered landlord. The young Duchessa was restless, casting many looks out of the window.

At last she heard the rattle of cartwheels.

'I am in need of a breath of air,' she said. 'I shall go and see how my cats are faring.' Taking only one guard, she stepped out into the night. She headed for the stables, where a weary Franco jumped down from the box and started to unharness the horses, who objected to the presence of the African cats in the stall next to them. Franco's young companion had been packed off back to Giglia at the last staging-post.

'Good evening, your Grace,' he said, bowing. 'You see that your statue follows you safely to Bellezza.'

'I am anxious to see if it is all right,' said Arianna.

'Certainly,' said Franco. He pulled back the canvas and pried open the crate with the crowbar, quite easily, for he had opened it a few times already on this journey and the lid was tacked only lightly into place.

The bodyguard's hand went to his sword when he saw a young man jump out, but the Duchessa laughed and Franco put out his hand to stop the guard drawing his weapon.

'Let us give them some time alone, my friend,' he said, taking the guard by the arm and leading him out of the stable. 'The Duchessa is in no danger from that one. He would give his life for her – and very nearly did.'

'Luciano!' said Arianna. 'I am so pleased to see you safe.'

He took her in his arms and kissed her. And, unlike the statue, she responded warmly.

'Your hair is full of straw,' she said, when they pulled apart.

'I am altogether unworthy of your elegant and beautiful Grace,' said Luciano, holding her at arm's length. 'Do take off your mask so I can see your expression.'

'My guard will run you through if he catches you looking at my face,' said Arianna, untying the mask.

'I don't think so,' said Luciano. 'I think it might be treason to kill a Duke.'

'But you're not a Duke,' said Arianna.

'I will be if you marry me,' said Luciano and kissed her again. He could see her expression clearly now. 'Won't I? Duke Luciano of Bellezza, Consort of the beautiful Duchessa?'

'Yes,' said Arianna. 'You would be.'

'Would?'

'If you asked me.'

'I'm asking.'

'And if I accepted.'

'Do you?'

'I do,' said Arianna. 'With all my heart.'

And she threw her mask away.

A Note on the di Chimici and the Medici

The history of the Medici is as tightly bound up with the city of Florence as that of the di Chimici is with Giglia. The Medici, or de' Medici to give them their proper Italian name, were a family which might have had an ancestor who was a doctor ('medico'). The six red balls on their family crest *might* represent pharmaceutical pills – or that might all be part of the family legend. What is certain is that, like the di Chimici, the Medici owed their fortune to banking.

The first Medici banker was Giovanni (1360–1429), roughly equivalent to the di Chimici ancestor Ferdinando. The Medici family benefited when King Edward III of England failed to pay back a gigantic loan to two other Florentine banking families, the Bardi and the Peruzzi. They never recovered. Cosimo the Elder (1389–1464), who married a Bardi, commissioned Brunelleschi (who built the church of San Lorenzo in Florence and the dome for the city's huge cathedral) to design a palace for him on the Via Larga, or broad street.

The plans were considered too grand and Cosimo switched to Michelozzo Michelozzi, whose palazzo (Medici-Riccardi) can still be visited on the Via Cavour (the modern name of the Via Larga). I stayed one block up the road from it when starting to write *City of Flowers*. It houses the fabulous Benozzo Gozzoli fresco of the journey of the Magi in its chapel, which is supposed to include portraits of prominent Medici family members.

Piero de' Medici (1416–1469), roughly equivalent to Fabrizio di Chimici, first Duke of Giglia, was best known for being the father of Lorenzo the Magnificent. He ruled for only five years, but his son Lorenzo (1449–1492), equivalent to Alfonso di Chimici, Niccolò's father, was in power for twenty-three years.

Lorenzo de' Medici, 'il magnifico', is the one that most people think of when they hear the name Medici. He was a great patron of the arts, a scholar, poet, philosopher and soldier, as well as a great womaniser, though a fond husband, a good friend and an implacable enemy.

I have bestowed the title of Duke much earlier in the di Chimici family, on Fabrizio (1425–1485). In fact it was Alessandro, the illegitimate son of Pope Clement VII, who first called himself Duke of Florence, in 1532. But the Medici then catch up, because Cosimo I, great-grandson of Lorenzo the Magnificent, had himself made Grand Duke in 1569, ten years before Niccolò di Chimici had the same idea.

Several Medici were Popes, like Ferdinando di Chimici, Lenient VI, the first being Leo X (Giovanni de' Medici, 1475–1521), Lorenzo's oldest son. Leo was as fond of eating and drinking as Ferdinando di Chimici, once serving a twenty-five course meal for six hundred guests.

As for enemies, the Medici had far more than the di Chimici! The Albizzi family, the Pitti, the Pazzi, the Strozzi . . . Florentine history is littered with them. The Pazzi conspiracy of 1478 was supposed to kill both Lorenzo and his brother Giuliano. The younger brother was indeed stabbed to death, during Easter Mass in the cathedral, but Lorenzo was only wounded. All the Pazzi were killed, imprisoned or exiled as Lorenzo avenged his brother.

It wasn't the first assassination attempt on a de' Medici. The Pitti had engineered one on Piero in 1466, as a result of which they lost the grand palace being built for them on the far side of Arno, which bears their name to this day. Brunelleschi was their first architect, but building stopped for a hundred years. The restless Grand Duke Cosimo moved from the Medici palace on the Via Larga to the Palazzo Vecchio in 1539 and into the Pitti Palace nine years later, though that technically belonged to his wife Eleonora of Toledo. Grand Duke Niccolò made the equivalent moves in a few weeks.

Although his grandfather Alfonso is closest in dates to Lorenzo the Magnificent, Gaetano resembles the flower of the Medici family closely in being charming but ugly, courteous, learned and a lover of the arts, as well as a fine horseman and swordsman. (He will make a much more faithful husband, however.)

But there is no historical equivalent to Falco. He was invented by me, inspired by Giuseppe Tomasi di Lampedusa's account of his solitary childhood wandering through the vast emptiness of his family's palaces, and by my two distant cousins, William and Henry, devoted brothers, one of whom badly damaged his leg (though, being a twenty-first-century young man, not with such disastrous consequences as Falco). All the rest of the di Chimici are complete inventions.

The dukes and princes of the di Chimici gave all their sons and daughters the honorary titles of Principe (prince) and Principessa (princess). They soon became princes and dukes in their own right anyway, as the di Chimici acquired power in more city-states of Talia (see Dramatis Personae).

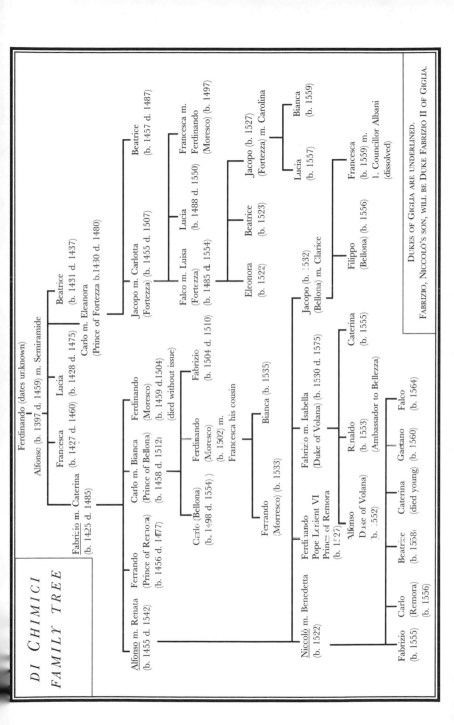

Dramatis Personae

 Stravaganti

William Dethridge, the Elizabethan who discovered
the art of stravagation. Known in Talia as
Guglielmo Crinamorte
Rodolfo Rossi, Regent of Bellezza
Luciano Crinamorte (formerly Lucien Mulholland),
foster-son of William Dethridge and Leonora. First
apprentice and then assistant to Rodolfo
Suliano Fabriano (Brother Sulien), pharmacist-friar at
Saint-Mary-among-the-Vines
Giuditta Miele, sculptor in Giglia
Sky Meadows (Celestino Pascoli, or Brother Tino),
sixth-former at Barnsbury Comprehensive
Georgia O'Grady, sixth-former at Barnsbury
Comprehensive
Nicholas Duke (formerly Falco di Chimici), Year 10
student at Barnsbury Comprehensive

 di Chimici

Niccolò, Duke of Giglia
Fabrizio, Niccolò's eldest son
Carlo, Niccolò's second son
Gaetano, Niccolò's third son
Beatrice, Niccolò's daughter
Ferdinando (Pope Lenient VI), Prince of Remora
Rinaldo, the Pope's chaplain and nephew, formerly

Reman Ambassador to Bellezza
Alfonso, Duke of Volana, Rinaldo's older brother
Caterina of Volana, Rinaldo's younger sister, engaged
to be married to Prince Fabrizio
Isabella, dowager Duchess of Volana, their mother
Jacopo, Prince of Fortezza
Princess Carolina, his wife
Lucia, their older daughter, engaged to be married to
Prince Carlo
Bianca, their younger daughter, engaged to be married
to Duke Alfonso of Volana
Francesca of Bellona, engaged to be married to Prince
Gaetano

 Nucci

Matteo Nucci, a rich wool merchant
Graziella, his wife
Camillo, their eldest son
Filippo, their second son
Davide, their youngest son
Anna and Lidia, their daughters

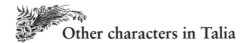 Other characters in Talia

Silvia Bellini, a wealthy 'widow' from Padavia
(formerly Duchessa of Bellezza)
Guido Parola, her servant and bodyguard
Susanna, her maid

Arianna Rossi, Duchessa of Bellezza, daughter of Silvia and Rodolfo

Barbara, her maid

Paola Bellini, Arianna's grandmother, a lace-maker on the island of Burlesca

Enrico Poggi, chief spy of Duke Niccolò

Sandro, an orphan, working for Enrico

Franco, Giuditta Miele's senior apprentice

Brother Tullio, cook-friar at Saint-Mary-among-the-Vines

Gabassi, Duke Niccolò's architect

Aurelio Vivoide, a Manoush, a harpist

Raffaella Vivoide, a Manoush, his companion

Fratello, a mongrel dog, adopted by Sandro

 **Other characters in England**

Rosalind Meadows, Sky's mother, an aromatherapist

Rainbow Warrior (aka Colin Peck), Sky's father

Gus Robinson, Rainbow Warrior's agent

Loretta, Rainbow Warrior's fourth wife

Gloria Peck, Rainbow Warrior's mother

Joyce Meadows, Rosalind's mother

Remedy, Sky's cat

Alice Greaves, Georgia's best friend

Paul Greaves, Alice's father

Jane Scott, Alice's mother, ex-wife of Paul Greaves

Laura, Rosalind's best friend, a House of Commons PA

Vicky Mulholland, Nicholas's foster-mother, a violin teacher

Mary Hoffman

Mary Hoffman lives in a big old converted barn in West Oxfordshire. Most of *City of Masks* was written in Mary's lovely study there, which is green and white, with French windows on to the garden, a silver mask on the notice board and a vase of peacock feathers in the fireplace.

City of Stars was encouraged by a terracotta tile of a flying horse, bought in Siena, and a shield featuring the ram of the Valdimontone district of that city, where the Palio horse race is held twice each summer.

For *City of Flowers*, Mary went to Florence for a month, then spent the next four months holed up in her study, sitting at the computer, putting on weight. She couldn't find a blue glass bottle just like the one on the cover, so had to make do with scent from Santa Maria Novella.

Mary goes to Italian literature classes each week in Oxford, produces four issues of the online children's book review magazine *Armadillo* every year, reads voraciously and plays with her Burmese cat, Kichri, a little red, who is her most devoted companion and has adapted well to life in the country (an Aga helps!)

www.stravaganza.co.uk
www.maryhoffman.co.uk
www.bloomsbury.com

WHERE BARTENDERS
DRINK

—

ADRIENNE STILLMAN

THE EXPERTS' GUIDE
TO THE BEST BARS
IN THE WORLD

CONTENTS

Introduction 6
Key 8

OCEANIA
Australia 14
    Sydney 16
    Melbourne 22
New Zealand 28

ASIA
Southwest Asia 38
South & Southeast Asia 42
    Singapore 50
China, Hong Kong,
    South Korea,
    & Taiwan 56
    Shanghai 60
    Hong Kong 64
Japan 70
    Tokyo 78

EUROPE
Iceland, Norway, Sweden,
    Denmark, & Finland 88
UK & Republic of Ireland 96
    London 100
The Netherlands
    & Belgium 122
    Amsterdam 126
France 132
    Paris 136
Spain & Portugal 148
    Barcelona 152
Germany & Switzerland 158
    Munich 164
Poland, The Czech
    Republic, Austria,
    & Hungary 170
Baltic States, Belarus,
    Romania, Greece,
    & Cyprus 176
The Russian Federation 184
Italy 190
    Milan 200
    Rome 206

AFRICA
South Africa 212

NORTH AMERICA
Canada 218
    Vancouver 226
USA West 232
    Los Angeles 248
    San Francisco 258
USA Midwest 268
    Chicago 274
USA South 286
    New Orleans 300
USA Northeast 308
    New York City 316

CENTRAL & SOUTH AMERICA
Central America
    & The Caribbean 344
South America North 352
South America South 358
    Buenos Aires 362

ESSAYS
Cocktails Down Under:
    Australia and
    New Zealand 12
Cocktails in Asia 36
Cocktails in Japan 72
Cocktails in Europe 86
From Mayfair to Shoreditch:
    Cocktails in London 104
Cocktails à la Française:
    Paris 138
The Art of Aperitivo:
    Cocktails in Italy 192
Cocktails in Canada 220
Cocktails in the
    United States 234
Cocktails in Los Angeles 250
Cocktails in San Francisco 260
The Windy City: Cocktails
    in Chicago 276
The Big Easy: Cocktails
    in New Orleans 302
Home of the Manhattan:
    Cocktails in
    New York City 318
Cocktails in Latin America 342

The Contributors 368
The Contributors'
    Recommendations 370
Index by Type 395
Index by Country 405
Index by Bar 413

INTRODUCTION

I discovered cocktails late one night in the fall of 2005. With a swoosh of the velvet curtain, I was ushered into Milk & Honey, one of the bars that sparked the cocktail revolution in New York City in the early 2000s. I was hooked at the first sip of my Gold Rush—a cocktail made with bourbon, lemon, and honey.

Over the past ten years, the cocktail scene has exploded around the globe. In some ways it's easy to see why: once you've tasted a great cocktail, you never go back.

Once there were only a handful of bars where you could get a proper Manhattan, now New York teems with them—and so do London and Paris, Tokyo and Singapore, Melbourne and Buenos Aires. Even more excitingly, great cocktail bars are no longer only a thing of metropolitan cities, they're cropping up in small towns and out-of-the-way places at a high rate. Slowly but surely the Old Fashioned has gone back to being a boozy whiskey drink instead of a fruit salad. Manhattans are stirred, not shaken. The Negroni has become a cocktail menu staple. People are rediscovering all kinds of spirits and liqueurs, and inventing new ones. It's an exciting time to be a discerning drinker.

The cocktail is an American invention—the first "Golden Age of Cocktails" occurred in the United States from the late 1800s to 1920. It was during these years that many of the classic drinks we know today, including the Manhattan and the Martini, were invented.

On January 16, 1920, however, cocktails were dealt a heavy blow: Prohibition—which banned the sale of alcoholic drinks in the United States—went into effect. As a result, many bartenders and their patrons escaped to Europe, especially Paris and London, helping to establish cocktail culture there.

Fast forward to the 1970s and the classics were all but forgotten, passed over in favor of drinks like the Long Island Iced Tea, designed to serve as much alcohol as possible while masking the flavor. Drinking ceased to be about enjoying something delicious and became about getting drunk as quickly as possible.

But by the mid 1980s, new glimmers of hope emerged with Dale DeGroff in New York, Dick Bradsell in London,

and Charles Schumann in Munich. Swapping sour mix for fresh citrus, bringing vermouth out from the cobwebs, and retiring those radioactive-red cherries, they planted the seeds for what has been called the second Golden Age of Cocktails that we are experiencing right now.

It must be said that without the chef movement that came before it—which spawned *Where Chefs Eat*, the first book in this series—there would be no cocktail movement. Our appreciation for and access to fine food has spilled into beverage: we are no longer content to drink a mediocre red wine with our Wagyu beef. We want more than a Jack and Coke. It is incredibly exciting to watch the cocktail world truly come into its own amid this highly creative environment.

This book is a collection of 700 bars recommended by close to 225 of the world's top bartenders, who are part of the incredible cocktail renaissance of the past twenty years. But they are not all cocktail bars. Far from it. As one bartender told me when I started my interviews, "You know your book is going to be all dive bars, right? Because that's where bartenders drink."

Certainly, many of the world's top cocktail destinations are included in these pages, but so are many dive bars and unsung neighborhood pubs. Because sometimes you want a perfectly executed Old Fashioned served over a perfectly clear cube of ice, and other times you want a shot or a cold beer—and maybe a hamburger. This diversity is the strength of the book: there is truly something for everyone and every mood.

It has been my great privilege to write and compile *Where Bartenders Drink*, to interview the many talented bartenders all over the world and showcase their exciting work in these pages. Throughout the process the bar community showed their enthusiasm and shared their knowledge and passion for their craft and each other. Obviously this book would not be possible without them, and I would like to thank all of them for sharing their favorite drinking spots with us.

ADRIENNE STILLMAN

KEY

For this guide, we asked our contributors to recommend their favorite bars around the world, according to the following classifications:

Late-Night
At the end of a long shift—or a long night out—this is where to go at 3:00 a.m.

Hotel
When traveling and in need of high quality libations, these hotels have you covered.

Neighborhood
The nondescript corner bar, the local dive, the homey pub: this is where bartenders go on their day off.

Local Must-Visit
If you leave without visiting these bars, you've done it wrong.

Worth the Travel
These are the places for which bartenders would gladly spend interminable hours in planes, trains, and automobiles to get to.

Wish I'd Opened
If the bartenders could go back in time and do it again, these are the places they wished they'd opened themselves.

Turn to page 370 for a full index of their global recommendations.

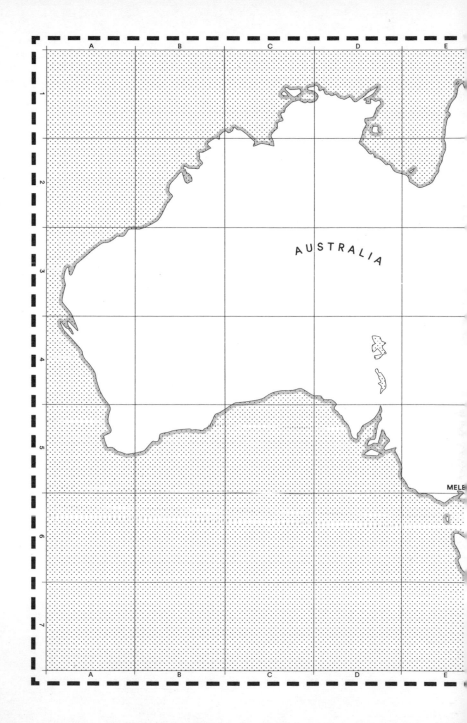

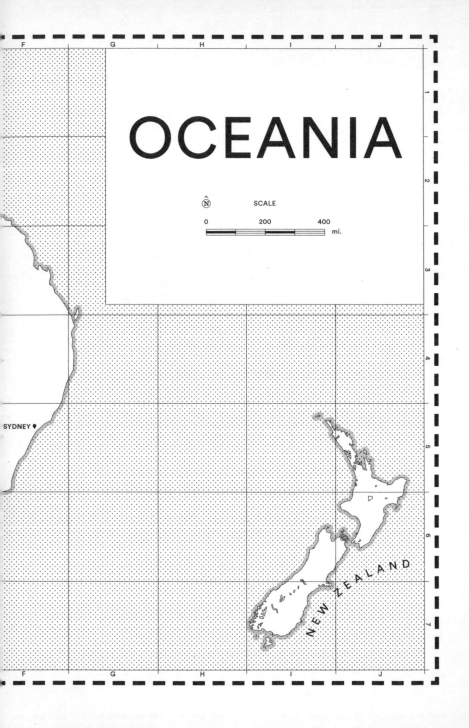

OCEANIA

$\hat{N}$ SCALE

0　　　200　　　400
mi.

SYDNEY ●

NEW ZEALAND

COCKTAILS DOWN UNDER: AUSTRALIA & NEW ZEALAND

Limes are a staple at cocktail bars. A key ingredient in classics like the Daiquiri or the Southside, along with lemons, they are the primary citrus used in cocktails. Imagine not being able to source any for three to four months a year. The remote island location of New Zealand means that when limes aren't in season locally, they aren't available.

Availability of products is one of the primary challenges—and a defining characteristic—of both Australia and New Zealand. Until recently, many liquor brands did not export there at all and specialty ingredients such as vermouth or amaro remain difficult to come by. As a result, locals have turned to their own devices and there are thriving local craft beer and spirits communities, as well as wine.

Australia

Sydney and Melbourne are the major cocktail hubs and home of internationally recognized bars such as the Black Pearl and the Baxter Inn. Sydney is a larger city, but cocktails first took hold of Melbourne in the early 2000s. Then in 2008, the liquor laws changed and suddenly a new group of bars started to spring up in Sydney. The eclectic selection ranges from American-style whiskey bar Shady Pines Saloon to ultra-seasonal Bulletin Place to Prohibition-style speakeasy Palmer & Co. The bar scene is weekend-centric, so Sunday to Wednesday nights are relatively quiet and a good time to go if you want to be able to chat with your bartender.

Practical Information:
- Cocktails range from AU$16 to AU$25.
- Tipping 10% to 15% is the norm.
- Beware of Sydney's 2:00 a.m. "lockout laws" that keep you from entering new bars after that time.

New Zealand

The cocktail scene here is more developed on the northern island in Auckland and Wellington. Because of its tourist industry, Queenstown in Otago offers a few bright spots, but after the devastating 2011 earthquake, Christchurch continues to struggle. Even more than Australia, product availability is a big challenge. The good news is that you'll find lots of interesting local ingredients such as kiwis, Manuka honey, and specialty citrus. Like in Australia, people tend to go out on the weekends more than midweek.

Practical Information:
- Cocktails range from NZ$16 to NZ$22.
- Tipping is not expected, but much appreciated, and may make you some new friends.

"AN INCREDIBLE AMOUNT OF DETAIL PUT INTO THE SMALLER THINGS … SIMPLE YET BOOZY, DELICATE BUT STRONG COCKTAILS."

PAIGE AUBERTON P.19

"A BAR CRAWL IN MELBOURNE WITHOUT THE CHARM OF THIS SMALL BAR MAKES LITTLE SENSE."

MIGUEL FERNANDEZ FERNANDEZ P.24

AUSTRALIA

"THE BACK BAR IS ENORMOUS, WITH TWO LIBRARY LADDERS EXTENDING TO THE CEILING."

JOE BALLINGER P.18

"WHETHER YOU'RE AFTER A PRIVATE BOOTH OR YOU WANT TO SHOW OFF YOUR DANCE MOVES, YOU'RE GUARANTEED A GREAT TIME HERE."

HANNAH KEIRL P.25

"THEY JUST DO EVERYTHING GOOD. COCKTAILS, PIZZA, COLD BEER, GREAT SERVICE, EPIC SUNDAY ROAST."

TIM PHILLIPS P.18

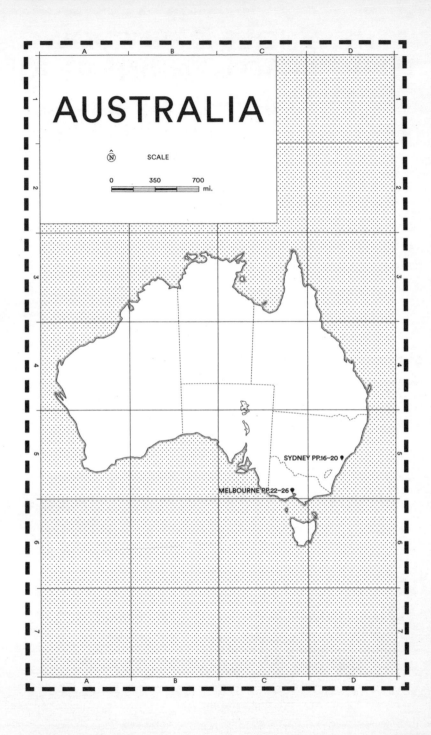

"THE WHOLE CREW DOWN THERE IS SO GENUINE THAT THEY'LL MAKE YOU FEEL LIKE A LOCAL EVEN IF IT'S YOUR FIRST TIME THERE."

PAIGE AUBERTON P.18

SYDNEY

"THIS BAR COMBINES TASTY, HIGH-QUALITY, LATE-NIGHT FOOD, GOOD COCKTAILS ... AND A SOLID RANGE OF BEERS."

TOM EGERTON P.19

"IT FEELS LIKE A BAR ROUND THE CORNER FROM YOUR HOME"

CHARLIE AINSBURY P.18

"FINALLY, A BAR IN SYDNEY WHERE YOU COULD JUST DRINK AND HAVE SOME FUN."

CHARLIE AINSBURY P.19

"IF YOU'RE SERIOUS ABOUT HEAVY BEER, LIGHT WHISKEY, AND FINE TUNES, THERE'S NO BETTER."

TOM EGERTON P.20

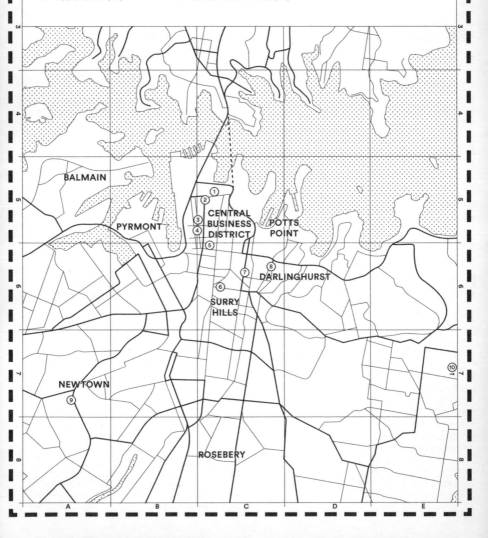

SYDNEY

SCALE

0   600   1200   1800
yd.

1. BULLETIN PLACE (P.18)
2. PALMER AND CO (P.19)
3. MOJO RECORD BAR (P.18)
4. THE BAXTER INN (P.18)
5. RAMBLIN' RASCAL TAVERN (P.19)
6. THE WILD ROVER (P.20)
7. SHADY PINES SALOON (P.19)
8. HENRIETTA SUPPER CLUB (P.19)
9. EARL'S JUKE JOINT (P.20)
10. THE CORNER HOUSE (P.18)

THE CORNER HOUSE

281 Bondi Road
Bondi
Sydney
New South Wales 2026
Australia
+61 280206698
www.thecornerhouse.com.au

Opening hours	Closed Monday
Reservation policy	Not accepted
Credit cards	Accepted
Price range	Affordable
Dress code	Casual
Style	Pizzeria and bar

"They just do everything good. Cocktails, pizza, cold beer, great service, epic Sunday roast."—Tim Philips

THE BAXTER INN

Basement Level
152-156 Clarence Street
Central Business District
Sydney
New South Wales 2000
Australia
www.thebaxterinn.com

Opening hours	Closed Sunday
Reservation policy	Not accepted
Credit cards	Accepted
Price range	Affordable
Dress code	Smart casual
Style	Speakeasy

"I travel to this bar at least three times a week. It may only be a two minute walk as it's a neighboring bar to my own, but my god, I'll be damned if I wouldn't go the distance anyway. Yes this place has whiskey, yes the back bar is mesmerizing but that's not what makes Baxter, Baxter's. It's the staff. From the top of its gorgeous head down to its toes you can't beat the team that works there."—Paige Auberton

"I visited this place a couple of times and it always surpassed anything I'd heard of. Like many places now, you pass through an anonymous alley and are ushered down some steps to a room which isn't overfilled and full of whiskey, jazz, and laughter. It's not the scale, or range of whiskey (which is the best I've ever seen), it's the atmosphere, achieved by the people inside."—Joe Ballinger

Baxter Inn was voted the best bar in Australia on the World's 50 Best Bars list in 2015, and has been in the top 10 globally since 2012.

BULLETIN PLACE

Level 1
10-14 Bulletin Place
Circular Quay
Central Business District
Sydney
New South Wales 2000
Australia
www.bulletinplace.com

Opening hours	Open 7 days
Reservation policy	Not accepted
Credit cards	Accepted
Price range	Affordable
Dress code	Smart casual
Style	Cocktail bar

"It's right in the thick of the financial district but it feels like a bar round the corner from your home. You will not get a shit drink here, any night of the week."—Charlie Ainsbury

"I really admire the philosophy and the bar vision of Tim D. Philips, the bar manager of the place. He always uses the freshest seasonal ingredients, keeps refreshing his cocktail menu, and still upgrades the venue with his own hands."—Igor Zernov

Bulletin Place has been included on the World's 50 Best Bars list since 2013.

MOJO RECORD BAR

Basement Level
73 York Street
Central Business District
Sydney
New South Wales 2000
Australia
+61 292624999
www.mojorecordbar.com

Opening hours	Closed Sunday
Reservation policy	Accepted
Credit cards	Accepted
Price range	Affordable
Dress code	Casual
Style	Cocktail bar

"Call me a sucker for basement bars, I don't give a damn. But if you're in town, head downstairs on York Street, have a quick flick through the record store and stumble through the back to the awesome bar that awaits you. Noble heads the team here and he is as effervescent as his smile is infectious. The whole crew down there are so genuine that they'll make you feel like a local even if it's your first time there." —Paige Auberton

PALMER AND CO

Abercrombie Lane
Central Business District
Sydney
New South Wales 2000
Australia
+61 292403000
www.merivale.com.au/palmerandco

Opening hours	Open 7 days
Reservation policy	Accepted
Credit cards	Accepted
Price range	Affordable
Dress code	Smart casual
Style	Speakeasy

"An incredible amount of detail put into the smaller things. A 1920s Prohibition-themed bar with a plethora of stellar international and home-grown bartenders working behind the stick. Simple yet boozy, delicate but strong cocktails. And a mac 'n' cheese that'll make you never want your mother's own recipe again." —Paige Auberton

RAMBLIN' RASCAL TAVERN

Basement Level
199 Elizabeth Street
Central Business District
Sydney
New South Wales 2000
Australia
www.ramblinrascaltavern.com

Opening hours	Closed Sunday
Reservation policy	Not accepted for drinks
Credit cards	Accepted
Price range	Affordable
Dress code	Casual
Style	Cocktail bar

"Like coming home . . . if home had charismatic men in overalls, an almost insurmountable range of Cognac, dark timber, and one of the best Daiquiri shakes in Sydney. Ask Cosmo for a Daiquiri, Charlie for some great chat and to play 'Call Me Maybe', and Dardan for a dirty joke. You won't be disappointed."—Paige Auberton

HENRIETTA SUPPER CLUB

Level 1
292–294 Victoria Road
Darlinghurst
Sydney
New South Wales 2010
Australia
www.henriettasupperclub.com.au

Opening hours	Open Tuesday–Saturday from 10 p.m.
Reservation policy	Accepted
Credit cards	Accepted
Price range	Affordable
Dress code	Casual
Style	Restaurant and bar

"Miraculously outside the draconian lock-out laws that have plagued Sydney and strictly catering to a hospitality crowd, this bar combines tasty, high-quality, late-night food, good cocktails, friendly service, mad beats, and a solid range of beers for when you've had a solid ass-kicking behind the bar and just want to sink something easy."—Tom Egerton

SHADY PINES SALOON

Shop 4
256 Crown Street
Darlinghurst
Sydney
New South Wales 2010
Australia
www.shadypinessaloon.com

Opening hours	Open 7 days
Reservation policy	Not accepted
Credit cards	Accepted
Price range	Affordable
Dress code	Casual
Style	Whiskey, beer, and cocktail bar

"American whiskey the breadth of the bar, beer from the most obscure craft to the cheapest tin of lager, rye and fresh Granny Smith juice for the neophyte, and enough taxidermy and country music to satisfy your inner cowboy. Sunday night is trade night in Sydney and it's the best time to see the best of Sydney's hospitality at their worst."—Tom Egerton

"Years ago, the Sydney bar scene was rather stale. A change in some regulations and the introduction of the Small Bars licence finally allowed people like us to take control of the drink offerings in our town. Jason Scott and Anton Forte led the way and opened up their first bar, Shadys. Finally, a bar in Sydney where you could just drink and have some fun. No poker machines, no TV screens, no plastic furniture, nothing generic about it. It was a bar for the people."
—Charlie Ainsbury

EARL'S JUKE JOINT

407 King Street
Newtown
Sydney
New South Wales 2042
Australia

Opening hours...Open 7 days
Reservation policy..Not accepted
Credit cards...Accepted
Price range..Affordable
Dress code..Smart casual
Style...Cocktail bar

"I nurse the pain of knowing I will never be the one to open Earl's in one hand while the other holds some ridiculously tasty classic cocktail. It does make it easier. The team at Earl's has a solid signatures list but my appreciation for the bar grew from the simple fact that I knew I could go there, anytime, any day (trading hours permitting obviously) and ask for any classic and have it made for me spot on. It seems simple but it's not. And these guys nail it. New Orleans inspired music ranging from blues to hip-hop and back again, and such hospitable service it makes me reach for another Negroni when I probably should have stopped two ago." —Paige Auberton

"Pasan helped bring two previous bars in Sydney to worldwide fame and took his work ethic and desire to create yet another fantastic cocktail bar in Sydney themed for his love of the Blues, which is also a love of my own. The pictures of blues musicians from the American South, which in turn spawned the Rolling Stones, Beatles, and Elvis, are laid out all across the walls of his bar . . . Juke Joint is a name for a gathering room for sharecroppers to listen to music and jam on the day they head off from the fields. Wonderful homage." —Chris Hannah

THE WILD ROVER

75 Campbell Street
Surry Hills
Sydney
New South Wales 2010
Australia
+61 292802235
www.thewildrover.com.au

Opening hours..Closed Sunday
Reservation policy................................Not accepted for drinks
Credit cards...Accepted
Price range..Affordable
Dress code...Casual
Style..Irish pub

"The ideal Irish pub, locked away behind the facade of a shirt pub and eschewing the usual trappings of shamrocks, rubbish ceilidh bands and Guinness branding, the Wild Rover boasts reams of good Irish whiskey, the best stout on handpull you'll find outside of St. James' Gate, and friendly folk behind the stick. If you're serious about heavy beer, light whiskey, and fine tunes, there's no better. And their St. Patrick's Day party will blow your socks off no doubt."—Tom Egerton

"PERFECT BAR TO SIT AND WATCH THE SUN GO DOWN WITH A COCKTAIL."

MICHAEL MADRUSAN P.24

"A BARTENDER'S HEAVEN WITH 200+ BITTERS AND OPEN UNTIL 3 A.M. EVERY DAY."

DAN BERGER P.24

MELBOURNE

"THIS IS WHAT A GOOD AUSSIE PUB IS ALL ABOUT."

TIM PHILIPS P.26

"BEAUTIFUL, CLASSIC COCKTAIL BAR IN MELBOURNE'S COOLEST NEIGHBORHOOD."

SAM ROSS P.26

"GOOD CHEESE, GOOD VIEWS, GREAT WINE, AND MARTINIS. WHAT ELSE COULD YOU WANT?"

TIM PHILIPS P.25

MELBOURNE

N̂   SCALE

0   500   1000   1500
yd.

1. BLACK PEARL (P.25)
2. NAPIER HOTEL (P.26)
3. EVERLEIGH (P.26)
4. SIGLO (P.25)

5. LILY BLACKS (P.24)
6. SECTION 8 (P.25)
7. HEARTBREAKER (P.24)
8. THE TOFF (P.25)

9. BAR AMERICANO (P.24)
10. LUI BAR (P.24)

BAR AMERICANO

20 Presgrave Place
Central Business District
Melbourne
Victoria 3000
Australia
www.baramericano.com

Opening hours	Closed Sunday
Reservation policy	Not accepted
Credit cards	Accepted but not AMEX
Price range	Affordable
Dress code	Smart casual
Style	Cocktail bar

"When I was in the Americano for the first time, I was overwhelmed/surprised: this small, unobtrusive bar in a side street . . . less than twenty spirits (not including the vermouth, of which they have more then fifty from around the world), no seating, very little room, soft music, only classic cocktails. But the charm of an Italian espresso bar (by the way the best espresso for me in a long time), a lot of attention to detail in the smallest space (the decanter of spirits, the drinks menu inspired by great cocktail books, Italian magazines . . .), perfectly balanced drinks, little hints of art, etc. . . . A bar crawl in Melbourne without the charm of this small bar makes little sense. A gem for connoisseurs and lovers of stylish understatement. *La dolce vita!*"—Miguel Fernandez Fernandez

HEARTBREAKER

234a Russell Street
Central Business District
Melbourne
Victoria 3000
Australia
+61 390410856
www.heartbreakerbar.com.au

Opening hours	Open 7 days
Reservation policy	Not accepted
Credit cards	Accepted
Price range	Affordable
Dress code	Smart casual
Style	Cocktail bar

"Great music, vibe, and drinks."—Michael Madrusan

LILY BLACKS

12 Meyers Place
Central Business District
Melbourne
Victoria 3000
Australia
+61 396544887
www.lilyblacks.com.au

Opening hours	Open 7 days
Reservation policy	Accepted
Credit cards	Accepted
Price range	Affordable
Dress code	Smart casual
Style	Cocktail bar

"My favorite bar in Australia. Tucked down a side street in the city center, this is a must see. A bartender's heaven with 200+ bitters and open until 3 a.m. every day. Worth the journey."
—Dan Berger

LUI BAR

Level 55, Rialto
525 Collins Street
Central Business District
Melbourne
Victoria 3000
Australia
+61 396913888
www.luibar.com.au

Opening hours	Open 7 days
Reservation policy	Not accepted
Credit cards	Accepted
Price range	Affordable
Dress code	Smart casual
Style	Cocktail bar

"Perfect bar to sit and watch the sun go down with a cocktail."—Michael Madrusan

SECTION 8

27-29 Tattersalls Lane
Central Business District
Melbourne
Victoria 3000
Australia
+61 430291588
www.section8.com.au

Opening hours	Open 7 days
Reservation policy	Not accepted
Credit cards	Not accepted
Price range	Affordable
Dress code	Casual
Style	Cocktail bar

"Such a simple street concept—a container bar, grungy, chilled out, and completely laid back. Outdoors. And even in winter you can't help but love it rugged up under small heaters with mulled cider. Always a guest DJ and smaller selection of awesome booze."—Hannah Keirl

SIGLO

Second Floor
161 Spring Street
The European Restaurant
Central Business District
Melbourne
Victoria 3000
Australia
+61 396546631
www.theeuropean.com.au

Opening hours	Open 7 days
Reservation policy	Not accepted for drinks
Credit cards	Accepted
Price range	Affordable
Dress code	Smart casual
Style	Cocktail bar

"Rooftop looking over Parliament House in Melbourne CBD. Good cheese, good views, great wine, and Martinis. What else could you want?"—Tim Philips

THE TOFF

Second Floor Curtin House
252 Swanston Street
Central Business District
Melbourne
Victoria 3000
Australia
+61 3 9639 8770
www.thetoffintown.com

Opening hours	Open 7 days
Reservation policy	Accepted
Credit cards	Accepted
Price range	Affordable
Dress code	Smart casual
Style	Nightclub and music venue

"Whether you're after a private booth or you want to show off your dance moves, you're guaranteed a great time here."—Hannah Keirl

BLACK PEARL

304 Brunswick Street
Fitzroy
Melbourne
Victoria 3065
Australia
+61 394170455
www.blackpearlbar.com.au

Opening hours	Open 7 days
Reservation policy	Accepted
Credit cards	Accepted but not AMEX
Price range	Affordable
Dress code	Smart casual
Style	Cocktail bar

"If people are heading to Melbourne I tell them to go here but I also tell them that when they do, they aren't going anywhere else. It's the black hole of bars, and I mean that in the best way possible. Stellar service, drinks are incredible . . . it feels like family with those guys."—Charlie Ainsbury

EVERLEIGH

Upstairs
150-156 Gertrude Street
Fitzroy
Melbourne
Victoria 3065
Australia
+61 394162229
www.theeverleigh.com

Opening hours	Open 7 days
Reservation policy	Not accepted
Credit cards	Accepted
Price range	Affordable
Dress code	Smart casual
Style	Cocktail bar

"My favorite bar room. Beautiful, classic cocktail bar in Melbourne's coolest neighborhood. Always classy."—Sam Ross

Founded by Michael Madrusan, an alumnus of New York's iconic Milk & Honey, PDT, and Little Branch bars, the Everleigh has been included in the World's 50 Best Bars list from 2013 to 2015. Additionally, Michael was nominated as Best International Bartender at Tales of the Cocktail in 2012.

NAPIER HOTEL

210 Napier Street
Fitzroy
Melbourne
Victoria 3065
Australia
+61 394194240
www.thenapierhotel.com

Opening hours	Open 7 days
Reservation policy	Not accepted for drinks
Credit cards	Accepted
Price range	Affordable
Dress code	Casual
Style	Gastropub

"This is what a good Aussie pub is all about. Great food, service, and independent beer selection. Get the Bogan Burger if you dare."—Tim Philips

"SIT OUT IN THE GARDEN WITH A FRESH HOPPED BEER FROM THEIR AMAZING REVOLVING SELECTION SURROUNDED BY MOUNTAINS, FOREST, AND STONE GOLD MINING COTTAGES AND YOU'LL UNDERSTAND."
PAUL SHIPMAN P.30

NEW ZEALAND

"SOLID COCKTAILS, GOOD CRAFT BEER, AND TASTY BAR SNACKS DON'T HURT EITHER, BUT REALLY IT'S THE VIEW YOU GO THERE FOR." PAUL SHIPMAN P.31

"A VENUE FOR OUT-OF-TOWNERS TO MEET THE CREATIVE CHARACTERS OF THE CITY."
JONNY MCKENZIE P.31

"THE ENVIRONMENT IS WELCOMING IN BOTH WINTER AND SUMMER, AND THE STAFF IS ALWAYS WILLING TO CHAT AND PROVIDE ADVICE. THE PERFECT NEIGHBORHOOD BAR."
JONNY MCKENZIE P.30

NEW ZEALAND

SCALE

0   80   160

mi.

AUCKLAND P.30 ●

●WELLINGTON PP.31–32

● CHRISTCHURCH P.30

QUEENSTOWN P.31 ●   ●ARROWTOWN P.30

DUNEDIN P.31 ●

THE FORK AND TAP

51 Buckingham Street
Arrowtown 9302
New Zealand
+64 34421860
www.theforkandtap.co.nz

Opening hours..Open 7 days
Reservation policy..............................Not accepted for drinks
Credit cards..............................Accepted but not AMEX
Price range...Affordable
Dress code...Casual
Style..Restaurant and bar

"Sit out in the beer garden with a fresh hopped beer from
their amazing revolving selection surrounded by mountains,
forest, and stone gold mining cottages and you'll understand.
This is the place where I meet friends, grab some Sunday
lunch, and work my way through the amazing beer list."—
Paul Shipman

THE GOLDEN DAWN

134 Ponsonby Road
Auckland 1011
New Zealand
+64 93769929
www.goldendawn.co.nz

Opening hours..Closed Monday
Reservation policy...Not accepted
Credit cards..Accepted
Price range...Affordable
Dress code...Casual
Style..Cocktail bar

MEA CULPA

3/175 Ponsonby Road
Auckland 1011
New Zealand
+64 93764460

Opening hours..Closed Monday
Reservation policy...Not accepted
Credit cards..Accepted
Price range...Affordable
Dress code..Smart casual
Style..Cocktail bar

MOLTEN

422 Mount Eden Road
Auckland 1024
New Zealand
+64 96387263
www.molten.co.nz

Opening hours..Closed Sunday
Reservation policy..Accepted
Credit cards..Accepted
Price range...Affordable
Dress code...Casual
Style..Wine bar

"Molten has packaged up a delicious menu with a fantastic
wine list, carefully selected beer list, and a few well-balanced
cocktails. The environment is welcoming in both winter and
summer, and the staff is always willing to chat and provide
advice. The perfect neighborhood bar."—Jonny Mckenzie

CIVIL & NAVAL

16 London Street
Lyttelton
Christchurch 8082
New Zealand
+64 33287206
www.civilandnaval.co.nz

Opening hours..Open 7 days
Reservation policy..............................Not accepted for drinks
Credit cards..................Accepted but not AMEX or Mastercard
Price range...Affordable
Dress code...Casual
Style..Tapas restaurant and bar

POMEROY'S PUB

292 Kilmore Street
Christchurch 8011
New Zealand
+64 33651523
www.pomspub.co.nz

Opening hours..Closed Monday
Reservation policy..Accepted
Credit cards..Accepted
Price range...Affordable
Dress code...Casual
Style..Beer bar

TOAST BAR

59 Princes Street
Dunedin 9016
New Zealand
+64 34792177
www.toastbar.co.nz

Opening hours	Open Wednesday–Saturday
Reservation policy	Accepted but not AMEX
Credit cards	Accepted
Price range	Affordable
Dress code	Casual
Style	Cocktail bar

EICHARDT'S BAR

2 Marine Parade
Eichardt's Private Hotel
Queenstown 9348
New Zealand
+64 34410450
www.eichardtsbar.com.nz

Opening hours	Open 7 days
Reservation policy	Not accepted for drinks
Credit cards	Accepted
Price range	Affordable
Dress code	Smart casual
Style	Lounge

"This was a very old and very bad pub in New Zealand's Alpine party town, before it was almost destroyed in a serious flood. A brave owner took the insurance, and an influx of money from the filming of *The Lord of the Rings*, and used it to create one of the most perfect small hotels, and hotel bars, anywhere on earth. After a hard day's skiing, you get a chair by the fire, order a whiskey or a glass of local Pinot Noir, look out at the lake, and realize there is nowhere else you would want to be."—Jacob Briars

PUBLIC KITCHEN & BAR

Ground Floor
Steamer Wharf
Beach Street
Queenstown
New Zealand
+64 34425969
www.publickitchen.co.nz

Opening hours	Open 7 days
Reservation policy	Accepted
Credit cards	Accepted
Price range	Affordable
Dress code	Casual
Style	Restaurant and bar

"Grab a table next to the lake (so close you can touch it) and you're wrapped in 360-degree mountain views. Go at sunset anytime of the year with a glass of local Pinot Noir for a spectacular sundowner. Solid cocktails, good craft beer, and tasty bar snacks don't hurt either, but really it's the view you go there for."—Paul Shipman

HAWTHORN LOUNGE

2/82 Tory Street
Wellington 6011
New Zealand
+64 48903724
www.hawthornlounge.co.nz

Opening hours	Open 7 days
Reservation policy	Not accepted for drinks
Credit cards	Accepted
Price range	Affordable
Dress code	Smart casual
Style	Speakeasy

"Hawthorn welcomes everybody. The staff makes you feel welcome and the challenge of finding this venue is all part of the experience. A venue for out-of-towners to meet the creative characters of the city."—Jonny Mckenzie

MATTERHORN

106 Cuba Street
Wellington 6146
New Zealand
+64 43843359
www.matterhorn.co.nz

Opening hours..Open 7 days
Reservation policy....................................Not accepted for drinks
Credit cards...Accepted
Price range...Affordable
Dress code...Casual
Style...Lounge

"This is where I started bartending when at law school, and it remains one of my favorite bars on earth. Wellington is a very compact city, the central city just a few blocks across, the city itself is a neighborhood, with Cuba Street running through the heart of it. Matterhorn acts as both the village pub and the town square. Locals arrive for coffee early, have a glass of wine with lunch, then move on to a cider or a Gin and Tonic in the courtyard, and cocktails in the evening. It has a very natural, organic feeling of being in tune with both the day and the city. And if you sit there long enough, you will see everyone you needed to see that day. It's a great place to combine business and pleasure!"—Jacob Briars

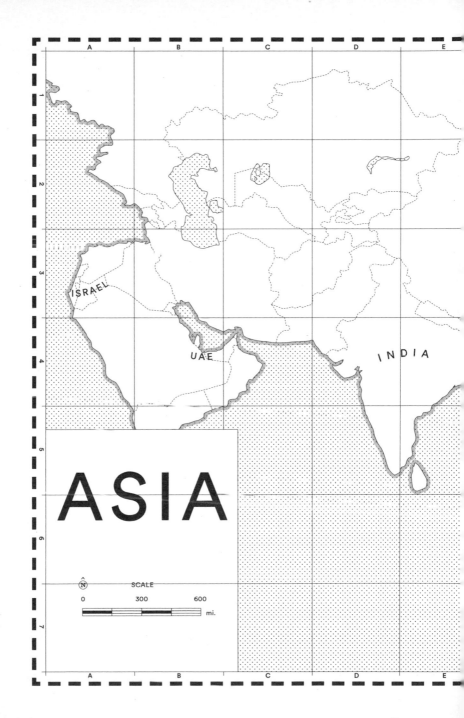

ASIA

ISRAEL

UAE

INDIA

N

SCALE

0   300   600
                              mi.

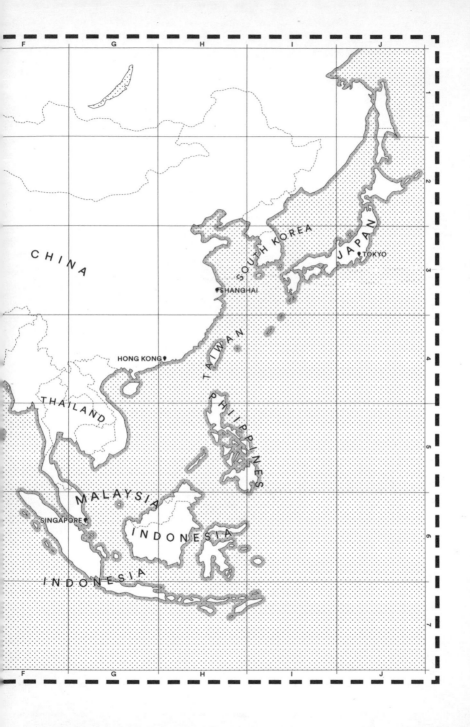

COCKTAILS IN ASIA

The young cocktail scene in Asia is one of the most rapidly evolving in the world. Cocktails have little to no history in most of the region, but as China has opened up, more cocktail bars have begun popping up.

Singapore, the birthplace of the Singapore Sling, has a new generation of bartenders reinvigorating the tiny island. Here you'll find ultra-luxe hotel bars like Manhattan Bar and the Long Bar at Raffles, as well as cutting-edge spots like 28 Hongkong Street and the sustainability-minded Operation Dagger.

Practical Information:
- Cocktails range from SG$14 to SG$31 at the very high end.
- Tipping is usually included in a 15% service charge; otherwise a 15% to 20% tip is standard.

Perhaps the biggest shift in Asia in recent years has been in mainland China and the bar scenes in Shanghai and Beijing. Outside these two cities, however, cocktails are harder to find. The bars are diverse, borrowing from New York speakeasies, high-end hotel bars, and Ginza cocktail dens, mashing them together with a local spin. More bartenders are incorporating local flavors—such as tea, Chinese medicinal herbs, and rice wine—into their cocktails as well as focusing on the classic canon.

Practical Information:
- Prices range from ¥60 to ¥160; tipping is not customary.
- Most places accept credit cards, but you should carry a few hundred yuan just in case.
- The social aspect of bartending is less developed in China and it is not as common for patrons to sit at a bar as it is to sit at a table.

Unlike mainland China, Hong Kong (under British rule for over one hundred years) and Taiwan have been open longer to Western cocktail culture and have international bar scenes. In Taiwan, the biggest focus is single malt whiskey. In addition to the cocktail scene, don't miss out on the local tradition of re chao, an assortment of stir-fried dishes with cold beer—a must after an evening of cocktails.

Southeast Asia and South Korea are rapidly evolving as well. In Thailand, Vietnam, Indonesia, and Malaysia, many of the best bars are in hotels. South Korea has historically been more focused on local products such as rice wine and shochu, and is just beginning to discover cocktails and Western spirits.

"THE BAR SELECTION IS THE BEST YOU CAN FIND, DRINKS ARE WELL MADE, AND THE OVERALL EXPERIENCE IS GOOD."

ANGUS MCGREGOR P.40

"GREAT COCKTAILS, TRENDY LOCATION, AND ALWAYS BUSY."

ANGUS MCGREGOR P.40

SOUTHWEST ASIA

"A VERY COOL BAR IN THE CITY THAT HAS A LIMITED NIGHTLIFE." BAR SHIRA P.40

"ALWAYS FULL OF PRETTY PEOPLE, GOOD FOOD, AND FAST DRINKS."

BAR SHIRA P.40

"THE DECOR IS WARM AND BEAUTIFUL, AND THE BAR FOOD IS DELICIOUS AND MATCHES THE EXPERTISE IN THE COCKTAIL PROGRAM."

CARINA SOTO VELASQUEZ P.40

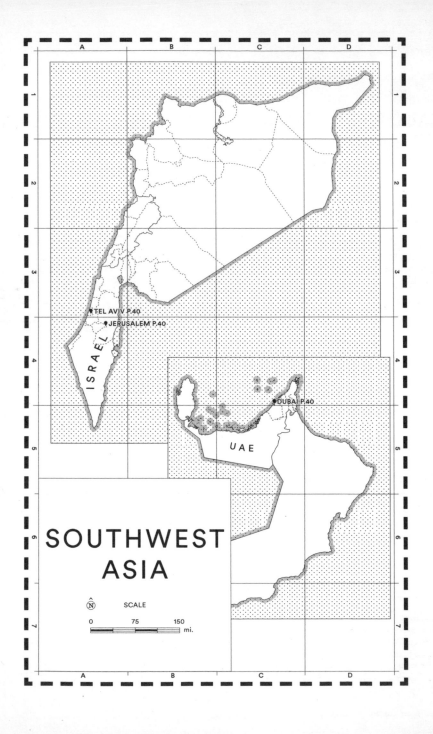

SOUTHWEST ASIA

 N   SCALE

0   75   150   mi.

GATSBY
Hillel 18
Jerusalem 94581
Israel
+972 548147143

Opening hours	Open 7 days
Reservation policy	Accepted
Credit cards	Accepted
Price range	Affordable
Dress code	Smart casual
Style	Restaurant and cocktail bar

"A very cool bar in the city that has a limited nightlife."
—Bar Shira

223
223 Dizengoff Street
Tel Aviv 6311602
Israel
+972 35446537
www.223tlv.com

Opening hours	Open 7 days
Reservation policy	Accepted
Credit cards	Accepted
Price range	Affordable
Dress code	Smart casual
Style	Cocktail bar

IMPERIAL CRAFT COCKTAIL BAR
66 HaYarkon Street
Imperial Hotel
Tel Aviv 63255
Israel
+972 732649464
www.imperialtlv.com

Opening hours	Open 7 days
Reservation policy	Accepted
Credit cards	Accepted
Price range	Affordable
Dress code	Smart casual
Style	Cocktail bar

"The hotel is unpretentious and small, and when you walk in you will never imagine the beautiful bar that is inside. The decor is warm and beautiful, and the bar food is delicious and matches the expertise in the cocktail program. Imperial is a hotel bar but not only for people that stay in the hotel, it is also for the locals and is a fantastic addition to the fun Tel Aviv nightlife."—Carina Soto Velasquez

"My favorite bar in Israel." —Gabe Orta

PORT SAID
Har Sinai 5
Tel Aviv 65815
Israel
+972 36207436

Opening hours	Open 7 days
Reservation policy	Not accepted for drinks
Credit cards	Accepted
Price range	Affordable
Dress code	Smart casual
Style	Restaurant and bar

"Always full of pretty people, good food, and fast drinks."
—Bar Shira

HAKKASAN
Sheikh Zayed Road
Jumeirah Emirates Towers Hotel
Dubai
United Arab Emirates
+971 43848484
www.hakkasan.com/locations/hakkasan-dubai

Opening hours	Open 7 days
Reservation policy	Not accepted for drinks
Credit cards	Accepted
Price range	Expensive
Dress code	Smart casual
Style	Restaurant and bar

"Hakkasan set a standard in the early 2000s and has maintained it to date. The bar selection is the best you can find, drinks are well made, and the overall experience is good."—Angus McGregor

ZUMA
Dubai International Financial Centre
Gate Village 06
Dubai
United Arab Emirates
+971 44255660
www.zumarestaurant.com

Opening hours	Open 7 days
Reservation policy	Not accepted for drinks
Credit cards	Accepted
Price range	Expensive
Dress code	Smart casual
Style	Japanese restaurant and bar

"Great cocktails, trendy location, and always busy."
—Angus McGregor

"ONE OF BANGKOK'S COOLEST LATE-NIGHT COCKTAIL SPOTS."
COLIN TAIT P.46

"GREAT ENVIRONMENT AND CONCEPT, BEST COCKTAILS IN PETALING JAYA."
ANDREW TAN P.48

"LIKE BEING IN A BAR IN ASIA IN THE 1950s, WITH ECLECTIC AND QUIRKY DECOR." COLIN TAIT P.46

SOUTH & SOUTHEAST ASIA

"THEIR SPECIAL CONCOCTIONS, PREPARED FROM HOMEMADE BITTERS AND LIQUEURS FLAVORED WITH ROSEMARY AND INDIAN SPICES, HOMEMADE RED WINE VINEGAR, ARE FAMOUS IN DELHI."
GAURAV DHYANI P.44

"STUNNING AMBIENCE WITH ITS INTERNATIONAL LOOK, FEEL, AND CONTEMPORARY CUTTING-EDGE DESIGN."
GAURAV DHYANI P.44

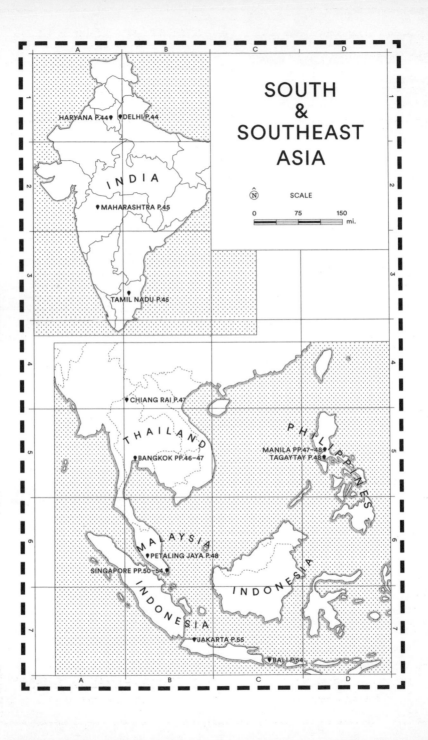

SOUTH
&
SOUTHEAST
ASIA

Ⓝ   SCALE

0   75   150
                        mi.

HARYANA P.44 ♦ ♦DELHI P.44

I N D I A

♦ MAHARASHTRA P.45

TAMIL NADU P.45

♦ CHIANG RAI P.47

T H A I L A N D

♦ BANGKOK PP.46–47

P H I L I P P I N E S

MANILA PP.47–48 ♦
TAGAYTAY P.48 ♦

M A L A Y S I A

♦ PETALING JAYA P.48

SINGAPORE PP.50–54 ♦

I N D O N E S I A

I N D O N E S I A

♦ JAKARTA P.55

♦ BALI P.54

ATM (À TA MAISON)

First Floor
21 Sundar Nagar Market
New Delhi
Delhi 110003
India
+91 9999449977
www.atamaison.com

Opening hours	Open 7 days
Reservation policy	Members only
Credit cards	Accepted
Price range	Expensive
Dress code	Smart casual
Style	Private club

"It is a very nice bar in Delhi, with an extremely comfortable setting on two floors with a nice terrace, a lovely restaurant, and a small great bar and bartenders. They cater for the upper-middle classes who travel and are used to great bars and restaurants around the world, and have created the first cool trendy members bar. India has a long history of members clubs due to their old British connection, but this one is redefining that."—Dimi Lezinska

BLUE BAR

Sardar Patel Marg Diplomatic Enclave
Taj Palace New Delhi
New Delhi
Delhi 110021
India
+91 1126110202
www.taj.tajhotels.com/en-in/taj-palace-new-delhi/
restaurants/the-blue-bar/

Opening hours	Open 7 days
Reservation policy	Not accepted for drinks
Credit cards	Accepted
Price range	Affordable
Dress code	Smart casual
Style	Lounge

"Stunning ambience with its international look, feel, and contemporary cutting-edge design . . . Blue Bar has got an array of flavours including different homemade liquor infusions and homemade bitters. Exclusive luxury cocktails and a collection of more than fifty-two different malts makes the menu special."—Gaurav Dhyani

RICK'S

1 Mansingh Road
The Taj Mahal Hotel
New Delhi
Delhi 110011
India
+91 1166566162
https://taj.tajhotels.com/en-in/the-taj-mahal-hotel-new-delhi/restaurants/ricks-bar/

Opening hours	Open 7 days
Reservation policy	Not accepted for drinks
Credit cards	Accepted
Price range	Affordable
Dress code	Smart casual
Style	Cocktail bar

"Rick's is an urban lounge bar at The Taj Mahal Hotel. It is famous for its innovative cocktail menu and delicious Southeast Asian cuisine . . . Their special concoctions, prepared from homemade bitters and liqueurs flavored with rosemary and Indian spices, and their homemade red wine vinegar. This bar has also introduced the concept of aged cocktails in the city."—Gaurav Dhyani

COCKTAIL AND DREAMS SPEAKEASY

Sector 15
Part II Market
Gurgaon
Haryana 122001
India
+91 9810104439
www.cndspeakeasy.com

Opening hours	Open 7 days
Reservation policy	Accepted
Credit cards	Not accepted
Price range	Budget
Dress code	Smart casual
Style	Speakeasy

"One of my favorite bars (and as the name suggests it's a speakeasy). What makes it unique is the staff and ambience. It's the one and only bartenders' bar in the country, everyone in service staff, including manager Anurag Dhingra, renowned bartender of Delhi, fixes great cocktails . . . They also have an uncommon collection of liqueurs and bitters which you can't find anywhere in India." —Gaurav Dhyani

BIG NASTY

Second Floor
Shatranj Napoli Building
12 Union Park
Khar West
Mumbai
Maharashtra 400052
India
+91 9821524563

Opening hours..Open 7 days
Reservation policy.....................Not accepted for drinks
Credit cards..Accepted
Price range...Budget
Dress code...Casual
Style..Lounge

"It is just a great mix of the expat and local community of Bombay. Very comfortable setting in the heart of Bandra (Bombay) with simple bar snacks. Don't go there for cocktails but just a good night out. Pricing is very cheap, which is very important for Bombay. Exported brands make drinking so expensive (due to high duty taxes) and the Big Nasty positions itself very well by offering great value for money."
—Dimi Lezinska

THE BOMBAY CANTEEN

Unit-1 Process House
S.B. Road, Lower Parel
Kamala Mills
Mumbai
Maharashtra 400013
India
+91 2249666666
www.thebombaycanteen.com

Opening hours..Open 7 days
Reservation policy...Accepted
Credit cards..Accepted
Price range..Affordable
Dress code...Casual
Style..Cafe and bar

"It is a contemporary interpretation of Indian nostalgic cuisine by a top US-based Indian chef. As a Westerner living in India I always thought it was a great idea to offer the city a modern perspective of their own culinary heritage, executing this with subtlety, without completely turning it on its head, but someone already did it and did it very well."
—Dimi Lezinska

"This place is notable for the creativity and constancy of cocktails and unique use of ingredients in cocktails as well as style of service."—Varun Sudhakar

ELLIPSIS

B-1 Amarchand Mansion
16 Madame Cama Road
Colaba
Mumbai
Maharashtra 400001
India
+91 2266213333
www.ellipsisrestaurant.com

Opening hours..Open 7 days
Reservation policy...Accepted
Credit cards..Accepted
Price range..Affordable
Dress code..Smart casual
Style..Restaurant and bar

"This bar is one of the best bars in India because it was set up by the Death & Co. team [from New York City], so the foundations were really solid. At any point you can get a great consistent cocktail by hungry, humble, passionate bartenders who are very happy to respond to any guest's request."—Dimi Lezinska

TRANQUEBAR

63, Mount Road
ITC Grand Chola Hotel
Guindy
Chennai
Tamil Nadu 600032
India
+91 4422200000
www.itchotels.in/Hotels/itcgrandchola/tranquebar-restaurant.aspx

Opening hours..Open 7 days
Reservation policy...Accepted
Credit cards..Accepted
Price range..Affordable
Dress code..Smart casual
Style..Cocktail bar

"The only cocktail bar in Chennai, chilled out and playful."
—Hannah Keirl

THE BAMBOO BAR

48 Oriental Avenue
Mandarin Oriental Hotel Bangkok
Bangkok 10500
Thailand
+66 26599000
www.mandarinoriental.com/bangkok

Opening hours...Open 7 days
Reservation policy...................Not accepted for drinks
Credit cards...Accepted
Price range..Affordable
Dress code...Smart casual
Style...Lounge

"The Bamboo Bar is a classy joint. Just recently it underwent a major renovation, yet it still retains an old-school charm, a lot of wood styling, and comfy chairs. The bar is beautiful to sit at and the guys here have some real talent and some interesting takes on classics."—Colin Tait

SMALLS

186/3 Suan Phlu Soi 1
Bangkok 10120
Thailand
+66 955851398

Opening hours.................................Closed Tuesday
Reservation policy...Accepted
Credit cards...Accepted
Price range..Affordable
Dress code...Casual
Style...Lounge

"I love this place, it's like being in a bar in Asia in the 1950s, with eclectic and quirky decor, very Parisian café culture styling. There is always some sort of live music . . . The second floor is a great place to hang out with a cold pint."—Colin Tait

SUGAR RAY | YOU'VE JUST BEEN POISONED

Ekkamai 21
Bangkok 10110
Thailand
+66 944179898

Opening hours................................Open Wednesday–Saturday
Reservation policy...Accepted
Credit cards..Not accepted
Price range..Affordable
Dress code...Casual
Style..Speakeasy

"This is a fantastic little hideaway of a bar, a little difficult to find but way worth the effort . . . There is no main bar to speak of, just two big shared tables where the bartender is set at the end to take your orders: it's almost is if you are sitting in your own kitchen with your buddies—you can't beat that homey feeling."—Colin Tait

U.N.C.L.E.

149 Sathorn Soi 12
Bangkok 10500
Thailand
+66 26350406
www.avunculus.com

Opening hours.................................Closed Sunday
Reservation policy...Accepted
Credit cards...Accepted
Price range..Affordable
Dress code...Smart casual
Style...Cocktail bar

"This is one of Bangkok's coolest late-night cocktail spots . . . It's probably best described as a hidden bar above a restaurant kind of affair—small, dark yet super welcoming. The emphasis at the moment is rum-driven tiki drinks but they will make anything with great chat thrown in."
—Colin Tait

VOLKSWAGEN BUS BARS
Bangkok
Thailand

Reservation policy	Not accepted
Credit cards	Not accepted
Price range	Budget
Dress code	Casual
Style	Mobile bar

"These mobile bars can be found in different areas of the city, especially Sukhumvit Soi 11. They're all colorful, unique, individually decorated. They're a lot of fun, and it's a nice change to sit outside and watch all the action on the street. And if you've even been to Bangkok, you know there's a lot to see."—Franky Marshall

BURMA BAR
Four Seasons Tented Camp Golden Triangle
Chiang Rai 57150
Thailand
+66 53910200
www.fourseasons.com/goldentriangle

Opening hours	Open 7 days
Reservation policy	Hotel guests only
Credit cards	Accepted
Price range	Expensive
Dress code	Casual
Style	Lounge

"They have a nice bar with wonderful sights of the peninsula that the Four Seasons maintains as an elephant reserve. Sitting down there enjoying the sunset, with a good cocktail and surrounded by nature, is an amazing and relaxing experience."—Javier de las Muelas

THE BLIND PIG
227 Salcedo Street
Makati City
Metropolitan Manila 1229
Philippines
+63 9175492264

Opening hours	Open 7 days
Reservation policy	Accepted
Credit cards	Accepted
Price range	Affordable
Dress code	Smart casual
Style	Speakeasy

"Located in central Manila, it's super fantastic, and very quiet."—Jericson Co

BUGSY'S BAR & BISTRO
Unit 1 Paseo Parkview Tower
142 Valero Street
Makati City
Metropolitan Manila 1227
Philippines
+ 63 25015203

Opening hours	Open 7 days
Reservation policy	Accepted
Credit cards	Accepted
Price range	Affordable
Dress code	Casual
Style	Bistro and bar

"The place is quiet with an ambience of a Prohibition-era bar."—Allanking Roxas

EDSA BEVERAGE DESIGN STUDIO
209 EDSA CLMC Building
Greenhills-Mandaluyong
Metropolitan Manila 1550
Philippines
+63 26319035
www.edsa-bdg.com

Opening hours	Open 7 days/Cocktail bar closed Sunday
Reservation policy	Accepted
Credit cards	Accepted
Price range	Affordable
Dress code	Casual
Style	Cafe and bar

"These guys roast their own coffee, and make their own sodas and bottled cocktails. It's an open studio: during the day they serve coffee and nonalcoholic drinks and they open at night as a regular bar."—Jericson Co

LONG BAR
1 Raffles Drive
Makati Avenue
Raffles Hotel Makati
Makati City
Metropolitan Manila 1224
Philippines
+63 25559840
www.raffles.com/makati

Opening hours	Open 7 days
Reservation policy	Not accepted for drinks
Credit cards	Accepted
Price range	Affordable
Dress code	Smart casual
Style	Cocktail bar

NINER ICHI NANA
The Globe Tower
32nd Street corner 7th Avenue
Taguig
Metropolitan Manila 1634
Philippines
+63 9178769999

Opening hours..Closed Sunday
Reservation policy...Accepted
Credit cards...Accepted
Price range..Affordable
Style...Cocktail bar

"They are very experimental—for example they do weird things with fruit, like dehydration. They make a cocktail inside a watermelon, and they have cocktails based on *Game of Thrones*. It's a very open, spacious, welcoming place—one of the sexier rooms in Manila."—Jericson Co

SAGE BAR
Ayala Avenue corner Makati Avenue
Makati Shangri-La Hotel
Makati City
Metropolitan Manila 1200
Philippines
+63 28142580
www.shangri-la.com/manila/makatishangrila

Opening hours.. Open 7 days
Reservation policy...Accepted
Credit cards...Accepted
Price range..Affordable
Dress code..Smart casual
Style...Cocktail bar

"Elegant and nice ambience."—Allanking Roxas

LANAI LOUNGE
Purok 138
Barangay Neogan
Tagaytay City 4120
Philippines
+63 9188992866
www.antoniosrestaurant.ph/lanai-lounge

Opening hours...Closed Monday
Reservation policy.................................Not accepted for drinks
Credit cards...Accepted
Price range..Affordable
Dress code..Smart casual
Style...Lounge

"This bar is a lounge attached to a restaurant called Antonio's, about 68 miles from metro Manila. It's a beautiful garden where you can have fantastic drinks on a hidden farm outside the city, and offers a Michelin-level experience."—Jericson Co

GERRY'S
Abreeza Mall
J.P. Laurel Avenue
Davao City
Philippines
+63 0823210960
www.gerrysgrill.com/ph

Opening hours...Open 7 days
Reservation policy..................................Not accepted for drinks
Credit cards...................................Accepted but not AMEX
Price range..Affordable
Dress code...Casual
Style...Bar and grill

"This is the place to go to for a hard-core Filipino experience. It's cafeteria style, with a long table down the middle, sand on the floor, and cheap buckets of beer."—Jericson Co

HYDE AT 53M
53M Jalan SS21/1A
Damansara Utama
Petaling Jaya 47400
Selangor D.E.
Malaysia
+60 1766801357

Opening hours...Closed Monday
Reservation policy...Accepted
Credit cards...Accepted
Price range..Affordable
Dress code..Smart casual
Style...Cocktail bar

"Friendly and attentive staff, great environment and concept, best cocktails in Petaling Jaya, and good variety of drinks and bar snacks."—Andrew Tan

"THEY TAKE THEIR TIME HERE, BUT IT'S WORTH THE WAIT."

PAIGE AUBERTON P.53

"A FORWARD-THINKING BAR, CHALLENGING CONVENTION WITHIN THE SINGAPORE BAR SCENE, WHICH IS EVIDENT IN THE OWNERS' RESPECTIVE PERSONALITIES."

NICK KOUMBARAKIS P.54

SINGAPORE

"THE TEAM IS SOME OF THE NICEST PEOPLE IN THE INDUSTRY."

PAMELA WIZNITZER P.53

"THE STAFF IS GREAT, WITH A LOT OF KNOWLEDGE. FRIENDLY ATMOSPHERE AND GREAT SERVICE."

KAMIL FOLTAN P.53

"WELL KNOWN FOR ITS PROGRESSIVE AND INNOVATIVE APPROACH."

KAMIL FOLTAN P.54

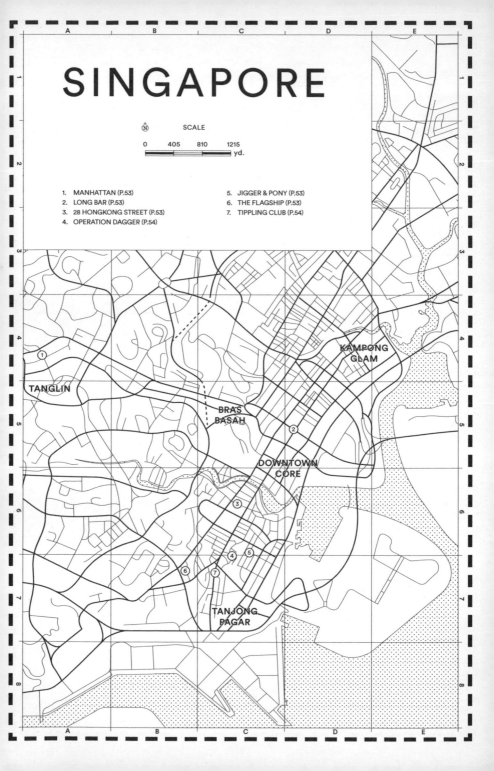

SINGAPORE

N̂

SCALE

0   405   810   1215
yd.

1. MANHATTAN (P.53)
2. LONG BAR (P.53)
3. 28 HONGKONG STREET (P.53)
4. OPERATION DAGGER (P.54)

5. JIGGER & PONY (P.53)
6. THE FLAGSHIP (P.53)
7. TIPPLING CLUB (P.54)

KAMPONG GLAM

TANGLIN

BRAS BASAH

DOWNTOWN CORE

TANJONG PAGAR

SINGAPORE SLING

One of the few classic cocktails that traces its roots to Asia, the Singapore Sling was created around 1915 by Ngiam Tong Boon at the Long Bar at the Raffles Hotel in Singapore. It combines a veritable smorgasbord of ingredients including gin, pineapple, lemon or lime juice, Cointreau, and Bénédictine—and different recipes claiming to be the original abound. Rumor has it the bar makes 1,400 Singapore Slings every day.

THE FLAGSHIP
18–20 Bukit Pasoh Road
Singapore
089834
www.theflagship.sg

Opening hours	Closed Sunday
Reservation policy	Accepted
Credit cards	Accepted
Price range	Affordable
Dress code	Casual
Style	Dive bar

"A fun dive bar."—Zdenek Kastanek

28 HONGKONG STREET
28 Hongkong Street
Singapore
059667
+65 83180328
www.28hks.com

Opening hours	Closed Sunday
Reservation policy	Accepted
Credit cards	Accepted
Price range	Affordable
Dress code	Smart casual
Style	Cocktail bar

"The staff is great with a lot of knowledge. Friendly
atmosphere and great service from opening till close."
—Kamil Foltan

JIGGER & PONY
101 Amoy Street
Singapore
069921
+65 62239101
www.jiggerandpony.com

Opening hours	Closed Sunday
Reservation policy	Accepted
Credit cards	Accepted
Price range	Affordable
Dress code	Smart casual
Style	Cocktail bar

"Japanese classic bar in a modern coat."—Zdenek Kastanek

"The team is some of the nicest people in the industry."
—Pamela Wiznitzer

LONG BAR
1 Beach Road
Raffles Hotel Singapore
Singapore
189673
+65 64121816
www.raffles.com/singapore

Opening hours	Open 7 days
Reservation policy	Not accepted for drinks
Credit cards	Accepted
Price range	Expensive
Dress code	Casual
Style	Cocktail bar

"This beautiful bar is where the famous Singapore Sling
cocktail was born."—Tenzin Samdo

MANHATTAN
1 Cuscaden Road
Regent Hotel
Singapore
249715
+65 67253377
www.regenthotels.com/en/Singapore

Opening hours	Open 7 days
Reservation policy	Accepted
Credit cards	Accepted
Price range	Affordable
Dress code	Smart casual
Style	Cocktail bar

"To one side of the entrance you have a barrel room, to the
other an ingredients room. Rows and rows of countless jars
filled with everything and anything to inspire their seasonal
cocktail menu. After you've climbed out of the rabbit hole
you jumped in, make your way back out to the dark melting
room, up to the bar, and ask for one of their signatures.
They take their time here, but it's worth the wait."—Paige
Auberton

"Interior is stunning and friendly staff on the floor and behind
the bar love the place and want to make it all happen for you . . .
They do amazing brunch on Sundays."—George Nemec

OPERATION DAGGER

7 Ann Siang Hil
Singapore
069791
www.operationdagger.com

Opening hours	Closed Sunday and Monday
Reservation policy	Accepted
Credit cards	Accepted
Price range	Affordable
Dress code	Smart casual
Style	Cocktail bar

"Luke Whearty—formally of Tippling Club, Der Raum, and Trink Tank—along with Aki Nishikura have executed something unique here. A forward-thinking bar, challenging convention within the Singapore bar scene, which is evident in the owners' respective personalities, yet instilling the importance of hospitality within their establishment. I have no doubt this bar will be the catalyst for a different approach to bartending within an exploding bar scene here in Singapore. Definitely worth the visit."—Nick Koumbarakis

TIPPLING CLUB

38 Tanjong Pagar Road
Singapore
088461
+65 64752217
www.tipplingclub.com

Opening hours	Closed Sunday
Reservation policy	Not accepted for drinks
Credit cards	Accepted
Price range	Affordable
Dress code	Smart casual
Style	Restaurant and cocktail bar

"Tippling Club is well known for its progressive and innovative approach. As it is part of the restaurant it does allow you to experience some unexpected moments with attention to every detail."—Kamil Foltan

KU DE TA

Jalan Kayu Aya 9
Seminyak
Bali 80361
Indonesia
+62 361736969
www.kudeta.net

Opening hours	Open 7 days
Reservation policy	Not accepted for drinks
Credit cards	Accepted
Price range	Affordable
Dress code	Casual
Style	Beach bar

"If you have ever dreamed of sipping a cocktail while watching the sunset in a paradisiac setting, Ku De Ta is the place to go. Their service is great and their cocktails are to die for. I highly recommend it if you are around the area."—Guillaume Le Dorner

WOO BAR

Jalan Petitenget Kerobokan
W Retreat & Spa Hotel
Seminyak
Denpasar
Bali 80361
Indonesia
+62 3614738106
www.wretreatbali.com/en/woobar_bali

Opening hours	Open 7 days
Reservation policy	Not accepted for drinks
Credit cards	Accepted
Price range	Affordable
Dress code	Smart casual
Style	Beach bar

"Good ambience, good beach, good DJ, and of course the cocktails never disappoint."—Budiman "Tom" Atmaja

LOEWY
Ground Floor
Jalan Lingkar Mega Kuningan E4.2 1
Oakwood Premier Cozmo
Jakarta 12950
Indonesia
+62 2125542378
www.loewyjakarta.com

Opening hours	Open 7 days
Reservation policy	Not accepted for drinks
Credit cards	Accepted
Price range	Affordable
Dress code	Smart casual
Style	American restaurant and cocktail bar

"It's classy, homey, and somehow when I get there there's always something that makes me excited about the bar, from the styles of the drinks to classic, modern gastronomy, and the collection of whiskey they never let me down. Overall they have reliable pricing and friendly barmen. If you come to Jakarta but don't go to Loewy, it's like you haven't accomplished your trip."—Budiman "Tom" Atmaja

UNION
Ground Floor
Plaza Senayan Courtyard
Jalan Asia Afrika 8
Jakarta 10270
Indonesia
+62 2157905861
www.unionjkt.com

Opening hours	Open 7 days
Reservation policy	Accepted
Credit cards	Accepted
Price range	Affordable
Dress code	Smart casual
Style	American restaurant and cocktail bar

"Warm, enchanting atmosphere and nice food."
—Budiman "Tom" Atmaja

"UNIQUE DESIGN, HIGH CEILINGS, GREAT COCKTAILS, FUN MUSIC, AND CONSISTENTLY GOOD SERVICE." ETHAN LIU P.58

"BEST ROOFTOP BAR IN BEIJING: GREAT MUSIC, IBIZA-STYLE SET-UP, AND SMASHING SUMMER DRINKS."
ETHAN LIU P.58

CHINA, HONG KONG, SOUTH KOREA, & TAIWAN

"A NICE, QUIET BAR, WITH GOOD AMBIENCE, NICE VIEW, REASONABLE PRICES, AND AN ENCHANTING ATMOSPHERE."
BUDIMAN "TOM" ATMAJA P.66

"BUCKETS OF BEER... POOL TABLES AND DART BOARDS... A GOOD PLACE TO DECOMPRESS AFTER A LONG WEEK."
RYAN NIGHTINGALE P.67

"THE LEVEL OF SERVICE AND HOSPITALITY IS EQUAL TO WHAT ONE COULD EXPERIENCE AT A MICHELIN THREE-STAR RESTAURANT." EDWARD HONG P.68

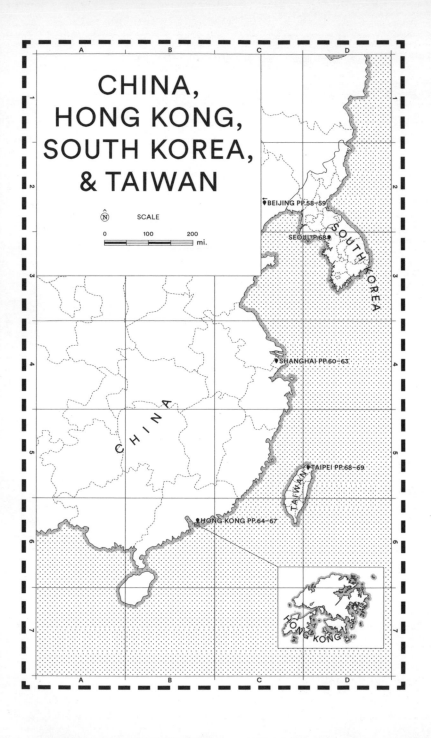

CHINA,
HONG KONG,
SOUTH KOREA,
& TAIWAN

N̂

SCALE

0   100   200 mi.

BEIJING PP.58–59

SEOUL P.68

SOUTH KOREA

SHANGHAI PP.60–63

CHINA

TAIPEI PP.68–69

TAIWAN

HONG KONG PP.64–67

HONG KONG

ATMOSPHERE BAR

Eightieth Floor
1 Jianguomenwai Avenue
China World Summit Wing Hotel
Beijing
Beijing 100004
China
+86 1065052299
www.shangri-la.com/beijing/chinaworldsummitwing

Opening hours	Open 7 days
Reservation policy	Accepted
Credit cards	Accepted
Price range	Affordable
Dress code	Smart casual
Style	Lounge

D LOUNGE

4 Gongti Bei Lu
Beijing
China
+86 1065937710
www.dlounge.com.cn

Opening hours	Open 7 days
Reservation policy	Not accepted for drinks
Credit cards	Accepted but not AMEX
Price range	Expensive
Dress code	Smart casual
Style	Cocktail bar

"D Lounge has been one of the best lounge/cocktail bars in Beijing for six years now, with unique design, high ceilings, great cocktails, fun music, and consistently good service. A great mixture of local people and foreign guests. You can dance and chill at the same time."—Ethan Liu

DA DONG ROAST DUCK

Multiple locations
Beijing
China
www.dadongdadong.com

Opening hours	Open 7 days
Reservation policy	Not accepted for drinks
Credit cards	Accepted
Price range	Affordable
Dress code	Casual
Style	Restaurant

"For wine and crispy duck!"—Marshall Altier

HIDDEN HOUSE

39 Xindong Lu
Beijing
China
+86 1084185718

Opening hours	Open 7 days
Reservation policy	Accepted
Credit cards	Not accepted
Price range	Affordable
Dress code	Smart casual
Style	Speakeasy

JANES + HOOCH

Building 10
4 Gongti Bei Lu
Beijing
China
+86 1065032757
www.janeshooch.com

Opening hours	Open 7 days
Reservation policy	Not accepted
Credit cards	Accepted but not AMEX
Price range	Affordable
Dress code	Casual
Style	Cocktail bar

MIGAS

Sixth Floor
Nali Patio
81 Sanlitun
Beijing
Beijing 100027
China
+86 1052086061
www.migasbj.com

Opening hours	Open 7 days
Reservation policy	Not accepted for drinks
Credit cards	Accepted
Price range	Affordable
Dress code	Smart casual
Style	Spanish restaurant and bar

"Best rooftop bar in Beijing: great music, Ibiza-style set-up, and smashing summer drinks!"—Ethan Liu

MOKIHI
Third Floor
C12 Haoyun Jie (Lucky Street)
Beijing
China
+86 1058670244

Opening hours	Open 7 days
Reservation policy	Accepted
Credit cards	Not accepted
Price range	Affordable
Dress code	Smart casual
Style	Cocktail bar

XIAN BAR
22 Jiuxianqiao Lu
EAST Beijing
Beijing
Beijing 100016
China
+86 1084149810
www.xian-bar.com

Opening hours	Open 7 days
Reservation policy	Accepted
Credit cards	Accepted
Price range	Affordable
Dress code	Smart casual
Style	Hotel lounge

"IT'S LIKE A NEIGHBORHOOD BAR, IT'S NOT PRETENTIOUS AND THEY MAKE REALLY GOOD DRINKS."
THEO WATT P.63

"AN AMERICAN BAR AND CHOP HOUSE WITH AN OLD-FILM FEEL, AND DARK GREEN LEATHER COUCHES."
THEO WATT P.63

SHANGHAI

"IT'S A MODERN DIVE. IT'S ABOUT THE ATMOSPHERE AND THE COOL PEOPLE."
THEO WATT P.62

"LOVE THE INTIMATE ATMOSPHERE OF THIS SMOKY LITTLE ROOM. IT'S A SHANGHAI CLASSIC."
MARSHALL ALTIER P.62

"THEY DON'T HAVE A MENU, YOU GO IN AND SAY WHAT YOU LIKE AND THEY MAKE YOU SOMETHING."
THEO WATT P.63

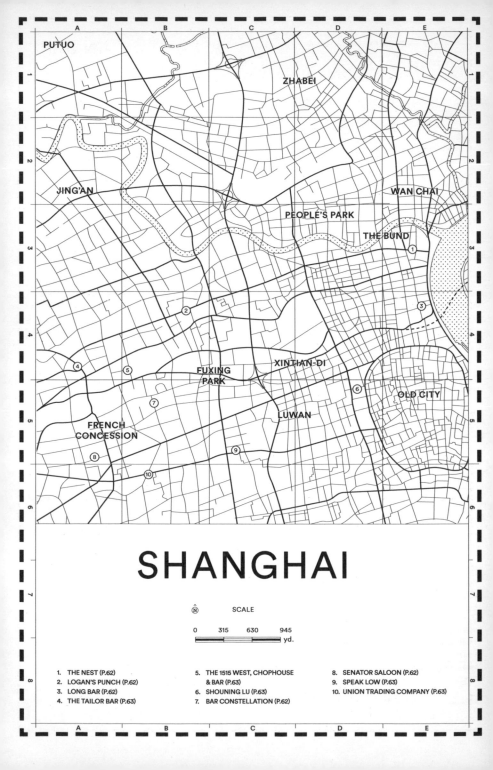

SHANGHAI

PUTUO

ZHABEI

JING'AN

WAN CHAI

PEOPLE'S PARK

THE BUND

FUXING PARK

XINTIAN-DI

LUWAN

FRENCH CONCESSION

OLD CITY

N̂   SCALE

0   315   630   945
                        yd.

1. THE NEST (P.62)
2. LOGAN'S PUNCH (P.62)
3. LONG BAR (P.62)
4. THE TAILOR BAR (P.63)

5. THE 1515 WEST, CHOPHOUSE & BAR (P.63)
6. SHOUNING LU (P.63)
7. BAR CONSTELLATION (P.62)

8. SENATOR SALOON (P.62)
9. SPEAK LOW (P.63)
10. UNION TRADING COMPANY (P.63)

BAR CONSTELLATION

86 Xinle Lu
Shanghai
China
+86 2154040970

Opening hours	Open 7 days
Reservation policy	Accepted
Credit cards	Accepted but not AMEX
Price range	Affordable
Dress code	Smart casual
Style	Cocktail bar

"It is my favorite. Love the intimate atmosphere of this smoky little room. It's a Shanghai classic."—Marshall Altier

LOGAN'S PUNCH

Second Floor
99 Taixing Road
Shanghai 200041
China
+86 18616814701
www.loganspunch.com

Opening hours	Open 7 days
Reservation policy	Accepted
Credit cards	Accepted
Price range	Affordable
Dress code	Casual
Style	Cocktail bar

"It's a modern dive. It's about the atmosphere and the cool people. It's nicely designed and they have some good bites."
—Theo Watt

LONG BAR

2 Zhongshan Dong Yi Road
Waldorf Astoria Shanghai on the Bund
Shanghai
Shanghai 200002
China
+86 2163229988
www.waldorfastoriashanghai.com

Opening hours	Open 7 days
Reservation policy	Accepted
Credit cards	Accepted
Price range	Expensive
Dress code	Smart casual
Style	Cocktail bar

"A classic."—Marshall Altier

THE NEST

Sixth Floor
130 Beijing Dong Lu
Shanghai
Shanghai 200085
China
+86 2163087669

Opening hours	Open 7 days
Reservation policy	Not accepted for drinks
Credit cards	Accepted
Price range	Affordable
Dress code	Smart casual
Style	Lounge

"Nest is a really good halfway house between a restaurant, a lounge, and a cocktail bar. They've got really good Nordic, Scandinavian-style food . . . The drinks are very easy, it's a high-volume bar with quality drinks. I'll probably go there and have simple Gin and Tonics. The food is good, the music is nice, the aesthetic design is lovely—and they do a dozen oysters for US$15."—Theo Watt

SENATOR SALOON

98 Wuyuan Lu
Shanghai
Shanghai 200031
China
+86 2154231330
www.senatorsaloon.com

Opening hours	Open 7 days
Reservation policy	Accepted
Credit cards	Accepted but not AMEX
Price range	Affordable
Dress code	Smart casual
Style	Cocktail and whiskey bar

"American-style classic cocktail bar."—Marshall Altier

SHOUNING LU

Shouning Lu
Shanghai
Shanghai 200000
China

Opening hours	Open 7 days
Reservation policy	Not accepted for drinks
Credit cards	Not accepted
Price range	Budget
Dress code	Casual
Style	Street food

"My favorite thing to do is go eat street food and drink beer after a night out."—Marshall Altier

SPEAK LOW

579 Fuxing Zhong Lu
Shanghai
Shanghai 200003
China
+86 2164160133

Opening hours	Open 7 days
Reservation policy	Not accepted
Credit cards	Accepted but not AMEX
Price range	Affordable
Dress code	Smart casual
Style	Speakeasy

THE TAILOR BAR

Fourth Floor
2 Huashan Road
Shanghai
Shanghai 200040
China
+86 18301977360

Opening hours	Open 7 days
Reservation policy	Accepted
Credit cards	Not accepted
Price range	Affordable
Dress code	Smart casual
Style	Cocktail bar

"Eddie Yang has a really nice little bar called Tailor, which is just opposite Jing'an Temple on the fourth floor of a Chinese medicine building. They don't have a menu, you go in and say what you like and they make you something. He's a very famous Chinese bartender and a great ambassador of Chinese bartending. The drinks are classically driven, but he also incorporates local flavors."—Theo Watt

UNION TRADING COMPANY

Building 2
64 Fen Yang Road
Shanghai
Shanghai 200031
China
+86 2164183077

Opening hours	Open 7 days
Reservation policy	Not accepted for drinks
Credit cards	Accepted
Price range	Affordable
Dress code	Smart casual
Style	Cocktail bar

"Owned partly by Yao Lu, of Shanghai origin, who also lived in San Francisco and Houston. He started this bar with some partners and a local famous chef, Austin Hu. It's like a neighborhood bar, it's not pretentious and they make really good drinks. It's in the French Concession part of Shanghai and was just included in Asia's 50 Best Bars."—Theo Watt

THE 1515 WEST, CHOPHOUSE & BAR

1218 Yan'an Middle Road
Jing An Kerry Centre
West Nanjing Road
Jing'an Shangri-La
Shanghai
Shanghai 200040
China
+86 2122038889
www.shangri-la.com/shanghai/jinganshangrila

Opening hours	Open 7 days
Reservation policy	Not accepted for drinks
Credit cards	Accepted
Price range	Expensive
Dress code	Formal
Style	Restaurant and bar

"It's an American bar and chop house with an old-film feel, and dark green leather couches. They're heavy on classic cocktails and whiskey, and for awhile they had their own label with Evan Williams bourbon."—Theo Watt

"A GOOD PLACE TO DECOMPRESS AFTER A LONG WEEK."

RYAN NIGHTINGALE P.67

"TRULY OLD-SCHOOL HOTEL BAR ... THEY'LL EVEN SERVE YOU A MARTINI IN ONE OF THEIR SILVER V-GLASSES."

RYAN NIGHTINGALE P.66

HONG KONG

"A REALLY ARTSY, YET SIMPLE, LOCAL BAR ... RECOMMENDED SPOT FOR OUT-OF-TOWNERS VISITING WAN CHAI."

RYAN NIGHTINGALE P.67

"THE KIND OF PLACE WHERE YOU HAVE LONG, PHILOSOPHICAL DISCUSSIONS WITH STRANGERS OR END UP PLAYING 'LIAR'S DICE' FOR DRINKS WITH YOUR FRIENDS."

RYAN NIGHTINGALE P.66

"A GOOD PLACE TO GET A BIT LOOSE."

RYAN NIGHTINGALE P.67

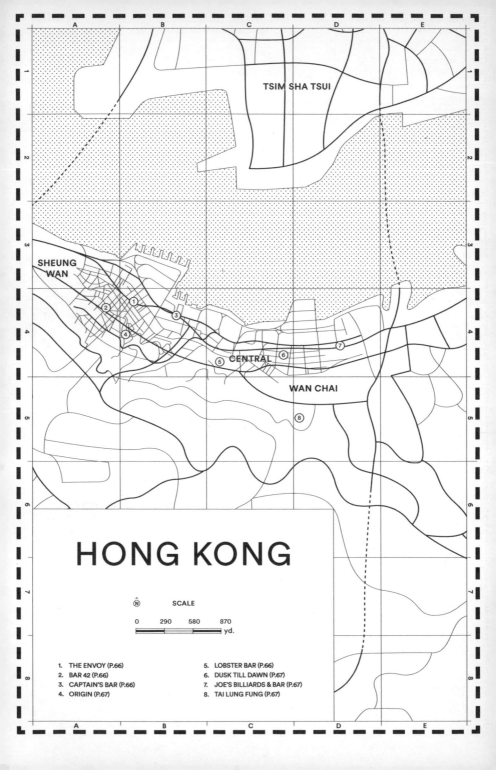

BAR 42

42 Staunton Street
Central
Hong Kong Island
Hong Kong S.A.R., China
+852 25401881

Opening hours	Open 7 days
Reservation policy	Not accepted
Credit cards	Accepted
Price range	Budget
Dress code	Casual
Style	Bar

"Another late night hangout. The kind of place where you have long, philosophical discussions with strangers or end up playing 'Liar's Dice' for drinks with your friends."
—Ryan Nightingale

CAPTAIN'S BAR

5 Connaught Road
Mandarin Oriental Hotel Hong Kong
Central
Hong Kong Island
Hong Kong S.A.R., China
+852 28254006
www.mandarinoriental.com/hongkong

Opening hours	Open 7 days
Reservation policy	Not accepted for drinks
Credit cards	Accepted
Price range	Expensive
Dress code	Smart casual
Style	Cocktail bar

"Truly old-school hotel bar. Sit at the bar, where you can rest your elbows on a cushioned rail. Draft beer is served in cool silver tankards and if you ask nicely, they'll even serve you a Martini in one of their silver V-glasses."
—Ryan Nightingale

THE ENVOY

Third Floor
74 Queen's Road
The Pottinger Hotel
Central
Hong Kong Island
Hong Kong S.A.R., China
+852 21693311
www.theenvoy.hk

Opening hours	Open 7 days
Reservation policy	Accepted
Credit cards	Accepted
Price range	Expensive
Dress code	Smart casual
Style	Restaurant and cocktail bar

LOBSTER BAR

Sixth Floor
Pacific Place
Supreme Court Road
Island Shangri-La Hong Kong
Central
Hong Kong Island
Hong Kong S.A.R., China
+852 28208560
www.shangri-la.com/hongkong/islandshangrila

Opening hours	Open 7 days
Reservation policy	Accepted
Credit cards	Accepted
Price range	Affordable
Dress code	Smart casual
Style	Restaurant and bar

"Due to the wonderful service and a few too many shots of Irish whiskey, Lobster Bar has become an industry hangout for Hong Kong's food and beverage staff. A great place to catch up with some friends over classic cocktails."
—Ryan Nightingale

"A nice, quiet bar, with good ambience, nice view, reasonable prices, and an enchanting atmosphere."
—Budiman "Tom" Atmaja

ORIGIN
48 Wyndham Street
Central
Hong Kong Island
Hong Kong S.A.R., China
+852 26685583
www.originbar.hk

Opening hours	Closed Sunday
Reservation policy	Accepted
Credit cards	Accepted
Price range	Affordable
Dress code	Smart casual
Style	Cocktail bar

DUSK TILL DAWN
76 Jaffe Road
Wan Chai
Hong Kong Island
Hong Kong S.A.R., China
+852 25284689
www.liverockmusic247.com

Opening hours	Open 7 days
Reservation policy	Accepted
Credit cards	Accepted
Price range	Budget
Dress code	Casual
Style	Nightclub

"A good place to get a bit loose. Live cover bands, crowded dance floors, cold beers, and late-night nachos (made with Doritos!)"—Ryan Nightingale

JOE'S BILLIARDS & BAR
Second Floor
303 Jaffe Road
King's Hotel
Wan Chai
Hong Kong Island
Hong Kong S.A.R., China
+852 31881470
www.joesbilliards.com

Opening hours	Open 7 days
Reservation policy	Accepted
Credit cards	Accepted
Price range	Budget
Dress code	Casual
Style	Pool hall and bar

"Buckets of beer, cheap (but well-maintained) pool tables and dart boards, and a good place to decompress after a long week."—Ryan Nightingale

TAI LUNG FUNG
5-9 Hing Wan Street
Wan Chai
Hong Kong Island
Hong Kong S.A.R., China
+852 25720055

Opening hours	Open 7 days
Reservation policy	Accepted
Credit cards	Accepted
Price range	Affordable
Dress code	Casual
Style	Restaurant and bar

"Located near some heritage buildings and a temple, this is a really artsy, yet simple, local bar. Relatively new, but with decor representing an era in Hong Kong history, this is often a recommended spot for out-of-towners visiting Wan Chai."—Ryan Nightingale

SPEAKEASY MORTAR

73-4 Han nam dong
Seoul 140-885
South Korea
+82 7042887168

Opening hours	Closed Sunday
Reservation policy	Accepted
Credit cards	Accepted
Price range	Affordable
Dress code	Smart casual
Style	Cocktail bar

"The bar has a team of strong personalities. They refuse all unauthorized photo taking with an iPhone and web posting or a small cover charge is added. But they obviously make you feel happy and comfortable. The bartenders are all specialized in cocktails and whiskey."—Taeeun Yoon

VAULT +82

95-15 Cheongdam-dong
Gangnam gu
Seoul 060-15
South Korea
+82 25449234

Opening hours	Open 7 days
Reservation policy	Accepted
Credit cards	Accepted
Price range	Expensive
Dress code	Smart casual
Style	Whiskey bar

"This bar is for high rollers with money to drop, but the level of service and hospitality is equal to what one could experience at a Michelin three-star restaurant. They mainly focus on premium single malts (which is perhaps the most popular craft spirit in Korea). A complimentary shoe shine and Havana Club rum daiquiris were two of many reasons I enjoyed my evening imbibing at Vault +82."—Edward Hong

ALCHEMY

Second Floor
16-1, Section 5, Xinyi Road
Xinyi District
Taipei 110
Taiwan
+886 227200080

Opening hours	Open 7 days
Reservation policy	Accepted
Credit cards	Accepted
Price range	Affordable
Dress code	Smart casual
Style	Speakeasy

"The Taiwanese bar scene is heavily influenced by Japanese-style bartending, and Alchemy is a great place to see Taiwanese bartenders putting their own unique spin on the Japanese style. Much of the credit for this is due to the bar manager Angus Zou . . . But remember to make a reservation, or your fortune may run out and there may not be space for you." —Payman Bahmani

MOD SEQUEL

7, Lane 11, Leli Road
Da'an District
Taipei 106
Taiwan
+886 227372955

Opening hours	Open 7 days
Reservation policy	Accepted
Credit cards	Accepted
Price range	Affordable
Dress code	Smart casual
Style	Lounge

"Good ambience and a pretty decent whiskey selection. Plus, the bartenders are friendly and the drinks are well-built Japanese-style classics. "—Spencer Huang

THE SPEAKEASY
554, Guāngfù South Road
Da'an District
Taipei 106
Taiwan
+886 227050300

Opening hours	Open 7 days
Reservation policy	Not accepted for drinks
Credit cards	Accepted
Price range	Affordable
Dress code	Casual
Style	Irish bar

"Nothing beats a late-night pint at Speakeasy. Great
atmosphere with some awesome people—especially Helen,
she's a sweetheart. The decor is homey, reminding me of a
good ol' fashioned pub in the midst of Taipei's bustling city.
Highly recommended if you need a brew at 2 or 3 a.m."
—Spencer Huang

TICKLE MY FANTASY
8, Section 2, Anhe Road
Da'an District
Taipei 106
Taiwan
+886 2 27090106

Opening hours	Open 7 days
Reservation policy	Accepted
Credit cards	Accepted
Price range	Affordable
Dress code	Casual
Style	Dive bar

"A late-night neighborhood hangout . . . Elaine is known
across the city for her wickedly strong Long Island Iced Teas,
which have at least eight or nine ounces of booze in them . . .
Always amicable and always ready to pour you free shots of
crappy scotch, you'd be hard-pressed to leave Tickle with
your sobriety intact . . . The food's not bad here either,
especially the roasted sweet Taiwanese pork sausages served
with raw sliced garlic . . . And then there are the . . . um . . .
inhabitants of Tickle, perhaps the most special aspect of the
bar: the owner's dogs and cats . . . It's not uncommon to find
a cat walking on the bar, a cat sleeping behind the bar, one
perched atop the ice machine. As far as dogs, I've counted
two, possibly three."—Payman Bahmani

> "THE MENU BOASTS MORE THAN TWO HUNDRED ORIGINAL COCKTAILS AS WELL AS A STRONG MASTERY OF CLASSICS."
>
> JUAN CORONADO P.75

> "SOLID VIBE. THIS IS A GREAT WHISKEY BAR WITH SOME VERY NICE PRIVATE ROOMS UPSTAIRS."
>
> NEYAH WHITE P.76

JAPAN

> "INCREDIBLE VIBE. DIM BAR WITH DECENT COCKTAILS AND VINTAGE VINYL."
>
> NEYAH WHITE P.76

> "THEIR ICE GAME IS ON POINT. THEY HAVE A GREAT COLLECTION OF JAPANESE WHISKEYS."
>
> FRANK CISNEROS P.80

> "COCKTAIL-MAKING IS ELEVATED TO AN ART FORM HERE AND EXHIBITS THE TRULY INCREDIBLE ARTISTRY OF JAPANESE BAR SERVICE."
>
> LYNNETTE MARRERO P.80

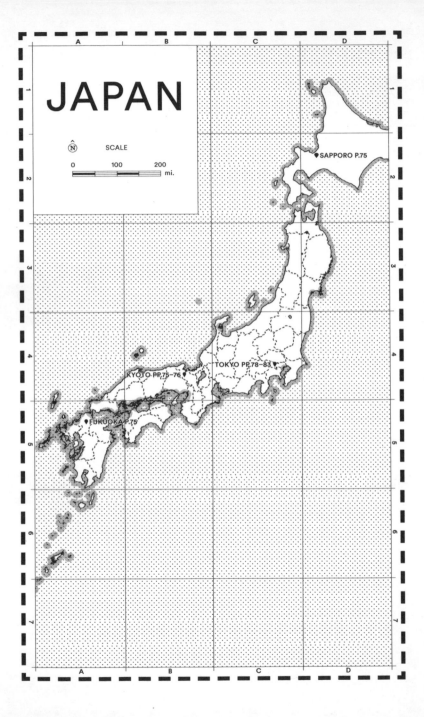

COCKTAILS IN JAPAN

Cocktails first came to Japan in the 1880s, fully taking root after World War II with the proliferation of American officers' clubs. This legacy is preserved as if in a time capsule in Tokyo's Ginza neighborhood, where these small, hushed bars are steeped in tradition and centered around a profound respect for the ritual of mixing drinks. Here you'll find Manhattans and Martinis executed to perfection by a tuxedo-clad bartender accompanied by a classic jazz soundtrack. In this rarefied bar world, the act of preparing the cocktail is equally as important as how it tastes, and rather than focus on innovation, Ginza's bartender elite turn their attention to perfecting what already exists.

Elsewhere in Tokyo and across Japan, younger bartenders, influenced by their Western contemporaries, are beginning to change things up. You'll find more innovative cocktails, using local ingredients, molecular mixology, and more at bars like Gen Yamamoto and Ishino Hana. In Kyoto, expect a more laid-back atmosphere, and more sake and whiskey bars than cocktail dens.

Don't forget to sample the other end of the Japanese drinking spectrum, however. You shouldn't leave without visiting a stand-up beer hall and eating takoyaki, a hot, unctuous ball of fried octopus.

Practical Information:

— The average price of a cocktail in Japan ranges from ¥1,500 to ¥3,000 when you factor in any cover charges and service fees.

— Some bars, especially in Ginza, may have a cover charge, usually around ¥1,500. You may also be charged for an otoshi, or small snack, around ¥800.

— Although bars may accept credit cards, many prefer cash and you should be prepared.

— Tipping is not customary.

— Japanese addresses can be confusing, so leave plenty of time to find the bar you are looking for. Bars are often not on the ground floor and may be located in the basement or five floors up. This is especially important if you have a reservation, as most bars will only hold your table for fifteen minutes.

— Don't expect to find extensive whiskey lists at a cocktail bar; if you are looking for whiskey on the rocks, go to a whiskey bar.

GINZA COCKTAIL BARS

The experience at a Ginza cocktail bar is like a three-star Michelin restaurant: the service and cocktails are impeccably correct, but there are also certain codes of conduct. The environment is more formal than many bars; for example, standing is not permitted. If you arrive at a bar and no seats are available, you will likely not be admitted. Ginza bars are therefore perfect for a quiet evening for two, but not so much for a party scene. Like Michelin restaurants, you don't go because you're hungry, you go for the entire experience.

JAPANESE WHISKEY

If you're looking to buy or taste Japanese whiskey in Japan, here are a few tips from expert Neyah White, a former brand ambassador for Suntory, producer of some of Japan's best known whiskeys, including Yamazaki and Hibiki:
– The better whiskey shops will sell you small tastes before you buy. If you see an open bottle, chances are they're selling drams of it.
– It's expensive! Be prepared.
– Don't be afraid of ice. Japanese whiskeys are designed for it.
– Don't expect to find great whiskeys in cocktail bars, as most do not have extensive whiskey lists. Similarly, don't order a cocktail in a whiskey bar.

BAR LAPIN

First Floor
Matsushima Building
2-2-13 Nakasu
Hakata-ku
Fukuoka 810-0801
Japan
+81 922721101

Opening hours...Closed Sunday
Reservation policy..Accepted
Credit cards...Accepted
Price range...Affordable
Dress code..Smart casual
Style..Cocktail bar

High quality local cocktail bar. You can also order food for
delivery from a local nearby pub.

BAR OSCAR

6th Floor
1-10-29 Daimyo
Chuo-ku
Fukuoka 810-0041
Japan
+81 927215352

Opening hours...Closed Sunday
Reservation policy..Not accepted
Credit cards...Accepted
Price range...Affordable
Dress code..Smart casual
Style..Cocktail bar

BAR YAMAZAKI

Fourth Floor
Katsumi Building
Minami 3 Nishi 3
Chuoku
Sapporo
Hokkaido 064-0820
Japan
+81 112217363
www.bar-yamazaki.com

Opening hours...Closed Sunday
Reservation policy..Accepted
Credit cards...Accepted
Price range...Affordable
Dress code..Smart casual
Style..Cocktail bar

"Mister Yamazaki is ninety-four years old, he only works
one day a week for three hours, but when he's there, it's
incredible. He is one of the very first bartenders in Japan.
The menu boasts more than two hundred original cocktails
as well as a strong mastery of classics."—Juan Coronado

Bar owner Tatsuro Yamazaki, in addition to many bar industry
accolades, received the Imperial Prize of the Japan Academy
in 1993, the first time this honor had been conferred on a
bartender.

BAR K6

Second Floor
Varuzubiru
Higashilri Higashiikesu cho 481
Chukyo-ku
Kyoto 604-0922
Japan
+81 752555009
www.ksix.jp

Opening hours...Open 7 days
Reservation policy.....................................Not accepted for drinks
Credit cards...Accepted
Price range...Expensive
Dress code..Smart casual
Style...Whiskey bar

"One of the best whiskey bars I have ever been in."
—Neyah White

BAR ROCKING CHAIR

434-2 Yamaguchi
Shimogyo-ku
Kyoto 600-8044
Japan
+81 754968679
www.bar-rockingchair.jp

Opening hours..Closed Tuesday
Reservation policy..................................Not accepted for drinks
Credit cards...Accepted
Price range...Affordable
Dress code..Smart casual
Style...Cocktail bar

"This cocktail bar is owned by one of Ueno-San's (of Bar High Five in Tokyo) pupils. Great lineage, great bar."
—Neyah White

HELLO DOLLY

Matsumoto cho 161
Nakagyo-ku
Kyoto 604-8013
Japan
+81 752411728
www.hellodolly.hannnari.com

Opening hours..Open 7 days
Reservation policy..Accepted
Credit cards..Accepted
Price range..Affordable
Dress code...Smart casual
Style..Cocktail bar

"Incredible vibe. Dim bar with decent cocktails and vintage vinyl."—Neyah White

THE DOOR

Multiple locations
Kyoto
Japan
www.bar-door.com

Opening hours..Open 7 days
Credit cards..Accepted
Reservation policy..Accepted
Price range..Expensive
Dress code...Smart casual
Style..Whiskey bar

"Solid vibe. This is a great whiskey bar with some very nice private rooms upstairs."—Neyah White

"THE CRAFT OF THE COCKTAIL HERE HAS BEEN STUDIED AND THE MASTER IS AT WORK— BLENDING, POURING, AND CHECKING THE TEMPERATURE WITH A THERMOMETER."
LYNNETTE MARRERO P.80

"A CIVILIZED RESPITE FROM THE BUSTLE OUTSIDE, A GUEST HERE IS TREATED TO THE UNPARALLELED HOSPITALITY AND EXPERTISE OF HISASHI KISHI."
JOAQUIN SIMO P.81

TOKYO

"THE BEST JAPANESE-STYLE COCKTAILS ANYWHERE, BAR NONE."
PIP HANSON P.81

"THE MOST AVANT-GARDE BARTENDER IN JAPAN RIGHT NOW. HE'S NOT AFRAID OF MOLECULAR GASTRONOMY AND HIS GARNISH GAME IS UNBELIEVABLE."
NEYAH WHITE P.82

"IT HAS THIS FEEL LIKE YOU'RE HANGING OUT IN YOUR GRANDPARENTS' BASEMENT IF THEY WERE HIP TOKYOITES IN THE 1970s."
FRANK CISNEROS P.80

TOKYO

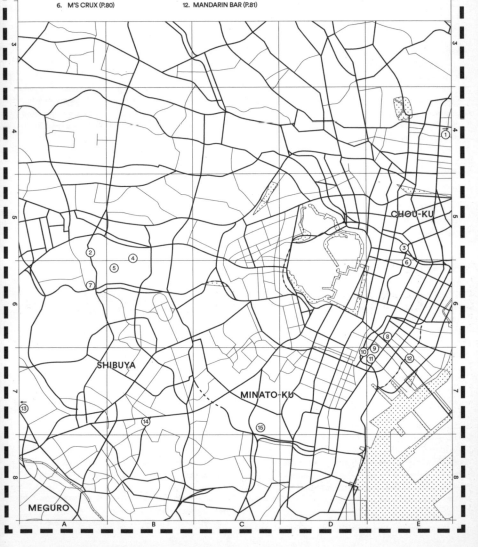

N

SCALE

0   585   1170   1755
yd.

1. BAR DORAS (P.83)
2. ZATTA (P.83)
3. KANDA 65 (P.80)
4. BAR HERMIT (P.82)
5. BEN FIDDICH (P.83)
6. M'S CRUX (P.80)

7. THE PEAK LOUNGE (P.83)
8. STAR BAR (P.81)
9. BAR HIGH FIVE (P.80)
10. LITTLE SMITH (P.80)
11. TENDER BAR (P.81)
12. MANDARIN BAR (P.81)

13. LADY JANE BOOZE & JAZZ (P.82)
14. ISHINO HANA (P.82)
15. GEN YAMAMOTO (P.82)

CHOU-KU

SHIBUYA

MINATO-KU

MEGURO

KANDA 65
Okuno Building 2F
1-3-7 Kaji-cho
Chiyoda-ku 101-0044
Tokyo
Japan
+81 335258705
www.kanda65.com

Opening hours	Closed Sunday
Reservation policy	Accepted
Credit cards	Accepted
Price range	Affordable
Dress code	Casual
Style	Restaurant and bar

"It's open till 7 a.m.! That's pretty special when you're coming off a shift at anywhere between 2 a.m. and 5 a.m. They have an amazing selection of two hundred international beers and they serve really good food right up till 7 a.m., traditional Japanese food, good Italian, and even Mexican food as well. It's a decidedly Japanese place, the staff speak little to no English, the menu is in Japanese but the fact that you can get a piece of home makes it really special. It's run by some of the greatest people on earth. The owner, Hiro San, is a huge Taylor Swift fan and loves European football. We hit it off from day one."—Frank Cisneros

M'S CRUX
Tsubaki Building B1
1-7-1 Kaji-cho
Chiyoda-ku
Tokyo 101-0044
Japan
+81 364275085

Opening hours	Open 7 days
Reservation policy	Not accepted for drinks
Credit cards	Accepted
Price range	Affordable
Style	Restaurant and cocktail bar

"The owner is a formally trained Japanese chef so they're constantly putting out some of the sickest traditional inspired Japanese food from their postage stamp-sized kitchen till 5 a.m. Their ice game is on point. They have a great collection of Japanese whiskeys. It has this feel like you're hanging out in your grandparents' basement if they were hip Tokyoites in the 1970s. It has all the underpinnings of an izakaya but it's decidedly modern and international perhaps without even knowing it. I often tell the owner that he had better come to New York City and start a bar with me because if not I'm just straight-up ripping him off. I'm serious too!"—Frank Cisneros

BAR HIGH FIVE
Efflore Ginza 5 Building BF
5-4-1 Ginza
Chuo-ku
Tokyo 104-0061
Japan
+81 335715815
www.barhighfive.com

Opening hours	Closed Sunday
Reservation policy	Not accepted for drinks
Credit cards	Accepted
Price range	Affordable
Dress code	Smart casual
Style	Cocktail bar

"Barman Hidetsugu Ueno is the host with the most."
—Jim Meehan

"Cocktail-making is elevated to an art form here and exhibits the truly incredible artistry of Japanese bar service. Drinks are mixed with care and precision by incredible barman and mentor Hidetsugo Ueno. The craft of the cocktail here has been studied and the master is at work—blending, pouring, and checking the temperature with a thermometer, judging every element as he goes. Every aspect of the experience has been taken into account, including the snacks, the music, the glassware, the ice."—Lynnette Marrero

"Easily one of the best bars in Japan."—Ago Perrone

LITTLE SMITH
KN Building B2F
6-4-12 Ginza
Chuo-ku
Tokyo 104-0061
Japan
+81 355681993
www.littlesmith.net

Opening hours	Closed Sunday
Reservation policy	Accepted
Credit cards	Accepted
Price range	Affordable
Dress code	Smart casual
Style	Cocktail bar

"There are a couple of bars that Westerners think of when they think of Japan, but like anywhere else in the world there are bars that local bartenders love and they tend to be the best of the best. This place really embodies what Japanese bartending is all about. Amazing space, basement level 3, no menu, awesome cocktails, great vibe, but to me the most important thing is that it's almost always devoid of Westerners. Learn a few Japanese phrases (no English

here unlike other well-known Japanese cocktail bars) and you will have one of the best cocktail experiences of your life."—Frank Cisneros

MANDARIN BAR

2-1-1 Nihonbashi Muromachi
Mandarin Oriental Tokyo
Chuo-ku
Tokyo 103-8328
Japan
+81 332708188
www.mandarinoriental.com/tokyo

Opening hours	Open 7 days
Reservation policy	Not accepted for drinks
Credit cards	Accepted
Price range	Expensive
Dress code	Smart casual
Style	Lounge

"Tokyo is unlike many U.S. cities. The hotel bar scene here has been strong for decades. Nowhere is it stronger than the decade-old Mandarin Bar. It has consistently pushed the envelope, has a staff of mostly women, has produced some of Japan's top bartenders including the head bartender Kurihara San and is always innovating. My introduction to the bar was when Noma was doing a pop-up thirty feet away . . . It's a truly inspirational place. And the view, oh my god." —Frank Cisneros

STAR BAR

Sankosha Building B1F
1-5-13 Ginza
Chuo-ku
Tokyo 104-0061
Japan
+81 335358005
www.starbar.jp

Opening hours	Open 7 days
Reservation policy	Not accepted
Credit cards	Accepted
Price range	Expensive
Dress code	Smart casual
Style	Cocktail bar

"It is the epitome of perfection!"—Charles Schumann

"An outpost of wonderful whiskeys, incredible hospitality, and some of the world's most pitch-perfect cocktails. Kishi San and his bartenders bring a whimsical warmth to this hushed den, which would seem so peculiar anywhere else in the world. It really is worth traveling for, getting lost and seeking out."—Ryan Chetiyawardana

"Tiny basement bar in Ginza with only two tables and ten bar stools. Dark wooden paneling decor with soft tango music in the background. Mr. Kishi, the owner, can be spotted often behind the bar and if you're lucky you'll get the best bar seat, which is at the far end from the entrance, right in front of where Mr. Kishi is always working. Great Highballs and Dry Martinis. Service is nothing but all about the details." —Erik Lorincz

"Ginza bars are pretty intimidating for foreigners, seeing as how they tend to be buried in faceless monolithic office buildings and charge staggering cover fees to enter. But there is no other feeling but warmth and comfort when you enter Star Bar. A civilized respite from the bustle outside, a guest here is treated to the unparalleled hospitality and expertise of Hisashi Kishi. I have rarely encountered such a respected professional who embodies humility and hospitality quite like him. The drinks are exemplary, but I'll happily return for a simple beer and that amazing service."—Joaquin Simo

TENDER BAR

Fifth Floor
Nogakudo Building
6-5-15 Ginza
Chuo-ku
Tokyo 104-0061
Japan
+81 335718343

Opening hours	Closed Sunday
Reservation policy	Accepted
Credit cards	Accepted
Price range	Expensive
Dress code	Formal
Style	Cocktail bar

"Bartender Kazuo Uyeda San absolutely makes the difference. Every cocktail is a performance—the magic of the light that involves all the liturgy and his humility." —Javier de las Muelas

"Elegance, sprezzatura, hospitality, amazing bartenders." —Massi Viaggiatore Dell'assurdo Stronati

"The best Japanese-style cocktails anywhere, bar none. Mr. Uyeda is a total badass."—Pip Hanson

"The Gimlet is amazing."—Tsuyoshi Miyazaki

GEN YAMAMOTO

Anniversary Building 1F
1-6-4 Azabu-Juban
Minato-ku
Tokyo 106-0045
Japan
+81 364340652
www.genyamamoto.jp

Opening hours	Closed Monday
Reservation policy	Accepted
Credit cards	Accepted
Price range	Expensive
Dress code	Smart casual
Style	Cocktail bar

"Gen Yamamoto is an eight-seat bar, with only the guy himself working. He has taken the Japanese way of working with seasonal products called 'shiki,' into a bar in a more traditional, yet still innovative way than I have ever seen. Do the menu course with five cocktails, super subtle tastes, and a big variation in texture. This is not a place you go for a party, this is for the experience." —Halvor Skiftun Digernes

"A must visit for any cocktail connoisseur."—Alex Kratena

Reservations are highly recommended for this tiny 8-seat bar carved out of a 500-year-old Mongolian oak tree; cocktails are served in flights of 4 or 6.

LADY JANE BOOZE & JAZZ

5-31-14 Daizawa
Setagaya-ku
Tokyo 155-0032
Japan
+81 334123947
www.bigtory.jp

Opening hours	Closed Monday
Reservation policy	Not accepted for drinks
Credit cards	Accepted
Price range	Budget
Dress code	Casual
Style	Lounge

"Unfiltered Casters and Yoichi on a glassy sphere; first-edition Pharoah Sanders records and black wood in a deserted Shimokita jazz club at 3 a.m."—Pip Hanson

ISHINO HANA

The Second Yago Building B1
3-6-2 Shibuya
Shibuya-ku
Tokyo 150-0002
Japan
+81 354858405
www.ishinohana.com

Opening hours	Closed Sunday
Reservation policy	Accepted
Credit cards	Accepted
Price range	Expensive
Dress code	Smart casual
Style	Cocktail bar

"Shinobu Ishigaki is the most avant-garde bartender in Japan right now. He's not afraid of molecular gastronomy and his garnish game is unbelievable. The garnishes don't just perch on the rim of the glass, they wrap around the stem. He's an innovative bartender, but it's worth it just to see the garnishes."—Neyah White

BAR HERMIT

Konwa Center Building BI
3-26-3
Shinjuku-ku
Tokyo 160-0000
Japan
+81 353251369

Opening hours	Open 7 days
Reservation policy	Accepted
Credit cards	Accepted
Price range	Affordable
Dress code	Smart casual
Style	Whiskey and cocktail bar

"Bourbon soda."—Hiroyasu Kayama

BEN FIDDICH

Ninth Floor
Yamatoya Building
1-13-7 Nishishinjuku
Shinjuku-ku
Tokyo 160-0023
Japan
+81 36279 4223

Opening hours	Closed Sunday
Reservation policy	Accepted
Credit cards	Accepted
Price range	Expensive
Dress code	Smart casual
Style	Cocktail bar

Presided over by bartender Hiroyasu Kayama, Ben Fiddich has quickly established a reputation as one of Tokyo's top cocktail bars. Hiroyasu often uses whole spices and herbs in his original cocktails, and makes many liqueurs in-house, including his take on Campari and Chartreuse.

THE PEAK LOUNGE

3-7-1-2 Nishi Shinjuku
Park Hyatt Tokyo
Shinjuku-Ku
Tokyo 163-1055
Japan
+81 353233461
www.tokyo.park.hyatt.com

Opening hours	Open 7 days
Reservation policy	Not accepted for drinks
Credit cards	Accepted
Price range	Affordable
Dress code	Smart casual
Style	Cocktail bar

"The view, wow."—Tony Conigliaro

"It's magical."—Toby Maloney

ZATTA

6-6-2 Nishishinjuku
Hilton Tokyo
Shinjuku-ku
Tokyo 160-0023
Japan
+81 353248039
www.tsunohazu-hilton.jp

Opening hours	Open 7 days
Reservation policy	Accepted
Credit cards	Accepted
Price range	Expensive
Dress code	Smart casual
Style	Lounge

BAR DORAS

2-2-6 Hanakawado
Taito
Tokyo 111-0033
Japan
+81 338475661
www.doras.exblog.jp

Opening hours	Open 7 days
Reservation policy	Accepted
Credit cards	Accepted
Price range	Affordable
Dress code	Smart casual
Style	Cocktail bar

"Very, very good!!"—Hiroyasu Kayama

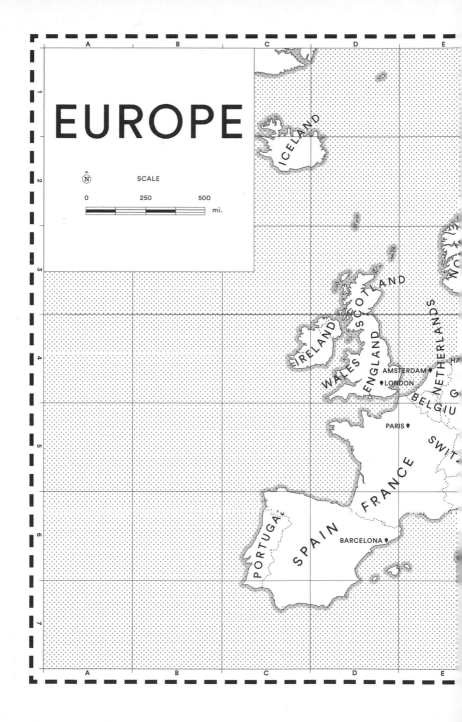

COCKTAILS IN EUROPE

One of the things that makes the European cocktail scene exciting is the rich historical context that exists there, from the cobblestone streets of Old Town Stockholm to London's formidable Mayfair hotels to the piazzas in Florence. The United States may lay claim to inventing the cocktail, but Europe is home to the history that precedes it—along with most of the base ingredients. Europe is also where much of America's bar talent escaped to after the enactment of Prohibition (which banned the sale of alcohol) in 1920.

London is the cocktail nerve center of Europe. With one of the deepest cocktail histories, its many bars—from posh hotel bars to cutting-edge cocktail laboratories—are among the continent's best. London is also where many young aspiring bartenders have come to learn their craft, and then returned home with their newfound knowledge.

In addition to London, Paris has emerged as another important European cocktail hub with a wave of new, trendy bars joining a handful of older, historic ones. Italy—home of amaro and the Negroni—and Germany also have strong cocktail communities. Often the cocktail zeitgeist is driven by the culinary one. On the heels of the rise of Nordic cuisine, the cocktail scene in Scandinavia has exploded over the past few years, in Stockholm in particular.

Although Europe is home to some of the world's most important food and beverage traditions, with a few notable exceptions, cocktail culture here is quite young. Beer, wine, and local spirits are all deeply ingrained, but there's quite an exciting energy among the close-knit bartending community—a feeling that they are creating something entirely new.

These new bars pop up right alongside the old ones, as in Barcelona, where the avant-garde Ohla Boutique Bar coexists with Boadas, Spain's first cocktail bar that remains largely unchanged since it opened in 1933. The juxtaposition makes for a very special experience where one moment you can be drinking history, and the next you're drinking the future.

"A COFFEE BAR DURING THE DAY AND COCKTAIL BAR IN THE EVENING, IT'S ALSO A LIVING SHOWROOM FOR NORWEGIAN DESIGN FROM THE 1970s–80s." MONICA BERG P.90

"ONE OF THE NEW COCKTAIL BARS IN OSLO, THEY FOCUS MAINLY ON FRESH AND HERBAL DRINKS, AND THEY HAVE TAKEN THE STEP TO ACTUALLY MAKE THEIR OWN GREENHOUSE IN THE BAR WHERE THEY CULTIVATE THEIR OWN HERBS." HALVOR SKIFTUN DIGERNES P.91

ICELAND, NORWAY, SWEDEN, DENMARK, & FINLAND

"GREAT COCKTAILS, GREAT SERVICE, GREAT DESIGN, GREAT COLLECTION OF SPIRITS, ESPECIALLY CHAMPAGNE, JUST AWESOME BAR, IT HAS EVERYTHING YOU MIGHT NEED." ALGIRDAS MULEVICIUS P.94

"BEST BAR TEAM IN SCANDINAVIA WILL ALWAYS SATISFY YOUR NEEDS; ROWDY BUT STILL ELEGANT!" EMIL ÅRENG P.94

"FINLAND'S FIRST SPEAKEASY AND HOW WELL IT OVERCOMES! TALENTED STAFF WHICH MIGHT BE THE BEST IN TOWN." JESSE TEERENMAA P.95

ICELAND,
NORWAY,
SWEDEN,
DENMARK,
& FINLAND

SCALE

0   90   180
                              mi.

ICELAND

REYKJAVÍK P.90

UMEÅ P.93

NORWAY

SWEDEN

FINLAND

OSLO PP.90–91

HELSINKI P.95

STOCKHOLM PP.91–93

DENMARK

AARHUS P.93

COPENHAGEN P.94

SLIPPBARINN

Mýrargata 2
Reykjavík 101
Iceland
+354 5608080
www.slippbarinn.is

Opening hours	Open 7 days
Reservation policy	Accepted
Credit cards	Accepted
Price range	Expensive
Dress code	Smart casual
Style	Restaurant and cocktail bar

"It started the cocktail scene in Iceland."
—Aðalsteinn Sigurðsson

FUGLEN

Universitetsgata 2
Oslo 0164
Norway
+47 22200000
www.fuglen.com

Opening hours	Cafe open 7 days, bar open Wednesday–Saturday
Reservation policy	Accepted
Credit cards	Accepted but not AMEX
Price range	Affordable
Dress code	Casual
Style	Cafe and bar

"A coffee bar during the day and cocktail bar in the evening, it's also a living showroom for Norwegian design from the 1970s–80s. The three owners each have different backgrounds: one of them is 'the guy' to go to for Scandinavian design of that era. The furniture they have is amazing, and you can buy everything. Another guy has been leading the barista coffee culture. And then you have Halvor, who is the cocktail guy. They've been in business together for many years. There is the original bar in Oslo and one in Tokyo."—Monica Berg

HIMKOK

Storgata 27
Oslo 0184
Norway
+47 22422202
www.himkok.no

Opening hours	Open 7 days
Reservation policy	Accepted
Credit cards	Accepted
Price range	Affordable
Dress code	Smart casual
Style	Cocktail bar

"Himkok means 'moonshine' in Norwegian. It's a distillery bar that produces most of its own spirits—vodka, gin, akvavit, and soon whiskey. The inventive cocktails incorporate many locally sourced ingredients and are inspired by the Norwegian palate—for example a dulce de leche flavored gin used to make a cocktail reminiscent of the traditional local breakfast dish. Physically, it's housed in a large space with two courtyards; there's also a barbershop, a small forty-seat cocktail bar, and a larger area upstairs where they serve 'tap-tails' (cocktails on tap) on the weekends."—Monica Berg

NO. 19

Møllergata 23
Oslo 0179
Norway
www.no-19.no

Opening hours	Closed Monday/open Friday–Sunday in summer
Reservation policy	Accepted
Credit cards	Accepted
Price range	Affordable
Dress code	Smart casual
Style	Cocktail bar

"No. 19 is your classic bar joint, packed with party people during the weekend , but a nice place to have your cocktail on a late lazy night. They have a nice signature menu, but are also very good at classics."—Halvor Skiftun Digernes

THE THIEF BAR

Landgangen 1
The Thief Hotel
Oslo 0252
Norway
+47 24004000
www.thethief.com

Opening hours..Open 7 days
Reservation policy.............................Not accepted for drinks
Credit cards...Accepted
Price range...Affordable
Dress code...Smart casual
Style...Cocktail bar

"One of the coolest bars in the world, prepare to be amazed!"
—Emil Åreng

"The Thief Bar is in The Thief design hotel, which is one of
the newest hotels in town. It's located at Tjuvholmen, the
new city district with a one-and-a-half-mile seafront, worth
a trip if you want to see the more flashy part of downtown.
The bar itself is classic yet innovative, doing a lot of
collaborations with international bartenders and bars."
—Halvor Skiftun Digernes

TORGGATA BOTANISKE

Torggata 17b
Oslo 0183
Norway
+47 98610210

Opening hours..Open 7 days
Reservation policy.............................Not accepted for drinks
Credit cards...Accepted
Price range...Affordable
Dress code...Smart casual
Style...Cocktail bar

"This is also one of the new cocktail bars in Oslo, they focus
mainly on fresh and herbal drinks, and they have taken the
step to actually make their own greenhouse in the bar where
they cultivate there own herbs. Nice and warm atmosphere,
classic design, and lots of plants!"—Halvor Skiftun Digernes

BAR HOMMAGE

Krukmakargatan 22
Delikatessen Bistro Bar
Stockholm 118 49
Sweden
www.bar-hommage.com

Opening hours................................Closed Sunday and Monday
Reservation policy.............................Not accepted for drinks
Credit cards...Accepted
Price range...Affordable
Dress code...Smart casual
Style...Cocktail bar

"The cocktails were on point."—Andrew Rice

CORNER CLUB

Lilla Nygatan 16
Stockholm 111 28
Sweden
+46 8208583
www.cornerclub.se

Opening hours................................Closed Sunday and Monday
Reservation policy.............................Not accepted for drinks
Credit cards...Accepted
Price range...Affordable
Dress code...Smart casual
Style...Cocktail bar

"[Bottles and Corner Club are] two standout bars in the Old
Town in Stockholm you always have to visit when you get
there."—Emil Åreng

EAST

Stureplan 13
Stockholm 111 45
Sweden
+46 86114959
www.east.se

Opening hours..Open 7 days
Reservation policy.............................Not accepted for drinks
Credit cards...Accepted
Price range...Affordable
Dress code...Smart casual
Style...Asian restaurant and bar

"It's a late-night bar; good people and a lot of hospitality
workers end up here for a late tipple, which creates a good
vibe."—Adam Snook

LING LONG

Riddargatan 6
Story Hotel Riddargatan
Stockholm 114 35
Sweden
+46 854503940
www.ling-long.se

Opening hours	Open 7 days
Reservation policy	Not accepted for drinks
Credit cards	Accepted
Price range	Affordable
Dress code	Smart casual
Style	Restaurant and bar

LINJE TIO

Hornsbruksgatan 24
Stockholm 117 34
Sweden
+46 8220021
www.linjetio.com

Opening hours	Open 7 days
Reservation policy	Accepted
Credit cards	Accepted
Price range	Affordable
Dress code	Smart casual
Style	Restaurant and cocktail bar

"Always crowded, always great cocktails, food, and beer. Always kick-ass service."—Emil Åreng

"One of the best bars in Sweden . . . Great drinks and also a great wine bar called Hornstulls Bodega located inside the venue!"—Ola Yau Carlson

LITTLE QUARTER

Hornsgatan 66
Marie Laveau
Stockholm 118 21
Sweden
+46 8 668 85 00
www.marielaveau.se

Opening hours	Open Wednesday–Saturday/closed in summer
Reservation policy	Not accepted for drinks
Credit cards	Accepted
Price range	Affordable
Dress code	Smart casual
Style	Speakeasy

"The bar is staffed by Stockholm's most respected bartenders, cranking out drinks of exceptional quality at lightening speed, all in an informal environment. There isn't a person in that city who doesn't love it—for damn good reason . . . I've never felt more at home in a bar, and possibly never had a more hungover flight back to the United States."
—Alex Day

PARADISO

Timmermansgatan 24
Stockholm 118 55
Sweden
+46 87206151
www.paradisostockholm.se

Opening hours	Closed Monday
Reservation policy	Accepted
Credit cards	Accepted
Price range	Affordable
Dress code	Smart casual
Style	Restaurant and bar

"A great little rum bar with delicious Daiquiris."
—Andrew Rice

PHARMARIUM

Stortorget 7
Stockholm 111 29
Sweden
+46 8200810
www.pharmarium.se

Opening hours	Open 7 days
Reservation policy	Accepted
Credit cards	Accepted
Price range	Affordable
Dress code	Smart casual
Style	Cocktail bar

"They create some amazing infused spirits and the look of the venue is stunning. It's an old chemist shop."—Adam Snook

"Really nice and friendly staff—and they have a really interesting food menu that is combined with perfectly matched cocktails."—Ola Yau Carlson

RESTAURANG BANKOMAT

Odengatan 85
Stockholm 113 22
Sweden
+46 8305130
www.odenplan.restaurangbankomat.se

Opening hours..Open 7 days
Reservation policy...Accepted
Credit cards..Accepted
Price range...Affordable
Dress code..Casual
Style..Restaurant and bar

"It's in my neighborhood, plays good music, and makes fine cocktails. Nice place to begin the night or anytime during the night."—Adam Snook

GOTTHARDS KROG

Storgatan 46
Stora Hotellet
Umeå 903 26
Sweden
+46 906903300
www.gotthardskrog.se

Opening hours..Open 7 days
Reservation policy.............................Not accepted for drinks
Credit cards..Accepted
Price range...Affordable
Dress code...Smart casual
Style..Restaurant and bar

"One of the world's most beautiful restaurants, classic cocktails, good beer, and high-class food. What else do you need?"—Emil Åreng

OPEN/CLOSED

Storgatan 44
Umeå 903 26
Sweden
+46 907800303
www.openclosed.se

Opening hours.................................Closed Sunday–Wednesday
Reservation policy.............................Not accepted for drinks
Credit cards.......................................Accepted but not AMEX
Price range...Affordable
Dress code...Smart casual
Style...Speakeasy

"This will blow your mind, literally!"—Emil Åreng

REX BAR & GRILL

Rådhustorget 1
Umeå 903 26
Sweden
+46 90706050
www.rexumea.se

Opening hours..Closed Sunday
Reservation policy.............................Not accepted for drinks
Credit cards..Accepted
Price range...Affordable
Dress code...Smart casual
Style..Restaurant and bar

"We try to go here as often as we can for a late after-work drink. When the mood is right in this place, you will have the best time of your life."—Emil Åreng

ST. PAULS APOTHEK

Jægergårdsgade 76
Aarhus 8000
Denmark
+45 86120833
www.stpaulsapothek.dk

Opening hours......................Closed Sunday and Monday
Reservation policy...Accepted
Credit cards..Accepted
Price range...Affordable
Dress code...Smart casual
Style..Restaurant and bar

"There's a special big-city vibe in the room with classic Danish furniture from the 1960s, raw walls, copper lamps, and amazing cocktails. The cocktail menu is in English and includes thirty-five cocktails. All of them are listed with different stories, both the classics and their award-winning signature cocktails."—Hasse Bank Johansen

THE BARKING DOG

Sankt Hans Gade 19
Copenhagen 2200
Denmark
+45 35361600
www.thebarkingdog.dk

Opening hours	Open 7 days
Reservation policy	Accepted
Credit cards	Accepted but not AMEX
Price range	Affordable
Dress code	Casual
Style	Cocktail bar

"Cozy place that works only with products from people who put heart in what they do."—Aðalsteinn Sigurðsson

K-BAR

Ved Stranden 20
Copenhagen 1061
Denmark
+45 33919222
www.k-bar.dk

Opening hours	Closed Sunday
Reservation policy	Accepted
Credit cards	Accepted
Price range	Affordable
Dress code	Smart casual
Style	Cocktail bar

"Great cocktails, great service, great design, great collection of spirits, especially Champagne. Just awesome bar, it has everything you might need."—Algirdas Mulevicius

OAK ROOM

Birkegade 10
Copenhagen 2200
Denmark
+45 38603860
www.oakroom.dk

Opening hours	Closed Sunday and Monday
Reservation policy	Accepted
Credit cards	Accepted
Price range	Affordable
Dress code	Smart casual
Style	Cocktail bar

"Nice place for a drink after work."—Aðalsteinn Sigurðsson

STRØM

Niels Hemmingsens Gade 32
Copenhagen 1153
Denmark
+45 81189421
www.strombar.dk

Opening hours	Closed Sunday
Reservation policy	Accepted
Credit cards	Accepted
Price range	Affordable
Dress code	Smart casual
Style	Cocktail bar

"Best bar team in Scandinavia will always satisfy your needs; rowdy but still elegant!"—Emil Åreng

"Awesome staff that gives new perspective to hospitality. Cocktails are classic and well made. My favorite bar by far."—Jesse Teerenmaa

LIBERTY OR DEATH

Erottajankatu 5
Helsinki 00130
Finland
+358 505424870
www.libertyordeath.bar

Opening hours	Closed Sunday
Reservation policy	Accepted
Credit cards	Accepted
Price range	Affordable
Dress code	Smart casual
Style	Cocktail bar

"I did a guest bartending shift here a few months ago, and it felt like I was at home in my own bar. The music, the clientele, the atmosphere. Love this bar."—Mal Spence

TEATTERI KELLOBAARI

Pohjoisesplanadi 2
Helsinki 00130
Finland
+358 961285005
www.teatteri.fi/kellobaari

Opening hours	Open Wednesday–Saturday
Reservation policy	Accepted
Credit cards	Accepted
Price range	Affordable
Dress code	Smart casual
Style	Lounge

"Head bartender Turo Kotajärvi knows his sh*t. They make technique-driven cocktails with seasonal ingredients. Try for example the Martinez which has been sous-vide aged for thirty-six hours."—Jesse Teerenmaa

TRILLBY & CHADWICK

Katariinankatu 1
Helsinki 00170
Finland
+358 401803199
www.trillbychadwick.fi

Opening hours	Closed Sunday
Reservation policy	Accepted
Credit cards	Accepted
Price range	Affordable
Dress code	Smart casual
Style	Speakeasy

"Finland's first speakeasy and how well it overcomes! Talented staff which might be the best in town. Atmosphere is tangible and cocktails are funky."—Jesse Teerenmaa

Themed as a local branch of a London detective agency tasked with enforcing prohibition laws, Trillby & Chadwick is hidden behind an unmarked wooden door on a small street. To gain entrance, you'll have to pick up the vintage telephone and make an appointment with Trillby. If there's space, you'll be invited into a charming small cocktail bar.

UK & REPUBLIC OF IRELAND

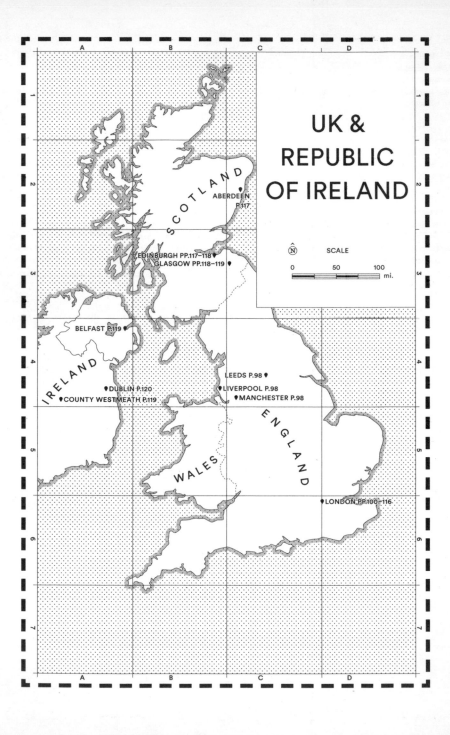

UK &
REPUBLIC
OF IRELAND

$\hat{N}$ SCALE

0   50   100
                              mi.

SCOTLAND

ABERDEEN
P.117

EDINBURGH PP.117–118
GLASGOW PP.118–119

BELFAST P.119

IRELAND

LEEDS P.98

DUBLIN P.120
COUNTY WESTMEATH P.119

LIVERPOOL P.98
MANCHESTER P.98

ENGLAND

WALES

LONDON PP.100–116

BERRY & RYE

48 Berry Street
Liverpool L1 4JQ
United Kingdom
+44 1513457271

Opening hours	Open 7 days
Reservation policy	Not accepted for drinks
Credit cards	Accepted
Price range	Affordable
Dress code	Casual
Style	Cocktail bar

"Definitely one of my favorite bars of all time, and hidden away in plain sight on the streets of Liverpool . . . With live musicians and cocktail menus hidden in classic literature, I can't express how much I love visiting Berry & Rye."
—Jamie Jones

FILTER + FOX

27 Duke Street
Liverpool L1 5AP
United Kingdom
+44 1517089458
www.filterandfox.co.uk

Opening hours	Open 7 days
Reservation policy	Not accepted for drinks
Credit cards	Accepted
Price range	Budget
Dress code	Casual
Style	Cafe and bar

"Perfect coffee, wine, and refined cocktails. This is everyone's favorite place for chilling on a free morning or afternoon. Whatever you choose to drink, it's always brilliant in a calm, inviting atmosphere."—Joe Ballinger

JENNY'S BAR

Fenwick Street
The Old Ropery
Liverpool L2 7NT
United Kingdom
+44 7557506660

Opening hours	Closed Monday and Tuesday
Reservation policy	Accepted
Credit cards	Accepted but not AMEX
Price range	Affordable
Dress code	Smart casual
Style	Cocktail bar

"It defines Liverpool perfectly. Funk and soul music, good times, and brilliant drinks. You can be looked after from your table or at the bar. A fun place to visit that isn't quite like anywhere else."—Joe Ballinger

MOJO

Liverpool, Leeds, Manchester
United Kingdom
+44 8456118643
www.mojobar.co.uk

Opening hours	Open 7 days
Reservation policy	Accepted
Credit cards	Accepted
Price range	Affordable
Dress code	Casual
Style	Cocktail bar and restaurant

"Rock and roll is what these guys do best. Loud tunes and quality liquor make it the perfect place to end your night or go after work. An industry favorite."—Joe Ballinger

"HAVING WON THE TITLE OF WORLD'S BEST BAR MORE THAN ONCE, YOU KNOW THAT SOMETHING SPECIAL IS GOING TO HAPPEN WHEN YOU VISIT THE ARTESIAN."

JAMIE JONES P.111

"FULL OF LIFE, LIVE MUSIC, IMPECCABLE SERVICE, ELEGANT ATMOSPHERE, GREAT COCKTAILS AND A TEAM WITH PASSION."

MIGUEL FERNANDEZ FERNANDEZ P.108

LONDON

"THERE IS SOMETHING VERY SPECIAL ABOUT DRINKING ONE OF THEIR WONDERFUL COCKTAILS BY THE THAMES."

GUILLAUME LE DORNER P.116

"THE FIRST TIME I WENT, I FELT LIKE I HAD DISCOVERED A SECRET NOBODY ELSE KNEW ABOUT."

JAMIE JONES P.109

"THIS BAR SHOWS OFF BRITISH DESIGN AT ITS BEST ... AN ICONIC SPACE AND A REAL PLEASURE TO VISIT."

AGO PERRONE P.110

LONDON
CENTRAL & WEST

0   360   720   1080
yd.

1. CHILTERN FIREHOUSE HOTEL (P.111)
2. ARTESIAN (P.111)
3. TRAILER HAPPINESS (P.113)
4. PUNCH ROOM (P.108)
5. MILK AND HONEY (P.115)
6. THE BLIND PIG (P.115)
7. LAB BAR (P.115)
8. BAR TERMINI (P.114)

9. THE 10 CASES (P.108)
10. CAFE PACIFICO (P.108)
11. THE FUMOIR (P.112)
12. EXPERIMENTAL COCKTAIL CLUB (P.107)
13. THE PINK CHIHUAHUA (P.115)
14. BEAUFORT BAR (P.108)
15. AMERICAN BAR (P.107)

16. THE CONNAUGHT BAR (P.112)
17. MR FOGG'S (P.113)
18. THE BAR AT THE DORCHESTER HOTEL (P.111)
19. DUKE'S BAR (P.112)
20. THE BLUE BAR (P.110)
21. THE LIBRARY BAR (P.110)

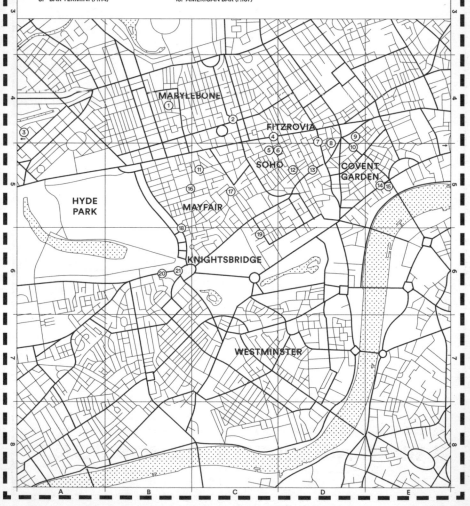

"A PERFECT EXAMPLE OF WHAT A GOOD HOTEL BAR SHOULD BE. EXCELLENT SERVICE AND CUSTOMER CARE, FINEST SELECTION OF SPIRITS IN THE WORLD, AND SUPERB COCKTAILS AND A BAR WHERE CUSTOMERS FROM ALL WALKS OF LIFE MAY FEEL AT HOME."

SALVATORE CALABRESE P.110

"THEY DO MY FAVORITE WINE BY THE GLASS. I LOVE THEIR WALNUT SALAMI AND THE FACT THAT YOU CAN EAT DINNER DOWN IN THE CELLAR."

TONY CONIGLIARO P.108

LONDON

"**THIS PLACE IS THE MOST SIMILAR TO MY DREAM BAR**"

TAEEUN YOON P.114

"IT'S GOT A CRAZY FEEL, WITH A SECRET DOOR AND DIFFERENT ENVIRONMENTS."

HONORIO OLIVEIRA P.113

"I NEVER WANT TO GO ANYWHERE ELSE FOR A DRY MARTINI."

LAURA SCHACHT P.108

"**THE MOST LAID-BACK HOTEL IN LONDON.**"

DAN BERGER P.113

LONDON
NORTH, EAST, & SOUTH

0   360   720   1080
yd.

22. HIGH WATER (P.116)
23. (69 COLEBROOKE ROW) (P.109)
24. WHITE LYAN (P.109)
25. SAGER + WILDE (P.109)
26. HAPPINESS FORGETS (P.109)
27. NIGHTJAR (P.114)
28. CALLOOH CALLAY (P.113)

29. ACE HOTEL (P.113)
30. SATAN'S WISKERS (P.107)
31. ZTH COCKTAIL LOUNGE (P.107)
32. LOUNGE BOHEMIA (P.114)
33. WORSHIP STREET WHISTLING SHOP (P.114)
34. DANDELYAN (P.116)

35. THE PROSPECT OF WHITBY (P.116)
36. THE HIDE BAR (P.110)

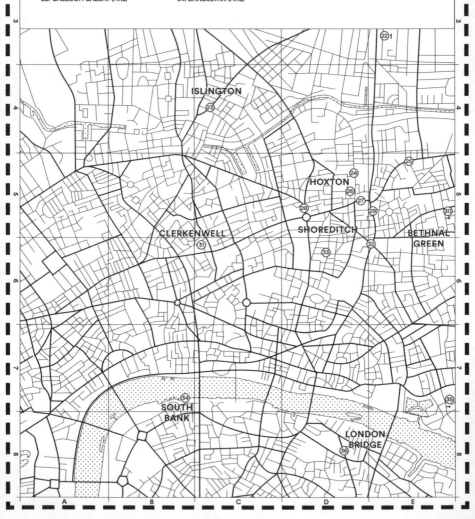

FROM MAYFAIR TO SHOREDITCH: COCKTAILS IN LONDON

The cocktail scene in London is anchored by the beautiful pomp and circumstance of the classic hotel bar on the one hand, and by a whimsical, avant-garde wave of boundary-pushing cocktail bars on the other.

As Jacob Briars, a longtime bartender originally from New Zealand who is now Global Advocacy Director at Bacardi, puts it, "London does hotel bars to a level that no other city does." Whether at the Savoy, Claridge's, Dukes, the Dorchester, or the Lanesborough, the service is impeccable, the ambiance pure luxury, and the drinks meticulous.

The American-style cocktail bar in London has its roots in American Prohibition, when both bartenders and their patrons escaped across the pond and set themselves up in hotels. One of the most famous examples of this is Harry Craddock, who became head bartender at the American Bar at the Savoy Hotel in 1920 and wrote *The Savoy Cocktail Book* in 1930. Here, the art of bartending has been kept alive and well up to the present day.

The more recent cocktail renaissance in London started in the 1980s with the late Dick Bradsell, whose last bartending post was at El Camion. The inventor of modern classics including the Bramble and the Espresso Martini, Bradsell inspired a new generation of bartenders who have taken cocktails far from the white-jacketed, pristine hotel bar ideal. Centered in East London's Shoreditch neighborhood, these bars include the wacky Callooh Callay, which was inspired by Lewis Carroll's poem "The Jabberwocky"; 69 Colebrooke Row, where your drink may include a lipstick-print garnish; and White Lyan, where all the drinks are premixed and there is no ice or citrus.

After New York City, London boasts the most cocktail bars of any city in this book—including the most recommended bar in this book: Artesian at the Langham Hotel—as well as some of the world's greatest bartending talent. Its influence is felt around the globe, and as the wave of experimental, high-concept bars shows no sign of waning, it will be fascinating to see what comes next.

Practical Information:
— Cocktails range from £10 to £25, with hotel bars coming in at the high end of the spectrum.
— Standard tipping is 10%.
— There is often an enforced dress code, especially at hotel bars, so be sure to check in advance.

HANKY PANKY

The Hanky Panky was created by Ada "Coley" Coleman, the head bartender at The Savoy Hotel in the early 1900s, for actor Charles Hawtrey who asked for something "with a kick." She combined gin with sweet vermouth and bitter, minty Fernet Branca, an Italian amaro. Hawtrey's reaction to her creation was to exclaim, "By Jove! That is the real hanky-panky!"

THE BRAMBLE

The Bramble was created in 1984 by Dick Bradsell, a leader of the cocktail revolution in London. It is a classic Gin Fix—gin and lemon—with the summery addition of either Crème de Mûre (blackberry liqueur) or fresh blackberries, served over crushed ice.

SATAN'S WHISKERS

343 Cambridge Heath Road
Bethnal Green
London E2 9RA
United Kingdom
+44 2077398362

Opening hours	Open 7 days
Reservation policy	Accepted
Credit cards	Accepted but not AMEX
Price range	Affordable
Dress code	Casual
Style	Cocktail bar

"A great neighborhood haven—and one I recommend when someone is doing the increasingly busy East End cocktail tour. Always relaxed, with a great local feel, the bar makes brilliantly executed versions of classic cocktails without any pomposity or fuss."—Ryan Chetiyawardana

EXPERIMENTAL COCKTAIL CLUB

13a Gerrard Street
Chinatown
London W1D 5PS
United Kingdom
www.chinatownecc.com

Opening hours	Open 7 days
Reservation policy	Accepted
Credit cards	Accepted but not AMEX
Price range	Affordable
Dress code	Smart casual
Style	Cocktail bar

"The bar is set on two floors with vintage decor. The selection of vintage cocktails and own creations are regularly updated. Great place to finish the evening."—Erik Lorincz

ZTH COCKTAIL LOUNGE

49-50 St John's Square
The Zetter Townhouse Clerkenwell
Clerkenwell
London EC1V 4JJ
United Kingdom
+44 2073244545
www.thezettertownhouse.com/clerkenwell/bar

Opening hours	Open 7 days
Reservation policy	Accepted
Credit cards	Accepted
Price range	Affordable
Dress code	Smart casual
Style	Cocktail bar

"This hotel bar's old school 'grandma' aesthetic is so captivating. 'Effortlessly cool.' The drinks and the bar food are innovative and satisfying. I've never had a better Scotch Egg. I visited three times during my London bar hop of 2013."—Eric Alperin

AMERICAN BAR

100 Strand
The Savoy
Covent Garden
London WC2R 0EU
United Kingdom
+44 2078364343
www.fairmont.com/savoy-london

Opening hours	Open 7 days
Reservation policy	Not accepted for drinks
Credit cards	Accepted
Price range	Expensive
Dress code	Smart casual
Style	Cocktail bar

"It's a historic London bar with an American heritage that epitomizes luxury and class."—Jim Meehan

"London does hotel bars to a level that no other city does. The Savoy has two of the best hotel bars: the American and the Beaufort Bar. It's very hard to top the American Bar at The Savoy: it's topped the international cocktail scene for forty plus years. Much like the ancient ruins, many of the ancient bars are not very good anymore, but the American Bar is as intact and important and fantastic as it was in 1930. It is both timeless and contemporary."—Jacob Briars

"Erik Lorincz has been the bar manager for the last five years and he is a true charmer. I just love sitting at his bar and watching him mix up the best classic Savoy cocktails or one of his own creations."—Tess Posthumus

The #3 most-recommended bar in this book (along with New York's Dead Rabbit), the American Bar was founded in the late 1800s. The legendary Ada "Coley" Coleman, inventor of the Hanky Panky cocktail, was head bartender there from 1903-1924. She was succeeded by Harry Craddock, an American bartender who left the United States to escape Prohibition and authored *The Savoy Cocktail Book*, which remains one of the definitive texts for today's cocktail bartenders. Head Bartender Erik Lorincz won International Bartender of the Year in 2011, the same year that the American Bar won World's Best Hotel Bar at the Tales of the Cocktail Spirited Awards. It is one of the top 10 bars of all time on the the World's 50 Best Bars.

BEAUFORT BAR

100 Strand
The Savoy
Covent Garden
London WC2R 0EU
United Kingdom
+44 2078364343
www.fairmont.com/savoy-london

Opening hours...Closed Sunday
Reservation policy...Accepted
Credit cards...Accepted
Price range..Expensive
Dress code..Smart casual
Style...Cocktail bar

"Classic. Everything. From atmosphere, to service, to drinks and charm. I never want to go anywhere else for a Dry Martini."—Laura Schacht

"Full of life, live music, impeccable service, elegant atmosphere, great cocktails, and a team with passion . . . Welcome to the Beaufort Bar!!"
—Miguel Fernandez Fernandez

CAFE PACIFICO

5 Langley Street
Covent Garden
London WC2H 9JA
United Kingdom
+44 2073797728
www.cafe-pacifico.com

Opening hours..Open 7 days
Reservation policy.............................Not accepted for drinks
Credit cards...Accepted
Price range...Affordable
Dress code..Casual
Style.....................................Mexican restaurant and tequila bar

"The first ever tequila bar in London. It's a tequila bar and restaurant and they have one of the largest collections of tequila in the world . . . You always have so much fun there—it's easy, not pretentious . . . One of the owners is Tom Estes, one of only three global tequila ambassadors, and the key cocktail is Tommy's Margarita with tequila, agave, and lime juice."—Giuseppe Gallo

THE 10 CASES

16 Endell Street
Covent Garden
London WC2H 9BD
United Kingdom
+44 2078366801
www.10cases.co.uk

Opening hours...Closed Sunday
Reservation policy.............................Not accepted for drinks
Credit cards...Accepted
Price range...Affordable
Dress code..Casual
Style...Wine bar

"They do my favorite wine by the glass. I love their walnut salami and the fact that you can eat dinner down in the cellar."—Tony Conigliaro

PUNCH ROOM

10 Berners Street
The London Edition
Fitzrovia
London W1T 3NP
United Kingdom
+44 2079087949
www.editionhotels.com/london

Opening hours..Open 7 days
Reservation policy..Required
Credit cards...Accepted
Price range...Affordable
Dress code..Smart casual
Style...Cocktail bar

"I have always found the atmosphere and drinks perfect. I've had quite intimate nights in there, and raucous parties. Reservations are essential."—Stu Bale

SAGER + WILDE

193 Hackney Road
Hackney
London E2 8JL
United Kingdom
+44 2081277330
www.sagerandwilde.com

Opening hours	Open 7 days
Reservation policy	Accepted
Credit cards	Accepted
Price range	Affordable
Dress code	Casual
Style	Wine bar

"Whenever I have a night off in London, this is the most likely place you'll find me. I love the relaxed atmosphere and the amazing wine by the glass menu, which changes daily. They always have very interesting selections, and should you feel hungry, they do great bar food as well."—Monica Berg

HAPPINESS FORGETS

8-9 Hoxton Square
Hoxton
London N1 6NU
United Kingdom
www.happinessforgets.com

Opening hours	Open 7 days
Reservation policy	Accepted
Credit cards	Accepted but not AMEX
Price range	Affordable
Dress code	Casual
Style	Cocktail bar

"Hands down, my favourite cocktail bar."—Ryan Nightingale

"A real hidden gem. The setting is casual and relaxed, with low lighting and just a handful of seats and bar stools, but the cocktails are truly excellent."—Ago Perrone

"The first time I went, I felt like I had discovered a secret nobody else knew about. It reminded me of a locals bar in Spain or France. Exposed brick walls, not an over-filled back bar, just select, great bottles of liquor. Drinks are simple and elegant, and damn moreish. Too moreish."—Jamie Jones

WHITE LYAN

153-155 Hoxton Street
Hoxton
London N1 6PJ
United Kingdom
+44 2030111153
www.whitelyan.com

Opening hours	Open 7 days
Reservation policy	Accepted
Credit cards	Accepted
Price range	Affordable
Dress code	Smart casual
Style	Cocktail bar

"Unique concept, unique flavors, only perfect drinks." —Oliver Ebert

"A really interesting, almost revolutionary view at making drinks … their experiments will determine what other bars will do in the next decade."—Ivar de Lange

White Lyan is the brainchild of Ryan Chetiyawardana, aka "Mr. Lyan." The inventive cocktail list features house spirits and ingredients, eschewing ice, perishables and brands. You can also purchase off-menu cocktails to take home. At the Tales of the Cocktail Spirited Awards, Chetiyawardana was named International Bartender of the Year in 2015 and White Lyan won Best New International Cocktail Bar in 2014. The bar has also been included in the World's 50 Best Bars list since it opened.

69 Colebrooke Row
Islington
London N1 8AA
United Kingdom
+44 7540528593
www.69colebrookerow.com

Opening hours	Open 7 days
Reservation policy	Accepted
Credit cards	Accepted
Price range	Affordable
Dress code	Smart casual
Style	Speakeasy

"Tony Conigliaro was one of the first to apply molecular science to libations. All the research is done in his lab above the bar, so cool. What's better than sitting down in a room inspired by a 1950s Italian café, and sipping on a champagne cocktail that has somehow reconstructed the famous Chanel No. 5 scent."—Vincent Stipo

"It's the kind of place where you can have all these drinks that have gone through the rotovap . . . and yet there's a tranny band playing, or a honky-tonk piano guy. And I like that, I like a good bit of fun mixed in with my serious."—Dave Arnold

Another frequent listing on the World's 50 Best Bar list, owner Tony Conigliaro is an icon in the cocktail world. The only sign is a numbered lantern outside. Commonly referred to as "69 Colebrooke Row", officially the bar has no name. The cocktails are a full sensorial experience, like the Prairie Oyster, that looks like an oyster, served in a shell, made with a tomato "yolk."

THE BLUE BAR

Wilton Place
The Berkeley Hotel
Knightsbridge
London SW1X 7RL
United Kingdom
+44 2072356000
www.the-berkeley.co.uk

Opening hours..Open 7 days
Reservation policy...................Not accepted for drinks
Credit cards..Accepted
Price range...Expensive
Dress code..Smart casual
Style...Cocktail bar

"This bar shows off British design at its best. Designed by the late David Collins, it is an iconic space and a real pleasure to visit, while their signature cocktail, The Berkeley, is the perfect combination of champagne and Grand Marnier."
—Ago Perrone

THE LIBRARY BAR

Hyde Park Corner
The Lanesborough Hotel
Knightsbridge
London SW1X 7TA
United Kingdom
+44 2072595599
www.lanesborough.com

Opening hours..Open 7 days
Reservation policy...................Not accepted for drinks
Credit cards..Accepted
Price range...Expensive
Dress code..Smart casual
Style...Cocktail bar

"The Library Bar holds a special place in my heart and it is a perfect example of what a good hotel bar should be. Excellent service and customer care, finest selection of spirits in the world, and superb cocktails and a bar where customers from all walks of life may feel at home."
—Salvatore Calabrese

It was here that Salvatore Calabrese famously created the Breakfast Martini which combines gin, lemon juice, and English marmalade.

THE HIDE BAR

39-45 Bermondsey Street
London Bridge
London SE1 3XF
United Kingdom
+44 2074036655
www.thehidebar.com

Opening hours...............................Closed Sunday and Monday
Reservation policy...Accepted
Credit cards..Accepted
Price range...Affordable
Dress code..Smart casual
Style..Cocktail bar

"Just a friendly neighborhood bar, where the bartenders take their drinks seriously. The decor is very cozy, and service is always good."—Ethan Liu

ARTESIAN

1C Portland Place
The Langham
Marylebone
London W1B 1JA
United Kingdom
+44 2076361000
www.artesian-bar.co.uk

Opening hours	Open 7 days
Reservation policy	Not accepted for drinks
Credit cards	Accepted
Price range	Expensive
Dress code	Smart casual
Style	Cocktail bar

"When it comes to bars, there's really no one that does it quite like Artesian. The bar is elegant and quite posh, but as soon as you get inside, they greet you like an old friend. It's always such a treat coming here, and their innovative takes on drinks are sure to blow your mind! Do try the Colada, or the Langham Martini."—Monica Berg

"Well, having won the title of World's Best Bar more than once, you know that something special is going to happen when you visit the Artesian. Not only is it beautiful, it's almost like watching a painting in real time. The energy, the chitchat, the ballet that takes place behind the bar, it is just a sensory experience. And that's all before you even take a sip of the modern art in a glass that will inevitably end up in front of you. Just simply exceptional."—Jamie Jones

"The Artesian was my hotel bar when I stayed for a week at The Langham hotel in 2013. At the time, the Artesian had won best bar in the world an unprecedented two times in a row. (They subsequently won last year as well, basically making them the Noma of the bar world.) Upon walking up to the bar, I was immediately served an amuse-bouche of sparkling wine and chips. The bartender handed me a metal disc menu with a tab to move the cocktails in a hole in the menu. The drinks were organized by flavor profile. I had never seen a commitment to excellence in a beverage menu before. I knew they must have spent some money putting this thing together because it was absolutely gorgeous. The care that the staff puts into their service is matched only by their technical skill in making drinks. This was the highest level of tending the bar I have seen in the world. Every cocktail we had was wonderful. The drinks were well thought out, whimsical, and innovative. I was on this trip to tour the best bars in London. I really only had to look as far as downstairs at my trusty hotel bar from that point on."—Julian Cox

The most recommended bar in this book by far by bartenders from around the globe, Artesian has won numerous industry awards and was voted #1 on the prestigious World's 50 Best Bars list an unprecedented four years in a row (2012-2015). It also won Best International Cocktail Bar in 2015 and World's Best Cocktail Bar in 2014 at the Tales of the Cocktail Spirited Awards.

CHILTERN FIREHOUSE HOTEL

1 Chiltern Street
London W1U 7PA
Marylebone
United Kingdom
+44 20 7073 7676
www.chilternfirehouse.com

Opening hours	Open 7 days
Reservation policy	Not accepted for drinks
Credit cards	Accepted
Price range	Affordable
Dress code	Smart casual
Style	Restaurant bar

"Beautiful people, beautiful decor makes you feel like you're in *The Great Gatsby*. Once you're in you completely lose control of time. Great bar snacks from Hugo Mendes and drinks made by the professional bar team impeccably dressed in white jackets."—Erik Lorincz

THE BAR AT THE DORCHESTER

53 Park Lane
The Dorchester
Mayfair
London W1K 1QA
United Kingdom
+44 2076298888
www.dorchestercollection.com/en/london/the-dorchester

Opening hours	Open 7 days
Reservation policy	Not accepted for drinks
Credit cards	Accepted
Price range	Expensive
Dress code	Smart casual
Style	Cocktail bar

"Giuliano Morandin has been the bar manager here for more than twenty years. It's not a bar that many industry bartenders know about, but they have an extraordinary high standard of service, and really deserve more attention. They have all bespoke glassware and very cutting edge cocktails. Giuliano is a real gentleman and a host. The cocktails are completely spot on all the time and they have one of the most incredible spirit collections in the world. It is a place to visit when you are in London."—Giuseppe Gallo

CONNAUGHT BAR

Carlos Place
The Connaught
Mayfair
London W1K 2AL
United Kingdom
+44 2073143419
www.the-connaught.co.uk

Opening hours	Open 7 days
Reservation policy	Not accepted for drinks
Credit cards	Accepted
Price range	Expensive
Dress code	Smart casual
Style	Cocktail bar

"The bar at The Connaught hotel is possibly my favorite room in the world. There's no other place that possesses such decorous decadence, instantly urging me to commence an immediate celebration. Perhaps it's the giant silver bucket filled with iced champagne sitting on the bar, or the pressed linen napkins your impeccable drinks are placed on. Most likely it's allowing the experience of the beauty and grace of the staff's refined technique and service to effortlessly transport you . . . The very first time I went to The Connaught Bar, Ago Perrone left me humbled and awed."—Joaquin Simo

"The first classic hotel bar inside of a five-star establishment that ever dared the 'twist on classic,' this place was our point of reference and a great example to follow. The great host and head bartender there is Agostino Perrone."
—Simone Caporale

"Makes you feel like you are going back in time and like you don't care how much you would pay for a simple and delicious Gin and Tonic."—Caitlin Laman

DUKES BAR

35 St James's Place
Dukes London
Mayfair
London SW1A 1NY
United Kingdom
+44 2074914840
www.dukeshotel.com/dukes-bar

Opening hours	Open 7 days
Reservation policy	Not accepted for drinks
Credit cards	Accepted
Price range	Expensive
Dress code	Smart casual
Style	Cocktail bar

"I've always felt quite special suiting up for an ice-cold Martini at this quiet oasis in London. There's something about the room and the service that makes it magical every time."
—Martin Cate

"This is where the Martini cocktail became a legend. It's the bar where Ian Fleming used to drink Dry Martinis and where he invented the Vesper Martini. It's the last bar in the world without music. You don't need music there, the vibe is so incredible. The key cocktail is the Dry Martini, made with gin or vodka straight from the freezer. They add three to four dashes of dry vermouth, then the gin or vodka straight into a chilled glass (the secret is they don't dry the glasses after they wash them, so there is always a little bit of water left on them to slightly dilute the drink), and serve with a big lemon twist from a true Amalfi Coast lemon, which is as big as a watermelon. Legendary bartenders like Salvatore Calabrese, Giuliano Morandin, and Gilberto Preti have all trained there. It's a very English bar, with a lot of Italian bartenders."
—Giuseppe Gallo

THE FUMOIR

49 Brook Street
Claridge's
Mayfair
London W1K 4HR
United Kingdom
+44 2076298860
www.claridges.co.uk

Opening hours	Open 7 days
Reservation policy	Not accepted for drinks
Credit cards	Accepted
Price range	Expensive
Dress code	Smart casual
Style	Cocktail bar

"Anyone who comes to London must go to Claridge's at least once and The Fumoir is the ideal place to stop for a pre- or post-evening drink. The decor is a rich, glamorous slice of Art Deco, all velvet seating and low lights, with vintage photographs on the wall, and the drinks are classic and well mixed—it's the perfect place to soak up the very best of London."—Ago Perrone

MR FOGG'S

15 Bruton Lane
Mayfair
London W1J 6JD
United Kingdom
+44 2070360608
www.mr-foggs.com

Opening hours	Open 7 days
Reservation policy	Accepted
Credit cards	Accepted
Price range	Affordable
Dress code	Smart casual
Style	Cocktail bar

TRAILER HAPPINESS

177 Portobello Road
Notting Hill
London W11 2DY
United Kingdom
+44 2070419833
www.trailerhappiness.com

Opening hours	Open 7 days
Reservation policy	Accepted
Credit cards	Accepted
Price range	Affordable
Dress code	Smart casual
Style	Tiki bar

"Good atmosphere and friendly people. If you are in the city for business and are going out alone for a drink, this is definitely the best neighborhood bar."
—Hasse Bank Johansen

ACE HOTEL

100 Shoreditch High Street
Shoreditch
London E1 6JQ
United Kingdom
+44 2076139800
www.acehotel.com/london

Opening hours	Open 7 days
Reservation policy	Not accepted for drinks
Credit cards	Accepted
Price range	Affordable
Dress code	Casual
Style	Restaurant, bar, and nightclub

"The most laid-back hotel in London. You don't feel out dressed and out of place and the drinks are to a high standard. There are different bars to suit your mood, including a basement club and a seventh-floor events terrace."—Dan Berger

CALLOOH CALLAY

65 Rivington Street
Shoreditch
London EC2A 3AY
United Kingdom
+44 2077394781
www.calloohcallaybar.com

Opening hours	Open 7 days
Reservation policy	Accepted
Credit cards	Accepted
Price range	Affordable
Dress code	Smart casual
Style	Cocktail bar

"It's got a crazy feel, with the secret door and different enviroments. Great drinks and very friendly staff. Also very good music selection."—Honorio Oliveira

"Pure hospitality. Each time I'm in London I drop by for a quirky cocktail or a delicious beer. The crew is friendly and always has great banter waiting for you."—Hannah Keirl

Calloob Callay takes its name —and its decor inspiration — from Lewis Carroll's "Jabberwocky" poem. You'll have to climb through the wardrobe to get to the more intimate upstairs Jubjub Bar. They won Best Cocktail Menu at the Spirited Awards in 2012 and are a regular on the World's 50 Best Bars list.

LOUNGE BOHEMIA

1e Great Eastern Street
Shoreditch
London EC2A 3EJ
United Kingdom
+44 7720707000
www.loungebohemia.com

Opening hours	Open 7 days
Reservation policy	Required
Credit cards	Accepted but not AMEX
Price range	Affordable
Dress code	Casual
Style	Cocktail bar

"Lounge Bohemia is owned and run by an amazing character, Paul Tvaroh, a great inspiration for me in the world of bartending."—Bek Narzi

NIGHTJAR

129 City Road
Shoreditch
London EC1V 1JB
United Kingdom
+44 2072534101
www.barnightjar.com

Opening hours	Open 7 days
Reservation policy	Accepted
Credit cards	Accepted
Price range	Affordable
Dress code	Smart casual
Style	Cocktail bar

"The most inspiring and creative place in the world."
—Marc Alvarez Safont

"From the moment you descend the stairs into Nightjar, you know the next few hours will be a little special. It's not just the impeccable service, or the ever-changing, perfectly crafted cocktail list, or the whimsical garnishes, it's the feeling that you've found your little hidden den, where you can step away from the craziness of Central London and just pause."—Paul Shipman

Internationally celebrated, Nightjar is on the cutting edge of the cocktail industry and has won numerous awards including six years on the World's 50 Best Bar list, coming in at #3 in 2015. It is the 6th most-recommended bar in this book, together with Bar High Five in Tokyo. Reservations are highly recommended and are often sold out weeks in advance.

WORSHIP STREET WHISTLING SHOP

63 Worship Street
Shoreditch
London EC2A 2DU
United Kingdom
+44 2072470015
www.whistlingshop.com

Opening hours	Closed Sunday
Reservation policy	Accepted
Credit cards	Accepted
Price range	Affordable
Dress code	Smart casual
Style	Cocktail bar

"They have an amazing, creative menu, laboratory, team work, and a great relationship with guests. So, this place is the most similar to my dream bar."—Taeeun Yoon

BAR TERMINI

7 Old Compton Street
Soho
London W1D 5JE
United Kingdom
+44 7860945018
www.bar-termini.com

Opening hours	Open 7 days
Reservation policy	Accepted
Credit cards	Accepted
Price range	Affordable
Dress code	Smart casual
Style	Coffee and cocktail bar

"I love the concept of Bar Termini. One of the only places in the world where you can have both great coffees and great cocktails. It's an aperitivo bar so if you like your Negronis and other Italian aperitifs, you should definitely pay a visit to Bar Termini."—Guillaume Le Dorner

THE BLIND PIG

58 Poland Street
Soho
London W1F 7NR
United Kingdom
+44 2079933251
www.socialeatinghouse.com

Opening hours	Closed Sunday
Reservation policy	Accepted
Credit cards	Accepted
Price range	Affordable
Dress code	Smart casual
Style	Speakeasy

"The Blind Pig is situated above the Social Eating House . . . and pretty much inconspicuous other than the sign outside the building stating 'optometrist.' One can't really call it a speakeasy, as it is so well known that everyone is talking about this copper-laden bar serving drinks with names loaded with typical British humor puns! The bar team is on point, the drinks are creative and edgy, and the ambience is exactly what one expects in a 1920s-theme dram house, but with some modern edge splashed here and there."
—Denzel Heath

LAB BAR

12 Old Compton Street
Soho
London W1D 4TQ
United Kingdom
+44 2074377820
www.labbaruk.com

Opening hours	Open 7 days
Reservation policy	Accepted
Credit cards	Accepted
Price range	Affordable
Dress code	Smart casual
Style	Cocktail bar

"A festive atmosphere in a modern and trendy bar. They serve the best Porn Star Martini worldwide."—Nicolas Berger

MILK & HONEY

61 Poland Street
Soho
London W1F 7NU
United Kingdom
+44 2070656800
www.mlkhny.com

Opening hours	Closed Sunday
Reservation policy	Accepted
Credit cards	Accepted
Price range	Expensive
Dress code	Smart casual
Style	Cocktail bar

"Always a good bar to go to with impeccable service. The guys there know how to make you comfortable. There is a real dedication and passion about the way things are done at Milk & Honey."—Guillaume Le Dorner

THE PINK CHIHUAHUA

25-27 Brewer Street
El Camion Mexicano
Soho
London W1F 0RR
United Kingdom
+44 2077347711
www.elcamion.co.uk/soho/

Opening hours	Closed Sunday
Reservation policy	Accepted
Credit cards	Accepted
Price range	Affordable
Dress code	Casual
Style	Mexican restaurant and bar

"There's nothing better than slamming a few shots of tequila with spicy pomegranate. Fun drinks in a fun environment. The perfect after-work spot!"—Dan Berger

"It is just the best. Tequila, mezcal, good music, good vibes, and insane times . . . Every time I go to London it is a MUST stop."—Ivy Mix

DANDELYAN

20 Upper Ground
Mondrian London
South Bank
London SE1 9PD
United Kingdom
+44 2037471063
www.morganshotelgroup.com/mondrian/mondrian-london

Opening hours	Open 7 days
Reservation policy	Accepted
Credit cards	Accepted
Price range	Affordable
Dress code	Smart casual
Style	Cocktail bar

"The setting is great—there is something very special about drinking one of their wonderful cocktails by the Thames river. Also, they have a great playlist; it's my go-to place on those days when I am in need of a good drink."
—Guillaume Le Dorner

HIGH WATER

23 Stoke Newington Road
Stoke Newington
London N16 8BJ
United Kingdom
+44 2072411984
www.highwaterlondon.com

Opening hours	Open 7 days
Reservation policy	Accepted
Credit cards	Accepted
Price range	Affordable
Dress code	Smart casual
Style	Cocktail bar

"High Water was our first project back in London and we love that little bar."—Mia Johansson

THE PROSPECT OF WHITBY

57 Wapping Wall
Wapping
London E1W 3SH
United Kingdom
+44 2074811095
www.taylor-walker.co.uk/pub/prospect-of-whitby-wapping/c8166

Opening hours	Open 7 days
Reservation policy	Not accepted for drinks
Credit cards	Accepted
Price range	Budget
Dress code	Casual
Style	Pub

"My favorite riverfront pub in London . . . A cozy warren of rooms, filled with great nautical decor, beautiful views over the water, and well-kept real ale. Perfect for a long, peaceful afternoon."—Martin Cate

NINETY-NINE BAR & KITCHEN

1 Back Wynd
Aberdeen
Scotland AB10 1JN
United Kingdom
+44 1224631640
www.99aberdeen.com

Opening hours..Open 7 days
Reservation policy...Accepted
Credit cards..............................Accepted but not AMEX
Price range..Affordable
Dress code...Casual
Style...Pub

"The staff are relaxed yet professional and knowledgable, the bar itself is open yet cozy, the food is excellent, and the spirit and beer selection is vast."—Sian Buchan

THE BON VIVANT

55 Thistle Street
Edinburgh
Scotland EH2 1DY
United Kingdom
+44 1312253275
www.bonvivantedinburgh.co.uk

Opening hours..Open 7 days
Reservation policy....................Not accepted for drinks
Credit cards...Accepted
Price range..Affordable
Dress code...Casual
Style...Gastropub

"Staffed by awesome people, a solid local following, incredible wine list, a deli next door, a small but perfectly formed spirit collection, and some of the best food to be found in Edinburgh, all housed in a beautiful Victorian building. This is the bar that you could spend the rest of your life welcoming friends into."—Paul Shipman

BRAMBLE

16A Queen Street
Edinburgh
Scotland EH2 1JE
United Kingdom
+44 1312266343
www.bramblebar.co.uk

Opening hours..Open 7 days
Reservation policy....................Not accepted for drinks
Credit cards...Accepted
Price range..Affordable
Dress code...Smart casual
Style...Cocktail bar

"Bramble channels every aspect of a great bar: amazing atmosphere, music, service, staff, drinks . . . but it does so with such effortless aplomb. It feels great to simply be a part of the atmosphere—like you've stumbled into something that will bring forth one of those rare, memorable nights that FOMO personifies. Consistently great, always ahead of the curve, and remains a true pioneer after almost ten years."
—Ryan Chetiyawardana

THE CANNY MAN'S

237 Morningside Road
Edinburgh
Scotland EH10 4QU
United Kingdom
+44 1314471484
www.cannymans.co.uk

Opening hours..Open 7 days
Reservation policy...Accepted
Credit cards..............................Accepted but not AMEX
Price range..Affordable
Dress code...Casual
Style...Pub

"A pilgrimage worth making for any interested drinker. This ancient family pub carries more than a few eccentric characteristics, but it is a living museum to Scotland's—and the world's—drinking histories. A cacophonous collection of all things drinks-related lines every inch, lending a charm that can't be replicated. The pub literally pours history, and you can enjoy their own whiskey, or one of an amazing selection of malts, and a perfect pint of Guinness in incredible—and quite unique—surroundings." —Ryan Chetiyawardana

GARIBALDI'S
97A Hanover Street
Edinburgh
Scotland EH2 1DJ
United Kingdom
+44 1312203007

Opening hours..Open 7 days
Reservation policy..................................Not accepted for drinks
Credit cards...Accepted
Price range..Budget
Dress code...Casual
Style...Dive bar

"This is a proper dive club that seriously needs a lick of paint and a mop bucket or four. But that's exactly what makes it so popular among Scottish bartenders . . . Pass around jugs of Piña Colada and knock back Mexican lager and tequila to the tune of cheesy music and I promise it's a right barrel-load of fun!"—James Kemp

PANDA & SONS
79 Queen Street
Edinburgh
Scotland EH2 4NF
United Kingdom
+44 1312200443
www.pandaandsons.com

Opening hours..Open 7 days
Reservation policy...Accepted
Credit cards...Accepted
Price range..Affordable
Dress code...Smart casual
Style..Speakeasy

"From the entrance to the welcome you get from the staff, this place is excellent. The drinks are amazing, the staff are awesome, the menu is quirky and fun . . . Just a fab place to spend an evening."—Sian Buchan

VILLAGER
49-50 George IV Bridge
Edinburgh
Scotland EH1 1EJ
United Kingdom
+44 1312262781
www.villagerbar.com

Opening hours..Open 7 days
Reservation policy...Accepted
Credit cards..................................Accepted but not AMEX
Price range..Affordable
Dress code...Casual
Style..Restaurant and bar

"Just a great hangout spot, very relaxed . . . a good vibe to it, not pretentious."—Angus McGregor

THE FINNIESTON BAR & RESTAURANT
1125 Argyle Street
Glasgow
Scotland G3 8ND
United Kingdom
+44 1412222884
www.thefinniestonbar.com

Opening hours..Open 7 days
Reservation policy..................................Not accepted for drinks
Credit cards..................................Accepted but not AMEX
Price range..Affordable
Dress code...Smart casual
Style...Gastropub

"Outside of my own bar, Kelvingrove Café, the next place I recommend is located just a few doors down. Specializing in gin and seafood, the bartenders here are really hospitable and knowledgeable."—Mal Spence

THE POT STILL
154 Hope Street
Glasgow
Scotland G2 2TH
United Kingdom
+44 1413330980
www.thepotstill.co.uk

Opening hours..Open 7 days
Reservation policy..................................Not accepted for drinks
Credit cards..................................Accepted but not AMEX
Price range..Affordable
Dress code...Casual
Style...Whiskey bar

"The Pot Still is simply the best whiskey bar in the world. With hundreds and hundreds of whiskeys from all over the world to select from, the old man pub atmosphere makes for a truly authentic Scottish pub experience. However, it is the people who run it that make this pub truly outstanding. 'Big Frank' Murphy (never to be seen without his trademark kilt, utility belt, hammer, and goatee) and his father, also Frank, run their bar with such enthusiasm and friendliness that their second-to-none whiskey knowledge almost seems like part of their biology. After one of Big Frank's famous hugs (dished out upon request), sit with a choice of whiskey recommended by the staff, a beer, and one of their famous homemade pies with beans. A true taste of what Glasgow is all about: fun, friendliness, 'banter,' and hundreds of whiskey."
—James Kemp

THE SALON

11 Blythswood Square
Blythswood Square Hotel
Glasgow
Scotland G2 4AD
United Kingdom
+44 1412488888
www.townhousecompany.com/blythswoodsquare/the-salon

Opening hours...Open 7 days
Reservation policy.......................................Accepted
Credit cards...Accepted
Price range...Affordable
Dress code...Smart casual
Style...Cocktail bar

"I spent three years of my life behind the bar here, shaping it from a building site into one of the best bars in the country."
—Mal Spence

DUKE OF YORK

7-11 Commercial Court
Belfast BT1 2NB
United Kingdom
+44 28 9024 1062
www.dukeofyorkbelfast.com

Opening hours...Open 7 days
Reservation policy....................Not accepted for drinks
Credit cards...........................Accepted but not AMEX
Price range...Affordable
Dress code...Casual
Style...Pub

THE HUDSON BAR

10-14 Gresham Street
Belfast BT1 1JN
United Kingdom
+44 2890232322
www.hudsonbelfast.com

Opening hours...Open 7 days
Reservation policy.......................................Accepted
Credit cards...........................Accepted but not AMEX
Price range...Affordable
Dress code...Smart casual
Style...Pub

KELLY'S CELLARS

30-32 Bank Street
Belfast BT1 1HL
United Kingdom
+44 2890246058
www.kellyscellars.com

Opening hours...Open 7 days
Reservation policy....................Not accepted for drinks
Credit cards...Accepted
Price range...Affordable
Dress code...Casual
Style...Pub

"It's my local in Belfast. One of the oldest bars to boot. Real gritty Belfast people, great pint of Guinness, and welcoming staff. My happy place."—Jack McGarry

SEAN'S BAR

13 Main Street
Althone
County Westmeath
Republic of Ireland
+353 906492358
www.seansbar.ie

Opening hours...Open 7 days
Reservation policy....................Not accepted for drinks
Credit cards...........................Accepted but not AMEX
Price range...Affordable
Dress code...Casual
Style...Pub

THE BRAZEN HEAD

20 Bridge Street Lower
Dublin 8
Republic of Ireland
+353 16779549
www.brazenhead.com

Opening hours..Open 7 days
Reservation policy...Accepted
Credit cards..................................Accepted but not AMEX
Price range...Affordable
Dress code...Casual
Style...Pub

JOHN KAVANAGH "THE GRAVEDIGGERS"

1 Prospect Square
Glasnevin
Dublin 9
Republic of Ireland
+353 872963713

Opening hours..Open 7 days
Reservation policy...................................Not accepted for drinks
Credit cards...Not accepted
Price range...Budget
Dress code...Casual
Style...Pub

"Best pint in Ireland. Historical venue and located beside the
resting place of Ireland's 1916 heroes."—Alan Kavanagh

THE LIQUOR ROOMS

5 Wellington Quay
Dublin 3
Republic of Ireland
+353 873393688
www.theliquorrooms.com

Opening hours..Open 7 days
Reservation policy...Accepted
Credit cards...Accepted
Price range...Affordable
Dress code...Smart casual
Style...Cocktail bar

"Great staff, unique decor, and always a friendly welcoming
atmosphere. Classic cocktails with a modern twist."
—Alan Kavanagh

SHELBOURNE HOTEL

27 St. Stephen's Green
Dublin 2
Republic of Ireland
+353 16634500
www.marriott.com/hotels/travel/dubbr-the-
shelbourne-dublin-a-renaissance-hotel

Opening hours..Open 7 days
Reservation policy...................................Not accepted for drinks
Credit cards...Accepted
Price range...Affordable
Dress code...Smart casual
Style...Lounge

"A fantastic historical building located in the heart of Dublin.
Every type of personality within the walls of the venue. Great
service."—Alan Kavanagh

"THE FIRST COCKTAIL BAR OUTSIDE OF AMSTERDAM [IN THE NETHERLANDS], IT HAS BEEN, AND STILL IS, A PIONEER FOR THE DUTCH COCKTAIL SCENE." IVAR DE LANGE P.124

THE NETHERLANDS & BELGIUM

"ONE OF THE BEST AND OLDEST CAFÉS IN HOLLAND."

IVAR DE LANGE P.124

"YOU JUST ENJOY YOUR BEER AND ORDER ANOTHER AND PROBABLY ANOTHER, BECAUSE ONCE YOU FORGET WHERE YOU ARE, YOU ARE BOUND TO LOSE TRACK OF TIME."

OLIVIER JACOBS P.130

"LOVE, LOVE, LOVE THESE GUYS! ALL THE GENTLEMEN THAT WORK THERE ARE INSPIRING, KIND, AND POSSESS GREAT SKILLS AND KNOWLEDGE ... PROUD TO BE BELGIAN WHEN I'M THERE!"

HANNAH VAN ONGEVALLE P.130

"BURGERS, BEERS, AND BOURBON, WHAT ELSE IS THERE TO SAY?"

OLIVIER JACOBS P.130

THE NETHERLANDS & BELGIUM

SCALE

0   250   500
mi.

♦ AMSTERDAM PP.126–129

THE NETHERLANDS

♦ NIJMEGEN P.124

♦ GHENT P.130

BELGIUM

THE BAR AT HOTEL CREDIBLE

Hertogstraat 1
Hotel Credible
Nijmegen 6511 RV
The Netherlands
+31 243220498
www.in-credible.nl

Opening hours...Open 7 days
Reservation policy.................................Not accepted for drinks
Credit cards.................................Accepted but not AMEX
Price range...Budget
Dress code..Casual
Style..Lounge

"It's nice and cozy and the service is very good."
—Ivar de Lange

CAFÉ IN DE BLAAUWE HAND

Achter de Hoofdwacht 3
Nijmegen 6511 VW
The Netherlands
+31 243232066
www.indeblaauwehand.nl

Opening hours...Closed Monday
Reservation policy.................................Not accepted for drinks
Credit cards...Accepted
Price range...Affordable
Dress code..Casual
Style..Pub

"De Blaauwe Hand because it is one of the best and oldest
cafés in Holland. An experience you can't have in any other
place."—Ivar de Lange

DEMAIN

Lange Hezelstraat 58a
Nijmegen 6511 CL
The Netherlands
+31 243243345
www.cafedemain.nl

Opening hours..Closed Monday
Reservation policy.................................Not accepted for drinks
Credit cards...Accepted
Price range...Affordable
Dress code..Smart casual
Style...Cocktail bar

"The first cocktail bar outside of Amsterdam [in The
Netherlands], it has been, and still is, a pioneer for
the Dutch cocktail scene."—Ivar de Lange

"THIS PLACE IS A MUST FOR ALL PEOPLE THAT APPRECIATE AN OLD-SCHOOL GENTLEMAN BEHIND THE BAR."
LAURA SCHACHT P.128

"WHAT MAKES THIS MY FAVORITE LATE-NIGHT BAR IS THAT THEY MAKE GREAT COCKTAILS AND ALSO HAVE A LATE-NIGHT BAR SNACK MENU."
TESS POSTHUMUS P.129

AMSTERDAM

"WHISKEY BAR WITH OVER 1,400 (!) WHISKEYS."
TIMO JANSE P.129

"THIS TIME-WORN BAR IS THE PLACE TO GIVE THE TRADITIONAL DUTCH KOPSTOOTJE A TRY."
TESS POSTHUMUS P.129

"THEY HAVE THE REQUISITE HIDDEN DOOR, ANTIQUE BARWARE, TIN CEILING, AND SOPHISTICATED ATMOSPHERE." TAEEUN YOON P.128

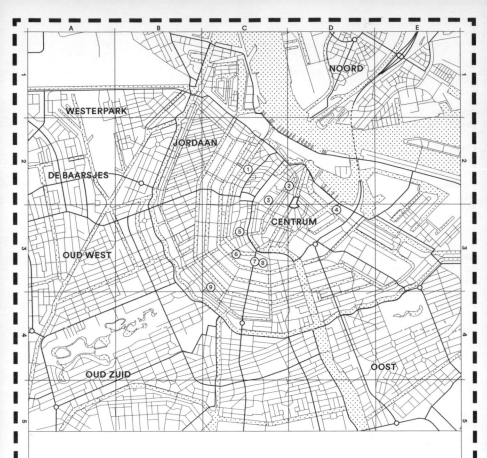

WESTERPARK

JORDAAN

DE BAARSJES

CENTRUM

OUD WEST

NOORD

OUD ZUID

OOST

AMSTERDAM

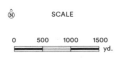

N̂

SCALE

0   500   1000 1500

yd.

1. TALES & SPIRITS (P.129)
2. EXCALIBUR (P.128)
3. WYNAND FOCKINK (P.129)

4. HIDING IN PLAIN SIGHT (P.128)
5. CAFÉ DE DOKTER (P.128)
6. SNAPPERS RESTO-BAR (P.129)

7. FEIJOA (P.128)
8. DOOR 74 (P.128)
9. WHISKY CAFÉ L&B (P.129)

CAFÉ DE DOKTER

Rozenboomsteeg 4
Amsterdam 1012 PR
The Netherlands
+31 206264427
www.cafe-de-dokter.nl

Opening hours	Closed Sunday and Monday
Reservation policy	Not accepted for drinks
Credit cards	Not accepted
Price range	Affordable
Dress code	Smart casual
Style	Cafe and bar

"This place is a must for all people that appreciate an old-school gentleman behind the bar, a good beer, and a small venue . . . Dusty, very likely not cleaned since hundreds of years, it is one of the oldest brown bars in Amsterdam. Some of the bottles are really old, but he is clever enough not to sell them to you, he knows what treasures he has in his back bar."
—Laura Schacht

"Authentic classic bar. No cocktails, just a small awesome bar." —Timo Janse

DOOR 74

Reguliersdwarsstraat 74I
Amsterdam 1017 BN
The Netherlands
+31 634045122
www.door-74.com

Opening hours	Open 7 days
Reservation policy	Accepted
Credit cards	Accepted
Price range	Affordable
Dress code	Smart casual
Style	Speakeasy

"'Find what you love, and let it kill you.' The bartenders that work at this bar are hard, passionate, and inspiring."
—Hannah Van Ongevalle

"Door 74 is the first speakeasy-style cocktail bar in The Netherlands. They have the requisite hidden door, antique barware, tin ceiling, and sophisticated atmosphere, plus delicious and perfectly balanced creations from Timo Janse, Tess [Posthumus], and the best bar team in Amsterdam."
—Taeeun Yoon

The first speakeasy-style bar in the Benelux, Door 74 is a staple of the World's 50 Best Bar list.

EXCALIBUR

Oudezijds Achterburgwal 48
Amsterdam 1012 DP
The Netherlands
+31 207708345
www.excaliburcafe.nl

Opening hours	Open 7 days
Reservation policy	Not accepted for drinks
Credit cards	Accepted but not AMEX
Price range	Budget
Dress code	Casual
Style	Dive bar

"Great biker bar in the red light district. Tough but fair!"
—Timo Janse

FEIJOA

Vijzelstraat 39
Amsterdam 1017 HE
The Netherlands
+31 621710434

Opening hours	Open 7 days
Reservation policy	Accepted
Credit cards	Accepted
Price range	Affordable
Dress code	Smart casual
Style	Cocktail bar

"Neo-classic cocktail bar. Great fun!"—Timo Janse

HIDING IN PLAIN SIGHT (HPS)

Rapenburg 18
Amsterdam 1011 TX
The Netherlands
+31 625293620
www.hpsamsterdam.com

Opening hours	Open 7 days
Reservation policy	Accepted
Credit cards	Accepted
Price range	Affordable
Dress code	Smart casual
Style	Cocktail bar

"Great drinks, super menu, great atmosphere, friendly bar staff, very nice crowd, and located outside the beaten path."
—Timo Janse

SNAPPERS RESTO-BAR

Reguliersdwarsstraat 21
Amsterdam 1017 BJ
The Netherlands
+31 208458144
www.snappers-amsterdam.nl

Opening hours	Open 7 days
Reservation policy	Not accepted for drinks
Credit cards	Accepted but not AMEX
Price range	Affordable
Dress code	Casual
Style	Restaurant and cocktail bar

"Relaxed food, relaxed drinks. Great value for money."
—Timo Janse

TALES & SPIRITS

Lijnbaanssteeg 5-7
Amsterdam 1012 TE
The Netherlands
+31 6 55356467
www.talesandspirits.com

Opening hours	Closed Monday
Reservation policy	Not accepted for drinks
Credit cards	Accepted
Price range	Affordable
Dress code	Smart casual
Style	Restaurant and cocktail bar

"Great cocktail bar, great food. Must visit! "—Timo Janse

"Tales & Spirits is a restaurant owned by two bartenders. They serve very good food and excellent drinks. What makes this my favorite late-night bar is that they make great cocktails and also have a late-night bar snack menu. This isn't very common in Amsterdam as most places stop serving food after 11 p.m. Once you're there, you should definitely try their Old Fashioned cocktail with truffle."—Tess Posthumus

WHISKY CAFÉ L&B

Korte Leidsedwarsstraat 82-84
Amsterdam 1017 RD
The Netherlands
+31 206252387
www.whiskyproeverijen.nl

Opening hours	Open 7 days
Reservation policy	Not accepted for drinks
Credit cards	Not accepted
Price range	Affordable
Dress code	Casual
Style	Whiskey bar

"Whiskey bar with over 1,400 (!) whiskeys."—Timo Janse

WYNAND FOCKINK

Pijlsteeg 31
Amsterdam 1012 HH
The Netherlands
+31 206392695
www.wynand-fockink.nl

Opening hours	Open 7 days
Reservation policy	Not accepted for drinks
Credit cards	Accepted but not AMEX
Price range	Affordable
Dress code	Casual
Style	Distillery and tasting room

"This small genever and liqueur distillery has been there for ages and it includes a tasting room. Located just behind Dam Square, this time-worn bar is the place to give the traditional Dutch Kopstootje a try. A Kopstootje is a small glass of genever with a draft beer on the side."—Tess Posthumus

CAFÉ DEN TURK

Botermarkt 3
Ghent 9000
Belgium
+32 92330197
www.denturk.be

Opening hours	Open 7 days
Reservation policy	Not accepted for drinks
Credit cards	Not accepted
Price range	Affordable
Dress code	Casual
Style	Cafe and bar

"It is one of the oldest bars of our city, they do tap the best 'pintjes' (flemish for a pils beer) but really it's just a regular Belgian cafe. Still it has something magical, you don't get bothered if you don't want to, the bar is full of regulars, and the bartender knows what they are having. You just enjoy your beer and order another and probably another because once you forget where you are, you are bound to lose track of time."—Olivier Jacobs

JIGGER'S

Oudburg 16
Ghent 9000
Belgium
+32 93357025
www.jiggers.be

Opening hours	Closed Sunday and Monday
Reservation policy	Accepted
Credit cards	Not accepted
Price range	Affordable
Dress code	Smart casual
Style	Cocktail bar

"Love, love, love these guys! All the gentlemen that work there are inspiring, kind, and possess great skills and knowledge. I've been a fan since the beginning and even though they are very successful in Belgium and with international bartenders, they keep their feet on the ground and serve great drinks. Proud to be Belgian when I'm there!"—Hannah Van Ongevalle

MINOR SWING

Ottogracht 56
Ghent 9000
Belgium
+32 494906483

Opening hours	Open 7 days
Reservation policy	Not accepted for drinks
Credit cards	Not accepted
Price range	Affordable
Dress code	Casual
Style	Jazz club

"It's a no nonsense bar just around our corner. They are usually open just a little later than we are so we can catch them for a last quaffing before hitting the hay. No cocktails on the menu, just beer, wine, and a good atmosphere."
—Olivier Jacobs

UNCLE BABE'S

Sluizekenstraat 2
Ghent 9000
Belgium
+32 92788919
www.unclebabes.com

Opening hours	Closed Monday
Reservation policy	Not accepted for drinks
Credit cards	Accepted
Price range	Affordable
Dress code	Casual
Style	Burger joint and bar

"Burgers, beer, and bourbon, what else is there to say? The owner, Abe, makes the best burgers of Belgium, the back bar is endless, and the beer cellar changes regularly. Vitas the bartender is still young but already very talented, he makes exquisite drinks although I plead guilty and usually go straight for beer when I am there."—Olivier Jacobs

"IT'S THE PLACE IN WHICH I WOULD LIKE NOTHING TO CHANGE ... IT'S 'HORS DU TEMPS,' TIMELESS, COMFORTABLE, GREAT JAZZ MUSIC, FOOD, COCKTAILS, WHISKEY."

MARC BONNETON P.134

"A PLACE I CAN HANG OUT EASILY, HAVE A GREAT COCKTAIL OR A SHOT, AND IT'S PERFECT."

NICO DE SOTO P.141

FRANCE

"IT'S DARK, COZY AND EASY TO GET LOST IN THE ARRAY OF INGREDIENTS, SPIRITS, AND BARTENDER TECHNIQUES."

JONATHAN POGASH P.142

"SMALL, PERSONAL, INSPIRING, AMAZING COCKTAILS AND THE PERFECT ICE."

DIRK HANY P.142

"THE BARTENDERS COULD BE IN AN INDIE ROCK BAND OR PAINTERS FROM THE NINETEENTH CENTURY; THEY ARE MYSTERIOUS, FILLED WITH KNOWLEDGE, AND A LOT OF FUN."

HANNAH VAN ONGEVALLE P.144

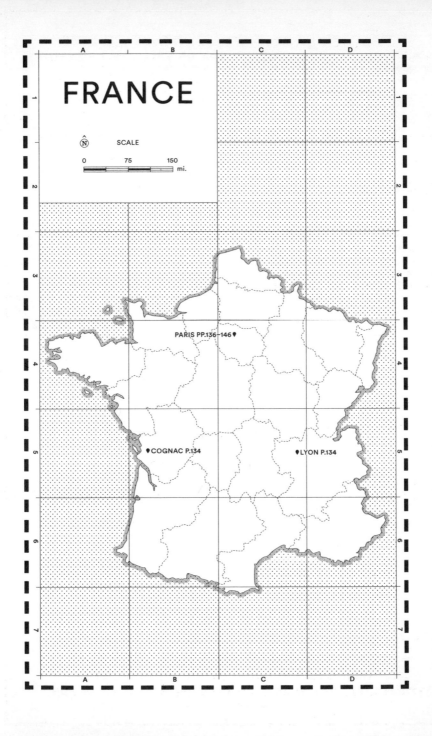

FRANCE

N

SCALE

0   75   150
               mi.

PARIS PP.136–146

COGNAC P.134

LYON P.134

BAR LOUISE

3 Place François 1er
Hôtel François 1er
Cognac 16100
France
+33 545808080
www.hotelfrancoispremier.fr

Opening hours..................................Closed Sunday and Monday
Reservation policy...Accepted
Credit cards...Accepted
Price range..Affordable
Dress code...Smart casual
Style..Cocktail bar

"This is the hotel you stay in [in Cognac]. It was recently
renovated and has a great little cocktail bar in the lobby
overseen by Alexandre Lambert. Late night when all the
other bars in the city are closed and there is a special event
for bartenders, there are a lot of behind-the-bar antics."
—Shawn Soole

L'ANTIQUAIRE

20 Rue Hippolyte Flandrin
Lyon 69001
France
+33 634215465
www.bdgandcie.com

Opening hours...............Open 7 days/closed Sunday in summer
Reservation policy.............................Not accepted for drinks
Credit cards...............................Accepted but not AMEX
Price range..Affordable
Dress code...Smart casual
Style..Cocktail bar

"It's the place in which I would like nothing to change . . .
it's 'hors du temps,' timeless, comfortable, great jazz music,
food, cocktails, whiskey."—Marc Bonneton

"A creative young team with whom I share the same ideas
about bartending. Some magic encounter between old-
school and new-school cocktails."—Nicolas Berger

BOSTON CAFÉ

8 Place des Terreaux
Lyon 69001
France
+33 478234290

Opening hours...Open 7 days
Reservation policy...................Not accepted for drinks
Credit cards...........................Accepted but not AMEX
Price range..Budget
Dress code...Casual
Style..Pub

"Friendship, people you meet, nothing special to drink
there . . . but close to where we work and open until very
late, so we have after-work beers there."—Marc Bonneton

"CANDELARIA IS A TOP-NOTCH BAR WITH GREAT DRINKS AND THE KIND OF VIBE THAT ONLY THE FRENCH CAN PULL OFF."

NEAL BODENHEIMER P.142

"GREAT TIKI BAR IN THE MIDDLE OF PARIS WITH AN EXCELLENT BAR TEAM."

GABE ORTA P.143

PARIS

"FOR ME, THIS BAR IS ABSOLUTELY PERFECT: COCKTAILS THAT SURPRISE WITH THEIR INTERESTING 'EXPERIMENTAL' COMBINATIONS, AND BARTENDERS WHO DON'T STOP, EVEN FOR A SECOND."

LIZAVETA MOLYAVKA P.141

"THIS BAR IS A TRUE PIECE OF PARIS, A GEM, OLDEST COCKTAIL BAR IN PARIS STILL OPEN."

MARC BONNETON P.141

"A MENU THAT UTILIZES ONLY FRENCH SPIRITS AND INGREDIENTS!"

AMANDA BOUCHER P.145

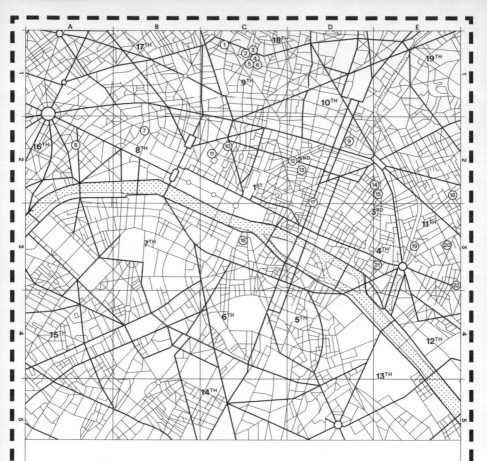

PARIS

N   SCALE

0   500   1000   1500
                           yd.

1. HOTEL MAISON SOUQUET
    + BAR (P.144)
2. GLASS (P.144)
3. LULU WHITE (P.144)
4. DIRTY DICK (P.143)
5. L'ENTRÉE DES ARTISTES
    PIGALLE (P.143)
6. RESTAURANT & BAR À VINS (P.144)
7. LE BAR DU BRISTOL (P.143)

8. LE BAR (P.143)
9. COPPER BAY (P.145)
10. HARRY'S NEW YORK BAR (P.141)
11. HEMINGWAY BAR (P.141)
12. MABEL (P.141)
13. EXPERIMENTAL COCKTAIL
    CLUB (P.141)
14. LITTLE RED DOOR (P.142)
15. CANDELARIA (P.142)

16. LA BUVETTE (P.145)
17. LE SYNDICAT (P.145)
18. THE BAR (P.142)
19. MOONSHINER (P.146)
20. MEDUSA (P.145)
21. SHERRY BUTT (P.142)
22. RED HOUSE (P.146)

COCKTAILS À LA FRANÇAISE: PARIS

A favorite destination of American expats in the early 1900s, Paris has a long and illustrious history as a cocktail city. By most accounts, it began in 1911 with Harry's New York Bar where Harry MacElhone (a Scotsman) served as head bartender and later bought the business. It was here that the Bloody Mary was invented, along with classics like the Sidecar and the White Lady. Paris was also a favorite destination of American bartenders during Prohibition, and it was here and in London that classic cocktail culture was kept alive during the 1920s.

More recently, Paris, like New York and London, has seen a cocktail renaissance. It started in 2007 when the Experimental Cocktail Club opened to great acclaim, and since then more than fifty cocktail bars have popped up around the city—most of them in up-and-coming neighborhoods such as Pigalle or Place de la République. This new, highly creative movement draws inspiration from New York in particular, but adds a distinctive French touch with high attention to detail and a desire to push the boundaries. Mostly owner-operated bars, each one has its own raison d'être. Le Syndicat only stocks French products, Glass has a light-up floor and slushy cocktails, and Dirty Dick is a tiki bar.

The final part of the Paris cocktail triptych is the luxury hotel bar, epitomized by the Hemingway Bar at The Ritz. Here, and at the Hotel George V or Le Bristol, you'll experience French luxury at its finest.

Practical Information:
– Cocktails in Paris range from €9 at the low end, €13 at the mid-range, and €20 or more at the high end (particularly at hotels).
– Tipping is not customary, though at higher-end establishments you might leave €1 or €2.
– Many bars will start to really fill up at 9:00 or 10:00 p.m.

THE BEE'S KNEES

One of the delicious cocktails created by longtime barman Fritz Meier at The Ritz Paris in the 1930s, the Bee's Knees is a gin sour (gin and lemon) with honey. Calling something the bee's knees at that time was considered quite a compliment.

BLOODY MARY

The Bloody Mary, the classic "hair of the dog" reviver, was in fact invented in Paris in the 1920s at Harry's New York Bar by Fernand "Pete" Petiot. After Prohibition was repealed in 1933, he moved to New York and introduced the drink to The King Cole bar at the St. Regis hotel.

HEMINGWAY BAR
15 Place Vendôme
Ritz Paris
1st Arrondissement
Paris 75001
France
+33 143163030
www.ritzparis.com

Opening hours	Open 7 days
Reservation policy	Not accepted for drinks
Credit cards	Accepted
Price range	Expensive
Dress code	Smart casual
Style	Cocktail bar

"Because it's a beautiful, iconic room, and it's been closed since 2012 and set to reopen in 2016. I'd love to be there to see the renovation, and sit at the bar to experience Mr. Colin Field back at the helm."—Franky Marshall

"Unique ambience and cozy atmosphere, feeling of discrete luxury, lovely glassware, and details."—Marc Bonneton

"Head bartender Colin Field is enormously talented."
—Dale DeGroff

A historic bar purportedly "liberated" by Ernest Hemingway ahead of the Allied forces in 1944, and so named for him.

EXPERIMENTAL COCKTAIL CLUB
37 Rue Saint-Sauveur
2nd Arrondissement
Paris 75002
France
+33 145088809
www.experimentalevents.com

Opening hours	Open 7 days
Reservation policy	Not accepted for drinks
Credit cards	Accepted
Price range	Affordable
Dress code	Smart casual
Style	Cocktail bar

"Because it's where everything started, including for myself."
—Nico de Soto

"Experimental Cocktail Club is a place that fascinated me from the very first minute and I go there every time I come to Paris. For me, this bar is absolutely perfect: cocktails that surprise with their interesting 'experimental' combinations, bartenders who don't stop, even for a second, a place which is small and cozy, and unites all those people who come to drink! But keep in mind that it's hard to find the bar, because

you won't see a huge sign . . . but a specific sign that will tell you that you are really close to the truth is a strong and very serious security guard at the entrance, who will never tell that behind the door you will find an amazing bar. In any case, good luck! And by the way, if you don't like the cocktail's 'experiment,' the bartenders will replace the drink immediately, free of charge. However, such a bar policy is an omen that it must be good!"
—Lizaveta Molyavka

HARRY'S NEW YORK BAR
5 Rue Daunou
2nd Arrondissement
Paris 75002
France
+33 142617114
www.harrysbar.fr

Opening hours	Open 7 days
Reservation policy	Not accepted for drinks
Credit cards	Accepted
Price range	Affordable
Dress code	Smart casual
Style	Cocktail bar

"The birthplace of the French 75 in the most beautiful city in the world. What's not to love?"—Beau Edgington

"It's a classic. An absolute must-visit for any bartender and it's located in the most beautiful city in the world. You feel like you're drinking in history."—Keely Edgington

"Really out of time, great feeling, old-school bartenders . . . this bar is a true piece of Paris, a gem, oldest cocktail bar in Paris still open."—Marc Bonneton

MABEL
58 Rue d'Aboukir
2nd Arrondissement
Paris 75002
France
+33 142332433
www.mabelparis.com

Opening hours	Closed Sunday
Reservation policy	Not accepted for drinks
Credit cards	Accepted but not AMEX
Price range	Affordable
Dress code	Casual
Style	Cocktail bar

"I'm not so much a beer and a shot guy, I always go for a cocktail. This is one of my best friend's bars. It's a place I can hang out easily, have a great cocktail or a shot, and it's perfect."—Nico de Soto

CANDELARIA

52 Rue de Saintonge
3rd Arrondissement
Paris 75003
France
+33 142744128
www.candelariaparis.com

Opening hours	Open 7 days
Reservation policy	Accepted
Credit cards	Accepted
Price range	Affordable
Dress code	Smart casual
Style	Cocktail bar and taqueria

"Candelaria is a top-notch bar with great drinks and the kind of vibe that only the French can pull off."—Neal Bodenheimer

"It's one of the spots that has brought quality cocktails to the forefront of the Paris drinks scene. It's dark, cozy, and easy to get lost in the array of ingredients, spirits, and bartender techniques being put on right before your very eyes. I try and visit every time I go to Europe."—Jonathan Pogash

LITTLE RED DOOR

60 Rue Charlot
3rd Arrondissement
Paris 75003
France
+33 142711932
www.lrdparis.com

Opening hours	Open 7 days
Reservation policy	Not accepted for drinks
Credit cards	Accepted but not AMEX
Price range	Affordable
Dress code	Smart casual
Style	Cocktail bar

"I haven't really had the chance to travel globally but when I was in France, the Little Red Door made me feel at home. The bartenders make amazing drinks and are incredibly friendly. Victor and Peter really took care of us. They even gracious enough to take us out, along with the one and only Remy Savage, to some of their favorite bars. What a cool scene they have there."—Jayson Wilde

SHERRY BUTT

20 Rue Beautreillis
4th Arrondissement
Paris 75004
France
+33 983384780
www.sherrybuttparis.com

Opening hours	Open 7 days
Reservation policy	Accepted
Credit cards	Accepted
Price range	Affordable
Dress code	Casual
Style	Cocktail bar

"Sherry Butt is the best bar, where the guys work with a perfect Japanese style! Good atmosphere and perfectly served drinks. I love this place."—Andre Pintz

"Small, personal, inspiring, amazing cocktails, and the perfect ice. When I visited this bar, it had all my visions of my own bar and much more! This is exactly how I would like to present my bar."—Dirk Hany

THE BAR

13 Rue des Beaux Arts
L'Hotel
6th Arrondissement
Paris 75006
France
+33 144419900
www.l-hotel.com

Opening hours	Open 7 days
Reservation policy	Not accepted for drinks
Credit cards	Accepted
Price range	Expensive
Dress code	Smart casual
Style	Cocktail bar

"This is where Oscar Wilde stayed and died in 1900. The bar became famous while Guy Louis Deboucheron was the owner—Anthony Quinn, Madonna, Sean Penn, and Isabelle Adjani were all regulars. I mean REGULARS. After Guy Louis disappeared the hotel became quite a disappointment. New owners have taken over and although the bar is no longer in its original position and the dungeon bar has been replaced by a spa, there is still a mysterious, uncanny feeling of immense class, and of magical stories with magical people around an enchanted fountain that was by the bar in the restaurant."—Colin Field

LE BAR

31 Avenue George V
Four Seasons Hotel George V
8th Arrondissement
Paris 75008
France
+33 149527000
www.fourseasons.com/paris

Opening hours	Open 7 days
Reservation policy	Not accepted for drinks
Credit cards	Accepted
Price range	Expensive
Dress code	Smart casual
Style	Cocktail bar

"Top-quality service, class and elegance."—Nicolas Berger

LE BAR DU BRISTOL

112 Rue du Faubourg Saint-Honoré
Le Bristol Paris
8th Arrondissement
Paris 75008
France
+33 153434241
www.lebristolparis.com

Opening hours	Open 7 days
Reservation policy	Not accepted for drinks
Credit cards	Accepted
Price range	Expensive
Dress code	Smart casual
Style	Cocktail bar

"The cutest hotel bar in the world, in my opinion, where I've spent really good moments and where I always want to go back to is the bar of Hotel 'Le Bristol' in Paris. Maxime Hoerth (Meilleur Ouvrier de France in 2011) is one of the most stylish guys whom I have seen work . . . It is a very elegant place to forget reality for a while. And the Maxime's Old Fashioned is a masterpiece."—Fede Cuco

DIRTY DICK

10 Rue Frochot
9th Arrondissement
Paris 75009
France

Opening hours	Open 7 days
Reservation policy	Accepted
Credit cards	Accepted but not AMEX
Price range	Affordable
Dress code	Casual
Style	Tiki bar

"Great tiki bar in the middle of Paris with an excellent bar team."—Gabe Orta

L'ENTRÉE DES ARTISTES PIGALLE

30-32 Rue Victor Massé
9th Arrondissement
Paris 75009
France
+33 145231193
lentreedesartistespigalle.com

Opening hours	Closed Sunday and Monday
Reservation policy	Not accepted for drinks
Credit cards	Accepted
Price range	Affordable
Dress code	Casual
Style	Lounge

"The décor, the vibe, the spirits selection. Chilled out atmosphere. Perfect for a drink after a long night's work!"—Amanda Boucher

GLASS

7 Rue Frochot
9th Arrondissement
Paris 75009
France
+33 980729883
www.glassparis.com

Opening hours	Open 7 days
Reservation policy	Not accepted for drinks
Credit cards	Accepted
Price range	Affordable
Dress code	Smart casual
Style	Cocktail bar

"One of the most memorable spots in Paris. DJs ignite the crowd with a mix of music that matches the venue's anything-goes vibe. Whether having champagne, a slushy, cocktails on tap, or shot-and-beer pairing—everything is offered at this fresh and feisty place. It is crowded and sweaty but you won't care, you will definitely dance. It is rare to leave before sunrise!"—Lynnette Marrero

"An incredible late-night bar for dancing and partying. Its light-up floor is just fun and the staff is unpretentious."
—Ezra Star

"Glass is not just any bar, it's a proper textbook late-night hangout. It's a tiny little place, which disregarding the day of the week, absorbs you, eats you, and spits you out in the morning (typically very drunk). It's one of those bars where time becomes irrelevant and there's no night that finishes early. Typically you get out in the morning wondering: 'how the hell did this just happen?'"—Alex Kratena

HOTEL MAISON SOUQUET BAR

10 Rue de Bruxelles
Hôtel Maison Souquet
9th Arrondissement
Paris 75009
France
+33 148785555
www.maisonsouquet.com

Opening hours	Open 7 days
Reservation policy	Accepted
Credit cards	Accepted
Price range	Affordable
Dress code	Casual
Style	Cocktail bar

"The hotel is like a maison clos. The bar is cozy and the cocktails are delicious. The crowd tends to be beautiful dancers from the Moulin Rouge, which is less than 300 feet away, and American tourists."—Colin Field

LULU WHITE

12 Rue Frochot
9th Arrondissement
Paris 75009
France
+33 983589332
www.luluwhite.bar

Opening hours	Closed Sunday
Reservation policy	Accepted
Credit cards	Accepted
Price range	Affordable
Dress code	Smart casual
Style	Cocktail bar

"Paris Pigalle-style with international class. The bartenders could be in an indie rock band or painters from the nineteenth century; they are mysterious, filled with knowledge, and a lot of fun. So why am I jealous? The name (seriously, Lulu White—best name ever), the bartenders, their simple but innovative cocktail menu, the location."—Hannah Van Ongevalle

RESTAURANT & BAR À VINS

29 Rue Victor Massé
Grand Pigalle Hotel
9th Arrondissement
Paris 75009
France
+33 185731200
www.grandpigalle.com

Opening hours	Open 7 days
Reservation policy	Accepted
Credit cards	Accepted
Price range	Affordable
Dress code	Smart casual
Style	Restaurant and wine bar

"Nice hotel which also has a nice little bar. Staff is lovely and atmosphere is out of this world. They also serve a few handcrafted cocktails in the rooms."—Jesse Teerenmaa

COPPER BAY

5 Rue Bouchardon
10th Arrondissement
Paris 75010
France
www.copperbay.fr

Opening hours	Closed Sunday and Monday
Reservation policy	Not accepted for drinks
Credit cards	Accepted
Price range	Affordable
Dress code	Smart casual
Style	Cocktail bar

"Design is SPOT ON. An old workshop transformed into an absolutely beautiful space with an island bar. There is no speakeasy influence here and thank god for that! In addition to inexpensive, well-made cocktails you can order pitchers of Ricard and Mauresque. Really fun!"—Amanda Boucher

LE SYNDICAT

51 Rue du Faubourg Saint-Denis
10th Arrondissement
Paris 75010
France
www.syndicatcocktailclub.com

Opening hours	Open 7 days
Reservation policy	Accepted
Credit cards	Accepted but not AMEX
Price range	Affordable
Dress code	Smart casual
Style	Cocktail bar

"A menu that utilizes only French spirits and ingredients! Sullivan and his team always welcome you with a smile and a desire to have you discover what France has to offer outside of Chartreuse Verte and Picon. The actual space is quite eccentric though very well put together."—Amanda Boucher

LA BUVETTE

67 Rue Saint-Maur
11th Arrondissement
Paris 75011
France
+33 983569411

Opening hours	Closed Monday and Tuesday
Reservation policy	Not accepted for drinks
Credit cards	Accepted but not AMEX
Price range	Affordable
Dress code	Casual
Style	Wine bar

"There are too many places that you must visit, there are charming cafés, neighborhood bars, and sophisticated places, but what you must do is a wine bar. I love this place because of Camille Fourmont—not only is she young, talented, and a fantastic sommelier, but she understands what hospitality is. When you go to her wine store/wine bar you are at her house; her selection of little dishes of local French-Mediterranean products is delicious. She works with small producers and can tell you amazing stories about what you drink and eat."—Carina Soto Velasquez

MEDUSA

48 Rue Basfroi
11th Arrondissement
Paris 75011
France
+33 606983545
www.medusaparis.com

Opening hours	Open 7 days
Reservation policy	Accepted
Credit cards	Accepted but not AMEX
Price range	Affordable
Dress code	Casual
Style	Cocktail bar

"Great music, very laid back and not pretentious with very delicious highballs. That's their thing: very simple cocktails with three to four ingredients, very well executed."
—Carina Soto Velasquez

MOONSHINER

5 Rue Sedaine
11th Arrondissement
Paris 75011
France
+33 950731299

Opening hours	Open 7 days
Reservation policy	Not accepted for drinks
Credit cards	Accepted but not AMEX
Price range	Affordable
Dress code	Smart casual
Style	Speakeasy

"The personnel are sincere and take good care of the clients.
The bar is a speakeasy with a good space for smoking too.
Lovely crowd."—Colin Field

RED HOUSE

1 bis Rue de la Forge Royale
11th Arrondissement
Paris 75011
France
+33 674393220

Opening hours	Open 7 days
Reservation policy	Accepted
Credit cards	Accepted but not AMEX
Price range	Budget
Dress code	Casual
Style	Cocktail bar

"Favorite neighborhood bar by far. I'm lucky enough to live
in the same neighborhood as this quirky place. Cocktails are
spot on, beer flows on tap, and Negronis are €5. The vibe is
great as well, music, clientele (usually), and the staff. Oh, the
staff. What else can you ask for?!"—Amanda Boucher

"THE OLDEST SHERRY BAR IN THE WORLD. GO WHEN THEY OPEN AT 11 A.M., BECAUSE BY NOON IT'S FULL OF BUSINESS PEOPLE HAVING A SHERRY BEFORE LUNCH."
JUAN CORONADO P.150

"A SUPER COOL COCKTAIL LOUNGE, HIDDEN IN ONE OF THE QUIETEST NEIGHBORHOODS OF THE CITY, WITH FIFTY-FIVE DIFFERENT COCKTAILS TO CHOOSE FROM, COMPLEMENTED BY A RANGE OF SPIRITS, WINES, AND CHAMPAGNES."
ANDRE PEIXE P.156

SPAIN & PORTUGAL

"FIRST REAL SPEAKEASY BAR IN LISBON. GREAT BARTENDERS."
HONORIO OLIVEIRA P.156

"BE BLOWN AWAY BY THE VIEW FROM THIS TERRACE ON THE 9TH FLOOR OF HOTEL MUNDIAL."
ANDRE PEIXE P.156

"A CLASSIC, AUTHENTIC COCKTAIL BAR, STEEPED IN HISTORY"
DRE MASSO P.154

LE CABRERA

Calle Bárbara de Braganza 2
Madrid 28004
Spain
+34 913199457
www.lecabrera.com

Opening hours	Open 7 days
Reservation policy	Accepted
Credit cards	Accepted
Price range	Affordable
Dress code	Smart casual
Style	Cocktail bar and restaurant

Avant-garde tapas are served alongside classic and house cocktails in this trendy restaurant and bar.

MUSEO CHICOTE

Calle Gran Vía 12
Madrid 28013
Spain
+34 915326737
www.museo-chicote.com

Opening hours	Open 7 days
Reservation policy	Not accepted for drinks
Credit cards	Accepted
Price range	Affordable
Dress code	Smart casual
Style	Cocktail bar and restaurant

LA VENENCIA

Calle Echegaray 7
Madrid 28014
Spain
+34 914297313

Opening hours	Open 7 days
Reservation policy	Not accepted for drinks
Credit cards	Not accepted
Price range	Budget
Dress code	Casual
Style	Sherry bar

"This is the oldest sherry bar in the world. Go when they open at 11 a.m., because by noon it's full of business people having a sherry before lunch. Their staff is incredibly knowledgeable about sherry."—Juan Coronado

"THIS IS WHAT I CALL A SPEAKEASY!"

MIGUEL FERNANDEZ FERNANDEZ P.155

"CLASSIC COCKTAILS, INTIMATE ATMOSPHERE."

JOSE ANTONIO FEMENIA LUIS P.155

BARCELONA

"THE COCKTAIL BARTENDERS' MEETING PLACE IN BARCELONA."

JOSE ANTONIO FEMENIA LUIS P.155

"A VERY SPECIAL PLACE ... THE BEST NEGRONI IN TOWN."

MARC ALVAREZ SAFONT P.155

"A SMALL BAR WORTH DISCOVERING, RANGING FROM CLASSIC COCKTAILS TO THE MOST ADVANCED TECHNIQUES."

JOSE ANTONIO FEMENIA LUIS P.154

BARCELONA

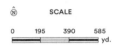

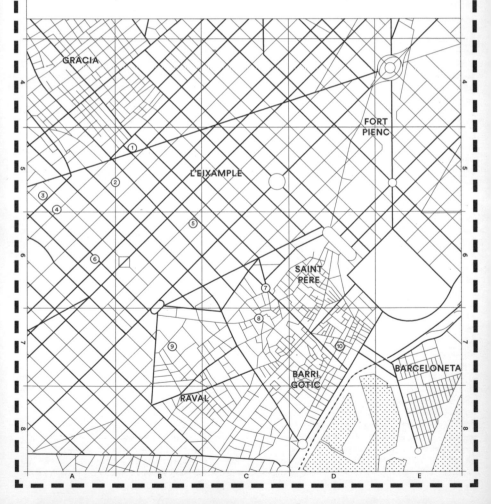

SCALE

0   195   390   585
                         yd.

1. MUTIS (P.155)
2. BOCA CHICA (P.154)
3. SLOW BARCELONA (P.155)
4. DRY MARTINI (P.154)

5. BANKER'S BAR (P.154)
6. TANDEM COCKTAIL BAR (P.155)
7. OHLA BOUTIQUE BAR (P.155)
8. BOADAS (P.154)

9. NEGRONI (P.155)
10. COLLAGE ART & COCKTAIL
    SOCIAL CLUB (P.154)

BANKER'S BAR

Passeig de Gràcia 38-40
Mandarin Oriental
Barcelona 08007
Spain
+34 931518782
www.mandarinoriental.com/barcelona

Opening hours..Open 7 days
Reservation policy..................................Not accepted for drinks
Credit cards...Accepted
Price range..Affordable
Dress code..Smart casual
Style...Cocktail bar

"Creative cocktails. Luxury service. Terrace for smokers."
—Jose Antonio Femenia Luis

BOADAS

Las Ramblas
Carrer dels Tallers 1
Barcelona 08001
Spain
+34 933189592
www.boadascocktails.com

Opening hours..Closed Sunday
Reservation policy..................................Not accepted for drinks
Credit cards...Accepted
Price range..Affordable
Dress code..Smart casual
Style...Cocktail bar

"Boadas is old-school. A classic, authentic cocktail bar,
steeped in history and paused in time. Situated on a quiet
side road steps away from the frenetic pace of Las Ramblas,
Boadas has been going strong for over seventy years.
The tobacco-stained walls are dotted with photographic
memorabilia archiving the history of the bar and its
bartenders. The original bartender and owner Miguel
Boadas learned his trade in La Floridita, one of the famous
cocktail bars in Havana, Cuba. He returned to Barcelona
and in 1933 opened his doors to the discerning drinker.
Among his clientele were Joan Miró, the surrealist painter
and sculptor, and George Orwell. In 1967 when Miguel
Boadas passed, his daughter (born in the year the bar
opened) succeeded her father in the theater of Boadas.
María Dolores can occasionally be found wowing customers
with her skillful throwing technique, passing liquid through
the air in an arc from one glass to another, without spilling
a drop (a technique I have often tried to replicate without
success). The experienced bar team will construct any
cocktail with the utmost precision. I would recommend
the *cóctel del día* (the cocktail of the day)."—Dre Masso

BOCA CHICA

Passatge de la Concepció 12
Barcelona 08003
Spain
+34 934675149
www.bocagrande.cat/en/boca-chica

Opening hours..Open 7 days
Reservation policy..................................Not accepted for drinks
Credit cards...Accepted
Price range..Affordable
Dress code..Smart casual
Style...Cocktail bar

"Nice bar, nice people . . . Ambience in a retro-style bar."
—Marc Alvarez Safont

COLLAGE ART & COCKTAIL SOCIAL CLUB

Carrer dels Consellers 4
Barcelona 08003
Spain
+34 931793785
www.mixologymobile.com/collage

Opening hours..Open 7 days
Reservation policy...Accepted
Credit cards..Accepted but not AMEX
Price range..Affordable
Dress code...Casual
Style...Cocktail bar

"A small bar worth discovering, ranging from classic cocktails
to the most advanced techniques, such as molecular
mixology."—Jose Antonio Femenia Luis

DRY MARTINI

Carrer Aribau 162
Barcelona 08036
Spain
+34 932175072
www.drymartiniorg.com

Opening hours..Open 7 days
Reservation policy..................................Not accepted for drinks
Credit cards...Accepted
Price range..Affordable
Dress code..Smart casual
Style...Cocktail bar

"A classic bar focusing on the Dry Martini cocktail. It
has beautiful decor, with a small dining room and a great
selection of spirits . . . The fact that when you order you
receive your own certificate with a number of the Martini
is awesome."—Kamil Foltan

Dry Martini is the brainchild of Javier de las Muelas, an icon in the European cocktail community. It is one of only five bars to have been named to the prestigious World's 50 Best Bars list seven years in a row (as of 2015) and is a staple of the Barcelona bar scene.

MUTIS

438 Avenida Diagonal
Barcelona 08037
Spain
+34 675749038

Opening hours	Open Wednesday–Saturday
Reservation policy	Accepted
Credit cards	Accepted
Price range	Affordable
Dress code	Smart casual
Style	Speakeasy

"Mutis means to mute. This speakeasy is so hidden inside a residential building that nobody knows it's there."
—Juan Coronado

"This is what I call a speakeasy! It's all quiet . . . until the door to the apartment opens. Inside it rages like during Prohibition. A small jazz band plays in the middle of the space, people are dancing everywhere . . . Champagne and fantastic cocktails in each hand. Bar chef Velasquez and his team celebrate the fun in life every night! Rarely have I seen a bar pulsate so and still exude elegance."
—Miguel Fernandez Fernandez

NEGRONI

Carrer de Joaquín Costa 46
Barcelona 08001
Spain
+34 619429271
www.negronicocktailbar.com

Opening hours	Open 7 days/closed Sunday and Monday in summer
Reservation policy	Not accepted for drinks
Credit cards	Accepted but not AMEX
Price range	Affordable
Dress code	Smart casual
Style	Cocktail bar

"Classic cocktails, intimate atmosphere."
—Jose Antonio Femenia Luis

OHLA BOUTIQUE BAR

Via Laietana 49
Ohla Barcelona
Barcelona 08003
Spain
+34 933415050
www.ohlahotel.com

Opening hours	Open 7 days
Reservation policy	Not accepted for drinks
Credit cards	Accepted
Price range	Expensive
Dress code	Smart casual
Style	Cocktail bar

Some of the best cocktails in Barcelona, served in a trendy, modern setting. Whimsical cocktails might include gold leaf, or be served in a seashell.

SLOW BARCELONA

Carrer de París 186
Barcelona 08036
Spain
+34 933681455
www.slowbarcelona.es

Opening hours	Closed Sunday
Reservation policy	Accepted
Credit cards	Accepted
Price range	Affordable
Dress code	Smart casual
Style	Cocktail bar

"The cocktail bartenders' meeting place in Barcelona."
—Jose Antonio Femenia Luis

TANDEM COCKTAIL BAR

Carrer d'Aribau 86
Barcelona 08036
Spain
+34 934514330
www.tandemcocktail.com

Opening hours	Open 7 days
Reservation policy	Not accepted for drinks
Credit cards	Accepted
Price range	Affordable
Dress code	Smart casual
Style	Cocktail bar

"A very special place, classic cocktails very well done . . . the best Negroni in town."—Marc Alvarez Safont

BAR FOXTROT
Travessa Santa Teresa 28
Lisbon 1200-405
Portugal
+351 213952697
www.barfoxtrot.pt

Opening hours	Open 7 days
Reservation policy	Accepted
Credit cards	Accepted
Price range	Affordable
Dress code	Casual
Style	Pub

"A bar where the great feature is its thirty-eight-year-old existence to serve several generations and with a spirit of the English pubs. One of the oldest bars in Lisbon."—Andre Peixe

CINCO LOUNGE
Rua Ruben A. Leitão 17-A
Lisbon 1200-392
Portugal
+351 213424033
www.cincolounge.com

Opening hours	Open 7 days
Reservation policy	Accepted
Credit cards	Not accepted
Price range	Affordable
Dress code	Smart casual
Style	Cocktail bar

"This is a super cool cocktail lounge, hidden in one of the quietest neighborhoods of the city, with fifty-five different cocktails to choose from, complemented by a range of spirits, wines and champagnes. There's also a selection of tapas if you're feeling hungry. But if you really want something different, ask the bartender for a signature cocktail, and there you will have the reality of how the secret is not only the spirits of the bottles, but in the hands and head of the bartender, here we discover new tastes and new directions."—Andre Peixe

PARK BAR
Calçada do Combro 58
Lisbon 1200-115
Portugal
+351 215914011

Opening hours	Closed Sunday
Reservation policy	Not accepted for drinks
Credit cards	Accepted but not AMEX
Price range	Affordable
Dress code	Smart casual
Style	Lounge

"Park is actually a rooftop parking lot turned into a hip, elevated garden terrace. Enjoy 180-degree views of Lisbon on a sunny afternoon or by starlight through the evening. Potted plants and wooden patio furniture provide a natural ambience and casual comfort . . . The cocktail menu is seasonal."—Andre Peixe

RED FROG
Rua do Salitre 5A
Lisbon 1250-196
Portugal
+351 215831120
www.redfrog.pt

Opening hours	Open 7 days
Reservation policy	Not accepted for drinks
Credit cards	Accepted but not AMEX
Price range	Affordable
Dress code	Smart casual
Style	Speakeasy

"First real speakeasy bar in Lisbon. Great bartenders."
—Honorio Oliveira

ROOFTOP BAR
Praça Martim Moniz 2
Hotel Mundial
Lisbon 1100-341
Portugal
+351 218842000
www.hotel-mundial.pt

Opening hours	Open 7 days/closed Monday in winter
Reservation policy	Not accepted for drinks
Credit cards	Accepted
Price range	Affordable
Dress code	Smart casual
Style	Lounge

"Be blown away by the view from this terrace on the 9th floor of Hotel Mundial. The castle is so close you can almost touch

it, and you can see almost all of downtown and Chiado.
It opens for pre-dinner drinks but also invites you to end the
night with a cocktail to the sound of jazz."—Andre Peixe

TABIK RESTAURANT
Avenida da Liberdade 29A
Lisbon 1250-139
Portugal
+351 213470549
www.tabikrestaurant.com

Opening hours..Closed Sunday
Reservation policy..Accepted
Credit cards...Accepted
Price range...Affordable
Dress code...Smart casual
Style...Restaurant and bar

"Great location, great bartenders, and great drinks."
—Honorio Oliveira

PUB BONAPARTE
Avenida do Brasil 130
Porto 4150-151
Portugal
+351 226188404
www.bonaparteporto.net

Opening hours..Open 7 days
Reservation policy.................................Not accepted for drinks
Credit cards...Accepted
Price range...Affordable
Dress code...Casual
Style..Pub

"It's a place where people from all over the city go."
—Honorio Oliveira

PORTA 22 CLUB
Avenida 25 de Abril 22
Vila Nova de Famalicão 4760-101
Portugal
+351 916203844

Opening hours..Closed Sunday
Reservation policy..Accepted
Credit cards...Accepted but not AMEX
Price range...Affordable
Dress code...Smart casual
Style..Lounge

An interior design concept space, cafe, and bar.

"**PERFECT DRINKS AND ATMOSPHERE. ALWAYS WORTH A VISIT.**"

BETTINA KUPSA P.160

"**THEIR SPIRIT LIST CONTAINS FIFTY-FIVE PAGES OF AWESOMENESS.**"

JESSE TEERENMAA P.160

GERMANY & SWITZERLAND

"IT IS THE PERFECT MIX OF A DIVE BAR WITH GOOD DRINKS THAT MAKE IT SPECIAL. ALWAYS CROWDED, ALWAYS FRIENDLY SERVICE." MARIO KAPPES P.162

"**THE MENU IS A TRIP AROUND THE WORLD WITH SMALL STOPS IN EACH CITY.**"

ANDRE PINTZ P.163

"**IT'S THE WARMEST, FRIENDLIEST, AND AT THE SAME TIME, MOST LUXURIOUS COCKTAIL BAR IN EUROPE.**"

JEFFREY MORGENTHALER P.163

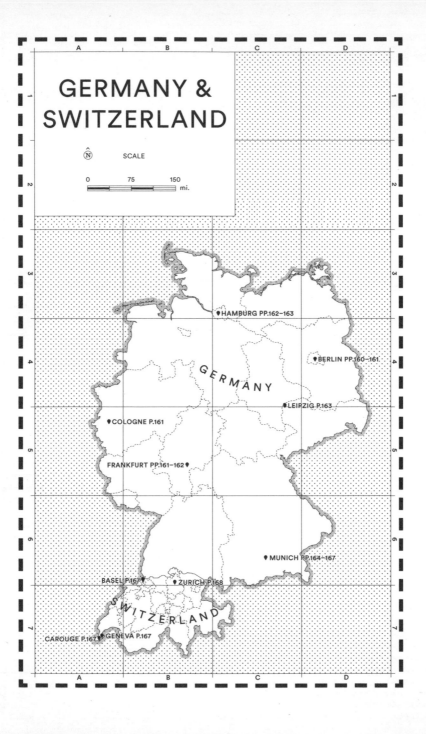

GERMANY & SWITZERLAND

N   SCALE

0   75   150
mi.

HAMBURG PP.162–163

BERLIN PP.160–161

G E R M A N Y

LEIPZIG P.163

COLOGNE P.161

FRANKFURT PP.161–162

MUNICH PP.164–167

BASEL P.167   ZURICH P.168

S W I T Z E R L A N D

CAROUGE P.167   GENEVA P.167

BADFISH
Stargarderstraße 14
Berlin 10437
Germany
+49 3054714788
www.badfishbarberlin.com

Opening hours	Open 7 days
Reservation policy	Accepted
Credit cards	Not accepted
Price range	Budget
Dress code	Casual
Style	Dive bar

"Good bourbon, few good beers, and open till very late."
—Oliver Ebert

BAR IMMERTREU
Christburger Strasse 6
Berlin 10405
Germany
+49 15785921221
www.bar-immertreu.de

Opening hours	Closed Sunday
Reservation policy	Accepted
Credit cards	Not accepted
Price range	Affordable
Dress code	Smart casual
Style	Cocktail bar

"Antique spirits used for perfect drinks."—Oliver Ebert

BUCK AND BRECK
Brunnenstraße 177
Berlin 10119
Germany
+49 17632315507
www.buckandbreck.com

Opening hours	Open 7 days
Reservation policy	Not accepted for drinks
Credit cards	Not accepted
Price range	Affordable
Dress code	Smart casual
Style	Cocktail bar

"Gonçalo de Sousa Monteiro is one of the most special bartenders I have ever meet. He built a very special and intimate place in the heart of Berlin. Just fourteen seats around the bar always gets people connected in a very special way. Perfect drinks and atmosphere. Always worth a visit."—Bettina Kupsa

"Incredible concept and execution in great style."
—Tomek Roehr

LEBENSSTERN
Kurfürstenstraße 58
Café Einstein
Berlin 10785
Germany
+49 3026391922
www.lebensstern-berlin.de

Opening hours	Open 7 days
Reservation policy	Accepted
Credit cards	Accepted
Price range	Affordable
Dress code	Smart casual
Style	Cocktail bar

"Their spirit list contains fifty-five pages of awesomeness. Head bartender Thomas Pflanz knows hostmanship. While sipping some of the best whiskeys I've had and puffing smoke into the air I could imagine myself in the 1930s."
—Jesse Teerenmaa

LOST IN GRUB STREET
Jägerstraße 34
Berlin 10117
Germany
+49 3020603780
www.lostingrubstreet.de

Opening hours	Closed Sunday and Monday
Reservation policy	Accepted
Credit cards	Accepted but not AMEX
Price range	Affordable
Dress code	Smart casual
Style	Cocktail bar

"Big bowls of punch if you are a bigger group, cocktails from true local boutique distillers if you are a cocktail nerd."
—Oliver Ebert

RUM TRADER

Fasanenstraße 40
Berlin 10719
Germany
+49 308811428

Opening hours	Closed Sunday
Reservation policy	Accepted
Credit cards	Not accepted
Price range	Affordable
Dress code	Smart casual
Style	Cocktail bar

"Its absolute authenticity, the all-encompassing hospitality of its owner-bartender Mr. Gregor Scholl, and the charm and warm welcome extended to all who come through its doors by regulars and staff alike."—Philip Duff

SPIRITS BAR

Engelbertstraße 63
Cologne 50674
Germany
+49 22120538044
www.spiritsbar.de

Opening hours	Closed Sunday
Reservation policy	Accepted
Credit cards	Accepted but not AMEX
Price range	Affordable
Dress code	Smart casual
Style	Cocktail bar

"The Spirits Bar is a unique place to enjoy the beats and breaks with a good connection to balanced drinks. When you like to feel the blues, jazz, and hip-hop, and see what the bartender is making, you are in the right place."
—Marian Krausz

JIMMY´S BAR

Friedrich-Ebert-Anlage 40
Grandhotel Hessischer Hof
Frankfurt 60325
Germany
+49 69 75400
www.jimmys-frankfurt.de

Opening hours	Open 7 days
Reservation policy	Accepted
Credit cards	Accepted
Price range	Affordable
Dress code	Smart casual
Style	Lounge

"Mr. Amador has been the host of this classic bar for forty years. Here, time seems to stand still . . . thankfully! Hardly anything has changed in the sixty years of the bar. It feels like an English Gentlemen's Room with live music, cigars, and a nice whiskey. The stories and the hospitality of the grand monsieur top it off!"—Miguel Fernandez Fernandez

THE PARLOUR

Zwingergasse 6
Frankfurt 60313
Germany
+49 6990025808
www.theparlour.de

Opening hours	Closed Sunday
Reservation policy	Accepted
Credit cards	Accepted but not AMEX
Price range	Affordable
Dress code	Smart casual
Style	Cocktail bar

"At a certain time (2 a.m.) one thing can help you to detect whether a bar still makes sense: many restaurateurs! The bar where the bartenders work is little more than a large table. And around it sit the guests, in front of the bartender or right next to him . . . no secrets! Beer or shots, or at least an experimental cocktail, a flavor roller coaster! With Mr. Yared Hagos, owner of the bar, and a charming crew you can gladly let the hours pass. And the audience: completely mixed! The best evenings are not planned. For me, a beer and a mezcal and wait and see what happens. Love it!"—Miguel Fernandez Fernandez

ROOMERS BAR

Gutleutstraße 85
Roomers Design Hotel Frankfurt
Frankfurt 60329
Germany
+49 69271342815
www.roomers-frankfurt.com

Opening hours	Open 7 days
Reservation policy	Accepted
Credit cards	Accepted
Price range	Affordable
Dress code	Smart casual
Style	Cocktail bar

"Frankfurt was known for its old-school piano and Cognac hotel bars, but when Roomers opened they said they wanted to have a new design. The bartenders all wear suits, there's a hip-hop DJ playing in the corner. Hip-hop music doesn't mean the bartender can't make a proper Vieux Carre or Sazerac, but he can also party with you. They are one of the pioneers of the German market."
—Miguel Fernandez Fernandez

SEVEN SWANS & THE TINY CUP

Mainkai 4
Frankfurt 60311
Germany
+49 1788539718
www.thotinyoup.do

Opening hours	Closed Sunday and Monday
Reservation policy	Not accepted for drinks
Credit cards	Accepted but not AMEX
Price range	Affordable
Dress code	Smart casual
Style	Cocktail bar

"The head bartender and owner, Mr. Sven Riebel, created something really special! In the same house as the fine dining restaurant Seven Swans you can find this Tiny Cup . . . with minimalist design and charming details (the surface is covered with warm leather, tubs set into the counter, subdued lighting) and classic cocktails. Groups of up to twenty people can be found in the basement of the Gin & Tonic Room . . . Mr. Riebel is also one of the most charming hosts you could meet at a bar and accompanies guests of all kinds with a smile through the evening."
—Miguel Fernandez Fernandez

BAR DACAIO

Barcastraße 3
The George Hotel
Hamburg 22087
Germany
+49 402800301810
www.thegeorge-hotel.de

Opening hours	Open 7 days
Reservation policy	Accepted
Credit cards	Accepted
Price range	Affordable
Dress code	Smart casual
Style	Cocktail bar

"They do a very special 'Martini Cocktail Service.' The bar manager, Giovanni, always gives you a very warm welcome. In summer time they have the most beautiful rooftop bar in the city. Have a Sundowner there and enjoy the view."
—Bettina Kupsa

BOILERMAN BAR

Eppendorfer Weg 211
Hamburg 20253
Germany
www.boilerman.de

Opening hours	Open 7 days
Reservation policy	Not accepted for drinks
Credit cards	Not accepted
Price range	Affordable
Dress code	Smart casual
Style	Whiskey bar

"It is the perfect mix of a dive bar with good drinks that make it special. Always crowded, always friendly service."
—Mario Kappes

3FREUNDE COCKTAILBAR

Clemens-Schultz-Straße 66
Hamburg 20359
Germany
+49 4053262639
www.3freunde-hamburg.de

Opening hours...Open 7 days
Reservation policy...Accepted
Credit cards..Not accepted
Price range...Affordable
Dress code...Casual
Style...Cocktail bar

"Easygoing lounge bar in the middle of St. Pauli. Monthly changing cocktail menu and really good value for price!"
—Bettina Kupsa

JAHRESZEITEN BAR

Neuer Jungfernstieg 9 - 14
Fairmont Hotel Vier Jahreszeiten
Hamburg 20354
Germany
+49 4034943360
www.hvj.de

Opening hours...Open 7 days
Reservation policy.................Not accepted for drinks
Credit cards...Accepted
Price range...Affordable
Dress code..Smart casual
Style...Cocktail bar

"Small, perfect service, intimate atmosphere, smoking is allowed—classic, classic, classic."—Mario Kappes

LE LION BAR DE PARIS

Rathausstraße 3
Hamburg 20095
Germany
+49 40334753780
www.lelion.net

Opening hours...Open 7 days
Reservation policy...Accepted
Credit cards...Accepted
Price range...Affordable
Dress code..Smart casual
Style...Cocktail bar

"It's the warmest, friendliest, and at the same time, most luxurious cocktail bar in Europe, I think."
—Jeffrey Morgenthaler

"Very cozy classic cocktail bar that always makes you forget time. Always gives me the feeling of diving into the past. Go there and have a Gin Basil Smash."—Bettina Kupsa

"Very good atmosphere, friendly bartenders, and outstanding drinks."—Hidetsugu Ueno

Led by the highly regarded Jörg Meyer, Le Lion Bar de Paris is one of only five bars to have been included in the World's 50 Best Bars list every year since its inception (2009-2015).

IMPERII

Brühl 72
Leipzig 04109
Germany
+49 34196283789
www.imperii.de

Opening hours...Closed Sunday
Reservation policy...Accepted
Credit cards.............................Accepted but not AMEX
Price range...Affordable
Dress code..Smart casual
Style...Cocktail bar

"The menu is a trip around the world with small stops in each city."—Andre Pintz

MADRIGAL

Käthe-Kollwitz-Straße 10
Leipzig 04109
Germany
+49 15786255141
www.bar-madrigal.de

Opening hours.................................Closed Sunday and Monday
Reservation policy...Accepted
Credit cards.............................Accepted but not AMEX
Price range...Affordable
Dress code..Smart casual
Style...Cocktail bar

"ONE OF THE MOST IMPORTANT HISTORIC HOTELS IN MUNICH. THE BAR IS IN THE MIDDLE OF THE LOBBY, LOCATED UNDER HIGH CEILINGS WITH A STUNNING AMBIENCE."

MAURO MAHJOUB P.166

"YOU NEVER HEAR ANYTHING ABOUT IT IN THE PRESS; IT'S A LOCAL SECRET."

MAURO MAHJOUB P.166

MUNICH

"THE FIRST AMERICAN BAR IN GERMANY, IT OPENED FORTY YEARS AGO, AND IS OPEN UNTIL 3 A.M."

MAURO MAHJOUB P.166

"AN ELEGANT ENVIRONMENT, THIS BAR CATERS TO THE WHO'S WHO IN MUNICH."

KYLE FORD P.167

"ONE OF THE IMPORTANT BARS THAT ALLOWED US TO DRINK THE WAY WE DO TODAY."

JACOB BRIARS P.167

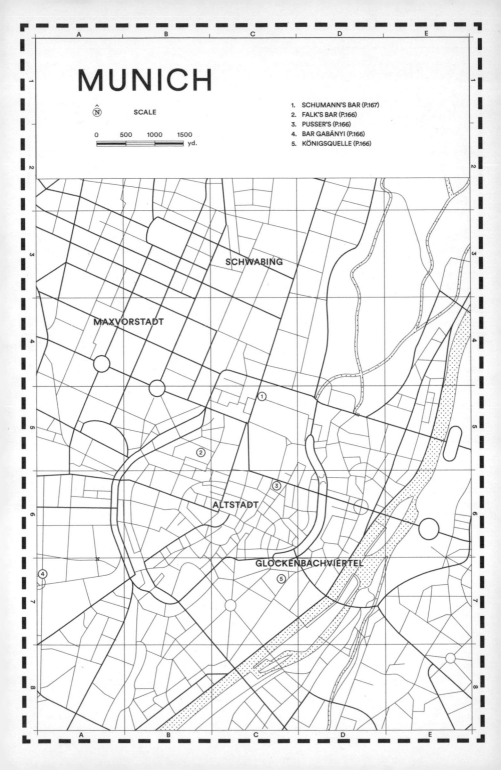

BAR GABÁNYI

Beethovenplatz 2
Munich 80336
Germany
+49 8951701805
www.bar-gabanyi.de

Opening hours	Closed Monday and Tuesday
Reservation policy	Accepted
Credit cards	Not accepted
Price range	Affordable
Dress code	Smart casual
Style	Cocktail bar

"It's an American bar, small, with a nice atmosphere, and they serve cocktails and food, with a whiskey specialty. It's not a speakeasy but it has an underground 'speakeasy-like' vibe. They are open til 5 a.m. on weekends."—Mauro Mahjoub

FALK'S BAR

Promenadeplatz 2-6
Hotel Bayerischer Hof
Munich 80333
Germany
+49 892120956
www.bayerischerhof.de

Opening hours	Open 7 days
Reservation policy	Accepted
Credit cards	Accepted
Price range	Affordable
Dress code	Smart casual
Style	Cocktail bar

"This is one of the most important historic hotels in Munich. The bar is in the middle of the lobby, located under high ceilings with a stunning ambience. Also, downstairs there is a Trader Vic's."—Mauro Mahjoub

KÖNIGSQUELLE

Baaderplatz 2
Munich 80469
Germany
+49 89220071
www.koenigsquelle.com

Opening hours	Open 7 days
Reservation policy	Not accepted for drinks
Credit cards	Accepted but not AMEX
Price range	Affordable
Dress code	Casual
Style	Restaurant and bar

"A classic bar that is not too large—they have a small kitchen and good spirits selection. You never hear anything about it in the press; it's a local secret."—Mauro Mahjoub

PUSSER'S

Falkenturmstraße 9
Munich 80331
Germany
+49 89220500
www.pussersbar.de

Opening hours	Open 7 days
Reservation policy	Accepted
Credit cards	Accepted
Price range	Affordable
Dress code	Smart casual
Style	Cocktail bar

"The first American bar in Germany, it opened forty years ago, and is open until 3 a.m. The specialty cocktail is the Painkiller with Pusser's Rum, and their pastrami sandwich is very nice. There is a live piano player two to three times a week. It is a very classic bar."—Mauro Mahjoub

SCHUMANN'S BAR

Odeonsplatz 6-7
Munich 80539
Germany
+49 89229060
www.schumanns.de

Opening hours..Open 7 days
Reservation policy...Accepted
Credit cards...Accepted but not AMEX
Price range...Affordable
Dress code..Smart casual
Style...Cocktail bar

"Swank, hospitality, and Charles Schumann. The cocktails? Decisively classic and served in custom glassware. An elegant environment, this bar caters to the who's who in Munich. After a few rounds, we left with a signed copy of his cocktail book, enamored with the German style of bartending, and with much love for this Münchner gem." —Kyle Ford

"Charles Schumann is one of the fathers of our profession. He hires really good chefs to work with him so his food is amazing. When you drink at Schumann's you are surrounded by the 1 per cent of Germans; it's very classy. Every bartender is a server and vice versa, so that the person who takes your order then goes behind the bar to make your drinks. It's really an experience. They only have male staff and they all wear bistro aprons, jackets, and ties. When I am in Munich, I am there every night."—Dushan Zaric

"One of the important bars that allowed us to drink the way we do today. In the 1980s, which was not a high point for cocktail culture in the United Kingdom or the United States, bars like Schumann's kept the craft alive. But it's no museum piece; it is just as good today as it ever has been, and has influenced bars all over Europe and the world."—Jacob Briars

BAR LES TROIS ROIS

Blumenrain 8
Grand Hotel Les Trois Rois
Basel 4001
Switzerland
+41 612605050
www.lestroisrois.com

Opening hours..Open 7 days
Reservation policy...............................Not accepted for drinks
Credit cards..Accepted
Price range..Expensive
Dress code..Smart casual
Style...Cocktail bar

Located in the 5-star luxury Grand Hotel Les Trois Rois on the banks of the Rhine, this posh, classic cocktail bar is much celebrated and is the recipient of many awards including *Mixology* magazine's Swiss Bar Of The Year in 2015.

CHAT NOIR

Rue Vautier 13
Carouge 1227
Switzerland
+41 223071040
www.chatnoir.ch

Opening hours.................................Closed Sunday and Monday
Reservation policy.................................Not accepted for drinks
Credit cards..Accepted
Price range...Affordable
Dress code..Smart casual
Style...Nightclub

"A high-quality bar in a legendary venue in Geneva. Keziah Jones played there years ago, but now he comes as a customer almost every time he's in town. Something new happens every night. It's just impossible to get bored there." —Nicolas Berger

L'APOTHICAIRE COCKTAIL CLUB

Boulevard Georges-Favon 16
Geneva 1204
Switzerland
+41 223281510

Opening hours.................................Closed Sunday and Monday
Reservation policy...Accepted
Credit cards..Accepted
Price range...Affordable
Dress code..Smart casual
Style...Cocktail bar

"I have great memories of some guest bartending there." —Nicolas Berger

GRÄBLI BAR

Niederdorfstrasse 66
Zürich 8001
Switzerland
+41 442519595
www.graebli-bar.ch

Opening hours	Open 7 days
Reservation policy	Not accepted for drinks
Credit cards	Accepted
Price range	Affordable
Dress code	Casual
Style	Cafe and bar

"This bar is fun. Late at night especially. Shots, beers, shots. Bar snacks? Boiled eggs. Flipper, jukebox, old and rare figures of Johnny Walker, Black and White Whiskey, and others. It is a melting pot of a city of artists, bankers, extremely rich, and extremely poor. You'll find all of them there. It is closed for one hour a day, from 5 to 6 a.m."—Laura Schacht

HOTEL RIVINGTON & SONS

Hardstrasse 201
Prime Tower
Zürich 8005
Switzerland
+41 433669082
www.hotelrivingtonandsons.ch

Opening hours	Closed Sunday
Reservation policy	Accepted
Credit cards	Accepted
Price range	Affordable
Dress code	Smart casual
Style	Restaurant and bar

"Beautiful location, great drinks and bartenders."
—Markus Blattner

KRONENHALLE

Rämistrasse 4
Zürich 8001
Switzerland
+41 442629911
www.kronenhalle.ch

Opening hours	Open 7 days
Reservation policy	Accepted
Credit cards	Accepted
Price range	Expensive
Dress code	Smart casual
Style	Cocktail bar

TALES BAR

Selnaustrasse 29
Zürich 8001
Switzerland
+41 445423802
www.tales-bar.ch

Opening hours	Closed Sunday
Reservation policy	Accepted
Credit cards	Accepted
Price range	Affordable
Dress code	Smart casual
Style	Cocktail bar

"Open until early morning, with a great spirit, cocktail, wine, and champagne selection, the Tales Bar is the place to have your 'bartender after-work drink' when finishing your shift. The bar food is homemade, stretching from fresh pasta to pulled pork sandwiches, currywurst, and cold cuts and cheese. The hospitality is very welcoming and the seating is very comfortable."—Dirk Hany

WIDDER BAR

Rennweg 7
Widder Hotel
Zürich 8001
Switzerland
+41 442242526
www.widderhotel.com

Opening hours	Open 7 days
Reservation policy	Not accepted for drinks
Credit cards	Accepted
Price range	Expensive
Dress code	Smart casual
Style	Cocktail bar

"A traditional hotel bar with live piano every day. Great hosts and bartenders! Outstanding spirit collection . . . One of the most beautiful locations I know!"—Markus Blattner

> "ONE OF THE OLDEST COCKTAIL BARS IN VIENNA WITH THE LARGEST VARIETY OF SPIRITS."
>
> KAN ZUO P.173

> "NOT EASY TO FIND, THIS BAR IS EXACTLY WHAT YOU EXPECT FROM A SPEAKEASY BAR."
>
> DIRK HANY P.174

POLAND, THE CZECH REPUBLIC, AUSTRIA, & HUNGARY

> "GREAT COCKTAILS, AWESOME SERVICE. WHEN YOU COME IN, YOU FEEL YOU'RE IN THE 1960s, THE ONLY THING MISSING IS JAMES BOND BY YOUR SIDE."
>
> ALGIRDAS MULEVICIUS P.172

> "A SPIRITS SELECTION THAT IS NEXT TO NONE."
>
> TOMEK ROEHR P.172

> "GREAT TEAM, A VERY UNIQUE AND SATISFYING MENU, AND BEAUTIFUL SETTINGS."
>
> JAMIE JONES P.174

COCKTAIL BAR MAX

Ulica Krucza 16/22
Warsaw 00-525
Poland
+48 691710000
www.barmax.pl

Opening hours	Open 7 days
Reservation policy	Accepted
Credit cards	Accepted
Price range	Affordable
Dress code	Smart casual
Style	Cocktail bar

"A spirits selection that is next to none."—Tomek Roehr

KITA KOGUTA

Ulica Krucza 6/14
Warsaw 00-950
Poland
+48 512307284
www.kitakoguta.pl

Opening hours	Closed Monday
Reservation policy	Accepted
Credit cards	Accepted but not AMEX
Price range	Affordable
Dress code	Smart casual
Style	Cocktail bar

"World class drinks in a clubby setting. All-round good-time bar."— Tomek Roehr

BLACK ANGEL'S BAR

Staroměstské náměstí 29
Hotel U Prince
Prague 110 00
The Czech Republic
+420 737261842
www.blackangelsbar.cz

Opening hours	Open 7 days
Reservation policy	Accepted
Credit cards	Accepted
Price range	Affordable
Dress code	Smart casual
Style	Cocktail bar

"It has a fantastic ambiance, nooks to hide in, two beautiful bars, and the service is wonderful. I spent a couple of memorable nights there hanging out with the staff and closing down the bar."—Franky Marshall

BUGSY'S BAR

Pařížská 10
Prague 110 00
The Czech Republic
+420 224810287
www.bugsysbar.com

Opening hours	Open 7 days
Reservation policy	Accepted
Credit cards	Accepted
Price range	Affordable
Dress code	Smart casual
Style	Cocktail bar

"It's the very first cocktail bar that opened after the Velvet Revolution. It's been open for twenty years now and it's still one of the top three bars in Prague."—Jiri George Nemec

"Great cocktails, awesome service. When you come in, you feel you're in the 1960s, the only thing missing is James Bond by your side. Just a great bar to be at."—Algirdas Mulevicius

CASH ONLY BAR

Liliová 218/3
Prague 110 00
The Czech Republic
+420 778087117
www.cashonlybar.cz

Opening hours	Open 7 days
Reservation policy	Not accepted for drinks
Credit cards	Not accepted
Price range	Affordable
Dress code	casual
Style	Cocktail bar

"It's the only bar where I can walk in in my shorts, open my lap top, have an awesome Margarita or espresso, and listen to great music all at once. Staff is young and great and interior unpretentious."— Jiri George Nemec

"More casual atmosphere and good music."—Ales Puta

HEMINGWAY BAR

Karolíny Světlé 26
Prague 110 00
The Czech Republic
+420 773974764
www.hemingwaybar.cz/bar-prague

Opening hours..Open 7 days
Reservation policy...Accepted
Credit cards...............................Accepted but not AMEX
Price range...Affordable
Dress code..Smart casual
Style..Cocktail bar

"Concept of the bar is based on Ernest Hemingway and his flamboyant lifestyle. Decor of the bar is beautiful, the team is very knowledgeable. Selection of spirits and cocktails are very unique. The bar by itself is small and very friendly in the middle of the romantic center of Prague."—Kamil Foltan

BARFLY'S

Esterhazygasse 33
Hotel Fürst Metternich
Vienna 1060
Austria
+43 15860825
www.castillo.at

Opening hours..Open 7 days
Reservation policy...Accepted
Credit cards...Accepted
Price range...Affordable
Dress code..Smart casual
Style..Cocktail bar

"One of the oldest cocktail bars in Vienna with the largest variety of spirits."—Kan Zuo

HALBESTADT

Stadtbahnbogen 155
Währinger Gürtel 144
Vienna 1090
Austria
+43 13194735
www.halbestadt.at

Opening hours...............................Closed Sunday and Monday
Reservation policy...Accepted
Credit cards...Accepted
Price range...Affordable
Dress code..Smart casual
Style..Cocktail bar

"Great hospitality, wide range of spirits."—Kan Zuo

NIGHTFLY'S CLUB AMERICAN BAR

Dorotheergasse 14
Vienna 1010
Austria
+43 15129979
www.nightflys.at

Opening hours..Closed Sunday
Reservation policy...Accepted
Credit cards...Accepted
Price range...Affordable
Dress code..Smart casual
Style..Cocktail bar

"Great hospitality, nice, down-to-earth atmosphere."
—Kan Zuo

TÜR 7

Buchfeldgasse 7
Vienna 1080
Austria
+43 6645463717
www.tuer7.at

Opening hours	Closed Sunday
Reservation policy	Required
Credit cards	Accepted but not AMEX
Price range	Affordable
Dress code	Smart casual
Style	Speakeasy

"What a surprise! Not easy to find, this bar is exactly what you expect from a speakeasy bar. The concept of feeling like being in your own home is a great success. Slippers await you at the entrance, where you will be personally let in by your bartender. The bar counter would be the kitchen where you enjoy cocktails by recommendations. Living room, smokers' lounge, and bathroom are nicely furnished. The very comfortable seating makes you want to stay all night."—Dirk Hany

THE BAR AT BARAKA

Dorottya Utca 6
Budapest 1051
Hungary
+36 12000817
www.barakarestaurant.hu

Opening hours	Closed Sunday
Reservation policy	Not accepted for drinks
Credit cards	Accepted
Price range	Affordable
Dress code	Smart casual
Style	Restaurant and bar

"It has a nice range of different cocktails in a nice chilled-out environment."—Zoltan Nagy

BOUTIQ BAR

Paulay Ede Utca 5
Budapest 1061
Hungary
+36 305542323
www.boutiqbar.hu

Opening hours	Closed Sunday and Monday
Reservation policy	Accepted
Credit cards	Not accepted
Price range	Affordable
Dress code	Casual
Style	Cocktail bar

"I definitely recommend Boutiq Bar, it reminds me very much of Happiness Forgets in London."—Jamie Jones

KOLLÁZS

Széchenyi István tér 5-6
Four Seasons Hotel Gresham Palace
Budapest 1051
Hungary
+36 12685184
www.kollazs.hu

Opening hours	Open 7 days
Reservation policy	Accepted
Credit cards	Accepted
Price range	Affordable
Dress code	Smart casual
Style	Brasserie and bar

"Great team, a very unique and satisfying menu, and beautiful settings."—Jamie Jones

"THE ONLY PLACE IN TALLINN THAT HAS HAD THE SAME INTERIOR FROM ITS OPENING DAY IN THE 1970s."

ANGELIKA LARKINA P.178

"NICE MUSIC, BEAUTIFUL PEOPLE, IT'S SMALL, IT'S COZY, AND IT HAS SUPER TASTY COCKTAILS FROM ONE OF THE MOST CREATIVE BARMEN FROM LITHUANIA."

REMI BEINORAS P.179

BALTIC STATES, BELARUS, ROMANIA, GREECE, & CYPRUS

"THE IDEAL BAR FOR THOSE WHO APPRECIATE CLASSIC DRINKS, INTERIOR, DISCREET SERVICE, QUIET JAZZ." LIZAVETA MOLYAVKA P.180

"EVERYTHING COMES TOGETHER IN THAT PLACE. GREAT PLACE TO PRE-PARTY OR EVEN STAY AND PARTY ALL NIGHT LONG."

ALGIRDAS MULEVICIUS P.179

"THE COZY BAR IN THE CENTER OF MINSK, WITH THE PERFECT COMBINATION OF FRIENDLY ATMOSPHERE, INTERESTING DRINKS, AND OPEN-MINDED BARTENDERS."

LIZAVETA MOLYAVKA P.179

BALTIC STATES, BELARUS, ROMANIA, GREECE, & CYPRUS

$\hat{N}$ SCALE

0   140   280   mi.

ESTONIA

TALLINN P.178

RIGA PP.178–179

LATVIA

KLAIPEDA P.179

LITHUANIA

VILNIUS P.179

MINSK PP.179–180

BELARUS

BUCHAREST P.180

ROMANIA

CLUJ-NAPOCA PP.180–181

GREECE

KHALANDRI P.182
ATHENS PP.181–182

CYPRUS

NICOSIA P.182

BUTTERFLY LOUNGE
Vana-Viru 13
Aia 4
Tallinn 10148
Estonia
+372 56903703
www.kokteilibaar.ee

Opening hours	Closed Sunday
Reservation policy	Accepted
Credit cards	Accepted
Price range	Affordable
Dress code	Smart casual
Style	Cocktail bar

"There are good cocktails, wonderful music, and great staff."
—Angelika Larkina

HORISONT BAR
Tornimäe 3
Swissotel Tallinn
Tallinn 10145
Estonia
+372 6243000
www.swissotel.com/hotels/tallinn

Opening hours	Open 7 days
Reservation policy	Accepted
Credit cards	Accepted
Price range	Affordable
Dress code	Smart casual
Style	Cocktail bar

"It is in the Swissotel top floor (30) and has a really beautiful view over Tallinn's Old Town and the Baltic Sea."
—Angelika Larkina

VALLI BAAR
Müürivahe 14
Tallinn 10146
Estonia
+372 6418379

Opening hours	Open 7 days
Reservation policy	Not accepted for drinks
Credit cards	Accepted but not AMEX
Price range	Budget
Dress code	Casual
Style	Dive bar

"It is the only place in Tallinn that has had the same interior from its opening day in the 1970s. The bartender and the clientele seem like they're from the past. Real Soviet Era bar! Locals go there to try their special shot MilliMallikas (Jellyfish in English)."—Angelika Larkina

BALZAMBĀRS
Torņa iela 4-1B
Riga 1050
Latvia
+371 67214494
www.balzambars.lv

Opening hours	Open 7 days
Reservation policy	Accepted
Credit cards	Accepted
Price range	Budgot
Dress code	Smart casual
Style	Restaurant and cocktail bar

"Cocktails, food, and balsam cocktails."—Inguss Reizenbergs

B BAR
Doma Laukums 2
Riga 1050
Latvia
+371 67228842
www.bbars.lv

Opening hours	Open 7 days
Reservation policy	Accepted
Credit cards	Accepted
Price range	Affordable
Dress code	Smart casual
Style	Restaurant and cocktail bar

THE LEFT DOOR BAR
Antonijas iela 12
Riga 1010
Latvia
+371 26300368

Opening hours	Open 7 days
Reservation policy	Accepted
Credit cards	Accepted
Price range	Affordable
Dress code	Smart casual
Style	Cocktail bar

"Great cocktails, nice atmosphere. Blue Blazer!"—Remi Beinoras

HARD SHAKE
Žvejų gatvė 10
Klaipeda 91240
Lithuania
+370 60861007

Opening hours	Closed Monday and Tuesday
Reservation policy	Accepted
Credit cards	Accepted but not AMEX
Price range	Affordable
Dress code	Smart casual
Style	Cocktail bar

"One of few cocktail bars in Lithuania, but this one is special because it's in the city by the seaside, and there are no bars like this. The music, the cocktails, the vibe, everything comes together in that place. Great place to pre-party or even stay and party all night long."—Algirdas Mulevicius

DREAM BAR
Gaono gatvė 7
Stikliai Hotel
Vilnius 01131
Lithuania
+370 52649595
www.stikliai.com/hotel-vilnius/hotels-facilities/hotels
-bar-vilnius/

Opening hours	Closed Sunday and Monday
Reservation policy	Not accepted for drinks
Credit cards	Accepted
Price range	Affordable
Dress code	Smart casual
Style	Cocktail bar

"Nice music, beautiful people, it's small, it's cozy, and it has super tasty cocktails from one of the most creative barmen from Lithuania, Robertas Janovskis."—Remi Beinoras

MATÉRIALISTE
Vilniaus gatvė 25
Vilnius 01402
Lithuania
+370 65999286
www.materialiste.lt

Opening hours	Open Friday and Saturday
Reservation policy	Accepted
Credit cards	Accepted but not AMEX
Price range	Affordable
Dress code	Smart casual
Style	Cocktail bar

"Exactly the bar for late-night drinks. Run by Rapolas Vareika, one of the best bartenders in Lithuania. Great drinks for each taste, fun place to be and to meet new people."
—Remi Beinoras

HEROES BAR
Vulica Kazlova 3
Minsk 220034
Belarus
+375 445441144

Opening hours	Open 7 days
Reservation policy	Not accepted for drinks
Credit cards	Accepted but not AMEX
Price range	Affordable
Dress code	Smart casual
Style	Cocktail bar

"The cozy bar in the center of Minsk, with the perfect combination of friendly atmosphere, interesting drinks, and open-minded bartenders. Over the weekend, the bar is always full of visitors: a lot of foreigners and local bartenders . . . In summer, the bar opens up the most beautiful terrace in the city, at the weekend barbecue parties with live music are always waiting for you. Coming into this bar for 'the last' drink, you never know when and where you will end the evening."—Lizaveta Molyavka

SWEET & SOUR

Vulica Karla Marksa 14
Minsk 220030
Belarus
+375 296282593
www.sweetandsour.by

Opening hours	Closed Sunday
Reservation policy	Accepted
Credit cards	Accepted but not AMEX
Price range	Affordable
Dress code	Smart casual
Style	Cocktail bar

"The ideal bar for those who appreciate classic drinks, interior, discreet service, quiet jazz. Bar has strict rules, which are exactly observed since the early days. I would prefer to go alone to this bar, where you would have an opportunity to be alone with your thoughts, but if you change your mind, you can always find really good company, often an artist, a traveler, or just an extremely inquisitive stranger with whom you can talk about everything. This bar has its own style and charm, which should impress everyone who comes to the capital, especially for the first time."—Lizaveta Molyavka

ACUARELA

Strada Polonă 40
Bucharest 010503
Romania
+40 745662889
www.acuarelabistro.ro

Opening hours	Open 7 days
Reservation policy	Accepted
Credit cards	Accepted but not AMEX
Price range	Affordable
Dress code	Casual
Style	Bistro and bar

"This is a different kind of place . . . the name comes from the Romanian term for 'watercolor' and it is indeed a work of art, joyful and childish in a good way! It is a small bistro in Bucharest, a place that talks joy and freedom throughout all the amazing details! It is wonderland! A place for creativity, colors, and joy, this small bistro is dressed with works of art, umbrellas, and very friendly people. It is a place for cultural events, with art exhibitions, jazz concerts, and theater plays and it is in an old house, with reconditioned objects, a beautiful terrace, and a very cozy loft. It has good wines, fantastic food, and it makes you feel like a child again."
—Aida Ashor

FLAIR ANGEL

Calea Rahovei 147-153
Palatul Bragadiru
Bucharest 050892
Romania
+40 723334931
www.flairangel.ro

Opening hours	Closed Sunday–Tuesday
Reservation policy	Not accepted for drinks
Credit cards	Accepted
Price range	Affordable
Dress code	Smart casual
Style	Cocktail bar

"A place where I feel like I'm home . . . A cozy cocktail bar! . . . Named after the stage name of Bogdan Costiniu, a great, very creative, and ambitious Romanian bartender, who left us a few years ago . . . In the bar you can find a few theatrical drawings: in the first room there are two paintings: one of Bogdan Costiniu and one of Jerry Thomas, the father of mixology . . . The second room named 'The Monkeys Room' is not called that for nothing! In the same style as the other two drawings, you will find five monkeys on the wall here. They represent five human characters and at the same time the five members of the Exquisite Bar Solutions bartending agency. One is dancing, another thinking, and they even have names! . . . Here people are not clients but guests and they hear beautiful stories about the fantastic and creative drinks they taste!"—Aida Ashor

JOBEN BISTRO

Strada Avram Iancu 29
Cluj-Napoca 400083
Romania
+40 720222800
www.jobenbistro.ro

Opening hours	Open 7 days
Reservation policy	Not accepted for drinks
Credit cards	Accepted but not AMEX
Price range	Affordable
Dress code	Smart casual
Style	Bistro

"Created with passion, in a steampunk style, this bar is unique in Romania and is one of the top twenty in Europe for the amazing design. At the entrance you are welcomed by a talking robot that is saying 'Hello!' And since that moment you enter another world! A Jules Verne world with a Zeppelin on the ceiling, amazing handmade steampunk details on the walls, with wheels and hats everywhere, this place surprises people also with great food, a nice collection of single malts and gins, and extraordinary cocktails."—Aida Ashor

SUBMARINE
Strada Piaţa Unirii 2
Cluj-Napoca 400133
Romania
+40 732119396

Opening hours	Open 7 days
Reservation policy	Not accepted for drinks
Credit cards	Accepted but not AMEX
Price range	Affordable
Dress code	Smart casual
Style	Nightclub

"There are two bars, one in the control room, a big bar with fantastic drinks, and a smaller bar in the 'Engine Rum' area, with a menu like a map: you can choose your destination by choosing a rum from a country or island. The bar is designed to look like a submarine, hence the name."—Aida Ashor

360
Ifaistou 2
Athens 105 55
Greece
+30 2103210006
www.three-sixty.gr

Opening hours	Open 7 days
Reservation policy	Accepted
Credit cards	Accepted
Price range	Affordable
Dress code	Smart casual
Style	Cocktail bar

Rooftop bar with high quality cocktails and incredible views.

42 BAR
Kolokotroni 3
Athens 105 62
Greece
+30 6948242455

Opening hours	Open 7 days
Reservation policy	Not accepted for drinks
Credit cards	Accepted but not AMEX
Price range	Affordable
Dress code	Casual
Style	Cocktail bar

So named because 42 is the answer to the "Ultimate Question of Life, the Universe, and Everything" in *The Hitchhiker's Guide to the Galaxy* by Douglas Adams. Their focus is on homemade, seasonal ingredients.

BABA AU RUM
Klitiou 6
Athens 105 60
Greece
+30 2117109140
www.babaaurum.com

Opening hours	Open 7 days
Reservation policy	Not accepted for drinks
Credit cards	Not accepted
Price range	Affordable
Dress code	Smart casual
Style	Cocktail bar

THE CLUMSIES
Praxitelous 30
Athens 105 61
Greece
+30 2103232682
www.theclumsies.gr

Opening hours	Open 7 days
Reservation policy	Accepted
Credit cards	Accepted but not AMEX
Price range	Affordable
Dress code	Smart casual
Style	Cocktail bar

A bi-level bar helmed by two former Greek champions of the Diageo World Class cocktail competition, downstairs you can enjoy coffee & snacks during the day, and cocktails and DJs at night. Upstairs, "The Room" can accommodate up to 10 people—by advance booking only—for more formal service around a fireplace, billiard table, and vinyl LP collection. Opened in 2014, The Clumsies debuted as #22 on the World's 50 Best Bar list in 2015.

CV DISTILLER
Chatzigianni Mexi 7
Athens 115 28
Greece
+30 2107231767

Opening hours	Open 7 days
Reservation policy	Accepted
Credit cards	Accepted
Price range	Affordable
Dress code	Smart casual
Style	Whiskey bar

"A bar with an enormous collection of rare spirits, a bar where whiskey has a special place." —Theodoros Pirillos

THE GIN JOINT

Christou Lada 1
Athens 105 61
Greece
+30 2103218646
www.theginjoint.gr

Opening hours	Open 7 days
Reservation policy	Accepted
Credit cards	Accepted but not AMEX
Price range	Affordable
Dress code	Casual
Style	Cocktail bar

SEVEN JOKERS

Voulis 7
Athens 105 62
Greece
+30 2103219225

Opening hours	Open 7 days
Reservation policy	Not accepted for drinks
Credit cards	Accepted but not AMEX
Price range	Budget
Dress code	Casual
Style	Cocktail bar

"There's an eclectic mix of late revelers, great music, and the simplicity of a shot with a beer chaser."—Tony Conigliaro

"Most of the bartenders in Athens choose Seven Jokers to have their nightcap after their shift and so do I . . . that bar has probably the most beautiful ambience, the music is great. But the most important reason is the hospitable owners."—Theodoros Pirillos

THEORY BAR & MORE

Platonos 14
Khalándri 152 34
Greece
+30 2106801633
www.theorybar.gr

Opening hours	Open 7 days
Reservation policy	Not accepted for drinks
Credit cards	Accepted but not AMEX
Price range	Affordable
Dress code	Smart casual
Style	Cafe and bar

"[Theory, 360, The Clumsies, The Gin Joint, Baba Au Rum and Bar 42] are some of the bars that reflect the growth of the bar scene in Athens. Passionate teams of hospitable people. They serve great drinks and with their diversity, can cover every need and mood."—Theodoros Pirillos

LOST + FOUND DRINKERY

38 Lord Byron
Nicosia 1096
Cyprus

Opening hours	Closed Sunday
Reservation policy	Not accepted for drinks
Credit cards	Accepted but not AMEX
Price range	Affordable
Dress code	Smart casual
Style	Cocktail bar

"Forty-three thousand cocktails in a year and only open for four days week. Need I say more? Granted, these days Dinos Constantinides and his team open a couple more days a week. Their ice program is a must see, their back of house systems are out of this world, and I can confidently say that Dinos has secured the best bar team in the Mediterranean; they are simply magical to watch. You may have heard of the devastating fire that burned the first Lost + Found to the ground, but the Lost + Found that stands today is still the true original, built by the owner, his father, and the hands of the bartenders that work the stick. Their menu is simple in its complexity and caters to the well-seasoned drinker as well as the novice cocktail enthusiast."—Denzel Heath

"**GREAT COMBINATION OF A COCKTAIL BAR AND A NIGHT CLUB! ONE-OF-A-KIND IN RUSSIA!**"

ROMAN MILOSTIVY P.186

"THE PURE ESSENCE OF RUSSIAN HOSPITALITY IN A WORLD-RENOWNED HOTEL WITH A PERFECT BAR CREW."

IGOR ZERNOV P.186

THE RUSSIAN FEDERATION

"GREAT BARTENDERS WHO HAVE A GREAT SENSE OF HOSPITALITY. THEY MAKE YOU FEEL AT HOME AS SOON AS YOU WALK IN. DRINKS ARE DONE TO GREAT STANDARDS."

DIMI LEZINSKA P.187

"A TRULY UNIQUE BAR WITH THE TEAM ABSOLUTELY OBSESSED WITH THEIR CONCEPT AND CRAFT."

IGOR ZERNOV P.187

"**THIS IS THE PERFECT BAR TO ENJOY LATE AT NIGHT.**"

IGOR ZERNOV P.188

THE RUSSIAN
FEDERATION

SCALE

0   140   280
mi.

SAINT PETERSBURG PP.187–188

MOSCOW PP.186–187

CHAINAYA TEA & COCKTAILS

29-1 1st Tverskaya-Yamskaya
Moscow 125047
Russia
+7 4959673052

Opening hours..................................Closed Sunday and Monday
Reservation policy...Not accepted
Credit cards..Not accepted
Price range..Expensive
Dress code...Smart casual
Style....................................Cocktail bar and Chinese restaurant

"Its owner Roman Milostiy is a person whom I consider my true friend."—Fede Cuco

DELICATESSEN

Sadovaya-Karetnaya ulitsa 2
Moscow 127051
Russia
+7 4956993952

Opening hours...Closed Monday
Reservation policy..Accepted
Credit cards...Accepted but not AMEX
Price range..Affordable
Dress code...Smart casual
Style...Cocktail bar

"The staff greet you in a really nice and friendly way, like you are the very best guest at their home even if you come from far, far away. A true home-away-from-home!"—Igor Zernov

MENDELEEV BAR

Petrovka ulitsa 20/1
Moscow 111395
Russia
+7 4956253385
www.mendeleevbar.ru

Opening hours...Closed Monday
Reservation policy.............................Not accepted for drinks
Credit cards...Accepted but not AMEX
Price range..Affordable
Dress code...Smart casual
Style..Speakeasy

"Great combination of a cocktail bar and a night club! One-of-a-kind in Russia!"—Roman Milostiy

MOSKOVSKY BAR

Okhotnyy Ryad 2
Four Seasons Hotel Moscow
Moscow 109012
Russia
+7 4992777100
www.fourseasons.com/moscow

Opening hours..Open 7 days
Reservation policy..Accepted
Credit cards...Accepted
Price range..Affordable
Dress code...Smart casual
Style...Cocktail bar

"Three places to visit in Moscow for out-of-town guests: 1. Bolshoi Theatre 2. Red Square 3. Moskovsky Bar. The home of the authentic Moscow Mule and White Russian, located in the heart of Moscow by Kremlin and Red Square. Service and drinks are always top notch."—Bek Narzi

"The pure essence of Russian hospitality in a world-renowned hotel with a perfect bar crew."—Igor Zernov

NOOR BAR

Tverskaya ulitsa 23/12
Moscow 125009
Russia
+7 9031367686
www.noorbar.com

Opening hours..Open 7 days
Reservation policy................................Not accepted for drinks
Credit cards...Accepted
Price range..Affordable
Dress code...Smart casual
Style...Cocktail bar

"Unique atmosphere . . . great place to make acquaintances, good choice of music."—Roman Milostiy

PIVBAR

Tverskaya-Yamskaya 2
Moscow 125047
Russia
+7 9296730541

Opening hours	Open 7 days
Reservation policy	Not accepted for drinks
Credit cards	Not accepted
Price range	Budget
Dress code	Casual
Style	Pub

SAXON + PAROLE

Spiridonievskiy pereulok 12/9
Moscow 123104
Russia
+7 9037550343
www.saxonandparole.ru

Opening hours	Open 7 days
Reservation policy	Not accepted for drinks
Credit cards	Accepted
Price range	Affordable
Dress code	Smart casual
Style	Restaurant and bar

"Great bar team and consistently warm atmosphere."
—Bek Narzi

SUZURAN BAR

Sverchkov 8
Moscow 101000
Russia
+7 4956210756
www.suzuranbar.com

Opening hours	Open 7 days
Reservation policy	Accepted
Credit cards	Accepted
Price range	Affordable
Dress code	Casual
Style	Cocktail bar

"Great bartenders who have a great sense of hospitality.
They make you feel at home as soon as you walk in. Drinks
are done to great standards. It really is the people behind
that bar that would make me come back!"—Dimi Lezinska

"A beer pub with lots of beers on tap and delicious hot
dog snacks. Nothing pretentious, very relaxed atmosphere,
friendly staff, often new seasonal ales to try."
—Roman Milostivy

EL COPITAS

Kolokolnaya ulitsa 2
Saint Petersburg 191025
Russia
+7 8129417168

Opening hours	Open Thursday-Saturday
Reservation policy	Not accepted for drinks
Credit cards	Not accepted
Price range	Affordable
Dress code	Smart casual
Style	Cocktail bar

"This is a truly unique bar with the team absolutely obsessed
with their concept and craft, saying nothing about Mexican
cuisine and agave spirits. A bar that's reaaaally hard to find
without the booking call."—Igor Zernov

FIDDLER'S GREEN
Rubinshteyna ulitsa 5
Saint Petersburg 191025
Russia
+7 8123255550
www.hatgroup.ru/fiddlers-green/

Opening hours..Open 7 days
Reservation policy.....................................Not accepted for drinks
Credit cards...Not accepted
Price range..Affordable
Dress code...Casual
Style...Pub

"This is the perfect bar to enjoy late at night. The goal of
the owner was to re-create a bar with an early twentieth-
century atmospherecapturing the dark and gloomy mood of
sailors about to go on their last voyage. 'Fiddler's Green' is an
ancient legendary place where all the sailors go after their
death."—Igor Zernov

POISON
Lomonosova ulitsa 2
Saint Petersburg 191011
Russia
+7 9046091769

Opening hours..Open 7 days
Reservation policy.....................................Not accepted for drinks
Credit cards..Accepted
Price range..Budget
Dress code...Casual
Style...Karaoke bar

"Karaoke bar without Russian songs; only hard-rock karaoke.
Loud, tough, late. Just what I like!"—Timo Janse

"A CLASSIC VENETIAN HAUNT THAT WAS FREQUENTED BY HEMINGWAY BACK IN THE 1950s. FAMOUS FOR THE BELLINI WHICH WAS INVENTED THERE."

SEAN MULDOON P.198

"A CUTTING-EDGE COCKTAIL BAR IN TURIN. ONE OF THE TOP FAVORITE BARS OF BARTENDERS IN THE AREA."

GIUSEPPE GALLO P.196

ITALY

"THE SERVICE, THE QUALITY OF THE DRINKS, THE FRIENDLINESS OF THE OWNER, AND THE HUGE CHOICE OF GIN."

GIORGIO FADDA P.196

"AMBIENCE, QUIET SITE, HISTORICAL GARDENS, NATURAL FLAVORING, GREAT FRIENDLY SERVICE, LARGE CHOICE OF ULTRA-PREMIUM SPIRITS."

LUCA PICCHI P.196

"ONE OF THE MOST MAGICAL EXPERIENCES IN THE WORLD IS CAFFÈ RIVOIRE IN FLORENCE: IT IS THE PINNACLE OF THE NEGRONI." JACOB BRIARS P.197

TRENTINO P.196 ♥

MILAN PP.200–204 ♥   ♥VENETO PP.197–199

♥TURIN P.196

♥BOLOGNA P.195

FLORENCE PP.196–197 ♥

TUSCANY PP.196–197 ♥

♥GROSSETO P.195

ROME PP.206–209 ♥

NAPLES P.195 ♥

ITALY

(N̂)   SCALE

0   80   160
mi.

THE ART OF APERITIVO: COCKTAILS IN ITALY

The United States may be the original home of the cocktail, but Italy is home to some of the most important cocktail ingredients: vermouth and amaro. It is also the birthplace of one of the most important cocktails, the Negroni, first created in Florence around 1920.

One of the hallmarks of drinking culture in Italy is the aperitivo, or pre-dinner cocktail, which is accompanied by small snacks (served by most bars free of charge). Aperitivo cocktails are typically lower in alcohol and slightly bitter, like the Americano with sweet vermouth, Campari, and soda. The idea is to awaken the palate before moving on to dinner, the main event.

High cocktail culture arrived in Italy around 2008, largely inspired by what was happening in London—thus The Jerry Thomas Project in Rome, Nottingham Forest in Milan, Smile Tree in Turin, and the tiki bar Nu Lounge in Bologna. But this culture remains far from mainstream.

Rome, as a hot tourist destination, has historically been dominated by upscale hotel bars like the Hotel de Russie, but more recently has welcomed a raft of new "street bars" (not attached to a hotel) including Jerry Thomas and Co.So.

Milan, as the country's business capital, has more of a mix, with the high-fashion Bamboo Bar at the Armani Hotel and the ultra-modern Nottingham Forest where your cocktail may arrive in a syringe over dry ice.

Turin is the most traditional city, the home of Vermouth di Torino and the former seat of the House of Savoy. But here too things are changing, with Smile Tree as one of the most cutting-edge bars in the country.

Finally there is Venice, the original home of the Bellini and another tourist stronghold. The Veneto region is where the Spritz originated and the Aperol Spritz is the unofficial, ubiquitous drink of Venice. The two sides of the city are captured perfectly by Harry's Bar— where you'll pay €20 for a Bellini—and the Corner Pub—where you'll pay €1.50 for a simple Spritz.

Practical Information:
– A Negroni at a small café will cost around €5. Cocktail bars will charge between €8 and €15, and five-star hotels go up from there.
– Italy does not have a tipping culture. There is no need to leave a tip for an Aperol Spritz, but at a place like Jerry Thomas, you should leave a few euros.

NEGRONI

The Negroni is a simple cocktail—with equal parts gin, Campari, and sweet vermouth—but it is simultaneously endlessly complex as bitter, sweet, botanical, and citrus combine to create one of the pillars of the cocktail canon.

Legend has it that around 1920, at Bar Casoni in Florence, Count Camillo Negroni ordered his usual Americano but asked for barman Fosco Scarselli to make it stronger. Scarselli swapped the club soda for gin and the Negroni was born. In Italy, it is most often served on the rocks, perhaps with a slice of orange, while in the United States you will also find it served up with an orange twist.

The best place to enjoy the original is Caffè Rivoire in Florence, made by the hand of Luca Picchi, who has written a book, *Negroni Cocktail: An Italian Legend*, about the cocktail's history.

BELLINI

The Bellini was created in 1948 by Harry Cipriani and named for a fifteenth-century Italian painter. The recipe calls for only two ingredients, white peach puree and Prosecco, but when done right, it is a transporting experience. Drinking one at its birthplace in Venice is a must, even if it does set you back a pretty penny.

SPEAKEASY COCKTAIL BAR
Piazza Municipio 19
Pomigliano d'Arco
Naples
Campania 80038
Italy
+39 08119177557
www.speakeasybar.it

Opening hours	Open 7 days
Reservation policy	Accepted
Credit cards	Accepted but not AMEX
Price range	Affordable
Dress code	Smart casual
Style	Cocktail bar

"It is the landmark for bartenders of my city. Here some bartenders and I have tried innovative recipes and new interesting products."—Adriano Costigliola

NU LOUNGE BAR
Via de'Musei 6
Bologna
Emilia-Romagna 40124
Italy
+39 051222532
www.nuloungebar.com

Opening hours	Closed Sunday
Reservation policy	Accepted
Credit cards	Accepted
Price range	Affordable
Dress code	Smart casual
Style	Lounge

"Tiki cocktail culture and the one and only Daniele Dalla Pola."—Remi Beinoras

SWINEBAR
Via Righi Augusto 24
Bologna
Emilia-Romagna 40100
Italy
+39 051232631
www.swinefood.it

Opening hours	Closed for dinner on Monday/open 7 days in summer
Reservation policy	Accepted
Credit cards	Accepted but not AMEX
Price range	Affordable
Dress code	Smart casual
Style	Wine bar and restaurant

"On my first international trip I went to Italy and in my time there I spent a bit in Bologna. On an espresso-fueled night of food, wine, people watching, exploring, and soaking in all things Bologna, my friend and I stumbled upon Swinebar. I was intrigued by their collection of gin and array of agricole rums that I had never seen. We spent the duration of the evening excitedly tasting spirits, exchanging bartending stories, and befriending our amazing bartender." —Meghan Konecny

IL PELLICANO HOTEL BAR
Località Sbarcatello
Hotel Il Pellicano
Porto Ercole
Grosseto 58019
Italy
+39 0564858111
www.pellicanohotel.com

Opening hours	Open 7 days
Reservation policy	Not accepted for drinks
Credit cards	Accepted
Price range	Expensive
Dress code	Smart casual
Style	Cocktail bar

"I have looked all over the world for a bar that resembles the Hemingway Bar [at the Ritz Paris], and I realized when I was working in this bar that I was actually looking for the wrong things. No bar resembles the Hemingway Bar, but with Federico Morosi, the head bartender, there is an atmosphere between the guests and Federico which is very similar to the Hemingway Bar. There is a true appreciation of one another. Hemingway said 'If I die and go to heaven I would like it to resemble the bars of the Ritz'. My heaven is more like the bars of Il Pellicano."—Colin Field

THE MAD DOG

Via Maria Vittoria 35A
Turin
Piedmont 10123
Italy
www.themaddog.it

Opening hours	Closed Monday and Sunday
Reservation policy	Accepted
Credit cards	Accepted
Price range	Affordable
Dress code	Smart casual
Style	Speakeasy

"A speakeasy type bar with a late-night license until 3 a.m. (which is very rare in Turin). It's one of the few places you can go after midnight."—Giuseppe Gallo

To enter Mad Dog, you must either be a member or know the password of the day, which can be found on the bar's website.

SMILE TREE

Piazza della Consolata 9
Turin
Piedmont 10122
Italy
+39 3311848136
www.smiletree.it

Opening hours	Closed Monday
Reservation policy	Accepted
Credit cards	Accepted but not AMEX
Price range	Affordable
Dress code	Smart casual
Style	Cocktail bar

"A cutting-edge cocktail bar in Turin. One of the top favorite bars of bartenders in the area."—Giuseppe Gallo

Presided over by Dennis Zoppi, Smile Tree's creative menu favors whimsical, emotive one-liners. For example, "Magical Villages", a combination of tequila, orange balsamic, and pink pepper, is described as "powerful sensuality, rough and witty insight." Your cocktail might arrive in a shell nestled on a bed of ice in a cocktail coupe, or perhaps even in a paper bag.

RIVABAR

Largo Medaglie d'Oro
Riva del Garda
Trentino 38066
Italy
+39 0464551969
www.rivabar.it

Opening hours	Open 7 days
Reservation policy	Accepted
Credit cards	Accepted
Price range	Affordable
Dress code	Smart casual
Style	Cocktail bar and club

"The service, the quality of the drinks, the friendliness of the owner, and the huge choice of gin."—Giorgio Fadda

ART BAR

Via del Moro 4r
Florence
Tuscany 50123
Italy
+39 055287661

Opening hours	Closed Sunday
Reservation policy	Not accepted for drinks
Credit cards	Accepted
Price range	Affordable
Dress code	Casual
Style	Cocktail bar

"Very old-style bar, owned for more than thirty years by Paolo, no rush in this place, vintage classic and twisted cocktails, and lots of fresh fruit. Typical Italian bar, you'll always find people from all around the world to chat with." —Luca Angeli

ATRIUM BAR

Borgo Pinti 99
Four Seasons Hotel Firenze
Florence
Tuscany 50121
Italy
+39 05526261
www.fourseasons.com/florence

Opening hours	Open 7 days
Reservation policy	Not accepted for drinks
Credit cards	Accepted
Price range	Expensive
Dress code	Smart casual
Style	Lounge

"Ambience, quiet site, historical gardens, natural flavoring, great friendly service, large choice of ultra-premium spirits."—Luca Picchi

CAFFÈ RIVOIRE

Piazza della Signoria
Via Vacchereccia 4/r
Florence
Tuscany 50122
Italy
+39 055214412
www.rivoire.it

Opening hours	Closed Monday
Reservation policy	Not accepted for drinks
Credit cards	Accepted
Price range	Affordable
Dress code	Smart casual
Style	Cafe and cocktail bar

"One of the most magical experiences in the world is Caffè Rivoire in Florence: it is the pinnacle of the Negroni."
—Jacob Briars

THE FUSION BAR AND RESTAURANT

Vicolo dell'Oro 3
Gallery Hotel Art
Florence
Tuscany 50123
Italy
+39 05527266987
www.lungarnocollection.com/the-fusion

Opening hours	Open 7 days
Reservation policy	Not accepted for drinks
Credit cards	Accepted
Price range	Affordable
Dress code	Smart casual
Style	Bar and restaurant

"Friendly professional bartenders, large choice of spirits, very good advanced cocktails selection."—Luca Picchi

IL KIOSKO

Bastione Tognon 18
Peschiera del Garda
Veneto 37019
Italy
+39 3288378668
www.ilkiosko.com

Opening hours	Open 7 days
Reservation policy	Accepted
Credit cards	Not accepted
Price range	Affordable
Dress code	Smart casual
Style	Lounge

CLOAKROOM COCKTAIL LAB

Piazza Monte Pietá 4
Treviso
Veneto 31100
Italy
+39 3487289953
www.citylifestyle.it

Opening hours	Open 7 days
Reservation policy	Not accepted for drinks
Credit cards	Accepted
Price range	Affordable
Dress code	Smart casual
Style	Cocktail bar

"A lot of professionalism and innovation . . . a real cocktail workshop."—Giorgio Fadda

CORNER PUB

Calle della Chiesa 684
Venice
Veneto 30123
Italy
+39 3494576739

Opening hours...Open 7 days
Reservation policy..................................Not accepted for drinks
Credit cards...Accepted but not AMEX
Price range...Affordable
Dress code..Casual
Style..Pub

"This is a little hole in wall halfway between the Accademia and the Peggy Guggenheim Museum in Dorsoduro. People who haven't been to Venice often ask, 'How did the Spritz become so popular?' In a town where even a coffee costs more than a meal in some cities, you stumble across this tiny, divey bar, and get a large, cold Spritz for €1.5. That's how! Even better than a Spritz, but less typically Venetian, is the wonderful, bittersweet 'Negroni Sbagliato.' Both are a great introduction to the amazing, refreshing world of Italian aperitivo drinks."—Jacob Briars

HARRY'S BAR

San Marco
Calle Vallaresso 1323
Venice
Veneto 30124
Italy
+39 0415285777
www.harrysbarvenezia.com

Opening hours...Open 7 days
Reservation policy..................................Not accepted for drinks
Credit cards...Accepted
Price range...Expensive
Dress code..Smart casual
Style...Restaurant and bar

"A classic Venetian haunt that was frequented by Hemingway back in the 1950s. Famous for the Bellini which was invented there, this bar continues to attract droves of tourists on an hourly basis. It's small in size but delivers a perfect punch."
—Sean Muldoon

"It's the epitome of a tourist destination: to sit at the four-seat bar and eat little open-faced sandwiches and drink over-priced Bellinis. Maybe it's being in Venice, the anticipation, the history surrounding it, but there's a special feeling at this bar. The sun's shining, you took a water taxi to get there, you happen into Harry's Bar, and that's it! Sometimes you can almost feel like Hemingway is sitting next to you."—Tony Abou-Ganim

Giuseppe Cipriani opened Harry's Bar in 1931, with the goal of creating a high end hotel bar that was not in a hotel. It was named for and funded by Harry Pickering, a young American. In the 1930s, Cipriani invented the Bellini cocktail —a combination of white peach puree and Prosecco. Among the star-studded clientele are the upper crust of European royalty as well as celebrities ranging from Ernest Hemingway to Charlie Chaplin, Truman Capote, Orson Welles, and more.

"EVEN THOUGH IT IS A BIG PLACE, IT IS VERY COMFORTABLE AND COZY."

ADRIANO COSTIGLIOLA P.203

"THEY MAKE DELICIOUS DRINKS AND THE ATMOSPHERE IS VERY COMFORTABLE."

SILVIA GHIONI P.203

MILAN

"WHENEVER I'M IN MILAN I MAKE A POINT OF VISITING THIS HIDDEN GEM. A SMALL BAR OFFERING GREAT COCKTAILS AND AN EXCELLENT COLLECTION OF SPIRITS."

SALVATORE CALABRESE P.203

"IT'S THE EPITOME OF ELEGANCE."

SILVIA GHIONI P.204

"THIS BAR IS VERY MAGICAL, WHEN YOU ENTER INSIDE, IT'S LIKE A COUNTRY OF FAIRY TALES. IT'S THE PARADISE OF BARTENDERS."

SILVIA GHIONI P.204

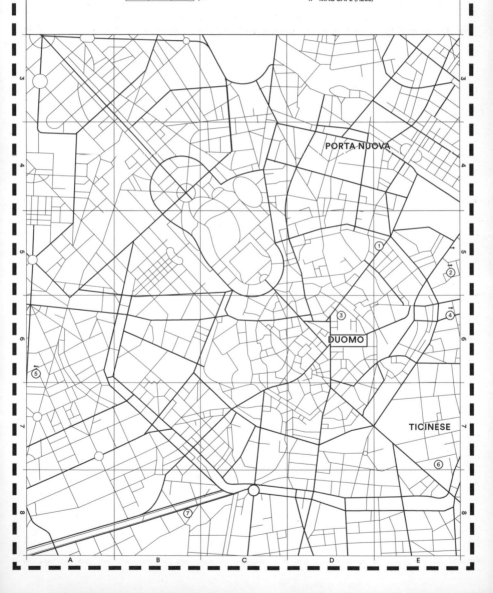

MILAN

SCALE

0   200   400   600
yd.

1. BAMBOO BAR (P.203)
2. NOTTINGHAM FOREST (P.204)
3. MIO BAR (P.204)
4. 1930 (P.203)
5. BAR 66 (P.203)
6. LACERBA (P.203)
7. MAG CAFÉ (P.203)

PORTA NUOVA

DUOMO

TICINESE

AMERICANO

The Americano is a delightfully refreshing aperitivo cocktail that combines equal parts Campari (from Milan) and sweet vermouth (from Turin), topped with club soda, and usually served with a slice of orange. It is an evolution of the Milano-Torino cocktail (the same recipe, without soda), and the precursor to the more famous Negroni, which swaps soda for gin.

1930

Via Pasquale Sottocorno
Cinque Giornate
Milan
Lombardy 20129
Italy

Opening hours	Open 7 days
Reservation policy	Not accepted for drinks
Credit cards	Not accepted
Price range	Expensive
Dress code	Smart casual
Style	Speakeasy

BAMBOO BAR

Via Manzoni 31
Armani Hotel Milano
Milan
Lombardy 20121
Italy
+39 0288838888
www.milan.armanihotels.com

Opening hours	Open 7 days
Reservation policy	Accepted
Credit cards	Accepted
Price range	Expensive
Dress code	Smart casual
Style	Lounge

BAR 66

Via Washington 66
Milan Marriott Hotel
Milan
Lombardy 20146
Italy
+39 0248522834
www.marriott.com/hotels/travel/milit-milan-marriott-hotel

Opening hours	Open 7 days
Reservation policy	Accepted
Credit cards	Accepted
Price range	Affordable
Dress code	Casual
Style	Lounge

"Entering the hotel you walk into a big lounge. Even though it is a big place, it is very comfortable and cozy. Walking through this room you can join the bar. The welcome is very special and it makes you feel at home."—Adriano Costigliola

LACERBA

Via Orti 4
Milan
Lombardy 20122
Italy
+39 025455475
www.lacerba.it

Opening hours	Closed Sunday
Reservation policy	Accepted
Credit cards	Accepted
Price range	Affordable
Dress code	Smart casual
Style	Restaurant and cocktail bar

"They make delicious drinks and the atmosphere is very comfortable."—Silvia Ghioni

MAG CAFÈ

Ripa di Porta Ticinese 43
Milan
Lombardy 20143
Italy
+39 0239562875

Opening hours	Open 7 days
Reservation policy	Accepted
Credit cards	Accepted but not AMEX
Price range	Affordable
Dress code	Smart casual
Style	Cocktail bar

"Whenever I am in Milan I make a point of visiting this hidden gem. A small bar offering great cocktails and an excellent collection of spirits. An unimposing venue, full of life and always busy with great customer care, they are always there to please."—Salvatore Calabrese

MIO BAR
Via Tommaso Grossi 1
Park Hyatt Milan
Milan
Lombardy 20121
Italy
+39 0288211234
www.milan.park.hyatt.com

Opening hours	Open 7 days
Reservation policy	Accepted
Credit cards	Accepted
Price range	Expensive
Dress code	Smart casual
Style	Lounge

"It's the epitome of elegance."—Silvia Ghioni

NOTTINGHAM FOREST
Viale Piave 1
Milan
Lombardy 20129
Italy
+39 02798311
www.nottingham-forest.com

Opening hours	Closed Monday
Reservation policy	Not accepted for drinks
Credit cards	Accepted
Price range	Affordable
Dress code	Smart casual
Style	Cocktail bar

"This bar is very magical, when you enter inside, it's like a country of fairy tales. It's the paradise of bartenders."
—Silvia Ghioni

"Dario Comini. He is the world's bartender landmark; he is always looking for new ideas. Behind his cocktails there are all the ingredients to success: passion, research, knowledge, professionalism, and courtesy."—Adriano Costigliola

"A LOVELY PLACE IN THE CENTER OF ROME ... GREAT ATMOSPHERE."

FEDERICO TOMASSELLI P.208

"LOCATED JUST NEXT TO THE COLOSSEUM OF ANCIENT ROME, IT IS A GIN 'COLOSSEUM'."

GIUSEPPE GALLO P.208

ROME

"'THE PLACE' IN ROME ... NO DETAIL IS LEFT UNNOTICED: EVEN THE DOOR HANDLES ARE IN THE SHAPE OF A COCKTAIL SHAKER ... ONE OF THE KEY COCKTAILS IS THE CARBONARA SOUR, MADE FROM VODKA INFUSED WITH PANCETTA."

GIUSEPPE GALLO P.208

"AMAZING BARTENDERS, PROHIBITION-ERA ATMOSPHERE, INCREDIBLE DRINKS."

MASSIMO STRONATI P.209

"THE AMBIENCE, THE ATMOSPHERE ARE FANTASTIC, THE QUALITY OF DRINKS: HIGH LEVEL."

LUCA ANGELI P.209

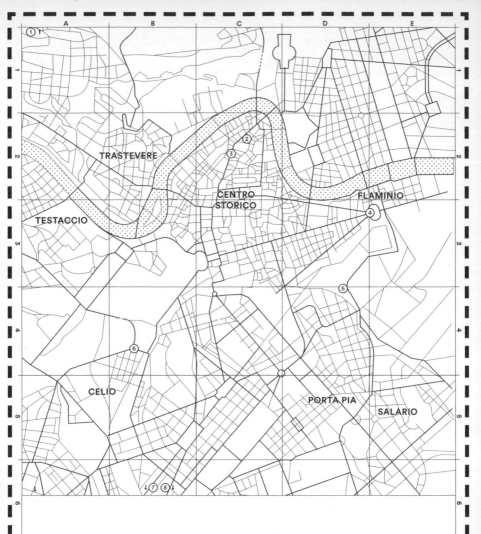

ROME

1. LE BON BOCK CAFÈ (P.208)
2. THE JERRY THOMAS PROJECT (P.209)
3. BARNUM CAFÈ (P.208)
4. STRAVINSKIJ BAR (P.209)
5. LA TERRASSE CUISINE & LOUNGE (P.209)
6. CAFFÈ PROPAGANDA (P.208)
7. SPIRITO (P.209)
8. CO.SO (P.208)

BARNUM CAFÈ

Via del Pellegrino 87
Rome
Lazio 00186
Italy
+39 0664760483
www.barnumcafe.com

Opening hours	Closed Sunday
Reservation policy	Accepted
Credit cards	Accepted
Price range	Affordable
Dress code	Casual
Style	Cocktail bar and cafe

"A lovely place in the center of Rome . . . Great atmosphere."
—Federico Tomasselli

LE BON BOCK CAFÈ

Circonvallazione Gianicolense 249
Rome
Lazio 00152
Italy
+39 065376806
www.lebonbock.com

Opening hours	Open 7 days
Reservation policy	Accepted
Credit cards	Accepted but not AMEX
Dress code	Casual
Style	Whiskey bar and brewery

"Huge selection of rare whiskey."—Leonardo Leuci

CAFFÈ PROPAGANDA

Via Claudia 15
Rome
Lazio 00184
Italy
+39 0694534255
www.caffepropaganda.it

Opening hours	Closed Monday
Reservation policy	Not accepted for drinks
Credit cards	Accepted
Price range	Affordable
Dress code	Smart casual
Style	Cocktail bar

"Located just next to the Colosseum of ancient Rome, it is a gin 'colosseum'."—Giuseppe Gallo

CO.SO.

Via Braccio da Montone 80
Rome
Lazio 00176
Italy
+39 0645435428

Opening hours	Closed Sunday
Reservation policy	Accepted
Credit cards	Accepted
Price range	Affordable
Dress code	Smart casual
Style	Cocktail bar

"'The place' in Rome. The concept is truly unique: it's totally handmade and personalized by owner Massimo D'Addezzio, formerly of the Hotel de Russie. No detail is left unnoticed: even the door handles are in the shape of a cocktail shaker. It is also very Roman. For example, one of the key cocktails is the Carbonara Sour, made from vodka infused with pancetta, an egg, and cracked pepper on top. It's just like the classic Spaghetti Carbonara, but in a cocktail. Or the Fern8 (pronounced Fernotto) with Fernet Branca and Chinotto soda, which takes inspiration from the popular Argentinian cocktail of Fernet and Coke, but Massimo makes it Roman by using the local San Pellegrino soda. They also have amari that you've never heard of and great local Roman food products. Inside the bar is the 'Speak-Co.So.' a small room for two people: to get into it you have to go into the bathroom and enter through the shower. And it's a proper late night bar because it doesn't have a closing time."—Giuseppe Gallo

THE JERRY THOMAS PROJECT

Vicolo Cellini 30
Rome
Lazio 00186
Italy
+39 0696845937
www.thejerrythomasproject.it

Opening hours	Closed Sunday and Monday
Reservation policy	Members only
Credit cards	Not accepted
Price range	Affordable
Dress code	Smart casual
Style	Speakeasy

"Amazing bartenders, Prohibition-era atmosphere, incredible drinks."—Massimo Stronati

"They got everything right that I got right with my own speakeasy cocktail bar, Door 74, but the addition of live music, and *la dolce vita* of Rome just makes it seem so much cooler and more beautiful. Also, they have bucketloads of good genever!"—Philip Duff

SPIRITO

Via Fanfulla da Lodi 53
Rome
Lazio 00176
Italy
+39 3272983900
www.club-spirito.com

Opening hours	Closed Tuesday
Reservation policy	Accepted
Credit cards	Accepted
Price range	Affordable
Dress code	Smart casual
Style	Cocktail bar

"Spirito is a place that is primarily run by women, and that's something that is hard to find around the world. What is immediately striking is the bar counter that represents a real roulette casino, fantastic."—Dennis Zoppi

STRAVINSKIJ BAR

Via del Babuino 9
Hotel de Russie
Rome
Lazio 00187
Italy
+39 0632888874
www.roccofortehotels.com/hotels-and-resorts/hotel-de-russie/restaurant-and-bar/

Opening hours	Open 7 days
Reservation policy	Not accepted for drinks
Credit cards	Accepted
Price range	Expensive
Dress code	Smart casual
Style	Cocktail bar

"They've got a beautiful garden out back, it's like a little oasis. There was a barman there a few years ago named Massimo d'Addezio who had trained a wonderful staff. It's very relaxed, very polite; you could be sitting next to Bruce Springsteen and not know it. I love that old-school European-style service you don't see that much in America."—Naren Young

"The ambience, the atmosphere are fantastic, the quality of drinks: high level. The hotel is close to Piazza del Popolo in Rome, and the location is amazing with a beautiful lounge bar."—Luca Angeli

LA TERRASSE CUISINE & LOUNGE

Via Lombardia 47
Sofitel Rome Villa Borghese
Rome
Lazio 00187
Italy
+39 06478022999
www.sofitel.com/gb/hotel-1312-sofitel-rome-villaborghese/index.shtml

Opening hours	Open 7 days
Reservation policy	Accepted
Credit cards	Accepted
Price range	Affordable
Dress code	Smart casual
Style	Cocktail bar

"A wonderful place in the center of Rome."
—Federico Tomasselli

AFRICA

$\hat{N}$

SCALE

0   350   700
                              mi.

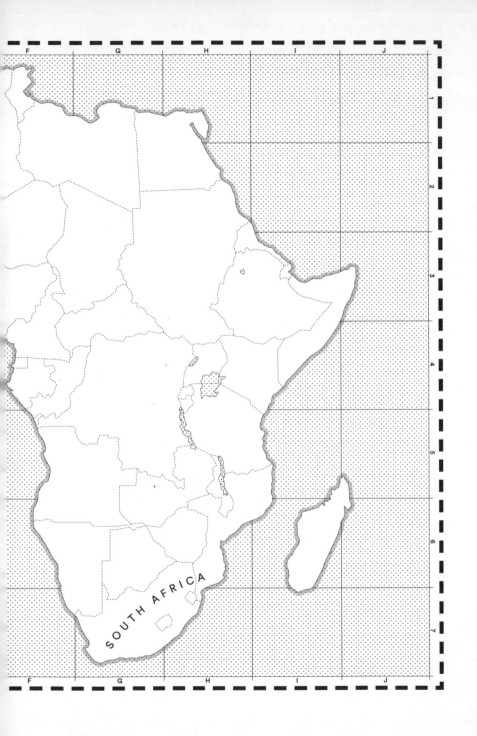

"THEIR WINE LIST BOASTS SOME OF SOUTH AFRICA'S FINEST WINES, AND THE COZY, CLASSIC RAND CLUB-INSPIRED INTERIOR MAKES IT THE PERFECT LIBATION STATION FOR ALL-WEATHER IMBIBING!"

DENZEL HEATH P.214

SOUTH AFRICA

"DO NOT BE FOOLED BY THE NAME, THIS DIVE BAR IS CERTAINLY ONE OF MY FAVORITES, ONE TO MARK OFF YOUR BUCKET LIST WHEN VISITING OUR SHORES." NICK KOUMBARAKIS P.214

"DEDICATED TO FINDING AND SHARING WINES FROM SUSTAINABLY FARMED VINEYARDS MADE WITH MINIMAL INTERVENTION IN THE CELLAR."

NICK KOUMBARAKIS P.214

"THIS BAR IS THE COOLEST IN THE WORLD: COFFEE SHOP BY DAY, BAR AND LIVE MUSIC BY NIGHT."

MAL SPENCE P.214

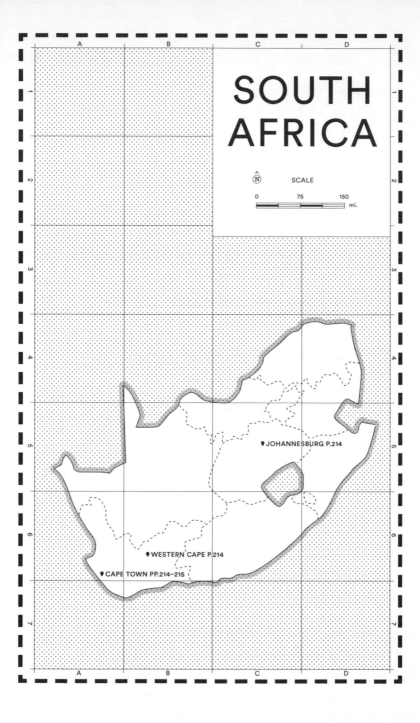

SOUTH AFRICA

SCALE

0   75   150
mi.

JOHANNESBURG P.214

WESTERN CAPE P.214

CAPE TOWN PP.214–215

THE LANDMARK

Bryanston Shopping Centre
William Nicol Drive and Ballyclare Drive
Johannesburg
Gauteng 2021
South Africa
+27 114635081
www.thelandmark.co.za

Opening hours...Closed Monday
Reservation policy...Accepted
Credit cards...Accepted
Price range...Affordable
Style...Cocktail bar

"The first bar of its kind in South Africa, where you can confidently walk up to the barkeep and order a Boulevardier, a Transvaal, or a Rob Roy and know that it will be flawless. Their menu is textbook—not in its size, but in its execution. And if you are not in the mood for one of Gareth Wainwright's (owner and head of mixology) immaculate creations, feel free to order from the one hundred classics on the famed wall menu. I would suggest trying one of their Afri Tiki cocktails which puts a local spin on tiki classics. Their wine list boasts some of South Africa's finest wines, and the cozy, classic Rand Club-inspired interior makes it the perfect libation station for all-weather imbibing!"—Denzel Heath

RONNIE'S SEX SHOP

Route 62
Barrydale
Western Cape 6750
South Africa

Opening hours.......................................Open 7 days in summer
Reservation policy..Not accepted
Credit cards...Not accepted
Dress code...Casual
Style..Dive bar

"Do not be fooled by the name, this dive bar is certainly one of my favorites, one to mark off your bucket list when visiting our shores. Take the scenic route along Route 62—you will not be disappointed."—Nick Koumbarakis

PUBLIK WINE BAR

81 Church Street
Cape Town
Western Cape 8001
South Africa
www.publik.co.za

Opening hours..Closed Sunday
Reservation policy.............................Not accepted for drinks
Credit cards...................................Accepted but not AMEX
Price range...Affordable
Dress code...Casual
Style..Wine bar

"Dedicated to finding and sharing wines from sustainably farmed vineyards made with minimal intervention in the cellar. Why? So you actually taste the land, not a winemaker's recipe. It's not being different just to be different, but these honest wines are exciting and don't get the recognition they deserve. The Wine Bar/Meat Merchants is a joint venture with Andy Fenner, a renowned and respected entrepreneur within the food industry, which includes Frankie Fenner Meat Merchants (FFMM) sourcing real meat that is clean, ethical, and sustainable."—Nick Koumbarakis

THE HOUSE OF MACHINES

84 Shortmarket Street
Cape Town
Western Cape 8000
South Africa
+27 214261400
www.thehouseofmachines.com

Opening hours..Closed Sunday
Reservation policy.............................Not accepted for drinks
Credit cards...................................Accepted but not AMEX
Price range...Affordable
Dress code...Casual
Style..Café and bar

"This bar is the coolest bar in the world: coffee shop by day, bar and live music by night. The venue is split into three, with the bar and café at the front; retail area in the middle selling merchandise, grooming products, and local designer collaborations; and in the back is a vintage motorbike shop. I'm obsessed with the T-shirts they sell. Bartenders Devin and Marshall are also top, top boys." —Mal Spence

THE POWER & THE GLORY

13B Kloof Nek Road
Cape Town
Western Cape 8001
South Africa
+27 214222108

Opening hours	Closed Sunday
Reservation policy	Not accepted for drinks
Credit cards	Accepted
Price range	Budget
Dress code	Casual
Style	Café & bar

A neighborhood bar serving sandwiches and hot dogs by day, with a bar that opens at 5pm each night. The house specialty is the pickleback, which comprises a shot of whisky followed by a shot of pickle juice.

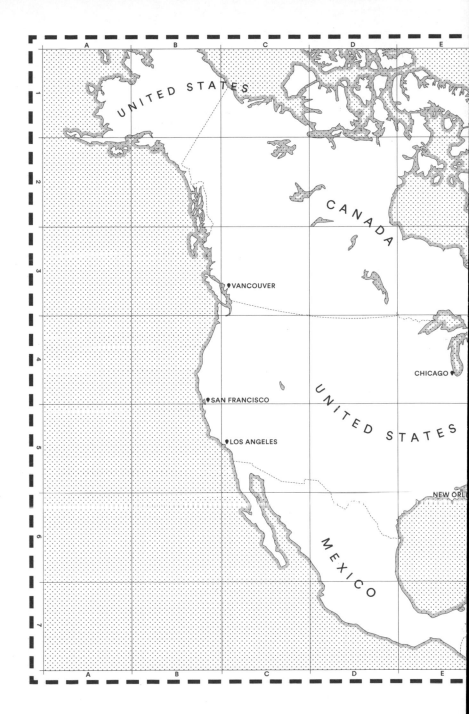

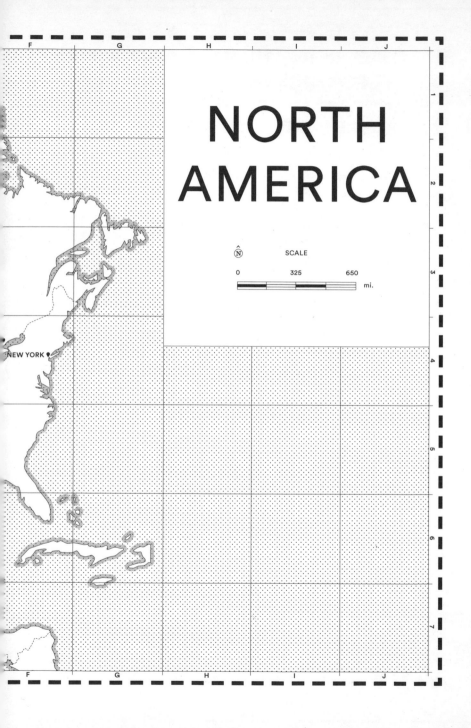

NORTH
AMERICA

N̂

SCALE

0   325   650

mi.

NEW YORK

"IT HAS ONE OF THE BEST BEER SELECTIONS IN THE CITY AND A TIDY LITTLE WHISKEY LIST." SHAWN SOOLE P.222

"THIS BAR IS ABSOLUTELY BEAUTIFUL, THE DETAILS AND CRAFTSMANSHIP OF THE ROOM ARE LIKE NO OTHER." EVELYN CHICK P.223

CANADA

"THE HARBORD ROOM IS A TINY HIDDEN GEM THAT HAS BEEN A STAPLE IN THE TORONTO BAR SCENE SINCE IT OPENED EIGHT YEARS AGO, BACK WHEN THE COCKTAIL SCENE WAS JUST STARTING TO DEVELOP." EVELYN CHICK P.223

"THE FIRST REAL COCKTAIL BAR THAT OPENED IN MONTREAL AND SINCE THEN THEY KEEP EVOLVING AND CREATING GREAT THINGS." JONATHAN HOMIER P.225

"SWEET, COZY SPOT WITH A BOULEVARD PATIO." SANDY DE ALMEIDA P.224

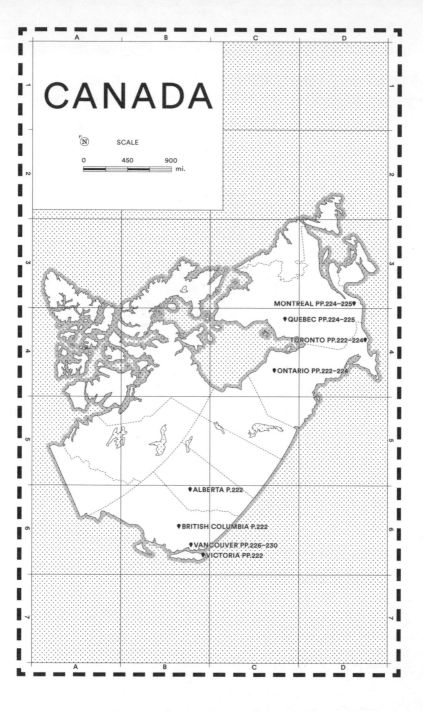

CANADA

N

SCALE

0 450 900
mi.

MONTREAL PP.224–225▼

♦QUEBEC PP.224–225

TORONTO PP.222–224♦

♦ONTARIO PP.222–224

♦ALBERTA P.222

♦BRITISH COLUMBIA P.222

♦VANCOUVER PP.226–230
♦VICTORIA PP.222

COCKTAILS IN CANADA

Since around 2005, Canada has been gaining momentum in its cocktail culture, with Vancouver, Toronto, and Montreal as the primary hubs.

Located on the West Coast, Vancouver puts a focus on local ingredients and the cocktails tend to be fresher and lighter in style, with plenty of vodka and gin. An important aspect of the local bar scene is that food service is required. You'll therefore find quite a few bars that are attached to or incorporated into restaurants. There's also a strong Asian influence here, as evidenced by Bao Bei and Keefer Bar, both located in Vancouver's Chinatown.

On the flip side, Toronto tends toward more whiskey-based, stirred cocktails, and draws influence from New York City (only an hour away by plane). This is encouraged by the fact that most Canadian whiskey is distilled in the east of the country. There is even a distillery district in the city and many bars stock a large selection of local brands.

Montreal, with its strong French heritage, is rooted in classics, but has a fair amount of experimentation going on as well, and a diverse bar scene.

Like its American cousins bourbon and rye, Canadian whiskey is experiencing quite the renaissance of its own. New small producers are experimenting with different grains and the category is quickly developing a reputation for quality. There are a number of Canadian gins as well—especially from British Columbia—that incorporate local botanicals.

Practical Information:
- Cocktails range from C$10–$19, with most coming in around C$14.
- Tipping is 15–20%.

MILK TIGER LOUNGE

1410 4 Street Southwest
Calgary
Alberta T2R 0Y1
Canada
+1 4032615009
www.milktigerlounge.ca

Opening hours..Open 7 days
Reservation policy..............................Not accepted for drinks
Credit cards...Accepted
Price range...Affordable
Dress code...Casual
Style...Lounge

"This is my favorite bar in my second home of Calgary, I love this place: the guys are super welcoming, you can easily wile away the hours here drinking beers, or spend hours talking all things cocktails and whiskey with Nathan and the team. A true inspiration, they definitely set the bar for all other cocktail programs in the city and offer genuine hospitality. A place for ladies, gentlemen, and scoundrels alike."
—Colin Tait

THE CHURCHILL

1140 Government Street
The Bedford Regency Hotel
Victoria
British Columbia V8W 1Y2
Canada
+1 2503846835
www.thechurchill.ca

Opening hours..Open 7 days
Reservation policy...Accepted
Credit cards...Accepted
Price range...Affordable
Dress code...Casual
Style..Pub

"It has one of the best beer selections in the city and a tidy little whiskey list. At the end of a fourteen-hour shift, a shot and a beer are all you really need. No sports on TVs, and awesome industry staff and guests make it a nice spot to have a quiet one even if the room is banging."—Shawn Soole

CLIVE'S CLASSIC LOUNGE

740 Burdett Avenue
Chateau Victoria Hotel & Suites
Victoria
British Columbia V8W 1B2
Canada
+1 2503615684
www.clivesclassiclounge.com

Opening hours..Open 7 days
Reservation policy..............................Not accepted for drinks
Credit cards...Accepted
Price range...Affordable
Dress code...Casual
Style...Lounge

"This is my old stomping ground, with amazing cocktails and a great selection of beer and spirits. Off the beaten track in a classic hotel, one of the resident bartenders (George) has been there for over twenty years and is the epitome of old-school charm and service."—Shawn Soole

BAR ISABEL

797 College Street
Toronto
Ontario M6G 1C7
Canada
+1 4165322222
www.barisabel.com

Opening hours..Open 7 days
Reservation policy..............................Not accepted for drinks
Credit cards...Accepted
Price range...Affordable
Dress code...Smart casual
Style..Tapas restaurant and bar

"Bar Isabel is right across the street from my house, with a wonderfully thought-out wine list, fantastic cocktails, and late-night food until 2 a.m. everyday. What makes a good neighborhood bar is definitely as much about the people as the quality of its products. Given that it is a VERY busy spot, any guest will still be able to walk in and feel right at home, whether you're having a water and some shishito peppers or just a fantastic sherry with your jamón ibérico de bellota. Great stuff!"—Evelyn Chick

BAR RAVAL

505 College Street
Toronto
Ontario M6G 1A4
Canada
www.thisisbarraval.com

Opening hours	Open 7 days
Reservation policy	Not accepted for drinks
Credit cards	Accepted
Price range	Affordable
Dress code	Casual
Style	Cafe, tapas restaurant, and bar

"You walk in and you're overwhelmed by the beauty of the space. 'How did they construct this place?' you ask. How the hell could they possibly make wood feel so . . . alive. But it's not just about looks. Bar Raval fires on all cylinders—from great cocktails, awesome sherry (my favorite!), and exceptional Spanish-inspired food, I can't think of a more perfect bar. If they'd let me live there, I might move in."
—Alex Day

"The most stellar of staffs in front and back of house. Some of the most beautiful bar and woodwork I've ever seen. Not to mention the exquisite food."—Jacyara De Oliveira

"This tiny 'bar' is open from 8 a.m. to 2 a.m. every day. They have incredible coffee and pastries in the morning; tapas all day long; amazing beer, wine, and spirits; a great sherry selection; and some of the best cocktails I've ever had. I wish I lived in Toronto just to be close to this bar."—David Kaplan

"This bar is absolutely beautiful, the details and craftsman-ship of the room are like no other. The owners are chefs and bartenders who have put a lot of thought in designing the Spanish-inspired menu and the venue . . . Stepping into this bar, you are immediately immersed in the depths of the little town of Raval in Spain."—Evelyn Chick

FAT CITY BLUES

890 College Street
Toronto
Ontario M6H 1A3
Canada
+1 6473458282
www.fatcityblues.com

Opening hours	Closed Monday
Reservation policy	Not accepted for drinks
Credit cards	Accepted but not AMEX
Price range	Affordable
Dress code	Casual
Style	Jazz bar

"New Orleans-inspired bar with late night food and a live jazz band every night. Things get pretty wild any night of the week and they make the best French 75 in the city. Also, one of the bartenders breathes fire."—Sandy de Almeida

THE HARBORD ROOM

89 Harbord Street
Toronto
Ontario M5S 1G4
Canada
+1 4169628989
www.theharbordroom.com

Opening hours	Open 7 days
Reservation policy	Accepted
Credit cards	Accepted but not AMEX
Price range	Affordable
Dress code	Smart casual
Style	Restaurant and bar

"The Harbord Room is a tiny hidden gem that has been a staple in the Toronto bar scene since it opened eight years ago, back when the cocktail scene was just starting to develop. Its menu focuses on local, farm-to-table ingredients foraged in and around the city, and the cocktails use the same principle with fresh, seasonal ingredients. The combination of both showcases a truly Canadian, great-time bar. Not to mention, the best patio in Toronto."—Evelyn Chick

HOOF COCKTAIL BAR

923 Dundas Street West
Toronto
Ontario M6J 1W3
Canada
+1 4167927511
www.hoofcocktailbar.com

Opening hours	Open 7 days
Reservation policy	Not accepted for drinks
Credit cards	Not accepted
Price range	Affordable
Dress code	Smart casual
Style	Cocktail bar

"Jen Agg has built the holy trinity of industry spots in this city. And of her three places, Cocktail Bar is my favorite . . . It's a great space. There are limited bar seats which makes the bartender/customer relationship super intimate. The bar's aesthetic is also very in line with my own . . . If there's anyone visiting from out of town, I know I'm putting them in good hands when I send them [here]. Always. Hands down."
—Sandy de Almeida

MIDFIELD WINE BAR & TAVERN

1434 Dundas Street West
Toronto
Ontario M6J 1Y7
Canada
+1 6473457005

Opening hours..Open 7 days
Reservation policy.................................Not accepted for drinks
Credit cards...............................Accepted but not AMEX
Price range...Affordable
Dress code...Casual
Style...Wine bar

"Sweet, cozy spot with a boulevard patio. Great wine selection curated by Christopher Sealy (co-owner and sommelier), amazing food by Leah Hannon, and the absolute best staff."—Sandy de Almelda

BAR DATCHA

98 Avenue Laurier Ouest
Montreal
Quebec H2T 2N4
Canada
+1 51427935
www.bardatcha.ca

Opening hours..................................Open Thursday–Saturday
Reservation policy...Accepted
Credit cards...Accepted
Price range...Affordable
Dress code...Smart casual
Style...Dance club

"On one side you have one of the best cocktail bars in the city (Kabinet), relaxed and laid-back, and on the other side you have a small club famous within the DJ community (Datcha) so you can party all night and still enjoy a great drink."
—Jonathan Homier

BAR KABINET

92 Avenue Laurier Ouest
Montreal
Quebec H2T 2N4
Canada
+1 5142793555
www.barkabinet.com

Opening hours..Open 7 days
Reservation policy...Accepted
Credit cards...Accepted
Price range...Affordable
Dress code...Casual
Style.......................................Coffee and cocktail bar

BISHOP & BAGG

52 Rue Saint Viateur Ouest
Montreal
Quebec H2T 2K8
Canada
+1 5142774400
www.bishopandbagg.com

Opening hours..Open 7 days
Reservation policy...Accepted
Credit cards...............................Accepted but not AMEX
Price range...Affordable
Dress code...Casual
Style...Pub

"It's a classic English pub with a large selection of tap, the largest selection of gin in Montreal, and fine scotch also. The food there is simply the best pub food in Montreal and the kitchen opens late."—Jonathan Homier

LA DISTILLERIE
Multiple Locations
Montreal
Quebec
Canada
+1 5144482461
www.pubdistillerie.com

Opening hours	Open 7 days
Reservation policy	Not accepted for drinks
Credit cards	Accepted but not AMEX
Price range	Affordable
Dress code	Smart casual
Style	Cocktail bar

"It's the first real cocktail bar that opened in Montreal and since then they keep evolving and creating great things. Also, the vibe there is always great, the staff is friendly and with their supersize 1-liter mason jar cocktail you sure will have a great time."—Jonathan Homier

L'GROS LUXE
Multiple Locations
Montreal
Quebec
Canada
+1 5144472227
www.lgrosluxe.com

Opening hours	Open 7 days
Reservation policy	Not accepted for drinks
Credit cards	Accepted but not AMEX
Price range	Affordable
Dress code	Smart casual
Style	Bistro

"They have been open for a little more than a year and they already have four locations with really different vibes and styles, but always the same idea of great cocktails, and great food for a super cheap price. (The only thing is that you need to order food to be able to drink because of their license, but even bartenders need to eat sometimes to keep on drinking!)"—Jonathan Homier

PLATEAU LOUNGE
901 Square Victoria
W Hotel
Montreal
Quebec H2Z 1R1
Canada
+1 5143953195
www.wmontrealhotel.com

Opening hours	Open Thursday–Saturday
Reservation policy	Accepted
Credit cards	Accepted
Price range	Affordable
Dress code	Smart casual
Style	Lounge

"When you imagine a trendy hotel bar you could see in a movie, you think of Plateau Lounge. You'll feel like a star drinking there. The cocktails are always great and the staff very professional."—Jonathan Homier

"PERFECT PLACE TO WALK TO FOR DRINKS AFTER WATCHING THE SUN SET AT SUNSET BEACH."

DANIELLE TATARIN P.230

VANCOUVER

"THEY MAKE A MEAN PIÑA COLADA BUT ALSO HAVE AN ARSENAL OF CLASSICALLY INSPIRED DRINKS THAT ARE INFLUENCED BY CHINATOWN."

DANIELLE TATARIN P.228

"YOU ALWAYS HAVE A GOOD TIME HERE."

GRANT SCENEY P.229

"A BEAUTIFUL BAR LIST RANGING FROM DELICIOUS NONALCOHOLIC DRINKS TO PREMIUM LOUIS VIII SAZERACS."

EVELYN CHICK P.229

"OPENED AND RUN BY BARTENDERS, IT'S BEEN A PLACE WHERE MANY OF THE CITY'S GREATS HAVE WORKED, OR DO WORK."

SHAUN LAYTON P.229

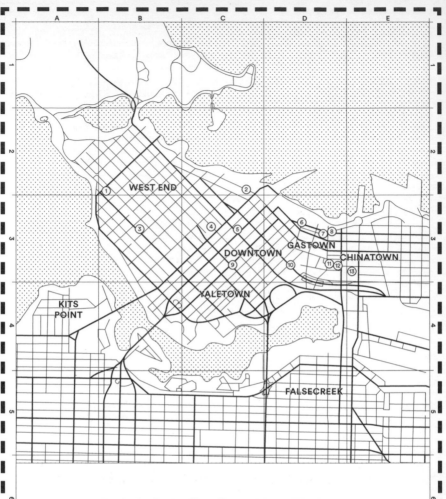

WEST END

DOWNTOWN

GASTOWN

CHINATOWN

KITS
POINT

YALETOWN

FALSECREEK

VANCOUVER

N̂   SCALE

0   275   550   825
▬▬▬▬▬▬▬▬▬▬▬ yd.

1. THE BAYSIDE LOUNGE (P.228)
2. THE LOBBY LOUNGE
   AND RAW BAR (P.229)
3. LOLITA'S (P.230)
4. GERARD LOUNGE (P.229)

5. HAWKSWORTH RESTAURANT (P.229)
6. POURHOUSE (P.230)
7. L'ABBATOIR (P.228)
8. MAMIE TAYLOR'S (P.230)
9. UVA WINE & COCKTAIL BAR (P.230)

10. CHAMBAR (P.228)
11. THE KEEFER BAR (P.229)
12. BAO BEI (P.228)
13. THE DIAMOND (P.228)

L'ABATTOIR

217 Carrall Street
Vancouver
British Columbia V6B 2J2
Canada
+1 6045681701
www.labattoir.ca

Opening hours	Open 7 days
Reservation policy	Not accepted for drinks
Credit cards	Accepted
Price range	Affordable
Dress code	Smart casual
Style	Restaurant and bar

L'Abattoir is located in what used to be Vancouver's first jail, next to the historic meatpacking district from which it draws its name (*abbatoir* means slaughterhouse in French). It serves French-inspired food alongside an eclectic wine list and innovative, original cocktails such as the Avocado Gimlet.

BAO BEI

163 Keefer Street
Vancouver
British Columbia V6A 1X3
Canada
+1 6046880876
www.bao-bei.ca

Opening hours	Open 7 days
Reservation policy	Not accepted for drinks
Credit cards	Accepted but not AMEX
Price range	Affordable
Dress code	Casual
Style	Chinese restaurant and bar

"They make a mean Piña Colada but also have an arsenal of classically inspired drinks that are influenced by Chinatown —the food is amazing! Vancouver's Chinatown is going through a revival and Bao Bei is a jumping off point for many restaurants and bars within a four-block radius. Food and drink combination that I love: Guavinez Cocktail and Sticky Rice Cakes."—Danielle Tatarin

THE BAYSIDE LOUNGE

1755 Davie Street
Best Western Plus Sands Hotel
Vancouver
British Columbia V6G 1W5
Canada
+1 6046821831
www.baysidelounge.ca

Opening hours	Open 7 days
Reservation policy	Accepted
Credit cards	Accepted
Price range	Affordable
Dress code	Casual
Style	Lounge

"It's upstairs right in the middle of English Bay so the views are spectacular. Better yet, a lot of locals and tourists don't even know it's there, so seats are usually available. It has a round sunken bar and huge round banquettes that flank the room. It's kind of stuck in the 1980s, which is awesome. Not a cocktail spot, but sure could be!"—Shaun Layton

CHAMBAR

568 Beatty Street
Vancouver
British Columbia V6B 2L3
Canada
+1 6048797119
www.chambar.com

Opening hours	Open 7 days
Reservation policy	Not accepted for drinks
Credit cards	Accepted
Price range	Affordable
Dress code	Smart casual
Style	Restaurant and bar

"A local, unpretentious Belgian brasserie, situated between several major venues downtown. Its location is perfect for any hockey game, soccer, or concert pre-event. Pull up to the bar, where they have great mussels and a solid all-around beverage program, including wine, cocktails, and Belgian beers. However, you don't need any kind of event as an excuse to visit here."—Grant Sceney

THE DIAMOND

6 Powell Street
Vancouver
British Columbia V6A 167
Canada
www.di6mond.com

Opening hours	Open 7 days
Reservation policy	Not accepted for drinks
Credit cards	Accepted
Price range	Affordable
Dress code	Smart casual
Style	Restaurant and bar

"If you visit Vancouver, you have to visit historic Gastown, and it works out perfectly that there is a kick-ass cocktail bar right in the heart of it."—Grant Sceney

"Opened and run by bartenders, it's been a place where many of the city's greats have worked, or do work. Always a fun room, great tunes, and fun smashing cocktails. In a great neighborhood too."—Shaun Layton

GERARD LOUNGE

845 Burrard Street
Sutton Place Hotel
Vancouver
British Columbia V6Z 2K6
Canada
+1 6046422900
www.suttonplace.com

Opening hours	Open 7 days
Reservation policy	Not accepted for drinks
Credit cards	Accepted
Price range	Affordable
Dress code	Smart casual
Style	Lounge

"The Gerard never really changes, though it did recently undergo renovations. It's not a famous cocktail destination, just a dark old-school bar with lots of wood—my kind of place for an afternoon drink."—Shaun Layton

HAWKSWORTH RESTAURANT

801 West Georgia Street
Rosewood Hotel Georgia
Vancouver
British Columbia V6C 1P7
Canada
+1 6046737000
www.hawksworthrestaurant.com

Opening hours	Open 7 days
Reservation policy	Not accepted for drinks
Credit cards	Accepted
Price range	Affordable
Dress code	Smart casual
Style	Restaurant and bar

"Hawksworth is more of your traditional-style hotel bar . . . It's a small room connected to the restaurant but they have a great team, warm service from very knowledgeable staff, and an impressive back bar with drinks to match."
—Grant Sceney

THE KEEFER BAR

135 Keefer Street
Vancouver
British Columbia V6A 1X3
Canada
+1 6046881961
www.thekeeferbar.com

Opening hours	Open 7 days
Reservation policy	Accepted
Credit cards	Accepted but not AMEX
Price range	Affordable
Dress code	Casual
Style	Cocktail bar

"You always have a good time here: it's a great small Chinese apothecary-style cocktail bar that also does live music and burlesque shows on varying nights throughout the week. You can go there for a quiet beer, cocktail, or a celebration with a group of friends. Good industry bar crowd and the bartenders also make this place a pretty fun spot to hang out."—Grant Sceney

THE LOBBY LOUNGE AND RAW BAR

1038 Canada Place
The Fairmont Pacific Rim
Vancouver
British Columbia V6C 0B9
Canada
+ 1 6046955502
www.lobbyloungerawbar.com

Opening hours	Open 7 days
Reservation policy	Not accepted for drinks
Credit cards	Accepted
Price range	Expensive
Dress code	Smart casual
Style	Lounge

"The Fairmont Pacific Rim hotel bar is attached to a gorgeous lounge in the busiest lobby in Vancouver. To be a great hotel bar, the drinks must satisfy the palates of people from all walks of life. Pacific Rim has a beautiful bar list ranging from delicious nonalcoholic drinks to premium Louis VIII Sazeracs. The bartenders are always friendly and accommodating—truly a great spot."—Evelyn Chick

In the words of head bartender Grant Sceney, "Known affectionately by locals as the Pac Rim ... Live music 6 nights a week in a gorgeous long white marble lobby. A very talented and dedicated bar team, alongside a fresh rawbar."

LOLITA'S

1326 Davie Street
Vancouver
British Columbia V6E 1N5
Canada
+1 6046969996
www.lolitasrestaurant.com

Opening hours	Open 7 days
Reservation policy	Not accepted for drinks
Credit cards	Accepted
Price range	Affordable
Dress code	Casual
Style	Mexican restaurant and bar

"It's a cozy room with tacos, tequila, and beer. Perfect place to walk to for drinks after watching the sun set at Sunset beach. Nuff said."—Danielle Tatarin

MAMIE TAYLOR'S

251 East Georgia Street
Vancouver
British Columbia V6A 1Z6
Canada
+1 6046208818
www.mamietaylors.ca

Opening hours	Open 7 days
Reservation policy	Not accepted for drinks
Credit cards	Accepted
Price range	Affordable
Dress code	Casual
Style	Restaurant and bar

"Mamie's is owned by two Vancouver bartenders. I usually drink beer there, but am confident the cocktails are always proper."—Shaun Layton

POURHOUSE

162 Water Street
Vancouver
British Columbia V6B 1B2
Canada
+1 6045687022
www.pourhousevancouver.com

Opening hours	Open 7 days
Reservation policy	Not accepted for drinks
Credit cards	Accepted
Price range	Affordable
Dress code	Smart casual
Style	Restaurant and bar

"It's got a very Prohibition-era look to it, which may sometimes lead to pretension, but quite the opposite here. The bar staff is always friendly and on point with spirit knowledge and cocktails. Pair that with great beers and one of the best burgers in the city."—Shaun Layton

UVA WINE & COCKTAIL BAR

900 Seymour Street
Moda Hotel
Vancouver
British Columbia V6B 3L9
Canada
+1 6046329560
www.uvavancouver.com

Opening hours	Open 7 days
Reservation policy	Not accepted for drinks
Credit cards	Accepted
Price range	Affordable
Dress code	Smart casual
Style	Wine and cocktail bar

"Delicious cocktails, great wine and beer selection, and friendly staff."—Danielle Tatarin

"WALKING IN IS LIKE STEPPING BACK IN TIME."

SUMMER JANE BELL P.237

"ONE OF MY FAVORITE PLACES TO END THE NIGHT. IT'S A PIANO BAR WITH A GUY WHO'S BEEN PLAYING FOR THIRTY YEARS."

MORGAN SCHICK P.237

USA WEST

"THE FUN, LOOSE ATMOSPHERE OF A GREAT LOCAL BAR WITH THE MIND-SET OF A CRAFT COCKTAIL BAR."

SEAN KENYON P.236

"THIS BAR IS IN MY TOP THREE FAVORITE BARS EVER ... THIS BAR HAS THAT DIVE FEEL BUT CAN MAKE YOU SOME OF THE BEST DRINKS."

JAYSON WILDE P.239

"ONE OF THE FIRST LOCAL DIVE BARS TO DO REALLY COOL MICROBREWS ON TAP."

ERICK CASTRO P.239

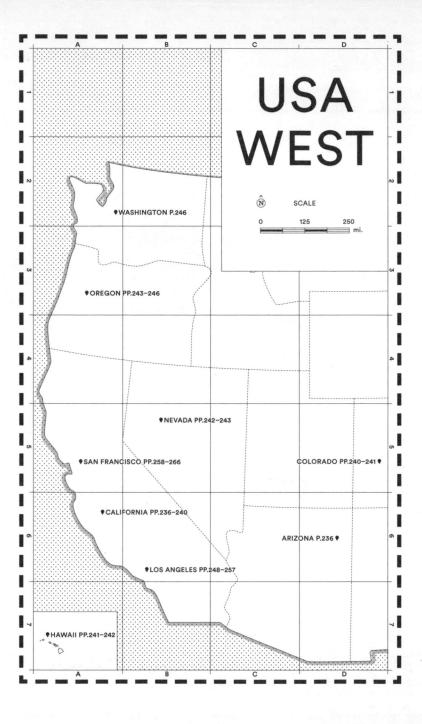

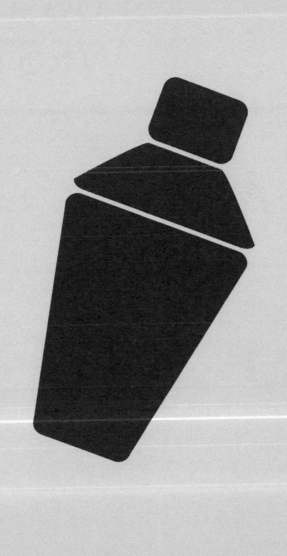

COCKTAILS IN THE UNITED STATES

The cocktail is one of the few culinary inventions that can be laid squarely at the doorstep of the United States. It is uniquely American. Most of the classic cocktails we drink today—including the Manhattan, the Martini, and the Old Fashioned—were invented in the United States during the first Golden Age of cocktails in the run-up to Prohibition, from the late 1800s until 1920.

And nowhere has cocktail culture experienced more of a renaissance in the twenty-first century than in the United States. Introduced in the 1980s by Dale DeGroff in New York City's the Rainbow Room, it was kick-started in 1999 with the opening of Milk & Honey by Sasha Petraske on the Lower East Side of Manhattan. Since then, cocktails have spread like wildfire, reigniting cities with deep histories of their own like San Francisco and New Orleans, taking root in new places like Los Angeles and Miami, and now springing up in cities like Nashville, Tennessee; Cleveland, Ohio; and Birmingham, Alabama.

It is fitting, therefore, that many of the bars profiled in this book are in the United States. Of course, drinking culture in the United States encompasses much more than cocktails. From grungy dive bars to swanky cocktail lounges, the United States is a true melting pot of drinking traditions, and you'll find that range in these pages.

Practical Information:
— Cocktail prices range widely across the country. In general, the low end will be around US$8, mid-range US$12 to US$15, and higher end up to US$25 or US$30. Prices are higher in large cities, especially New York.
— Tipping is expected and 15% to 20% (or US$2 to US$3 per drink) is the norm.

BITTER & TWISTED COCKTAIL PARLOUR

1 West Jefferson Street
Phoenix
Arizona 85003
United States
+1 6023401924
www.bitterandtwistedaz.com

Opening hours	Closed Sunday and Monday
Reservation policy	Accepted
Credit cards	Accepted
Price range	Affordable
Dress code	Smart casual
Style	Cocktail bar

"The whole experience is setting a benchmark for the Phoenix community. Ross Simon and the staff do a great job of making each experience memorable for every guest. Catch them on a Tuesday and have one of their boozy cupcakes—best snack ever for your inner drunken fat kid! I have to add: Ross DOES make a mean Ramos Gin Fizz."—Clint Spotleson

CRUDO

3603 East Indian School Road
Phoenix
Arizona 85018
United States
+1 6023588666
www.crudoaz.com

Opening hours	Closed Sunday and Monday
Reservation policy	Not accepted for drinks
Credit cards	Accepted
Price range	Affordable
Dress code	Smart casual
Style	Restaurant and cocktail bar

"The pig ears are my favorite bar snack of all time and I crave them all the time. Micah also has an awesome whiskey collection and usually is the first in the city to get most of the new ones, so there's always something new to taste!"
—Clint Spotleson

SHADY'S FINE ALES AND COCKTAILS

2701 East Indian School Road
Phoenix
Arizona 85016
United States
+1 6029568998

Opening hours	Open 7 days
Reservation policy	Not accepted for drinks
Credit cards	Accepted
Price range	Budget
Dress code	Casual
Style	Lounge

"It's got a 'divey' feel to it without being a dive. Shady's has a killer jukebox and is the kind of place where you can get a good beer and a shot, or a classic cocktail if you're in the mood. They always have the most random Netflix movie possible on the TV, which has led to many a night of subtitling what you think the actors are saying. Plus there's always an industry crowd, so you can find a friend there."
—Clint Spotleson

PRIZEFIGHTER

6702 Hollis Street
Emeryville
California 94608
United States
www.prizefighterbar.com

Opening hours	Open 7 days
Reservation policy	Accepted
Credit cards	Accepted
Price range	Affordable
Dress code	Casual
Style	Cocktail bar

"Prizefighter has achieved what I always wanted in a bar. The fun, loose atmosphere of a great local bar with the mind-set of a craft cocktail bar. It is open and airy with a great patio. The beer selection is fantastic. They serve punch by the bowl and the cocktails are top-notch. And the bartenders are hospitable and talented. PLUS, they have shuffleboard."
—Sean Kenyon

THE DAGGER BAR

16278 Pacific Coast Highway
Don the Beachcomber
Huntington Beach
California 92649
United States
+1 5625921321
www.donthebeachcomber.com

Opening hours	Open 7 days
Reservation policy	Accepted
Credit cards	Accepted
Price range	Affordable
Dress code	Casual
Style	Tiki bar

"I wish I would have opened it because the life of Don The Beachcomber has always fascinated me. This way I could continue and revitalize his ideas."—Adriano Costigliola

THE ALLEY

3325 Grand Avenue
Oakland
California 94610
United States
+1 5104448505

Opening hours	Open 7 days
Reservation policy	Not accepted for drinks
Credit cards	Not accepted
Price range	Budget
Dress code	Casual
Style	Dive bar

"This is one of my favorite places to end the night. It's a piano bar with a guy who's been playing for thirty years. It's a bar where it always feels like late night, as though perhaps you're in a slightly odd Edward Hopper painting. It has a little bit of that desolation, but feels old and timeless, with a history of people drinking there late at night."—Morgan Schick

HEINOLD'S FIRST AND LAST CHANCE SALOON

48 Webster Street
Oakland
California 94607
United States
+1 5108396761

Opening hours	Open 7 days
Reservation policy	Not accepted for drinks
Credit cards	Accepted but not AMEX
Price range	Budget
Dress code	Casual
Style	Dive bar

"Built in 1883 and it hasn't changed much, besides the extreme slope of the bar with the whole room sinking in toward the center. Walking in is like stepping back in time. Outside on the patio you'll find a diverse group of Oakland hipsters, families, professionals, and boatsmen enjoying pints and the Oakland waterfront. I frequent this place on Sunday afternoons and I've recommended it to travelers and other Bay Area residents looking to see a real slice of Oakland, California. During the 1920s, the ferry that ran between Alameda and Oakland stopped next to Heinold's. Alameda was a dry city at the time, and this bar was truly a commuter's first and last chance for a refreshment. As the years wore on, many servicemen left for overseas from the Port of Oakland, and the First and Last tradition stuck, so the name of the saloon was officially changed to Heinold's First and Last Chance."—Summer Jane Bell

RADIO BAR

435 13th Street
Oakland
California 94612
United States
+1 5104512889

Opening hours	Open 7 days
Reservation policy	Not accepted for drinks
Credit cards	Accepted
Price range	Budget
Dress code	Casual
Style	Dive bar

"Radio Bar is just straight up FUN. The music bumps with rotating DJs playing rock and roll or hip-hop. They serve till the bitter end. And I always run into people I know from different stages in my career. Coming here late night is like coming home to an awesome house party."
—Summer Jane Bell

PAPPY+HARRIET'S PIONEERTOWN PALACE

53688 Pioneertown Road
Pioneertown
California 92268
United States
+17603655956
www.pappyandharriets.com

Opening hours	Closed Tuesday and Wednesday
Reservation policy	Not accepted for drinks
Credit cards	Accepted
Price range	Affordable
Dress code	Casual
Style	Restaurant and bar

"It's a juke joint in an Old West-style town that was built for the Hollywood of the 1940s. They serve up awesome pit barbecue, cold beer, strong drinks and there's a live music set every night, often from nationally-touring acts. Once you've had your fill and danced your face off, you step outside to the patio and look up to see more stars than you knew existed."
—Andrew and Briana Volk

BACK DOOR LOUNGE

1112 Firehouse Alley
Old Sacramento Merchants
Sacramento
California 95814
United States
+1 9164425751

Opening hours	Open 7 days
Reservation policy	Not accepted for drinks
Credit cards	Accepted
Price range	Budget
Dress code	Casual
Style	Dive bar

"The Back Door is the raddest little hidden gem in Sacramento. It's in an alley in the historic tourist-heavy part of Old Sacramento. They have this guy, Lee Diamond, who does Sinatra-esque covers on the piano on weekends. I'm pretty sure that they don't hire anyone under fifty or their bartenders have been there since they were twenty. No frills here. Just a great place to hear great stories."—Jayson Wilde

SHADY LADY SALOON

1409 R Street
Sacramento
California 95811
United States
+1 9162319121
www.shadyladybar.com

Opening hours	Open 7 days
Reservation policy	Not accepted for drinks
Credit cards	Accepted
Price range	Affordable
Dress code	Smart casual
Style	Cocktail bar

"Shady Lady is where I cut my teeth. I spent twelve years working for an insurance company before jumping behind the bar to barback here. Within twenty minutes, I knew what I wanted to do with the rest of my life. Every time I walk through the door, even if don't know the bartenders, I always feel at home. They serve great food until midnight and their drink menu is both classic and progressive."—Jayson Wilde

BLIND LADY ALE HOUSE

3416 Adams Avenue
San Diego
California 92116
United States
+1 6192552491
www.blindlady.blogspot.com

Opening hours	Open 7 days
Reservation policy	Not accepted for drinks
Credit cards	Accepted
Price range	Affordable
Dress code	Casual
Style	Beer bar

"It's owned by one of the best beer brewers in the world, Lee Chase. He used to be the brewmaster for Stone Brewery when it opened, then he split to open his own little spot. He brews his own beers, it's incredible, he has amazing stuff on tap that no one else has. And they have incredible pizza. In my opinion it's one of the best beer bars in the world."
—Erick Castro

CANTINA MAYAHUEL

2934 Adams Avenue
San Diego
California 92116
United States
+1 6192836292

Opening hours	Open 7 days
Reservation policy	Not accepted for drinks
Credit cards	Accepted but not AMEX
Price range	Affordable
Dress code	Casual
Style	Mexican restaurant

"They make amazing Margaritas and Micheladas. They have great food and a killer tequila selection. All they have is tequila—no bourbon, no gin, only agave."—Erick Castro

COIN-OP GAME ROOM

3926 30th Street
San Diego
California 92104
United States
+1 6192558523
www.coinopsd.com

Opening hours...Open 7 days
Reservation policy............................Not accepted for drinks
Credit cards...Accepted
Price range..Budget
Dress code..Casual
Style...Bar and arcade

"At this point in my life I have fully embraced drinking while playing games. Yes, sure, I love catching up with a friend or just chatting with someone about the day, but in all honesty I would love to have that conversation while I'm beating them at NBA Jam or Buckhunter. Coin-Op has done this way too well: a room packed full of arcade games, mezcal for days, cocktails, and great bar food."—Trevor Easter

EL DORADO COCKTAIL LOUNGE

1030 Broadway
San Diego
California 92101
United States
+1 6192370550
www.eldoradobar.com

Opening hours...Open 7 days
Reservation policy..Accepted
Credit cards...Accepted
Price range..Budget
Dress code..Casual
Style..Cocktail bar

"This bar is in my top three favorite bars ever. There is something special about San Diego. This bar has that dive feel but can make you some of the best drinks. From what I can remember, I've never had a bad time there. I've guest bartended, blacked out, judged competitions, and made some of the dearest friends I have there."—Jayson Wilde

HOPE 46

2223 El Cajon Boulevard
The Lafayette Hotel
San Diego
California 92104
United States
+1 6197800358
www.lafayettehotelsd.com

Opening hours...Open 7 days
Reservation policy..Accepted
Credit cards...Accepted
Price range..Affordable
Dress code..Casual
Style..Restaurant and pool bar

"This places is great: just people hanging out having fun by the swimming pool. For decades, it was an old, classy hotel, but has now evolved into a happening spot for hipsters. You can get a decent classic, like a Gimlet or a Collins, but nothing too fancy. It's great people-watching and a fun place to hang out."—Erick Castro

LIVE WIRE

2103 El Cajon Boulevard
San Diego
California 92104
United States
+1 6192917450
www.livewirebar.com

Opening hours...Open 7 days
Reservation policy............................Not accepted for drinks
Credit cards...Accepted
Price range..Budget
Dress code..Casual
Style..Dive bar

"One of the first local dive bars to do really cool microbrews on tap. It might look like a shitty bar, but they've always been really serious about the beer program and they get all kinds of great stuff that no one else can get, like Pliny the Elder on tap. It's a beer bar: don't order a cocktail, don't ask for anything fancy. It's a killer spot that everybody parties at."—Erick Castro

NOBLE EXPERIMENT

777 G Street
San Diego
California 92101
United States
+1 6198884713
www.nobleexperimentsd.com

Opening hours	Closed Monday
Reservation policy	Accepted
Credit cards	Accepted
Price range	Affordable
Dress code	Smart casual
Style	Speakeasy

"The Noble Experiment: It's perfect because there's no windows so you never feel like you're out too late. It's the perfect place to escape the club scene of the Gaslamp District. It feels like a classic speakeasy where you kind of forget where you're at and it's very easy to lose track of time."—Erick Castro

POLITE PROVISIONS

4696 30th Street
San Diego
California 92116
United States
+1 6196773784
www.politeprovisions.com

Opening hours	Open 7 days
Reservation policy	Not accepted for drinks
Credit cards	Accepted
Price range	Affordable
Dress code	Casual
Style	Cocktail bar

ROCKY'S CROWN PUB

3786 Ingraham Street
San Diego
California 92109
United States
+1 8582739140
www.rockyburgers.com

Opening hours	Open 7 days
Reservation policy	Not accepted for drinks
Credit cards	Not accepted
Price range	Budget
Dress code	Casual
Style	Burger joint

"I don't care what anyone says, this place has the best burger in San Diego, and it doesn't hurt that they also have really good beer. The menu is pretty sparse, just burger and fries, that's it. If you want to be fancy you can order it with a slice of cheese. Go for the combo meal: burger, fries, and a beer."
—Erick Castro

TURF SUPPER CLUB

1116 25th Street
San Diego
California 92102
United States
+1 6192346363
www.turfsupperclub.com

Opening hours	Open 7 days
Reservation policy	Not accepted for drinks
Credit cards	Accepted
Price range	Affordable
Dress code	Casual
Style	Restaurant and bar

"Tucked up in South Park just up the hill from downtown San Diego, this old-school bar somehow landed here via a time machine, practically untouched since my Dad used to hang out here. What makes the place extra special is their famous blue bird bath cocktail called the 'Sneaky Tiki', the old horse racing decor, and the fact that when you order your steak or burger, you have to grill it yourself, drink in hand, rubbing elbows with the other guests."—Trevor Easter

THE BUCKHORN EXCHANGE

1000 Osage Street
Denver
Colorado 80204
United States
+1 3035349505
www.buckhorn.com

Opening hours	Open 7 days
Reservation policy	Accepted
Credit cards	Accepted
Price range	Affordable
Dress code	Casual
Style	Restaurant and bar

"The bar upstairs is 180 years old, and the restaurant is so replete with artifacts from the Wild West days that it resembles a cluttered museum. The food is campy: snake, alligator, and Rocky Mountain oysters. It's a must-see."
—Sean Kenyon

MY BROTHER'S BAR

2376 15th Street
Denver
Colorado 80202
United States
+1 3034559991
www.mybrothersbar.com

Opening hours	Closed Sunday
Reservation policy	Accepted
Credit cards	Accepted
Price range	Budget
Dress code	Casual
Style	Pub

"On any given night it is full with hospitality industry people, catching up after a shift, drinking whiskey and beer. They serve a great burger until 1 a.m."—Sean Kenyon

WILLIAMS & GRAHAM

3160 Tejon Street
Denver
Colorado 80211
United States
+1 3039978886
www.williamsandgraham.com

Opening hours	Open 7 days
Reservation policy	Accepted
Credit cards	Accepted
Price range	Affordable
Dress code	Smart casual
Style	Speakeasy

Considered the top cocktail bar in Denver, it is located behind a tiny bookstore facade, with entry via a bookshelf. Proprietor Sean Kenyon was named American Bartender of the Year at the 2012 Tales of the Cocktail Spirited Awards. The bar won Best American Cocktail Bar at those same awards in 2015 and was also named to the World's 50 Best Bar List in 2014.

L'APERITIF COCKTAIL BAR

2199 Kalia Road
La Mer
Halekulani Hotel
Honolulu
Hawaii 96815
United States
+1 8089232311
www.halekulani.com

Opening hours	Open 7 days
Reservation policy	Not accepted for drinks
Credit cards	Accepted
Price range	Expensive
Dress code	Formal
Style	Cocktail bar

"Henry makes L'Aperitif Bar classy. Great cocktails, well served, with a great atmosphere. Food pairing with the cocktails created by Vikram Garg make a great cocktail into a great experience."—Colin Field

HOUSE WITHOUT A KEY

2199 Kalia Road
Halekulani Hotel
Honolulu
Hawaii 96815
United States
+1 8442888022
www.halekulani.com

Opening hours	Open 7 days
Reservation policy	Not accepted for drinks
Credit cards	Accepted
Price range	Affordable
Dress code	Casual
Style	Beach bar

"It's on a beach under a tree with a view of the sunset." —Julie Reiner

LEWERS LOUNGE

2199 Kalia Road
Halekulani Hotel
Honolulu
Hawaii 96815
United States
+1 8089232311
www.halekulani.com

Opening hours	Open 7 days
Reservation policy	Not accepted for drinks
Credit cards	Accepted
Price range	Affordable
Dress code	Formal
Style	Lounge

"With a beverage program that Dale DeGroff reworked a number of years ago, this hidden gem inside the Halekulani Hotel is one of my favorite places to sneak away for a cocktail. When I'm feeling like treating myself to a great experience in a swanky environment, you can find me enjoying a well- crafted Negroni or sipping a whiskey at this great hotel bar."—Dave Newman

MURPHY'S BAR AND GRILL

2 Merchant Street
Honolulu
Hawaii 96816
United States
+1 8085310422
www.murphyshawaii.com

Opening hours	Open 7 days
Reservation policy	Not accepted for drinks
Credit cards	Accepted
Price range	Budget
Dress code	Casual
Style	Irish pub

"No other bar I have been to is as welcoming as Murphy's. The staff takes hospitality to the next level. Jonathan Schwalbenitz has been tending bar here for nearly a quarter century and instills his passion for hospitality in his crew. Everyone is treated the same whether you drink here three times a week or it's your first visit. They pour a mean pint and remember the way you like your Manhattan, not to mention your name."—Dave Newman

BUMBYE BEACH BAR

3550 Wailea Alanui Drive
The Andaz Maui at Wailea Resort
Wailea
Hawaii 96753
United States
+1 8085731234
www.maui.andaz.hyatt.com

Opening hours	Open 7 days
Reservation policy	Not accepted for drinks
Credit cards	Accepted
Price range	Affordable
Dress code	Casual
Style	Beach bar

"Because you can bartend and look out at the ocean. When that's your workspace, it's awesome. One day I want to retire there and only make Daiquiris."—Julie Reiner

HERBS & RYE

3713 West Sahara Avenue
Las Vegas
Nevada 89102
United States
+1 7029828036
www.herbsandrye.com

Opening hours	Closed Sunday
Reservation policy	Accepted
Credit cards	Accepted
Price range	Affordable
Dress code	Smart casual
Style	Restaurant and bar

"Herbs & Rye was the first truly craft cocktail bar to open in Vegas that embodies the cocktail movement we've been enjoying in the United States. Opened by Nectaly Mendoza in 2010, it's a great feel-good bar that makes fantastic cocktails and food. Plus, it's off the Strip and I love for our guests to experience all of Las Vegas, not just the Strip."—Tony Abou-Ganim

OAK & IVY

707 Fremont Street
Downtown Container Park
Las Vegas
Nevada 89101
United States
www.oakandivy.com

Opening hours	Open 7 days
Reservation policy	Not accepted for drinks
Credit cards	Accepted but not AMEX
Price range	Affordable
Dress code	Casual
Style	Cocktail bar

"When you think of Las Vegas, you think of the Strip, but there's an entire world and bartending community going on outside of that. When you get to the older portion of Vegas, they have a container park with old shipping containers converted into shop fronts. There's a cocktail bar there called Oak & Ivy that has maybe seven stools and a culinary-driven program and top bartending talent."—Rachel Ford

PETROSSIAN LOUNGE

3600 Las Vegas Boulevard South
Bellagio Hotel
Las Vegas
Nevada 89109
United States
+1 7026937111
www.bellagio.com

Opening hours	Open 7 days
Reservation policy	Not accepted for drinks
Credit cards	Accepted
Price range	Expensive
Dress code	Smart casual
Style	Lounge

"I opened the Bellagio in 1998 and this place holds a very special place in my heart. It's just off the casino floor, but it feels miles away. It's the kind of place where if you sit long enough, you'll see somebody you know, a great spot to escape the bells and whistles of Las Vegas."
—Tony Abou-Ganim

365 TOKYO

107 Las Vegas Boulevard South
Inspire Las Vegas
Las Vegas
Nevada 89101
United States
www.inspirelasvegas.com

Opening hours	Closed Sunday and Monday
Reservation policy	Members only
Credit cards	Accepted
Price range	Expensive
Dress code	Smart casual
Style	Cocktail bar

"365 Tokyo is comprised of only ten bar seats, is reservation only, and is completely mind blowing. The ice is beautifully hand chipped to order, some drinks are smoked with your choice of wood, and drinks such as the Amaretto Sour have elements that are even flambéed to order. It's flown under the radar despite being one of the best bars in the world."
—David Kaplan

BIT HOUSE SALOON

Southeast Grand Avenue
Portland
Oregon 97214
United States
+1 5039543913
www.bithousesaloon.com

Opening hours	Open 7 days
Reservation policy	Not accepted for drinks
Credit cards	Accepted
Price range	Affordable
Dress code	Casual
Style	Cocktail bar

"Everything about that place is 100%."—Will Hollingsworth

CLYDE COMMON

1014 Southwest Stark Street
Ace Hotel
Portland
Oregon 97205
United States
+1 5032283333
www.clydecommon.com

Opening hours	Open 7 days
Reservation policy	Not accepted for drinks
Credit cards	Accepted
Price range	Affordable
Dress code	Casual
Style	Restaurant and bar

"With a more laid-back approach than what is usually associated with a hotel bar, Clyde Common makes you feel right at home, even when you are very far away."
—Naomi Levy

"We met, fell in love, and got engaged at Clyde Common. Not to mention, the drinks are incredible, the staff is on point and it continues to be one of the standout places in Portland, Oregon. We travel back several times a year to drink here."
—Andrew and Briana Volk

HORSE BRASS PUB

4534 Southeast Belmont Street
Portland
Oregon 97215
United States
+1 5032322202
www.horsebrass.com

Opening hours	Open 7 days
Reservation policy	Not accepted for drinks
Credit cards	Accepted
Price range	Affordable
Dress code	Casual
Style	Pub

"This is where the craft beer revolution in this country started. It was where the folks who are now huge names in brewing got together and traded their love for beer. It's a piece of modern history."—Jeffrey Morgenthaler

HUBER'S CAFE

411 Southwest 3rd Avenue
Portland
Oregon 97204
United States
+1 5032285686
www.hubers.com

Opening hours	Open 7 days
Reservation policy	Accepted
Credit cards	Accepted
Price range	Affordable
Dress code	Smart casual
Style	Restaurant and bar

"Huber's is one of the oldest bars in Portland and they've been making their Spanish Coffee—a combination of 151, Triple Sec, Kahlua, and coffee served in a wine glass with a caramelized-sugar rim topped with whipped cream—since the mid 1970s . . . It's something you really have to experience when in Portland."—Jeffrey Morgenthaler

IMPERIAL

410 Southwest Broadway
Portland
Oregon 97205
United States
+1 5032287222
www.imperialpdx.com

Opening hours	Open 7 days
Reservation policy	Not accepted for drinks
Credit cards	Accepted
Price range	Affordable
Dress code	Smart casual
Style	Restaurant and bar

"To paraphrase Tennessee Williams, America only has two beverage towns: New York and Portland. Everywhere else is Cleveland. Imperial manages to tuck a true Portland bar into a Kimpton property in South West, and they do it very, very well. Casual, funny service, great drinks, great ice, and the feeling that you're where you deserve to be—which, even in a hotel bar, is a tough vibe to pull off." —Will Hollingsworth

MARY'S CLUB

129 Southwest Broadway
Portland
Oregon 97209
United States
+1 5032273023
www.marysclub.com

Opening hours	Open 7 days
Reservation policy	Not accepted for drinks
Credit cards	Accepted but not AMEX
Price range	Budget
Dress code	Casual
Style	Strip club

"It's Portland's oldest strip club, something of a local landmark. It's family owned and run entirely by women. There's a certain homey feel to it, if your home is the sort of place that screams with rock and roll and is crawling with strippers."—Jeffrey Morgenthaler

MULTNOMAH WHISKEY LIBRARY

1124 Southwest Alder Street
Portland
Oregon 97205
United States
+1 5039541381
www.mwlpdx.com

Opening hours	Closed Sunday
Reservation policy	Members only
Credit cards	Accepted
Price range	Affordable
Dress code	Smart casual
Style	Cocktail and whiskey bar

"The first time I walked into this bar I literally said, 'I bet this is what heaven looks like for whiskey drinkers.' Tommy Klus did an amazing job of putting this program together and the space is simply breathtaking. The whiskey selection alone would be worth the flight, but put it all together and I would be hard-pressed to find another bar that I would travel farther to enjoy."—Dave Newman

PEPE LE MOKO

407 Southwest 10th Avenue
Ace Hotel
Portland
Oregon 97205
United States
+1 5035468537
www.pepelemokopdx.com

Opening hours	Open 7 days
Reservation policy	Accepted
Credit cards	Accepted
Price range	Affordable
Dress code	Smart casual
Style	Cocktail bar

"While visiting Portland for cocktail week, my husband and I discovered this underground cocktail den and returned every evening for five days straight! What makes this bar so special? On our first visit, we were offered the sole available table, nicknamed the 'hot tub' for its rounded booth and private corner location, but were warned that some people find it too private. Not us! The 'hot tub' provided us with the perfect amount of solace while we enjoyed fresh West Coast oysters and expertly made cocktails and soaked up the dimly lit and cozy atmosphere."—Rachel Ford

RUM CLUB

720 Southeast Sandy Boulevard
Portland
Oregon 97214
United States
+1 5032658807
www.rumclubpdx.com

Opening hours	Open 7 days
Reservation policy	Not accepted for drinks
Credit cards	Accepted
Price range	Affordable
Dress code	Casual
Style	Cocktail bar

"In a city filled with amazing bars and great bartenders, it's pretty awesome to have an industry bar like Rum Club. People talk about how much the company you keep affects how you feel about the places you are in . . . but there is more to Rum Club than who you walk in with. Every time I have gone to this bar, I have run into so many familiar industry faces that I can't believe are in the same place at the same time. So for me, grabbing a late-night drink really can't beat my visits to Portland and my time sitting at the bar at Rum Club."—Dave Newman

SPIRIT OF 77

500 Northeast Martin Luther King Jr Boulevard
Portland
Oregon 97232
United States
+1 5032329977
www.spiritof77bar.com

Opening hours	Open 7 days
Reservation policy	Accepted
Credit cards	Accepted
Price range	Budget
Dress code	Casual
Style	Sports bar

"I've always admired American sports bars. I think they only really work in the United States because of the way sport is televised there. All year, there are at least two competitions running between baseball, basketball, soccer, hockey, and football. The teams mostly play six days a week and there are two time zones on the East and West coast. This means there's live sports ALL THE TIME. Spirit of 77 is the perfect place to watch said sports and drink great beer and cocktails. There are also tvs everywhere, and FREE basketball arcade games. Fun, without being tacky, dingy, or dirty."
—Tim Philips

TEARDROP LOUNGE

1015 Northwest Everett Street
Portland
Oregon 97209
United States
+1 5034458109
www.teardroplounge.com

Opening hours	Open 7 days
Reservation policy	Not accepted for drinks
Credit cards	Accepted
Price range	Affordable
Dress code	Smart casual
Style	Cocktail bar

"Daniel Shoemaker opened the first 'cocktail bar' in the city, and his team still serves some of the best drinks in town."—Jim Meehan

CANON

928 12th Avenue
Seattle
Washington 98122
United States
www.canonseattle.com

Opening hours	Open 7 days
Reservation policy	Accepted
Credit cards	Accepted
Price range	Affordable
Dress code	Smart casual
Style	Cocktail bar

"The biggest selection of spirits in the Western Hemisphere, amazing cocktails. Whenever I travel to Seattle, it is one of the places that I always make a trek to."—Shawn Soole

HAZLEWOOD

2311 Northwest Market Street
Seattle
Washington 98107
United States
+1 2067830478

Opening hours	Open 7 days
Reservation policy	Accepted
Credit cards	Accepted
Price range	Affordable
Dress code	Casual
Style	Cocktail bar

"Hazlewood is owned by rockers Drew Church and Ben Shepherd. Themed after a love for Lee Hazlewood, this place is perfect. Great location, perfect-sized bar, great drinks, giant cow skulls, and a great mezzanine. If you go upstairs there is a little peephole and when you press the button, an image becomes illuminated . . . but I guess you'll have to find out for yourself what it is."—Greg West

LIBERTY

517 15th Avenue East
Seattle
Washington 98102
United States
+1 2063239898
www.libertybars.com

Opening hours	Open 7 days
Reservation policy	Accepted
Credit cards	Accepted
Price range	Budget
Dress code	Casual
Style	Cocktail bar

"Say what you want about this neighborhood dive but this is the sort of spot I want to 'retire' with. Coffee shop by day, high-end cocktail bar by night. Relaxed, gritty, community supporting. 'Why do you have thirty-plus mezcals and Japanese whiskeys?' 'Because I want to.' There is no rhyme or reason to the place; it's what the owner wanted cause it was his —very liberating."—Shawn Soole

ROB ROY

2332 2nd Avenue
Seattle
Washington 98121
United States
+1 2069568423
www.robroyseattle.com

Opening hours	Open 7 days
Reservation policy	Accepted
Credit cards	Accepted
Price range	Affordable
Dress code	Smart casual
Style	Cocktail bar

"It's a cool neighborhood, cool locals that hang out there, and it's progressive enough to be a great cocktail bar, but also laid-back so you can have a beer with your friends, or a glass of wine."—Sother Teague

"A GREAT OLD HOLLYWOOD SALOON."

DALE DEGROFF P.253

LOS ANGELES

"IT'S A 70s-THEMED BAR, DECKED OUT TO LOOK LIKE YOUR HAIRY-CHESTED, OPEN-SHIRTED UNCLE'S APARTMENT."

PAYMAN BAHMANI P.253

"ALWAYS THE ADDED BONUS OF CATCHING AN A-LIST ROCK STAR OR CELEB ON THE TURNTABLES RIPPING INTO SOME VINYL."

TREVOR EASTER P.254

"ALMOST LIKE A CHOOSE-YOUR-OWN-ADVENTURE BAR!"

KAREN GRILL P.254

"A GREAT WAY TO FEEL LIKE YOU'RE IN THE HOLLYWOOD OF THE RAT PACK ERA."

ERIC ALPERIN P.255

LOS ANGELES

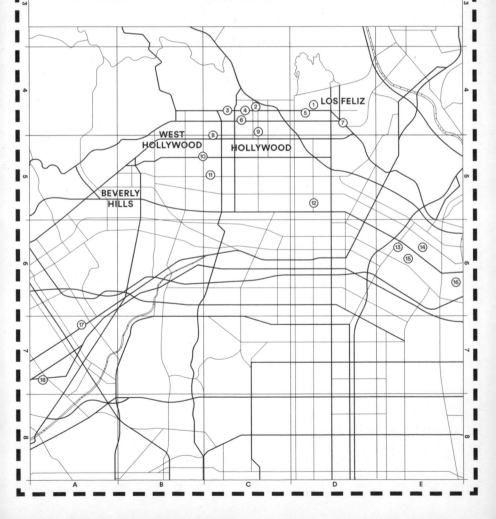

N

SCALE

0   1500   3000   4500

yd.

1. JUMBO'S CLOWN ROOM (P.254)
2. GOOD TIMES
   AT DAVEY WAYNE'S (P.253)
3. THE SPARE ROOM (P.256)
4. MUSSO & FRANK GRILL (P.255)
5. HARVARD & STONE (P.254)
6. BOARDNER'S (P.253)

7. TIKI-TI (P.256)
8. HARLOWE (P.254)
9. SASSAFRAS (P.256)
10. MELROSE UMBRELLA
    COMPANY (P.255)
11. PETTY CASH TAQUERIA (P.255)
12. THE WALKER INN (P.257)

13. THE CORNER DOOR (P.253)
14. THE VARNISH (P.257)
15. GOLDEN GOPHER (P.253)
16. TONY'S SALOON (P.256)
17. OLDFIELD'S LIQUOR ROOM (P.255)
18. HONEYCUT (P.254)

LOS FELIZ

WEST
HOLLYWOOD

HOLLYWOOD

BEVERLY
HILLS

COCKTAILS IN LOS ANGELES

The cocktail scene in Los Angeles is a relatively new one. Unbound by the deep historic influences that inform cities like San Francisco and New York, Los Angeles is gradually charting its own course. The Varnish was one of the first serious cocktail bars to hit the city in 2009, and since then a plethora of bars have popped up all over the city.

One of Los Angeles's defining characteristics is a laid-back atmosphere that doesn't take itself too seriously. You're far more likely to drink a great cocktail here while dancing on a light-up floor than quietly seated at a speakeasy. This attitude is reflected in the drinks themselves, which focus on fresh ingredients and tend toward the adventurous. Another hallmark of Los Angeles is that great cocktail programs are often found in restaurants.

Though many associate Los Angeles with Hollywood and the entertainment industry, it is in reality a sprawling collection of towns, with an incredible spread and pockets of communities of people from around the world. This diversity is reflected in its bar scene.

For glitz and glamour look no further than Beverly Hills and West Hollywood. Hollywood and East Hollywood have a rock-and-roll party scene with bars like Harvard & Stone. On the other hand Culver City, Silver Lake, and Los Feliz have a more casual vibe. Newly revitalized Downtown Los Angeles offers an incredibly diverse scene from casual neighborhood bars like Golden Gopher, to speakeasy-style The Varnish, to high-energy cocktail nightclub Honeycut. Whatever you do, don't leave town without having a Martini at Musso & Frank's.

Practical Information:
— Cocktails range from about US$12 to US$14 each.
— Standard tipping is 20%.

MOSCOW MULE

The Moscow Mule was invented in Los Angeles in 1941—the result of a bar with a surplus of ginger beer and marketing execs who were promoting Smirnoff vodka. It's traditionally served in a copper mug.

BOARDNER'S
1652 North Cherokee Avenue
Los Angeles
California 90028
United States
+1 3234629621
www.boardners.com

Opening hours	Open 7 days
Reservation policy	Not accepted for drinks
Credit cards	Accepted
Price range	Affordable
Dress code	Casual
Style	Cocktail bar

"A great old Hollywood saloon."—Dale DeGroff

THE CORNER DOOR
12477 West Washington Boulevard
Los Angeles
California 90066
United States
+1 3103135810
www.thecornerdoorla.com

Opening hours	Open 7 days
Reservation policy	Not accepted for drinks
Credit cards	Accepted
Price range	Affordable
Dress code	Smart casual
Style	Restaurant and bar

"The Corner Door is one of those places that will exceed expectations the moment you walk through the door. It's a simple-looking place, the kind of neighborhood haunt we're drawn to because it's so damn comfortable. But hiding inside is one of Los Angeles's best bar programs overseen by one of our city's best bartenders, Beau de Bois. It's not just great cocktails (though they're amazing), The Corner Door fires on all cylinders with a well-rounded bar and excellent food. I only wish I lived closer."—Alex Day

GOLDEN GOPHER
417 West 8th Street
Los Angeles
California 90014
United States
+1 2136148001
www.213nightlife.com/goldengopher

Opening hours	Open 7 days
Reservation policy	Not accepted for drinks
Credit cards	Accepted
Price range	Affordable
Dress code	Smart casual
Style	Lounge

"Golden Gopher opened in Downtown Los Angeles in 1905 and was the first liquor license in Downtown . . . This liquor license has the only off-premise condition, so on your way out, as long as it's not 2 a.m., you can cash and carry a six-pack and your favorite bottle of booze."—Eric Alperin

GOOD TIMES AT DAVEY WAYNE'S
1611 North El Centro Avenue
Los Angeles
California 90028
United States
+1 3239623804
www.goodtimesatdaveywaynes.com

Opening hours	Open 7 days
Reservation policy	Accepted
Credit cards	Accepted
Price range	Affordable
Dress code	Smart casual
Style	Cocktail bar

"When you walk into Davey Wayne's (which is essentially through a refrigerator door at the back of a vintage-threads stall), you basically walk into Jack Tripper's apartment. It's a 70s-themed bar, decked out to look like your hairy-chested, open-shirted uncle's apartment. Sometimes there's a funky band of some sort, but most often there's a DJ in the 'living room' playing all the most awesome classic rock songs of the 1960s and 1970s. And it always inspires dancing—I mean serious dancing . . . There's even a backyard with an Airstream fitted with a bar that sells boozy snowcones . . . I've never walked into Davey Wayne's and not had an awesome time."—Payman Bahmani

HARLOWE

7321 Santa Monica Boulevard
Los Angeles
California 90046
United States
+1 3238765839
www.harlowebar.com

Opening hours	Open 7 days
Reservation policy	Not accepted for drinks
Credit cards	Accepted
Price range	Affordable
Dress code	Smart casual
Style	Cocktail bar

An upscale cocktail bar inspired by Hollywood's Golden Age serving original and classic cocktails and bar snacks.

HARVARD & STONE

5221 Hollywood Boulevard
Los Angeles
California 90027
United States
+1 3234666063
www.harvardandstone.com

Opening hours	Open 7 days
Reservation policy	Accepted
Credit cards	Accepted
Price range	Affordable
Dress code	Smart casual
Style	Cocktail bar

"Cans of beer, dark industrial digs, burlesques dancers swinging from the rafters, rock and roll, and some of the best bartenders in the city. What's not to love about popping into this place at 12 a.m.? There is always the added bonus of catching an A-list rock star or celeb on the turntables ripping into some vinyl."—Trevor Easter

HONEYCUT

819 South Flower Street
Los Angeles
California 90017
United States
+1 2136880888
www.honeycutla.com

Opening hours	Closed Monday
Reservation policy	Accepted for groups of 8 or more
Credit cards	Accepted
Price range	Affordable
Dress code	Smart casual
Style	Cocktail bar and dance club

"It's almost like a choose-your-own-adventure bar! There's one side of the bar that is more like a dark cocktail lounge and one side that is a disco party, complete with light-up disco floor and draft cocktails."—Karen Grill

JUMBO'S CLOWN ROOM

5153 Hollywood Boulevard
Los Angeles
California 90027
United States
+1 3236661187
www.jumbos.com

Opening hours	Open 7 days
Reservation policy	Not accepted for drinks
Credit cards	Accepted
Price range	Affordable
Dress code	Casual
Style	Strip club

"A Los Angeles institution for a shot and a beer and a great line-up of burlesque dancers."—Eric Alperin

MELROSE UMBRELLA COMPANY

7465 Melrose Avenue
Los Angeles
California 90046
United States
+1 3239510709
www.melroseumbrellaco.com

Opening hours	Open 7 days
Reservation policy	Not accepted for drinks
Credit cards	Accepted
Price range	Affordable
Dress code	Smart casual
Style	Cocktail bar

"A bar where everyone is allowed in and the only requirement is that you have fun . . . Late night it's not a surprise to see bartenders standing on the bar pouring shots for the adoring crowd while listening to the sounds of legions of patrons singing along to Prince's 'Little Red Corvette'."—Julian Cox

OLDFIELD'S LIQUOR ROOM

10899 Venice Boulevard
Los Angeles
California 90034
United States
+1 3108428066
www.oldfieldsliquorroom.com

Opening hours	Open 7 days
Reservation policy	Accepted
Credit cards	Accepted
Price range	Affordable
Dress code	Smart casual
Style	Cocktail bar

"I swing by Oldfield's sometimes after work if I know one of my favorite bartenders, Robin Jackson, is working. Robin is the real deal . . . You could stop paying her, insist that she has no shifts, but you can bet your ass, she'll still be studying and swizzling top-notch drinks."—Beau du Bois

MUSSO & FRANK GRILL

6667 Hollywood Boulevard
Los Angeles
California 90028
United States
+1 3234677788
www.mussoandfrank.com

Opening hours	Closed Monday
Reservation policy	Not accepted for drinks
Credit cards	Accepted
Price range	Affordable
Dress code	Smart casual
Style	Restaurant and bar

"It's a great way to feel like you're in the Hollywood of the Rat Pack era. Sit at the bar and let Manny (twenty-year veteran bartender) make you a Martini."—Eric Alperin

PETTY CASH TAQUERIA

7360 Beverly Boulevard
Los Angeles
California 90036
United States
+1 3239335300
www.pettycashtaqueria.com

Opening hours	Open 7 days
Reservation policy	Not accepted for drinks
Credit cards	Accepted
Price range	Affordable
Dress code	Casual
Style	Taqueria

"It's a taqueria and a bar and it's awesome."—Dushan Zaric

SASSAFRAS

1233 North Vine Street
Los Angeles
California 90038
United States
+1 3234672800
www.sassafrashollywood.com

Opening hours	Open 7 days
Reservation policy	Accepted
Credit cards	Accepted
Price range	Affordable
Dress code	Casual
Style	Cocktail bar

"I've never seen an atmosphere come close to what they've built at Sassafras. Name another bar that has a large house inside it, surrounded by hanging moss. Combine the atmosphere with one the most creative bartenders I've ever met, Karen Grill, and you've got an experience that's just crazy enough to remind you that you're in Los Angeles."
—Beau du Bois

THE SPARE ROOM

7000 Hollywood Boulevard
The Hollywood Roosevelt Hotel
Los Angeles
California 90028
United States
+1 3237697296
www.spareroomhollywood.com

Opening hours	Closed Tuesday
Reservation policy	Not accepted for drinks
Credit cards	Accepted
Price range	Affordable
Dress code	Smart casual
Style	Gaming parlor and cocktail lounge

"Delicious cocktails, bowling, and board games are the three things that will get me off the couch and into an Uber."—Trevor Easter

"So much fun. And not boring like most hotel bars."
—Elad Zvi

TIKI-TI

4427 Sunset Boulevard
Los Angeles
California 90027
United States
+1 3236699381
www.tiki-ti.com

Opening hours	Open Wednesday–Saturday
Reservation policy	Not accepted for drinks
Credit cards	Not accepted
Price range	Affordable
Dress code	Casual
Style	Tiki bar

"Open only Wednesday through Saturday, with just twelve seats at the bar, this tiny room offers eighty-two impeccably mixed tropical drinks, many of them served just as they were at America's first tiki bar, Don The Beachcomber's of Hollywood. The Tiki-Ti was founded in 1961 by one of the Beachcomber's original 1934 bartenders, Ray Buhen; it's now run by his son, Mike, and grandson, Mike Jr., who maintain a relaxed, friendly, neighborhood vibe. No velvet rope here. The house specialty is the Ray's Mistake, a secret recipe that regulars have been trying to figure out for decades. You also can't go wrong with a Rum Barrel or a Puka Puka. If you're not driving, try a Great White Shark (which has a bite like one)."
—Jeff "Beachbum" Berry

TONY'S SALOON

2017 East 7th Street
Los Angeles
California 90021
United States
+1 2136225523
www.213nightlife.com/tonyssaloon

Opening hours	Open 7 days
Reservation policy	Not accepted for drinks
Credit cards	Accepted
Price range	Budget
Dress code	Casual
Style	Whiskey bar

"This is the perfect everyday, any day bar—in part because it's a short two-block walk from my Los Angeles home. They have great go-to cocktails, cheap drinks, a big outdoor space with a ping-pong table, and an outdoor bar on the weekend. Like any great neighborhood bar, it's open seven days a week and you know what you're getting every night."
—David Kaplan

THE VARNISH

118 East 6th Street
Los Angeles
California 90014
United States
+1 2132657089
www.213nightlife.com/thevarnish

Opening hours..Open 7 days
Reservation policy....................................Not accepted for drinks
Credit cards...Accepted
Price range...Affordable
Dress code...Smart casual
Style..Speakeasy

"The Varnish is Los Angeles's original craft cocktail house and
one that is still hard to beat. The drinks are brilliant and the
hospitality is always top-notch."—David Kaplan

THE WALKER INN

3612 West 6th Street
The Normandie Club
Hotel Normandie
Los Angeles
California 90005
United States
+1 2132632709
www.thewalkerinnla.com

Opening hours....................................Open Wednesday–Sunday
Reservation policy...Accepted
Credit cards...Accepted
Price range..Expensive
Dress code...Smart casual
Style..Speakeasy

"There are not enough words to describe this bar. From
the moment you ring the buzzer at the secret door, the
experience is exhilarating. The tableside service is perfect,
the cocktails are some of the most beautiful I've ever seen,
and the space is gorgeous. I've never had more bar envy in
my life."—Karen Grill

SAN FRANCISCO

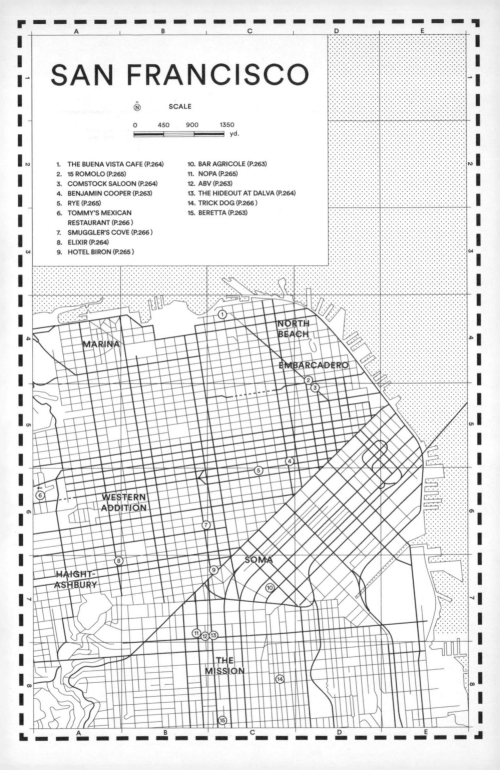

SAN FRANCISCO

N̂   SCALE

0   450   900   1350
yd.

1. THE BUENA VISTA CAFE (P.264)
2. 15 ROMOLO (P.265)
3. COMSTOCK SALOON (P.264)
4. BENJAMIN COOPER (P.263)
5. RYE (P.265)
6. TOMMY'S MEXICAN
   RESTAURANT (P.266)
7. SMUGGLER'S COVE (P.266)
8. ELIXIR (P.264)
9. HOTEL BIRON (P.265)
10. BAR AGRICOLE (P.263)
11. NOPA (P.265)
12. ABV (P.263)
13. THE HIDEOUT AT DALVA (P.264)
14. TRICK DOG (P.266)
15. BERETTA (P.263)

MARINA

NORTH
BEACH

EMBARCADERO

WESTERN
ADDITION

SOMA

HAIGHT-
ASHBURY

THE
MISSION

COCKTAILS IN
SAN FRANCISCO

The San Francisco bar scene runs the gamut from dive bar to tavern to speakeasy to tiki bar and everything in between. Its long and illustrious cocktail history has roots in the 1849 gold rush, which brought with it a multitude of thirsty miners and immigrants from around the world and spawned classics including the Martini. A century later, in 1944, tiki took root here, fostered by Vic Bergeron of Trader Vic's, inventor of the Mai Tai. And in the 2000s, the city has been at the vanguard of the modern cocktail renaissance.

This history is on display in the city's vast and varied bars. Comstock Saloon (located near what used to be known as the Devil's Acre because of the sheer density of bars) pays homage to the late 1800s with excellently executed classics. At Smuggler's Cove, which boasts the largest collection of rum in the country, the tiki tradition is alive and kicking. And at Trick Dog, in the Mission District, you'll find as inventive and innovative a cocktail selection as you can imagine.

The Californian focus on fresh, local ingredients is also reflected in its bar scene, where the citrus in your drink is as likely to be as local as the gin. Craft distilling was practically born here, when St. George Spirits set up shop in 1982. More recent additions include 209 Gin, Fernet Francisco (a local version of the popular Italian bitter liqueur Fernet-Branca), and Sutton Cellars vermouth.

In addition to the aforementioned bars, a visit to San Francisco is only complete with an Irish Coffee at The Buena Vista Café. This classic waterfront saloon may be a tourist destination, but it is also a pilgrimage site for bartenders and the perfect way to warm up on a gray, foggy day.

Practical Information:
- Cocktail prices start around US$10 and top out at US$16.
- Standard tipping is 20%, or US$2 to US$3 per drink.

TOMMY'S MARGARITA

The origins of the Margarita—the tequila, lime, and Cointreau classic—remain murky, but this variation, a bartender favorite, was created by Julio Bermejo in 1987 at his family's Tommy's Bar in San Francisco, where they substitute the traditional Cointreau for agave syrup.

MAI TAI

The Mai Tai is one of the most iconic of tiki cocktails, created by Vic Bergeron in 1944 at his eponymous Trader Vic's in Oakland in the Bay Area. The original recipe calls for the seventeen-year-old J. Wray & Nephew rum from Jamaica, combined with lime, orange curaçao, and orgeat, an almond syrup made with orange flower water.

Supposedly, Vic served it to a Tahitian friend who pronounced the drink *"Maita'i roa ae!"* or *"Very good!"* Trader Vic's is no longer around, but Smuggler's Cove is the perfect place to experience this tiki classic.

MARTINI / MARTINEZ

The Martini as we know it today—a combination of gin or vodka with varying amounts of dry vermouth—originated as the Martinez, with gin, maraschino, and sweet vermouth. Legend has it that this was first made in the town of Martinez, just north of San Francisco, for a thirsty gold miner in the mid-1800s. You can sip a perfect example of the original or its more modern offspring at the Comstock Saloon.

ABV

3174 16th Street
San Francisco
California 94103
United States
+1 4154004748
www.abvsf.com

Opening hours..Open 7 days
Reservation policy.................................Not accepted for drinks
Credit cards...Accepted
Price range...Affordable
Dress code...Casual
Style...Cocktail bar

"ABV in SF is my idea of a perfect neighborhood bar. Both the food and drinks are incredible. I never have to worry about my selection because EVERYTHING there is excellent. Every bartender there is somebody I could lose a few hours in front of."—Jayson Wilde

"Great mezcal selection, good beer and wine, great food served late. Plus they have a little bit of sherry."
—Caitlin Laman

"You can sit in the front bar area and sip on cocktails, or curated spirits, and eat delicious bar snacks. Through the front window you can see all your friends passing by and invite them in. It is a comfortable, unpretentious space with a graffiti logo on the walls. The spirits selection, particularly, the agave, is top-notch."—Lynnette Marrero

ABV has quickly become a local favorite and won Best New American Cocktail Bar at the 2015 Tales of the Cocktail Spirited Awards.

BAR AGRICOLE

355 11th Street
San Francisco
California 94103
United States
+1 4153559400
www.baragricole.com

Opening hours..Closed Sunday
Reservation policy.................................Not accepted for drinks
Credit cards...Accepted
Price range...Affordable
Dress code...Smart casual
Style...Restaurant and cocktail bar

"Because the drinks are so good and the service is wonderful."—Morgan Schick

BENJAMIN COOPER

398 Geary Street
Hotel G
San Francisco
California 94102
United States
+1 4159862000
www.benjamincoopersf.com

Opening hours..Closed Sunday
Reservation policy.................................Not accepted for drinks
Credit cards...Accepted
Price range...Affordable
Dress code...Smart casual
Style...Cocktail and oyster bar

"This new and tucked-away gem is owned by two bartenders I adore. They are the ultimate hosts, making everyone feel welcome and at ease while shaking up some of the most original yet approachable cocktails in town. Dealer's Choice is their specialty and I'm always wowed by the creativity and intuitive skill of Brian Felley and Mo Hodges. I love this place!" —Summer Jane Bell

BERETTA

1199 Valencia Street
San Francisco
California 94110
United States
+1 4156951199
www.berettasf.com

Opening hours..Open 7 days
Reservation policy...Accepted
Credit cards...Accepted
Price range...Affordable
Dress code...Smart casual
Style...Italian restaurant and cocktail bar

"This is the sort of buzzy neighborhood restaurant bar that you wish you had just down your street. They serve great food and brilliant drinks, but make no fuss about either. In a decade's time, when good drinks become a given in every neighborhood, I think every bar will look and feel a lot like Beretta."—Jacob Briars

THE BUENA VISTA CAFE

2765 Hyde Street
San Francisco
California 94109
United States
+1 4154745044
www.thebuenavista.com

Opening hours	Open 7 days
Reservation policy	Not accepted for drinks
Credit cards	Accepted
Price range	Affordable
Dress code	Casual
Style	Cafe and bar

"They do one thing and they do it great: Irish Coffee. Have a couple there, hopefully see the bartender do some magic, then order Irish Coffees 'to go' and walk along the water."
—Ryan Fitzgerald

COMSTOCK SALOON

155 Columbus Avenue
San Francisco
California 94133
United States
+1 4156170071
www.comstocksaloon.com

Opening hours	Open 7 days
Reservation policy	Not accepted for drinks
Credit cards	Accepted
Price range	Affordable
Dress code	Smart casual
Style	Restaurant and cocktail bar

"It's the perfect place to cap off your night with a fantastic staff, and a lively mix of regulars, tourists, and local eccentrics who give the place a convivial atmosphere. Sometimes you catch a little jazz combo swinging in the balcony as a bonus, which makes that last Old Fashioned taste all the better. Pulling up a stool with a drink in your hand as you watch the nightlife of North Beach go by through the panoramic windows is surely a defining San Francisco experience."—Martin Cate

"To be honest, I have only been there once (I live on the other side of the country), but the bar made such an impression on me that I have thought and/or spoken about it probably once a week for the intervening five years."—Phoebe Esmon

ELIXIR

3200 16th Street
San Francisco
California 94103
United States
+1 4155521633
www.elixirsf.com

Opening hours	Open 7 days
Reservation policy	Not accepted for drinks
Credit cards	Accepted
Price range	Affordable
Dress code	Casual
Style	Cocktail bar

"It is a staple in San Francisco and always full of locals. I often find myself here flying solo and I'm always welcomed by the regulars. You can get a great drink or just sip on a beer and soak up the local flavor in this vibrant neighborhood."
—Charles Joly

THE HIDEOUT AT DALVA

3121 16th Street
San Francisco
California 94103
United States
+1 4152527740
www.dalvasf.com/hideout

Opening hours	Open 7 days
Reservation policy	Not accepted for drinks
Credit cards	Not accepted
Price range	Affordable
Dress code	Casual
Style	Cocktail bar

"Punk rock cocktail bar—small bar with no pretense. Great, innovative cocktails and loud music—mostly restaurant industry crowd. Solid selection of tequila, mezcal, and scotch along with a variety of canned or bottled beer. No nonsense."
—Ryan Fitzgerald

HOTEL BIRON

45 Rose Street
San Francisco
California 94102
United States
+1 4157030403
www.hotelbiron.com

Opening hours	Open 7 days
Reservation policy	Not accepted for drinks
Credit cards	Accepted
Price range	Affordable
Dress code	Smart Casual
Style	Wine Bar

"This is a small, half-hidden wine bar that just hits on so many of my favorite touchpoints: a tight but very solid wine list, meats and cheeses, moody lighting, and a very cool crowd. I love it."—Neyah White

NOPA

560 Divisadero Street
San Francisco
California 94117
United States
+1 4158648643
www.nopasf.com

Opening hours	Open 7 days
Reservation policy	Not accepted for drinks
Credit cards	Accepted
Price range	Affordable
Dress code	Smart casual
Style	Restaurant and bar

"It's a restaurant with a full bar—always great cocktails, totally unfamiliar wines by the glass, with very knowledge-able staff. Outstanding food with lots of 'healthy' options. Serving that incredible food until 1 a.m. helps. Also, it's literally around the corner from my house. Don't know what I did before it opened."—Ryan Fitzgerald

15 ROMOLO

15 Romolo Place
The Basque Hotel
San Francisco
California 94133
United States
+1 4153981359
www.15romolo.com

Opening hours	Open 7 days
Reservation policy	Not accepted for drinks
Credit cards	Accepted
Price range	Affordable
Dress code	Smart casual
Style	Cocktail bar

"This bar will forever be my spirit animal. Curious concoctions delight those in search of something new, paired with late-night bar bites or a bibulous weekend brunch. Hidden up an alleyway in San Francisco's North Beach, right off of colorful Broadway, surrounded by strip clubs, this cocktail den has an awesome jukebox and photo booth to guarantee good times. With the proliferation of cocktail bars in the surrounding area, this is always a great place to start or end up."—Kyle Ford

RYE

688 Geary Street
San Francisco
California 94102
United States
+1 4154744448

Opening hours	Open 7 days
Reservation policy	Not accepted for drinks
Credit cards	Accepted
Price range	Affordable
Dress code	Casual
Style	Cocktail bar

"Rye is the epitome of an industry bar. Nestled comfortably in San Francisco's Tendernob, it's a central destination. Perhaps that's why everyone who is anyone in the restaurant and bar industry frequents this spot for late-night cocktails. With the hyperbolic mélange of ingredients found on cocktail menus these days, Rye keeps it simple. Fresh ingredients change daily and are incorporated into classically styled templates (i.e., their Basil Gimlet). It also happens to be my alma mater, where I first made my foray into craft cocktails. That said, it will always have a special place in my heart."
—Kyle Ford

SMUGGLER'S COVE

650 Gough Street
San Francisco
California 94102
United States
+1 4158691900
www.smugglerscovesf.com

Opening hours	Open 7 days
Reservation policy	Not accepted for drinks
Credit cards	Accepted
Price range	Affordable
Dress code	Smart casual
Style	Tiki bar

"If you're in San Francisco and you don't go to Smuggler's Cove, you've done something wrong."—Morgan Schick

"It's like teleporting to Pirates of the Caribbean at Disneyland except it's a tiki bar. With dozens of amazing tiki drinks and the largest selection of rum in North America . . . do not think you'll leave there standing upright!"—Greg West

TOMMY'S MEXICAN RESTAURANT

5929 Geary Boulevard
San Francisco
California 94121
United States
+1 4153874747
www.tommystequila.com

Opening hours	Closed Tuesday
Reservation policy	Not accepted
Credit cards	Accepted
Price range	Affordable
Dress code	Casual
Style	Restaurant and tequila bar

"Tommy's has become a real institution over the years. Its signature house cocktail (the Tommy's Margarita) is a modern twist on the classic Margarita, omitting the triple sec and replacing it with organic agave syrup. Lime is squeezed to order. This is the only cocktail they make at Tommy's, which boasts one of the largest collections of 100 percent agave tequila in the world and has a tequila club with more than 7,000 members."—Dre Masso

"Best tequila bar on earth. Run by one of the most important mentors of the San Francisco bartending community, Julio Bermejo. Best margaritas, best tequila selection, and unparalleled hospitality."—Ryan Fitzgerald

TRICK DOG

3010 20th Street
San Francisco
California 94110
United States
+1 4154712999
www.trickdogbar.com

Opening hours	Open 7 days
Reservation policy	Not accepted for drinks
Credit cards	Accepted
Price range	Affordable
Dress code	Casual
Style	Cocktail bar

"How innovative the menus are. How approachable the staff is. How great the food is. Trick Dog is solid gold."
—Jeffrey Cole

"I recently made a trip to San Francisco for the first time. I told my travel companion it was because I had never been there, but really it was pretty much to see this bar. And it did not disappoint. I love the fact that they change their menu concept when they want to change the drinks. I think the whole idea is so cool and I constantly look to them as a source of inspiration."—Steva Casey

> "GREAT, INVENTIVE COCKTAILS AND HOSPITABLE SERVICE EXECUTED BY BARTENDER BERTO SANTORO."
>
> KEELY EDGINGTON P.271

> "GREAT STAFF (WHERE EVERYBODY KNOWS YOUR NAME), AUTHENTIC FEEL ... AND PLENTY OF OLD OVERHOLT RYE WHISKEY AND COLD BEER."
>
> BEAU EDGINGTON P.271

USA MIDWEST

> "IT'S GOT THE CLASSIC FEEL OF A COCKTAIL BAR, BUT THEY ALSO DO A LOT OF BEERS AND THEY HAVE A HUGE WHISKEY LIST."
>
> TED KILGORE P.271

> "THE FEELING OF HOSPITALITY WAS INCREDIBLE AND THEY TAKE THEIR DRINKS VERY SERIOUSLY."
>
> RACHEL FORD P.273

> "IT'S MORE THAN A COCKTAIL BAR, IT'S MORE THAN A NEIGHBORHOOD BAR, IT'S A PLACE WHERE PEOPLE COME TOGETHER NIGHT AFTER NIGHT, YEAR AFTER YEAR, TO BE TOGETHER AND SHARE IN SOMETHING SPECIAL."
>
> JEFFREY MORGENTHALER P.273

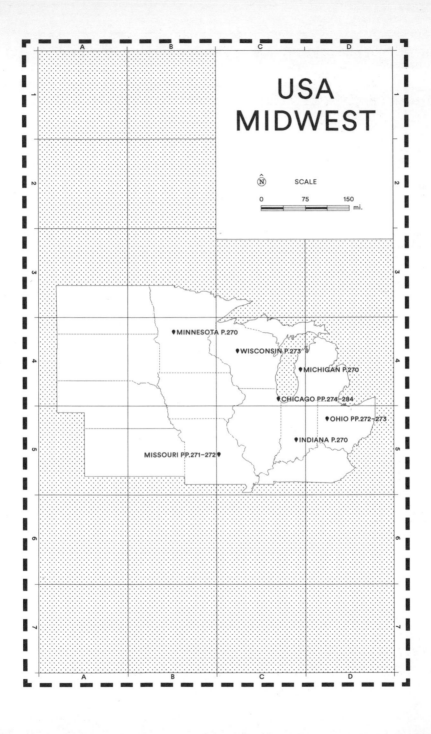

USA
MIDWEST

♦ MINNESOTA P.270

♦ WISCONSIN P.273

♦ MICHIGAN P.270

♦ CHICAGO PP.274–284

♦ OHIO PP.272–273

♦ INDIANA P.270

MISSOURI PP.271–272 ♦

THE HEOROT PUB AND DRAUGHT HOUSE

219 South Walnut Street
Muncie
Indiana 47305
United States
+1 7652870173
www.theheorotpub.com

Opening hours	Open 7 days
Reservation policy	Not accepted for drinks
Credit cards	Accepted
Price range	Budget
Dress code	Casual
Style	Beer bar

"Aside from the roaring fireplace and ancient weaponry adorned on the walls, the selection of over 350 beers is staggeringly impressive. I would never devalue that selection, but the real reason The Heorot has haunted my dreams since my days at Ball State is the wood oven personal pizzas. A couple of Belgian IPAs and pizza by the fire is my idea of undiluted paradise."—Beau du Bois

BRASS RAIL BAR

410 Huron Avenue
Port Huron
Michigan 48060
United States
+1 8109824592

Opening hours	Open 7 days
Reservation policy	Not accepted for drinks
Credit cards	Not accepted
Price range	Budget
Dress code	Casual
Style	Bar

"Opened in 1937 by my cousin Helen David, it is the definition of a neighborhood bar. Helen once told me 'more deals get done at the Brass Rail than in any office around town.' It's a true melting pot of people from all walks of life."
—Tony Abou-Ganim

DONNY DIRK'S ZOMBIE DEN

2027 North 2nd Street
Minneapolis
Minnesota 55411
United States
+1 6125889700
www.donnydirks.com

Opening hours	Open Thursday–Saturday
Reservation policy	Not accepted for drinks
Credit cards	Accepted but not AMEX
Price range	Affordable
Dress code	Casual
Style	Cocktail bar

"One of the most comfortable, cozy spaces in Minneapolis, if your definition of 'comfortable' can be stretched to include an emergency chainsaw on the wall. A fun bar to just be at."
—Pip Hanson

MARVEL BAR

50 North 2nd Avenue
Minneapolis
Minnesota 55401
United States
+1 6122063929
www.marvelbar.com

Opening hours	Open 7 days
Reservation policy	Not accepted for drinks
Credit cards	Accepted
Price range	Affordable
Dress code	Smart casual
Style	Cocktail bar

"From the floor tiling to the cozy booth seating, Marvel Bar is the epitome of a classic cocktail bar. Their drink execution is levels beyond other craft cocktail bars, and each bartender is able to show off his/her own creativity when given the opportunity to roll the dice. I start with a Morricone and then move on to an Agricole Daiquiri. Then Sherry Gimlets and the rest is blurry. If the bartender thinks I'm pretty, I usually get bonus Cheetos, but my doctor says a small tumbler should be my maximum. I'm not sure if they still do this, but they used to offer a Hamm's shotgun service, fully equipped with a Laguiole knife and clean cloth napkin."—Edward Hong

EXTRA VIRGIN

1900 Main Street
Kansas City
Missouri 64108
United States
+1 8168422205
www.extravirginkc.com

Opening hours..Closed Sunday
Reservation policy..................................Not accepted for drinks
Credit cards...Accepted
Price range...Affordable
Dress code...Casual
Style...Restaurant and bar

"Great, inventive cocktails and hospitable service executed by bartender Berto Santoro."—Keely Edgington

HARRY'S BAR & TABLES

501 Westport Road
Kansas City
Missouri 64111
United States
+1 8165613950
www.harrysbarandtables.com

Opening hours..Open 7 days
Reservation policy..................................Not accepted for drinks
Credit cards...Accepted
Price range..Budget
Dress code...Casual
Style...........................Cocktail and whiskey bar and beer garden

"Perfect for an after-shift shot and a beer. Takes the edge off. A bartender's bar."—Keely Edgington

"Great staff (where everybody knows your name), authentic feel, glassy-eyed patrons, and plenty of Old Overholt rye whiskey and cold beer."—Beau Edgington

MANIFESTO

1924 Main Street
Kansas City
Missouri 64108
United States
+1 8165361325
www.theriegerkc.com/manifesto

Opening hours..Closed Sunday
Reservation policy...Accepted
Credit cards...Accepted
Price range...Affordable
Dress code..Smart casual
Style...Speakeasy

"The entire experience is very special here: it's the personal service and interaction with the bartender that makes it so much more than just ordering a drink. It's very small and intimate and the cocktails are top-notch."—Ted Kilgore

THE PEANUT

5000 Main Street
Kansas City
Missouri 64112
United States
+1 8167539499
www.peanutkc.com

Opening hours..Open 7 days
Reservation policy..................................Not accepted for drinks
Credit cards...Accepted
Price range..Budget
Dress code...Casual
Style...Bar and grill

"Best wings in town, a rock-solid BLT, cold Coors Banquet beer, a down-to-earth staff, and the weirdest regular clientele in the city."—Beau Edgington

SCOTCH & SODA

310 South Avenue
Springfield
Missouri 65806
United States
+1 4177194224
www.thescotchandsoda.com

Opening hours....Closed Monday. Open Sunday (brunch only)
Reservation policy...Accepted
Credit cards...Accepted
Price range...Affordable
Dress code...Casual
Style..Cocktail bar

"It's got the classic feel of a cocktail bar, but they also do a lot of beers and they have a huge whiskey list."—Ted Kilgore

FOX & HOUNDS

6300 Clayton Road
The Cheshire Hotel
St. Louis
Missouri 63117
United States
+1 3146477300
www.cheshirestl.com

Opening hours	Open 7 days
Reservation policy	Not accepted for drinks
Credit cards	Accepted
Price range	Budget
Dress code	Casual
Style	Pub

"An old-school, English-style bar that's not super fussy like many hotel bars, and one of the first places in town where you could get old-school cocktails."—Ted Kilgore

FRIENDLY'S

3503 Roger Place
St. Louis
Missouri 63116
United States
+1 3147712040
www.friendlyssportsbar.com

Opening hours	Open 7 days
Reservation policy	Not accepted for drinks
Credit cards	Not accepted
Price range	Budget
Dress code	Casual
Style	Sports bar

"They have lots of games and they have the whole Four Roses lineup. You have to be careful though because they pour very heavy. It's a great place to play some Deer Hunter, eat some wings, and drink Four Roses Single Barrel."—Ted Kilgore

THE ROYALE

3132 South Kingshighway Boulevard
St. Louis
Missouri 63139
United States
+1 3147723600
www.theroyale.com

Opening hours	Open 7 days
Reservation policy	Not accepted for drinks
Credit cards	Accepted
Price range	Budget
Dress code	Casual
Style	Gastropub

"One of the first places in the city to do fresh juices, they spin records and there's an outdoor patio as well as a great beer selection."—Ted Kilgore

SANCTUARIA

4198 Manchester Avenue
St. Louis
Missouri 63110
United States
+1 3145359700
www.sanctuariastl.com

Opening hours	Closed Monday
Reservation policy	Accepted
Credit cards	Accepted
Price range	Affordable
Dress code	Smart casual
Style	Restaurant and bar

"In St. Louis there aren't a lot of places where simple cocktails are done well, and this is the only place you can get them done right until 3 a.m."—Ted Kilgore

PROSPERITY SOCIAL CLUB

1109 Starkweather Avenue
Cleveland
Ohio 44113
United States
+1 2169371938
www.prosperitysocialclub.com

Opening hours	Open 7 days
Reservation policy	Not accepted for drinks
Credit cards	Accepted
Price range	Affordable
Dress code	Smart casual
Style	Restaurant and bar

"It was built in the 30s as Dempsey's Paradise, a firefighters' bar. In the mid-2000s, Bonnie bought it and filled it with vintage Cleveland beer signs and tchotchkes, and despite being the kitschiest place imaginable, all the bartenders have been there for years, the food is heavy and delicious, and none of it feels put-on. It feels like a living document of Cleveland History. I love that bar."—Will Hollingsworth

THE SPOTTED OWL

710 Jefferson Avenue
Cleveland
Ohio 44113
United States
+1 2167955595
www.spottedowlbar.com

Opening hours	Closed Sunday
Reservation policy	Accepted
Credit cards	Accepted
Price range	Affordable
Dress code	Smart casual
Style	Cocktail bar

"I was very impressed by the cocktails in Cleveland—especially at The Spotted Owl. It's located in what looks like an old church, with religious stained glass. The feeling of hospitality was incredible and they take their drinks very seriously."—Rachel Ford

VELVET TANGO ROOM

2095 Columbus Road
Cleveland
Ohio 44113
United States
+1 2162418869
www.velvettangoroom.com

Opening hours	Closed Sunday
Reservation policy	Not accepted for drinks
Credit cards	Accepted
Price range	Affordable
Dress code	Smart casual
Style	Cocktail bar

"A marvelous place. One of the first craft bars in Cleveland, inspired by the Rainbow Room."—Dale DeGroff

FOREQUARTER

708 East Johnson Street
Madison
Wisconsin 53703
United States
+1 6086094717
www.forequartermadison.com

Opening hours	Open 7 days
Reservation policy	Not accepted for drinks
Credit cards	Accepted
Price range	Affordable
Dress code	Casual
Style	Restaurant and bar

"This restaurant is my former employer and is, in my opinion, the best restaurant Madison has to offer. The bar program focuses on seasonal ingredients, molecular back-of-house preparations, and makes the most out of its limited space. The bar staff consists of stair-climbing professionals, since they lack refrigeration behind the bar. I started my career in beverage service behind that bar, and it's always a pleasure to return and imbibe on the best side of the bar."—Edward Hong

WOODY & ANNE'S

2236 Winnebago Street
Madison
Wisconsin 53704
United States
+1 6082495157

Opening hours	Open 7 days
Reservation policy	Not accepted for drinks
Credit cards	Not accepted
Price range	Budget
Dress code	Casual
Style	Dive bar

"Woody & Anne's consists of an eighteen-seat elliptical bar that is tended by four lifetime bartenders. I come here after an opening shift to grab a cheap beer and some advice and stories from their veteran staff. They also have a shuffleboard, and that's always a thing."—Edward Hong

BRYANT'S COCKTAIL LOUNGE

1579 South 9th Street
Milwaukee
Wisconsin 53204
United States
+1 4143832620
www.bryantscocktaillounge.com

Opening hours	Closed Monday
Reservation policy	Not accepted for drinks
Credit cards	Accepted but not AMEX
Price range	Affordable
Dress code	Smart casual
Style	Cocktail bar

"It's more than a cocktail bar, it's more than a neighborhood bar, it's a place where people come together, night after night, year after year, to be together and share in something special."—Jeffrey Morgenthaler

"IT'S A PERFECT COMBINATION OF AMAZING STAFF, GOOD SELECTION OF BOOZE AND DOMESTIC BEERS, A SOLID JUKEBOX, AND GUARANTEED GOOD PEOPLE WATCHING." CHARLES JOLY P.281

CHICAGO

"DELILAH'S IS THE WHISKEY BAR THAT ALL OTHER WHISKEY BARS WANT TO BE LIKE WHEN THEY GROW UP." JOHN STANTON P.281

"HERE YOU DON'T DRINK COCKTAILS, YOU EXPERIENCE THEM." HASSE BANK JOHANSEN P.279

"THE PERFECT PLACE TO SIT BY YOURSELF AT THE BAR WITH A GLASS OF WINE ..." EDEN LAURIN P.280

"SMALL, ECLECTIC, WEIRD, AND HISTORIC. THE BEAUTY OF THIS BAR IS ACCENTUATED BY THE LADIES WHO RUN IT." JACYARA DE OLIVEIRA P.281

CHICAGO

SCALE

0 1000 2000 3000
yd.

1. THE GREEN MILL (P.281)
2. LOST LAKE (P.282)
3. LONGMAN & EAGLE (P.282)
4. BILLY SUNDAY (P.280)
5. ANALOGUE (P.279)
6. DELILAH'S (P.281)
7. CHARLESTON (P.280)
8. THE VIOLET HOUR (P.284)

9. ROOTSTOCK (P.282)
10. SALONE NICO (P.283)
11. THE MATCHBOX (P.282)
12. SPORTSMAN'S CLUB (P.283)
13. BAR DEVILLE (P.279)
14. CLARK STREET ALE HOUSE (P.281)
15. THE DRIFTER (P.281)
16. THE BERKSHIRE ROOM (P.279)

17. THREE DOTS AND A DASH (P.283)
18. SABLE KITCHEN & BAR (P.283)
19. THE AVIARY (P.279)
20. BOOZE BOX (P.280)
21. CINDY'S (P.280)

THE WINDY CITY:
COCKTAILS IN CHICAGO

In 2007, Chicago didn't quite know what to make of The Violet Hour, a small cocktail bar quite unlike anything else in the city at the time. Ten years later, Chicago has one of the most vibrant cocktail scenes in the United States and the world, with bars ranging from lowbrow to highbrow and whiskey to tiki.

Chicago has deep cocktail—and whiskey—roots. In the late 1800s it was home to many of the country's preeminent bars and is likely the birthplace of the Old Fashioned. It was also the epicenter of the Women's Christian Temperance Union, which fought for Prohibition. Accordingly, Repeal Day—which celebrates the repeal of the 18th Amendment that ended Prohibition on December 5, 1933—is staunchly observed.

Along with cocktail bars, new local distilleries are also popping up, like FEW Spirits (which takes its name from the initials of Women's Christian Temperance Union president Frances Elizabeth Willard). There's a heavy focus on whiskey, but vodka and gin are also represented, and you'll find many of them on menus across the city.

In addition to intimate cocktail dens like The Violet Hour, Chicago is also home to two great tiki bars—Three Dots and a Dash as well as Lost Lake, which both offer a welcome respite from the winter cold in the Windy City. On the other end of the spectrum is The Aviary—the highly conceptual, molecular cocktail bar owned by Chef Grant Achatz of Alinea. In between you'll find whiskey bars like Delilah's and relaxed neighborhood joints like the Charleston. All are worth a visit.

Practical Information:
- Cocktails range from US$8 to US$18.
- Standard tipping is 20%.
- Because of local liquor laws, most bars close at 2:00 a.m. with the last call around 1:15 a.m., and they must serve food up until then.

OLD FASHIONED

The earliest written definition of the cocktail describes the Old Fashioned as a combination of spirit, bitters, sugar, and water. This is also effectively the definition of the Old Fashioned, which calls for rye or bourbon, Angostura bitters, sugar, and ice. (Fruit salad, cherry syrup, lemon-lime soda, and sour mix are *not* part of the original recipe.)

The exact origins of the Old Fashioned—with the recipe we know today—is impossible to know, but it is likely that it originated in Chicago in the late 1800s. Located so close to bourbon country, it's not surprising that the Windy City would be the birthplace of this classic drink. It's the perfect way to warm up from the cold, blustery weather that gives the town its name.

ANALOGUE

2523 North Milwaukee Avenue
Chicago
Illinois 60647
United States
+1 7739048567
www.analoguechicago.com

Opening hours	Closed Monday
Reservation policy	Accepted
Credit cards	Accepted
Price range	Affordable
Dress code	Smart casual
Style	Cajun restaurant and cocktail bar

"Best new bar and restaurant in Chicago—specialised in Creole/Cajun fare that is all locally sourced, homemade, and completely addictive. The drinks are constantly pushing boundaries, including a frozen Ramos that churns in the daquiri machine on the bar, Purls (bittered beers), and Shandies. The place is the best."—Eden Laurin

THE AVIARY

955 West Fulton Market
Chicago
Illinois 60607
United States
www.theaviary.com

Opening hours	Open 7 days
Reservation policy	Accepted
Credit cards	Accepted
Price range	Expensive
Dress code	Smart casual
Style	Cocktail bar

"The way these guys approach cocktails is essentially molecular gastronomy for the glass. They take their ingredients and really research how they want to use them, present them, and preserve the flavors of each and every part of their cocktail."—Spencer Huang

"A lot of times high-concept drinks look great but don't taste great, but you know their team makes them taste great too."—Theo Lieberman

"Here you don´t drink cocktails, you experience them. They even have one man full-time creating the best ice. It is amazing."—Hasse Bank Johansen

The Aviary is part of Chef Grant Achatz's group of high-end Chicago destinations, alongside restaurants Alinea and Next. Known for its experimental, highly conceptual approach to cocktails, it has been highly awarded — including World's Best Cocktail Menu at the 2014 Tales of the Cocktail Spirited

Awards and winner of the James Beard Foundation Awards Outstanding Bar Program in the same year — and is one of the top 10 most-recommended bars in this book. Entrance is by ticketed reservation, with options ranging from $20 a la carte to a $165 per person "7 Course Kitchen Table Experience."

BAR DEVILLE

701 North Damen Avenue
Chicago
Illinois 60622
United States
+1 3129292349
www.bardeville.com

Opening hours	Open 7 days
Reservation policy	Not accepted
Credit cards	Not accepted
Price range	Affordable
Dress code	Smart casual
Style	Cocktail bar

"Bar Deville is special because it almost acts as a home base for a large portion of our industry family here in Chicago. It's the place we meet before going to a game or event, or the place we meet after; sometimes both! Any time you walk in you'll know someone behind the bar, at the door, or bellied up, which is an amazing thing when you've just finished a long grueling service."—Meghan Konecny

THE BERKSHIRE ROOM

15 East Ohio Street
ACME Hotel
Chicago
Illinois 60611
United States
+1 3128940945
www.theberkshireroom.com

Opening hours	Open 7 days
Reservation policy	Not accepted for drinks
Credit cards	Accepted
Price range	Affordable
Dress code	Smart casual
Style	Cocktail bar

"What makes it special is mainly the people who tend bar, but they also have well-crafted, interesting cocktails and an outstanding whiskey list. And you won't feel like you're at a hotel bar."—Larry Rice

BILLY SUNDAY

3143 West Logan Boulevard
Chicago
Illinois 60647
United States
+1 7736612485
www.billy-sunday.com

Opening hours	Open 7 days
Reservation policy	Not accepted for drinks
Credit cards	Accepted
Price range	Affordable
Dress code	Smart casual
Style	Cocktail bar

"This was the first bar I stepped into when I was visiting Chicago. The staff provide excellent service and are more than eager to welcome new and returning guests in through the door. The menu is exceptionally crafted, with both familiar and completely unique ingredients in the cocktails, allowing for seasoned and novice drinkers to be able to explore a little each time they order."—Julia Momose

CHARLESTON

2076 North Hoyne Avenue
Chicago
Illinois 60647
United States
+1 7734894757
www.charlestonbarchicago.com

Opening hours	Open 7 days
Reservation policy	Not accepted for drinks
Credit cards	Not accepted
Price range	Affordable
Dress code	Casual
Style	Cocktail bar

"The Charleston is a neighborhood bar, now managed by awesome folks that have careers but love spending a few nights a week throwing a kick-ass party. Rumor has it that all proceeds go to charity. But either way, its the perfect place to sit by yourself at the bar with a glass of wine or bring in a birthday party, your own pizza, and start a dance party."
—Eden Laurin

BOOZE BOX

823 West Randolph Street
Sushi Dokku
Chicago
Illinois 60607
United States
+1 3124558238
www.sushidokku.com/booze-box

Opening hours	Closed Sunday and Monday
Reservation policy	Accepted
Credit cards	Accepted
Price range	Affordable
Dress code	Casual
Style	Japanese bar

"Booze Box is at the bottom of a sushi resturant; I only see females working there. It has a clean-lined, simple menu, DJ music, but is not overly crowded despite being in a super busy neighborhood."—Eden Laurin

CINDY'S

12 South Michigan Avenue
Chicago Athletic Association Hotel
Chicago
Illinois 60603
United States
+1 3127923502
www.cindysrooftop.com

Opening hours	Open 7 days
Reservation policy	Not accepted for drinks
Credit cards	Accepted
Price range	Affordable
Dress code	Smart casual
Style	Gastropub

"Run by an amazing woman, Nandini Khaund, Cindy's is THE hotel bar, on a rooftop and part of an incredibly dynamic building—full of history and contemporary businesses, all run by folks that respect the history and trendset by pushing the industry forward."—Eden Laurin

CLARK STREET ALE HOUSE

742 North Clark Street
Chicago
Illinois 60654
United States
+1 3126429253
www.clarkstreetalehouse.com

Opening hours	Open 7 days
Reservation policy	Accepted
Credit cards	Accepted
Price range	Affordable
Dress code	Casual
Style	Beer bar

"It's a perfect combination of amazing staff, good selection of booze and domestic beers, a solid jukebox, and guaranteed good people watching. It's always open and close to everything downtown, but just far enough away from the late night mess to keep it from going too far."—Charles Joly

DELILAH'S

2771 North Lincoln Avenue
Chicago
Illinois 60614
United States
+1 7734722771
www.delilahschicago.com

Opening hours	Open 7 days
Reservation policy	Not accepted for drinks
Credit cards	Accepted
Price range	Budget
Dress code	Casual
Style	Whiskey bar

"Delilah's is the whiskey bar that all other whiskey bars want to be like when they grow up. Punk rock, esoteric German, Belgian, and microbrewed beers, and the deepest, most insane whiskey list you could possibly imagine. Go and sip some Port Ellen or extinct bourbon while listening to loud punk music and watching old kung fu movies."
—John Stanton

THE DRIFTER

676-8 North Orleans Street
Chicago
Illinois 60654
United States
+1 3126313887
www.thedrifterchicago.com

Opening hours	Open Wednesday–Saturday
Reservation policy	Not accepted for drinks
Credit cards	Accepted
Price range	Affordable
Dress code	Smart casual
Style	Speakeasy

"Small, eclectic, weird, and historic. The beauty of this bar is accentuated by the ladies that run it."—Jacyara De Oliveira

THE GREEN MILL

4802 North Broadway Street
Chicago
Illinois 60640
United States
+1 7738785552
www.greenmilljazz.com

Opening hours	Open 7 days
Reservation policy	Not accepted for drinks
Credit cards	Not accepted
Price range	Affordable
Dress code	Casual
Style	Jazz club

"This place is a survivor. Dating back to the early 1900s, the bar has seen it all and stuck around against all odds. Still a valuable part of the live jazz scene in Chicago, you have to make time to stop by here. I prefer it on a quieter weeknight. Cover is always reasonable, the stay always a little surly, and the beer is fairly cold."—Charles Joly

LONGMAN & EAGLE

2657 North Kedzie Avenue
Chicago
Illinois 60647
United States
+1 7732767110
www.longmanandeagle.com

Opening hours	Open 7 days
Reservation policy	Not accepted for drinks
Credit cards	Accepted
Price range	Affordable
Dress code	Casual
Style	Restaurant and bar

"One of the best things about living in Chicago, is that my neighborhood bar has a Michelin star. Longman & Eagle has an impeccably curated whiskey list, beautiful cocktails, and no side eyes if all you want is a PBR. The staff, as with all good Chicago hospitality stewards, are warm and unpretentiously knowledgeable. Not to mention you can get a pretty good bite to eat as well."—Meghan Konecny

LOST LAKE

3154 West Diversey Avenue
Chicago
Illinois 60647
United States
+1 7739617475
www.lostlaketiki.com

Opening hours	Open 7 days
Reservation policy	Not accepted for drinks
Credit cards	Accepted
Price range	Affordable
Dress code	Smart casual
Style	Tiki bar

"It is the first perfect bar I have seen in a long while. I am not even a tiki freak, but I couldn't get enough of this place. I just didn't want to leave. The decor, the staff, the menu, the Chinese restaurant next door. It's all perfect."—Caitlin Laman

"What every tiki bar inspires toward and few manage to meet."—Ezra Star

THE MATCHBOX

770 North Milwaukee Avenue
Chicago
Illinois 60642
United States
+1 3126669292
www.thesilverpalmrestaurant.com/TheMachBox.php

Opening hours	Open 7 days
Reservation policy	Not accepted for drinks
Credit cards	Accepted
Price range	Affordable
Dress code	Casual
Style	Cocktail bar

"This neighborhood bar is in such a small space, it actually becomes narrower the further you walk in. There is an impressive back bar with little to no repetition of bottles whatsoever. The bartenders remember their regulars and have their cocktail/shot/beer waiting for them by the time they walk through the red door and squeeze onto a seat at the bar. This place is truly unique."—Julia Momose

"The greatest smallest bar on earth. Order a confectioners' sugar Daiquiri. THE BEST."—Ivy Mix

ROOTSTOCK

954 North California Avenue
Chicago
Illinois 60622
United States
+1 7732921616
www.rootstockbar.com

Opening hours	Open 7 days
Reservation policy	Not accepted for drinks
Credit cards	Accepted but not AMEX
Price range	Affordable
Dress code	Casual
Style	Wine and beer bar

"Rootstock is AWESOME. Food is served until late night; it feels like a secret spot for lovers and late-night businesses, and it has an amazing management team—often the owners are serving tables and pouring wines that will blow your tongue right off, they are so good."—Eden Laurin

SABLE KITCHEN & BAR

505 North State Street
Hotel Palomar
Chicago
Illinois 60654
United States
+1 3127559704
www.sablechicago.com

Opening hours	Open 7 days
Reservation policy	Not accepted for drinks
Credit cards	Accepted
Price range	Affordable
Dress code	Smart casual
Style	Restaurant and cocktail bar

"It's all about the people who work there: Mike Ryan has done a great job. It's hard to run a hotel bar because you have to cater to people who are into the cocktail scene, as well as guests who may not be interested in what you're trying to do as a bar."—Sother Teague

SALONE NICO

1015 North Rush Street
Nico Osteria
Chicago
Illinois 60611
United States
+1 3129947100
www.nicoosteria.com

Opening hours	Open 7 days
Reservation policy	Not accepted for drinks
Credit cards	Accepted
Price range	Affordable
Dress code	Smart casual
Style	Italian restaurant and bar

"Beautiful lounge area and bar room. Living wall is exceptionally gorgeous. Cocktails and food are always good."—Jacyara de Oliveira

SPORTSMAN'S CLUB

948 North Western Avenue
Chicago
Illinois 60622
United States
+1 8722068054
www.sportsmans.squarespace.com

Opening hours	Open 7 days
Reservation policy	Not accepted for drinks
Credit cards	Not accepted
Price range	Affordable
Dress code	Casual
Style	Cocktail bar

"Sportsman's Club has everything I would want for a bar of my own. A warm, welcoming decor and sense of hospitality. A rotating cocktail and beer list to keep drinking options fresh. Killer tunes on a reel to reel. A space that lends itself to all four seasons. And rosé on tap!"—Meghan Konecny

THREE DOTS AND A DASH

435 North Clark Street
Chicago
Illinois 60654
United States
+1 3126104220
www.threedotschicago.com

Opening hours	Open 7 days
Reservation policy	Accepted
Credit cards	Accepted
Price range	Affordable
Dress code	Smart casual
Style	Tiki bar

"It's a killer spot: amazing uniforms, gorgeous drinks, great munchies, and always a great time (sit back and watch a sucker order the treasure chest)."—Eden Laurin

"It's the place with the most incredible bartenders, just two ladies working hard in the best mix between bar and club. The tiki style there is awesome, the glassware, the music, everything has a lot of details that make a memorable experience."—Jose Leon

THE VIOLET HOUR

1520 North Damen Avenue
Chicago
Illinois 60622
United States
+1 7732521500
www.theviolethour.com

Opening hours	Open 7 days
Reservation policy	Not accepted for drinks
Credit cards	Accepted
Price range	Affordable
Dress code	Smart casual
Style	Cocktail bar

"The Violet Hour always has beautifully refined cocktails in an almost magical setting. For a bar geek like myself, it's a wonderful place to go to be inspired and do a little homework. For an out of town guest, it is an amazing place to have one of the most gracious hospitality teams wow you with attentive service, impressive product knowledge (without being pretentious), and mind blowing, thoughtful cocktails."—Meghan Konecny

Winner for Outstanding Bar Program at the 2015 James Beard Awards, The Violet Hour is one of Chicago's premiere cocktail establishments. The bar program is helmed by Toby Maloney, a veteran of the industry, and is anchored in the classics. Every day from 6-8 p.m. they host "L'heure Verte", the "Green Hour", celebrating Absinthe. Reservations are not accepted and the wait can be long, so try to arrive as close to opening as possible (6 p.m.). The Violet Hour takes its name from *The Waste Land* by T.S. Eliot.

"GREAT CLASSIC AND CREATIVE COCKTAILS FROM SOME OF THE BEST BARTENDERS IN THE CITY."

DEREK BROWN P.289

"SUPER CLASSY... TINY BAR WITH INCREDIBLY KNOWLEDGEABLE BARTENDERS."

JOHN MAHER P.289

USA SOUTH

"I THINK IT'S THE BEST BAR IN AMERICA RIGHT NOW: THEY'VE NAILED IT ... IT'S VERY NON-MIAMI, IN THAT THE DRINKS ARE CHEAP AND IT'S VERY UNPRETENTIOUS."

NAREN YOUNG P.290

"THIS BAR IS A STEP BACK IN TIME, FEATURING ONLY CLASSIC COCKTAILS."

ROB FERRARA P.291

"THIS IS NOT WHERE I GO TO DRINK COCKTAILS, IT'S WHERE I GO TO DRINK WHISKEY, SPECIFICALLY JAPANESE MALT WHISKEYS AND SCOTCH."

KELLIE THORN P.291

USA
SOUTH

SCALE

0   75   150
mi.

DISTRICT OF COLUMBIA PP.288–290 ♥

MARYLAND P.294 ♥

KENTUCKY PP.293–294 ♥

♥ VIRGINIA P.299

OKLAHOMA P.294 ♥

TENNESSEE P.296 ♥

SOUTH CAROLINA P.295 ♥

TEXAS PP.296–299 ♥

ALABAMA P.288 ♥

♥ GEORGIA PP.291–293

♥ NEW ORLEANS PP.300–307

♥ FLORIDA PP.290–291

THE COLLINS

2125 2nd Avenue North
Birmingham
Alabama 35203
United States
+1 2053237995
www.thecollinsbar.com

Opening hours	Closed Monday
Reservation policy	Accepted
Credit cards	Accepted
Price range	Affordable
Dress code	Smart casual
Style	Cocktail bar

"Collins is the hot ticket in town right now. And it's pretty special . . . The jam there is that there is no drink menu. You tell the bartenders what you're in the mood for and they whip something up for you. Everything is a Dealer's Choice. It's an adventure for sure, but the staff is great and ultimately just want to make you happy."—Steva Casey

LOU'S PUB

726 29th Street South
Birmingham
Alabama 35233
United States
+1 2053227005
www.louspub.com

Opening hours	Open 7 days
Reservation policy	Not accepted for drinks
Credit cards	Accepted
Price range	Affordable
Dress code	Casual
Style	Bar and liquor store

"Lou's is part bar, part package store. So it's the best of both worlds. If you are out of something in your home bar, you go there and pick it up. And while you're there, you might as well have a drink. Mike Carpri, the owner, is one of the nicest guys in the world, who calls everyone by name as they walk in the door. You feel like you're home every time you walk in there."
—Steva Casey

MARTY'S PM

1813 10th Court South
Birmingham
Alabama 35205
United States

Opening hours	Open 7 days
Reservation policy	Not accepted for drinks
Credit cards	Accepted
Price range	Budget
Dress code	Casual
Style	Dive bar

"Marty's was owned for many years by a man named Marty Eagle who created the best dive bar in the world. When he passed away, Marsha and Phil Mims bought it and kept the tradition of patty melts and beers until 5 a.m. alive. The bar starts serving food at 11 p.m. and continues until 5 a.m. And it's really good food. Patty melts that are commonly referred to as 'party melts' around these parts. There is also a 'Recession Special' of a fried bologna sandwich and PBR for $5, so really is there a better dive bar out there? And of course, because of the hours, it's definitely an industry bar."
—Steva Casey

ALL SOULS

725 T Street Northwest
District of Columbia 20001
United States
+1 2027335929
www.allsoulsbar.com

Opening hours	Open 7 days
Reservation policy	Not accepted for drinks
Credit cards	Accepted
Price range	Affordable
Dress code	Casual
Style	Bar

"Laid-back bartender-owned bar. You can get a shot and beer, cocktail, or wine and they're all going to be good. But nothing is ostentatious or over the top. This is a bar for drinkers, not weekend warriors or 'cocktail enthusiasts.' Just good old-fashioned drinkers."—Derek Brown

BARMINI

501 9th Street Northwest
District of Columbia 20004
United States
+1 2023934451
www.minibarbyjoseandres.com

Opening hours	Closed Sunday and Monday
Reservation policy	Accepted
Credit cards	Accepted
Price range	Expensive
Dress code	Smart casual
Style	Cocktail bar

The cocktail counterpoint to Spanish Chef José Andrés' adjacent minibar restaurant, barmini is an avant-garde cocktail bar as well as a research lab for his restaurant group. Drinks range from the traditional to the whimsical and esoteric.

BOURBON STEAK

2800 Pennsylvania Avenue Northwest
The Four Seasons Hotel
District of Columbia 20007
United States
+1 2029442026
www.bourbonsteakdc.com

Opening hours	Open 7 days
Reservation policy	Not accepted for drinks
Credit cards	Accepted
Price range	Expensive
Dress code	Smart casual
Style	Restaurant and bar

"Great classic and creative cocktails from some of the best bartenders in the city."—Derek Brown

COLUMBIA ROOM

124 Blagden Alley Northwest
District of Columbia 20001
United States
+1 2023169396
www.columbiaroomdc.com

Opening hours	Closed Sunday and Monday
Reservation policy	Accepted
Credit cards	Accepted
Price range	Affordable
Dress code	Smart casual
Style	Cocktail bar

The much beloved Columbia Room re-opened in early 2016 in a new location featuring three spaces: the Spirits Library, the Punch Garden and the Tasting Room. In the first, guests can taste rare, antique spirits such as a cognac dating to 1811 as well as moderately priced cocktails. The Punch Garden is a rooftop deck that opens seasonally, while the Tasting Room offers a three or five course cocktail prix-fixe tasting menu by ticketed reservation. The Columbia Room is owned by Derek Brown, a spirits and cocktail expert and revered bartender. He was named *Imbibe* magazine's Bartender of the Year in 2015, and is also Chief Spirits Advisor at the National Archive. His Drink Company owns a number of other local favorites including Mockingbird Hill, Southern Efficiency, and Eat The Rich.

MOCKINGBIRD HILL

1843 7th Street Northwest
District of Columbia 20001
United States
+1 2023169396
www.drinkmoresherry.com

Opening hours	Closed Sunday
Reservation policy	Not accepted for drinks
Credit cards	Accepted
Price range	Affordable
Dress code	Casual
Style	Sherry bar

"Sherry and jamón, and garlic juice shots. Small, intimate, and hyperfocused."—John Stanton

The only sherry bar in this book outside of Spain, created by Washington, D.C. bartender Derek Brown. In his own words, "It's a little geeky, but it's perfect for someone with an urge to drink and just a little bit of curiosity."

QUILL

1200 16th Street Northwest
The Jefferson Hotel
District of Columbia 20036
United States
+1 2024482300
www.jeffersondc.com

Opening hours	Open 7 days
Reservation policy	Not accepted for drinks
Credit cards	Accepted
Price range	Affordable
Dress code	Smart casual
Style	Cocktail bar

"Super classy . . . tiny bar with incredibly knowledgeable bartenders."—John Maher

SHOWTIME
113 Rhode Island Avenue Northwest
District of Columbia 20001
United States

Opening hours	Open 7 days
Reservation policy	Not accepted for drinks
Credit cards	Not accepted
Price range	Budget
Dress code	Casual
Style	Dive bar

"Great jukebox curated by owner/DJ Paul Vivari with plenty of funk, soul, and obscure artists. Best part: the jukebox is free! Otherwise, you can get a combo of Bourbon and Natty Boh for $5. The bartenders are great and the environment is cozy. That's all I need."—Derek Brown

THE MOLOKAI BAR
3599 North Federal Highway
Mai Kai
Fort Lauderdale
Florida 33308
United States
+1 9545633272
www.maikai.com

Opening hours	Closed Monday
Reservation policy	Not accepted for drinks
Credit cards	Accepted
Price range	Affordable
Dress code	Casual
Style	Tiki bar and restaurant

"It is the Mecca of my people: the last of the great Polynesian Pop Palaces. Filled to capacity with stunning rare decor, beautiful gardens, exotic cocktails, and great food. A true journey through time to the Golden Era of Tiki."—Martin Cate

"Complete with indoor waterfalls, outdoor jungle gardens, live Tahitian fire-dancers, and seven tiki-filled dining rooms —perfectly preserved, as if you're time-traveling back to opening day in 1956. Start your evening at the Molokai Bar, designed to give you the feeling that you're in a sunken eighteenth-century sailing ship: water streams down the slanted windows as flickering lanterns cast shadowy light on the layered nautical decor. Of the fifty-one tropical drinks on the menu, two standouts are the Mutiny and the Black Magic."—Jeff "Beachbum" Berry

THE BROKEN SHAKER
2727 Indian Creek Drive
The Freehand Miami
Miami Beach
Florida 33140
United States
+1 3055312727
www.thefreehand.com/miami/venues/the-broken-shaker

Opening hours	Open 7 days
Reservation policy	Not accepted for drinks
Credit cards	Accepted
Price range	Affordable
Dress code	Casual
Style	Cocktail bar

"I think it's the best bar in America right now: they've nailed it. The drinks are awesome. It's very non-Miami, in that the drinks are cheap and it's very unpretentious. They're almost like a bunch of artists or hippies. No one's trying to impress anyone. They've got this little oasis with a pool, table tennis, and barbecues going on. It's just awesome."—Naren Young

"This former pop-up bar is found inside a hostel in Miami Beach. Herbs from the garden and a menu that changes every few weeks really keeps a finger on the pulse of the cocktail world."—Rob Ferrara

"It's just one of the happiest places . . . It's definitely one of my top bars are in the country."—Kellie Thorn

MAC'S CLUB DEUCE
222 14th Street
Miami Beach
Florida 33139
United States
+1 3055316200
www.macsclubdeuce.com

Opening hours	Open 7 days
Reservation policy	Not accepted for drinks
Credit cards	Not accepted
Price range	Budget
Dress code	Casual
Style	Dive bar

"One of the most iconic dive bars in the state—bikers, tattoo artist, models, and plenty of shenanigans in the middle of South Beach."—Gabe Orta

PURDY LOUNGE

1811 Purdy Avenue
Miami Beach
Florida 33139
United States
+1 3055314622
www.purdylounge.com

Opening hours	Open 7 days
Reservation policy	Not accepted for drinks
Credit cards	Accepted
Price range	Affordable
Dress code	Casual
Style	Lounge

"Because that's Miami! Sexy, crazy, shady, but with a lot of soul and heart!"—Elad Zvi

THE REGENT COCKTAIL CLUB

1690 Collins Avenue
Gale Hotel
Miami Beach
Florida 33139
United States
+1 7869752555
www.regentcocktailclub.com

Opening hours	Open 7 days
Reservation policy	Not accepted for drinks
Credit cards	Accepted
Price range	Affordable
Dress code	Smart casual
Style	Cocktail bar

"This bar is a step back in time, featuring only classic cocktails. The service and attention to detail is bar none. Ask for Julio Cabrera and you'll see what I'm talking about." —Rob Ferrara

REPOUR BAR

1650 James Avenue
The Albion Hotel
Miami Beach
Florida 33139
United States
+1 3059131000
www.repourbar.com

Opening hours	Open 7 days
Reservation policy	Not accepted for drinks
Credit cards	Accepted
Price range	Affordable
Dress code	Casual
Style	Cocktail bar

"They stay open late for industry professionals like myself. Repour has a cozy indoor bar and a spacious outdoor courtyard, where you can sip handcrafted cocktails inspired by family, grander fresh herbs, seasonal ingredients, and the creative imaginations of Isaac and his crew."—Rob Ferrara

SWEET LIBERTY

237-B 20th Street
Miami Beach
Florida 33139
United States
+1 3057638217
www.mysweetliberty.com

Opening hours	Open 7 days
Reservation policy	Not accepted for drinks
Credit cards	Accepted
Price range	Affordable
Dress code	Casual
Style	Cocktail bar

"Owned by John Lermayer, it opened last year and is already a bartender hangout."—Dale DeGroff

BOOKHOUSE PUB

736 Ponce De Leon Avenue Northeast
Atlanta
Georgia 30306
United States
+1 4042541176
www.thebookhousepub.net

Opening hours	Open 7 days
Reservation policy	Not accepted for drinks
Credit cards	Accepted
Price range	Budget
Dress code	Casual
Style	Pub

"My favorite little neighborhood bar on Ponce, and another industry favorite in the city. If you don't know the show *Twin Peaks* it's still an awesome bar, but if you do, you'll get all the fun references. As in, the Bookhouse Boys. But it's not cheesy and it's not overdone: the bar is dark wood and there are stained glass windows. This is not where I go to drink cocktails, it's where I go to drink whiskey, specifically Japanese malt whiskeys and Scotch. They have an incredible selection. The bartenders are attentive with just the right amount of irreverence and sass. It's a really fun bar with a great vibe."—Kellie Thorn

EMPIRE STATE SOUTH

999 Peachtree Street Northeast
Atlanta
Georgia 30309
United States
+1 4045411105
www.empirestatesouth.com

Opening hours	Open 7 days
Reservation policy	Not accepted for drinks
Credit cards	Accepted
Price range	Affordable
Dress code	Casual
Style	Restaurant and bar

"In all my travels I've never felt more at home than here. They serve great coffee and pastries in the morning, awesome lunch and dinner options. Kellie Thorn's bar programming is perfect for the space: amazing selections of cocktails and booze nerd stuff, as well as a fantastic wine program. They are the all-arounder joint, whatever you want and with a gracious staff."—Kirk Estopinal

THE RIGHTEOUS ROOM

1051 Ponce De Leon Avenue Northeast
Briarcliff Plaza Shopping Center
Atlanta
Georgia 30306
United States
+1 4048740939
www.stayrighteous.com

Opening hours	Open 7 days
Reservation policy	Not accepted for drinks
Credit cards	Accepted but not AMEX
Price range	Budget
Dress code	Casual
Style	Dive bar

"When I want a Fernet and Coke or a whiskey, I go to The Righteous Room. It's a smokey little dive bar next to Atlanta's oldest operating movie theater. It still has a nonelectronic jukebox loaded with great music. It's a low-key bar and it's always populated with industry people."—Kellie Thorn

VICTORY SANDWICH BAR

913 Bernina Avenue Northeast
Atlanta
Georgia 30307
United States
+1 4049631742
www.vicsandwich.com

Opening hours	Open 7 days
Reservation policy	Not accepted for drinks
Credit cards	Accepted
Price range	Budget
Dress code	Casual
Style	Sandwich hop and bar

"This is an unpretentious and fun bar where they serve their well-thought-out and balanced cocktails in Mason jars and there's a Jack and Coke slushy on tap all the time."
—Kellie Thorn

KIMBALL HOUSE

303 East Howard Avenue
Decatur
Georgia 30030
United States
+1 4043783502
www.kimball-house.com

Opening hours	Open 7 days
Reservation policy	Not accepted for drinks
Credit cards	Accepted
Price range	Affordable
Dress code	Smart casual
Style	Restaurant and bar

"That's the bar that I take everybody to when they come to visit me. It's in Decatur, fifteen minutes from the center of Atlanta. It's run by Miles Macquarrie and he is really talented and passionate and hospitality driven. His cocktails are beautiful; the restaurant is beautiful. To give you an idea of their attention to detail, they have somebody who is devoted to curating their oyster menu, which is always incredible."
—Kellie Thorn

THE GREY

109 Martin Luther King Jr Boulevard
Savannah
Georgia 31401
United States
+1 9126625999
www.thegreyrestaurant.com

Opening hours	Closed Monday
Reservation policy	Not accepted for drinks
Credit cards	Accepted
Price range	Affordable
Dress code	Smart casual
Style	Restaurant and bar

"The Grey is a beautiful restaurant in an old Greyhound bus station in Savannah that *Bon Appétit* magazine named best designed restaurant of the year. Cody Henson runs the bar program and he's doing a really great job. It's a classics-driven bar, the kind of place you can go in and order a Gin Martini and trust that it will be perfect."—Kellie Thorn

FREDDIE'S 220

220 West Broadway
Louisville
Kentucky 40202
United States
+1 5025829123

Opening hours	Open 7 days
Reservation policy	Not accepted for drinks
Credit cards	Not accepted
Price range	Budget
Dress code	Casual
Style	Dive bar

"It's the kind of place where the 'new guy' on staff is seventy-five years old and has been there for forty years. They have cold beer in bottles and great whiskey on the back bar. It has that neighborhood bar thing that involves drinking with a wide array of people, which to me is what makes a neighborhood bar special; that's what they're for."
—Morgan Schick

NACHBAR

969 Charles Street
Louisville
Kentucky 40204
United States
+1 5026374377

Opening hours	Open 7 days
Reservation policy	Not accepted for drinks
Credit cards	Accepted
Price range	Budget
Dress code	Casual
Style	Beer and whiskey bar

"Casual, friendly, great jukebox, cheap beer AND great beer, huge outdoor patios, neighborhood folks, great whiskey, and lots of smiles. Also look for their House Rules . . . they're the only ones to do it right."—John Stanton

SERGIO'S WORLD BEERS

1605 Story Avenue
Louisville
Kentucky 40206
United States
+1 5026182337
www.sergiosworldbeers.com

Opening hours	Open 7 days
Reservation policy	Not accepted for drinks
Credit cards	Not accepted
Price range	Affordable
Dress code	Casual
Style	Beer bar

"This is the ultimate beer-nerd bar. Mind-shredding tap list and bottle selection; secret, locked rooms filled with the REALLY good stuff; a staff that's as knowledgeable as anywhere; Miller Lite cans in the bathroom marked '$27.00.' The least interesting thing they'll have on tap will be more interesting than the most amazing thing at most beer bars. Sergio and his staff are just beer weirdos, and it shows. They get really excited about the whole world of craft beer and that translates into the service and selection at the bar."
—Will Groves

THE SILVER DOLLAR

1761 Frankfort Avenue
Louisville
Kentucky 40206
United States
+1 5022599540
www.whiskeybythedrink.com

Opening hours	Open 7 days
Reservation policy	Accepted
Credit cards	Accepted
Price range	Affordable
Dress code	Casual
Style	Whiskey bar

"I've never been to Louisville just to go to the Silver Dollar, but if I did nothing else, going here would make it worth the trip. Owner Larry Rice is a very special fellow. The first time I walked in, I thought 'Oh, somebody made a bar for me.' There was great music on, they have one of the most impressive American whiskey selections I've ever seen, everyone is really nice, it's low key and comfortable, and the food is good. It's everything I care about in a bar."
—Morgan Schick

"Bourbon. BBQ. Record player. All in an old firehouse and they do it well. It's everything awesome in the world and then some. Plus it is so casual . . . it just feels right. If I lived in Louisville I would be there all the time. Hospitality is bar none. I think I could write paragraphs about the place, but the best way to sum it up is I have their 'Whiskey by the Drink' stickers slapped on a dozen things in my house!"
—Clint Spotleson

BAD DECISIONS

1928 Fleet Street
Baltimore
Maryland 21231
United States
+1 4109795161
www.makeabaddecision.com

Opening hours	Open 7 days
Reservation policy	Not accepted for drinks
Credit cards	Accepted
Price range	Budget
Dress code	Casual
Style	Cocktail bar

"It's everything a bar should be. They go low, they go high. They make drinking fun but also make great drinks."
—Derek Brown

THE HILO CLUB

1221 Northwest 50th Street
Oklahoma City
Oklahoma 73118
United States
+1 4058431722
www.hilookc.com

Opening hours	Open 7 days
Reservation policy	Not accepted for drinks
Credit cards	Accepted but not AMEX
Price range	Budget
Dress code	Casual
Style	Dive bar

"The HiLo is legendary. They say that if Freddy Mercury, Mae West, and Che Guevara had a love child, she and her girlfriend would come here. It's that bar. Not quite a gay bar, not quite a metal bar, not quite a speakeasy, it just is The HiLo. Burlesque shows every Friday night, impossibly small square footage, darts, a jukebox that doesn't quit, strongest drinks in town, and walls that could write a dozen novels. The HiLo was connected via an underground tunnel to an office building across the street and was supposedly a brothel and speakeasy for a long time. The tunnel still exists, although it is walled off today. Just an insane amount of debauchery and history in one place. It's so human."—Jeffrey Cole

THE OTHER ROOM

3009 Paseo
Oklahoma City
Oklahoma 73103
United States
+1 4056022002
www.picassosonpaseo.com

Opening hours	Open 7 days
Reservation policy	Not accepted for drinks
Credit cards	Accepted
Price range	Budget
Dress code	Casual
Style	Cocktail bar

"This was my first favorite bar . . . The people in the bar are really what make a late-night bar special and if there ever was an after-work *Cheers* type spot for me, this is it. Chefs, bartenders, servers, you name it, that's the watering hole most visit after their long shift. The Other Room exists in the middle of a neighborhood I lived and worked in for years called The Paseo, which is home to an arts district of the same name."—Jeffrey Cole

THE BELMONT

511 King Street
Charleston
South Carolina 29403
United States
www.thebelmontcharleston.com

Opening hours..Open 7 days
Reservation policy........................Not accepted for drinks
Credit cards...Accepted
Price range...Affordable
Dress code...Casual
Style...Cocktail bar

"The Belmont is unpretentious, straight-forward drinking for spirit lovers. Their selection of Amari and whiskey is unmatched in the city, and the barmen, clad in white shirts and black ties, ply their craft quickly, kindly, and with an enthusiasm for the guest."—Brooks Reitz

BIN 152

152 King Street
Charleston
South Carolina 29401
United States
+1 8435777359
www.bin152.com

Opening hours..Open 7 days
Reservation policy........................Not accepted for drinks
Credit cards...Accepted
Price range...Affordable
Dress code...Casual
Style...Wine bar

"While they serve only beer and wine, the space, outfitted with vintage French antiques, is insanely pleasing. And the location—on a sleepy, forgotten stretch of King Street, dotted mostly with retail—is an escape from an otherwise busy, bustling city."—Brooks Reitz

THE GIN JOINT

182 East Bay Street
Charleston
South Carolina 29401
United States
+1 8435776111
www.theginjoint.com

Opening hours..Open 7 days
Reservation policy..Accepted
Credit cards...Accepted
Price range...Affordable
Dress code...Casual
Style...Cocktail bar

"The small size and the small corner bar make this a special spot. The food is exactly what you'd expect from a modern Charleston eatery and the cocktails complement the city very well. I was first introduced to 'bespoke' bartending here with their Bartender's Choice list of flavors to choose from."
—Jeffrey Cole

A gin-focused cocktail bar with, as they put it, "one of the largest collections of gin in the galaxy."

THE RAREBIT

474 King Street
Charleston
South Carolina 29403
United States
+1 8439745483
www.therarebit.com

Opening hours..Closed Monday
Reservation policy........................Not accepted for drinks
Credit cards...Accepted
Price range...Affordable
Dress code...Casual
Style...Restaurant and bar

"One of the best Gin and Tonics I've ever had."—Kyle Ford

NO. 308

407 Gallatin Avenue
Nashville
Tennessee 37206
United States
+1 6156507344
www.bar308.com

Opening hours	Open 7 days
Reservation policy	Not accepted for drinks
Credit cards	Accepted
Price range	Affordable
Dress code	Casual
Style	Cocktail bar

"The hospitality is great, the cocktails are fantastic, and it's a fun space to hang out."—Kyle Ford

OLD GLORY

1200 Villa Place
Nashville
Tennessee 37212
United States
+1 6156790509

Opening hours	Open 7 days
Reservation policy	Not accepted for drinks
Credit cards	Accepted
Price range	Affordable
Dress code	Casual
Style	Cocktail bar

They serve standards as well as innovative cocktails.

PINEWOOD SOCIAL

33 Peabody Street
Nashville
Tennessee 37210
United States
+1 6157518111
www.pinewoodsocial.com

Opening hours	Open 7 days
Reservation policy	Accepted
Credit cards	Accepted
Price range	Affordable
Dress code	Casual
Style	Coffee shop, restaurant, and bar

An eclectic bar that is also a coffee shop during the day and features a pool, Airstream bar, and six bowling lanes. They serve creative cocktails alongside pitchers of beer and wine.

ROBERT'S WESTERN WORLD

416B Broadway
Nashville
Tennessee 37203
United States
+1 6152449552
www.robertswesternworld.com

Opening hours	Open 7 days
Reservation policy	Not accepted for drinks
Credit cards	Accepted
Price range	Budget
Dress code	Casual
Style	Dive bar

"A cool old-style, honky-tonk bar where you can go to eat a fried bologna sandwich with a shot and a beer at midnight." —Kyle Ford

HALF STEP

75 ½ Rainey Street
Austin
Texas 78701
United States
+1 5123911877
www.halfstepbar.com

Opening hours	Open 7 days
Reservation policy	Not accepted for drinks
Credit cards	Accepted
Price range	Affordable
Dress code	Casual
Style	Cocktail bar

"Great bar located in one of the coolest areas in town, tons of bars and food trucks all around but Half Step is the best of all."—Gabe Orta

SECOND BAR + KITCHEN

200 Congress Avenue
Austin
Texas 78701
United States
+1 5128272750
www.secondbarkitchen.com

Opening hours	Open 7 days
Reservation policy	Accepted
Credit cards	Accepted
Price range	Affordable
Dress code	Smart casual
Style	Restaurant and bar

A New American restaurant with a serious bar program offering craft cocktails, wine & beer, as well as a non-alcoholic mocktail menu created by bar director Jason Stevens.

FOE (FRATERNAL ORDER OF EAGLES)

8500 Arturo Drive
Dallas
Texas 75228
United States
+1 2143279563

Opening hours..Open 7 days
Reservation policy....................Not accepted for drinks
Credit cards..Accepted
Price range...Budget
Dress code..Casual
Style...Pool bar

"It's a booze-soaked oasis that's the summer camp from *Meatballs* crossed with a VFW hall. Add patronage from the local motorcycle gangs and you get one helluva time."
—Chad Solomon

MIDNIGHT RAMBLER

1530 Main Street
Joule Hotel
Dallas
Texas 75201
United States
+1 2142614601
www.midnightramblerbar.com

Opening hours..Open 7 days
Reservation policy....................Not accepted for drinks
Credit cards..Accepted
Price range..Affordable
Dress code..Casual
Style..Cocktail bar

"This beautiful bar located below the Joule Hotel is everything you could hope for in a hotel bar and so much more. Chad Solomon and Christy Pope, brilliant minds behind the bar, have long been on the leading edge of cocktail culture and it shows through here. The drinks are laser focused, fun, and served in a room sexy enough to encourage any imbiber to end the night by getting a room upstairs. Pro-tip: some of the rooms have round beds."
—David Kaplan

PROOF + PANTRY

1722 Routh Street
Dallas
Texas 75201
United States
+1 2148809940
www.proofandpantry.com

Opening hours...............................Closed Monday
Reservation policy....................Not accepted for drinks
Credit cards..Accepted
Price range..Affordable
Dress code...Smart casual
Style..Restaurant and cocktail bar

Serves inventive cocktails — including a "no proof" (mocktail) and low-proof section —alongside an eclectic food menu.

VICTOR TANGOS

3001 North Henderson Avenue
Dallas
Texas 75206
United States
+1 2142528595
www.victortangos.com

Opening hours................................Closed Sunday
Reservation policy.............................Not accepted
Credit cards..Accepted
Price range..Affordable
Dress code...Smart casual
Style.............................Tapas restaurant and cocktail bar

"Because everybody knows your name, the tunes are good, and the beer and Amaro flow freely."—Christy Pope

THE CHAT ROOM

1263 West Magnolia Avenue
Fort Worth
Texas 76104
United States
+1 8179228319
www.thechatroompub.com

Opening hours..Open 7 days
Reservation policy....................Not accepted for drinks
Credit cards..Accepted
Price range...Budget
Dress code..Casual
Style...Dive bar

"Easy drinks . . . Easy people . . . that get even easier and busier as the night gets later!"—Christy Pope

LA CARAFE

813 Congress Avenue
Houston
Texas 77002
United States
+1 7132299399

Opening hours	Open 7 days
Reservation policy	Not accepted for drinks
Credit cards	Not accepted
Price range	Affordable
Dress code	Casual
Style	Wine bar

Located in the oldest commercial building in Houston — and thought to be the oldest bar in the city — La Carafe offers a rotating selection of wines and what is commonly considered the best jukebox in town.

JULEP

1919 Washington Avenue
Houston
Texas 77007
United States
+1 7138694383
www.julephouston.com

Opening hours	Open 7 days
Reservation policy	Not accepted for drinks
Credit cards	Accepted
Price range	Affordable
Dress code	Smart casual
Style	Cocktail bar

"I visited Alba Huerta's bar Julep last year for the first time and fell in love completely. It's so unique and convivial. It is very 'Alba' with this elegant Southern charm. The drinks are perfectly executed, as is the food. It's a big contrast for Houston, it really sticks out from the other bars in the city. Alba's bourbon selection is amazing, and she also has very good Cognacs. There is a specific section of Juleps on the menu that changes seasonally. Then she has a lot of other classic cocktails, and her own creations. The wine selection is also very strong. The role of a bar is to be part of the community and to be exciting, and Alba has done this very well."—Carina Soto Velasquez

NOTSUOH

314 Main Street
Houston
Texas 77002
United States
+1 7133210824
www.notsuoh.com

Opening hours	Open 7 days
Reservation policy	Not accepted for drinks
Credit cards	Accepted
Price range	Budget
Dress code	Casual
Style	Rock club

"A late-night/after-hours Houston institution where the night crawlers go bump."—Chad Solomon

POISON GIRL

1641 Westheimer Road
Suite B
Houston
Texas 77006
United States
+1 7135279929

Opening hours	Open 7 days
Reservation policy	Not accepted for drinks
Credit cards	Accepted
Price range	Budget
Dress code	Casual
Style	Whiskey bar

"A shot and a beer bar, it's always accessible and affordable, and it really reflects the neighborhood . . . Poison Girl is the greatest whiskey bar ever invented."—Alba Huerta

WEST ALABAMA ICE HOUSE

1919 West Alabama Street
Houston
Texas 77098
United States
+1 7135286874

Opening hours	Open 7 days
Reservation policy	Not accepted for drinks
Credit cards	Accepted
Price range	Budget
Dress code	Casual
Style	Dive bar

"The greatest place ever."—Alba Huerta

JETT'S GRILL

207 North Highland Avenue
Hotel Paisano
Marfa
Texas 79843
United States
+1 4327293838
www.hotelpaisano.com

Opening hours	Open 7 days
Reservation policy	Not accepted for drinks
Credit cards	Accepted
Price range	Affordable
Dress code	Casual
Style	Restaurant and bar

"I like to stop there for a hot meal and a cold beverage after a long stretch on US-90. The air about the place is peaceful and calm, especially around sunset. Comfortable beds upstairs."—Richard Boccato

LEMAIRE

101 West Franklin Street
The Jefferson Hotel
Richmond
Virginia 23220
United States
+1 8046494629
www.lemairerestaurant.com

Opening hours	Open 7 days
Reservation policy	Not accepted for drinks
Credit cards	Accepted
Price range	Affordable
Dress code	Smart casual
Style	Restaurant and bar

"The Jefferson Hotel is one of the most significant pieces of architecture in Richmond. Lemaire, which is the more premium of two restaurants in the hotel, is full of polished wood and marble, great food and drink. The service is always friendly and professional, and they have a surprisingly good happy hour at the bar for such a high-end hotel."
—Mattias Hagglund

THE ROOSEVELT

623 North 25th Street
Richmond
Virginia 23223
United States
+1 8046581935
www.rooseveltrva.com

Opening hours	Open 7 days
Reservation policy	Not accepted for drinks
Credit cards	Accepted
Price range	Affordable
Dress code	Casual
Style	Restaurant and bar

"Food, cocktails, beer, and a Virginia-exclusive wine list make this a place I would happily go to for any occasion. It feels comfortable and charming, and I always know that whatever I order here it will be delicious. Whether just stopping in for a drink, a quick snack, dinner, or a special occasion, they always hit the mark."—Mattias Hagglund

SAISON

23 West Marshall Street
Richmond
Virginia 23220
United States
+1 8042693689
www.saisonrva.com

Opening hours	Open 7 days
Reservation policy	Accepted
Credit cards	Accepted
Price range	Affordable
Dress code	Casual
Style	Gastropub

"A cocktail and beer bar that stays open to 2 a.m. every night, with excellent drinks and a friendly staff. Saison is hip, fun, and welcoming to all."—Mattias Hagglund

> ## "AN INTEGRAL PART OF THE QUARTER WITH A RICH HISTORY."
> FRANKY MARSHALL P.305

NEW ORLEANS

> ## "THE BAR PROGRAM IS RUN BY AN INDUSTRY VETERAN WHO'S RESPECTED BY HIS PEERS, THE SPACE IS COMFORTABLE, THE FOOD SPOT ON."
> ANDREW AND BRIANA VOLK P.305

> ## "I'VE NEVER HAD A BAD DRINK HERE, BUT I'VE HAD PLENTY OF AMAZING ONES."
> JEFF "BEACHBUM" BERRY P.306

> ## "A PIECE OF NEW ORLEANS HEAVEN ON EARTH."
> ABIGAIL GULLO P.305

> ## "A SOULFUL, GRITTY BAR THAT DESPITE BEING LOCATED IN AN EXTREMELY HIP HOTEL, FEELS LIKE A NEIGHBORHOOD JOINT."
> CHAD SOLOMON P.307

NEW ORLEANS

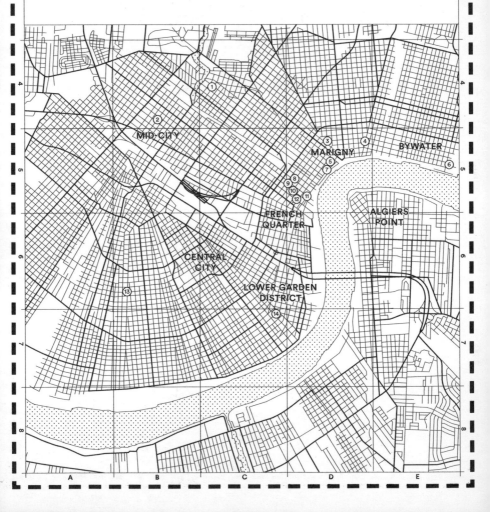

SCALE

0   655   1310   1965   yd.

1. PAL'S LOUNGE (P.307)
2. FINN MCCOOL'S (P.306)
3. R BAR (P.307)
4. CANE & TABLE (P.305)
5. MIMI'S (P.307)
6. BACCHANAL WINE (P.305)

7. MOLLY'S AT THE MARKET (P.307)
8. ERIN ROSE (P.306)
9. ARNAUD'S FRENCH 75 BAR (P.305)
10. OLD ABSINTHE HOUSE (P.307)
11. BEACHBUM BERRY'S
    LATITUDE 29 (P.305)

12. THE CAROUSEL BAR
    & LOUNGE (P.306)
13. CURE (P.306)
14. THE SAINT (P.307)

THE BIG EASY: COCKTAILS IN NEW ORLEANS

New Orleans is a bastion of cocktail history. The birthplace of the Sazerac and the Ramos Gin Fizz, as well as Peychaud's Bitters, it is also home to some of the country's most iconic bars, where you truly feel as though you are drinking history.

As a result, cocktails here are deeply rooted in classics, and almost all bars in the city pay homage to this tradition. At the same time, the Crescent City is one of stark contrast: upscale destinations coexist alongside dive bars, and both are quintessentially New Orleans. One of the best examples of this is the French Quarter, where Arnaud's French 75 Bar—a wood-paneled, cigar-smoke-filled lounge presided over by head bartender Chris Hannah in a perfectly white dinner jacket—is a few steps away from Erin Rose—an Irish dive bar that specializes in frozen Irish Coffee.

The modern history of New Orleans has been hugely shaped by Hurricane Katrina, which devastated the city in 2005. In the wake of the destruction, an influx of investment has revitalized certain neighborhoods and breathed new life into the city's cocktail culture.

New bars like Cure—opened by Neal Bodenheimer and Kirk Estopinal in 2009—and Beachbum Berry's Latitude 29—a tiki bar created by "The Beachbum" himself in 2014—are prime examples. Older neighborhoods like the Bywater and the Marigny have also seen explosive growth.

Practical Information:
— Cocktails start at US$6 during happy hour, and go up to US$15 at the higher-end hotels.
— Standard tipping is 20%.
— New Orleans has open-container laws that allow you to drink cocktails on the street. Many bars, even fancy ones, will give you a to-go cup if you haven't finished your drink.

SAZERAC

One of the most famous drinks to come out of New Orleans is the Sazerac. Served neat in a rocks glass, it was originally made with Cognac, but in the late 1800s, American rye was used instead. It was most famously served at the Sazerac Coffee House. A defining ingredient in the Sazerac is Peychaud's Bitters, created by a Creole apothecary in New Orleans in the 1830s. The anise flavor in the bitters is amplified by the absinthe used to rinse the glass.

FRENCH 75

Named for a World War I field gun that took 75mm shells, the French 75 is in fact a very elegant drink made with gin, lemon, and Champagne. It may have been created in Europe in the late 1910s, or in the United States in the 1920s, but its exact origins remain unknown. In any case, one of the best places to enjoy a French 75 is at the eponymous bar Arnaud's French 75 Bar in New Orleans, where head barman Chris Hannah favors cognac over the more commonly referenced gin.

RAMOS GIN FIZZ

The Ramos Gin Fizz is a beautiful, frothy breakfast drink. It was invented in the late 1800s in New Orleans by Henry Ramos, who famously employed a line of shaker boys to ensure each drink reached the perfect consistency. It is effectively a gussied up Gin Fizz with heavy cream and orange flower water, which lend it a luxurious texture and floral aroma. There are few things as delicious as a perfectly shaken Ramos Gin Fizz on a hot day in New Orleans.

ARNAUD'S FRENCH 75 BAR

813 Bienville Street
New Orleans
Louisiana 70112
United States
+1 5045235433
www.arnaudsrestaurant.com

Opening hours	Open 7 days
Reservation policy	Not accepted for drinks
Credit cards	Accepted
Price range	Affordable
Dress code	Smart casual
Style	Cocktail bar

"In New Orleans, I suggest everyone visit Arnaud's French 75 Bar. It's a beautiful room, an integral part of the Quarter with a rich history, and if you're lucky enough to be there when head barman Chris Hannah is working, you'll be all set."
—Franky Marshall

"French 75 is an island of quality in the shitstorm that can be Bourbon Street. The bar program is run by an industry veteran who's respected by his peers, the space is comfortable, the food spot on. Additionally, they'll serve you cigars while you drink."—Andrew and Briana Volk

One of New Orleans' most iconic cocktail (and cigar) bars, the barmen are dressed in white dinner jackets and service is top notch. Chris Hannah runs the show and can be found behind the bar on most nights. There's only one thing to order: the bar's namesake French 75 — with cognac, not gin. Make sure to check out the Mardi Gras Museum located upstairs, too.

BACCHANAL WINE

600 Poland Avenue
New Orleans
Louisiana 70117
United States
+1 5049489111
www.bacchanalwine.com

Opening hours	Open 7 days
Reservation policy	Not accepted for drinks
Credit cards	Accepted
Price range	Affordable
Dress code	Casual
Style	Wine bar

"This indie wine shop evolved over the years to a piece of New Orleans heaven on earth. Fairy lights, great food, live music, interesting people, and a killer cocktail program with unusual spirits. It IS New Orleans to me."—Abigail Gullo

"It's one of the best places in the world."—Morgan Schick

BEACHBUM BERRY'S LATITUDE 29

321 North Peters Street
Bienville House Hotel
New Orleans
Louisiana 70130
United States
+1 5046093811
www.latitude29nola.com

Opening hours	Open 7 days
Reservation policy	Accepted
Credit cards	Accepted
Price range	Affordable
Dress code	Casual
Style	Tiki bar

"Jeff 'Beachbum' Berry is the reason tiki drinks and tiki culture are currently enjoying a resurgence in popular culture . . . As a tiki geek, this is THE bar. Cocktail menu, decor, food menu, and everything else has been created and curated by the man who is the reason for the season, so to speak. Tiki drinks are like every other cocktail, but more fun. Cocktail culture has gotten very precious and pretentious, and you can't be that serious while you're holding a drink that's on fire in a skull-shaped mug."—Will Groves

CANE & TABLE

1113 Decatur Street
New Orleans
Louisiana 70116
United States
+1 5045811112
www.caneandtablenola.com

Opening hours	Open 7 days
Reservation policy	Not accepted for drinks
Credit cards	Accepted
Price range	Affordable
Dress code	Casual
Style	Tiki bar

Opened in summer 2013, Cane & Table is a "Rustic Colonial Cuisine and Proto-Tiki" bar and restaurant led by Neal Bodenheimer (of local favorites Cure and Bellocq) and Nick Detrich (also of Cure). Upon entering, you feel as though you've stepped into Old Havana: the room is anchored by a long marble bar that runs the entire length of one distressed-plaster wall. The menu is rum-centric and tiki-inspired, but the team has added their own special twists; take for example the Boss Colada, a riff on the Piña Colada, with Bäska Snaps, a bitter Swedish-style spirit.

THE CAROUSEL BAR & LOUNGE

214 Royal Street
Hotel Monteleone
New Orleans
Louisiana 70130
United States
+1 5045233341
www.hotelmonteleone.com

Opening hours	Open 7 days
Reservation policy	Not accepted for drinks
Credit cards	Accepted
Price range	Affordable
Dress code	Casual
Style	Cocktail bar

"Usually I'm in New Orleans for Tales of the Cocktail and during this festival it's a great place to sit and chat with bartenders and spirits industry folk from all over the world. I was introduced to my favorite cocktail here many years ago: the Vieux Carre."—Danielle Tatarin

Located in one of New Orleans' oldest hotels, The Carousel Bar is a must for any cocktail aficionado. The hotel is the home of the original Vieux Carre (French for "Old Square" and the historic name of the French Quarter neighborhood in which it is located). The 25-seat Carousel Bar does in fact spin — one revolution every 15 minutes. It also has a rich literary history: Truman Capote claimed he was born in the Hotel Monteleone and authors including Ernest Hemingway, Tennessee Williams, and William Faulkner are among its distinguished guests.

CURE

4905 Freret Street
New Orleans
Louisiana 70115
United States
+1 5043022767
www.curenola.com

Opening hours	Open 7 days
Reservation policy	Accepted
Credit cards	Accepted
Price range	Affordable
Dress code	Smart casual
Style	Cocktail bar

"Neil Bodenheimer opened Cure in 2009, and it quickly changed the cocktail landscape of the city, ushering it into the twenty-first-century craft cocktail renaissance. When I'm showing New Orleans to visitors from the cocktail capitals of Europe, such as London or Berlin, this is always my first stop. Cure is indisputably world-class. I have never had a bad drink here, but I've had plenty of amazing ones. —Jeff "Beachbum" Berry

ERIN ROSE

811 Conti Street
New Orleans
Louisiana 70112
United States
+1 5045223573
www.erinrosebar.com

Opening hours	Open 7 days
Reservation policy	Not accepted for drinks
Credit cards	Accepted
Price range	Budget
Dress code	Casual
Style	Irish pub

"A no-frills Irish pub in the heart of the French Quarter. Outrageously awesome prices, killer po' boys, and frozen Irish coffees (to-go if you desire). Not to mention the friendly, dressed-down staff that's no stranger to a stiff pour of whiskey."—Beau Edgington

FINN MCCOOL'S

3701 Banks Street
New Orleans
Louisiana 70119
United States
+1 5044869080
www.finnmccools.com

Opening hours	Open 7 days
Reservation policy	Not accepted for drinks
Credit cards	Accepted
Price range	Budget
Dress code	Casual
Style	Irish pub

"Top to bottom, the owners to the bartenders and their love of the neighborhood they chose to open their bar in. They even came back in force after it was flooded by Hurricane Katrina. They have always worked with their neighborhood of Mid-City, New Orleans, and they represent it well." —Chris Hannah

MIMI'S
2601 Royal Street
New Orleans
Louisiana 70117
United States
+1 5048729868
www.mimismarigny.com

Opening hours..Open 7 days
Reservation policy............................Not accepted for drinks
Credit cards..Accepted
Price range...Budget
Dress code..Casual
Style...Dive bar

"Very cool . . . dive bar on the first floor and a chic tapas bar on the top."—Chris Hannah

MOLLY'S AT THE MARKET
1107 Decatur Street
New Orleans
Louisiana 70116
United States
+1 5045255169
www.mollysatthemarket.net

Opening hours..Open 7 days
Reservation policy............................Not accepted for drinks
Credit cards..Accepted
Price range...Budget
Dress code..Casual
Style...Dive bar

"Always someone there that you know. Social atmosphere and sense of community."—Kirk Estopinal

OLD ABSINTHE HOUSE
240 Bourbon Street
New Orleans
Louisiana 70112
United States
+1 5045233181
www.ruebourbon.com/oldabsinthehouse

Opening hours..Open 7 days
Reservation policy............................Not accepted for drinks
Credit cards..Accepted
Price range...Budget
Dress code..Casual
Style...Dive bar

Purportedly the birthplace of the Absinthe Frappe (absinthe with sugar, water & ice) in 1874; still the iconic drink to order.

PAL'S LOUNGE
949 North Rendon Street
New Orleans
Louisiana 70119
United States
+1 5044887257

Opening hours..Open 7 days
Reservation policy............................Not accepted for drinks
Credit cards..Accepted
Price range...Budget
Dress code..Casual
Style..Lounge

"Pal's is cocktail in plastic cups with air hockey, naked pictures in the toilets, and dogs roaming the bar. Yes. A thousand times yes to all these things."—Abigail Gullo

R BAR
1431 Royal Street
Royal Street Inn
New Orleans
Louisiana 70116
United States
+1 5049487499
www.royalstreetinn.com

Opening hours..Open 7 days
Reservation policy............................Not accepted for drinks
Credit cards..Accepted
Price range...Budget
Dress code..Casual
Style...Dive bar

"R Bar is a soulful, gritty bar that despite being located in an extremely hip hotel, feels like a neighborhood joint."
—Chad Solomon

THE SAINT
961 Saint Mary Street
New Orleans
Louisiana 70130
United States
+1 5045230050
www.thesaintneworleans.com

Opening hours..Open 7 days
Reservation policy............................Not accepted for drinks
Credit cards..Accepted
Price range...Budget
Dress code..Casual
Style...Dive bar

"Upbeat . . . the best dive bar in the city."— Chris Hannah

"THEY HAVE NO SET MENU, YOU TELL THE BARTENDERS A FEW ADJECTIVES LIKE 'SMOKEY', 'CITRUS', 'TROPICAL', ETC., WITH YOUR PREFERENCE OF SPIRIT AND THEY WILL DO THE MAGIC."

TENZIN SAMDO P.310

"TEXAS-INSPIRED ATMOSPHERE WITH A LARGE MEZCAL AND TEQUILA SELECTION."

EZRA STAR P.311

USA NORTHEAST

"THE FACT THAT THEY HAVE THE BEST BEER SELECTION IN THE AREA FEELS LIKE A HAPPY ACCIDENT."

WILL GROVES P.312

"GREAT WINE LIST, GREAT COCKTAILS, AND YOU CAN GET CHEAP BEER IN A CAN ON TOP OF ALL THAT."

WILL GROVES P.314

"THE STAFF IS SUPER WARM AND FRIENDLY, THE COCKTAILS AND DRAFT LIST ARE GREAT, THE WINE LIST IS CURATED BY AN INCREDIBLE SOMMELIER, AND THE SPACE IS COZY AND INVITING."

WILL GROVES P.314

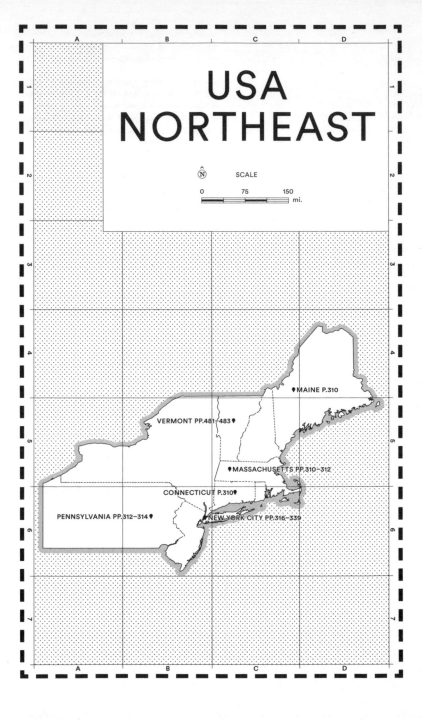

USA
NORTHEAST

N

SCALE

0   75   150

mi.

MAINE P.310

VERMONT PP.481–483

MASSACHUSETTS PP.310–312

CONNECTICUT P.310

PENNSYLVANIA PP.312–314

NEW YORK CITY PP.316–339

ORDINARY

990 Chapel Street
New Haven
Connecticut 06510
United States
+1 2039070238
www.ordinarynewhaven.com

Opening hours..Closed Sunday
Reservation policy....................................Not accepted for drinks
Credit cards...Accepted
Price range..Affordable
Dress code..Smart casual
Style...Cocktail bar

The Ordinary is housed in a building that's been a tavern or bar since the 1700s. It's a homey bar serving classic cocktails including a barrel-aged Stinger variation. On Wednesdays they host "Cocktail Lab" nights where they share new drinks based on a theme or ingredient, for example "Maverick vs Iceman" with drinks inspired by the film, *Top Gun*.

EVENTIDE OYSTER CO.

86 Middle Street
Portland
Maine 04101
United States
+1 2077748538

Opening hours..Open 7 days
Reservation policy....................................Not accepted for drinks
Credit cards...Accepted
Price range..Affordable
Dress code..Smart casual
Style...Cocktail bar

DRINK

348 Congress Street
Boston
Massachusetts 02210
United States
+1 6176951806
www.drinkfortpoint.com

Opening hours..Open 7 days
Reservation policy....................................Not accepted for drinks
Credit cards...Accepted
Price range..Affordable
Dress code..Smart casual
Style...Cocktail bar

"Drink has been one of my favorite craft-cocktail bars, not only in Boston but in the world. They have no set menu, you tell the bartenters a few adjectives like 'smokey,' 'citrus,' 'tropical,' etc, with your preference of spirit and they will do the magic. I encourage you to go there earlier in the night because of the limited capacity, creating a queue down the sidewalk. Their collection of vintage barware and tools is very impressive. Every guest sips cocktails from unique vintage glasses and mugs. Never had a bad drink from this bar." —Tenzin Samdo

"Since they opened, Drink has some of the best drinks and some of the best service we've ever experienced. They're amazing at reading guests and tailoring their service style to each individual. You want to geek out on cocktails? They do that. You want to impress a date? They'll help. You want to be left alone? Consider it done. You want to trade raunchy jokes? They're right there with you."—Andrew and Briana Volk

EASTERN STANDARD

528 Commonwealth Avenue
Boston
Massachusetts 02215
United States
+1 6175329100
www.easternstandardboston.com

Opening hours..Open 7 days
Reservation policy....................................Not accepted for drinks
Credit cards...Accepted
Price range..Affordable
Dress code..Smart casual
Style.......................................Restaurant and cocktail bar

"It is rare to find a large-scale space that is able to be so much to so many. It is open three hundred and sixty-four days a year, nineteen hours a day. One day you may sit on the patio for a tasting menu with some of the best natural wines in the city; another, snag a table on the patio for oysters and champagne; the next, grab a burger and a beer before a Sox game; and the next, come in late at night for crazy snacks and handcrafted drinks from a list of over seventy. ES is James Beard-nominated for best service and a benchmark for how to execute quality within the industry."—Vincent Stipo

THE HAWTHORNE
500A Commonwealth Avenue
Hotel Commonwealth
Boston
Massachusetts 02215
United States
+1 6175329150
www.thehawthornebar.com

Opening hours	Open 7 days
Reservation policy	Accepted
Credit cards	Accepted
Price range	Affordable
Dress code	Smart casual
Style	Cocktail bar

"The Hawthorne, tucked in the basement of Hotel Commonwealth, is the creation of legendary Boston bartender Jackson Cannon. Here you will find the finest on-the-spot concoctions crafted by some of the city's finest bartenders. The place is intimate and their expansive cocktail menu is filled with nouveau classics, rediscovered gems, and daily changing creations."—Tenzin Samdo

"Whether you're starting or ending your evening, this is a must when in Boston. Spot-on cocktails, hospitality, and you can walk (or be walked to) your room. On top of it, the place is flanked by two other killer spots: Eastern Standard and Island Creek Oysters. It's a built-in bar crawl."—Charles Joly

TAVERN ROAD
343 Congress Street
Boston
Massachusetts 02210
United States
+1 6177900808
www.tavernroad.com

Opening hours	Closed Sunday
Reservation policy	Not accepted for drinks
Credit cards	Accepted
Price range	Affordable
Dress code	Casual
Style	Restaurant and cocktail bar

"Tavern Road is a high-energy restaurant and cocktail bar . . . Entertaining, energetic, knowledgeable bartenders who are very great on keeping the guests entertained for almost eleven hours. Also, one of my city's top-industry, late-night spots for food and beverage and last-minute fun and memorable experiences."—Tenzin Samdo

BRICK & MORTAR
567 Massachusetts Avenue
Cambridge
Massachusetts 02139
United States
+1 6174910016
www.brickmortarltd.com

Opening hours	Open 7 days
Reservation policy	Accepted
Credit cards	Accepted
Price range	Affordable
Dress code	Smart casual
Style	Speakeasy

"Amazing good time. Music-driven with great cocktails in a unique space."—Ezra Star

LONE STAR TACO BAR
635 Cambridge Street
Cambridge
Massachusetts 02141
United States
+1 8572856179
www.lonestar-boston.com

Opening hours	Open 7 days
Reservation policy	Not accepted for drinks
Credit cards	Accepted
Price range	Affordable
Dress code	Casual
Style	Taco restaurant and bar

"Texas-inspired atmosphere with a large mezcal and tequila selection."—Ezra Star

STATE PARK

Building 300
1 Kendall Square
Cambridge
Massachusetts 02139
United States
+1 6178484355
www.statepark.is

Opening hours	Open 7 days
Reservation policy	Not accepted for drinks
Credit cards	Accepted
Price range	Budget
Dress code	Casual
Style	Dive bar

"This upscale dive, opened by the folks behind award-winning Hungry Mother, has the comfort of the neighborhood, but with great food and drinks, not to mention pinball and shuffleboard."—Naomi Levy

BACKBAR

7 Sanborn Court
Somerville
Massachusetts 02143
United States
+1 6177180249
www.backbarunion.com

Opening hours	Open 7 days
Reservation policy	Accepted
Credit cards	Accepted
Price range	Affordable
Dress code	Smart casual
Style	Cocktail bar

"Awesome, small bar with innovative, award-winning cocktails."—Ezra Star

TRINA'S STARLITE LOUNGE

3 Beacon Street
Somerville
Massachusetts 02143
United States
+1 6175760006
www.trinastarlitelounge.com

Opening hours	Open 7 days
Reservation policy	Not accepted for drinks
Credit cards	Accepted but not AMEX
Price range	Affordable
Dress code	Casual
Style	Restaurant and lounge

"The laid-back drinks and the brunch. They do an industry brunch every Monday and the food is killer. Chicken and waffles and some Fernet Branca for me, please."
—Jonathan Pogash

HOUSE OF 1000 BEERS

357 Freeport Street
New Kensington
Pennsylvania 15068
United States
+1 7243377666
www.houseof1000beers.com

Opening hours	Open 7 days
Reservation policy	Accepted
Credit cards	Accepted
Price range	Affordable
Dress code	Casual
Style	Beer bar

"This place is in a far-flung suburb of Pittsburgh called New Kensington. It's a former steel town that is a little rough around the edges. In a lot of important ways, House of 1000 Beers (Ho1kB) feels like any other slightly divey bar in a suburb of Pittsburgh. The fact that they have the best beer selection in the area feels like a happy accident. You can always find some gems at Ho1kB from the likes of Mikkeler, Prairie Artisan Ales, Evil Twin, Maine Beer Co., HaandBryggeriet, and other breweries no one else in the area ever gets. Service is always really friendly and fun. This place could be so snobby if they wanted it to be, but they don't want to be and never are. Also, when you play Black Sabbath on the jukebox for almost an hour straight, no one seems to mind."
—Will Groves

THE 700

700 North 2nd Street
Philadelphia
Pennsylvania 19123
United States
+1 2154133181
www.the700.org

Opening hours	Open 7 days
Reservation policy	Not accepted for drinks
Credit cards	Accepted but not AMEX
Price range	Affordable
Dress code	Casual
Style	Nightclub

"I still work behind the bar several nights a week, so I don't get a lot of late-night chances to go out , but on my nights off or if I am magically cut early, I am likely to stop into The 700 club in the Northern Liberties neighborhood of Philadelphia (just down the street from Emmanuelle). There are invariably a mixed bag of characters there, no one takes themselves too seriously, and there is a decent lineup of amari, whiskeys, and a great beer list. One of my favorite parts is that there is almost always someone there (sometimes a DJ, sometimes the bartender) playing really good records."—Phoebe Esmon

THE GOOD KING TAVERN

614 South 7th Street
Philadelphia
Pennsylvania 19147
United States
+1 2156253700
www.thegoodkingtavern.com

Opening hours	Open 7 days
Reservation policy	Not accepted for drinks
Credit cards	Accepted
Price range	Affordable
Dress code	Casual
Style	Gastropub

"A French-inspired neighborhood bar run by a father/ daughter team. Inspired by their years in Aix-en-Provence, they offer a full French menu until 1 a.m. and have staffed the bar with seasoned professionals who love nothing more than stirring a Sazerac, while pouring a draft and yelling over an album from The Roots playing in the background. Neighborhood bars are those few places that fill up first on Mondays and Tuesdays, offer an escape from those cold rainy days, and where the stool is yours as long as you need it." —Vincent Stipo

LOCO PEZ

2401 East Norris Street
Philadelphia
Pennsylvania 19125
United States
+1 2678868061
www.locopez.com

Opening hours	Open 7 days
Reservation policy	Not accepted for drinks
Credit cards	Not accepted
Price range	Affordable
Dress code	Casual
Style	Mexican restaurant and bar

A casual taco joint and bar specializing in Mexican and local beers, and over 25 tequilas.

MACE'S CROSSING

1714 Cherry Street
Philadelphia
Pennsylvania 19103
United States
+1 2155645203

Opening hours	Open 7 days
Reservation policy	Not accepted for drinks
Credit cards	Accepted
Price range	Affordable
Dress code	Casual
Style	Bar

"It's a classic shotgun-barrel bar in the middle of Center City. After 9pm, the neighborhood is empty except for everyone who's at Mace's, mostly industry people. Jameson & Yards Pale, and if you have the right way about you, Gary will let you stay late." —Will Hollingsworth

THE ALLEGHENY WINE MIXER

5326 Butler Street
Pittsburgh
Pennsylvania 15201
United States
+1 4122522337
www.alleghenywinemixer.com

Opening hours	Closed Monday
Reservation policy	Not accepted for drinks
Credit cards	Accepted
Price range	Affordable
Dress code	Casual
Style	Wine bar

"It's a wine bar with none of the trappings of what people think of as a 'wine bar.' It's really approachable and really fun. It was opened and is staffed by beverage nerds. Great wine list, great cocktails, and you can get cheap beer in a can on top of all that. It's what every wine bar should be, but very few are. Sunday night is service industry night and it's always a solid crowd of chefs and bartenders."—Will Groves

BAR 11

1101 Bradish Street
Pittsburgh
Pennsylvania 15203
United States
+1 4123810899

Opening hours	Closed Sunday–Tuesday
Reservation policy	Not accepted for drinks
Credit cards	Accepted
Price range	Budget
Dress code	Casual
Style	Dive bar

"This bar is the most ridiculous collection of gimmicks, and it winds up being so over the top that it works. Fire-breathing, mystery-beer vending machine, laser lights, foam machines, fog machines, shot wheel, and a drum kit suspended over the bar that the bartender plays from time to time. The drinks are terrible and deceptively strong, but they do come with candy necklaces and little plastic doodads. Not for the faint of heart or seekers of peace and quiet but it must be seen to be believed."—John Stanton

BUTTERJOINT

214 North Craig Street
Pittsburgh
Pennsylvania 15213
United States
+1 4126212700
www.thebutterjoint.com

Opening hours	Closed Sunday
Reservation policy	Not accepted for drinks
Credit cards	Accepted
Price range	Affordable
Dress code	Smart casual
Style	Cocktail bar

"Best burger in Pittsburgh. Simple as that. Also the staff is super warm and friendly, the cocktails and draft list are great, the wine list is curated by an incredible sommelier, and the space is cozy and inviting. But really, if you come to Pittsburgh and don't eat a Butterjoint burger, you did it wrong."—Will Groves

"IT'S BEEN AROUND FOR SIX YEARS AND IT'S SUCH A STAPLE IN CLEAN, CLASSIC COCKTAILS. THE ROOMS ARE BEAUTIFUL AND THE DRINKS ARE AMAZING."

THEO LIEBERMAN P.320

"IT WAS THE MOST INFAMOUS SPEAKEASY IN NEW YORK DURING PROHIBITION AND IT'S STILL THERE ... ENJOY A GIANT MARTINI IN STYLE, IN A SETTING THAT HAS REMAINED TIMELESS."

KYLE FORD P.321

NEW YORK CITY

"THE BARTENDERS AND THE BIG ICE. IT ALL MAKES YOU FEEL AT HOME AND THE COCKTAILS ARE AT THE TOP OF THE GAME."

ERIC ALPERIN P.339

"IT'S BEEN AROUND FOR 130 YEARS ... FRIENDLY OLD-SCHOOL BARTENDERS WHO REMEMBER YOUR REGULAR DRINK AND ASK HOW YOUR FAMILY IS (BY NAME)."

SAM ROSS P.321

"YOU'LL FIND SOME OF THE MOST RESEARCHED AND TALENTED BARTENDERS, CRAFTING FORGOTTEN CLASSICS AND SQUEEZING FRESH JUICE TO ORDER."

RACHEL FORD P.322

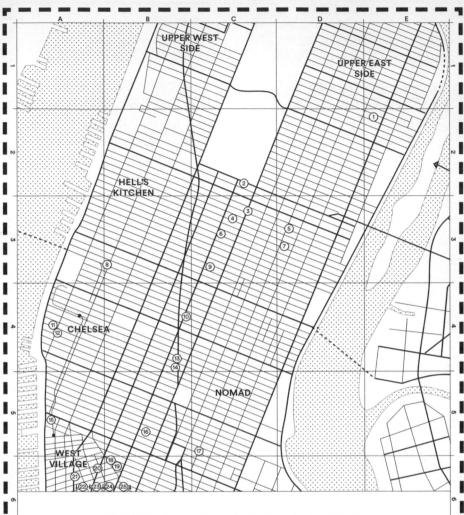

NEW YORK CITY

MANHATTAN UPTOWN & CHELSEA

N̂

SCALE

0   290   580   870
yd.

1. SEAMSTRESS (P.324)
2. THE PALM COURT (P.322)
3. KING COLE BAR (P.322)
4. 21 CLUB (P.321)
5. P.J. CLARKE'S (P.322)
6. RAINBOW ROOM (P.323)
7. HUDSON MALONE (P.321)
8. HOLLAND BAR (P.321)
9. LANTERN'S KEEP (P.322)

10. KEENS STEAKHOUSE (P.321)
11. PORCHLIGHT (P.320)
12. GALLOW GREEN (P.320)
13. THE BRESLIN (P.323)
14. THE NOMAD BAR (P.323)
15. THE TOP OF THE STANDARD (P.326)
16. THE RAINES LAW ROOM (P.320)
17. DEAR IRVING (P.320)
18. SLOWLY SHIRLEY (P.325)

19. THE HAPPIEST HOUR (P.325)
20. WILFIE & NELL (P.326)
21. EMPLOYEES ONLY (P.324)
22. LITTLE BRANCH (P.325)
23. DADDY-O (P.324)
24. DANTE (P.324)
25. ZZ'S CLAM BAR (P.326)

HOME OF THE MANHATTAN: COCKTAILS IN NEW YORK CITY

New York City is the epicenter of both the current cocktail renaissance, as well as the first golden era of cocktails of the late 1800s. It was here that Jerry Thomas, legendary bartender and author of the very first cocktail guide, *Bartenders Guide*, mixed drinks in the 1860s in modern day NoHo. In the 1980s, one hundred years after Thomas's death, Dale DeGroff reintroduced New York to great cocktails at the Rainbow Room. And on New Year's Eve 1999, a bar called Milk & Honey quietly opened and sparked the modern cocktail revolution.

Now-iconic bars such as Pegu Club, PDT, Death & Co, and Employees Only soon followed, and by the early 2010s great cocktails had become mainstream again. Along with the bar explosion, a plethora of local distilleries have popped up, such as the New York Distilling Company in Brooklyn. Their wares can be sampled in the adjoining bar The Shanty.

Of course, in addition to some of the world's top cocktail establishments, New York is also home to a rich tapestry of drinking traditions ranging from old-school dives to ritzy hotel bars to casual neighborhood joints, and everything in between. And, true to its nickname as The City That Never Sleeps, most are open until 4:00 a.m.

The southern half of Manhattan and Brooklyn have the highest concentration of cocktail bars. On the Lower East Side and in the East Village there's one on every corner—ranging from reservation-only PDT to laid-back Holiday Cocktail Lounge—alongside classic dives like Lucy's and pieces of New York history like McSorley's Ale House. Move uptown toward Madison Square Park and you'll find chic destinations such as The Raines Law Room and The NoMad Bar. New York institutions including 21 Club, the King Cole Bar, and P.J. Clarke's dominate midtown Manhattan. As soon as you move out to Brooklyn, things become more relaxed. Williamsburg echoes the Lower East Side with its wide variety and Cobble Hill offers great neighborhood destinations such as Clover Club. Long Island City, Queens—home of Dutch Kills—is an up-and-coming destination, alongside other areas of Brooklyn.

Although Jerry Thomas's Broadway bar is long gone, and Milk & Honey is no more, their legacies continue to impact bars not only in New York, but all over the world. To drink a classic cocktail today is to experience their influence.

Practical Information:
— Cocktails start around US$10, average US$14 to US$15, and max out around US$25.
— Standard tipping is 20%.

GALLOW GREEN

542 West 27th Street
The McKittrick Hotel
Chelsea
New York
New York 10001
United States
+1 2125641662
www.mckittrickhotel.com/gallow-green

Opening hours	Open seasonally in the summer
Reservation policy	Accepted
Credit cards	Accepted
Price range	Affordable
Dress code	Smart casual
Style	Rooftop bar and lounge

"I love the secret garden feel of Gallow Green, and it has a stunning view of the Hudson and downtown Manhattan. It's a really lovely place to take visitors and let them soak up the views, and it's always great people-watching."
—Meaghan Dorman

PORCHLIGHT

271 11th Avenue
Chelsea
New York
New York 10001
United States
+1 2129816188
www.porchlightbar.com

Opening hours	Closed Sunday
Reservation policy	Not accepted for drinks
Credit cards	Accepted
Price range	Affordable
Dress code	Casual
Style	Cocktail bar

Danny Meyer's first stand-alone bar, Porchlight combines his signature hospitality with top notch cocktails and bar snacks to match. A short, well-curated cocktail list includes the iconic Gun Metal Blue, with mezcal, peach brandy, and blue curaçao and a brilliant aqua hue as well as more classic riffs. The large footprint on 11th Avenue offers ample space for groups, too.

THE RAINES LAW ROOM

48 West 17th Street
Flatiron
New York
New York 10011
United States
www.raineslawroom.com

Opening hours	Open 7 days
Reservation policy	Accepted
Credit cards	Accepted
Price range	Affordable
Dress code	Smart casual
Style	Speakeasy

"It's been around for six years and it's such a staple in clean, classic cocktails. The rooms are beautiful and the drinks are amazing. What Meaghan has done there has elevated modern, classic cocktails."—Theo Lieberman

The Raines Law Room —named after an 1896 New York state law that restricted the service of alcoholic beverages on Sundays — is a gem of the New York cocktail scene. Head Bartender Meaghan Dorman presides over an intimate room full of mismatched Victorian sofas and a handful of small banquettes surrounded by sheer curtains. To enter, walk down the small flight of stairs and ring the bell on the unmarked door. Reservations are available Sunday through Thursday only and the wait list can top two hours on busy nights. A small garden is open in nice weather and offers an especially romantic setting.

DEAR IRVING

55 Irving Place
Gramercy
New York
New York 10003
United States
www.dearirving.com

Opening hours	Open 7 days
Reservation policy	Accepted
Credit cards	Accepted
Price range	Affordable
Dress code	Smart casual
Style	Cocktail bar

"Dear Irving is my favorite cocktail bar that's opened in the last couple of years."—Andrew Rice

A seductive bar with top notch cocktails headed up by Meaghan Dorman, also of The Raines Law Room.

21 CLUB

21 West 52nd Street
Midtown
New York
New York 10019
United States
+1 2125827200
www.21club.com

Opening hours	Closed Sunday
Reservation policy	Not accepted for drinks
Credit cards	Accepted
Price range	Expensive
Dress code	Smart casual
Style	Restaurant and bar

"It was the most infamous speakeasy in New York during Prohibition and it's still there. Think not of the dark, dingy, basement neo-speakeasies of the 2000s. The 21 Club is a New York institution, very much defined by its eclectic and well-to-do clientele. Gentlemen, jacket please. Did I mention that jeans and t-shirts are strictly prohibited? Enjoy a giant Martini in style, in a setting that has remained timeless. It is the only place I know of in town where you can still order pomme soufflés. If you make friends with the bartender, you may even get a tour of their famed wine cellar, hidden behind a brick wall and two-ton door in their basement. Where else can you tour the remnants of Prohibition's past?"—Kyle Ford

HOLLAND BAR

532 Ninth Avenue
Midtown
New York
New York 10018
United States
+1 2125024609

Opening hours	Open 7 days
Reservation policy	Not accepted for drinks
Credit cards	Not accepted
Price range	Budget
Dress code	Casual
Style	Dive bar

"I used to be a regular at this bar. It's a good place, the kind that has pictures on the walls of the regulars, where it may look kind of scary, but everyone's super friendly."
—Dave Arnold

HUDSON MALONE

218 East 53rd Street
Midtown
New York
New York 10022
United States
+1 2123556607
www.hudsonmalone.com

Opening hours	Open 7 days
Reservation policy	Not accepted for drinks
Credit cards	Accepted
Price range	Affordable
Dress code	Casual
Style	Restaurant and bar

"A recreated P.J. Clarke's located around the corner by Doug Quinn, the original P.J. Clarke bartender."—Dale DeGroff

KEENS STEAKHOUSE

72 West 36th Street
Midtown
New York
New York 10018
United States
+1 2129473636
www.keens.com

Opening hours	Open 7 days
Reservation policy	Not accepted for drinks
Credit cards	Accepted
Price range	Affordable
Dress code	Smart casual
Style	Restaurant and bar

"It's been around for 130 years. It's a restaurant primarily but the bar room is the place to be. Friendly old-school bartenders who remember your regular drink and ask how your family is (by name) despite the fact that it is three-deep and you haven't been by in six months. Amazing Scotch list too."—Sam Ross

KING COLE BAR

2 East 55th Street
St. Regis Hotel
Midtown
New York
New York 10022
United States
+1 2127534500
www.kingcolebar.com

Opening hours	Open 7 days
Reservation policy	Not accepted for drinks
Credit cards	Accepted
Price range	Expensive
Dress code	Smart casual
Style	Cocktail bar

"Another place bartenders pay tribute at is the King Cole Bar. Everyone wants to see the King Cole triptych mural by Mayfield Parrish. Sitting in front of that mural is really a sight to behold. Great bartenders have stood in front of that bar, including Harry Craddock who went on to write *The Savoy Cocktail Book*. They have a wonderful cognac collection and do great Martinis and Manhattans."—Dale DeGroff

LANTERN'S KEEP

49 West 44th Street
The Iroquois Hotel
Midtown
New York
New York 10036
United States
+1 2124534287
www.iroquoisny.com/lanternskeep

Opening hours	Closed Sunday
Reservation policy	Not accepted for drinks
Credit cards	Accepted
Price range	Affordable
Dress code	Smart casual
Style	Cocktail bar

"While this dark and cozy cocktail haven is usually packed to the gills from 5 p.m. on, it turns into our little secret in the late hours of the night. When the suits have fled and a few scattered couples, deep in conversation, lean in to each other over cocktails, I prefer to sit at the bar. There, you'll find some of the most researched and talented bartenders, crafting forgotten classics and squeezing fresh juice to order. It is in these quieter hours that you'll find other bartenders trickling in, eager to enjoy a perfectly executed cocktail—that they themselves didn't have to make."—Rachel Ford

THE PALM COURT

5th Avenue at Central Park South
The Plaza Hotel
Midtown
New York
New York 10019
United States
+1 2125465300
www.theplazany.com

Opening hours	Open 7 days
Reservation policy	Not accepted for drinks
Credit cards	Accepted
Price range	Expensive
Dress code	Smart casual
Style	Cocktail bar

"The Palm Court is high tea and Eloise and Gatsby and Trader Vic. Historic cocktails, finely crafted and beautifully presented."—Abigail Gullo

P. J. CLARKE'S

915 3rd Avenue
Midtown
New York
New York 10022
United States
+1 2123171616
www.pjclarkes.com

Opening hours	Open 7 days
Reservation policy	Not accepted for drinks
Price range	Affordable
Dress code	Casual
Style	Burger joint and bar

"A bartender's bar, open three hundred and sixty-five days a year. They used to close for only two hours each day, to mop the floors. New Year's Day, Christmas Day: it's always open and there are always people."—Dale DeGroff

RAINBOW ROOM

30 Rockefeller Plaza
Midtown
New York
New York 10112
United States
+1 2126325000
www.rainbowroom.com

Opening hours	Rainbow Room is open Sunday and Monday only/SixtyFive is open Monday–Friday
Reservation policy	Accepted
Credit cards	Accepted
Price range	Expensive
Dress code	Formal
Style	Restaurant and bar

"I almost hesitate to share this secret . . . New York's iconic Rainbow Room (Dale DeGroff's alma mater) reopened recently for Sunday brunch and Monday dinner. What many don't know, however, is that SixtyFive, the adjoining bar, is open for service in the evenings during the week. From the Top of the Rock, you can enjoy a delicious cocktail while taking in breathtaking panoramic views of Manhattan.

This gem is infinitely better than any double decker bus or viewing platform."—Rachel Ford

THE BRESLIN

16 West 29th Street
Ace Hotel
NoMad
New York
New York 10001
United States
+1 2126791939
www.thebreslin.com

Opening hours	Open 7 days
Reservation policy	Not accepted for drinks
Credit cards	Accepted
Price range	Affordable
Dress code	Casual
Style	Gastropub

"I love a place where you can get a great drink and hearty cuisine. I would go anywhere to eat April Bloomfield's food, but here I can take part in my favorite activity (sitting at a bar) and order off of a menu created by Chef Bloomfield. Bonus."—Sean Kenyon

THE NOMAD BAR

10 West 28th Street
NoMad
New York
New York 10001
United States
+1 3474725660
www.thenomadhotel.com

Opening hours	Open 7 days
Reservation policy	Not accepted for drinks
Credit cards	Accepted
Price range	Affordable
Dress code	Smart casual
Style	Cocktail bar

"NoMad is a special place for number of reasons. It is one of the very few places where to me everything is just perfect. Each of the bar rooms has stunning, yet different design . . . It's friendly and relaxed, yet extremely professional, the most delicious bar food ever and drinks from an award-winning team. The cocktails are interesting, great flavors, and the guys bang them out fast! If a cocktail is not your cup of tea the wine list will delight you and don't forget to try Nomader Weisse beer with basil and fennel syrup!"—Alex Kratena

"There's nothing about the NoMad that isn't killing it. From food to drinks to service, this crew is of a professional caliber that no other bar on the planet can match . . . Try to leave and not feel like the bartender is your best friend, I dare you."—Alex Day

"The NoMad Bar is near blissful perfection . . . there is perhaps nothing better than snagging a table on the balcony above with a dry Martini in hand and watching the convivial atmosphere below."—Kyle Ford

The NoMad Bar is actually comprised of three separate bars within the NoMad Hotel: the Library Bar is open to hotel guests only; the Elephant Bar welcomes guests before dinner in the restaurant; and the main bar is accessible via its own entrance on 28th Street which spans two floors. The NoMad Bar was named the World's Best Hotel Bar in 2013 and the Best American Restaurant Bar in 2014 at the Spirited Awards and won Outstanding Bar Program at the James Beard Awards also in 2014. It is also the #5 most-recommended bar in this book. Beverage Director Leo Robitschek oversees the program here and at sister property Eleven Madison Park.

SEAMSTRESS

339 East 75th Street
Upper East Side
New York
New York 10021
United States
+1 2122888033
www.seamstressny.com

Opening hours	Open 7 days
Reservation policy	Not accepted for drinks
Credit cards	Accepted
Price range	Affordable
Dress code	Casual
Style	Restaurant and bar

"The team behind this spot are good friends—and they've done a pretty amazing job with it. It combines all of my favorite elements: history, just enough kitsch, amazing cocktails, and great food. It's an all-around amazing spot on the Upper East Side, which before now, was never a cocktail destination. But now it is, thanks to Seamstress and a couple of other spots in that area."—Jonathan Pogash

DADDY-O

44 Bedford Street
West Village
New York
New York 10014
United States
+1 2124148884
www.daddyonyc.com

Opening hours	Open 7 days
Reservation policy	Not accepted for drinks
Credit cards	Accepted
Price range	Affordable
Dress code	Casual
Style	Bar

"Phil Casceli stocks an amazing selection of spirits and hires hospitable bartenders who will happily pour you a perfect pint of Guinness."—Jim Meehan

DANTE

79-81 Macdougal Street
West Village
New York
New York 10012
United States
+1 2129825275
www.dante-nyc.com

Opening hours	Open 7 days
Reservation policy	Not accepted for drinks
Credit cards	Accepted
Price range	Affordable
Dress code	Casual
Style	Cafe and bar

"Dante is one of those rare renovations that manages to feel timeless and yet 'so on trend.' It is leading a reappraisal of vermouth and aperitif drinks, as well as the fresh, culinary cocktails of which bar manager Naren Young is the master. It's the sort of perfect place where you can come for lunch and stay for drinks and dinner. It has the all-day buzz of a cocktail loving Balthazar. Dante manages to be both international and quintessentially New York City at the same time, which means it's the perfect place to drink whatever your mood."—Jacob Briars

EMPLOYEES ONLY

510 Hudson Street
West Village
New York
New York 10014
United States
+1 2122423021
www.employeesonlynyc.com

Opening hours	Open 7 days
Reservation policy	Not accepted for drinks
Credit cards	Accepted
Price range	Affordable
Dress code	Smart casual
Style	Cocktail bar

"Employees Only has a famous ability to stop time, like a casino for cocktail lovers. A running joke in the industry is that you never remember leaving EO, or more realistically, you will always stay twice as long as you meant to. It's not because of the cocktails, though they are excellent, of course. It is more that they have created this remarkable ambience, a combination of high service and high spirits, fueled by the incredible energy of the staff. Normally in a bar or restaurant, the service wanes as the night drags on, and it becomes obvious when you are supposed to leave. In EO, the service never flags, whether it is opening or last call, which is probably why the bar remains so busy from the moment the

doors open. When the check arrives, it's a shock, as if you can't believe it's time to go. 'You can't close now, we're all having too much fun!'"—Jacob Briars

"Late-night cocktails can be hard to find. But late-night cocktails with steak tartare and chicken soup to ease you out the door at 4 a.m.? I still find this hard to beat. Oh that I still lived stumbling distance away . . ."—Abigail Gullo

"When I walked into EO I thought 'This is it: this is the bar I'd like to open.' It's always remained fun, it's always busy, there's never a limit of how many people can come in. You don't have to sit down and turn your cell phone off. And so many great protégées have come out of there. I think that's a hallmark of a great bar, when people have gone on to do great things because of it."—Tony Abou-Ganim

One of the original bars that sparked the cocktail renaissance in New York City, Employees Only is an industry and local favorite. The entrance is marked only by the "EO" symbol on the awning, set above a neon "Psychic" sign in the front window. Led by a team that includes industry icon Dushan Zaric, the bar celebrated its 10th birthday in December 2014 and has won many awards including Best American Bar Team and Best American High Volume Cocktail Bar at the 2015 Tales of the Cocktail Spirited Awards. It has appeared on the World's 50 Best Bars list every year since its inception in 2009, coming in at #4 in 2015 and #2 overall since the awards were invented. It is also the second most-recommended bar in this book.

THE HAPPIEST HOUR

121 West 10th Street
West Village
New York
New York 10011
United States
+1 2122432827
www.happiesthournyc.com

Opening hours...Open 7 days
Reservation policy...Accepted
Credit cards...Accepted
Price range...Affordable
Dress code..Casual
Style...Restaurant and bar

"The sheer amount of volume happening here with the execution of deliciously crafted cocktails is amazing. The very exposed bar has bartenders working in 'round'. The menu is cleverly creative to assist in execution with a 'choose' your booze option on the upstairs menu, slushies, and no joke bar food. The vibe is retro 1950s fun, the music makes you smile. The new Slowly Shirley (downstairs) is the lab. The large cocktail menu explores many different styles of cocktails including the controversial room-temp cocktails. Its era is 1940s Hollywood so it is more cocktail formal with

some clever drink vessels and unique flavor combinations. The fact that you can have both experiences in the same venue is one of the reasons why it should not be missed."
—Lynnette Marrero

LITTLE BRANCH

20 7th Avenue South
West Village
New York
New York 10011
United States
+1 2129294360

Opening hours..Open 7 days
Reservation policy.....................Not accepted for drinks
Credit cards..Not accepted
Price range...Affordable
Dress code..Smart casual
Style...Cocktail bar

"They serve till 3 a.m. The drinks are always amazing, the staff only seems to get better as the night goes on, and there's live jazz during the week."—Theo Lieberman

One of the bars from the late industry pioneer Sasha Petraske, Little Branch offers an underground cocktail oasis in the heart of the West Village. Expect long lines on the weekends and at peak times, but the cocktails and service never disappoint.

SLOWLY SHIRLEY

Downstairs
121 West 10th Street
West Village
New York
New York 10011
United States
+1 2122432827
www.slowlyshirley.com

Opening hours.........................Closed Sunday and Monday
Reservation policy...Accepted
Credit cards...Accepted
Price range...Affordable
Dress code..Smart casual
Style...Speakeasy

"Located in the basement of The Happiest Hour, they've got great 1970s decor and a very relaxed vibe. You can get a great cocktail or a beer and they have one of the best drinks-men in the city in charge, Jim Kearns."—Naren Young

THE TOP OF THE STANDARD

848 Washington Street
The Standard Hotel
West Village
New York
New York 10014
United States
+1 2126457600
www.standardhotels.com/new-york

Opening hours...Open 7 days
Reservation policy...Accepted
Credit cards...Accepted
Price range...Expensive
Dress code...Formal
Style...Lounge

"It's the most beautiful bar in the world for me."—Elad Zvi

WILFIE & NELL

228 West 4th Street
West Village
New York
New York 10014
United States
+1 2122422990
www.wilfieandnell.com

Opening hours...Open 7 days
Reservation policy.........................Not accepted for drinks
Credit cards...Accepted
Price range..Affordable
Dress code...Casual
Style..Gastropub

"I love the location of Wilfie & Nell in the West Village,
and its big windows and airy feel. I love to get there early
afternoon and snag a seat by the window. The bartenders
are always so nice even when it's the wee hours, it just has
a great vibe."—Meaghan Dorman

ZZ'S CLAM BAR

169 Thompson Street
West Village
New York
New York 10012
United States
www.zzsclambar.com

Opening hours...............................Closed Sunday and Monday
Reservation policy...Accepted
Credit cards...Accepted
Price range...Expensive
Dress code..Smart casual
Style...Cocktail bar

"It's a twelve-seat jewel box."—Chad Solomon

"A MARVELOUS REINTERPRETATION OF A HISTORIC BAR THAT NAILS THE CURRENT BOOZY ZEITGEIST."

JOAQUIN SIMO P.334

"THE DRINKS ARE MAGNIFICENT, THE ROOM IS COZY AND SEXY, THE MENU BEGUILINGLY UNENDING IN LENGTH AND VARIETY." JOAQUIN SIMO P.331

NEW YORK CITY

"ONE OF THE OLDEST BARS IN NEW YORK. IT'S PROPER OLD-SCHOOL. LIGHT AND DARK ALE, SAWDUST STREWN FLOORS, AND FEROCIOUS STAFF —JUST AS MCSORLEY WAS HIMSELF."

JACK MCGARRY P.333

"THE DRINKS ARE ALWAYS AMAZING, THE STAFF ONLY SEEMS TO GET BETTER AS THE NIGHT GOES ON, AND THERE'S LIVE JAZZ DURING THE WEEK."

THEO LIEBERMAN P.325

"ONE OF THE MOST BEAUTIFUL BARS THAT ALMOST TAKES YOU BACK TO A DIFFERENT TIME AND PLACE." MONICA BERG P.338

NEW YORK CITY

MANHATTAN DOWNTOWN, BROOKLYN, & QUEENS

SCALE

0   290   580   870   yd.

1. THE CORNER BAR (P.339)
2. DUTCH KILLS (P.339)
3. BLUE RIBBON (P.335)
4. MCSORLEY'S OLD ALE HOUSE (P.332)
5. PDT (P.333)
6. HOLIDAY COCKTAIL LOUNGE (P.332)
7. BUA (P.331)
8. LUCY'S (P.332)
9. DONOSTIA (P.331)
10. SWIFT HIBERNIAN LOUNGE (P.333)
11. MAYAHUEL (P.332)
12. MACE (P.332)
13. DEATH & CO (P.331)
14. AMOR Y AMARGO (P.331)
15. THE WAYLAND (P.333)

16. PEGU CLUB (P.336)
17. ANGEL'S SHARE (P.331)
18. THE EAR INN (P.335)
19. MOTHER'S RUIN (P.335)
20. ATTABOY (P.334)
21. NITECAP (P.334)
22. MAISON PREMIERE (P.338)
23. IONA (P.337)
24. EXTRA FANCY (P.337)
25. THE LEADBELLY (P.334)
26. 169 BAR (P.334)
27. BUSHWICK COUNTRY CLUB (P.336)
28. THE LONG ISLAND BAR (P.338)
29. THE DEAD RABBIT GROCERY
    AND GROG (P.335)

30. MONTERO BAR & GRILL (P.338)
31. DONNA (P.337)
32. THE MAYFLOWER (P.338)
33. GRAND ARMY (P.337)
34. THE BROOKLYN INN (P.336)
35. SUNNY'S BAR (P.338)
36. FORT DEFIANCE (P.337)
37. CLOVER CLUB (P.336)
38. BUTTERMILK (P.336)

PENICILLIN

A modern classic, the Penicillin is a variation of the Whiskey Sour, made with blended Scotch, lemon, honey, ginger, and a float of peated Scotch, resulting in the perfect combination of smoke, citrus, and spice. It was created in 2005 by Sam Ross at Milk & Honey, where Attaboy now stands and where Sam is also partner. If you're lucky, you may be able to drink one created by the man himself.

SOUTHSIDE

The origins of the Southside (or South Side) are the matter of some debate. A refreshing combination of gin, lime, and mint, most likely it was created at the Southside Sportsmen's Club on Long Island. Some say it hails from the South Side of Chicago during Prohibition—or it may have been invented at New York's 21 Club, which, regardless, is the perfect place to drink one.

MANHATTAN

The exact origins of the Manhattan are unknown, but it is definitely from New York City, and perhaps from the now-defunct Manhattan Club. By the mid-1880s it was commonplace in bars across the city. A combination of rye whiskey and sweet vermouth (the exact proportions vary, but are usually 2:1), it should never be shaken, always stirred, and garnished with a brandied cherry.

The Manhattan is one of the most enduring classic cocktails and has spawned a vast range of drinks, including the Martini, which is in effect a gin Manhattan with dry instead of sweet vermouth.

AMOR Y AMARGO

443 East 6th Street
East Village
New York
New York 10009
United States
+1 2126146818
www.amoryamargony.com

Opening hours...Open 7 days
Reservation policy.......................Not accepted for drinks
Credit cards...Accepted
Price range...Affordable
Dress code...Casual
Style...Cocktail bar

"Die-hard classic tiny cocktail bar with NO FRUIT juices, only spirit, bitter and bitters."—Timo Janse

ANGEL'S SHARE

8 Stuyvesant Street
East Village
New York
New York 10003
United States
+1 2127775415

Opening hours...Open 7 days
Reservation policy.......................Not accepted for drinks
Credit cards...Accepted
Price range...Affordable
Dress code...Smart casual
Style..Speakeasy

To find Angel's Share, walk upstairs, turn left through Village Yokocho (a Japanese restaurant) and look for an unmarked door. Behind it lies an intimate cocktail den that only seats parties of 4 or fewer, with no standing allowed. The menu of original cocktails draws heavily on East Asian ingredients including yuzu, matcha tea, and plum wine.

BUA

122 St. Marks Place
East Village
New York
New York 10009
United States
+1 2129796276
www.buabar.com

Opening hours...Open 7 days
Reservation policy...Accepted
Credit cards...Accepted
Price range...Affordable
Dress code...Casual
Style...Bar

"Bua isn't a dive bar but it has the comfort and familiarity of one, and it isn't a fancy cocktail bar but the barkeeps know their classics and can mix you a fine one."—Payman Bahmani

DEATH & CO

433 East 6th Street
East Village
New York
New York 10009
United States
+1 2123880882

Opening hours...Open 7 days
Reservation policy......................................Not accepted
Credit cards...Accepted
Price range...Affordable
Dress code...Smart casual
Style...Cocktail bar

"Death & Co will always feel like home to me, and the experience of entering that nearly pitch-black room still sends shivers down my spine, no matter how many times I have done it. The drinks are magnificent, the room is cozy and sexy, the menu beguilingly unending in length and variety. The menu and the room have been copied all over the world, and so many of today's young bartenders credit their first visit to D&C as the turning point of their hospitality careers."—Joaquin Simo

DONOSTIA

155 Avenue B
East Village
New York
New York 10009
United States
+1 6462569773
www.donostianyc.com

Opening Hours...Open 7 days
Reservation Policy...Accepted
Credit Cards...Accepted
Price Range...Affordable
Dress Code...Casual
Style...Tapas & Sherry Bar

"The vibe. The cider. The sherry and low-alcohol cocktails. The food is also amazing. Well appointed tapas like you'd have in San Sebastián."—Kirk Estopinal

HOLIDAY COCKTAIL LOUNGE

75 St. Marks Place
East Village
New York
New York 10003
United States
+1 2127779637
www.holidaycocktaillounge.nyc

Opening hours	Open 7 days
Reservation policy	Not accepted for drinks
Credit cards	Accepted
Price range	Affordable
Dress code	Casual
Style	Cocktail bar

"It's full of industry, I feel like Norm from *Cheers* when I walk in there."—Sother Teague

LUCY'S

135 Avenue A
East Village
New York
New York 10009
United States
+1 2126733824

Opening hours	Open 7 days
Reservation policy	Not accepted for drinks
Credit cards	Not accepted
Price range	Budget
Dress code	Casual
Style	Dive bar

"Lucy's is a classic dive—one of a few left. Lucy, a seventy-plus- year-old Polish woman, owns the bar and is running the show almost every night, often with her twenty-six-year-old grand-daughter. The bar has everything you could need—a great jukebox, two pool tables, buck hunter, no pretense, and a bartender your grandma's age who will make you feel like drinking until 4 a.m. every night is more than ok. Occasionally she closes to go back to Poland and leaves a little handwritten note on the door."
—David Kaplan

MACE

649 East 9th Street
East Village
New York
New York 10009
United States
www.macenewyork.com

Opening hours	Open 7 days
Reservation policy	Accepted
Credit cards	Accepted
Price range	Affordable
Dress code	Casual
Style	Cocktail bar

Each cocktail on Mace's menu derives its name from a spice, jars of which also line the walls, having been collected by partner Greg Boehm on his many international travels. After a drink in the cozy, exposed-brick-walled space, head around the corner to continue your cocktail crawl on Avenue C, home to the Wayland, among others.

MAYAHUEL

304 East 6th Street
East Village
New York
New York 10003
United States
+1 2122535888
www.mayahuelny.com

Opening hours	Open 7 days
Reservation policy	Accepted
Credit cards	Accepted
Price range	Affordable
Dress code	Casual
Style	Tequila bar

"One of the most beautiful places I have ever seen. Super cool choice of tequilas and mezcal with best Mexican food. I totally adore Mayahuel!"—Bettina Kupsa

MCSORLEY'S OLD ALE HOUSE

15 East 7th Street
East Village
New York
New York 10003
United States
+1 2124739148
www.mcsorleysoldalehouse.nyc

Opening hours	Open 7 days
Reservation policy	Not accepted for drinks
Credit cards	Not accepted
Price range	Budget
Dress code	Casual
Style	Irish pub

"One of the oldest bars in New York. It's proper old-school. Light and Dark ale, sawdust strewn floors, and ferocious staff—just as McSorley was himself. In a modern, ever-changing city, it's a must-see."—Jack McGarry

"Make sure to order a cheese platter, which is still just some slices of cheddar, onions, and a stack of saltines. Remember they only serve beers in pairs, and there are only two valid orders: two dark or two light."—Dave Arnold

PDT

113 St. Marks Place
East Village
New York
New York 10009
United States
+1 2126140386
www.pdtnyc.com

Opening hours	Open 7 days
Reservation policy	Accepted
Credit cards	Accepted
Price range	Affordable
Dress code	Smart casual
Style	Speakeasy

"So many trends and standards were either started at this bar or perfected here, be it the speakeasy concept, bacon-infused bourbon, or simply the notion that great hospitality is equal in import to the quality of cocktails you put out. If you have a speakeasy in your town that opened up in the last five years, it was most likely directly influenced by PDT."
—Payman Bahmani

"One of my favourite moments was visiting in 2007 with my sister and friends and having quite the perfect moment sitting at the bar eating a Wylie Dog and some tater tots, sipping a Jack Rose cocktail. I remember being content and jealous in equal measure."—Ryan Chetiyawardana

"The hot dogs and the telephone booth are a must experience for any out-of-towner."—Sean Muldoon

SWIFT HIBERNIAN LOUNGE

34 East 4th Street
East Village
New York
New York 10003
United States
+1 2122279438
www.swiftnycbar.com

Opening hours	Open 7 days
Reservation policy	Accepted
Credit cards	Accepted
Price range	Affordable
Dress code	Casual
Style	Irish pub

With an extensive beer selection, small plates, and a large space, Swift is a good spot for groups at any time of the evening and especially for late-night as they are open til 4am.

THE WAYLAND

700 East 9th Street
East Village
New York
New York 10009
United States
+1 2127777022
www.thewaylandnyc.com

Opening hours	Open 7 days
Reservation policy	Not accepted for drinks
Credit cards	Accepted
Price range	Affordable
Dress code	Casual
Style	Cocktail bar

"I love The Wayland because I am always comfortable there. The hospitality is gracious without being obsequious, the drinks are tasty but not precious, and it always has good energy without feeling like a meat market. Also, they serve amazing food until 3:30 a.m. every night, which is critical when you have been working all night on an empty stomach. A couple dozen oysters, sausage bread with ricotta, and a dressed Tecate to wash it all down? That's a glorious end to a night."—Joaquin Simo

169 BAR

169 East Broadway
Lower East Side
New York
New York 10002
United States
+1 2126410357 (text only)
www.169barnyc.com

Opening hours	Open 7 days
Reservation policy	Not accepted for drinks
Credit cards	Accepted
Price range	Budget
Dress code	Casual
Style	Dive bar

"It's one of those places where everything goes and everyone in there is always happy."—Yana Volfson

ATTABOY

134 Eldridge Street
Lower East Side
New York
New York 10002
United States

Opening hours	Open 7 days
Reservation policy	Not accepted for drinks
Credit cards	Accepted
Price range	Affordable
Dress code	Casual
Style	Cocktail bar

"What Sam Ross and Michael McIlroy were able to pull off with their amazing bar Attaboy is nothing short of amazing. They respected the bar they worked at for eight years, but didn't slavishly copy it when it was time for their update. A marvelous reinterpretation of a historic bar that nails the current boozy zeitgeist."—Joaquin Simo

"Attaboy is great late night for several reasons. First: handsome bartenders with beards and accents, enough said. Second: best Dark 'n' Stormys around. Also they play a lot of Fleetwood Mac, which I love, and there is always a friendly crowd at the bar, so it's perfect for rolling in solo after a shift for a drink or two."—Meaghan Dorman

"Between Sammy and Mickey, they are a motley crew of testosterone. You know you're going to have a good time if you go there."—Julie Reiner

"I'm sure I don't need to repeat the incredible history of this bar, or the outsize role it has played, as both Milk & Honey and Attaboy, in twenty-first-century bar life. But aside from all that, it's a perfect bar. It has a timeless feel now, part 1950s Americana, part turn-of-the-century cocktail den. The best time to go is about 2 a.m. when the crowd moves from cocktail lovers to cocktail makers, and becomes an industry hang out. Going at this hour allows you a couple of hours of their brilliant cocktails, then you walk out the door at 4 a.m. Leaving Attaboy may be one of the most iconic moments in the city, you walk out with the taste of a Penicillin fresh in your mind, into the quiet street, and as your eyes get used to the dark street, the first thing you see (apart from the trash cans, perhaps) is the Chrysler Building due north. I love this feeling of leaving one New York City icon to look up at another, and as you start your walk home at 4 a.m., you feel you have the city all to yourself. It's a magical moment."
—Jacob Briars

Opened in 2013 by long-time Milk & Honey bartenders Sam Ross and Michael McIlroy, Attaboy occupies the original Milk & Honey space on the Lower East Side. It has been included in the World's 50 Best Bars list since it opened in 2013 and is the #6 most-recommended bar in this book.

THE LEADBELLY

14 Orchard Street
Lower East Side
New York
New York 10002
United States
+1 6465969142

Opening hours	Open 7 days
Reservation policy	Not accepted for drinks
Credit cards	Accepted
Price range	Affordable
Dress code	Casual
Style	Cocktail bar

"I love the design of The Leadbelly—a ramshackle explorer's den so different from every other cocktail bar in New York City. It's worn, honest, comfortable, and fun. But for me, what really sells it is the music: I've heard some of the finest DJs in my life spin records in this tiny room, and the feel is classic, sexy New York City in a room meant for a new generation."
—Brooks Reitz

NITECAP

Downstairs
120 Rivington Street
Lower East Side
New York
New York 10002
United States
+1 2124663361
www.nitecapnyc.com

Opening hours	Open 7 days
Reservation policy	Accepted
Credit cards	Accepted
Price range	Affordable
Dress code	Casual
Style	Cocktail bar

"I don't think these guys can do anything wrong. I love everything about them. The drinks, the bar, the decor, the vibe. It's all amazing. Impeccable is a pretty good word to use."—John Maher

THE DEAD RABBIT GROCERY AND GROG

30 Water Street
Lower Manhattan
New York
New York 10004
United States
+1 6464227906
www.deadrabbitnyc.com

Opening hours	Open 7 days
Reservation policy	Not accepted for drinks
Credit cards	Accepted
Price range	Affordable
Dress code	Smart casual
Style	Irish pub and cocktail bar

"Dead Rabbit is simply the best experience I've ever had in any bar. The Taproom downstairs is great fun with really enthusiastic and friendly bar staff, the beer selection is brilliant . . . whilst the cocktails are simple and delicious—their signature Irish Coffee is a must try. Then there is The Parlor. This upstairs bar is darkly lit with beautiful mini oil lamps and red lamp shades . . . Quiet Irish folk music plays from the speakers as customers peruse the beautifully crafted and cleverly composed cocktail book . . . I genuinely cannot recommend this bar highly enough. Sean Muldoon and Jack McGarry have really raised the bar here. I'd happily hop on a plane from Glasgow just to go for a night."
—James Kemp

"For non-cocktailians there's one of the best Irish bars anywhere on the ground floor, certainly one of the very best and boundary-breaking cocktail bars on the first floor, and the Occasional Room upstairs from that for even more shenanigans."—Philip Duff

MOTHER'S RUIN

18 Spring Street
Nolita
New York
New York 10012
United States
www.mothersruinnyc.com

Opening hours	Open 7 days
Reservation policy	Not accepted for drinks
Credit cards	Accepted
Price range	Budget
Dress code	Casual
Style	Cocktail bar

"I love the rickety old bar top behind which super laid-back bar staff fire out really excellent drinks. I really like the juxtaposition of a run down dive bar feel that serves excellent food and drinks. In the ultrafashionable Soho district, the bar is always full of interesting, friendly, and colourful people and the staff have just as much fun as their customers. Really, really good bar."—James Kemp

BLUE RIBBON

97 Sullivan Street
SoHo
New York
New York 10012
United States
+1 2122740404
www.blueribbonrestaurants.com/restaurants/blue-ribbon-brasserie

Opening hours	Open 7 days
Reservation policy	Not accepted for drinks
Credit cards	Accepted
Price range	Affordable
Dress code	Smart casual
Style	Restaurant

"I worked in New York from 1993–95, shortly after Blue Ribbon opened, at Mario Batali's first restaurant, Po, as the first bartender. It was a regular haunt for industry folks after they got off work: you could have a duck club and cheese fondue at 3:30 a.m. with a fantastic cocktail, beer or great glass of wine."—Tony Abou-Ganim

THE EAR INN

326 Spring Street
SoHo
New York
New York 10013
United States
+1 2122269060
www.earinn.com

Opening hours	Open 7 days
Reservation policy	Not accepted for drinks
Credit cards	Accepted
Price range	Affordable
Dress code	Casual
Style	Pub

"A long, long running neighborhood bar. It's a saloon, divey kind of place. A wonderful bar."—Dale DeGroff

PEGU CLUB

77 West Houston Street
SoHo
New York
New York 10012
United States
+1 2124737348
www.peguclub.com

Opening hours	Open 7 days
Reservation policy	Accepted
Credit cards	Accepted
Price range	Affordable
Dress code	Smart casual
Style	Cocktail bar

"Pegu Club was inspirational to me when I first got into the cocktail bar scene. The ethos of the bar encapsulated a sense of purpose to what they were offering and the way they went about it. Well-balanced drinks and polished environment."
—Jonny McKenzie

THE BROOKLYN INN

148 Hoyt Street
Brooklyn
New York 11217
United States
+1 7185222525

Opening hours	Open 7 days
Reservation policy	Not accepted for drinks
Credit cards	Not accepted
Price range	Budget
Dress code	Casual
Style	Bar

"The Brooklyn Inn isn't exactly a dive, nor is it by any means fancy, but it's perhaps the oldest bar in Brooklyn and feels, well, well-worn. I lived down the street from it for years and it's still one of the places that I'm excited to go back to and have a shot and a beer when I'm in town for business. It's really just a great neighborhood bar (just ask David Wondrich)."—Michael Pazdon

BUSHWICK COUNTRY CLUB

618 Grand Street
Brooklyn
New York 11211
United States
+1 7183882114
www.bushwickcountryclub.com

Opening hours	Open 7 days
Reservation policy	Not accepted for drinks
Credit cards	Accepted
Price range	Budget
Dress code	Casual
Style	Dive bar

"I lived across the street from this bar for years and also had the pleasure of working there. It really embodies the whole concept of a 'third place' so well . . . No matter where my career and travels take me, I always know I can come back to BCC at any time, see a half dozen familiar faces, and have a cold beer and a shot of Fernet waiting for me."
—Frank Cisneros

This is the alleged birthplace of the Pickleback (a shot of Jameson and a shot of pickle juice). It's a dive bar, not a country club, but they do have a 6-hole mini-golf course out back.

BUTTERMILK

577 5th Avenue
Brooklyn
New York 11215
United States
+1 7187886297

Opening hours	Open 7 days
Reservation policy	Not accepted for drinks
Credit cards	Accepted
Price range	Budget
Dress code	Casual
Style	Dive bar

"It's a local neighborhood dive: you can bring your own potato chips and they have Miller High Life and Fernet."
—Theo Lieberman

CLOVER CLUB

210 Smith Street
Brooklyn
New York 11201
United States
+1 7188557939
www.cloverclubny.com

Opening hours	Open 7 days
Reservation policy	Accepted
Credit cards	Accepted
Price range	Affordable
Dress code	Smart casual
Style	Cocktail bar

"It's the epitome of perfection. Julie and Sue saw the need in their neighborhood for a cocktail bar, and they created not just a cocktail bar, but a great bar all around."
—Pam Wiznitzer

DONNA

27 Broadway
Brooklyn
New York 11249
United States
+1 6465686622
www.donnabklyn.com

Opening hours	Open 7 days
Reservation policy	Accepted
Credit cards	Accepted
Price range	Affordable
Dress code	Casual
Style	Cocktail bar

"Great simple cocktails in classic formulas."—Jacob Briars

EXTRA FANCY

302 Metropolitan Avenue
Brooklyn
New York 11211
United States
+1 3474220939
www.extrafancybklyn.com

Opening hours	Open 7 days
Reservation policy	Not accepted for drinks
Credit cards	Accepted
Price range	Affordable
Dress code	Casual
Style	Seafood restaurant and cocktail bar

"This bar is directly on my way home, and I've had a lot of great late nights here."—Nick Bennett

FORT DEFIANCE

365 Van Brunt Street
Brooklyn
New York 11231
United States
+1 3474536672
www.fortdefiancebrooklyn.com

Opening hours	Open 7 days
Reservation policy	Not accepted for drinks
Credit cards	Accepted
Price range	Affordable
Dress code	Casual
Style	Restaurant and cocktail bar

"I worked there for years. Red Hook, Brooklyn is a little hard to get to unless you're dedicated. But once you are there, it is AMAZING and Fort Defiance serves as a local bar for people in the neighborhood. It is a little corner of New York City that doesn't feel like you're there. St John Frizzell owns it and it's just my favorite place on earth."—Ivy Mix

GRAND ARMY

336 State Street
Brooklyn
New York 11217
United States
+1 7184227867
www.grandarmybar.com

Opening hours	Open 7 days
Reservation policy	Accepted
Credit cards	Accepted
Price range	Affordable
Dress code	Casual
Style	Cocktail bar

"Grand Army Bar is in my hood and it's my most frequent stop. I love oysters and they have great wine options for when I'm not in a cocktail mood."—Meaghan Dorman

IONA

180 Grand Street
Brooklyn
New York 11211
United States
+1 7183845008
www.ionabrooklyn.com

Opening hours	Open 7 days
Reservation policy	Not accepted for drinks
Credit cards	Accepted
Price range	Budget
Dress code	Casual
Style	Dive bar

"Iona is a dive bar around the corner from me and I know when I go here I'm either watching a Manchester United game or just chilling out with my wife. No cocktail talk is permitted."—Jack McGarry

THE LONG ISLAND BAR

110 Atlantic Avenue
Brooklyn
New York 11201
United States
+1 7186258908
www.thelongislandbar.com

Opening hours	Open 7 days
Reservation policy	Not accepted for drinks
Credit cards	Accepted
Price range	Affordable
Dress code	Casual
Style	Cocktail bar

"When I first moved to New York City a decade ago, the coolest bar in the city was Passerby. After a greedy landlord shuttered it in a vain attempt to jack up the rent, Toby Cecchini spent the next five years trying to find his next bar. The long wait was worth it. He took over a long-defunct Art Deco-styled diner in Boerum Hill and opened up a new neighborhood staple. The food is decadent and delicious, the bartenders are knowledgeable and efficient, and the vibe is eternally comfortable."—Joaquin Simo

MAISON PREMIERE

298 Bedford Avenue
Brooklyn
New York 11211
United States
+1 3473350446
www.maisonpremiere.com

Opening Hours	Open 7 days
Reservation Policy	Not accepted for drinks
Credit Cards	Accepted
Price Range	Affordable
Dress Code	Smart casual
Style	Cocktail bar

"This is one of the most beautiful bars that almost takes you back to a different time and place. I still remember the first time I walked into Maison Premiere and was just stunned by the amazing room. Go early, have some oysters, enjoy the cocktails, stay into the evening, and finish off with champagne and absinthe. It's the recipe for the perfect night!"—Monica Berg

THE MAYFLOWER

132 Greene Avenue
Brooklyn
New York 11238
United States
+1 7185763584
www.aitarestaurant.com

Opening hours	Open 7 days
Reservation policy	Not accepted for drinks
Credit cards	Accepted
Price range	Affordable
Dress code	Casual
Style	Cocktail bar

"It's just around the corner."—Yana Volfson

MONTERO BAR & GRILL

73 Atlantic Avenue
Brooklyn
New York 11201
United States
+1 6467294129

Opening hours	Open 7 days
Reservation policy	Not accepted for drinks
Credit cards	Not accepted
Price range	Budget
Dress code	Casual
Style	Dive bar

"This bar is a timeless remnant of the industrial roots mired along the South Brooklyn waterfront. Memories of the longshoremen and sailors who frequented the place prior to and after World War II can still be found and felt throughout. Coldest bottle of Budweiser in New York City."
—Richard Boccato

SUNNY'S BAR

253 Conover Street
Brooklyn
New York 11231
United States
+1 7186258211
www.sunnysredhook.com

Opening hours	Closed Monday
Reservation policy	Not accepted for drinks
Credit cards	Not accepted
Price range	Budget
Dress code	Casual
Style	Bar

"An institution on the water in Red Hook. It's been around forever and you can feel that walking in the door. On any night there are a rotating cast of local musicians playing bluegrass in the back room. An experience, every time."
—Sam Ross

"I finally made it to this spot after hearing about it for years, and it didn't disappoint. It's got a great atmosphere, outdoor seats, live music, and cheap beer. I sat on the bench outside watching the sunset on a lazy Sunday afternoon with a drink in hand, and it was fantastic. This is the type of bar every neighborhood needs."—Franky Marshall

"Serving the people of Red Hook for 126 years, Sunny's is an inimitable treasure. It is the most important bar that I have ever been to, hands down—a touchstone as far as drinking establishments are concerned. I visit as often as I can. I'll be there tonight."—Richard Boccato

"The first place I ever tended bar, run by my uncle in my hometown of Sag Harbor. It's been in my family for thirty-plus years; it's a local sports bar, beers on tap, shots, free pour —a decent selection of Budweiser and Bud Lites. There are photos on the wall of people who used to be the regulars from when they first opened and have since passed on. That's the kind of vibe I love, that kind of style."—Nick Bennett

DUTCH KILLS

27-24 Jackson Avenue
Long Island City, Queens
New York 11101
United States
+1 7183832724
www.dutchkillsbar.com

Opening hours	Open 7 days
Reservation policy	Not accepted for drinks
Credit cards	Accepted
Price range	Affordable
Dress code	Casual
Style	Cocktail bar

"The bartenders and the big ice. It all makes you feel at home and the cocktails are at the top of the game, but they don't frown upon you for ordering a shot and a beer. It's been in business since 2009, but has a timeless feel, which when you're in Long Island City, you feel like Dutch Kills has been there forever."—Eric Alperin

THE CORNER BAR

1 Main Street
Sag Harbor, Long Island
New York 11963
United States
+1 6317259760
www.cornerbarsagharbor.com

Opening hours	Open 7 days
Reservation policy	Not accepted for drinks
Credit cards	Accepted
Price range	Affordable
Dress code	Casual
Style	Pub

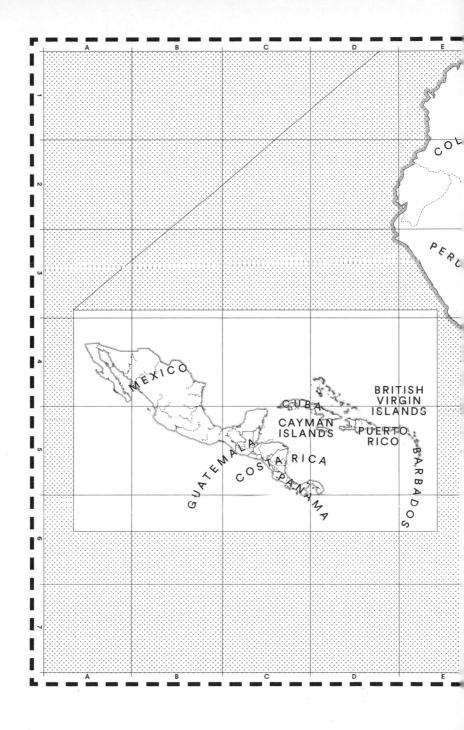

CENTRAL
& SOUTH
AMERICA

BRAZIL

CHILE

ARGENTINA

◆BUENOS AIRES

N̂ SCALE

0   300   600 mi.

COCKTAILS IN
LATIN AMERICA

Latin America is one of the most exciting regions for cocktails right now, with a vibrant food and beverage scene. Mexico City, Buenos Aires, and Lima are the centers of cocktail culture, taking inspiration from New York and Europe, and adding local traditions, spirits, and flavors. Here you'll find a wide variety of bars, demonstrating a mash-up of local and global influences.

Mexico
Mexico City's cocktail scene got started when Licorería Limantour opened in 2011. Since then, others have followed suit, creating a patchwork of high-end cocktail bars. Classic and original drinks use local tequila and mezcals, along with other more obscure spirits.

Mexico's most-recommended bar in this book is La Capilla, in the town of Tequila, where the signature drink is tequila, lime, and Coke.

Practical Information:
- Cocktails range from about Mex$130 to Mex$210.
- Standard tipping is 15%.
- The bar scene starts late, typically filling up at 9:00 or 10:00 p.m.

Peru
Lima has one of the oldest cocktail traditions in South America, evidenced by American expat Victor Martin who invented the Pisco Sour here around 1916. The Pisco Sour, still ubiquitous, now takes on additional flavorings; and pisco itself—delicious sipped straight—is a symbol of national pride. An unaged grape brandy, pisco is made from freshly fermented grapes grown in the Ica Valley.

Practical Information:
- Cocktails range from PEN20 to PEN40.
- A 10% service charge is sometimes included and leaving an additional 10% is customary at higher-end places.

Argentina
Buenos Aires draws much of its drinking influence from Europe. The bar Florería Atlántico takes its inspiration from the European immigrants that flowed into the country in the early 1900s. You'll find plenty of Italian amaro here—particularly the deeply bitter Fernet-Branca which, mixed with Coke, is a nightclub staple.

Practical Information:
- Cocktails range from AR$85 to AR$120.
- Standard tipping is 10%.
- The bar scene here tends to start and end later.

"EXTENSIVE VINTAGE RUM AND CIGAR COLLECTION WITH GOOD DRINKS. IF YOU EVER VISIT BARBADOS, IT IS A MUST!"

GRANT SCENEY P.351

"GREAT LOCATION, THE BEST PIÑA COLADA IN THE CARIBBEAN, AND FRIENDLY BARTENDERS. WHAT ELSE DO YOU NEED?"

SIMON CROMPTON P.349

CENTRAL AMERICA & THE CARIBBEAN

"INCREDIBLE, CREATIVE DRINKS. BEST HOSTING THAT I'VE HAD FOR AGES, COOL BAR CREW, AND BEST ATMOSPHERE."

MARIO KAPPES P.347

"THE HOME OF THE DAIQUIRI, IF YOU ARE LOOKING FOR OLD-SCHOOL ELEGANCE IN HAVANA, THIS CAN'T BE BEAT."

SIMON CROMPTON P.348

"TEQUILA MECCA. HEAVEN ON EARTH."

IVY MIX P.347

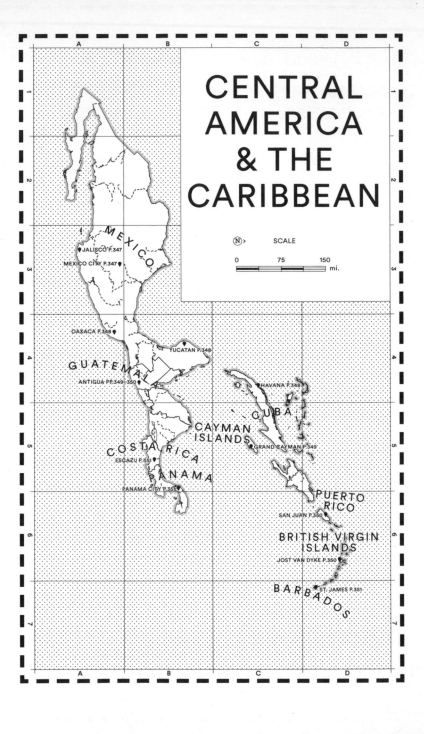

CENTRAL AMERICA & THE CARIBBEAN

SCALE

0   75   150 mi.

A B C D

1 2 3 4 5 6 7

MEXICO

JALISCO P.347

MEXICO CITY P.347

OAXACA P.348

YUCATAN P.348

GUATEMALA

ANTIGUA PP.349-350

HAVANA P.348

CUBA

CAYMAN ISLANDS

GRAND CAYMAN P.349

COSTA RICA

ESCAZU P.351

PANAMA

PANAMA CITY P.351

PUERTO RICO

SAN JUAN P.350

BRITISH VIRGIN ISLANDS

JOST VAN DYKE P.350

BARBADOS

ST. JAMES P.351

DAIQUIRI

Created in 1896 in Cuba by an American expat bartender, the Daiquiri was perfected at Havana's El Floridita Bar by the cocktail king, Constantino Ribalaigua Vert, who is reputed to have made more than ten million of them. It became Ernest Hemingway's cocktail of choice with a slight variation—the addition of maraschino liqueur and grapefruit juice. A classic Daiquiri contains rum, lime, and sugar and is not blended with ice, but shaken and served in a cocktail coupe.

BALTRA

Iztaccíhuatl 36-D
Mexico City
Federal District 06700
Mexico
+52 5552641279

Opening hours	Closed Sunday
Reservation policy	Accepted
Credit cards	Accepted
Price range	Affordable
Dress code	Smart casual
Style	Cocktail bar

"I really enjoy small cozy bars, where you can chat with the bartenders. It is a very small bar with a very well-executed cocktail menu and good atmosphere."—Luis Iriarte

LICORERÍA LIMANTOUR

Álvaro Obregón 106
Mexico City
Federal District 06700
Mexico
+52 5552644122
www.limantour.tv

Opening hours	Open 7 days
Reservation policy	Accepted
Credit cards	Accepted
Price range	Affordable
Dress code	Smart casual
Style	Cocktail bar

"Incredible, creative drinks. Best hosting that I've had for ages, cool bar crew, and best atmosphere."—Mario Kappes

Mexico's first craft cocktail bar, Licorería Limantour is home to many of the city's finest bar staff. Their creative cocktail list features a wide range of tequila and mezcal cocktails showcasing local flavors, like the Margarita al Pastor inspired by the flavors of al pastor tacos. They opened a second location in the Polanco neighborhood of Mexico City a few years ago. In 2015 Licorería Limantour was the only bar in Latin America to be named to the World's 50 Best Bars, at #20. As head bartender Jose Leon says, it's "a beautiful place that was made with a lot of love."

PARKER & LENOX

Milán 14
Mexico City
Federal District 06600
Mexico
+52 5555466979

Opening hours	Closed Sunday and Monday
Reservation policy	Accepted
Credit cards	Accepted
Price range	Affordable
Dress code	Smart casual
Style	Cocktail bar

"It's a kind of speakeasy, it's a beautiful place and has live jazz. The drinks are OK but the atmosphere is incredible."—Jose Leon

LA CAPILLA

Calle Miguel Hidalgo 31
Tequila
Jalisco 46400
Mexico

Opening hours	Open 7 days
Reservation policy	Not accepted for drinks
Credit cards	Not accepted
Price range	Budget
Dress code	Casual
Style	Tequila bar

"Tequila mecca. Heaven on earth."—Ivy Mix

"Eighty-something-year-old barman, Don Javier Delgado Corona, exudes the magic of hospitality, has the coy smile of a saint, and welcomes thirsty bartenders from all over the world to pull up a chair."—Charles Joly

"[Don Javier Delgado Corona's] wise, wrinkled hands effortlessly assemble his home recipe, La Batanga, a cocktail made with tequila, fresh lime, and cola served tall over ice with a crunchy sea-salt rim and stirred with a long knife. Intrigued bartenders and tourists alike travel from far and wide on a 'spiritual' pilgrimage to sample Don Javier's drinks and warm hospitality. Kids ride by on horseback and big old American 4×4 vehicles cruise by, booming out traditional mariachi music. His regular clientele are a combination of farm workers and distillery owners."—Dre Masso

PARE DE SUFRIR TOME MEZCAL

Calle Argentina 66
Guadalajara
Jalisco 44160
Mexico
+52 3338261041

Opening hours	Closed Sunday–Tuesday
Reservation policy	Not accepted for drinks
Credit cards	Not accepted
Price range	Affordable
Dress code	Casual
Style	Mezcal bar

"Best bar in the world. Unparalleled mezcal selection, great crowd dancing like there's no tomorrow. Some of the best tunes you've never heard. All run by the inimitable Pedro Jimenez. Always, always a great time."—Ryan Fitzgerald

"Amazing selection of traditional mezcals, raicilla (another name for mezcal from Jalisco), and Mexican craft beers. Not much else. You can drink this one-of-a-kind agave spirits selection and dance to Cumbia music, a Colombian dance music, while chomping on beef jerky with lime and hot sauce. I had no idea how awesome this would be until I went."—Derek Brown

MEZCALOTECA

Reforma 506
Oaxaca Centro
Oaxaca 68000
Mexico
+52 9515140082
www.mezcaloteca.com

Opening hours	Closed Sunday
Reservation policy	Required
Credit cards	Accepted but not AMEX
Price range	Affordable
Dress code	Casual
Style	Mezcal bar

"It's one of the most unique places to try incredible mezcal. Oaxaca is for me one of the most powerful cities in the world; their culture and identity is so unique it makes an exceptional trip. I will travel around the world for a sip of the best mezcal made in the traditional way, and the Mezcaloteca has a beautiful selection working closely with mezcaleros from different villages and having unusual products that respect the values of mezcal and the traditional way of making it."
—Carina Soto Velasquez

LA ZEBRA

Carretera Tulum a Boca Paila Km 8.2
Ejido Pino Suarez
Tulum
Yucatán 77780
Mexico
+52 19841154728
www.lazebratulum.com

Opening hours	Open 7 days
Reservation policy	Not accepted for drinks
Credit cards	Accepted
Price range	Affordable
Dress code	Casual
Style	Beach bar

"Not only is it located on the beach in one of the most beautiful places in the world, but they also know how to mix up a cocktail. Sipping on a fresh strawberry and coconut Miami Vice while watching a huge crowd salsa dancing with my toes in the sand is my idea of a good time . . . Stepping into a bar should be a vacation, but this bar is so great it's a vacation within your vacation."—Trevor Easter

EL FLORIDITA

Obispo 557
Havana 10100
Cuba
+53 78671300
www.floridita-cuba.com

Opening hours	Open 7 days
Reservation policy	Accepted
Credit cards	Not accepted
Price range	Affordable
Dress code	Casual
Style	Restaurant and bar

"I love Cuba, I love that period in time, it's a magical place."
—Tony Conigliaro

"On the one occasion I was able to visit this historic venue, it was a time warp into the 1930s. The way we were hosted to a pre-dinner cocktail that would set our palate for the seafood feast was perfect. The service in the restaurant was welcoming and the food was incredible. Our cigars were chosen to suit the evening and then the atmosphere of the bar kicked in with humorous chats and creative beverages. All with no music, just the sound of laughter. Would definitely travel the world to go back to that special place."—Jonny Mckenzie

"The home of the Daquiri; if you are looking for old-school elegance in Havana, this can't be beat. Best to count how many Daiquiris you have as they can fly down a little bit too easily!"—Simon Crompton

LA FUENTE

Calle 13, entre F y G
Havana
Cuba

Reservation policy	Not accepted
Credit cards	Not accepted
Price range	Budget
Dress code	Casual
Style	Café and bar

"This is by far my favorite bar in Havana. It's not for cocktails, it's a locals bar for drinking Havana Club and Coke, and eating barbecued pork. It's always my first stop in Havana."—Stu Bale

AGUA RESTAURANT & LOUNGE
Unit 1–3
Galleria Plaza
Seven Mile Beach
Galleria Plaza
Grand Cayman KY1-1207
Cayman Islands
+1 3459492482
www.agua.ky

Opening hours	Open 7 days
Reservation policy	Accepted
Credit cards	Accepted
Price range	Affordable
Dress code	Smart casual
Style	Restaurant and bar

"The best cocktail bartenders on the island who use a lot of local produce from local farmers' markets. Always imaginative drinks with a great variety of spirits, and with an amazing array of ceviches and small-plate appetizers available till late in the night, another great stop for a late-night drink and snack on the island."—Simon Crompton

BAR JACK
Ritz Carlton
Seven Mile Beach
Grand Cayman
Grand Cayman KY1-1209
Cayman Islands
+1 3459439000
www.ritzcarlton.com/GrandCayman

Opening hours	Open 7 days
Reservation policy	Not accepted for drinks
Credit cards	Accepted
Price range	Affordable
Dress code	Casual
Style	Beach bar

"Great location, the best piña colada in the Caribbean, and friendly bartenders. What else do you need?"
—Simon Crompton

CALICO JACK'S BAR AND GRILL
Seven Mile Beach
Grand Cayman KY1-1201
Cayman Islands
+1 3459457850

Opening hours	Open 7 days
Reservation policy	Not accepted for drinks
Credit cards	Accepted
Price range	Budget
Dress code	Casual
Style	Beach bar

"Best bar staff on the island, great live music on some nights, ice-cold beers and shots, perfect in the Caribbean on a hot night after work, or during the day with your feet in the sand and looking out over the Caribbean Sea."—Simon Crompton

CAFÉ NO SÉ
1a Avenida Sur 11C
Antigua 03001
Guatemala
+502 78320563
www.cafenose.com

Opening hours	Open 7 days
Reservation policy	Not accepted for drinks
Credit cards	Accepted
Price range	Affordable
Dress code	Casual
Style	Mezcal and cocktail bar

"I worked here for four years and that's where I started bartending. SERIOUSLY the best bar on earth. I love it there."—Ivy Mix

"There's a mezcal bar out the back that's got a two-drink-per-person minimum. As much as it tries to not be a bar for tourists, they still flock there. The drinks are simple, essentially mezcal or beer. There's live music most nights, and the place is always too dark, but I love it. The fact it's in the valley of Antigua, a place time has forgotten, with its cobblestone streets, and steep volcanoes adds to the charm."—Tim Philips

"With a speakeasy style, Café No Sé is a required stop when visiting Antigua . . . The real charm is the relaxed atmosphere and of course the mezcal Bar. Go after 8 p.m. to see it in action."—Raul Cojolon

LUCKY RABBIT

5a Avenida Sur 8
Antigua 01059
Guatemala
+502 78325099

Opening hours	Open 7 days
Reservation policy	Not accepted for drinks
Credit cards	Accepted
Price range	Budget
Dress code	Casual
Style	Dive bar and game room

"Enjoy the party and games accompanied by great music: Beer Pong, Giant Jenga Arcade Punching Machine, Ping-Pong and more! If you're hungry, Segafredo Antigua next door serves delicious wood-fired pizza and gourmet burgers with a great view on the balcony." —Raul Cojolon

LA REUNION GOLF RESORT AND RESIDENCES

Ruta Nacional CA 14, Km. 91.5
Alotenango, Sacatepequez
Antigua 03001
Guatemala
+502 78731400
www.lareunion.com.gt

Opening hours	Open 7 days
Reservation policy	Not accepted for drinks
Credit cards	Accepted
Price range	Affordable
Dress code	Smart casual
Style	Lounge

"A place to relax, to have fun, in a private setting, away from the city with class, style, and personalized service. This place is not just one more place to go to relax . . . this is THE PLACE to go to relax."—Raul Cojolon

LAS VIBRAS DE LA CASBAH

5a Avenida Norte 30
Antigua 03001
Guatemala
+502 78322640
www.lasvibrasantigua.com

Opening hours	Closed Sunday and Monday
Reservation policy	Accepted
Credit cards	Accepted
Price range	Budget
Dress code	Smart casual
Style	Nightclub

"It was created in 1994 with the idea of establishing in Antigua a place with good music, a different atmosphere, and unusual decor, taking advantage of its location amid some old ruins—a combination that creates a contrast between the old and the new."—Raul Cojolon

LA FACTORIA

Calle San Sebastián 148
San Juan 00901
Puerto Rico
+1 7874124251

Opening hours	Open 7 days
Reservation policy	Not accepted for drinks
Credit cards	Accepted but not AMEX
Price range	Affordable
Dress code	Casual cocktail bar

"This bar is fantastic. It's in Old San Juan and it's this small bar, then you go through a door and you're in a little wine bar, and then you go through another door to a larger room with a DJ. It's not a pushed-speakeasy feel though, and if you didn't know about the other rooms you wouldn't feel like you were missing anything. It has a great old Latin feel. It's the kind of bar you could hang out at for hours."—Kellie Thorn

EL FAROLITO BAR

Calle Sol 277
San Juan 00901
Puerto Rico

Opening hours	Open 7 days
Reservation policy	Not accepted for drinks
Credit cards	Accepted
Price range	Budget
Dress code	Casual
Style	Dive bar

"It feels like home, it's mostly industry people after 4 a.m. and you need to know the bartenders."—Mario Seijo Rivera

SOGGY DOLLAR BAR

White Bay
Jost Van Dyke
British Virgin Islands
+1 2844959888
www.soggydollar.com

Opening hours	Open 7 days
Reservation policy	Not accepted for drinks
Credit cards	Accepted but not AMEX
Price range	Affordable
Dress code	Casual
Style	Beach bar

"Half the fun is getting there. A flight, a ferry ride, a private boat/catamaran/yacht, and then a swim to shore, just to get to one of the most beautiful bar locations in the world. Great atmosphere and a potent and appropriately tropical concoction, the Painkiller. Totally worth the effort and results in all-day beach drinking. Makes the swim back to the boat a little interesting."—Keely Edgington

THE CLIFF

Derricks
St. James
Barbados BB24110
+1 2464321922
www.thecliffbarbados.com

Opening hours	High Season: Open 7 days.
	Low Season: Closed Sunday
Reservation policy	Not accepted for drinks
Credit cards	Accepted
Price range	Expensive
Dress code	Smart casual
Style	Restaurant and bar

"Three-level high-end bar and restaurant literally hanging off the side of a cliff. Extensive vintage rum and cigar collection with good drinks. If you ever visit Barbados, it is a must!"
—Grant Sceney

POCKET FOOD AND DRINK

Centro Comercial Plaza Ciclón
Escazú 398-1250
Costa Rica
+506 22893432

Opening hours	Closed Sunday
Reservation policy	Accepted
Credit cards	Accepted
Price range	Budget
Dress code	Casual
Style	Restaurant and bar

"Located in an unremarkable tiny shopping mall, with less than sixty seats . . . this place is no doubt one of the happiest bars I've been to in my life. Everybody there is absolutely crazy about making you feel at home . . . and even crazier about their beloved gin. And it's not only that they have a wonderful selection, but if you happen to engage in a conversation with one of the owners (who also happens to be the bartender!) it's a sure thing you're going to end up sampling and even making your own drinks behind the bar! No pretensions, always willing to give and mostly learn from their guests, this tiny little bar is by now a legend in San José and I guess will soon become famous all over the globe."—Daniel Estremadoyro

RESTAURANT CABANA

Torre Yoo
6th Floor
Avenida Balboa
Panama City
Panama
+507 3948496

Opening hours	Open 7 days
Reservation policy	Accepted
Credit cards	Accepted
Price range	Expensive
Dress code	Smart casual
Style	Restaurant and bar

"Outside terrace with a view of all the city´s bay. Mind-blowing menu of signature drinks that pair so well with the Mediterranean-style dishes. Beautiful decoration following Yoo Tower´s style. If you have the opportunity I recommend the 'Citronella', a Tanqueray Ten-based cocktail that you will love!"—Enrique Ignacio Auvert

"OVERSIZED COCKTAILS ARE SERVED IN HAND-DECORATED CERAMIC JUGS, GLASS JARS."

DRE MASSO P.355

"THE ATMOSPHERE OF THIS BAR IS UNIQUE, SURROUNDED BY PRICELESS ARTWORK, IT IS AN EXPERIENCE TO ENJOY DELICIOUS COCKTAILS AND ESCAPE THE CITY."

JOSE LUIS VALENCIA P.356

SOUTH AMERICA NORTH

"A BOLD RESTAURANT THAT TAKES ITS INSPIRATION FROM THE PERUVIAN AMAZON WITH UNIQUE DRINKS THAT INTRIGUE AND SURPRISE."

JOSE LUIS VALENCIA P.356

"THIS BAR IS HISTORIC IN LIMA. IT HAS BEEN AROUND FOR MORE THAN ONE HUNDRED YEARS."

AARON DIAZ OLIVOS P.357

"THIS PLACE IS AN ICON OF THE NIGHTLIFE IN COLOMBIA."

CARINA SOTO VELASQUEZ P.355

A · B · C · D

1

2

CUNDINAMARCA P.355

COLOMBIA

3

PERU

4

LIMA PP.356–357

5

6

7

SOUTH
AMERICA
NORTH

N̂   SCALE

0   225   450 mi.

PISCO SOUR

The Pisco Sour was perhaps created in San Francisco—where pisco was popular before Prohibition—or by California expat Victor Morris at his bar in Lima, Peru, around 1916. It is a variation of the Whiskey Sour using Peru's flagship spirit pisco—an unaged grape brandy—with lime juice and an egg white. It's perfectly refreshing and ubiquitous in its home city.

CLICK CLACK HOTEL

Carrera 11 93-77
Bogota
Cundinamarca
Colombia
+57 17430404
www.clickclackhotel.com

Opening hours	Open 7 days/Apache Bar is closed Sunday
Reservation policy	Not accepted for drinks
Credit cards	Accepted
Price range	Affordable
Dress code	Smart casual
Style	Lounge

"This hotel is fantastic. Everything around you radiates talent and personality. I think the owners are animal lovers because animals are depicted everywhere in very extravagant and modern forms. The rooms are fanciful and every detail is designed to be remembered over time. The food is always delicious ... with curious, original, and enjoyable proposals."—Dennis Zoppi

ANDRÉS CARNE DE RES

Calle 3 11A-56
Chia
Cundinamarca
Colombia
+57 18612233
www.andrescarnederes.com

Opening hours	Open 7 days
Reservation policy	Accepted
Credit cards	Accepted
Price range	Affordable
Dress code	Casual
Style	Steakhouse and bar

"This place is an icon of the nightlife in Colombia; it represents everything that we Colombians love and how proud we feel of our culture, including great music, a lot of dancing, food, and aguardiente! All that in an unpretentious and crazy market-feeling decor. They suggest drivers to get you back home because it is outside the city, this way you don't drink and drive (smart)."—Carina Soto Velasquez

"While visiting Colombia a few years back, I had the best bar and restaurant experience of my life. Andrés Carne de Res started more than twenty-five years ago as a small shack selling burgers. It is now a legendary, uber-cool hangout on the outskirts of Bogota, which seamlessly handles upwards of 1,000 covers per night. Prime beef is flown in directly from Argentina, food is served on chopping boards, and mouthwatering steaks are sliced with Rambo-sized steak knives. Oversized cocktails are served in hand-decorated ceramic jugs, glass jars, and coconut shells. Everything inside and outside the venue is recycled and crafted with their own fair hands, from drinks coasters to door frames, chandeliers, and dining tables, and the walls groan under layers of art and artifacts. Staff entertain the customers with enchanting theatrical performances throughout the evening, take my word for it. If you order a bottle of spirit for the table it is served in a unique way and comes dressed with their individual branding. Andrés Carne de Res is an unforgettable, out-of-this-world adventure. It has a personality that is larger than life. It is colorful, vibrant, warm, and infectious. Not somewhere you'd go if you're planning a quiet night!"—Dre Masso

HOTEL B

Sáenz Peña 204
Barranco
Lima 15063
Peru
+51 12060800
www.hotelb.pe

Opening hours	Open 7 days
Reservation policy	Not accepted for drinks
Credit cards	Accepted
Price range	Affordable
Dress code	Smart casual
Style	Cocktail bar

"The atmosphere of this bar is unique, surrounded by priceless artwork, it is an experience to enjoy delicious cocktails and escape the city. Located in the bohemian district of Barranco, the bar at Hotel B offers a diverse menu of gin cocktails based on artisanal processes and 'perfumology'. Located in a 1920s summer house that has been rescued to offer luxury service to every visitor."
—Jose Luis Valencia

SIBARIS RESTO BAR

Jiron 28 de Julio 206-B
Barranco
Lima 15063
Peru
+51 12470263
www.sibarisperu.com

Opening hours	Closed Sunday and Monday
Reservation policy	Accepted
Credit cards	Accepted
Price range	Affordable
Dress code	Casual
Style	Peruvian restaurant and cocktail bar

"Very friendly and special comfortable place."
—Joel Chirinos Durand

AMAZ

Avenida la Paz 1079
Miraflores
Lima 15074
Peru
+51 12219393
www.amaz.com.pe

Opening hours	Open 7 days
Reservation policy	Not accepted for drinks
Credit cards	Accepted
Price range	Affordable
Dress code	Smart casual
Style	Peruvian restaurant and bar

"A bold restaurant that takes its inspiration from the Peruvian Amazon with unique drinks that intrigue and surprise . . . each sip is a direct trip to the Amazon."—Jose Luis Valencia

OPEN BAR

Francisco de Paula Camino 280
Miraflores
Lima 15074
Peru
+51 4456318

Opening hours	Closed Sunday and Monday
Reservation policy	Accepted
Credit cards	Accepted
Price range	Affordable
Dress code	Smart casual
Style	Tapas restaurant and bar

"The place is nice, has good music, and their cocktails are good."—Aaron Diaz Olivos

ANTIGUA TABERNA QUEIROLO

Avenida San Martin 1090
Pueblo Libre
Lima 15063
Peru
+51 14600441
www.antiguatabernaqueirolo.com

Opening hours	Open 7 days/closed for dinner on Sunday
Reservation policy	Accepted
Credit cards	Accepted
Price range	Affordable
Dress code	Casual
Style	Tavern

"This bar is historic in Lima. It has been around for more than one hundred years. Their food is very much tavern-like. You can prepare your cocktail on the table called Res and it closes at eleven at night."—Aaron Diaz Olivos

ASTRID & GASTON CASA MOREYRA
Avenida Paz Soldán 290
San Isidro
Lima 15073
Peru
+51 14422775
www.en.astridygaston.com

Opening hours	Open 7 days/closed for dinner on Sunday
Reservation policy	Accepted
Credit cards	Accepted
Price range	Affordable
Dress code	Smart casual
Style	Restaurant and cocktail bar

"The one-of-a-kind bar at Astrid & Gaston possesses a team that not only prepares good cocktails, but also specializes in each area—a conceptual cocktail bar which will make you fall in love with every drink. Simply otherworldly cocktails."—Jose Luis Valencia

BOTTEGA DASSO
Calle Miguel Dasso 155
San Isidro
Lima 15073
Peru
+51 12223418
www.bottegadasso.com

Opening hours	Open 7 days
Reservation policy	Accepted
Credit cards	Accepted
Price range	Affordable
Dress code	Smart casual
Style	Mediterranean restaurant and bar

"Sophisticated bar with Italian inspiration offering Mediterranean dishes and well-balanced cocktails. Located in the heart of the business district of San Isidro, it has captivated its clients since it opened with new labels and constant innovation of its cocktail program."
—Jose Luis Valencia

SUPERBA
Avenida Petit Thouars 2884
San Isidro
Lima 15046
Peru
+51 12217185

Opening hours	Closed Sunday
Reservation policy	Accepted
Credit cards	Accepted
Price range	Affordable
Dress code	Smart casual
Style	Bar

"It is a casual, relaxed place where you will always find a hug upon arrival by the family that owns the bar. It has a lot of variety of craft beers and classic sandwiches."
—Aaron Diaz Olivos

> "WHERE EVERYBODY KNOWS WHAT YOU NEED, WHEN YOU NEED IT, AND HOW YOU WANT IT."
>
> DANIEL ESTREMADOYRO P.360

> "THIS IS A PLACE YOU GO TO DRINK BEER AND EAT FRIED FISH ... IT HAS AN INCREDIBLE ATMOSPHERE TO WATCH THE BEAUTIFUL PEOPLE OF RIO WALK TO AND FROM THE BEACH."
>
> JACOB BRIARS P.360

SOUTH AMERICA SOUTH

> "GOOD SERVICE AND COCKTAILS THAT DATE BACK TO THE PROHIBITION ERA." ALEX MESQUITA P.360

> "A PLACE WHERE YOU CAN JUST GO TO HAVE AN EXCELLENT CLASSIC, LIKE A NEGRONI, OLD FASHIONED, OR A JULEP, AND SHARE SOME TIME WITH FRIENDS."
>
> MATIAS SUPAN P.361

> "EXQUISITE FOOD WITH A TENDENCY FOR MOROCCAN CUISINE, GREAT COCKTAILS, AND THE DECORATION IS UNIQUE IN SANTIAGO."
>
> RICARDO GUERRERO P.361

SOUTH
AMERICA
SOUTH

LA COVA DEL DRAC

Belgrano 896
Córdoba
Córdoba 5000
Argentina
+54 3514699505

Opening hours...............................Closed Monday and Tuesday
Reservation policy...Accepted
Credit cards...Accepted but not AMEX
Price range...Affordable
Dress code..Casual
Style..Cocktail bar

"Where everybody knows what you need, when you need it, and how you want it. Not to mention the head bartender and owner, Matías Leonoz, for sure one of the best in the country. The place is absolutely packed with fine spirits and even oddities worth discovering and tasting. Certainly a place to have a wonderful and enlightening bar experience any time you want."—Daniel Estremadoyro

BELMOND COPACABANA PALACE

Avenida Atlântica 1702
Rio de Janeiro
Rio de Janeiro 22021-001
Brazil
+55 2125487070
www.belmond.com/copacabana-palace-rio-de-janeiro

Opening hours...Open 7 days
Reservation policy...............................Not accepted for drinks
Credit cards...Accepted
Price range..Affordable
Dress code...Smart casual
Style...Lounge

"Old-style decoration and near the beach of Copacabana."
—Alex Mesquita

JOBI

Avenida Ataulfo de Paiva 1166
Rio de Janeiro
Rio de Janeiro 22440-035
Brazil
+55 2122740547

Opening hours...Open 7 days
Reservation policy...............................Not accepted for drinks
Credit cards...Accepted
Price range..Affordable
Dress code..Casual
Style..Café and bar

"This is a place you go to drink beer and eat fried fish. It's on the main street and you sort of drop in and have a half glass of very cold beer. It has an incredible atmosphere to watch the beautiful people of Rio walk to and from the beach."
—Jacob Briars

FRANK BAR

Alameda Campinas 150
Maksoud Plaza Hotel
São Paulo
São Paulo 01404-900
Brazil
+55 1131458000
www.maksoud.com.br

Opening hours...Open 7 days
Reservation policy...............................Not accepted for drinks
Credit cards...Accepted
Price range..Affordable
Dress code...Smart casual
Style..Cocktail bar

"The reinterpretations of classic cocktails, the attendants give a class on cocktails while preparing them. Moreover, the unique presentations of these cocktails. Splendid hospitality of the bartenders."—Laércio de Souza Silva (Zulu)

"This bar is under the command of a great professional and has just been revitalized by it. Good cocktails and good food."—Alex Mesquita

SUB ASTOR

Rua Delfina 163
São Paulo
São Paulo 05443-010
Brazil
+55 1138151364
www.subastor.com.br

Opening hours...............................Closed Sunday and Monday
Reservation policy...............................Not accepted for drinks
Credit cards...Accepted
Price range..Affordable
Dress code...Smart casual
Style..Cocktail bar

"Good service and cocktails that date back to the Prohibition era."—Alex Mesquita

BARBAZUL

Avenida Vitacura 9257
Santiago
Región Metropolitana de Santiago 7500000
Chile
+56 222245292
www.barbazul.cl

Opening hours	Open 7 days
Reservation policy	Accepted
Credit cards	Accepted
Price range	Budget
Style	Restaurant and bar

"Long drinks that are outrageously high in alcohol."
—Ricardo Guerrero

KY

Avenida Perú 631
Santiago
Región Metropolitana de Santiago 8420000
Chile
+56 227777245
www.restobarky.cl

Opening hours	Closed Sunday and Monday
Reservation policy	Accepted
Credit cards	Accepted
Price range	Affordable
Dress code	Smart casual
Style	Restaurant and bar

"Exquisite food with a tendency for Moroccan cusine, great cocktails, and the decoration is unique in Santiago."
—Ricardo Guerrero

POLLUELO AMARILLO

General Flores 47
Santiago
Región Metropolitana de Santiago 7500000
Chile
+56 228804480
www.barpolluelo.cl

Opening hours	Closed Sunday
Reservation policy	Not accepted for drinks
Credit cards	Accepted
Price range	Affordable
Dress code	Casual
Style	Tapas bar

"It is a bar to meet friends and drink a delicious drink. Whenever you go you meet new people."—Ricardo Guerrero

W LOUNGE

Isidora Goyenechea 3000
W Hotel Santiago
Santiago
Región Metropolitana de Santiago 7550000
Chile
+56 227700000
www.starwoodhotels.com/whotels/property/dining/index.html?propertyID=1979

Opening hours	Open 7 days
Reservation policy	Accepted
Credit cards	Accepted
Price range	Affordable
Dress code	Smart casual
Style	Lounge

"Maybe the most trendy bar in my city. You can go there and have a great drink, dance, meet some people from a lot of countries. They also have an amazing twenty-fourth floor view. It is a must-visit."—Matias Supan

THE WHITE RABBIT

Antonia Lopez de Bello 0118
Santiago
Región Metropolitana de Santiago 7520288
Chile
+56 225034246
www.thewhiterabbitstgo.com

Opening hours	Open 7 days/closed for dinner on Sunday
Reservation policy	Accepted
Credit cards	Accepted
Price range	Affordable
Dress code	Smart casual
Style	Restaurant and bar

"A place where you can just go to have an excellent classic, like a Negroni, Old Fashioned, or a Julep, and share some time with some friends. Service and people are great, and you can feel comfortable in there . . . Just a neighborhood bar."—Matias Supan

"IT'S A CLASSIC OF THE CITY, AN EXCELLENT COCKTAIL BAR."
SEBASTIAN ATIENZA P.364

"A WONDERFUL BASEMENT BAR, WITH AN ENTRANCE THROUGH A REFRIGERATOR DOOR."
NAOMI LEVY P.366

BUENOS AIRES

"A SPEAKEASY, HIDDEN BEHIND THE FAÇADE OF A RESTAURANT WITH A SUSHI BAR."
RICARDO GUERRERO P.365

"THE OWNER IS A LOVER OF INDIE FILMS AND MUSIC. I COULD SPEND ALL MY NIGHTS AT THAT BAR."
FEDERICO CUCO P.364

"I LOVE THE ENERGY IN THAT PLACE, AND THE MUSIC, PEOPLE, AND EVERYTHING IS PERFECT."
MATIAS SUPAN P.365

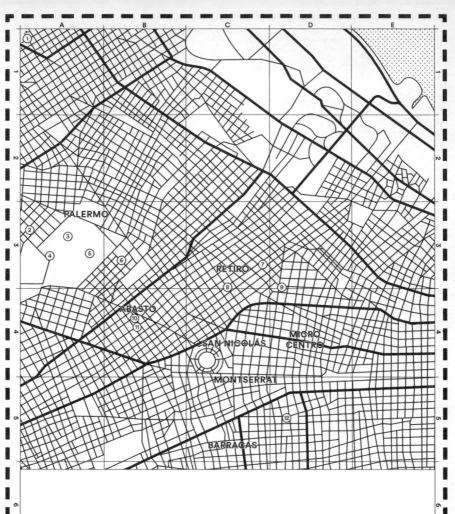

BUENOS AIRES

SCALE

0   425   850   1275
                        yd.

1. KOROVA CINE BAR (P.364)
2. FRANK'S BAR (P.365)
3. KIKA (P.365)
4. 878 (P.364)
5. THE HARRISON SPEAKEASY (P.365)
6. VERNE CLUB (P.365)
7. FLORERÍA ATLÁNTICO (P.366)
8. MILION (P.366)
9. PLAZA BAR (P.366)
10. PIZZERIA KENTUCKY (P.364)
11. SANATA BAR (P.364)
12. DOPPELGÄNGER BAR (P.366)

PIZZERIA KENTUCKY

Avenida Corrientes 3599
Abasto
Buenos Aires 1194
Argentina
+54 1148625377
www.pizzeriaskentucky.com

Opening hours..Open 7 days
Reservation policy...............................Not accepted for drinks
Credit cards..Not accepted
Price range..Budget
Dress code...Casual
Style...Pizzeria

"Usually after work I'll drink a beer and eat a slice of pizza, in a very old pizzeria called Kentucky, opened in 1942. It has the virtue of being open twenty-four hours. The pizza is always delicious, and even better with a draft beer. In this place I always run into several colleagues, and cooks, waiters and bartenders from other restaurants and bars."
—Federico Cuco

SANATA BAR

Sarmiento 3501
Abasto
Buenos Aires 1196
Argentina
+54 1148615761
www.sanatabar.com

Opening hours..Open 7 days
Reservation policy..Accepted
Credit cards..Accepted
Price range...Affordable
Dress code..Smart casual
Style...Restaurant and Tango club

"Friendly atmosphere; it is a tango club, and there is beautiful music and live bands."—Sebastian Atienza

KOROVA CINE BAR

Eduardo Ramseyer 1475
Olivos
Buenos Aires 1636
Argentina
+54 1147906191

Opening hours...Closed Monday
Reservation policy...............................Not accepted for drinks
Credit cards..Not accepted
Price range..Affordable
Dress code...Casual
Style..Cocktail bar

"Korova is three blocks from the Quinta de Olivos, the Argentine president's residence. It's an unpretentious bar, selling everything from beer to Japanese malt whiskeys, classic cocktails, and signature drinks. It is a bar I saw growing up. 'Popi' (the owner) is the perfect landlord, knows the names of all customers, and always has something to make you feel welcome. The owner is a lover of indie films and music. I could spend all my nights at that bar. But beware, they do not serve anything to eat, only drinks."—Federico Cuco

878

Thames 878
Palermo
Buenos Aires 1414
Argentina
+54 1147731098
www.878bar.com.ar

Opening hours..Open 7 days
Reservation policy..Accepted
Credit cards..Accepted
Price range...Affordable
Dress code..Smart casual
Style...Restaurant and cocktail bar

"It's a classic of the city, an excellent cocktail bar."
—Sebastian Atienza

FRANK'S BAR
Arévalo 1445
Palermo
Buenos Aires 1414
Argentina

Opening hours...................................Closed Sunday-Tuesday
Reservation policy...Accepted
Credit cards...Accepted
Price range...Expensive
Dress code...Smart casual
Style...Speakeasy

"In my humble opinion Frank's is the best cocktail bar in Buenos Aires. I love the energy in that place, and the music, people, and everything is perfect."—Matias Supan

"Luxurious and surprising, everything is big at Frank's. If you can make your way in, through passwords and hidden doors, you'll find yourself inside of one of the best bars in Buenos Aires for the last five years, and even when the place is packed, and the music is making the house tremble and the drink orders are flying, you'll note there's always someone trying to make you feel comfortable and amused. The cocktails are great and the crowd is the best. An unforgettable experience every night."—Daniel Estremadoyro

THE HARRISON SPEAKEASY
Malabia 1764
Palermo
Buenos Aires 1414
Argentina
+54 1148310519

Opening hours...............................Closed Sunday and Monday
Reservation policy...................Not accepted for drinks
Credit cards...Accepted
Price range..Affordable
Dress code...Smart casual
Style...Speakeasy

"A speakeasy, hidden behind the façade of a restaurant with a sushi bar. The sushi is good and the cocktails delicious and very well served."—Ricardo Guerrero

KIKA
Honduras 5339
Palermo
Buenos Aires 1743
Argentina
+54 1148339171
www.kikaclub.com.ar

Opening hours....................................Closed Monday
Reservation policy...................Not accepted for drinks
Credit cards...Accepted
Price range..Affordable
Dress code...Smart casual
Style...Nightclub

"I do not go so often to party, but if I wanted to dance until dawn, without hesitation I would go to Kika, a disco that closes when the sun comes up."—Federico Cuco

VERNE CLUB
Avenida Medrano 1475
Palermo
Buenos Aires 1179
Argentina
+54 1148220980
www.vernecocktailclub.com

Opening hours...Open 7 days
Reservation policy...Accepted
Credit cards...Accepted
Price range..Affordable
Dress code...Smart casual
Style...Cocktail bar

"One could say that owning a bar is a 'labor of love'. That dream came true for its owner, the renowned bartender Federico Cuco, so everything has a purpose, time, and place in there . . . from the steampunk imagery, and the drinks inspired by Jules Verne's work, to the stories told by the staff, and the relaxed mood. It's really easy to stay to share their dream for hours and hours . . . while having a drink or three of course."—Daniel Estremadoyro

FLORERÍA ATLÁNTICO

Arroyo 872
Recoleta
Buenos Aires 1007
Argentina
+54 1143136093
www.floreriaatlantico.com.ar

Opening hours	Open 7 days
Reservation policy	Not accepted for drinks
Credit cards	Accepted
Price range	Affordable
Dress code	Smart casual
Style	Cocktail bar

"You would never expect to see a flower shop open until the wee hours of the night — best of all, hidden inside the shop is one of the best bars or Latin America. With a sea-voyager-style, Florería Atlántico highlights flavors of the sea, wine, and bitters, with long conversations and a cozy ambience."—Jose Luis Valencia

"A wonderful basement bar, with an entrance through a refrigerator door. From the decor to the drinks to the top-notch food, everything is on point, especially the welcoming hospitality."—Naomi Levy

"Florería Atlántico is an idea that I would have loved to have. You walk down a street where I'm sure you would never imagine a beautiful bar could be. There is a little flower market and in there a hidden door, where you´ll find a flight of stairs. Walk down and you will see the underground of an old building with an amazing bar."—Matias Supan

Florería Atlántico was voted the top bar in South America on the World's 50 Best Bars list in 2014 and 2013.

MILION

Paraná 1048
Recoleta
Buenos Aires 1018
Argentina
+54 1148159925
www.milion.com.ar

Opening hours	Open 7 days
Reservation policy	Accepted
Credit cards	Accepted
Price range	Affordable
Dress code	Smart casual
Style	Restaurant and cocktail bar

"Nice atmosphere, beautiful location, and good prices."
—Sebastián Atienza

PLAZA BAR

Plaza Hotel Buenos Aires
Florida 1005
Retiro
Buenos Aires 1005
Argentina
+54 1143183000
www.plazahotelba.com

Opening hours	Open 7 days
Reservation policy	Accepted
Credit cards	Accepted
Price range	Affordable
Dress code	Smart casual
Style	Lounge

"In my town the bar at the Plaza Hotel is almost perfect, it is hidden in the basement, there is always a pianist playing. Gabriel Santinelli (the bartender) has been working there since he was a teenager. He prepares great classics and always has a smile and a good story to share."
—Federico Cuco

DOPPELGÄNGER BAR

Avenida Juan de Garay 500
San Telmo
Buenos Aires 1153
Argentina
+54 1143000201
www.doppelgänger.com.ar

Opening hours	Closed Sunday and Monday
Reservation policy	Not accepted for drinks
Credit cards	Accepted
Price range	Affordable
Dress code	Smart casual
Style	Cocktail bar

"To feel what it is to drink in Buenos Aires I would recommend Doppelgänger Bar or 878 cocktail bar, and drinking Fernet with Coke at any corner bar. And find out where my favorite bartenders—Luis Miranda, Chicho Bruno Sebastián García, and Sebastián Atienza—are working."—Federico Cuco

THE CONTRIBUTORS

ARGENTINA
Sebastian Atienza, Federico Cuco, Daniel Estremadoyro, Ricardo Guerrero, Naomi Levy, Jose Luis Valencia, Matias Supan.

AUSTRALIA
Charlie Ainsbury, Joe Ballinger, Dan Berger, Tom Egerton, Miguel Fernandez Fernandez, Chris Hannah, Hannah Keirl, Michael Madrusan, Tim Philips, Sam Ross, Igor Zernov.

AUSTRIA
Dirk Hany, Kan Zuo.

BARBADOS
Grant Sceney.

BELARUS
Lizaveta Molyavka.

BELGIUM
Olivier Jacobs, Hannah Van Ongevalle.

BRAZIL
Alex Mesquita, Laércio de Souza Silva (Zulu).

CAYMAN ISLANDS
Simon Crompton.

CANADA
Sandy De Almeida, Evelyn Chick, Alex Day, Jonathan Homier, David J. Kaplan, Shaun Layton, Jacyara de Oliveira, Grant Sceney, Shawn Soole, Colin Tait, Danielle Tatarin.

CHILE
Ricardo Guerrero, Matias Supan.

CHINA
Marshall Altier.

COLOMBIA
Dre Masso, Carina Soto Velasquez, Dennis Zoppi.

COSTA RICA
Daniel Estremadoyro.

CUBA
Tony Conigliaro, Simon Crompton, Jonny Mckenzie.

CYPRUS
Tony Conigliaro, Simon Crompton, Jonny Mckenzie.

CZECH REPUBLIC
Kamil Foltan, Franky Marshall, Algirdas Mulevičius, Jiri George Nemec, Aleš Půta.

DENMARK
Emil Åreng, Hasse Bank Johansen, Algirdas Mulevičius, Aðalsteinn Sigurðsson, Jesse Teerenmaa.

ESTONIA
Angelika Larkina.

FINLAND
Mal Spence, Jesse Teerenmaa.

FRANCE
Nicolas Berger, Marc Bonneton, Amanda Boucher, Keely Edgington, Dirk Hany, Alex Kratena, Lynnette Marrero, Franky Marshall, Lizaveta Molyavka, Gabe Orta, André Pintz, Jonathan Pogash, Shawn Soole, Nico de Soto, Carina Soto Velasquez, Ezra Star, Jesse Teerenmaa, Hannah Van Ongevalle, Jayson Wilde.

GERMANY
Philip Duff, Oliver Ebert, Miguel Fernandez Fernandez, Kyle Ford, Mario Kappes, Bettina Kupsa, Mauro Mahjoub, Jeffrey Morgenthaler, André Pintz, Tomek Roehr, Charles Schumann, Jesse Teerenmaa, Hidetsugu Ueno, Dushan Zaric.

GREECE
Tony Conigliaro, Theodoros Pirillos.

GUATEMALA
Raul Cojolon, Ivy Mix, Tim Philips.

HONG KONG
Budiman "Tom" Atmaja, Ryan Nightingale.

HUNGARY
Jamie Jones, Zoltan Nagy.

ICELAND
Aðalsteinn Sigurðsson.

INDIA
Gaurav Dhyani, Hannah Keirl, Dimi Lezinska, Varun Sudhakar.

INDONESIA
Budiman "Tom" Atmaja, Guillaume Le Dorner.

IRELAND
Alan Kavanagh.

ISRAEL
Gabe Orta, Bar Shira, Carina Soto Velasquez.

ITALY
Luca Angeli, Remigijus Beinoras, Salvatore Calabrese, Adriano Costigliola, Philip Duff, Giorgio Fadda, Giuseppe Gallo, Silvia Ghioni, Meghan Konecny, Leonardo Leuci, Luca Picchi, Massimo Stronati, Federico Tomasselli, Naren Young, Dennis Zoppi.

JAPAN
Ryan Chetiyawardana, Frank Cisneros, Tony Conigliaro, Juan Coronado, Pip Hanson, Hiroyasu Kayama, Alex Kratena, Erik Lorincz, Toby Maloney, Lynnette Marrero, Jim Meehan, Tsuyoshi Miyazaki,

Javier de las Muelas, Charles Schumann, Joaquín Simó, Halvor Skiftun Digernes, Massimo Stronati, Hidetsugu Ueno, Neyah White.

LATVIA
Remigijus Beinoras, Inguss Reizenbergs.

LITHUANIA
Remigijus Beinoras, Algirdas Mulevičius.

MALAYSIA
Andrew Tan.

MEXICO
Derek Brown, Trevor Easter, Ryan Fitzgerald, Luis C. Iriarte, Charles Joly, Mario Kappes, Jose Luis Leon, Dre Masso, Ivy Mix, Carina Soto Velasquez.

THE NETHERLANDS
Ivar de Lange, Timo Janse, Tess Posthumus, Laura Schacht, Hannah Van Ongevalle, Taeeun Yoon.

NEW ZEALAND
Jonny Mckenzie, Paul Shipman.

NORWAY
Emil Åreng, Monica Berg, Halvor Skiftun Digernes.

PANAMA
Enrique Ignacio Auvert.

PERU
Joel Chirinos Durand, Aaron Diaz Olivos, Jose Luis Valencia.

PHILIPPINES
Jericson Co, Allanking Roxas.

POLAND
Tomek Roehr.

PORTUGAL
Honorio Oliveira, André Manuel Duarte Peixe.

PUERTO RICO
Mario Seijo Rivera, Kellie Thorn.

ROMANIA
Aida Ashor.

THE RUSSIAN FEDERATION
Timo Janse, Dimi Lezinska, Roman Milostivy, Bek Narzi, Igor Zernov.

SINGAPORE
Kamil Foltan, Nick Koumbarakis, Pamela Wiznitzer.

SOUTH AFRICA
Denzel Heath, Nick Koumbarakis, Mal Spence.

SOUTH KOREA
Taeeun Yoon.

SPAIN
Marc Alvarez Safont, Juan Coronado, Jose A. Femenia Luis, Miguel Fernandez Fernandez, Kamil Foltan, Dre Masso.

SWEDEN
Emil Åreng, Alex Day, Adam Snook, Ola Yau Carlson.

SWITZERLAND
Nicolas Berger, Markus Blattner, Dirk Hany, Laura Schacht.

TAIWAN
Payman Bahmani, Spencer Huang.

THAILAND
Franky Marshall, Javier de las Muelas, Colin Tait.

UNITED ARAB EMIRATES
Angus McGregor.

UNITED KINGDOM
Eric Alperin, Marc Alvarez Safont, Dave Arnold, Joe Ballinger, Hasse Bank Johansen, Monica Berg, Dan Berger, Nicolas Berger, Sian Buchan, Salvatore Calabrese, Simone Caporale, Martin Cate, Ryan Chetiyawardana, Tony Conigliaro, Julian Cox, Guillaume Le Dorner, Oliver Ebert, Miguel Fernandez Fernandez, Giuseppe Gallo, Denzel Heath, Mia Johansson, Jamie Jones, Hannah Keirl, James Kemp, Caitlin Laman, Ivar de Lange, Ethan Liu, Erik Lorincz, Jack McGarry, Angus McGregor, Jim Meehan, Ivy Mix, Bek Narzi, Ryan Nightingale, Honorio Oliveira, Agostino Perrone,

Tess Posthumus, Laura Schacht, Paul Shipman, Joaquín Simó, Nico de Soto, Mal Spence, Vincent Stipo, Taeeun Yoon.

UNITED STATES OF AMERICA
Tony Abou-Ganim, Eric Alperin, Dave Arnold, Payman Bahmani, Hasse Bank Johansen, Summer-Jane Bell, Nick Bennett, Monica Berg, Jeff "Beachbum" Berry, Richard Boccato, Neal Bodenheimer, Beau du Bois, Derek Brown, Jackson Cannon, Steva Casey, Erick Castro, Martin Cate, Ryan Chetiyawardana, Frank Cisneros, Jeffrey Cole, Adriano Costigliola, Julian Cox, Alex Day, Meaghan Dorman, Philip Duff, Trevor Easter, Keely Edgington, Phoebe Esmon, Kirk F. Estopinal, Ryan Fitzgerald, Kyle Ford, Rachel Ford, Karen Grill, Will Groves, Abigail Gullo, Mattias Hägglund, Chris Hannah, Pip Hanson, Edward Hong, Spencer Huang, Alba Huerta, Timo Janse, Charles Joly, David J Kaplan, James Kemp, Sean Kenyon, Ted Kilgore, Meghan Konecny, Alex Kratena, Bettina Kupsa, Caitlin Laman, Eden Laurin, Naomi Levy, Theo Lieberman, John Maher, Lynnette Marrero, Franky Marshall, Dre Masso, Jack McGarry, Jonny Mckenzie, Jim Meehan, Ivy Mix, Julia Momose, Jeffrey Morgenthaler, David Newman, Jacyara de Oliveira, Gabe Orta, Michael Jack Pazdon, Tim Philips, Jonathan Pogash, Christy Pope, Julie Reiner, Brooks Reitz, Larry Rice, Sam Ross, Mike Ryan, Morgan Schick, Joaquín Simó, Chad Solomon, Shawn Soole, Carina Soto Velasquez, Clint Spotleson, Ezra Star, Vincent Stipo, Danielle Tatarin, Sother Teague, Kellie Thorn, Yana Volfson, Greg West, Neyah White, Jayson Wilde, Naren Young, Dushan Zaric.

THE CONTRIBUTORS' RECOMMENDATIONS

TONY ABOU-GANIM
Owner, The Modern Mixologist
www.modernmixologist.com

Blue Ribbon 335	Late-Night
Petrossian Lounge 243	Hotel
Herbs & Rye 242	Local Must-Visit
Harry's Bar 198	Worth the travel
Employees Only 324	Wish I'd opened

COSTIGLIOLA ADRIANO
Ambassador, Tequila Patron Italia
www.patrontequila.com

Nottingham Forest 204	Late-Night
Bar 66 203	Hotel
Speakeasy Cocktail Bar 195	Local Must-Visit
Beachbum Berry's Latitude 29 305	Worth the travel

CHARLIE AINSBURY
Owner/Operator, This Must Be The Place
239 Oxford Street, Darlinghurst

Bulletin Place 18	Neighborhood
Black Pearl 25	Local Must-Visit
Tommy's Mexican Restaurant 266	Worth the travel
Shady Pines Saloon 19	Wish I'd opened

ERIC ALPERIN
Proprietor & Bartender,
The Varnish/Half Step/Penny Pound Ice, Los Angeles

Jumbo's Clown Room 254	Late-Night
Dutch Kills 339	Neighborhood
Musso & Frank Grill 255	Local Must-Visit
Zth Cocktail Lounge 107	Worth the travel
Golden Gopher 253	Wish I'd opened

MARSHALL ALTIER
Managing Director, Spirit House Consultants
www.spirithouseconsultants.com

Shouning Lu 63	Late-Night
Bar Constellation 62	Local Must-Visit

LUCA ANGELI
Head Bartender, Hotel Four Seasons Florence
Borgo Pinti 99, Florence

Nightjar 114	Late-Night
Stravinskij Bar 209	Hotel
Art Bar 196	Local Must-Visit
PDT 333	Worth the travel

EMIL ÅRENG
Bartender, Open/Closed
Storgatan 44, Umeå

Linje Tio 92	Late-Night
Strøm 94	Late-Night
Gotthards Krog 93	Hotel
The Thief Bar 91	Hotel
Corner Club 91	Neighborhood
Rex Bar & Grill 93	Neighborhood
Open/Closed 93	Local Must-Visit
Bulletin Place 18	Worth the travel
American Bar 107	Wish I'd opened

DAVE ARNOLD
Owner, Booker and Dax
207 2nd Avenue, New York City

Old Absinthe House 307	Late-Night
Holland Bar 321	Neighborhood
Porchlight 320	Local Must-Visit
69 Colebrooke Row 109	Worth the travel
The NoMad Bar 323	Wish I'd opened

AIDA ASHOR
Bartender
www.aidaashor.com

Submarine 181	Late-Night
Flair Angel 180	Neighborhood
Joben Bistro180	Local Must-Visit
Acuarela 180	Worth the travel

SEBASTIÁN ATIENZA
Bar Manager, Florería Atlántico
Arroyo 872, Buenos Aires

Milion 366	Late-Night
Artesian 111	Hotel
Sanata Bar 364	Neighborhood
878 (bar) 364	Local Must-Visit
The Dead Rabbit Grocery and Grog 335	Worth the travel

BUDIMAN "TOM" ATMAJA
Bar Superivisor, Vin+ Group
www.vinplus.co

Loewy 55	Late-Night
Woo Bar 54	Hotel
Union 55	Neighborhood
Loewy 55	Local Must-Visit
American Bar 107	Worth the travel
PDT 333	Worth the travel
Lobster Bar 66	Wish I'd opened

PAIGE AUBORT
Manager, The Lobo Plantation
209 Clarence Street, Basement, Sydney

Palmer and Co 19	Late-Night
Manhattan (Singapore) 53	Hotel
Ramblin' Rascal Tavern 19	Neighborhood
Mojo 98	Local Must-Visit
The Baxter Inn 18	Worth the travel
Earl's Juke Joint 20	Wish I'd opened

ENRIQUE IGNACIO AUVERT
Head Bartender, Estudio Millesime Panama
www.millesimeworld.com/panama/estudio-millesime/

Employees Only 324	Late-Night
Artesian 111	Hotel
Restaurant Cabana 351	Local Must-Visit
Bar High Five 80	Worth the travel
Milk & Honey (now Attaboy 334)	Wish I'd opened

PAYMAN BAHMANI
Bar Czar, Crafty
Singapore

Bua 331	Late-Night
Tickle My Fantasy 69	Neighborhood
Alchemy 68	Local Must-Visit
PDT 333	Worth the travel
Good Times at Davey Wayne's 253	Wish I'd opened

STUART BALE
Bartender, Strange Hill
20a Brownlow Mews, London

Punch Room 108	Hotel
69 Colebrooke Row 109	Local Must-Visit
La Fuente 348	Worth the travel
The Pot Still 118	Wish I'd opened

JOE BALLINGER
Bar Manager, Berry and Rye
48 Berry Street, Liverpool

Mojo 98	Late-Night
Artesian 111	Hotel
Filter + Fox 98	Neighborhood
Jenny's Bar 98	Local Must-Visit
The Baxter Inn 18	Worth the travel
Happiness Forgets 109	Wish I'd opened

REMIGIJUS BEINORAS
Former Bacardi Brand Ambassador for the Baltics
Vilnius

Matérialiste 179	Late-Night
Dream Bar 179	Neighborhood
The Left Door Bar 179	Local Must-Visit
Employees Only 324	Worth the travel
Nu Lounge Bar 195	Wish I'd opened

SUMMER-JANE BELL
President USBG SF, Co-Founder TrophyCocktail, National Brand Ambassador for Suerte Tequila
Oakland

Radio Bar 237	Late-Night
Benjamin Cooper 263	Hotel
Heinold's First and Last Chance Saloon 237	Local Must-Visit

NICK BENNETT
Head Bartender, Porchlight
271 11th Avenue, New York City

Extra Fancy 337	Late-Night
Holiday Cocktail Lounge 332	Late-Night
The NoMad Bar 323	Hotel
The Corner Bar 339	Neighborhood
Dutch Kills 339	Local Must-Visit
The Brazen Head 120	Worth the travel
Sean's Bar 119	Worth the travel

MONICA BERG
Bartender; Co-Founder, P(OUR)
www.pourdrink.org

Glass 144	Late-Night
Sager + Wilde 109	Neighborhood
Artesian 111	Local Must-Visit
Fuglen 90	Local Must-Visit
Himkok 90	Local Must-Visit
The NoMad Bar 323	Worth the travel
Maison Premiere 338	Wish I'd opened

NICOLAS BERGER
Co-Owner/Head Bartender, Little Barrel
15 Rue du Lac, Geneva

Chat Noir 167	Late-Night
Le Bar 143	Hotel
L'Antiquaire 134	Neighborhood
L'Apothicaire Cocktail Club 167	Local Must-Visit
Artesian 111	Worth the travel
Happiness Forgets 109	Worth the travel
Lab Bar 115	Wish I'd opened

DAN BERGER
Bar Manager, Ace Hotel London
100 Shoreditch High Street, London

Ace Hotel 113	Hotel
Happiness Forgets 109	Local Must-Visit
Lily Blacks 24	Worth the travel

JEFF "BEACHBUM" BERRY
Owner, Beachbum Berry's Latitude 29
321 North Peters Street, New Orleans

Tiki-Ti 256	Neighborhood
Cure 306	Local Must-Visit

MARKUS BLATTNER
Owner/Bar Manager, Old Crow
Schwanengasse 4, Zurich

Hotel Rivington & Sons 168	Late-Night
Widder Bar 168	Hotel
Kronenhalle 168	Local Must-Visit
Tür 7 174	Worth the travel

RICHARD BOCCATO
Partner, Dutch Kills/Fresh Kills Bar/Hundredweight Ice
New York City

Montero Bar & Grill 339	Late-Night
Jett's Grill 299	Hotel
Sunny's Bar 338-39	Neighborhood
Sunny's Bar 338-39	Local Must-Visit
Sunny's Bar 338-39	Worth the travel

NEAL BODENHEIMER
Owner, Cure/Bellocq/Cane & Table
New Orleans

Employees Only 324	Late-Night
American Bar 107	Hotel
Cure 306	Local Must-Visit
Candelaria 142	Worth the travel
Maison Premiere 338	Wish I'd opened

MARC BONNETON
Owner, L'Antiquaire/RedWood
Lyon

Boston Café 134	Late-Night
Hemingway Bar (Paris) 141	Hotel
L'Antiquaire 134	Local Must-Visit
Attaboy 334	Worth the travel
Harry's Bar 198	Wish I'd opened

AMANDA BOUCHER
Head Bartender, Pas de Loup
108 Rue Amelot, Paris

L'Entrée des Artistes Pigalle 143	Late-Night
Red House 146	Neighborhood
Le Syndicat 145	Local Must-Visit
Artesian 111	Worth the travel
Copper Bay 145	Wish I'd opened

JACOB BRIARS
Global Advocacy Director, Bacardi
www.bacardi.com

Attaboy 334	Late-night
Employees Only 324	Late-Night
American Bar 107	Hotel
Beaufort Bar 108	Hotel
Eichardt's Bar 51	Hotel
Jobi 360	Neighborhood
Matterhorn 32	Neighborhood
Smuggler's Cove 266	Neighborhood
Dante 324	Local Must-Visit
Artesian 111	Worth the travel
Caffè Rivoire 197	Worth the travel
PDT 333	Worth the travel
ABV 263	Wish I'd opened
Beretta 263	Wish I'd opened
Canon 246	Wish I'd opened
Clyde Common 243	Wish I'd opened
Donna 337	Wish I'd opened
Schumann's Bar 167	Wish I'd opened

DEREK BROWN

President/Owner, Drink Company (Mockingbird Hill,
Eat the Rich, Southern Efficiency, Columbia Room)
1825 7th Street NW, Washington, D.C.

Showtime 290	Late-Night
Bourbon Steak 289	Hotel
All Souls 288	Neighborhood
Mockingbird Hill 289	Local Must-Visit
Bad Decisions 294	Wish I'd opened

SIAN BUCHAN

Ambassador, The Drink Cabinet UK
Glasgow Collective, 15 East Campbell Street, Glasgow

Bramble 117	Late-Night
American Bar 107	Hotel
Panda & Sons 118	Local Must-Visit
Employees Only 324	Worth the travel

SALVATORE CALABRESE

Bar Owner/Bartender; former President,
United Kingdom Bartenders' Guild
www.salvatore-calabrese.co.uk

Mag Cafè 203	Late-Night
The Library Bar 110	Hotel
Tommy's Mexican Restaurant 266	Worth the travel

JACKSON CANNON

Owner, The Hawthorne; Bar Director, Island Creek
Oyster   Bar/Eastern Standard Kitchen & Drinks
Boston

Drink 310	Late-Night
The Broken Shaker 290	Hotel
Happiness Forgets 109	Neighborhood
Mockingbird Hill 289	Worth the travel
Trick Dog 266	Worth the travel
The Varnish 257	Worth the travel
Glass 144	Wish I'd opened

SIMONE CAPORALE

Bartender
www.simonecaporale.com, London

Boadas 154	Late-Night
Dukes Bar 112	Hotel
Connaught Bar 112	Local Must-Visit
El Floridita 348	Worth the travel

OLA YAU CARLSON

Bar Manager, Bar Hommage
Krukmakargatan 22, Stockholm

Attaboy 334	Late-Night
Linje Tio 92	Neighborhood
Open/Closed 93	Local Must-Visit
Pharmarium 92	Local Must-Visit
Mace 332	Worth the travel
Happiness Forgets 109	Wish I'd opened

STEVA CASEY

Bar Manager/Bartender, Saturn
200 41st Street South, Birmingham

Marty's PM 288	Late-Night
Lou's Pub 288	Neighborhood
The Collins 288	Local Must-Visit
Multnomah Whiskey Library 245	Worth the travel
Trick Dog 266	Wish I'd opened

ERICK CASTRO

Bartender/Proprietor, Boilermaker/Polite Provisions;
Founder, Possessed By Spirits
www.possessedbyspirits.com, New York and San Diego

Noble Experiment 240	Late-Night
Hope 46 (bar) 239	Hotel
Cantina Mayahuel 238	Neighborhood
Live Wire 239	Local Must-Visit
Rocky's Crown Pub 240	Local Must-Visit
Turf Supper Club 240	Local Must-Visit
Blind Lady Ale House 238	Worth the travel
Amor y Amargo 331	Wish I'd opened

MARTIN CATE

Owner, Smuggler's Cove/Whitechapel
www.martincate.com, San Francisco

Comstock Saloon 264	Late-Night
Dukes Bar 112	Hotel
Heinold's First and Last Chance Saloon 237	Local Must-Visit
The Molokai Bar 290	Worth the travel
The Prospect of Whitby 116	Wish I'd opened

RYAN CHETIYAWARDANA

Owner, White Lyan/Dandelyan
London

Bramble 117	Late-Night
Satan's Whiskers 107	Neighborhood
The Canny Man's 117	Local Must-Visit
Star Bar 81	Worth the travel
PDT 333	Wish I'd opened

EVELYN CHICK
Bar Manager, Pretty Ugly
237 Queen Street West, Toronto

Employees Only 324	Late-Night
The Lobby Lounge and Raw Bar 229	Hotel
Bar Isabel 222	Neighborhood
The Harbord Room 223	Local Must-Visit
Artesian 111	Worth the travel
Bar Raval 223	Wish I'd opened

FRANK CISNEROS
Former Bartender, Mandarin Oriental, Tokyo; Bartender,
Dram/The Shanty; Co-Owner, The Drink
Brooklyn

Kanda 65 (bar) 80	Late-Night
Mandarin Bar 81	Hotel
Little Smith 80-1	Local Must-Visit
Bushwick Country Club 336	Worth the travel
M's Crux 80	Wish I'd opened

JERICSON CO
Owner, The Curator
134 Legazpi Street, Corner C, Palanca Street, Makati
Metropolitan Manila

The Blind Pig 47	Late-Night
Long Bar (Singapore) 53	Hotel
Gerry's 48	Neighborhood
Edsa Beverage Design Studio 47	Local Must-Visit
Lanai Lounge 48	Local Must-Visit
Lanai Lounge 48	Worth the travel

HECTOR RAUL COJOLON
Head Bartender, Bar El Conquistador Porta Hotels
8va. Calle Poniente No. 1, Antigua

Café No Sé 349	Late-Night
Lucky Rabbit 350	Neighborhood
La Reunion Golf Resort and Residences 350	Local Must-Visit
The Dead Rabbit Grocery and Grog 335	Worth the travel
Las Vibras de la Casbah 350	Wish I'd opened

JEFFREY COLE
Bar Manager, O Bar at the Ambassador Hotel
1200 North Walker Avenue, Oklahoma City

The Other Room 294	Late-Night
Midnight Rambler 297	Hotel
The Hilo Club 294	Local Must-Visit
The Gin Joint 295	Worth the travel
Trick Dog 266	Wish I'd opened

TONY CONIGLIARO
Owner, 69 Colebrooke Row; Co-Founder, The Drink Factory
69 Colebrooke Row, London

Seven Jokers 182	Late-Night
The Peak Lounge 83	Hotel
The 10 Cases 108	Local Must-Visit
Midnight Rambler 297	Worth the travel
El Floridita 348	Wish I'd opened

JUAN CORONADO
Co-Founder, The Pour Group
www.thepourgroup.com, New York City

Ohla Boutique Bar 155	Hotel
La Venencia 150	Neighborhood
Bar Lapin 75	Local Must-Visit
Barmini 289	Local Must-Visit
Ben Fiddich 83	Local Must-Visit
La Factoria 350	Local Must-Visit
Le Cabrera 150	Local Must-Visit
Licorería Limantour 347	Local Must-Visit
Mutis 155	Local Must-Visit
Bar Oscar 75	Worth the travel
Bar Yamazaki 75	Worth the travel
Angel's Share 331	Wish You'd Opened

JULIAN COX
Beverage Director, Three Dots and a Dash; Co-Founder/
Partner, Soigné Group
435 North Clark, Chicago

Artesian 111	Hotel bar
Tippling Club 54	Worth the travel
Melrose Umbrella Company 255	Late-Night

SIMON CROMPTON
Diageo Reserve Brand Ambassador for Cayman
and the Caribbean
www.diageo.com

Calico Jack's Bar and Grill 349	Late-Night
Bar Jack 349	Hotel
Agua Restaurant & Lounge 349	Neighborhood
El Floridita 348	Local Must-Visit
The Dead Rabbit Grocery and Grog 335	Worth the travel
Little Branch 325	Worth the travel
Employees Only 324	Wish I'd opened

FEDERICO CUCO
Co-Owner/Head Bartender, Verne Club
Avenue Medrano 1475, Buenos Aires

Kika 365	Late-Night
Pizzeria Kentucky 364	Late-Night
Le Bar du Bristol 143	Hotel
Korova Cine Bar 364	Neighborhood
878 (bar) 364	Local Must-Visit
Doppelgänger Bar 292	Local Must-Visit
Chainaya Tea & Cocktails 186	Worth the travel

GIAN CARLO D'URSO
General Manager, CATCH
1st Level, Fairmont Dubai, Sheikh Zayed Road, Trade Centre
  Area,
Dubai

Nightjar 114	Late-Night

ALEX DAY
Partner, Proprietors LLC (Death & Co, Nitecap, 151, Honeycut,
  The Normandie Club, The Walker Inn)
Los Angeles

Little Quarter 92	Late-Night
The NoMad Bar 323	Hotel
Prizefighter 236	Neighborhood
Attaboy 334	Local Must-Visit
The Corner Door 253	Local Must-Visit
Bar Raval 223	Worth the travel
Bar Raval 223	Wish I'd opened

SANDY DE ALMEIDA
Bartender, The Drake Hotel
1150 Queen Street West, Toronto

Fat City Blues 223	Late-Night
Midfield Wine Bar & Tavern 224	Neighborhood
Bar Raval 223	Worth the travel

IVAR DE LANGE
Master Bartender, Lucas Bols
Paulus Potterstraat 12, Amsterdam

Demain 124	Late-Night
The Bar at Hotel Credible 124	Hotel
Café in de Blaauwe Hand 124	Local Must-Visit
Demain 124	Local Must-Visit
White Lyan 109	Wish I'd opened
Bar High Five 80	Worth the travel
Black Pearl 25	Worth the travel
Operation Dagger 54	Wish I'd opened

JAVIER DE LAS MUELAS
CEO, Dry Martini
www.drymartiniorg.com

Burma Bar 47	Late-Night
American Bar 107	Hotel
Artesian 111	Hotel
King Cole Bar 322	Hotel
Boadas 154	Local Must-Visit
Tender Bar 81	Worth the travel
Museo Chicote 150	Wish I'd opened

JACYARA DE OLIVEIRA
Bartender, Sportsman Club
948 North Western Avenue, Chicago

Clark Street Ale House 281	Late-Night
The The Green Mill 281	Local Must-Visit
Bar Raval 223	Worth the travel
The Drifter 281	Wish I'd opened

NICO DE SOTO
Head Bartender/Co-Owner, Mace
649 East 9th Street, New York City

Mabel 141	Late-Night
Artesian 111	Hotel
The Dead Rabbit Grocery and Grog 335	Neighborhood
The Dead Rabbit Grocery and Grog 335	Local Must-Visit
Experimental Cocktail Club (Paris) 141	Local Must-Visit
The Aviary 279	Worth the travel
69 Colebrooke Row 109	Wish I'd opened

DALE DEGROFF
Bartender; Founding President, Museum of the
  American Cocktail
www.kingcocktail.com

American Bar 107	Hotel
The Broken Shaker 290	Hotel
Dukes Bar 112	Hotel
Hemingway Bar (Paris) 141	Hotel
King Cole Bar 322	Hotel
The Ear Inn 335-6	Neighborhood
The Green Mill 281	Neighborhood
Hudson Malone 321	Neighborhood
McSorley's Old Ale House 332-3	Neighborhood
Swift Hibernian Lounge 333	Neighborhood
Arnaud's French 75 Bar 305	Local Must-Visit
Boadas 154	Local Must-Visit
Boardner's 253	Local Must-Visit
Cafe Pacifico 108	Local Must-Visit
Dry Martini 154	Local Must-Visit
Employees Only 324	Local Must-Visit
Erin Rose 306	Local Must-Visit
Harry's New York Bar 141	Local Must-Visit
Musso & Frank Grill 255	Local Must-Visit

Pegu Club 336...Local Must-Visit
Sweet Liberty 291..Local Must-Visit
Velvet Tango Room 273.......................................Local Must-Visit
P. J. Clarke's 322...Wish I'd opened

GAURAV DHYANI
Head Bartender, Grappa at the Shangri-La Hotel
19 Ashoka Road, Connaught Place, New Delhi
Rick's 44..Hotel
Cocktail and Dreams Speakeasy 44......................Neighborhood
Blue Bar (Delhi) 44...Local Must-Visit

HALVOR SKIFTUN DIGERNES
Co-Founder, Fuglen
www.fuglen.com/nightlife/cocktail-bar
No. 19 90..Late-Night
The Thief Bar 91...Hotel
Torggata Botaniske 91..Local Must-Visit
Gen Yamamoto 82...Worth the travel
Fuglen 90...Wish I'd opened

MEAGHAN DORMAN
Bar Director, Raines Law Room/Dear Irving/The Bennett
New York City
Attaboy 334..Late-Night
The NoMad Bar 323...Hotel
Grand Army 337..Neighborhood
Gallow Green 320...Local Must-Visit
Ordinary 310...Local Must-Visit
Everleigh 26..Worth the travel
Wilfie & Nell 326..Wish I'd opened

BEAU DU BOIS
Head Bartender, The Corner Door
12477 West Washington Boulevard, Los Angeles
Oldfield's Liquor Room 255....................................Late-Night
The Heorot Pub and Draught House 270...............Neighborhood
Sassafras 256...Local Must-Visit
Bar High Five 80...Worth the travel
The Varnish 257..Wish I'd opened

PHILIP DUFF
Spirits Educator/Director, Liquid Solutions Consulting;
    Director of Education, Tales of the Cocktail
www.liquidsolutions.org
Mother's Ruin 335..Late-Night
The NoMad Bar 323...Hotel
The Dead Rabbit Grocery and Grog 335...............Local Must-Visit
Rum Trader 161...Worth the travel
The Jerry Thomas Project 209...............................Wish I'd opened

JOEL CHIRINOS DURAND
Bar Consultant/Beverage Manager, Hanasumi Restaurant
Avenue Conquistadores 1087, San Isidro
Sibaris Resto Bar 357...Late-Night
Artesian 111...Hotel
Bar High Five 80...Worth the travel

TREVOR EASTER
Manager, Noble Experiment; Co-Founder, Revelry Cocktail Co.
San Diego
Harvard & Stone 254..Late-Night
The Spare Room 256...Neighborhood
Turf Supper Club 240...Local Must-Visit
La Zebra 348...Worth the travel
Coin-op Game Room 239..Wish I'd opened

OLIVER EBERT
Bartender, Becketts Kopf
Pappelallee 64, Berlin
Bar Immertreu 160..Late-Night
Badfish 160...Neighborhood
Lost in Grub Street 160...Local Must-Visit
White Lyan 109..Worth the travel
Milk & Honey (now Attaboy 334)...........................Wish I'd opened

KEELY EDGINGTON
Owner, Julep
4141 Pennsylvania Avenue, Kansas City
Harry's Bar & Tables 271...Late-Night
Harry's Bar 198...Wish I'd opened

TOM EGERTON
Bar Manager, Eau de Vie
1 Malthouse Lane, Melbourne
Henrietta Supper Club 19.......................................Late-Night
The Wild Rover 20...Neighborhood
Shady Pines Saloon 19...Local Must-Visit
The Dead Rabbit Grocery and Grog 335...............Worth the travel

VITALIK EKIMENKO
Bartender, Funny Cabany
ulitsa Malaya Dmitrovka, 5/9, Moscow
Chainaya Tea & Cocktails 186................................Late-Night
Moskovsky Bar 186...Hotel
69 Colebrook Row 109..Local Must-Visit
American Bar 107..Worth the travel

PHOEBE ESMON
Partner, Spirit Animal LLC; Founding President, United States Bartenders' Guild; Consultant, The Yachtsman Tiki
Philadelphia

The 700 (bar) 313	Late-Night
The Carousel Bar & Lounge 306	Hotel
Loco Pez 313	Neighborhood
Comstock Saloon 264	Neighborhood
Pare de Sufrir Tome Mezcal 347-8	Worth the travel

KIRK F. ESTOPINAL
Owner/Operator, Cure/Bellocq/Cane & Table
New Orleans

Molly's at the Market 307	Late-Night
Arnaud's French 75 Bar 305	Local Must-Visit
Empire State South 292	Worth the travel
Donostia 331	Wish I'd opened

DANIEL ESTREMADOYRO
Owner, Mixing Glass Bartending School; Beverage Director, The Rooftop Guemes Bar
General Manuel Belgrano 731 Planta Alta, Güemes, Córdoba

Verne Club 365	Late-Night
La Cova del Drac 361	Neighborhood
Frank's Bar 365	Local Must-Visit
Pocket Food and Drink 351	Worth the travel

GIORGIO FADDA
Bar Manager, Bar Tiepolo at The Westin Europa & Regina
San Marco 2159, Venice

Rivabar 196	Late-Night
Cloakroom Cocktail Lab 197	Neighborhood
The Jerry Thomas Project 209	Worth the travel

ANTHONY FARRELL
Love & Death Inc/Aether & Echo/APOC
10a Ann Street, Belfast

The Hudson Bar 119	Late-Night
Zth Cocktail Lounge 107	Hotel
John Kavanagh "The Gravediggers" 120	Neighborhood
Duke of York 119	Local Must-Visit
Boadas 154	Worth the travel
Boadas 154	Wish I'd opened

MIGUEL FERNANDEZ FERNANDEZ
Bar Manager, Ozone at The Ritz Carlton
Level 118, International Commerce Ctr., 1 Austin Road West, Kowloon, Hong Kong

The Parlour 161	Late-Night
Beaufort Bar 108	Hotel
Jimmy's Bar 161	Hotel
Roomers Bar 162	Local Must-Visit
Seven Swans & The Tiny Cup 162	Local Must-Visit
Mutis 155	Worth the travel
Bar Americano 24	Wish I'd opened

ROBERT FERRARA
Bar Director, Lure Fishbar/The Rum Line
1601 Collins Avenue, Miami Beach

Repour Bar 291	Late-Night
The Regent Cocktail Club 291	Hotel
The Broken Shaker 290	Local Must-Visit
Bar High Five 80	Worth the travel

COLIN PETER FIELD
Executive Head Bartender, Hotel Ritz Paris
15 Place Vendôme, Paris

Moonshiner 146	Late-Night
Hotel Maison Souquet Bar 144	Hotel
The Bar of L'Hotel 142	Local Must-Visit
Lewers Lounge 241	Worth the travel
L'Aperitif Cocktail Bar 241	Worth the travel
Il Pellicano Hotel Bar 195	Wish I'd opened

RYAN FITZGERALD
Owner, ABV
3174 16th Street, San Francisco

The Hideout at Dalva 264	Late-Night
Nopa 265	Neighborhood
The Buena Vista Cafe 264	Local Must-Visit
Tommy's Mexican Restaurant 266	Local Must-Visit
Pare de Sufrir Tome Mezcal 347-8	Worth the travel
ABV 26	Wish I'd opened

KAMIL FOLTAN
Group Bar Manager, Potato Head Family
Bali

28 Hongkong Street 53	Late-Night
Manhattan (Singapore) 53	Hotel
Tippling Club 54	Local Must-Visit
Hemingway Bar 141	Worth the travel
Dry Martini 154	Wish I'd opened

KYLE FORD

Cocktail & Spirits Expert, Remy Cointreau; Co-Owner, Ford Marketing Lab
www.fordmarketinglab.com

No. 308 (bar) 296...Late-Night
Robert's Western World 296.........................Late-Night
Rye 265...Late-Night
The NoMad Bar 323...Hotel
21 Club 321...Local Must-Visit
Old Glory 296.......................................Local Must-Visit
Pinewood Social 296............................Local Must-Visit
The Rarebit 295....................................Local Must-Visit
Schumann's Bar 167.............................Worth the travel
15 Romolo 265......................................Wish I'd opened

RACHEL FORD

Owner, Ford Mixology Lab
www.fordmarketinglab.com

Lantern's Keep 322..Late-Night
Pepe Le Moko 245...Hotel
Oak & Ivy 242.......................................Local Must-Visit
Rainbow Room 323................................Local Must-Visit
The Spotted Owl 272-3.........................Local Must-Visit
Schumann's Bar 167,............................Worth the travel
15 Romolo 265......................................Wish I'd opened

GIUSEPPE GALLO

Italian Spirits Expert; Co-Owner; Gastrovino & Bar8
257 Kings Road, London

The Bar at the Dorchester 111..............................Hotel
American Bar 107..Hotel
Caffè Propaganda 208..........................Local Must-Visit
Co.So. 208...Local Must-Visit
The Mad Dog 196..................................Local Must-Visit
Nightjar 114...Local Must-Visit
Smile Tree 196.......................................Local Must-Visit
Dukes Bar 112.......................................Worth the travel

SILVIA GHIONI

Bartender, Chateau Monfort
Corso Concordia 1, Milan

Mio Bar 204...Hotel bar
Bar High Five 80...................................Worth the travel
Nottingham Forest 204.........................Local Must-Visit
Lacerba 203...Late-Night

WALTER GOSSO

Mad Dog Speakeasy
Via Maria Vittoria, 35A, Turin

Employees Only 324.......................................Late-Night
Artesian 111..Hotel
1930 (bar) 203.......................................Local Must-Visit
The Dead Rabbit Grocery and Grog 335...........Worth the travel
The Mad Dog 196...................................Wish I'd opened

KAREN GRILL

Attache, The Bon Vivants
www.bonvivants.com, Los Angeles

Harvard & Stone 254......................................Late-Night
Live Wire 239... Neighborhood
Honeycut 254..Local Must-Visit
Black Pearl 25,......................................Worth the travel
The Walker Inn 257...............................Wish I'd opened

WILL GROVES

Bar Program Director, Smallman Gallery
54 21st Street, Pittsburgh

The Allegheny Wine Mixer 313.....................Late-Night
House of 1000 Beers 312....................... Neighborhood
Butterjoint 314......................................Local Must-Visit
Beachbum Berry's Latitude 29 (bar) 305............Worth the travel
Sergio's World Beers 293......................Wish I'd opened

RICARDO GUERRERO

Mixologist; Director, Bar Academy Santiago
Mensia de los Nidos No. 1129, Santiago

Polluelo Amarillo................................... Neighborhood
KY 361..Local Must-Visit
Employees Only 324.............................Worth the travel
Barbazul 360...Wish I'd opened

ABIGAIL GULLO

Bar Manager, Compère Lapin
535 Tchoupitoulas Street, New Orleans

Employees Only 324.......................................Late-Night
The Palm Court 322..Hotel
Julep 298... Neighborhood
Pal's Lounge 307................................... Neighborhood
Bacchanal Wine 305.............................Local Must-Visit
Extra Virgin 241....................................Local Must-Visit
American Bar 107..................................Worth the travel
Soggy Dollar Bar 350–1.........................Worth the travel
The Long Island Bar 338........................Wish I'd opened

MATTIAS HÄGGLUND
Owner/Bartender, Heritage
1627 West Main Street, Richmond

Saison 299	Late-Night
Lemaire 299	Hotel bar
The Roosevelt 299	Neighborhood
The Violet Hour 284	Worth the travel
The Dead Rabbit Grocery and Grog 335	Wish I'd opened

CHRIS HANNAH
Bartender, French 75 Bar
813 Bienville Street, New Orleans

Erin Rose 306	Late-Night
Finn McCool's 306	Neighborhood
The Saint 307	Local Must-Visit
Earl's Juke Joint 20	Worth the travel
Mimi's 307	Wish I'd opened

PIP HANSON
Head Bartender, Artesian
1C Portland Place, London

Lady Jane Booze & Jazz 82	Late-Night
The Carousel Bar & Lounge 306	Hotel bar
Donny Dirk's Zombie Den 270	Local Must-Visit
Tender Bar 81	Worth the travel
Arnaud's French 75 Bar 305	Wish I'd opened

DIRK HANY
Bar Manager, Widder Bar
Widdergasse 6, Zurich

Tales Bar 168	Late-Night
Widder Bar 168	Hotel
Bar les Trois Rois 167	Local Must-Visit
Kronenhalle 168	Local Must-Visit
Tür 7 174	Worth the travel
Sherry Butt 142	Wish I'd opened

DENZEL HEATH
Head, MMI Bar Academy
Dubai

The NoMad Bar 323	Hotel
The Landmark 214	Local Must-Visit
Lost + Found Drinkery 182	Worth the travel
The Blind Pig 115	Wish I'd opened

WILL HOLLINGSWORTH
Proprietor, The Spotted Owl
710 Jefferson Avenue, Cleveland

The Wayland 333	Late-Night
Mace 332's Crossing 313	Neighborhood
Prosperity Social Club 272	Local Must-Visit
Bit House Saloon 243	Worth the travel
Polite Provisions 240	Wish I'd opened

JONATHAN HOMIER
Quebec Brand Ambassador, Jack Daniels
www.jackdaniels.com

Bar Datcha 224	Late-Night
Bar Kabinet 224	Late-Night
Plateau Lounge 225	Hotel bar
Bishop & Bagg 224	Neighborhood
La Distillerie 225	Local Must-Visit
The Dead Rabbit Grocery and Grog 335	Worth the travel
L'Gros Luxe 225	Wish I'd opened

EDWARD HONG
General Manager, Gib's
1380 Williamson Street, Madison

Marvel Bar 270	Late-Night
Woody & Anne's 273	Neighborhood
Forequarter 273	Local Must-Visit
Vault +82 (bar) 68	Worth the travel
The NoMad Bar 323	Wish I'd opened

SPENCER HUANG
Co-Founder/Head Bartender, R&D Craft Cocktail Lab
#36 JiaXing Street, Taipei

The Speakeasy 69	Late-Night
Mod Sequel 68	Neighborhood
The Aviary 279	Worth the travel

ALBA HUERTA
Owner/Operator, Julep
Houston

Midnight Rambler 297	Hotel
Poison Girl 298	Neighborhood
Half Step 296	Local Must-Visit
La Carafe 298	Local Must-Visit
Proof + Pantry 297	Local Must-Visit
Second Bar + Kitchen 296	Local Must-Visit
West Alabama Ice House 298	Local Must-Visit
Glass 144	Worth the travel

LUIS C. IRIARTE
Bartender, Bar Systems
www.barsystems.com.mx, Mexico City

King Cole Bar 322	Hotel
PDT 333	Late-Night
Baltra 347	Local Must-Visit
Bar High Five 80	Worth the travel
Employees Only 324	Wish I'd opened

OLIVIER JACOBS
Bartender, Jigger's--The Noble Drugstore
Oudburg 16, Ghent

Uncle Babe's 130	Neighborhood
Bar High Five 80	Worth the travel
Café den Turk 130	Local Must-Visit
Harry's Bar 198	Wish I'd opened
Minor Swing 130	Late-Night

TIMO JANSE
Manager, Door 74; Owner, Perfect Serve Barshow
Reguliersdwarsstraat 74I, Amsterdam

Poison 188	Late-Night
The Carousel Bar & Lounge 306	Hotel
Hiding in Plain Sight (HPS) 128	Neighborhood
Café de Dokter 128	Local Must-Visit
Excalibur 128	Local Must-Visit
Feijoa 128	Local Must-Visit
Snappers Resto-Bar 129	Local Must-Visit
Tales & Spirits 129	Local Must-Visit
Whisky Café L&B 129	Local Must-Visit
Wynand Fockink 129 129	Local Must-Visit
Amor y Amargo 331	Worth the travel
Employees Only 324	Wish I'd opened

HASSE BANK JOHANSEN
Owner, St. Pauls Apothek
Jægergårdsgade 76, Aarhus

Nightjar 114	Late-Night
Trailer Happiness 113	Neighborhood
St. Pauls Apothek 93	Local Must-Visit
The Aviary 279	Worth the travel
Artesian 111	Wish I'd opened

MIA JOHANSSON
Independent Bartender
London

Employees Only 324	Late-Night
Artesian 111	Hotel bar
Happiness Forgets 109	Local Must-Visit
The Dead Rabbit Grocery and Grog 335	Worth the travel
High Water 116	Wish I'd opened

CHARLES JOLY
Owner, Crafthouse Cocktails
www.crafthousecocktails.com, Chicago

Clark Street Ale House 281	Late-Night
The Hawthorne 311	Hotel
Elixir 264	Neighborhood
The The Green Mill 281	Local Must-Visit
La Capilla 347	Worth the travel

JAMIE JONES
Bartender, No Fixed Abode; Group Bars Executive,
   The Social Company
www.thesocialcompany.co.uk

Boutiq Bar 174	Late-Night
Happiness Forgets 109	Late-Night
Artesian 111	Hotel
Berry & Rye 98	Local Must-Visit
Bar High Five 80	Worth the travel
The Dead Rabbit Grocery and Grog 335	Wish I'd opened

DAVID J. KAPLAN
Partner, Proprietors LLC/Death & Co/Nitecap/151/Honeycut/
   The Normandie Club/The Walker Inn
Los Angeles

Lucy's 332	Late-Night
Midnight Rambler 297	Hotel bar
Tony's Saloon 256	Neighborhood
The Varnish 257	Local Must-Visit
Tokyo 365	Worth the travel
The Varnish 257	Local Must-Visit

MARIO KAPPES
Head Bartender, Le Lion Bar de Paris
Rathausstraße 3, Hamburg

Le Bar 143	Hotel bar
Licorería Limantour 347	Worth the travel
Buck and Breck 160	Local Must-Visit
Le Lion Bar de Paris 163	Wish I'd opened
Boilerman Bar 162	Late-Night

ZDENEK KASTANEK
28 Hongkong Street / Proof & Company
28 Hongkong Street, Singapore

Manhattan (Singapore) 53	Late-Night
Black Pearl 25	Neighborhood
28 Hongkong Street 53	Local Must-Visit
The Flagship 53	Local Must-Visit
Jigger & Pony 53	Local Must-Visit
Maison Premiere 338	Worth the travel
Employees Only 324	Wish I'd opened

ALAN KAVANAGH
Advocacy Development Manager, Edward Dillon & Co.;
Owner/Managing Director, Total Cocktail Solutions
Dublin
Shelbourne Hotel 120..Hotel
John Kavanagh "The Gravediggers" 120..............Local Must-Visit
The Liquor Rooms 120.......................................Late-Night

HIROYASU KAYAMA
Head Bartender, Ben Fiddich
1 Chome–13–7, Tokyo
Bar Hermit 82..Late-Night
Zatta 83...Hotel
Bar Doras 83.......................................Local Must-Visit
Speak Low 63.....................................Worth the travel

HANNAH KEIRL
Director, Global Bartender Exchange
www.globalbartenderexchange.com
The Toff 25...Late-Night
The NoMad Bar 323..Hotel
Tranquebar 45.....................................Local Must-Visit
Callooh Callay 113...............................Worth the travel
Section 8 (bar) 25...............................Wish I'd opened

JAMES KEMP
Bartender, The Finnieston Bar & Restaurant
1125 Argyle Street, City Centre, Glasgow
Garibaldi's 118...Late-Night
Artesian 111..Hotel
The Pot Still 118..................................Local Must-Visit
The Dead Rabbit Grocery and Grog 335..............Worth the travel
Mother's Ruin 335...............................Wish I'd opened

SEAN KENYON
Proprietor, Williams & Graham
3160 Tejon Street, Denver
My Brother's Bar 241...Late-Night
The Breslin 323..Hotel
The Buckhorn Exchange 240................Local Must-Visit
Artesian 111...Worth the travel
Prizefighter 236...................................Wish I'd opened

TED KILGORE
Owner, Planter's House
1000 Mississippi Avenue, St. Louis
Sanctuaria 272...Late-Night
Fox & Hounds 272..Hotel
Friendly's 272.......................................Neighborhood
The Royale 272.....................................Local Must-Visit
Manifesto 271.......................................Worth the travel
Scotch & Soda 271................................Worth the travel
Clover Club 337....................................Wish I'd opened

MEGHAN KONECNY
Bar Manager, Scofflaw
3201 West Armitage Avenue, Chicago
Bar Deville 279...Late-Night
Longman & Eagle 282...........................Neighborhood
The Violet Hour 284..............................Local Must-Visit
Swinebar 195.......................................Worth the travel
Sportsman's Club 283...........................Wish I'd opened

NICK KOUMBARAKIS
Creative Director, Alchemist Says
www.alchemistsays.tumblr.com
The Power & The Glory 215....................Neighborhood
The House of Machines 214....................Local Must-Visit
Operation Dagger 54.............................Local Must-Visit
Publik Wine Bar 214..............................Local Must-Visit
Ronnie's Sex Shop 214...........................Local Must-Visit
Bar High Five 80....................................Worth the travel

ALEX KRATENA
Former Head Bartender, Artesian
www.alexkratena.com, London
Glass 144...Late-Night
The NoMad Bar 323...Hotel
Bar Termini 114.....................................Local Must-Visit
Gen Yamamoto 82.................................Worth the travel
The Aviary 279......................................Wish I'd opened

MARIAN KRAUSE
Bar Manager, ShakeKings Institute for Bar Culture
www.shakekings.com, Cologne
Spirits Bar 161..Late-Night
Spirits Bar 161......................................Local Must-Visit
28 Hongkong Street 53..........................Worth the travel
The Dead Rabbit Grocery and Grog 335..............Wish I'd opened

BETTINA KUPSA
Bartender, The Chug Club
Taubenstraße 13, Hamburg

3Freunde Cocktailbar 163	Late-Night
Bar Dacaio 162	Hotel
Le Lion Bar de Paris 163	Local Must-Visit
Cantina Mayahuel 238	Worth the travel
Buck and Breck 160	Wish I'd opened

ANTONIO LAI
Owner, Quinary
56-58 Hollywood Road, Central, Hong Kong

Lobster Bar 66	Late-Night
The Envoy 66	Hotel
Origin 67	Local Must-Visit
Nottingham Forest 204	Worth the travel

CAITLIN LAMAN
Bartender, Trick Dog
3010 20th Street, San Francisco

ABV 263	Late-Night
Connaught Bar 112	Hotel
Smuggler's Cove 266	Local Must-Visit
Lost Lake 282	Worth the travel

ANGELIKA LARKINA
Training Center Manager, Estonian Bartenders Association
www.barman.ee

Butterfly Lounge 178	Late-Night
Horisont Bar 178	Hotel
Valli Baar 178	Local Must-Visit
Artesian 111	Worth the travel

EDEN LAURIN
Managing Partner, The Violet Hour
520 North Damen Avenue, Chicago

Booze Box 280	Late-Night
Rootstock 282	Late-Night
Cindy's 280	Hotel
Charleston 280	Neighborhood
Analogue 279	Local Must-Visit
Angel's Share 331	Worth the travel
Three Dots and a Dash 283	Wish I'd opened

SHAUN LAYTON
Bar Manager at Juniper
Lietzenburger Strasse 13, Berlin

Pourhouse 230	Late-Night
Gerard Lounge 229	Hotel
Mamie Taylor's 230	Neighborhood
The Diamond 228	Local Must-Visit
Dukes Bar 112	Worth the travel
The Bayside Lounge 228	Wish I'd opened

GUILLAUME LE DORNER
Bar Manager, The Bar with No Name
69 Colebrooke Row, London

Milk & Honey 115	Late-Night
Dandelyan 116	Hotel
Ku De Ta 54	Worth the travel
Happiness Forgets 109	Wish I'd opened

JOSE LUIS LEON
Bartender, Licorería Limantour/Baltra Bar
Álvaro Obregón 106, Cuauhtémoc, Roma Nte., Mexico City

Parker & Lenox 347	Late-Night
Three Dots and a Dash 283	Worth the travel
The Dead Rabbit Grocery and Grog 335	Wish I'd opened

LEONARDO LEUCI
Bartender, Jerry Thomas Speakeasy
Vicolo Cellini, 30, Rome

El Copitas 187	Late-Night
Connaught Bar 112	Hotel
Canon 246	Worth the travel

NAOMI LEVY
Bar Manager, Eastern Standard Kitchen and Drinks
528 Commonwealth Avenue, Boston

Employees Only 324	Late-Night
Clyde Common 243	Hotel
State Park 312	Neighborhood
Eastern Standard 310	Local Must-Visit
Florería Atlántico 366	Worth the travel

DIMI LEZINSKA
Beverage Consultant, Co-Host, Cocktail Kings
www.dimilezinska.com, Mumbai

ATM (À Ta Maison) 44	Late-Night
Big Nasty 45	Neighborhood
Ellipsis 45	Local Must-Visit
Suzuran Bar 187	Worth the travel
The Bombay Canteen 45	Wish I'd opened

THEO LIEBERMAN
Head Sommelier, Compagnie des Vins Surnaturels; Former Head Bartender, Milk & Honey/Eleven Madison Park
249 Centre Street, New York City
Little Branch 325...Late-Night
Lantern's Keep 322...Hotel
Buttermilk 336..Neighborhood
The Raines Law Room 320...................Local Must-Visit
The Aviary 279......................................Worth the travel
The NoMad Bar 323.............................Wish I'd opened

ETHAN LIU
Reserve Brand Amabassdor, Diageo China
www.diageo.com
Migas 58...Late-Night
Atmosphere Bar 58..Hotel
Janes + Hooch 58.............................Neighborhood
Mokihi 59..Neighborhood
D Lounge 58...................................Local Must-Visit
The Dead Rabbit Grocery and Grog 335.............Worth the travel
The Hide Bar 110................................Wish I'd opened

ERIK LORINCZ
Head Bartender, American Bar (The Savoy)
Strand, London
Experimental Cocktail Club (Paris) 141...........Late-Night
Chiltern Firehouse Hotel 111....................................Hotel
Nightjar 114..Local Must-Visit
Star Bar 81...Worth the travel

CHRIS LOWDER
Head Bartender, Four Seasons Hotel
97 Saemunan-ro, Jongno-gu, Seoul
Extra Fancy 337...Late-Night

JOSE A. FEMENIA LUIS
Head Bartender, Boadas Cocktail Bar
Carrer dels Tallers, 1, Barcelona
Slow Barcelona 155....................................Late-Night
Banker's Bar 154...Hotel
Negroni 155...Neighborhood
Collage Art & Cocktail Social Club 154.............Local Must-Visit
American Bar 107...............................Worth the travel
The Aviary 279...................................Wish I'd opened

MICHAEL MADRUSAN
Owner, The Everleigh
150-156 Gertrude Street, Melbourne
Heartbreaker 24...Late-Night
American Bar 107...Hotel
Lui Bar 24...Local Must-Visit
Attaboy 334.......................................Worth the travel
Milk & Honey.....................................Wish I'd opened

JOHN MAHER
Owner, The Rogue Gentlemen
618 North 1st Street, Richmond
Saison 299...Late-Night
Quill 289...Hotel
15 Romolo 265................................Worth the travel
Nitecap 334-5.................................Wish I'd opened

MAURO MAHJOUB
Owner/Head Bartender, Mauro's Negroni Club
Kellerstrasse 32, Munich
Bar Gabányi 166.......................................Late-Night
Königsquelle 166..............................Neighborhood
Pusser's 166......................................Local Must-Visit

TOBY MALONEY
Partner/Head Mixologist, The Violet Hour/The Patterson House
520 North Damen Avenue, Chicago
Mother's Ruin 335....................................Late-Night
Extra Fancy 337..................................Neighborhood
Attaboy 334.......................................Local Must-Visit
The Peak Lounge 83...........................Worth the travel
Milk & Honey (now Attaboy 334)..................Wish I'd opened

LYNNETTE MARRERO
Co-Founder, Speed Rack; Owner, DrinksAt6
www.drinksatsix.com
Glass 144...Late-Night
ABV 263..Neighborhood
The Happiest Hour 325.....................Local Must-Visit
Slowly Shirley 325............................Local Must-Visit
Bar High Five 80..............................Worth the travel
The Broken Shaker 290.....................Wish I'd opened

FRANKY MARSHALL
Beverage Director, Le Boudoir
135 Atlantic Avenue, Brooklyn
Volkswagen Bus Bars 47.................................Late-Night
Artesian 111..Hotel
Black Angel's Bar 172...................................Hotel
Sunny's Bar 338-39...............................Neighborhood
Arnaud's French 75 Bar 305...............Local Must-Visit
28 Hongkong Street 53........................Worth the travel
Hemingway Bar 141.............................Worth the travel
Bacchanal Wine 305.............................Wish I'd opened

DRE MASSO
Mixologist, Potato Head
Bali, Jakarta, and Singapore
Boadas 154...Late-Night
Tommy's Mexican Restaurant 266.............Neighborhood
La Capilla 347....................................Worth the travel
Andrés Carne de Res 355......................Wish I'd opened

JACK MCGARRY
Managing Partner, The Dead Rabbit
30 Water Street, New York City
Maison Premiere 338...................................Late-Night
The NoMad Bar 323......................................Hotel
Iona 338..Neighborhood
McSorley's Old Ale House 332-3............Local Must-Visit
Kelly's Cellars 119.............................Worth the travel

ANGUS MCGREGOR
Group Director of Beverage, Utopia
Emirates Towers Hotel, G Floor, Dubai
Panda & Sons 118.......................................Late-Night
Hakkasan 40..Hotel
Villager 118...Neighborhood
Zuma 40...Local Must-Visit
The Dead Rabbit Grocery and Grog 335.............Worth the travel

JONNY M.R. MCKENZIE
CEO, Posboss
www.posbosshq.com
Hawthorn Lounge 31....................................Late-Night
Toast Bar 31..Late-Night
Molten 30..Neighborhood
Pomeroy's Pub 30...................................Neighborhood
Civil & Naval 30 ....Local Must-Visit
The Golden Dawn 30..............................Local Must-Visit
Hawthorn Lounge 31.............................Local Must-Visit
Mea Culpa 30 ....Local Must-Visit
El Floridita 348...................................Worth the travel
Pegu Club 336......................................Wish I'd opened

JIM MEEHAN
Co-Founder, PDT
113 St. Marks Place, New York City
The Aviary 279...Late-Night
American Bar 107...Hotel
Daddy-O 324...Neighborhood
Teardrop Lounge 246...........................Local Must-Visit
Bar High Five 80.................................Worth the travel

ALEX MESQUITA
Head Bartender, Parisbar
Kantstrasse 152, Berlin
Sub Astor 360..Late-Night
Belmond Copacabana Palace 360...........................Hotel
Frank's Bar 365..................................Worth the travel
Frank Bar 360......................................Wish I'd opened

ROMAN MILOSTIVY
Owner, Chainaya Tea & Cocktails
1-ya Tverskaya-Yamskaya ulitsa, 29, 1, Moscow
Noor Bar 186...Late-Night
Pivbar 187..Neighborhood
Mendeleev Bar 186...............................Local Must-Visit
Tommy's Mexican Restaurant 266.............Worth the travel
Buck and Breck 160..............................Wish I'd opened

IVY MIX
Bar Owner, Leyenda
221 Smith Street, Brooklyn
The Pink Chihuahua 115................................Late-Night
The Matchbox 282...................................Neighborhood
Fort Defiance 337................................Local Must-Visit
Café No Sé 350....................................Worth the travel
La Capilla 347.....................................Wish I'd opened

TSUYOSHI MIYAZAKI
Bar Manager, Narahotel
1096 Takabatake-cho, Nara
Tender Bar 81..Late-Night
Brass Rail Bar 270.................................Neighborhood
American Bar 107..................................Worth the travel

LIZAVETA MOLYAVKA
Bartender, News Cafe
vulica Karla Marksa 34, Minsk
Heroes Bar 179...Late-Night
Sweet & Sour 180.................................Local Must-Visit
Nightjar 114.......................................Worth the travel
Experimental Cocktail Club (Paris) 141............Wish I'd opened

JULIA MOMOSE
Head Bartender, GreenRiver
259 East Erie Street, Chicago

Clark Street Ale House 281	Late-Night
The Matchbox 282	Neighborhood
Billy Sunday 280	Local Must-Visit
Bar High Five 80	Worth the travel
Rye 265	Wish I'd opened

JEFFREY MORGENTHALER
Bar Manager, Clyde Common & Pépé Le Moko
Portland

Mary's Club 244	Late-Night
Clyde Common 243	Hotel
Bryant's Cocktail Lounge 273	Neighborhood
Horse Brass Pub 244	Local Must-Visit
Huber's Cafe 244	Local Must-Visit
Le Lion Bar de Paris 163	Worth the travel
Prizefighter 236	Wish I'd opened

SEAN MULDOON
Managing Partner, The Dead Rabbit
30 Water Street, New York City

Employees Only 324	Late-Night
The NoMad Bar 323	Hotel
Duke of York 119	Neighborhood
PDT 333	Local Must-Visit
Artesian 111	Worth the travel
Harry's Bar 198	Wish I'd opened

ALGIRDAS MULEVIČIUS
Bartender, Trinity
LV-1010, Dzirnavu iela 67, Riga

K-Bar 94	Late-Night
Artesian 111	Hotel
Hard Shake 179	Local Must-Visit
Bugsy's Bar & Bistro 47	Worth the travel
Death & Co 331	Wish I'd opened

ZOLTAN NAGY
Head Bartender/Owner, Boutiq'Bar
Paulay Ede u., Budapest

Artesian 111	Late-Night
Mr Fogg's	Neighborhood
The Bar at Baraka 174	Local Must-Visit
The Aviary 279	Worth the travel
Callooh Callay 113	Wish I'd opened

BEK NARZI
Co-Owmer, Pachamama Restaurant Group
www.narzi.london

Saxon + Parole 187	Late-Night
Moskovsky Bar 186	Hotel
Moskovsky Bar 186	Local Must-Visit
El Copitas 187	Worth the travel
Lounge Bohemia 114	Wish I'd opened

GEORGE JIRI NEMEC
Global Brand Ambassador, Becherovka Original; Founder,
Bohemian Bar Club; Founder, AtBars
www.atbars.com

Manhattan (Singapore) 53	Hotel
Cash Only Bar 172	Neighborhood
Bugsy's Bar & Bistro 47	Local Must-Visit

DAVID NEWMAN
Owner, Pint + Jigger
1936 South King Street, Honolulu

Rum Club 245	Late-Night
Lewers Lounge 241	Hotel
Murphy's Bar and Grill 242	Neighborhood
Multnomah Whiskey Library 245	Worth the travel
The Varnish 257	Wish I'd opened

RYAN NIGHTINGALE
Bar Manager, Ham & Sherry/Wan Chai
1-7 Ship Street, Wan Chai, Hong Kong

Joe's Billiards & Bar 67	Late-Night
Tai Lung Fung 67	Late-Night
Captain's Bar 66	Hotel
Lobster Bar 66	Hotel
Bar 42 66	Neighborhood
Tai Lung Fung 67	Local Must-Visit
The Dead Rabbit Grocery and Grog 335	Worth the travel
Happiness Forgets 109	Wish I'd opened

HONORIO OLIVEIRA
Bar Manager, The Marriott Lisbon
Avenue dos Combatentes 45, Lisbon

Porta 22 Club 157	Late-Night
Red Frog 156	Late-Night
Cinco Lounge 156	Local Must-Visit
Pub Bonaparte 157	Local Must-Visit
Nightjar 114	Worth the travel
Callooh Callay 113	Wish I'd opened

AARON DIAZ OLIVOS

Beverage Director, Astrid & Gaston Casa Moreyra
Avenue Paz Soldán 290, San Isidro

Open Bar 356	Late-Night
Artesian 111	Hotel
Superba 357	Neighborhood
Antigua Taberna Queirolo 356–7	Local Must-Visit
The Aviary 279	Worth the travel

GABRIEL ORTA

Co-Founder, Bar Lab/The Broken Shaker
2727 Indian Creek Drive, Miami Beach

Mother's Ruin 335	Late-Night
American Bar 107	Hotel
Half Step 296	Neighborhood
Imperial 244	Local Must-Visit
Mac's Club Deuce 290	Local Must-Visit
Dirty Dick 143	Worth the travel
Employees Only 324	Wish I'd opened

MATTIA PASTORI

Bar Manager, Mandarin Oriental Milano
Via Andegari, 9, Milan

1930 (bar) 203	Late-Night
Bamboo Bar 203	Hotel bar

MICHAEL JACK PAZDON

Proprietor/Bar Manager, The Wallingford
7 Wallingford Square #101, Kittery

Employees Only 324	Late-Night
Smuggler's Cove 266	Late-Night
The Brooklyn Inn 336	Neighborhood

ANDRÉ MANUEL DUARTE PEIXE

Head Bartender, Bar Esplanada Príncipe Real
Rua D. Pedro V No 56-D, Lisbon

Cinco Lounge 156	Late-Night
Rooftop Bar 156–7	Hotel bar
Park Bar 156	Local Must-Visit
Connaught Bar 112	Worth the travel
Bar Foxtrot 156	Wish I'd opened

CLAUDIO PERINELLI

Bar Manager, The Soda Jerk
Vicolo Quadrelli, 5, Verona

Zth Cocktail Lounge 107	Late-Night
Bar 66 203	Hotel
Artesian 111	Local Must-Visit
Il Kiosko 197	Worth the travel
Zth Cocktail Lounge 107	Wish I'd opened

AGOSTINO PERRONE

Director of Mixology, The Connaught
Carlos Place, London

Nightjar 114	Late-Night
The Blue Bar (London) 110	Hotel
Happiness Forgets 109	Neighborhood
The Fumoir 112	Local Must-Visit
Bar High Five 80	Worth the travel
Connaught Bar 112	Wish I'd opened

TIM PHILIPS

Co-Owner, Bulletin Place
10-14 Bulletin Place, Sydney

Siglo 25	Late-Night
The Corner House 18	Neighborhood
Napier Hotel 26	Local Must-Visit
Café No Sé 349	Worth the travel
Spirit of 77 245	Wish I'd opened

LUCA PICCHI

Bartender, Caffè Rivoire 872
Piazza della Signoria, 5, Florence

The Fusion Bar and Restaurant 197	Hotel
Atrium Bar 196	Local Must-Visit
Artesian 111	Worth the travel

ANDRÉ PINTZ

Bartender, Imperii
Brühl 72, Leipzig

Glass 144	Late-Night
Artesian 111	Hotel
Madrigal 163	Local Must-Visit
Sherry Butt 142	Worth the travel
Imperii 163	Wish I'd opened

THEODOROS PIRILLOS

Head Bartender, A for Athens
Miaouli 2, Athens

Seven Jokers 182	Late-Night
CV Distiller 181	Neighborhood
360 (bar) 181	Local Must-Visit
Baba au Rum 181	Local Must-Visit
Bar 42 66	Local Must-Visit
The Clumsies 181	Local Must-Visit
The Gin Joint 295	Local Must-Visit
Theory Bar & More 182	Local Must-Visit
El Floridita 348	Worth the travel

JONATHAN POGASH
President/CEO, The Cocktail Guru Inc
www.thecocktailguru.com

Employees Only 324	Late-Night
Candelaria 142	Worth the travel
Seamstress 324	Wish I'd opened

CHRISTY POPE
Owner/Operator, Cuffs & Buttons/Midnight Rambler
Dallas

The Chat Room 297	Late-Night
The Spare Room 256	Hotel
Victor Tangos 297	Neighborhood
Midnight Rambler 297	Local Must-Visit
69 Colebrooke Row 109	Worth the travel
Milk & Honey (now Attaboy 334)	Wish I'd opened

TESS POSTHUMUS
Bartender, Door 74
Reguliersdwarsstraat 74I, Amsterdam

Tales & Spirits 129	Late-Night
American Bar 107	Hotel
Wynand Fockink 129	Local Must-Visit
Artesian 111	Worth the travel
Door 74 (bar) 128	Wish I'd opened

ALEŠ PŮTA
Bartender, Hemingway Bar
Karoliny Svetlé 279/26, Prague

Callooh Callay 113	Late-Night
Artesian 111	Hotel
Bugsy's Bar & Bistro 47	Local Must-Visit
Drink 310	Worth the travel
Cash Only Bar 172	Wish I'd opened

JULIE REINER
Owner, Clover Club/Flatiron Lounge/Leyenda
New York City

The Dead Rabbit Grocery and Grog 335	Late-Night
House Without a Key 241	Hotel
Attaboy 334	Local Must-Visit
Artesian 111	Worth the travel
Bumbye Beach Bar 242	Wish I'd opened

BROOKS REITZ
Restaurateur Leon's Oyster Shop/Saint Alban/Jack Rudy
Cocktail Co.
Charleston

The Belmont 295	Late-Night
Bin 152 (bar) 295	Local Must-Visit
Artesian 111	Worth the travel
The Leadbelly 334	Wish I'd opened

INGUSS REIZENBERGS
Brand Ambassador, Monin
www.monin.com

Balzambārs 178	Late-Night
B Bar 178	Neighborhood
Balzambārs 178	Local Must-Visit

ANDREW RICE
General Manager, Attaboy
134 Eldridge Street, New York City

The Brooklyn Inn 336	Late-Night
The NoMad Bar 323	Hotel
Fort Defiance 337	Neighborhood
Bar Hommage 91	Local Must-Visit
Dear Irving 320	Local Must-Visit
Linje Tio 92	Local Must-Visit
Paradiso 92	Local Must-Visit

LARRY RICE
Proprietor, The Silver Dollar and El Camino
1761 Frankfort Ave, Louisville

Nachbar 293	Late-Night
The Berkshire Room 279	Hotel
Sable Kitchen & Bar 283	Hotel
Nachbar 293	Local Must-Visit
Trick Dog 266	Worth the travel
Delilah's 281	Wish I'd opened

MARIO SEIJO RIVERA
Bartender, La Factoria
148 Calle San Sebastián, San Juan

El Farolito Bar 350	Late-Night
The NoMad Bar 323	Hotel
La Factoria 350	Local Must-Visit
Nu Lounge Bar 195	Worth the travel
Employees Only 324	Wish I'd opened

TOMEK ROEHR
Bartender, Bar Wieczorny
Wiśniowa 46, Warsaw
Cocktail Bar Max 172.................................Late-Night
Artesian 111...Hotel
Kita Koguta 172................................Local Must-Visit
Buck and Breck 160............................Worth the travel
Dandelyan 116................................Wish I'd opened

SAM ROSS
Owner, Attaboy
134 Eldridge Street, New York City
Bua 331...Late-Night
Sunny's Bar 338-39.............................Neighborhood
Keens Steakhouse 321........................Local Must-Visit
Everleigh 26....................................Worth the travel

ALLANKING ROXAS
Operations Manager, Dillingers 1903 and Prohibition
Greenbelt 3, Esperaza, Makati, 1223 Metro Manila
Bugsy's Bar & Bistro (Manila) 47.................Late-Night
Sage Bar 48...Hotel
PDT 333.......................................Worth the travel

MARC ALVAREZ SAFONT
Group Bar Manager, elBarri
www.elbarriadria.com
Artesian 111...Hotel
Tandem Cocktail Bar 155.......................Neighborhood
Boca Chica 154................................Local Must-Visit
Nightjar 114.....................................Worth the travel
Gen Yamamoto 82 ....Wish I'd opened

TENZIN KONCHOK SAMDO
Beverage Director, Tavern Road
343 Congress Street, Boston
Tavern Road 311......................................Late-Night
The Hawthorne 311......................................Hotel
Long Bar (Singapore) 53....................Worth the travel
Drink 310...Local Must-Visit

GRANT SCENEY
Beverage Director, Tavern Road
343 Congress Street, Boston
The Keefer Bar 229.................................Late-Night
Hawksworth Restaurant 229.........................Hotel
The Lobby Lounge and Raw Bar 229...................Hotel
Chambar 228.....................................Neighborhood
The Diamond 228..............................Local Must-Visit
Artesian 111.....................................Worth the travel
The Cliff 351....................................Wish I'd opened

LAURA SCHACHT
Bar Manager, Hiding In Plain Sight
Rapenburg 18, Amsterdam
Gräbli Bar 168.......................................Late-Night
Beaufort Bar 108...Hotel
Café de Dokter 128.............................Local Must-Visit
Employees Only 324..........................Worth the travel
Hiding in Plain Sight (HPS) 128.............Wish I'd opened

MORGAN SCHICK
Creative Director, The Bon Vivants
San Francisco
The Alley 237...Late-Night
Clover Club 337......................................Late-Night
Freddie's 220 293.............................Neighborhood
Bar Agricole 263...............................Local Must-Visit
Comstock Saloon 264.........................Local Must-Visit
Smuggler's Cove 266...........................Local Must-Visit
The Silver Dollar 294.........................Worth the travel
Amor y Amargo 331............................Wish I'd opened
Bacchanal Wine 305...........................Wish I'd opened

CHARLES SCHUMANN
Owner, Schumann's Bar
Odeonsplatz 6-7, Munich
Artesian 11...Hotel
Le Lion Bar de Paris 163......................Neighborhood
Bar Gabányi 166.............................Local Must-Visit
Star Bar 81.....................................Worth the travel

PAUL SHIPMAN
Bartender, Sherwood
554 Frankton Road, Queenstown
Nightjar 114...Late-Night
The Fork and Tap 30............................Neighborhood
Public Kitchen & Bar 31.....................Local Must-Visit
The Aviary 279..................................Worth the travel
The Bon Vivant 117............................Wish I'd opened

BAR SHIRA
Owner, Imperial Craft cocktail Bar/La Otra
Ha-Yarkon Street 66, Tel Aviv-Yafo
Glass 144..Late-Night
Artesian 111...Hotel
Port Said 40.....................................Neighborhood
Gatsby 40..Local Must-Visit
The Broken Shaker 290........................Worth the travel
223 (bar) 40....................................Wish I'd opened

AÐALSTEINN SIGURÐSSON
Bartender, Kol Restaurant
40 Skolavoroustigur 40, Reykjavik

Oak Room 94	Late-Night
Slippbarinn 90	Hotel
Slippbarinn 90	Local Must-Visit
The Barking Dog 94	Worth the travel

LAÉRCIO ZULÚ SILVA
Custom Cocktails
www.customcocktails.com.br, Sao Paulo

Sub Astor 360	Late-Night
Frank Bar 360	Hotel
Sub Astor 360	Local Must-Visit
Artesian 111	Worth the travel
Venda do Zulu	Wish I'd opened

JOAQUÍN SIMÓ
Owner, Pouring Ribbons
225 Avenue B, New York City

The Wayland 333	Late-Night
Connaught Bar 112	Hotel
The Long Island Bar 338	Neighborhood
Death & Co 331	Local Must-Visit
Star Bar 81	Worth the travel
Attaboy 334	Wish I'd opened

ADAM SNOOK
Bartender, Bar39
Kungsholmen

East 91	Late-Night
Restaurang Bankomat 93	Neighborhood
Pharmarium 92	Local Must-Visit
La Capilla 347	Worth the travel
Nightjar 114	Wish I'd opened

CHAD SOLOMON
Owner/Operator, Cuffs & Buttons/Midnight Rambler
Dallas

Notsuoh 298	Late-Night
R Bar 307	Hotel
The Saint 307	Neighborhood
Foe (Fraternal Order of Eagles) 297	Local Must-Visit
69 Colebrooke Row 109	Worth the travel
ZZ's Clam Bar 326	Wish I'd opened

SHAWN SOOLE
Principal Consultant, S2 Hospitality Concepts
www.squaredhospitality.ca, Victoria

The Churchill 222	Late-Night
Bar Louise 134	Hotel
Clive's Classic Lounge 222	Hotel
The Harbord Room 223	Neighborhood
L'Abattoir 228	Local Must-Visit
Canon 246	Worth the travel
Liberty 246	Wish I'd opened

MAL SPENCE
Global Ambassador, Black Bottle Whisky; Kelvingrove Cafe
1161-1163 Argyle Street, Glasgow

Dutch Kills 339	Late-Night
The Salon 119	Hotel
The Finnieston Bar & Restaurant 118	Local Must-Visit
Liberty or Death 95	Worth the travel
The House of Machines 214	Wish I'd opened

CLINT SPOTLESON
Chief Mixologist, Renaissance Phoenix Downtown Hotel
100 North 1st Street, Phoenix

Shady's Fine Ales and Cocktails 236	Late-Night
Crudo 236	Neighborhood
Bitter & Twisted Cocktail Parlour 236	Local Must-Visit
Death & Co 331	Worth the travel
The Silver Dollar 294	Wish I'd opened

JOHN STANTON
Bartender
Chicago

Erin Rose 306	Late-Night
Sable Kitchen & Bar 283	Hotel
Nachbar 293	Neighborhood
Delilah's 281	Local Must-Visit
Bar 11 314	Worth the travel
Mockingbird Hill 289	Wish I'd opened

EZRA STAR
General Manager, Drink/Barbara Lynch Gruppo
348 Congress Street, Boston

Employees Only 324	Late-Night
Lost Lake 282	Neighborhood
Backbar 312	Local Must-Visit
Brick & Mortar 311	Local Must-Visit
Eastern Standard 310	Local Must-Visit
Lone Star Taco Bar 311	Local Must-Visit
Glass 144	Worth the travel
Attaboy 334	Wish I'd opened

VINCENT STIPO
Real Estate & Hospitality Consultant, MSC Retail
www.mscretail.com
The Good King Tavern 313......................................Neighborhood
69 Colebrooke Row 109...Worth the travel
Attaboy 334...Wish I'd opened

MASSIMO STRONATI
Founder of DrinkettiLab Mixology Trainings; Bar Consultant
Milan
The Jerry Thomas Project 209...............................Late-Night
American Bar 107...Hotel
Nottingham Forest 204..Local Must-Visit
Tender Bar 81...Worth the travel
Analogue 279...Wish I'd opened

VARUN SUDHAKAR
Bartender, The AER Bar and Lounge at Four Seasons
    Hotel Mumbai
1/136, 34th Floor, Dr. E. Moses Road, Worli, Mumbai
Nightjar 114...Late-Night
American Bar 107..Hotel
The Bombay Canteen 45...Local Must-Visit
El Floridita 348...Worth the travel
Manhattan (Singapore) 53......................................Wish I'd opened

MATÍAS SUPÁN
General Manager for Spirits, La Vinoteca
Santiago
Frank's Bar 365..Late-Night
The White Rabbit 361..Neighborhood
Artesian 111   ....Worth the travel
Florería Atlántico 366...Wish I'd opened

COLIN TAIT
Director, Brown Bottle
Bangkok
U.N.C.L.E. 46..Late-Night
The Bamboo Bar 46...Hotel
Smalls 46...Neighborhood
Sugar Ray | You've Just Been Poisoned 46..........Local Must-Visit
Milk Tiger Lounge 222..Worth the travel
Smuggler's Cove 266..Wish I'd opened

ANDREW TAN
Beverage Director, HYDE
Petaling Jaya
Hyde at 53M 48...Late-Night
Hyde at 53M 48...Neighborhood
Nightjar 114...Worth the travel
Manhattan (Singapore) 53......................................Wish I'd opened

DANIELLE TATARIN
Director of Operations, The Keefer Bar
135 Keefer Street, Vancouver
Uva Wine & Cocktail Bar 230.................................Late-Night
The Carousel Bar & Lounge 306............................Hotel
Lolita's 230...Neighborhood
Bao Bei 228..Local Must-Visit
Artesian 111..Worth the travel
Milk & Honey (now Attaboy 334)...........................Wish I'd opened

SOTHER TEAGUE
Beverage Director, Amor y Amargo/Cienfuegos/Mother
    of Pearl
New York City
Holiday Cocktail Lounge 332..................................Late-Night
Sable Kitchen & Bar 283...Hotel
Rob Roy 246...Neighborhood
McSorley's Old Ale House 332-3...........................Local Must-Visit
American Bar 107..Worth the travel
Canon 246...Wish I'd opened

JESSE JAMES TEERENMAA
Bar Manager, Grotesk Bar
Ludviginkatu 10, Helsinki
Teatteri Kellobaari 95...Late-Night
Restaurant & Bar à Vins 144..................................Hotel
Trillby & Chadwick 95...Local Must-Visit
Strøm 94...Worth the travel
Lebensstern 160..Wish I'd opened

KELLIE THORN
Beverage Director, Hugh Acheson; Bar Manager,
    Empire State South
999 Peachtree Street Northeast, Atlanta
The Righteous Room 292..Late-Night
Victory Sandwich Bar 292......................................Late-Night
The Broken Shaker 290..Hotel
Bookhouse Pub 291...Neighborhood
The Grey 293..Local Must-Visit
Kimball House 292...Local Must-Visit
Cane & Table 305...Worth the travel
La Factoria 350...Wish I'd opened

FEDERICO TOMASSELLI
Bar Manager, Porto Fluviale
Via del Porto Fluviale, 22, Rome

Barnum Cafè 208	Late-Night
La Terrasse Cuisine & Lounge 209	Hotel
PDT 333	Worth the travel

HIDETSUGU UENO
Owner, Bar High Five
Efflore Ginza5 Bldg. BF, 5-4-15 Ginza

Star Bar 81	Local Must-Visit
Le Lion Bar de Paris 163	Worth the travel

JOSE LUIS VALENCIA
Head Bartender, Hotel B
Sáenz Peña 204, Barranco, Lima

Hotel B 356	Late-Night
Bottega Dasso 357	Neighborhood
Amaz 356	Local Must-Visit
Astrid & Gaston Casa Moreyra 357	Worth the travel
Florería Atlántico 366	Wish I'd opened

HANNAH VAN ONGEVALLE
Co-Owner, The Pharmacy/The Antique Shop
Knokke-Heist

Door 74 (bar) 128	Late-Night
Artesian 111	Hotel
Jigger's 130	Local Must-Visit
Bar High Five 80	Worth the travel
Lulu White 144	Wish I'd opened

CARINA SOTO VELASQUEZ
CEO, Quixotic Projects (Candelaria, Glass, La Mary
  Celeste, Hero)
www.quixotic-projects.com, Paris

Glass 144	Late-Night
Imperial 244	Hotel
Medusa 145	Neighborhood
La Buvette 145	Local Must-Visit
Julep 298	Worth the travel
Mezcaloteca 348	Worth the travel
Andrés Carne de Res 355	Wish I'd opened

YANA VOLFSON
Beverage Director, Cosme
35 East 21st Street, New York City

169 Bar 334	Late-Night
The NoMad Bar 323	Hotel
The Mayflower 338	Neighborhood
Attaboy 334	Local Must-Visit
Star Bar 81	Worth the travel

ANDREW AND BRIANA VOLK
Owners, Portland Hunt + Alpine Club
75 Market Street, Portland

Arnaud's French 75 Bar 305	Late-Night
Clyde Common 243	Hotel
The Silver Dollar 294	Neighborhood
Eventide Oyster Co. 310	Local Must-Visit
Pappy & Harriet's Pioneertown Palace 238	Worth the travel
Drink 310	Wish I'd opened

THEO WATT
Publisher/Founder, Thirsty Work Productions/DRiNK
  Magazine
www.drinkmagazine.asia, Shanghai

Logan's Punch 62	Late-Night
The 1515 West, Chophouse Bar 63	Hotel
Union Trading Company 63	Neighborhood
The Tailor Bar 63	Local Must-Visit
Speak Low 63	Worth the travel
The Nest 62	Wish I'd opened

GREG WEST
General Manager, Bourbon & Branch
501 Jones Street, San Francisco

Rye 265	Late-Night
Smugglers Cove	Local Must-Visit
The Dead Rabbit Grocery and Grog 335	Worth the travel
Hazlewood 246	Wish I'd opened

NEYAH WHITE
Single Malt Specialist, Whyte & Mackay;
  Principal, OH Group
www.whyteandmackay.com

Rye 265	Late-Night
The NoMad Bar 323	Hotel
Bar Rocking Chair 76	Local Must-Visit
The Buena Vista Cafe 264	Local Must-Visit
The Door 76	Local Must-Visit
Hello Dolly 76	Local Must-Visit
Ishino Hana 82	Local Must-Visit
Hotel Biron 265	Wish I'd opened

GARRY WHITE
General Manager, Denmark on High
463 North High Street, 2nd Floor, Columbus
The Aviary 279...Wish I'd opened

JAYSON WILDE
Bartender/Owner, Bottle & Barlow
1120 R Street, Sacramento
Shady Lady Saloon 238.........................Late-Night
Clyde Common 243...................................Hotel
ABV 263...Neighborhood
Back Door Lounge 238..................Local Must-Visit
Little Red Door 142.....................Worth the travel
El Dorado Cocktail Lounge 239..............Wish I'd opened

BEAU WILLIAMS
Owner, Julep
4141 Pennsylvania Avenue, Kansas City
Harry's Bar & Tables 271........................Late-Night
The Peanut 271...............................Neighborhood
Julep 298....................................Local Must-Visit
Harry's New York Bar 141..................Worth the travel
Erin Rose 306...............................Wish I'd opened

PAMELA WIZNITZER
Creative Director, Seamstress
339 East 75th Street, New York City
Daddy-O 324....................................Late-Night
The NoMad Bar 323.................................Hotel
Lucy's 332....................................Neighborhood
McSorley's Old Ale House 332-3..........Local Must-Visit
Williams & Graham 241..................Local Must-Visit
Black Pearl 25............................Worth the travel
Jigger & Pony 53.........................Worth the travel
Clover Club 337...........................Wish I'd opened

TAEEUN YOON
Bartender, THE BEASTRO Seoul
358-32 Seogyo-dong, Mapo-gu, Seoul
Door 74 (bar) 128..............................Late-Night
American Bar 107..................................Hotel
Speakeasy Mortar 68.....................Local Must-Visit
Canon 246................................Worth the travel
Worship Street Whistling Shop 114.........Wish I'd opened

NAREN YOUNG
Proprietor, Dante
79-81 MacDougal Street, New York City
The Dead Rabbit Grocery and Grog 335..........Late-Night
Mother's Ruin 335..............................Late-Night
Slowly Shirley 325.............................Late-Night
Beaufort Bar 108..................................Hotel
Stravinskij Bar 209...............................Hotel
The Long Island Bar 338.....................Neighborhood
PDT 333....................................Local Must-Visit
The Broken Shaker 290....................Worth the travel
The Broken Shaker 290....................Wish I'd opened

DUSHAN ZARIC
Co-Founder, Employees Only; Partner, The 86 Co
510 Hudson Street, New York City
Harlowe 254....................................Late-Night
Swift Hibernian Lounge 333.....................Late-Night
The Varnish 257................................Late-Night
American Bar 107..................................Hotel
Petty Cash Taqueria 255....................Neighborhood
Cantina Mayahuel 238.....................Local Must-Visit
PDT 333....................................Local Must-Visit
The Varnish 257...........................Local Must-Visit
Schumann's Bar 167.......................Worth the travel

IGOR ZERNOV
Owner, El Copitas Bar
Kolokolnaya ulitsa, 2, Saint Petersburg
Fiddler's Green 188............................Late-Night
Moskovsky Bar 186.................................Hotel
Delicatessen 186............................Neighborhood
El Copitas 187.............................Local Must-Visit
Bulletin Place 18........................Worth the travel
Rainbow Room 323.........................Wish I'd opened

DENNIS ZOPPI
Bartender, Smile Tree
Piazza della Consolata, 9, Turin
Connaught Bar 112..............................Late-Night
Click Clack Hotel 335............................Hotel
Spirito 209...............................Local Must-Visit
Tender Bar 81............................Worth the travel
Smile Tree 196...........................Wish I'd opened

KAN ZUO
Bartender, The Sign Cocktaillounge
Liechtensteinstrasse 104-106, Vienna

Nightfly's American Bar 107..Late-Night
Halbestadt 173..Neighborhood
Barfly's 173...Local Must-Visit
Nightjar 114...Worth the travel
Nightjar 114...Wish I'd opened

ELAD ZVI
Owner, Bar Lab and The Broken Shaker
2727 Indian Creek Drive, Miami Beach

Lost Lake 282...Late-Night
The Spare Room 256...Hotel
Sportsman's Club 283..Neighborhood
Purdy Lounge 29...Local Must-Visit
Imperial 244..Worth the travel
The Top of the Standard 326..Wish I'd opened

INDEX BY TYPE

LATE-NIGHT

Argentina
  Kika 365
  Milion 366
  Pizzeria Kentucky 364
  Verne Club 365
Australia
  Heartbreaker 24
  Henrietta Supper Club 19
  Palmer and Co 19
  Siglo 25
  The Toff 25
Austria
  Nightfly's Club American Bar 173
Belarus
  Heroes Bar 179
Belgium
  Minor Swing 130
Brazil
  Sub Astor 360
Canada
  Bar Datcha 224
  The Churchill 222
  Fat City Blues 223
  The Keefer Bar 229
  Pourhouse 230
  Uva Wine & Cocktail Bar 230
Cayman Islands
  Calico Jack's Bar and Grill 349
China
  Dusk Till Dawn 67
  Joe's Billiards & Bar 67
  Lobster Bar 66
  Logan's Punch 62
  Migas 58
  Shouning Lu 63
Denmark
  K-Bar 94
  Oak Room 94
  Strøm 94
Estonia
  Butterfly Lounge 178
Finland
  Teatteri Kellobaari 95
France
  Boston Café 134
  Experimental Cocktail Club
    (Paris) 107

Glass 144
L'Entrée des Artistes
  Pigalle 143
  Mabel 141
  Moonshiner 146
Germany
  3Freunde Cocktailbar 163
  Bar Gabányi 166
  Bar Immertreu 160
  Boilerman Bar 162
  The Parlour 161
  Spirits Bar 161
Greece
  Seven Jokers 182
Guatemala
  Café No Sé 350
Hungary
  Boutiq Bar 174
India
  ATM (À Ta Maison) 44
Indonesia
  Loewy 55
Italy
  1930 (bar) 203
  Barnum Cafè 208
  The Jerry Thomas Project 209
  Lacerba 203
  Mag Cafè 203
  Nottingham Forest 204
  Rivabar 196
Japan
  Bar Hermit 82
  Lady Jane Booze & Jazz 82
  Tender Bar 81
Latvia
  Balzambārs 178
Lithuania
  Matérealiste 179
Malaysia
  Hyde at 53M 48
Mexico
  Parker & Lenox 347
The Netherlands
  Demain 124
  Door 74 128
  Tales & Spirits 129
New Zealand
  Hawthorn Lounge 31
Norway

No.19 (bar) 90
Peru
  Hotel B 356
  Open Bar 356
  Sibaris Resto Bar 357
Philippines
  Bugsy's Bar & Bistro 47
Poland
  Cocktail Bar Max 172
Portugal
  Cinco lounge 156
  Porta 22 Club 157
  Red Frog 156
Puerto Rico
  El Farolito Bar 350
Romania
  Submarine 181
Russia
  Chainaya Tea & Cocktails 186
  El Copitas 187
  Fiddler's Green 188
  Noor Bar 186
  Poison188
  Saxon + Parole 187
Singapore
  28 Hongkong Street 53
Spain
  Boadas 154
  Slow Barcelona 155
Sweden
  East 91
  Linje Tio 92
  Little Quarter 92
Switzerland
  Chat Noir167
  Gräbli Bar 168
  Hotel Rivington & Sons 168
  Tales Bar 168
Taiwan
  The Speakeasy 69
Thailand
  Burma Bar 47
  U.N.C.L.E. 46
  Volkswagen Bus Bars 47
United Kingdom & Republic
    of Ireland
  Artesian 111
  Bramble 117
  Callooh Callay 113

Connaught Bar 112
Experimental Cocktail Club
   (London) 107
Garibaldi's 118
Happiness Forgets 109
The Hudson 119
The Liquor Rooms 120
Milk & Honey (London) 115
Mojo 98
Nightjar 114
Panda & Sons 118
The Pink Chihuahua 115
United States
169 Bar 334
The 700 (bar) 313
ABV 263
The Allegheny Wine Mixer 313
The Alley 237
Arnuud's French 75 Bar 305
Attaboy 334
The Aviary 279
Bar Deville 279
The Belmont 295
Blue Ribbon 335
Booze Box 280
The Brooklyn Inn 336
Bua 331
The Chat Room 297
Clark Street Ale House 281
Clover Club 337
Comstock Saloon 264
Daddy-O 324
The Dead Rabbit Grocery
   and Grog 335 Drink 310
Dutch Kills 339
Employees Only 324
Erin Rose 306
Extra Fancy 337
Harlowe 254
Harry's Bar and Tables 271
Harvard & Stone 254
The Hideout at Davla 264
Holiday Cocktail Lounge 332
Jumbo's Clown Room 254
Lantern's Keep 322
Little Branch 325
Lost Lake 282
Lucy's 332
Maison Premiere 338
Marty's PM 288
Marvel Bar 270
Mary's Club 244
Melrose Umbrella Company 255
Molly's at the Market 307
Montero Bar & Grill 339
Mother's Ruin 335

My Brother's Bar 241
Nachbar 293
Noble Experiment 240
Notsuoh 298
Old Absinthe House 307
Oldfield's Liquor Room 255
The Other Room 294
PDT 333
Radio Bar 237
Repour Bar 291
The Righteous Room 292
Robert's Western World 296
Rootstock 282
Rum Club 245
Rye 265 Saison 299
Sanctuaria 272
Shady Lady Saloon 238
Showtime 290
Slowly Shirley 325
Smuggler's Cove 266
Swift Hibernian Lounge 333
Tavern Road 311
The Varnish 257
The Wayland 333
Victory Sandwich Bar 292

———————————————

HOTEL
Brazil
   Belmond Copacabana
      Palace 360
   Frank Bar 360
Canada
   Clive's Classic Lounge 222
   Gerard Lounge 229
   Hawksworth Restaurant 229
   The Lobby Lounge and Raw Bar
      229
   Plateau Lounge 225
Cayman Islands
   Bar Jack 349
China
   The 1515 West, Chophouse &
      Bar West at the Jingan
      Shangri-La 63
   Atmosphere Bar 58
   Captain's Bar 66
   The Envoy 66
   Lobster Bar 66
Colombia
   Click Clack Hotel 355
Czech Republic
   Black Angel's Bar 172
Estonia
   Horisont Bar 178
France

Bar Louise 134
Hemingway Bar (Paris) 141
Hotel Maison Souquet Bar 144
Le Bar du Bristol 143
Restaurant & Bar à Vins 144
Germany
   Bar Dacaio 162
   Jimmy's Bar 161
Iceland
   Slippbarinn 90
India
   Rick's 44
Indonesia
   Woo Bar 54
Italy
   Bar 66 203
   Bamboo Bar 203
   The Fusion Bar
      and Restaurant 197
   La Terrasse Cuisine & Lounge 209
   Mio Bar 204
   Stravinskij Bar 209
Japan
   Mandarin Bar 81
   The Peak Lounge 83
   Zatta 83
The Netherlands
   The Bar at Hotel Credible 124
New Zealand
   Eichardt's Bar 31
Norway
   The Thief Bar 91
Philippines
   Sage Bar 48
Portugal
   Rooftop Bar 156-7
Russia
   Moskovsky Bar 186
Singapore
   Long Bar 53
   Manhattan 53
Spain
   Ohla Boutique Bar 155
Sweden
   Gotthards Krog 93
Switzerland
   Widder Bar 168
United Arab Emirates
   Hakkasan 40
United Kingdom & Republic
   of Ireland
   Ace Hotel 113
   American Bar 107
   Artesian 111
   The Bar at the Dorchester 111
   Beaufort Bar 108

The Blue Bar (London) 110
Chiltern Firehouse Hotel 111
Connaught Bar 112
Dandelyan 116
Dukes Bar 112
The Library Bar 110
The Punch Room 108
The Salon 119
Shelbourne Hotel 120
Zth Cocktail Lounge 107
United States
Benjamin Cooper 263
Berkshire Room 279
Bourbon Steak 289
The Breslin 323
The Broken Shaker 290
The Carousel Bar & Lounge 306
Cindy's 280
Clyde Common 243
Fox & Hounds 272
The Hawthorne 311
Hope 46 239
House Without A Key 241
Imperial 244
Jett's Grill 299
King Cole Bar 322
Lantern's Keep 322
Lemaire 299
Lewers Lounge 241
Midnight Rambler 297
The NoMad Bar 323
The Palm Court 322
Pepe le Moko 113
Petrossian Lounge 243
Quill 289
R Bar 307
The Regent Cocktail Club 291
Sable Kitchen & Bar 283
The Spare Room 256

NEIGHBORHOOD
Argentina
Korova Cine Bar 364
La Cova del Drac 361
Sanata Bar 364
Australia
Black Pearl 25
Bulletin Place 18
The Corner House 18
Ramblin' Rascal Tavern 19
The Wild Rover 20
Austria
Halbestadt 173
Belgium
Uncle Babe's 130

Brazil
Jobi 360
Canada
Bar Isabel 222
Bishop & Bagg 224
Chambar 228
Harbord Room 223
Lolita's 230
Midfield Wine Bar & Tavern 224
Chile
Polluelo Amarillo 361
The White Rabbit 361
China
Bar 42 181
Janes + Hooch 58
Mamie Taylor's 230
Mokihi 59
Union Trading Company 63
Czech Republic
Cash Only Bar 172
France
L'Antiquaire 134
Medusa 145
Red House 146
Germany
Badfish 160
Königsquelle 166
Le Lion Bar de Paris 163
Greece
CV Distiller 181
Guatemala
Lucky Rabbit 350
India
Big Nasty 45
Cocktail and Dreams
Speakeasy 44
Indonesia
Union 55
Israel
Port Said 40
Italy
Cloakroom Cocktail Lab 197
Latvia
B Bar 178
Lithuania
Dream Bar 179
Malaysia
Hyde at 53M 48
The Netherlands
Hiding in Plain Sight (HPS) 128
New Zealand
The Fork and Tap 30
The Matterhorn 32
Molten 30
Pomeroy's Pub 30
Peru

Bottega Dasso 357
Superba 357
Philippines
Gerry's 48
Romania
Flair Angel 180
Russia
Delicatessen Bar 186
Pivbar 187
South Africa
The Power & the Glory 215
Spain
La Venencia 150
Negroni Cocktail Bar 155
Tandem Cocktail Bar 155
Sweden
Corner Club 91
Linje Tio 92
Restaurang Bankomat 93
Rex Bar & Grill 93
Taiwan
Mod Sequel 68
Tickle My Fantasy 69
Thailand
Smalls 46
United Kingdom & Republic of
Ireland
Cafe Pacifico 108
Duke of York 119
Filter + Fox 98
Happiness Forgets 109
John Kavanagh "The Grave-
diggers" 120
Mr Fogg's 113
Sager + Wilde 109
Satan's Whiskers 107
Trailer Happiness 113
Villager 118
United States
ABV 263
All Souls 288
Bookhouse Pub 291
Brass Rail Bar 270
The Brooklyn Inn 336
Bryant's Cocktail Lounge 273
Buttermilk 336
Cantina Mayahuel 238
Charleston 280
Comstock Saloon 264
Corner Bar 339
Crudo 236
Daddy-O 324
The Dead Rabbit Grocery and
Grog 335
Dutch Kills 339
The Ear Inn 335-6

Elixir 264
Extra Fancy 337
Finn McCools 306
Fort Defiance 337
Freddie's 220 (bar) 293
Friendly's 272
The Good King Tavern 313
Grand Army 337
The Green Mill 281
Half Step 296
The Heorot Pub and Draught
  House 270
Holland Bar 321
House of 1000 Beers 312
Hudson Malone 321
Iona 338
Julep 298
Live Wire 239
Loco Pez 313
The Long Island Bar 338
Longman & Eagle 282
Lost Lake 282
Lou's Pub 288
Lucy's 332
Mace's Crossing 313
The Matchbox 282
The Mayflower 338
McSorley's Old Ale House
  332-3
Murphy's Bar and Grill 242
Nachbar 293
Nopa 265
Pal's Lounge 307
The Peanut 271
Petty Cash Tanqueria 255
Poison Girl 298
Prizefighter 236
Rob Roy 246
The Roosevelt 299
The Saint 307
The Silver Dollar 294
Smuggler's Cove 266
The Spare Room 256
Sportsman's Club 283
State Park 312
Sunny's Bar 338-39
Swift Hibernian Lounge 333
Tiki-Ti 256
Tommy's Mexican
  Restaurant 266
Tony's Saloon 256
Victor Tangos 297
Woody & Anne's 273

LOCAL MUST-VISIT
Argentina
  878 (bar) 364
  Doppelgänger Bar 292
  Frank's Bar 365
Australia
  Black Pearl 25
  Lui Bar 24
  Mojo Record Bar 18
  Napier Hotel 26
  Shady Pines Saloon 19
Austria
  Barfly's 173
Belarus
  Sweet & Sour 180
Belgium
  Café den Turk 130
  Jigger's 130
Brazil
  Sub Astor 360
Canada
  Bao Bei 228
  The Diamond 228
  The Harbord Room 223
  L'Abattoir 228
  La Distillerie 225
Chile
  KY 361
  W Lounge 361
China
  Bar 42 66
  Bar Constellation 62
  D Lounge in Beijing 58
  Da Dong Roast Duck 58
  Hidden House 58
  Janes + Hooch 58
  Migas 58
  Origin 67
  Senator Saloon 62
  The Tailor Bar 63
  Tai Lung Fung 67
Cuba
  El Floridita 348
Denmark
  St. Pauls Apothek 93
Estonia
  Valli Baar 178
Finland
  Trillby & Chadwick 95
France
  Experimental Cocktail Club
    (Paris) 141
  Harry's New York Bar 141
  L'Antiquaire 134
  La Buvette 145

  Le Syndicat 145
Germany
  Bar Gabányi 166
  Buck & Breck 160
  Le Lion Bar de Paris 163
  Lost In Grub Street 160
  Madrigal 163
  Pusser's 166
  Roomers Bar 162
  Seven Swans & The Tiny
    Cup 162
  Spirits Bar 161
Greece
  360 (bar) 181
  Baba au Rum 181
  The Clumsies 181
  The Gin Joint 182
  Theory Bar & More 182
Guatemala
  La Reunion Golf Resort and
    Residences 350
Hungary
  The Bar at Baraka 174
Iceland
  Slippbarinn 90
India
  The Bombay Canteen 45
  Ellipsis 45
  Tranquebar 45
Indonesia
  Loewy 55
Israel
  Gatsby 40
Italy
  1930 (bar) 203
  Art Bar 196
  Atrium Bar 196
  Caffè Propaganda 208
  Co. So. 208
  Le Bon Bock Café 208
  The Mad Dog 196
  Notthingam Forest 204
  Smile Tree 196
  Speakeasy Cocktail Bar 195
  Spirito 209
Japan
  Bar High Five 80
  Bar Lapin 75
  Bar Rocking Chair 76
  Ben Fiddich 83
  The Door 76
  Hello Dolly 76
  Ishino Hana 82
  Little Smith 80-1
  Star Bar 81
Latvia

Balzâmbars 178
The Left Door Bar 179
Lithuania
Hard Shake 179
Mexico
Baltra 347
Licorería Limantour 347
The Netherlands
Café de Dokter 128
Café in de Blaauwe Hand 124
Demain 124
Excalibur 128
Feijoa 128
Snappers Resto-Bar 129
Tales & Spirits 129
Whisky Café L&B 129
Wynand Fockink 129
New Zealand
Civil & Naval 30
The Golden Dawn 30
Hawthorn Lounge 31
Mea Culpa 30
Public Kitchen & Bar 31
Norway
Fuglen 90
HIMKOK 90
Torggata Botaniske 91
Panama
Restaurant Cabana 351
Peru
Amaz 356
Antica Taberna Queirolo 356-7
Astrid & Gaston Casa
Moreyra 357
Philippines
Bugsy's Bar & Bistro 172
Edsa Beverage Design Studio 47
Niner Ichi Nana 48
Poland
Kita Koguta 172
Portugal
Cinco Lounge 156
Park Bar 156
Pub Bonaparte 157
Puerto Rico
La Factoria 350
Romania
Joben Bistro 180
Russia
El Copitas Bar 187
Mendeleev Bar 186
Moskovsky Bar 186
Singapore
28 Hongkong Street 53
The Flagship 53
Jigger and Pony 53

Operation Dagger 54
Tippling Club 54
South Africa
The House of Machines 214
Publik Wine Bar 214
Ronnie's Sex Shop 214
South Korea
Speakeasy Mortar 68
Spain
Boadas 154
Boca Chica 154
Collage Art & Cocktail Social
Club 154
Dry Martini 154
Le Cabrera 150
Mutis 155
Sweden
Bar Hommage 91
Linje Tio 92
Open/Closed 93
Paradiso 92
Pharmarium 92
Switzerland
Bar Les Trois Rois 167
Kronenhalle Bar 168
L'Apothicaire Cocktail Club 167
Taiwan
Alchemy 68
Thailand
Sugar Ray | You've Just Been
Poisoned 46
United Arab Emirates
Zuma 40
United Kingdom & Republic
of Ireland
The 10 Cases 108
69 Colebrooke Row 109
Artesian 111
Bar Termini 114
Berry & Rye 98
The Blue Bar 110
Cafe Pacifico 108
The Canny Man's 117
Connaught Bar 112
The Corner Door 253
Duke of York Belfast 119
The Finnieston Bar
& Restaurant 118
Happiness Forgets 109
Jenny's Bar 98
John Kavanagh "The Grave-
diggers" 120
Nightjar 114
Panda & Sons 118
The Pot Still 118
United States

21 Club 321
Analogue 279
Arnaud's French 75 Bar 305
Attaboy 334
Bacchanal Wine 305
Back Door Lounge 238
Backbar 312
Bar Agricole 263
Barmini 289
Billy Sunday 280
Bin 152 295
Bitter & Twisted Cocktail
Parlour 236
Boardner's 253
Brick & Mortar 311
The Broken Shaker 290
The Buckhorn Exchange 240
The Buena Vista Cafe 264
Butterjoint 314
Cantina Mayahuel 332
The Collins 288
Comstock Saloon 264
Cure 306
Dante 324
The Dead Rabbit Grocery and
Grog 335
Dear Irving 320
Death & Co 331
Delilah's 281
Donny Dirk's Zombie Den 270
Drink 310
Dutch Kills 339
Eastern Standard 310
Employees Only 324
Erin Rose 306
Eventide Oyster Co. 310
Extra Virgin 271
Foe (Fraternal Order
of Eagles) 297
Forequarter 273
Fort Defiance 337
Gallow Green 320
The Green Mill 281
The Grey 293
Half Step 296
The Happiest Hour 325
Heinold's First and Last Chance
Saloon 237
Herbs & Rye 242
The Hilo Club 294
Honeycut 254
Horse Brass Pub 244
Huber's Café 244
Imperial 244
Julep 298
Keens Steakhouse 321

Kimball House 292
La Carafe 298
Live Wire 239
Lone Star Taco Bar 311
McSorley's Old Ale House
 332-3
Midnight Rambler 297
Mockingbird Hill 289
Musso & Frank Grill 255
Nachbar 293
The NoMad Bar 323
Oak & Ivy 242
Old Glory 296
Ordinary 310
PDT 333
Pegu Club 336
Pinewood Social 296
Porchlight 320
Proof + Pantry 297
Prosperity Social Club 272
Purdy Lounge 291
The Raines Law Room 320
The Rarebit 295
Rainbow Room 323
The Royale 272
Sassafras 256
The Saint 307
Second Bar + Kitchen 296
Slowly Shirley 325
Smuggler's Cove 266
The Spotted Owl 272-3
Sunny's Bar 338-39
Sweet Liberty 291
Teardrop Lounge 246
Tommy's Mexican
 Restaurant 266
Trina's Starlite Lounge 312
Turf Supper Club 240
The Varnish 257
Velvet Tango Room 273
The Violet Hour 284
West Alabama Ice House 298
Williams & Graham 241

WORTH THE TRAVEL
Argentina
 Florería Atlántico 366
 Frank's Bar 365
Australia
 The Baxter Inn 18
 Black Pearl 25
 Bulletin Place 18
 Earl's Juke Joint 20
 Everleigh 26
 Lily Blacks 24

Austria
 Tür 7 174
British Virgin Islands
 Soggy Dollar Bar 350-1
Canada
 Bar Raval 223
 Milk Tiger Lounge 222
China
 Speak Low 63
Costa Rica
 Pocket Food and Drink 351
Cuba
 El Floridita 348
 La Fuente 349
Cyprus
 Lost + Found Drinkery 182
Czech Republic
 Bugsy's Bar 172
 Hemingway Bar (Prague) 173
Denmark
 The Barking Dog 94
 Strøm 94
Finland
 Liberty or Death 95
France
 Candelaria 142
 Dirty Dick 143
 Glass 144
 Harry's New York Bar 141
 Hemingway Bar (Paris) 141
 Little Red Door 142
 Sherry Butt 142
Germany
 Buck and Breck 160
 Le Lion Bar de Paris 163
 Rum Trader 161
 Schumann's Bar 167
Guatemala
 Café No Se 350
Indonesia
 Ku De Ta 54
Italy
 Caffè Rivoire 197
 Harry's Bar 198
 Il Kiosko 197
 The Jerry Thomas Project 209
 Nottingham Forest 204
 Nu Lounge Bar 195
 Swinebar 195
Japan
 Bar High Five 80
 Bar High Five Tokyo 80
 Bar Oscar 75
 Bar Yamazaki 75
 Gen Yamamoto 82
 Star Bar 81

Tender Bar 81
Mexico
 La Capilla 347
 La Zebra 348
 Licorería Limantour 347
 Mezcaloteca 348
 Pare de Sufrir Tome Mezcal
 347-8
Peru
 Astrid & Gaston Casa
 Moreyra 357
Philippines
 Lanai Lounge 48
Romania
 Acuarela 180
Russia
 Chainaya Tea & Cocktails 186
 El Copitas 187
 Suzuran Bar 187
Singapore
 28 Hongkong Street 53
 Jigger and Pony 53
 Tippling Club 54
South Korea
 Vault +82 (bar) 68
Spain
 Boadas 154
 Mutis 155
United Kingdom & Republic
 of Ireland
 69 Colebrooke Row 109
 American Bar 107
 Artesian 111
 The Brazen Head 120
 Callooh Callay 113
 Connaught Bar 112
 Dukes Bar 112
 Happiness Forgets 109
 Kelly's Cellars 119
 Nightjar 114
 Sean's Bar 119
 White Lyan 109
United States
 15 Romolo 265
 365 Tokyo 243
 Amor y Amargo 331
 Angel's Share 331
 Attaboy 334
 The Aviary 279
 Bar 11 314
 Beachbum Berry's Latitude 29
 (bar) 305
 Bit House Saloon 243
 Blind Lady Ale House 238
 The Broken Shaker 290
 Bushwick Country Club 336

Cane & Table 305
Canon 246
The Dead Rabbit Grocery
  and Grog 335
Death & Co 331
Drink 310
Empire State South 292
Employees Only 324
Imperial 244
Julep 298
L'Aperitif Cocktail Bar 241
Little Branch 325
Lost Lake 282
Mace 332
Maison Premiere 338
Manifesto 271
Mayahuel 332
Midnight Rambler 297
Mockingbird Hill 289
Multnomah Whiskey
  Library 245
The NoMad Bar 323
Pappy + Harriet's Pioneertown
  Palace 238
PDT 333
Scotch & Soda 271
The Silver Dollar 294
Sunny's Bar 338-39
Three Dots and a Dash 283
Tommy's Mexican
  Restaurant 266
Trick Dog 266
The Varnish 257
The Violet Hour 284

WISH I'D OPENED
Argentina
  Florería Atlántico 366
  Frank's Bar 365
Australia
  Bar Americano 24
  Earl's Juke Joint 20
  Section 8 (bar) 25
  Shady Pines Saloon 19
Barbados
  The Cliff 351
Canada
  Bar Raval 223
  The Bayside Lounge 228
  L'Gros Luxe 225
Chile
  Barbazul 360
China
  Lobster Bar 66
  The Nest 62

Colombia
  Andrés Carne de res 355
Cuba
  El Floridita 348
Czech Republic
  Cash Only Bar 172
France
  Copper Bay 145
  Experimental Cocktail Club
    (Paris) 141
  Glass 144
  Lulu White 144
  Sherry Butt 142
Germany
  Buck and Breck 160
  Imperii 163
  Le Lion Bar de Paris 163
  Lebensstern 160
  Schumann's Bar 167
Guatemala
  Las Vibras de la Casbah 350
India
  The Bombay Canteen 45
Israel
  223 (bar) 40
Italy
  Harry's Bar 198
  Il Pellicano 195
  The Jerry Thomas Project 209
  The Mad Dog 196
  Nu Lounge Bar 195
  Smile Tree 196
Japan
  Gen Yamamoto 82
  M's Crux 80
Mexico
  La Capilla 347
The Netherlands
  Door 74 (bar) 128
  Hiding in Plain Sight (HPS) 128
Norway
  Fuglen 90
Portugal
  Bar Foxtrot 156
Puerto Rico
  La Factoria 350
Singapore
  Manhattan (Singapore) 53
  Operation Dagger 54
South Africa
  The House Of Machines 214
Spain
  Boadas 154
  Dry Martini 154
  Museo Chicote 150
United Kingdom & Republic

  of Ireland
  69 Colebrooke Row 109
  American Bar 107
  Artesian 111
  The Blind Pig 115
  The Bon Vivant 117
  Callooh Callay 113
  Connaught Bar 112
  Dandelyan 116
  The Dead Rabbit Grocery
    and Grog 335
  Happiness Forgets 109
  The Hide Bar 110
  High Water 116
  Hotel Biron Ireland 265
  Lab Bar 115
  Lounge Bohemia 114
  Milk & Honey 115
  Nightjar 114
  Nitecap 334-5
  The Pot Still 118
  The Prospect of Whitby 116
  White Lyan 109
  Worship Street Whistling
    Shop 114
United States
  15 Romolo 265
  ABV 263
  Amor y Amargo 331
  Analogue Bar 279
  Angel's Share 331
  Arnaud's French 75 Bar 305
  Attaboy 334
  The Aviary 279
  Bacchanal Wine 305
  Bad Decisions 294
  Beretta 263
  The Broken Shaker 290
  Bumbye Beach Bar 242
  Canon 246
  Clover Club 337
  Clyde Common 243
  Coin-op Game Room 239
  The Dead Rabbit Grocery and
    Grog 335
  Death & Co 331
  Delilah's 281
  Donna 337
  Donostia 331
  The Drifter 281
  Drink 310
  El Dorado Cocktail Lounge 239
  Employees Only 324
  Erin Rose 306
  Golden Gopher 253
  Good Times at Davey

Wayne's 253
Hazlewood 246
The Leadbelly 332
Liberty 246
The Long Island Bar 338
Maison Premiere 338
McSorley's Old
Ale House 332-3
Mimi's 307
Mockingbird Hill 289
Mothers Ruin 335
The NoMad Bar 323
P. J. Clarke's 322
PDT 333
Pegu Club 336
Polite Provisions 240
Prizefighter 236
Rainbow Room 323
Rye 265
Seamstress 324
Sergio's World Beers 293
The Silver Dollar 294
Smugglers Cove 266
Spirit of 77 245
Sportsman's Club 283
Three Dots and a Dash 283
Trick Dog 266
The Varnish 257
The Walker Inn 257
Wilfie & Nell 326
ZZ's Clam Bar 326

INDEX BY COUNTRY

A

Argentina
 Buenos Aires
  878 (bar) 364
  Doppelgänger Bar 292
  Florería Atlántico 366
  Frank's Bar 365
  The Harrison Speakeasy 365
  Kika 365
  Korova Cine Bar 364
  Milion 366
  Pizzeria Kentucky 364
  Plaza Bar 366
  Sanata Bar 364
  Verne Club 365
 Córdoba
  La Cova del Drac 361
Australia
 Melbourne
  Bar Americano 24
  Black Pearl 25
  Everleigh 26
  Heartbreaker 24
  Lily Blacks 24
  Lui Bar 24
  Napier Hotel 26
  Section 8 25
  Siglo 25
  The Toff 25
 Sydney
  The Baxter Inn 18
  Bulletin Place 18
  The Corner House 18
  Earl's Juke Joint 20
  Henrietta Supper Club 19
  Mojo Record Bar 18
  Palmer and Co 19
  Ramblin' Rascal Tavern 19
  Shady Pines Saloon 19
  The Wild Rover 20
Austria
 Vienna
  Barfly's 173
  Halbestadt 173
  Nightfly's Club
   American Bar 173
  Tür 7 174

B

Barbados
 St. James
  The Cliff 351
Belarus
 Minsk
  Heroes Bar 179
  Sweet & Sour 180
Belgium
 Ghent
  Café den Turk 130
  Jigger's 130
  Minor Swing 130
  Uncle Babe's 130
Brazil
 Rio de Janeiro
  Belmond Copacabana
   Palace 360
  Jobi 360
 São Paulo
  Frank Bar 360
  Sub Astor 360
British Virgin Islands
 Jost Van Dyke
  Soggy Dollar Bar 350–1

C

Canada
 Calgary
  Milk Tiger Lounge 222
 Montreal
  Bar Datcha 224
  Bar Kabinet 224
  Bishop & Bagg 224
  La Distillerie 225
  L'Gros Luxe 225
  Plateau Lounge 225
 Toronto
  Bar Isabel 222
  Bar Raval 223
  Fat City Blues 223
  The Harbord Room 223
  Hoof Cocktail Bar 223
  Midfield Wine Bar
   & Tavern 224
 Vancouver
  L'Abattoir 228

  Bao Bei 228
  The Bayside Lounge 228
  Chambar 228
  The Diamond 228
  Gerard Lounge 229
  Hawksworth Restaurant 229
  The Keefer Bar 229
  The Lobby Lounge
   and Raw Bar 229
  Lolita's 230
  Mamie Taylor's 230
  Pourhouse 230
  Uva Wine & Cocktail
   Bar 230
 Victoria
  The Churchill 222
  Clive's Classic Lounge 222
Cayman Islands
 Grand Cayman
  Agua Restaurant
   & Lounge 349
  Bar Jack 349
  Calico Jack's Bar
   and Grill 349
Chile
 Santiago
  Barbazul 360
  KY 361
  Polluelo Amarillo 361
  W Lounge 361
  The White Rabbit 361
China
 Beijing
  Atmosphere Bar 58
  D Lounge 58
  Da Dong Roast Duck 58
  Hidden House 58
  Janes + Hooch 58
  Migas 58
  Mokihi 59
  Xian Bar 59
 Hong Kong
  Bar 42 66
  Captain's Bar 66
  Dusk Till Dawn 67
  The Envoy 66
  Joe's Billiards & Bar 67
  Lobster Bar 66
  Origin 67

Tai Lung Fung 67
Shanghai
  The 1515 West, Chophouse
    & Bar 63
  Bar Constellation 62
  Logan's Punch 62
  Long Bar 62
  The Nest 62
  Senator Saloon 62
  Shouning Lu 63
  Speak Low 63
  The Tailor Bar 63
  Union Trading Company 63
Colombia
  Bogota
    Click Clack Hotel 355
  Chia
    Andrés Carne de Res 355
Costa Rica
  Escazú
    Pocket Food and Drink 351
Cuba
  Havana
    El Floridita 348
    La Fuente 348
Cyprus
  Nicosia
    Lost + Found Drinkery 182
Czech Republic
  Prague
    Black Angel's Bar 172
    Bugsy's Bar 172
    Cash Only Bar 172
    Hemingway Bar 173

D
Denmark
  Aarhus
    St. Pauls Apothek 93
  Copenhagen
    The Barking Dog 94
    K-Bar 94
    Oak Room 94
    Strøm 94

E
England
  Liverpool
    Berry & Rye 98
    Filter + Fox 98
    Jenny's Bar 98
    Mojo 98
  London
    69 Colebrooke Row 109

The 10 Cases 108
Ace Hotel 113
American Bar 107
Artesian 111
The Bar at the Dorchester
  111
Bar Termini 114
Beaufort Bar 108
The Blind Pig 115
The Blue Bar 110
Cafe Pacifico 108
Callooh Callay 113
Chiltern Firehouse Hotel 111
Connaught Bar 112
Dandelyan 116
Dukes Bar 112
Experimental Cocktail
  Club 107
The Fumoir 112
Happiness Forgets 109
The Hide Bar 110
High Water 116
Lab Bar 115
The Library Bar 110
Lounge Bohemia 114
Milk & Honey 115
Mr Fogg's 113
Nightjar 114
The Pink Chihuahua 115
The Prospect of Whitby 116
Punch Room 108
Sager + Wilde 109
Satan's Whiskers 107
Trailer Happiness 113
White Lyan 109
Worship Street Whistling
  Shop 114
Zth Cocktail Lounge 107
Estonia
  Talinn
    Butterfly Lounge 178
    Horisont Bar 178
    Valli Baar 178

F
Finland
  Helsinki
    Liberty or Death 95
    Teatteri Kellobaari 95
    Trillby & Chadwick 95
France
  Cognac
    Bar Louise 134
  Lyon
    L'Antiquaire 134

Boston Café 134
Paris
  Le Bar 143
  Le Bar du Bristol 143
  The Bar 142
  La Buvette 145
  Candelaria 142
  Copper Bay 145
  Dirty Dick 143
  L'Entrée des Artistes
    Pigalle 143
  Experimental Cocktail Club 141
  Glass 144
  Harry's New York Bar 141
  Hemingway Bar (Paris) 141
  Hotel Maison Souquet Bar 144
  Little Red Door 142
  Lulu White 144
  Mabel 141
  Medusa 145
  Moonshiner 146
  Red House 146
  Restaurant & Bar à Vins 144
  Sherry Butt 142
  Le Syndicat 145

G
Germany
  Berlin
    Badfish 160
    Bar Immertreu 160
    Buck and Breck 160
    Lebensstern 160
    Lost in Grub Street 160
    Rum Trader 161
  Cologne
    Spirits Bar 161
  Frankfurt
    Jimmy's Bar 161
    The Parlour 161
    Roomers Bar 162
    Seven Swans & The
      Tiny Cup 162
  Hamburg
    3Freunde Cocktailbar 163
    Bar Dacaio 162
    Boilerman Bar 162
    Jahreszeiten Bar 163
    Le Lion Bar de Paris 163
  Leipzig
    Imperii 163
    Madrigal 163
  Munich
    Bar Gabányi 166
    Falk's Bar 166

Königsquelle 166
Pusser's 166
Schumann's Bar 167
Greece
Athens
42 Bar 181
360 (bar) 181
Baba au Rum 181
The Clumsies 181
CV Distiller 181
The Gin Joint 182
Seven Jokers 182
Khalándri
Theory Bar & More 182
Guatemala
Antigua
Café No Sé 349
Lucky Rabbit 350
La Reunion Golf Resort and
Residences 350
Las Vibras de la Casbah 350

H
Hungary
Budapest
The Bar at Baraka 174
Boutiq Bar 174
Kollázs 174

I
Iceland
Reykjavik
Slippbarinn 90
India
Chennai
Tranquebar 45
Delhi
ATM (À Ta Maison) 44
Blue Bar 44
Rick's 44
Haryana
Cocktail and Dreams
Speakeasy 44
Mumbai
Big Nasty 45
The Bombay Canteen 45
Ellipsis 45
Indonesia
Bali
Seminyak
Ku De Ta 54
Woo Bar 54
Jakarta
Loewy 55

Union 55
Ireland
Athlone
Sean's Bar 119
Dublin
The Brazen Head 120
John Kavanagh "The Grave-
diggers" 120
The Liquor Rooms 120
Shelbourne Hotel 120
Israel
Jerusalem
Gatsby 40
Tel Aviv
223 (bar) 40
Imperial Craft Cocktail Bar 40
Port Said 40
Italy
Bologna
Nu Lounge Bar 195
Swinebar 195
Florence
Art Bar 196
Atrium Bar 196
Caffè Rivoire 197
The Fusion Bar
and Restaurant 197
Grosseto
Il Pellicano Hotel Bar 195
Milan
1930 203
Bamboo Bar 203
Bar 66 203
Lacerba 203
Mag Cafè 203
Mio Bar 204
Nottingham Forest 204
Naples
Speakeasy Cocktail Bar 195
Peschiera del Garda
Il Kiosko 197
Rome
Barnum Cafè 208
Le Bon Bock Cafè 208
Caffè Propaganda 208
Co.So. 208
The Jerry Thomas Project 209
Spirito 209
Stravinskij Bar 209
La Terrasse Cuisine & Lounge
209
Trentino
Rivabar 196
Treviso
Cloakroom Cocktail Lab 197
Turin

The Mad Dog 196
Smile Tree 196
Venice
Corner Pub 198
Harry's Bar 198

J
Japan
Fukuoka
Bar Lapin 75
Bar Oscar 75
Kyoto
Bar K6 75
Bar Rocking Chair 76
The Door 76
Hello Dolly 76
Sapporo
Bar Yamazaki 75
Tokyo
Bar Doras 83
Bar Hermit 82
Bar High Five 80
Ben Fiddich 83
Gen Yamamoto 82
Ishino Hana 82
Kanda 65 80
Lady Jane Booze & Jazz 82
Little Smith 80–1
M's Crux 80
Mandarin Bar 81
The Peak Lounge 83
Star Bar 81
Tender Bar 81
Zatta 83

L
Latvia
Riga
B Bar 178
Balzambārs 178
The Left Door Bar 179
Lithuania
Klaipeda
Hard Shake 179
Vilnius
Dream Bar 179
Matérialiste 179

M
Malaysia
Selangor
Hyde at 53M 48
Mexico

Guadalajara
  Pare de Sufrir Tome
    Mezcal 347–8
Mexico City
  Baltra 347
  Licorería Limantour 347
  Parker & Lenox 347
Oaxaca
  Mezcaloteca 348
Tequila
  La Capilla 347
Tulum
  La Zebra 348

N
The Netherlands
  Amsterdam
    Café de Doktor 128
    Door 74 128
    Excalibur 128
    Feijoa 128
    Hiding in Plain Sight (HPS) 128
    Snappers Resto-Bar 129
    Tales & Spirits 129
    Whisky Café L&B 129
    Wynand Fockink 129
  Nijmegen
    The Bar at Hotel Credible 124
    Café in de Blaauwe Hand 124
    Demain 124
New Zealand
  Arrowtown
    The Fork and Tap 30
  Auckland
    The Golden Dawn 30
    Mea Culpa 30
    Molten 30
  Christchurch
    Civil & Naval 30
    Pomeroy's Pub 30
  Dunedin
    Toast Bar 31
  Queenstown
    Eichardt's Bar 31
    Public Kitchen & Bar 31
  Wellington
    Hawthorn Lounge 31
    Matterhorn 32
Northern Ireland
  Belfast
    Duke of York 119
    The Hudson Bar 119
    Kelly's Cellars 119
Norway
  Oslo

Fuglen 90
    Himkok 90
    No. 19 90
    The Thief Bar 91
    Torggata Botaniske 91

P
Panama
  Panama City
    Restaurant Cabana 351
Peru
  Lima
    Amaz 356
    Antigua Taberna Queirolo
      356–7
    Astrid & Gaston Casa
      Moreyra 357
    Bottega Dasso 357
    Hotel B 356
    Open Bar 356
    Sibaris Resto Bar 357
    Superba 357
Philippines
  Gerry's 48
  Manila
    The Blind Pig 47
    Bugsy's Bar & Bistro 47
    Edsa Beverage Design
      Studio 47
    Long Bar 47
    Nlner Ichi Nana 48
    Sage Bar 48
  Tagaytay City
    Lanai Lounge 48
Poland
  Warsaw
    Cocktail Bar Max 172
    Kita Koguta 172
Portugal
  Lisbon
    Bar Foxtrot 156
    Cinco Lounge 156
    Park Bar 156
    Red Frog 156
    Rooftop Bar 156–7
    Tabik Restaurant 157
  Porto
    Pub Bonaparte 157
  Vila Nova de Famalicão
    Porta 22 Club 157
Puerto Rico
  San Juan
    La Factoria 350
    El Farolito Bar 350

R
Romania
  Bucharest
    Acuarela 180
    Flair Angel 180
  Cluj-Napoca
    Joben Bistro 180
    Submarine 181
Russia
  Moscow
    Chainaya Tea & Cocktails 186
    Delicatessen 186
    Mendeleev Bar 186
    Moskovsky Bar 186
    Noor Bar 186
    Pivbar 187
    Saxon + Parole 187
    Suzuran Bar 187
  Saint Petersburg
    El Copitas 187
    Fiddler's Green 188
    Poison 188

S
Scotland
  Aberdeen
    Ninety-Nine Bar
      & Kitchen 117
  Edinburgh
    The Bon Vivant 117
    Bramble 117
    The Canny Man's 117
    Garibaldi's 118
    Panda & Sons 118
    Villager 118
  Glasgow
    The Finnieston Bar
      & Restaurant 118
    The Pot Still 118
    The Salon 119
Singapore
  28 Hongkong Street 53
  The Flagship 53
  Jigger & Pony 53
  Long Bar 53
  Manhattan 53
  Operation Dagger 54
  Tippling Club 54
South Africa
  Barrydale
    Ronnie's Sex Shop 214
  Cape Town
    The House of Machines 214
    The Power & The Glory 215

Publik Wine Bar 214
Johannesburg
  The Landmark 214
South Korea
  Seoul
    Speakeasy Mortar 68
    Vault +82 (bar) 68
Spain
  Barcelona
    Banker's Bar 154
    Boadas 154
    Boca Chica 154
    Collage Art & Cocktail Social
      Club 154
    Dry Martini 154
    Mutis 155
    Negroni 155
    Ohla Boutique Bar 155
    Slow Barcelona 155
    Tandem Cocktail Bar 155
  Madrid
    Le Cabrera 150
    Museo Chicote 150
    La Venencia 150
Sweden
  Stockholm
    Bar Hommage 91
    Corner Club 91
    East 91
    Ling Long 92
    Linje Tio 92
    Little Quarter 92
    Paradiso 92
    Pharmarium 92
    Restaurang Bankomat 93
  Umeå
    Gotthards Krog 93
    Open/Closed 93
    Rex Bar & Grill 93
Switzerland
  Basel
    Bar les Trois Rois 167
  Carouge
    Chat Noir 167
  Geneva
    L'Apothicaire Cocktail
      Club 167
  Zürich
    Gräbli Bar 168
    Hotel Rivington & Sons 168
    Kronenhalle 168
    Tales Bar 168
    Widder Bar 168

T
Taiwan
  Taipei
    Alchemy 68
    Mod Sequel 68
    The Speakeasy 69
    Tickle My Fantasy 69
Thailand
  Bangkok
    The Bamboo Bar 46
    Smalls 46
    Sugar Ray | You've Just Been
      Poisoned 46
    U.N.C.L.E. 46
    Volkswagen Bus Bars 47
  Chiang Rai
    Burma Bar 47

U
United Arab Emirates
  Dubai
    Hakkasan 40
    Zuma 40
United States
  Alabama
    Birmingham
      The Collins 288
      Lou's Pub 288
      Marty's PM 288
  Arizona
    Phoenix
      Bitter & Twisted Cocktail
        Parlour 236
      Crudo 236
      Shady's Fine Ales and
        Cocktails 236
  California
    Emeryville
      Prizefighter 236
    Huntington Beach
      The Dagger Bar 237
    Los Angeles
      Boardner's 253
      The Corner Door 253
      Golden Gopher 253
      Good Times at Davey
        Wayne's 253
      Harlowe 254
      Harvard & Stone 254
      Honeycut 254
      Jumbo's Clown Room 254
      Melrose Umbrella
        Company 255
      Musso & Frank Grill 255

      Oldfield's Liquor Room 255
      Petty Cash Taqueria 255
      Sassafras 256
      The Spare Room 256
      Tiki-Ti 256
      Tony's Saloon 256
      The Varnish 257
      The Walker Inn 257
    Oakland
      The Alley 237
      Heinold's First and Last
        Chance Saloon 237
      Radio Bar 237
    Pioneertown
      Pappy + Harriet's
        Pioneertown Palace 238
    Sacramento
      Back Door Lounge 238
      Shady Lady Saloon 238
    San Diego
      Blind Lady Ale House 238
      Cantina Mayahuel 238
      Coin-op Game Room 239
      El Dorado Cocktail
        Lounge 239
      Hope 46 239
      Live Wire 239
      Noble Experiment 240
      Polite Provisions 240
      Rocky's Crown Pub 240
      Turf Supper Club 240
    San Francisco
      15 Romolo 265
      ABV 263
      Bar Agricole 263
      Benjamin Cooper 263
      Beretta 263
      The Buena Vista Cafe 264
      Comstock Saloon 264
      Elixir 264
      The Hideout at Dalva 264
      Hotel Biron 265
      Nopa 265
      Rye 265
      Smuggler's Cove 266
      Tommy's Mexican
        Restaurant 266
      Trick Dog 266
  Colorado
    Denver
      The Buckhorn Exchange 240
      My Brother's Bar 241
      Williams & Graham 241
  Connecticut
    New Haven
      Ordinary 310

District of Columbia
  All Souls 288
  Barmini 289
  Bourbon Steak 289
  Columbia Room 289
  Mockingbird Hill 289
  Quill 289
  Showtime 290
Florida
  Fort Lauderdale
    The Molokai Bar 290
  Miami Beach
    The Broken Shaker 290
    Mac's Club Deuce 290
    Purdy Lounge 291
    The Regent Cocktail
      Club 291
    Repour Bar 291
    Sweet Liberty 291
Georgia
  Atlanta
    Bookhouse Pub 291
    Empire State South 292
    The Righteous Room 292
    Victory Sandwich Bar 292
  Decatour
    Kimball House 292
  Savannah
    The Grey 293
Hawaii
  Honolulu
    L'Aperitif Cocktail Bar 241
    House Without a Key 241
    Lewers Lounge 241
    Murphy's Bar and Grill 242
  Wailea
    Bumbye Beach Bar 242
Illinois
  Chicago
    Analogue 279
    The Aviary 279
    Bar Deville 279
    The Berkshire Room 279
    Billy Sunday 280
    Booze Box 280
    Charleston 280
    Cindy's 280
    Clark Street Ale House 281
    Delilah's 281
    The Drifter 281
    The Green Mill 281
    Longman & Eagle 282
    Lost Lake 282
    The Matchbox 282
    Rootstock 282
    Sable Kitchen & Bar 283

    Salone Nico 283
    Sportsman's Club 283
    Three Dots and a Dash 283
    The Violet Hour 284
Indiana
  Muncie
    The Heorot Pub and
      Draught House 270
Kentucky
  Louisville
    Freddie's 220 (bar) 293
    Nachbar 293
    Sergio's World Beers 293
    The Silver Dollar 294
Louisiana
  New Orleans
    Arnaud's French 75 Bar 305
    Bacchanal Wine 305
    Beachbum Berry's
      Latitude 29 (bar) 305
    Cane & Table 305
    The Carousel Bar
      & Lounge 306
    Cure 306
    Erin Rose 306
    Finn McCool's 306
    Mimi's 307
    Molly's at the Market 307
    Old Absinthe House 307
    Pal's Lounge 307
    R Bar 307
    The Saint 307
Maine
  Portland
    Eventide Oyster Co. 310
Maryland
  Baltimore
    Bad Decisions 294
Massachusetts
  Boston
    Drink 310
    Eastern Standard 310
    The Hawthorne 311
    Tavern Road 311
  Cambridge
    Brick & Mortar 311
    Lone Star Taco Bar 311
    State Park 312
  Somerville
    Backbar 312
    Trina's Starlite Lounge 312
Michigan
  Port Huron
    Brass Rail Bar 270
Minnesota
  Minneapolis

    Donny Dirk's Zombie
      Den 270
    Marvel Bar 270
Missouri
  Kansas City
    Extra Virgin 271
    Harry's Bar & Tables 271
    Manifesto 271
    The Peanut 271
  St. Louis
    Fox & Hounds 272
    Friendly's 272
    The Royale 272
    Sanctuaria 272
  Springfield
    Scotch & Soda 271
Nevada
  Las Vegas
    365 Tokyo 243
    Herbs & Rye 242
    Oak & Ivy 242
    Petrossian Lounge 243
New York
  New York City
    Brooklyn
      The Brooklyn Inn 336
      Bushwick Country Club 336
      Buttermilk 336
      Clover Club 337
      Donna 337
      Extra Fancy 337
      Fort Defiance 337
      Grand Army 337
      Iona 338
      The Long Island Bar 338
      Maison Premiere 338
      The Mayflower 338
      Montero Bar & Grill 339
      Sunny's Bar 338-39
    Manhattan
      Chelsea
        Gallow Green 320
        Porchlight 320
      East Village
        Amor y Amargo 331
        Angel's Share 331
        Bua 331
        Death & Co 331
        Donostia 331
        Holiday Cocktail
          Lounge 332
        Lucy's 332
        Mace 332
        McSorley's Old Ale
          House 332–3
        Mayahuel 332

PDT 333
Swift Hibernian
Lounge 333
The Wayland 333
Flatiron
The Raines Law Room 320
Gramercy
Dear Irving 320
Lower East Side
169 Bar 334
Attaboy 334
The Leadbelly 334
Nitecap 334-5
Lower Manhattan
The Dead Rabbit
Grocery and Grog 335
Midtown
21 Club 321
Holland Bar 321
Hudson Malone 321
Keens Steakhouse 321
King Cole Bar 322
Lantern's Keep 322
The Palm Court 322
P. J. Clarke's 322
Rainbow Room 323
Nolita
Mother's Ruin 335
NoMad
The Breslin 323
The NoMad Bar 323
SoHo
Blue Ribbon 335
The Ear Inn 335-6
Pegu Club 336
Upper East Side
Seamstress 324
West Village
Daddy-O 324
Dante 324
Employees Only 324
The Happiest Hour 325
Little Branch 325
Slowly Shirley 325
The Top of the
Standard 326
Wilfie & Nell 326
ZZ's Clam Bar 326
Queens
Long Island City
Dutch Kills 339
Sag Harbor, Long Island
The Corner Bar 339
Ohio
Cleveland
Prosperity Social Club 272

The Spotted Owl 272–3
Velvet Tango Room 273
Oklahoma
Oklahoma City
The Hilo Club 294
The Other Room 294
Oregon
Portland
Bit House Saloon 243
Clyde Common 243
Horse Brass Pub 244
Huber's Cafe 244
Imperial 244
Mary's Club 244
Multnomah Whiskey
Library 245
Pepe Le Moko 245
Rum Club 245
Spirit of 77 245
Teardrop Lounge 246
Pennsylvania
New Kensington
House of 1000 Beers 312
Philadelphia
The 700 313
The Good King Tavern 313
Loco Pez 313
Mace's Crossing 313
Pittsburgh
The Allegheny Wine
Mixer 313
Bar 11 314
Butterjoint 314
South Carolina
Charleston
The Belmont 295
Bin 152 295
The Gin Joint 295
The Rarebit 295
Tennessee
Nashville
No. 308 296
Old Glory 296
Pinewood Social 296
Robert's Western World 296
Texas
Austin
Half Step 296
Second Bar + Kitchen 296
Dallas
Foe (Fraternal Order of
Eagles) 297
Midnight Rambler 297
Proof + Pantry 297
Victor Tangos 297
Fort Worth

The Chat Room 297
Houston
La Carafe 298
Julep 298
Notsuoh 298
Poison Girl 298
West Alabama Ice
House 298
Marfa
Jett's Grill 299
Virginia
Richmond
Lemaire 299
The Roosevelt 299
Saison 299
Washington
Seattle
Canon 246
Hazlewood 246
Liberty 246
Rob Roy 246
Wisconsin
Madison
Forequarter 273
Woody & Anne's 273
Milwaukee
Bryant's Cocktail
Lounge 273

INDEX BY BAR

3Freunde Cocktailbar 163
The 10 Cases 108
15 Romolo 265
21 Club 321
28 Hongkong Street 53
42 Bar 181
69 Colebrooke Row 109
169 Bar 334
223 (bar) 40
360 (bar) 181
365 Tokyo 243
The 700 313
878 (bar) 364
The 1515 West, Chophouse
& Bar 63
1930 (bar) 203

A
L'Abattoir 228
ABV 263
Ace Hotel 113
Acuarela 180
Agua Restaurant & Lounge 349
Alchemy 68
All Souls 288
The Allegheny Wine Mixer 313
The Alley 237
Amaz 356
American Bar 107
Amor y Amargo 331
Analogue 279
Andrés Carne de Res 355
Angel's Share 331
Antigua Taberna Queirolo 356–7
L'Antiquaire 134
L'Aperitif Cocktail Bar 241
L'Apothicaire Cocktail Club 167
Arnaud's French 75 Bar 305
Art Bar 196
Artesian 111
Astrid & Gaston Casa
Moreyra 357
ATM (À Ta Maison) 44
Atmosphere Bar 58
Atrium Bar 196
Attaboy 334
The Aviary 279

B
B Bar 178
Baba au Rum 181
Bacchanal Wine 305
Back Door Lounge 238
Backbar 312
Bad Decisions 294
Badfish 160
Baltra 347
Balzambärs 178
The Bamboo Bar (Bangkok) 46
Bamboo Bar (Milan) 203
Banker's Bar 154
Bao Bei 228
Le Bar 143
Bar 11 314
Bar 42 66
Bar 66 203
Bar Agricole 263
Bar Americano 24
The Bar at Baraka 174
Le Bar du Bristol 143
Bar Constellation 62
Bar Dacaio 162
Bar Datcha 224
Bar Deville 279
Bar Doras 83
The Bar at the Dorchester
111
Bar Foxtrot 156
Bar Gabányi 166
Bar Hermit 82
Bar High Five 80
Bar Hommage 91
The Bar 142
The Bar at Hotel Credible 124
Bar Immertreu 160
Bar Isabel 222
Bar Jack 349
Bar K6 75
Bar Kabinet 224
Bar Lapin 75
Bar Louise 134
Bar Oscar 75
Bar Raval 223
Bar Rocking Chair 76
Bar Termini 114
Bar les Trois Rois 167

Bar Yamazaki 75
Barbazul 360
Barfly's 173
The Barking Dog 94
Barmini 289
Barnum Cafè 208
The Baxter Inn 18
The Bayside Lounge 228
Beachbum Berry's
Latitude 29 305
Beaufort Bar 108
Belmond Copacabana
Palace 360
The Belmont 295
Ben Fiddich 83
Benjamin Cooper 263
Beretta 263
The Berkshire Room 279
Berry & Rye 98
Big Nasty 45
Billy Sunday 280
Bin 152 295
Bishop & Bagg 224
Bit House Saloon 243
Bitter & Twisted Cocktail
Parlour 236
Black Angel's Bar 172
Black Pearl 25
Blind Lady Ale House 238
The Blind Pig (London) 115
The Blind Pig (Manila) 47
Blue Bar (Delhi) 44
The Blue Bar (London) 110
Blue Ribbon 335
Boadas 154
Boardner's 253
Boca Chica 154
Boilerman Bar 162
The Bombay Canteen 45
Le Bon Bock Café 208
The Bon Vivant 117
Bookhouse Pub 291
Booze Box 280
Boston Café 134
Bottega Dasso 357
Bourbon Steak 289
Boutiq Bar 174
Bramble 117
Brass Rail Bar 270

The Brazen Head 120
The Breslin 323
Brick & Mortar 311
The Broken Shaker 290
The Brooklyn Inn 336
Bryant's Cocktail Lounge 273
Bua 331
Buck and Breck 160
The Buckhorn Exchange 240
The Buena Vista Cafe 264
Bugsy's Bar (Prague) 172
Bugsy's Bar & Bistro (Manila) 47
Bulletin Place 18
Bumbye Beach Bar 242
Burma Bar 47
Bushwick Country Club 336
Butterfly Lounge 178
Butterjoint 314
Buttermilk 336
La Buvette 145

C
Le Cabrera 150
Café in de Blaauwe Hand 124
Café de Dokter 128
Café No Sé 350
Cafe Pacifico 108
Café den Turk 130
Caffè Propaganda 208
Caffè Rivoire 197
Calico Jack's Bar and Grill 349
Callooh Callay 113
Candelaria 142
Cane & Table 305
The Canny Man's 117
Canon 246
Cantina Mayahuel 238
La Capilla 347
Captain's Bar 66
La Carafe 298
The Carousel Bar & Lounge 306
Cash Only Bar 172
Chainaya Tea & Cocktails 186
Chambar 228
Charleston 280
Chat Noir 167
The Chat Room 297
Chiltern Firehouse Hotel 111
The Churchill 222
Cinco Lounge 156
Cindy's 280
Civil & Naval 30
Clark Street Ale House 281
Click Clack Hotel 355
The Cliff 351

Clive's Classic Lounge 222
Cloakroom Cocktail Lab 197
Clover Club 337
The Clumsies 181
Clyde Common 243
Cocktail and Dreams
  Speakeasy 44
Cocktail Bar Max 172
Coin-op Game Room 239
Collage Art & Cocktail Social
  Club 154
The Collins 288
Columbia Room 289
Comstock Saloon 264
Connaught Bar 112
El Copitas 187
Copper Bay 145
The Corner Bar 339
Cornor Club 91
The Corner Door 253
The Corner House 18
Corner Pub 198
Co.So. 208
La Cova del Drac 361
Crudo 236
Cure 306
CV Distiller 181

D
D Lounge 58
Da Dong Roast Duck 58
Daddy-O 324
The Dagger Bar 237
Dandelyan 116
Dante 324
The Dead Rabbit Grocery
  and Grog 335
Dear Irving 320
Death & Co 331
Delicatessen 186
Delilah's 281
Demain 124
The Diamond 228
Dirty Dick 143
La Distillerie 225
Donna 337
Donny Dirk's Zombie Den 270
Donostia 331
The Door 76
Door 74 128
Doppelgänger Bar 292
El Dorado Cocktail Lounge 239
Dream Bar 179
The Drifter 281
Drink 310

Dry Martini 154
Duke of York 119
Dukes Bar 112
Dusk Till Dawn 67
Dutch Kills 339

E
The Ear Inn 335-6
Earl's Juke Joint 20
East 91
Eastern Standard 310
Edsa Beverage Design Studio 47
Eichardt's Bar 31
Elixir 264
Ellipsis 45
Empire State South 292
Employees Only 324
L'Entrée des Artistes Pigalle 143
The Envoy 66
Erin Rose 306
Eventide Oyster Co. 310
Everleigh 26
Excalibur 128
Experimental Cocktail
  Club (London) 107
Experimental Cocktail
  Club (Paris) 141
Extra Fancy 337
Extra Virgin 271

F
La Factoria 350
Falk's Bar 166
El Farolito Bar 350
Fat City Blues 223
Feijoa 128
Fiddler's Green 188
Filter + Fox 98
Finn McCool's 306
The Finnieston Bar
  & Restaurant 118
The Flagship 53
Flair Angel 180
Florería Atlántico 366
El Floridita 348
Foe (Fraternal Order
  of Eagles) 297
Forequarter 273
The Fork and Tap 30
Fort Defiance 337
Fox & Hounds 272
Frank Bar (São Paulo) 360
Frank's Bar (Buenos Aires) 365
Freddie's 220 293

Friendly's 272
La Fuente 349
Fuglen 90
The Fumoir 112
The Fusion Bar and
   Restaurant 197

G
Gallow Green 320
Garibaldi's 118
Gatsby 40
Gen Yamamoto 82
Gerard Lounge 229
Gerry's 48
The Gin Joint (Athens) 182
The Gin Joint (Charleston) 295
Glass 144
The Golden Dawn 30
Golden Gopher 253
The Good King Tavern 313
Good Times at Davey
   Wayne's 253
Gotthards Krog 93
Gräbli Bar 168
Grand Army 337
The Green Mill 281
The Grey 293
L'Gros Luxe 225

H
Hakkasan 40
Halbestadt 173
Half Step 296
The Happiest Hour 325
Happiness Forgets 109
The Harbord Room 223
Hard Shake 179
Harlowe 254
The Harrison Speakeasy 365
Harry's Bar 198
Harry's Bar & Tables 271
Harry's New York Bar 141
Harvard & Stone 254
Hawksworth Restaurant 229
Hawthorn Lounge 31
The Hawthorne 311
Hazlewood 246
Heartbreaker 24
Heinold's First and Last Chance
   Saloon 237
Hello Dolly 76
Hemingway Bar (Paris) 141
Hemingway Bar (Prague) 173
Henrietta Supper Club 19

The Heorot Pub and Draught
   House 270
Herbs & Rye 242
Heroes Bar 179
Hidden House 58
The Hide Bar 110
The Hideout at Dalva 264
Hiding in Plain Sight (HPS) 128
High Water 116
The Hilo Club 294
Himkok 90
Holiday Cocktail Lounge 332
Holland Bar 321
Honeycut 254
Hoof Cocktail Bar 223
Hope 46 239
Horisont Bar 178
Horse Brass Pub 244
Hotel B 356
Hotel Biron 265
Hotel Maison Souquet Bar 144
Hotel Rivington & Sons 168
House of 1000 Beers 312
The House of Machines 214
House Without a Key 241
Huber's Cafe 244
The Hudson Bar 119
Hudson Malone 321
Hyde at 53M 48

I
Imperial 244
Imperial Craft Cocktail Bar 40
Imperii 163
Iona 338
Ishino Hana 82

J
Jahreszeiten Bar 163
Janes + Hooch 58
Jenny's Bar 98
The Jerry Thomas Project 209
Jett's Grill 299
Jigger & Pony 53
Jigger's 130
Jimmy's Bar 161
Joben Bistro 180
Jobi 360
Joe's Billiards & Bar 67
John Kavanagh
   "The Gravediggers" 120
Julep 298
Jumbo's Clown Room 254

K
K-Bar 94
Kanda 65 80
The Keefer Bar 229
Keens Steakhouse 321
Kelly's Cellars 119
Kika 365
Kimball House 292
King Cole Bar 322
Il Kiosko 197
Kita Koguta 172
Kollázs 174
Königsquelle 166
Korova Cine Bar 364
Kronenhalle 168
Ku De Ta 54
KY 361

L
Lab Bar 115
Lacerba 203
Lady Jane Booze & Jazz 82
Lanai Lounge 48
The Landmark 214
Lantern's Keep 322
The Leadbelly 332
Lebensstern 160
The Left Door Bar 179
Lemaire 299
Lewers Lounge 241
Liberty 246
Liberty or Death 95
The Library Bar 110
Licorería Limantour 347
Lily Blacks 24
Ling Long 92
Linje Tio 92
Le Lion Bar de Paris 163
The Liquor Rooms 120
Little Branch 325
Little Quarter 92
Little Red Door 142
Little Smith 80-1
Live Wire 239
The Lobby Lounge and Raw
   Bar 229
Lobster Bar 66
Loco Pez 313
Loewy 55
Logan's Punch 62
Lolita's 230
Lone Star Taco Bar 311
Long Bar (Manila) 47
Long Bar (Shanghai) 62

Long Bar (Singapore) 53
The Long Island Bar 338
Longman & Eagle 282
Lost + Found Drinkery 182
Lost in Grub Street 160
Lost Lake 282
Lounge Bohemia 114
Lou's Pub 288
Lucky Rabbit 350
Lucy's 332
Lui Bar 24
Lulu White 144

M
M's Crux 80
Mabel 141
Mac's Club Deuce 290
Mace 332
Mace's Crossing 313
McSorley's Old Ale House 332–3
The Mad Dog 196
Madrigal 163
Mag Cafè 203
Maison Premiere 338
Mamie Taylor's 230
Mandarin Bar 81
Manhattan (Singapore) 53
Manifesto 271
Marty's PM 288
Marvel Bar 270
Mary's Club 244
The Matchbox 282
Matérialiste 179
Matterhorn 32
Mayahuel 332
The Mayflower 338
Mea Culpa 30
Medusa 145
Melrose Umbrella Company 255
Mendeleev Bar 186
Mezcaloteca 348
Midfield Wine Bar & Tavern 224
Midnight Rambler 297
Migas 58
Milion 366
Milk & Honey 115
Milk Tiger Lounge 222
Mimi's 307
Minor Swing 130
Mio Bar 204
Mr Fogg's 113
Mockingbird Hill 289
Mod Sequel 68
Mojo 98
Mojo Record Bar 18

Mokihi 59
Molly's at the Market 307
The Molokai Bar 290
Molten 30
Montero Bar & Grill 339
Moonshiner 146
Moskovsky Bar 186
Mother's Ruin 335
Multnomah Whiskey Library 245
Murphy's Bar and Grill 242
Museo Chicote 150
Musso & Frank Grill 255
Mutis 155
My Brother's Bar 241

N
Nachbar 293
Napier Hotel 26
Negroni 155
The Nest 62
Nightfly's Club American Bar 173
Nightjar 114
Niner Ichi Nana 48
Ninety-Nine Bar & Kitchen 117
Nitecap 334-5
Noble Experiment 240
The NoMad Bar 323
Noor Bar 186
Nopa 265
Notsuoh 298
Nottingham Forest 204
Nu Lounge Bar 195
No. 19 90
No. 308 296

O
Oak & Ivy 242
Oak Room 94
Ohla Boutique Bar 155
Old Absinthe House 307
Old Glory 296
Oldfield's Liquor Room 255
Open Bar 356
Open/Closed 93
Operation Dagger 54
Ordinary 310
Origin 67
The Other Room 294

P
The Palm Court 322
Palmer and Co 19
Pal's Lounge 307

Panda & Sons 118
Pappy + Harriet's Pioneertown Palace 238
Paradiso 92
Pare de Sufrir Tome Mezcal 347–8
Park Bar 156
Parker & Lenox 347
The Parlour 161
PDT 333
The Peak Lounge 83
The Peanut 271
Pegu Club 336
Il Pellicano Hotel Bar 195
Pepe Le Moko 245
Petrossian Lounge 243
Petty Cash Taqueria 255
Pharmarium 92
Pinewood Social 296
The Pink Chihuahua 115
Pivbar 187
Pizzeria Kentucky 364
P. J. Clarke's 322
Plateau Lounge 225
Plaza Bar 366
Pocket Food and Drink 351
Poison 188
Poison Girl 298
Polite Provisions 240
Polluelo Amarillo 361
Pomeroy's Pub 30
Porchlight 320
Port Said 40
Porta 22 Club 157
The Pot Still 118
Pourhouse 230
The Power & The Glory 215
Prizefighter 236
Proof + Pantry 297
The Prospect of Whitby 116
Prosperity Social Club 272
Pub Bonaparte 157
Public Kitchen & Bar 31
Publik Wine Bar 214
Punch Room 108
Purdy Lounge 291
Pusser's 166

Q
Quill 289

R
R Bar 307
Radio Bar 237

Rainbow Room 323
The Raines Law Room 320
Ramblin' Rascal Tavern 19
The Rarebit 295
Red Frog 156
Red House 146
The Regent Cocktail Club 291
Repour Bar 291
Restaurang Bankomat 93
Restaurant & Bar à Vins 144
Restaurant Cabana 351
La Reunion Golf Resort and
  Residences 350
Rex Bar & Grill 93
Rick's 44
The Righteous Room 292
Rivabar 196
Rob Roy 246
Robert's Western World 296
Rocky's Crown Pub 240
Ronnie's Sex Shop 214
Rooftop Bar 156–7
Roomers Bar 162
The Roosevelt 299
Rootstock 282
The Royale 272
Rum Club 245
Rum Trader 161
Rye 265

S
Sable Kitchen & Bar 283
Sage Bar 48
Sager + Wilde 109
The Saint 307
St. Pauls Apothek 93
Saison 299
The Salon 119
Salone Nico 283
Sanata Bar 364
Sanctuaria 272
Sassafras 256
Satan's Whiskers 107
Saxon + Parole 187
Schumann's Bar 167
Scotch & Soda 271
Seamstress 324
Sean's Bar 119
Second Bar + Kitchen 296
Section 8 25
Senator Saloon 62
Sergio's World Beers 293
Seven Jokers 182
Seven Swans & The Tiny Cup 162
Shady Lady Saloon 238

Shady Pines Saloon 19
Shady's Fine Ales
  and Cocktails 236
Shelburne Hotel 120
Sherry Butt 142
Shouning Lu 63
Showtime 290
Sibaris Resto Bar 357
Siglo 25
The Silver Dollar 294
Slippbarinn 90
Slow Barcelona 155
Slowly Shirley 325
Smalls 46
Smile Tree 196
Smuggler's Cove 266
Snappers Resto-Bar 129
Soggy Dollar Bar 350–1
The Spare Room 256
Speak Low 63
The Speakeasy 69
Speakeasy Cocktail Bar 195
Speakeasy Mortar 68
Spirit of 77 245
Spirito 209
Spirits Bar 161
Sportsman's Club 283
The Spotted Owl 272–3
Star Bar 81
State Park 312
Stravinskij Bar 209
Strøm 94
Sub Astor 360
Submarine 181
Sugar Ray | You've Just Been
  Poisoned 46
Sunny's Bar 338-39
Superba 357
Suzuran Bar 187
Sweet & Sour 180
Sweet Liberty 291
Swift Hibernian Lounge 333
Swinebar 195
Le Syndicat 145

T
Tabik Restaurant 157
Tai Lung Fung 67
The Tailor Bar 63
Tales & Spirits 129
Tales Bar 168
Tandem Cocktail Bar 155
Tavern Road 311
Teardrop Lounge 246
Teatteri Kellobaari 95

Tender Bar 81
La Terrasse Cuisine
  & Lounge 209
Theory Bar & More 182
The Thief Bar 91
Three Dots and a Dash 283
Tickle My Fantasy 69
Tiki-Ti 256
Tippling Club 54
Toast Bar 31
The Toff 25
Tommy's Mexican
  Restaurant 266
Tony's Saloon 256
The Top of the Standard 326
Torggata Botaniske 91
Trailer Happiness 113
Tranquebar 45
Trick Dog 266
Trillby & Chadwick 95
Trina's Starlite Lounge 312
Tür 7 174
Turf Supper Club 240

U
U.N.C.L.E. 46
Uncle Babe's 130
Union 55
Union Trading Company 63
Uva Wine & Cocktail Bar 230

V
Valli Baar 178
The Varnish 257
Vault +82 68
Velvet Tango Room 273
La Venencia 150
Verne Club 365
Las Vibras de la Casbah 350
Victor Tangos 297
Victory Sandwich Bar 292
Villager 118
The Violet Hour 284
Volkswagen Bus Bars 47

W
W Lounge 361
The Walker Inn 257
The Wayland 333
West Alabama Ice House 298
Whisky Café L&B 129
White Lyan 109
The White Rabbit 361

Widder Bar 168
The Wild Rover 20
Wilfie & Nell 326
Williams & Graham 241
Woo Bar 54
Woody & Anne's 273
Worship Street
   Whistling Shop 114
Wynand Fockink 129

X
Xian Bar 59

Z
Zatta 83
La Zebra 348
Zth Cocktail Lounge 107
Zuma 40
ZZ's Clam Bar 326

Phaidon Press Limited
Regent's Wharf
All Saints Street
London N1 9PA

Phaidon Press Inc.
65 Bleecker Street
New York, NY 10012

www.phaidon.com

First published 2017
© 2017 Phaidon Press Limited

ISBN 978 0 7148 7315 2

As many establishments are closed Sunday and/or
Monday, and some change their opening hours in relation
to the seasons or close for extended periods at different
times of the year, it is always advisable to check opening
hours before visiting. All information is correct at the
time of going to print, but is subject to change.

Commissioning Editor: Emily Takoudes
Project Editor: Olga Massov
Production Controller: Adela Cory
Designed by Kobi Benezri and Julia Hasting

Printed in Italy

The publisher would like to thank all the participating
contributors for their generosity, time, and insightful
recommendations; Adrienne Stillman for her expertise
and commitment and Evelyn Battaglia, Vanessa Bird,
Jane Ellis, Marna Gilligan, Annie Kramer, Sophie Kullman,
Christopher Lacey, Lesley Malkin, Luisa Martelo, Cecilia
Molinari, João Mota, Jorge Sagradas, Kim Scott, Bav
Shah, Hans Stofregen, Tracey Smith, Ana Teodoro,
and Louise Wheeler for their contributions to the making
of this book.

Illustrations from thenounproject.com, based on original
artwork by: anbileru adaleru (mocktail, p.12); YuguDesign
(cocktail, p.36); Anthony Lui (whiskey, p.72); Clément
Thorez (Champagne flute, p.86); Travis Beckham
(martini glass, p.104 and cover); Pedrol Martínez Muñoz
(olive, p.138); João Miranda (liquor bottle, p.192);
Roberto Colombo (whiskey, p.220); Adam Simpson
(cocktail shaker, p.234); Julie E (jigger, p.250); Evan
Shuster (cocktail glass, p.276); Edward Boatman (cocktail,
p.302); Jake Duham (Empire State Building, p.318);
and Alex Bu (lemon, p.342).

About the author
Adrienne Stillman is the co-founder of Dipsology,
a curated digital guide and online community for New
York City cocktail enthusiasts. She works in marketing
for the wine industry. She studied economics at Barnard
College and is a Certified Sommelier through the Court
of Master Sommeliers. A native New Yorker, Adrienne
lives in Napa Valley, California with her husband Jacob
Krausz. Her favorite cocktail is the Silver Fox, made with
gin, orgeat, amaretto, lemon, and egg white.

Author acknowledgements
It has been a true privilege to guide *Where Bartenders
Drink* from idea to fruition. I am greatly indebted to the
225 bartenders all over the world, as well as numerous
cocktail-industry friends who were more than generous
with their time and insight.

I am particularly grateful to Theo Lieberman, Neyah
White, Nico de Soto, Pamela Wiznitzer, Jonny Mckenzie,
Theo Watt, Marshall Altier, Zdenek Kastanek, Frank
Cisneros, Carina Soto Velasquez, Giuseppe Gallo, Evelyn
Chick, Grant Sceney, Alex Day, David Kaplan, Martin
Cate, Eden Laurin, Ola Yau Carlson, Neal Bodenheimer,
Jose Luis Leon, Fede Cuco, Kellie Thorn, Monica Berg,
Simone Caporale, Alex Kratena, Kyle and Rachel Ford,
Gabriel Orta, Jeffrey Morgenthaler, Sean Muldoon,
Nate Whitehouse, Lizzie da Trindade-Asher, and Miguel
Fernandez Fernandez, for sharing their local knowledge
and helping make this book a truly global one.

Thank you to Emily Takoudes, executive commissioning
editor at Phaidon Press, and Emilia Terragni, Phaidon's
publisher, for entrusting me with this project; and to
project editor Olga Massov for making sure all the t's were
crossed and the i's dotted. I have also been fortunate to
rely on the good sense and guidance of my agent Sarah
Funke Butler.

I would not have been in a position to write *Where
Bartenders Drink* in the first place if not for Dipsology
co-founder Alexa Scordato, my partner in crime in many
a cocktail adventure. And I would never have gotten through
it without the unfailing support of my husband, Jacob
Krausz, and my parents, Stanley and Andrea Stillman.

Where Bartenders Drink is dedicated to everyone who
has ever searched for a great cocktail and discovered
something so much more.